THE COMPLETE TRILOGY

THE COMPLETE TRILOGY

REVAMPED AND REWRITTEN FROM THE ORIGINAL NOVELS

SCOTT R. ETTERS

THE DROPAS EFFECT

First Edition 2021

First Printing 2021

Cover Design: Scott R. Etters

Image Art: Timm Etters

Etters, Scott R.
    The Dropas : Complete Trilogy / Scott R. Etters.
        p. cm.   (The Dropas; Complete Trilogy)
        ISBN: 978-1-7363334-0-2
        1. Fantastic Fiction   I. Etters, Scott R. II. Title III. Series
813'.54 -- dc20
FIC

Printed in the United States of America

BREAKING THROUGH

THE WALLS

BOOK I

For those people who still believe we can make this planet a better place to live, I challenge you to make believers out of those who don't, so we may venture forth in great numbers to make it a reality.

Prologue

International governments and societies, consumed by capitalistic and materialistic beliefs, finally collapsed, resulting in the most devastating global war in history. The war eliminated nearly a third of the human population, flattened country infrastructures, and rendered numerous lands uninhabitable.

The near extinction of humanity was sparked by one man's detrimental spread of government secrets. The Special Intelligence Agency nicknamed him the Human Virus. That information leakage helped proliferate the greed and hatred toward each nation's leadership, greed and hatred that had been mounting for decades. Civilians around the world revolted against their authoritative parties in whatever way possible.

Initially, militaries defended their governments but later opted to repudiate their obligation due to the wide-spread corruption. Before long, people waged war on their own kind everywhere. The global conflict escalated to the point where no one knew whom they were fighting or for what purpose they fought. Using this as an opportunity to usurp international leadership, organized crime groups united. This new alliance called themselves the ForLords and was led by a man named Lord Ozone.

The ForLords accumulated a significant stockpile of Organic Destructors—biological armaments developed by the allied nations—and the only known supply of untested vaccines. Because the destructors were capable of emitting a deadly and extremely contagious virus, the ForLords designated it their primary weapon. They also seized the small stockpile of nuclear weapons that remained after the signing of the Global Nuclear Weapons Treaty five years earlier.

Administrations of nations eventually relinquished power to the global revolutionaries—a major faction seeking to restore universal peace. Focus shifted to eradicating the three million ForLords who had superseded the governments as the more threatening force to society. The usurpers fell with minimal resistance, having lost their only two advantages. They had detonated every nuclear warhead and exhausted the finite supply of Organic Destructors. The revolutionaries ultimately ended the human annihilation and Lord Ozone's stranglehold on the world.

Postwar casualties mounted from the nuclear aftermath and the effects of the biological weapons. It was later discovered that the virus emitted from the Organic Destructors had been classified as a rapidly attenuating one—the contagion quickly diminished over time. Its limited existence proved to be the only definitive cure and the resulting deaths subsequently ceased.

Damage assessment estimated the death count to be in the billions. Large portions of global regions were declared nuclear wastelands and habitation was forbidden, indefinitely. Entire cities had been leveled, and sickness, hunger, and homelessness persisted. The survivors contemplated the notion of whom the fortunate ones were: themselves or those who had perished. One characteristic was evident, individuals who endured were more resolute than ever to ensure that the human race perpetuated in a new harmonious world.

Representatives from the world's nations developed, signed, and implemented the Survival Treaty, the most comprehensive document humankind had ever written. It required six months to compose and was authored by the most brilliant minds of the time. The Treaty detailed selfless policies—uncustomary prior to the war—in an effort to achieve global harmony. Many of those same representatives formed the Global Governing Board, or GGB, and served to oversee the execution and sustenance of the Treaty provisions.

The world was long overdue for a Treaty of such magnitude, with near human extinction fresh in the minds of the war survivors. It inspired and promoted efforts of unity, presenting avenues to understand each other's differences rather than turning against each other for those differences. The Treaty contained clauses guaranteeing education of future generations regarding the events leading up to the war. It also included mandates to abolish weapons, pollution, crime, drugs, hunger, financial markets and usage of money altogether, and reverse global warming—all problems national leaders were supposed to solve while in office.

Citizens around the globe heartily embraced and accepted the Survival Treaty. They committed to fulfilling the Treaty directives and contributing to society in a positive way. As long as they did, they were compensated for their efforts by means of an unsophisticated credit system that replaced the monetary structure and capital exchange. This new program afforded individuals the essentials needed to live and the opportunity to enjoy life. Enforcement agencies consisting of GGB officers were established to apprehend policy violators and ForLord outliers. In all, the institution of the Treaty propelled the world into a global utopia whereby the human race, and all living things, could cherish their time on Earth and live peacefully for eternity.

The GGB also appointed regional liaisons across countries to act as the conduit between the board and the widespread public. The Treaty details were clearly communicated via the liaisons to the general populace. The less war-torn countries—specified by the number of survivors, available resources, and level of infrastructure—pledged to help the less fortunate ones. Weeks following the signing, the GGB established the Global News Station (GNS) to convey specifics regarding activities and progress in each region.

The rebuilding process and global synchronization progressed admirably, resulting in many demolished cities acquiring new infrastructures. Like ancestors of long ago, societies aspired to enrich their minds and souls as cultural activities were once again prevalent in everyday life. Liam Street, a former revolutionary who played a major role in ending the conflict, and his younger, artistic brother, Mason, restarted their pre-war art service that complemented the world-wide revitalization. Through Mason's art, the service educated the public and beautified the surroundings. His murals accentuated all types of buildings, helping to restore images lost during the war or creating new ones. However, they relished working in schools the most, inspiring students on a daily basis.

Past and Present

Six years before the war, the city lights of Manhattan illuminated the sky. A well-anticipated art show, featuring the ultra-controversial Leonard von Zonek, was set to occur. His unseen exhibit, *Life in the Underworld*, was already condemned by the media because it depicted Satan's netherworld as a glorified place for human existence. This condemnation stemmed from the already-biased journalists and art critics who wrote negatively about von Zonek's customary provocative and divisive artwork.

A large crowd of two factions gathered in the downtown art district. Aside from a few obscenities, the majority of von Zonek's opposers calmly mingled in the streets while his supporters eagerly awaited entrance into the Art Center. Anticipating potential rioting due to von Zonek's disparagers threatening to discredit him, the New York city police arrived en masse to oversee the event. Presently, the crowd showed no signs of disruptive activity and the rumored threats had not materialized. Atop the Art Center steps, two officers suspiciously observed the subdued behavior of the gathering crowd.

"I'm surprised at the calmness," the first officer commented.

"Me too," replied the superior officer. "I've been a part of too many of these. Just to be safe, raise the alert level. Something's going down tonight."

The first officer relayed the orders over his radio as he neared the entrance. Careful not to heighten anxiety, the police force working the area unobtrusively positioned themselves amid the crowd.

The Art Center doors opened. In a hurried, yet orderly manner, the art enthusiasts funneled inside—only a limited number would gain entrance. They proceeded through the hallways to the largest exhibit room.

Facing away from the incoming crowd, Leonard von Zonek spoke on stage to a horde of domestic and international reporters. Although the media were granted early admittance for the informal press conference, von Zonek prohibited them from previewing his work at the event. Floor-to-ceiling curtains covered the art and guards standing in front of roped stanchions protected it from curious attendees. Except for a handful of meticulously selected art pundits, von Zonek wanted all to view his art simultaneously. He showed no favoritism, not even to his closest friends who had implored him for a glimpse of the paintings before the public unveiling. The exhibit hall quickly filled to capacity, leaving thousands outside waiting.

As the doors closed, the ushers directed reporters to their designated seats, making von Zonek fully visible. Characterized as an eccentric, he was a tall, well-built, and imposing individual. His hooked nose was a prominent feature on his otherwise average-looking, pale face. He wore his hair long and combed back, not caring that the style unflatteringly accentuated his receding hairline.

Buzzing with anticipation, significantly more supporters than dissenters were in attendance.

The curator arrived at the podium and gestured to quiet the crowd. "Thank you. Welcome, art lovers, to this much-anticipated event. We're all excited to see Mr. von Zonek's latest creations."

The crowd reacted excitedly, but maintained control. The curator raised her hands, calming the attendees.

"Many of you are familiar with Mr. von Zonek's exceptional, but always controversial art. Behind those curtains is a collection of unique paintings in which he has brilliantly channeled his childhood struggles. This exhibit transcends mere controversy and you are here to formulate your own opinions. Without further ado, I am honored to introduce the renowned Mr. Leonard von Zonek."

The supporters enthusiastically applauded while the outnumbered opposers sat quietly. Von Zonek stepped to the podium and basked in the warm reception before silencing the crowd.

"Thank you for attending tonight. Because we all have waited a long time for this day, I will be brief. I learned early in my career not to concern myself with the majority of art pundits and, even more so, freelance or disreputable critics. The public is my audience. And those of you in attendance tonight will be the first to witness my latest work. I ask that you scrupulously view it, but examine it with an open mind."

The crowd cheered, this time more loudly. Smiling, von Zonek nodded at the curator. Raising her arm, she signaled to the attendants who readied themselves by the curtains.

"And without further delay, I unveil my latest art to the world," von Zonek announced.

The curator dropped her arm with a flourish. The attendants pulled the cords and the curtains ascended to the ceiling. The crowd gasped in horror, not in awe and appreciation as von Zonek expected. An expression of rage overtook his elated face. His supporters were stunned in silent disbelief and his disparagers snickered loudly in mockery.

"May you rot with the devil, von Zonek!" one bellowed.

"View that with an open mind!" another sneered.

"What have they done to my work?" von Zonek angrily shouted.

His art had been sabotaged by destructive chemicals. In despair, von Zonek leapt from the stage and ran to the closest painting. That noteworthy piece depicted a boyish von Zonek, searching for acceptance in the underworld as the spiritual images of his deceased parents guided him.

With chemical-laced paint dripping down the canvases and holes prominent throughout each piece of art, the mutilation had rendered the entire collection unidentifiable. He frantically rubbed his hands over the canvas, trying desperately to restore the damaged painting to its original state. Realizing he could do nothing to save it, he leaned against the wall, slid down, and buried his head in his hands. Although their words would provide little help, his supporters sought to console him as he screamed in pain while the chemicals ate through his flesh.

The security guards escorted the media and public attendees to the nearest exit. Outside, the antagonists chanted loudly. The catastrophic news spread through the crowd like wildfire. Police officers intervened and prevented small scuffles from escalating into a larger riot.

Moments later, the mild skirmishes abruptly halted as von Zonek burst through the Art Center doors, cradling his head in his palms and screaming in agony. Pulling away his skinless hands revealed von Zonek's partially-eaten face. It was a gruesome sight: exposed muscle tissue and even bone. The crowd silenced as he staggered from the doors to the top step. He spoke in spite of the excruciating pain.

His voice roared with rage. "You all believed my paintings depicted evil! None of you have witnessed pure evil yet, but you will! It will be worse than you can possibly imagine, that is, if you live to tell about it! Remember my name, because you can no longer recognize my face! I will return with a vengeance and make all of you suffer for this day!"

Leonard von Zonek collapsed and tumbled down the first tier of steps. Several devotees ran to his side, but the majority dispersed as the police officers methodically cleared the streets to make room for the ambulance.

Nine years after the war, Liam Street traveled with his much older sister, Sarah, to Athens, Greece—one of a small number of historical cities left virtually unscathed from the global conflict.

Liam's blue eyes, mustache, and long, thick, wavy hair—parted down the middle—were distinguishing features on an otherwise average body frame. He grew out his ashy brown locks after the war, preferring it to the short-cropped, military style he wore as a revolutionary. Standing six feet two, he was lean and toned—staying fit had always been a top priority.

The purpose of the trip was two-fold. First and foremost, Liam hoped the excursion would deliver closure to his prolonged mourning. Athens is where Liam honeymooned with his late wife, Ashley, who lost her life shortly after the ForLords surrendered. Second, he had a strong desire to visit the city, a befitting site for the GGB headquarters, and tour the monumental building.

Liam's anger resurfaced when he occasionally reflected on the idiocy of previous governments and the collective role they played in precipitating the war, the war that ultimately took his beloved wife. For Liam to proceed with his life and be fully productive, he had to experience a spiritual cleansing. Up to that point, all his efforts were unsuccessful.

Aboard the return flight to the United States, Liam stared out the window, his thoughts disconnected and scattered.

"Liam?" Sarah rested her hand on his forearm. "You okay?"

"Huh? Yeah, I'm all right. Just thinking about Ash—the Survival Treaty."

"It's all right, Liam. You didn't come to Greece to forget her."

"Ashley will always be a part of me. This is where we began our life as one."

"No need to explain."

"Thanks for traveling with me. I truly believe this is what I needed."

"Of course." Sarah changed the subject. "You said you were also thinking about the Survival Treaty. Isn't it remarkable how societies around the world have united since its inception?"

Liam sighed. "Yes, it is. Unfortunately, it's a shame we all had to face possible extinction before accepting individual differences."

"Consider the changes," Sarah replied positively. "The credit system is far better than any financial system we had. And the crime, drugs, hunger, pollution—"

"I understand. That's all but eradicated."

"Today, we all enjoy and cherish our time on Earth. We're closer to a utopian existence than anyone could have imagined."

"I agree. The GGB is doing a phenomenal job reuniting the world."

"You speak with less conviction than you have before."

"I've grown a bit concerned after witnessing extreme negativity on this trip. And I frequently encountered instances of greed, similar to what was prevalent prior to the war."

"Liam, please tell me this oversensitivity is because you're feeling sentimental about Ashley."

"Perhaps...but I don't think it is."

Back Home

Athens wasn't the only place where strange events were happening. Peculiar incidents were also occurring back home.

It was two-thirty in the morning. Mason sat upright in bed, awakened by another asthma attack. Slimmer and an inch shorter than Liam, Mason also sported a mustache. He wore his thin hair at medium length to hide the onset of a receding hairline. Some people noted facial similarities between the two brothers, while others remarked that they saw no resemblance whatsoever. Desiring to stay in shape, Mason wanted to partake in physical activities, but his allergies and asthma often were a major deterrent. This prompted Mason to immerse himself in art instead of sports as a child.

Sweating profusely, his hands and arms trembled. The late-night attacks were not uncommon, but Mason was troubled over the frequency of the recent episodes. It had been the fourth consecutive night.

Mason fumbled around on the nightstand for his inhaler. Two quick pumps accompanied by two deep breaths made up the usual routine. He leaned against the headboard, waiting for the medicine to take effect as the relief he sought came slowly. An hour passed before Mason fell back to sleep.

BEEP! BEEP! BEEP! Mason mustered enough energy to completely turn off the alarm, having already depressed the snooze button several times. Almost eight-thirty, Pockets would be arriving at nine. Like most mornings, even with extra sleep, Mason felt like a truck ran over him. The majority of artists dislike waking early, that is, any time before lunch. Artists need to ease into the new day before they present themselves to the world. At least Mason did.

He flung off the covers. Before his feet met the ground, he realized that his morning ritual would require navigating the numerous laundry piles in the bedroom, hallway, and bathroom.

Pockets steered his electric car into a vacant parking spot. The dashboard clock displayed 8:57 a.m. Always punctual, he kept Mason on schedule.

* * * * *

Pockets was a unique and interesting person, contrary to his average physical features. Standing five feet ten, he had a full head of black hair, brown eyes, and was always clean-shaven. Stocky but not overweight, he did sport a small pot belly. Jeans or shorts, in the summer months, accompanied by a tucked-in, collared shirt with a pocket on the left side comprised his typical attire.

Pockets met Mason three years earlier. One summer day he introduced himself and asked Mason if he needed an assistant. Liam and Mason had oftentimes discussed hiring one, but Mason had grown accustomed to working solo. After a lengthy conversation, Pockets convinced Mason that having a co-worker would improve the productivity of the art service. Mason could spend more time painting and minimal time prepping for a job.

Pockets had very little art or painting experience, but closely followed Mason's work. Formerly employed as a stock person at a local grocery store, he lost his position when the family owners retired. Thereafter, Pockets performed various jobs, each less interesting than the previous one. That's when he approached Mason about working as an assistant. Pockets described himself as a fast learner, and he didn't disappoint. Not involved in a romantic relationship also allowed Pockets to willingly work whenever, wherever, and for as long as Mason needed him.

Mason candidly described the lack of gratification the position brought: cleaning equipment, mixing paints, rigging airbrushes, base-coating walls, and performing other menial tasks. Pockets didn't mind. As Liam and Mason grew closer to Pockets, they discovered he rarely had a problem with anything. He went through life at his own pace, taking each day as it came.

Pockets' most endearing quality, a heart of gold, was evident in schools where Mason painted the majority of his murals. Pockets acquainted himself with the staff and parents, and related incredibly well to the students. He patiently answered their questions and enthusiastically discussed with them the artistic symbolism present in the designs. He also discreetly diverted the students' interest away from Mason when Mason needed to detail a section of the mural.

Pockets once aspired to be a teacher, but admitted he lacked the book smarts to make it through college. It's a shame, because he would have made an excellent one. He frequently described to the children how an airbrush worked, once he learned how to operate it himself, and demonstrated how to use it on their hands. They always found it cool to have a painted tattoo to show off to friends, siblings, and parents.

Pockets and Mason worked extremely well together and shared the same philosophy regarding children. Although it sometimes hindered the overall schedule, spending extra time with them played an essential part of the art service. Oftentimes, a young individual needed an impartial adult to confide in during a difficult time of their life. Besides offering guidance and conversation, Mason and Pockets taught the students that art was more than just paint covering a wall.

* * * * *

Pockets strolled to the sliding door, whistling and twirling his car keys. He rapped on the glass loud enough for Mason to hear.

"It's open!" Mason shouted from the bathroom.

Pockets entered the apartment, shaking his head at the miscellaneous piles in the living-dining area and the mound of dirty dishes in the kitchen. "Hey, Mason. Are you ready?" Pockets carefully navigated his way to the hallway, stopping in front of Mason's studio.

"Almost done shaving."

Pockets stepped into the art room. It, too, was cluttered with a small air compressor, paint supplies, airbrushes, paint cans, etc. Furnishings included a messy desk, a drawing table, shelves, and a cabinet with knickknacks, used baseballs, and childhood toys. Near the far corner was an easel with a partially-completed canvas painting. Colored doodles covered the wall to the left of the easel where Mason tested his airbrushes after changing colors.

Pockets approached Mason's drawing table. He peeked over his shoulder at the doorway, leaned above the table, and gently pulled open his shirt pocket.

"Are you looking for something?" Mason asked from the doorway.

Startled, Pockets quickly stood erect, fumbling to button his pocket. "Uh, yes," Pockets replied hesitantly before raising Mason's keys from the table, "your keys…of course."

"That's where I left them. What would I do without you?"

"Difficult to say." Pockets tossed the keys to Mason. "Are you ready to head to the school?"

"Let me grab a quick bite to eat. You want anything?"

"No thanks, I already ate."

In the kitchen, Mason searched the cabinets for a clean bowl. He selected a small mixing bowl from the cupboard, emptied the last bit of cereal from the box, crumbs and all, and reached into the refrigerator for the near-empty jug. "Darn it! I forgot to buy milk last night." Mason slowly drizzled the residual liquid over the contents, trying in vain to make it fill the entire bowl.

"You realize that won't work," Pockets laughed.

"It was worth a shot." Mason poured himself a tall glass of juice to help wash down the dry cereal.

"Will we finish the mural today?"

"That's the plan."

"Those kids will miss us after we leave."

"They usually do." Mason ate the last spoonful, smug that he had a tiny amount of milk left.

"It is different this time," Pockets added.

"Why?"

"Most students and teachers generally acquire a changed perspective after you paint a mural. School spirit is lifted and your symbolism has a positive effect. The impact has not been the same lately. I've observed over recent jobs that a number of students and staff have developed negative attitudes."

"I guess I haven't noticed it quite as much as you." Unable to rinse his glass and bowl due to the precariously stacked dishes in the sink, Mason set them on the counter alongside the overflow.

"I have also seen this negative attitude outside the schools," Pockets added.

"In what way?"

"Things have been progressing smoothly since the Treaty went into effect. I realize certain individuals had difficulty transitioning, but they willingly made sacrifices necessary for us all to continue living on this planet. Lately, it seems that a fair amount are reverting to selfish attitudes prevalent before the war."

"I can't dispute that." Mason grabbed his phone and keys on the way to the door. "A lot of good things are happening."

Pockets was already outside. "That is true. I am not saying every person is changing, but it seems to me that the number of those with negative attitudes is increasing."

"To paraphrase Liam, you can always find a silver lining," Mason offered as he drove out of the parking lot. "Sometimes you must search a little harder. What keeps us all going are the positive attitudes. We survived the war because the majority wanted it to end and they honestly believed things could change."

"Your brother's influence is apparent in what you're telling me, but what I'm seeing concerns me. All I ask is that you pay closer attention and tell me if what I have described is true or not."

"Absolutely." Mason changed the subject. "Did you order—"

"Two gallons of clearcoat, right?"

"Yep."

Mason steered into the school lot and parked the van in the only available spot, farthest from the primary entrance. He hopped out and was ready to close the door when Pockets jingled the keys.

"Right, I may need those. Thanks."

"Hey, Joe," Mason cordially greeted his art supply rep who was impatiently waiting at the main door.

"I wish you guys would place bigger orders in the future," Joe admonished and thrust two gallons of clearcoat at Pockets. "It's hardly worth my effort."

Before Mason responded to the unexpected outburst, Joe marched to his car. Mason and Pockets exchanged dumbfounded expressions.

"Man! What's up with him?"

"See what I mean, Mason?"

"Totally. Joe is one of the friendliest guys around, even after a tough day."

They entered the school during passing period. Students swarming through the halls to their next class welcomed Mason and Pockets with waves or high fives.

"You two missed a good one this morning." Lauren, a senior and student council president, was one of Mason's biggest fans and couldn't wait to impart the latest news. "A nasty fight broke out in the commons. GGB officers came and questioned more than a dozen students."

"Seriously?" Mason inquired. "How did it start?"

"A group of guys sprayed paint on the walls and several baseball players intervened. Bodies flew all over the place. It was really scary. Luckily, teachers and other staff members broke up the brawl."

"Anyone hurt?" Pockets asked.

"No, but we have a play-off game tonight and our best players may not be able to participate."

"That's not good," Mason said.

"Come on," Lauren insisted, "I'll show you the damage."

When they arrived, Mason and Pockets were stunned. Pockets set down the two cans of clearcoat to examine the vandalism. The paint had partially eaten away sections of a brick wall, exposing the cinder block behind it.

"Are you sure they used paint?" Pockets extended his hand.

"Don't touch it!" Mason yanked Pockets' arm away from the wall. "If it's wet, it could eat right through your skin."

"Thanks." Pockets stepped back. "Even after working together this long, I still have a hard time determining if breaks in walls are real or painted by you."

"I assure you, I had nothing to do with this."

"In answer to your question, Pockets, what they used sure looked like normal spray paint," Lauren offered.

"Did the staff confiscate any cans?" Mason questioned.

"No, they disintegrated."

"Disintegrated?"

"When the room cleared out, one teacher discovered only spray can bases and tops on the floor." Lauren glanced at the wall clock. "Holy cow, I need to prepare for my next class, but I wanted to tell you what happened. I'm sure Mr. Barnaby will have a different version. Principals always tend to filter information."

"Thanks for showing us," Pockets acknowledged.

"No problem. I'll swing by the mural later." Lauren scurried off to her locker.

"Pockets, let's get the principal's take on this."

Pockets grabbed the cans of clearcoat, and unbeknownst to Mason, inserted them in his shirt pocket. "That was pretty destructive paint, or whatever it was."

"You're telling me. The scary thing about it is—" Mason paused.

"The scary thing about it, is what?"

They turned right, down the main hallway closest to Principal Mike Barnaby's office.

"The scary thing is, this incident seems familiar," Mason recalled.

"In what way?"

"I remember seeing or hearing about a similar form of vandalism, but I can't remember where." Mason scratched his temple. "Where was that?"

"Maybe your brother knows," Pockets suggested. "We can ask him when he returns from Greece."

"Good idea. Speaking of my brother, what is today?"

"It's Friday, June 2."

"Liam gets home tomorrow. Wait, he gets home today."

"Yes, he does," Pockets affirmed.

"That reminds me." Mason patted his pockets. "Where's that paper with the flight information? I meant to enter it in my phone."

"Not again."

"What?" Mason exclaimed innocently.

"It amazes me the number of things you misplace. It is probably in the van. Practically everything you own passes through your van." Pockets tugged on his shirt pocket. "You need to get yourself one of these."

Mason chuckled and then changed the subject. "Will you stay behind to clearcoat the mural and pack up the supply box?"

"No problem."

"We'll pick it up tomorrow." Mason confirmed, somewhat puzzled.

"What's wrong?"

"Where are the cans of clearcoat?"

"Must you ask?" Pockets inquired amusingly. "The convenience of my pocket never gets old."

"To this day, I don't understand how you fit all that stuff in there."

Pockets simply grinned and kept walking. They reached the main office as Mike Barnaby approached from another hallway.

"Good morning, Mike," Mason and Pockets said.

"Morning, gentlemen. The *good* part is questionable today."

Two GGB officers exited as Mike opened the door.

"Mason, why don't you and Pockets take a seat in my office," Mike requested. "I'll be right with you."

"Sure thing."

Inside Mike's office, the wall décor reflected a high level of school spirit: pennants, framed newspaper articles and photos, awards, etc.

Mike entered moments later, closed the door, and sat behind his desk. "Did you hear what happened this morning?"

"Bits and pieces," Mason replied. "Lauren showed us the damage."

"In all my years of working in the education system, I have never experienced anything like this." Mike leaned back in his chair. "Those kids could have been seriously hurt. What puzzles me most is, it was started by three of our best students. I understand exams are a stressful time, but those kids have never acted like this in the past."

"I doubt testing is the cause of this incident." Pockets could no longer suppress his concern.

"What do you mean?"

Pockets explained what he had shared with Mason about attitudes changing. He also included Joe's earlier incident as another example. Mike didn't find Pockets' observations unusual.

"Come to think of it, a handful of students, and faculty for that matter, have been acting strangely. Why is it happening?"

"Not sure, but we'll pay closer attention to this type of behavior." Mason rose from his seat.

"I will too."

"We expect to finish the mural project today."

"Great. I'll submit your contribution credit by the end of the day."

"Perfect."

Mason and Pockets each shook Mike's hand.

"Thank you, guys. We appreciate all you do here. It's been a tremendous uplift for school spirit and, as always Mason, your artwork is magnificent."

"Thanks, Mike."

"Before I forget." Pockets reached into his shirt pocket and withdrew a large set of photos, books, and other school paraphernalia Mike had lent them to use as references for the mural.

Befuddled, Mike accepted the resources.

Mason shrugged. "Don't even ask."

Mike patted Pockets on the shoulder as they left. "Take care, guys."

Mason had finished all the detail work and touch-ups. He took advantage of various opportunities to say good-bye to students and get their contact information. Roberto wanted to hook up with him over the summer to learn dance moves Mason performed years ago. Lauren briefly visited to invite Mason and Pockets to the upcoming graduation ceremony. Most of all, the kids just came by to compliment Mason on the mural. It was a typical last day for the artist and his assistant.

Mason drove Pockets back to the apartment to retrieve his car. Pockets then returned to the school to clearcoat the mural and pack up the supply box. Meanwhile, Mason found the missing travel information in his van, of course, and drove to the airport.

The view of Lake Michigan and rebuilt sections of the Chicago skyline welcomed Liam home. The sun shone brightly and the temperature hovered in the low seventies.

Liam and Sarah departed the plane and navigated through customs. Unfortunately, she had another long flight to Oregon.

"Thanks for accompanying me, Sarah. I bet Jack and the kids weren't thrilled with your lengthy trip away from them."

"I'd do anything for you, Liam. And even though I missed them dearly, I benefited from the break too."

"Have a safe trip and call or text me when you get home."

"I will."

They shared a warm embrace. Sarah backed away and eyed Liam.

"What is it?" Liam inquired.

"You seem different than when we first left, in a good way."

"I feel better." Liam smiled. "The time away was therapeutic."

Sarah reciprocated the smile and proceeded to her gate.

Speculating as to whether his ride had promptly arrived at the airport, Liam strolled to the baggage claim area and phoned Mason. "Hey, are you close by…on your way to arrivals." Liam glanced at the exit doors. "Perfect. I'll be standing on the second median. See you in a bit."

Talking about the vacation made the ride home pass quickly. Remnants of the war destruction remained visible, but far less than what could be seen immediately after it ended. New buildings and structures were much more abundant and land had been prepared for new parks and recreational facilities— further evidence of human resiliency.

Throughout the conversation, Mason brought up the discussion he had with Pockets pertaining to changing attitudes. He recounted details of his unusual experience with Joe that morning and what happened in the school commons. Liam couldn't blame a distraught Mason, and the situation troubled Mason more after hearing about Liam's encounters with individuals demonstrating similar types of behavior in Greece.

Liam ruled out the possibility of the instances being merely coincidental and hypothesized that the recent chain of events was happening on a global scale rather than just locally. Too many commonalities existed. Attitudes had to remain strong and positive during the sustained rebuilding of the new world. The lack of positive attitudes was one of many catalysts that sparked the war. The return of negativity was not a good sign. It appeared the cycle had begun to repeat itself. But why? Had the implementation of the Survival Treaty run its course? Liam and Mason agreed to gather additional information.

Mason drove into the parking lot of Liam's apartment complex. As part of the healing process, Liam had downsized months earlier, moving out of the house where he and Ashley built most of their life together. Somehow it survived the war, as did the memories.

Uncovering The Secret

It was approaching seven o'clock when Liam arrived at Mason's apartment and sauntered to the unlocked sliding screen door. He let himself in and announced his entrance. "Mason!"

"I'll be there in a minute!" Mason yelled from his bedroom.

Liam set a carefully-packed box containing a vase on the cluttered dining table. Mason navigated the hallway laundry piles as if they didn't exist.

"Hey there," Mason said. "How are you feeling?"

"Better. I power napped after unpacking. The jet lag will eventually subside."

"That's good."

"I like what you've done with the place," Liam quipped. "I hope our books are better kept."

"Believe me, cleaning is on my to-do list. Not sure about the books."

"Those can wait. There's something more important." Liam slid the box closer to Mason. "You'll need to open this first."

Elated, Mason reached for the carton. "For me?"

"It's actually for both of us."

Mason retrieved a dirty knife from the kitchen sink. He eagerly slit the tape securing the flaps, forcing them open. "T-shirts? This is what's so important?"

"Those are mine." Liam removed the shirts encasing the artifact.

Mason lifted the vase out of the box. "Wow. This…is amazing." Amused, he ran his finger over the inscriptions. "Those little guys are cool."

"Have a seat, it's story time."

Eyes fixated on the artwork, Mason set the vase on the table and sat across from Liam who gently plucked the vase from Mason's hands and slid it to the center.

"Right. Story time." Mason had difficulty containing his excitement. "I'm listening."

"I was near the Acropolis…"

* * * * *

Liam and Sarah leisurely strolled through the crowded Plaka, or open market of Athens, enjoying each other's company and mingling with the locals.

"That's interesting," Sarah commented on a Greek clothing shop that caught her eye. "Maybe there's something in there for the kids."

"I pass. Meet you here in an hour. I want to explore the area."

Always curious, Liam was accustomed to wandering off on his own to seek unique attractions. Leaving the crowded streets behind him, he spotted an isolated shop a fair distance from the central activity—an appropriate destination for his inquisitive nature.

As Liam surveyed the interior, he perceived an ambience unlike other Plaka shops. To the left of the door, an old man sat quietly, stirring a concoction in a small, clay bowl. Immersed in the activity, he was outwardly unaware that Liam stood in front of him. Spread out on the table were ancient crucibles sealed with small lids. Liam peeked inside the uncovered ones. From his vantage point, each contained an unidentifiable, colored liquid that he deemed uninteresting. Papers, broken pottery, and miscellaneous knickknacks cluttered the rest of the table.

The old man broke his concentration and focused on Liam above his half lenses. Liam detected an odd, glaze-like substance over the old man's green eyes. Liam presumed it was due to the many years of hovering over those solutions. After shifting looks between Liam and the bowl, the old man cleared his throat and spoke in heavily-accented English.

"I am Demitrius. I was told you would be coming."

"Demitrius? Wait...what? Who told you I was coming?" Liam questioned with paranoia. He had never met that man and it was unlikely they had any mutual acquaintances.

"Who, does not matter." Demitrius rose from his chair. "Come with me."

Liam's initial impression proved correct. That shop was not like any other, yet he followed without hesitation. They walked to the rear of the building, carefully avoiding the stacked crates of trinkets. Once there, they stopped in front of an old wooden door barred shut with a large piece of lumber. Demitrius struggled to lift the board out of the iron brackets, but with considerable determination, he dislodged the beam and set it down behind him. The rusted hinges, which were in dire need of lubrication, squeaked as he opened the door. A cool breeze escaped from the other side, bringing with it a fair amount of dust that scattered the sunlight streaming in from the window to the right. Liam imagined the door had not been opened in hundreds of years, maybe even a thousand. Markedly shorter than Liam, Demitrius strained to reach a lantern resting high on a shelf.

Demitrius lit the wick, increased the flame height, and beckoned Liam to follow him through the doorway onto the dirt floor. Demitrius easily cleared the first crossbeam. Conversely, Liam had to duck six inches to avoid bumping his head and maintain a semi-erect posture throughout the journey. Cobwebs dangled from the ceiling and flanked shelves, becoming entangled in Liam's hair and ears as he trailed Demitrius down a dimly lit passageway. The dusty racks held countless, ancient vases decorated with art or inscribed with Greek writing.

Liam gazed at the endless pottery, perpetually removing the silky strands from his head. Unexpectedly, he felt Demitrius' hand on his elbow. Liam nearly jumped out of his shorts and whacked his head on the low ceiling.

"We must keep moving." Demitrius disregarded Liam's pain.

Liam rubbed his head as he resumed the adventure. "What's the hurry?"

Demitrius said nothing. Although not yet understanding the purpose of the quest, Liam didn't resist his escort's desire to march onward. They walked for some time, allowing Liam to hone his proficiency at brushing away cobwebs.

Liam nearly bowled over Demitrius who stopped abruptly at the final destination. His curiosity heightened as they entered a chamber or sacred tomb. Free of dust and cobwebs, etched stones lined the walls and floor. Demitrius dimmed the lantern. The limited lighting made it difficult to focus on the anticipated attraction in front of them.

Briefly wondering if Sarah was worried about him, Liam made no attempt to leave. Absent a light source to guide him through the darkened passageway, he willingly stayed for whatever it was Demitrius wanted to show him.

Patience was a strong suit of Liam, but the longer they waited with nothing happening, the more that trait was tested. Regardless, they endured the silence inside the dim chamber throughout the lengthy interlude.

Suddenly, a glowing, star-shaped object materialized from the front wall. Liam fixated on the object once his eyes adjusted to the brightness.

It wasn't a star at all, but rather the helmet of Athena, the Greek goddess of war, wisdom, and the arts. Her glimmering headpiece shined brightly above the vase resting on a table. Slightly larger than the ones Liam had passed earlier, that artifact had a crescent moon shaped handle on its lid and the base depicted inscriptions of artists painting a mural. They were the most peculiar artists Liam had ever seen. The nonhuman figures resembled connected liquid drops holding long paint brushes. Seated alongside the artists, a woman strummed her harp. Overseeing the artists and the musician was Athena herself, donned in armor and holding a spear. She wore an expression of peace and contentment.

Demitrius gently rotated and lifted the lid before leaning it against the vase. From the glowing helmet, an intense light beam descended into the artifact. After reaching the contents, the single beam transformed into spectral arches of brilliant colors that burst out of the vase like a miniature fireworks show. Liam finally dropped to one knee as his back and shoulders cramped from hunching over for such a long period of time. As the light beam faded, it carried the helmet impression with it. Demitrius handed Liam the lantern, replaced the lid, and securely positioned the vase under his arm.

Upon leaving the chamber, Liam pondered the significance of what he had witnessed. The vase inscriptions correlated with the art service back home. Mason, a mural artist, listened to music when he painted, and their service logo included Athena. While contemplating that, Liam gagged on a mouthful of cobwebs and smacked his head on a crossbeam. Again, Demitrius ignored him.

Liam squinted as he stepped into the shop, his eyes reacting to the sunlit room. Demitrius sealed the door, extinguished the lantern flame, and led Liam to a nearby table. There rested a bowl of fresh fruit someone had brought out prior to their return. The timing was perfect as Liam desired something a bit more filling than cobwebs. Next to the bowl were two small plates, cloth napkins, and a sharp paring knife. Demitrius set the vase on the table close to his side, and he and Liam sat down to eat.

Demitrius spread the napkin over his lap and carefully picked through the produce. Too hungry to bypass even the bruised fruit, Liam was uncharacteristically not as meticulous as his host. They both ate in silence and savored each bite, consuming every piece except three grapes approaching raisinhood. Demitrius slid the tableware and linen to the end of the table and situated the vase in the center.

Liam had a hundred questions, and as he started asking them, Demitrius silenced the curious visitor by placing his right index finger over his lips.

"I am sure you desire many answers," Demitrius spoke in a serious tone, "but you are not here to ask questions. You are here to listen to, receive, and follow my instructions. Do you understand?"

Liam nodded hesitantly.

"What I am giving you is vital to the existence of the human race."

With that profound opening, he undeniably had Liam's attention.

Demitrius didn't waste time detailing the story of the vase contents. He went straight to the point and revealed specific instructions. "Take this with you and mix eleven drops with each quart of paint your brother uses on his murals."

How did this guy know about Mason, let alone that he painted murals? What are these drops? Why us? Vital to the human race?

As those questions tumbled around Liam's mind, Demitrius sensed the barrage of unspoken inquiries. He gestured with his hands, signaling Liam to listen. Liam trusted the answers would present themselves at the appropriate time as the adventure progressively grew more interesting.

"I repeat, eleven drops for every quart of paint. No more, no less. One drop in the protective coating. No more, no less. The vase contains enough drops for a lifetime of painting." Demitrius handed Liam the vase. "Protect it with your life and follow my instructions. I have done all I can. It is in your hands now."

Liam offered a polite thank you and secured the artifact under his arm. Demitrius resumed his activities at the table where the two first met. A dumbfounded Liam left the shop, contemplating the recent events. Overcome by a strange sensation, he pivoted. The area was barren and the shop had vanished.

* * * * *

"Totally gone?" Mason slid the vase closer, removed the lid, and examined the contents. "Vital to the human race? It looks like plain liquid to me."

"Perhaps, but something must happen when mixed with the mural paint."

"A good puzzle. That's right up your alley." Mason adjusted the angle, allowing more light to shine into the vase. He swirled the substance, seeing nothing that he regarded critical to saving humanity. "I'm sure you'll solve it."

"I will, indeed."

Mason replaced the lid. He and Liam discussed the mysterious liquid for a bit longer without resolution. Liam was tiring but not ready to leave. Effects of jet lag and the actual vacation itself had exhausted him. Only his curiosity about the importance of the liquid to human survival kept him temporarily energized.

"Speaking of puzzles. Come check out my latest artwork."

Leaning upon Mason's studio easel was an unfinished canvas painting. It depicted a gradient blue sky with clouds and a rainbow—the only element Mason added during Liam's vacation.

"What can I add to this? It's very frustrating when I get these creative blocks."

"The good thing is you always overcome them," Liam said encouragingly. "Have you considered your trademark broken wall?"

"That's the block. I want something new and different."

Liam and Mason examined the painting. "The vase," they chimed in unison.

Liam retrieved the artifact and prepared a quart of paint using eleven drops of the liquid. He transferred a small amount into an airbrush bottle and appropriately thinned it with water before handing it to Mason.

Mason connected the bottle to an airbrush and sprayed the wall section displaying the colored doodles. Paint unexpectedly discharged into a wide splatter containing traces of different colors. The clogged airbrush dispersed paint on the wall, the nearby table, and a section of the canvas.

"Seriously?" Mason raised his arms in the air.

Liam snatched a rag from a bin and hurried to the kitchen sink. He wet the cloth, wrung out the excess water, and threw it through the studio doorway to Mason who frantically wiped the spatters off the table. Both disregarded the odd-shaped drops on the wall—tending to the mishap took precedence.

"I don't get it," Mason said. "This airbrush has a new needle and tip in it."

Mason sprayed the airbrush on another area of the wall. This time, the paint flowed smoothly, covering the area evenly. He painted another cloud over the spatters on the canvas, leaned back, and stared at it in anticipation.

"Is that it?" Mason asked, even more befuddled.

"Hmm, no light beam or fireworks. I'm not sure what should happen. And, frankly, I'm too tired to wait around for it." Liam replaced the lid on the vase and sealed the can containing the mixture.

"Maybe it needs to sit overnight." Mason disconnected the airbrush, capped the bottle, and rinsed the airbrush with water. In normal fashion, he sprayed the contents on his pants.

Detecting no distinct differences to the painting, they retreated to the kitchen.

"Do you have enough energy for our meeting?" Mason asked.

"A quick one. I'm not sure how much longer I can stay awake."

"You thirsty?"

"What are my choices?"

Mason opened the door to the refrigerator, shaking his head at the lack of food and beverages. "Grape juice or ice water."

"Juice, please." Liam chuckled as he sifted through the pile of dishes. "Should I wash a couple of glasses?"

"No," Mason laughed, recognizing that Liam was teasing him again about his messy apartment. "I have clean ones in the cabinet. Back to your trip. Did the locals speak much English?"

"Some more than others, but I enjoyed the challenge of conversing with those who didn't. It was humorous at times. We should all work that diligently to communicate, even when we speak the same language. Perhaps it would help everyone understand each other better."

"You'll get no argument from me." Mason handed Liam his juice. "Welcome back!" He clinked Liam's glass.

"It's good to be home." Liam retrieved various tracking logs from the briefcase he had lent Mason while on vacation. "Is everything in order?"

"Not even close," Mason admitted. "Have I ever told you I truly don't like the management responsibilities you handle for our service? I just want to paint."

"More than once. I'll take care of that part tomorrow. Moving on. What is the current job status?"

"Pockets and I are ready for the next mural. We're meeting in the morning to pick up the supply box. By the way, where is the next job?"

Liam reviewed the schedule. "A community center." He handed Mason the project data sheet and the address to enter into his phone.

"Cool. I have great ideas for that one."

"Did you hear that?" Liam whispered after hearing a soft rustling sound.

"No," Mason replied, "what was it?"

Liam held an index finger to his lips. "There it is again."

They both listened and quietly rose from their chairs.

"Now I do." Mason tilted his head.

"It sounds like it originated in your studio."

"Any ideas what it could be?"

"It wouldn't surprise me if it was a laundry mouse," Liam quipped.

"Yeah, right," Mason replied, puzzled. "A laundry mouse?" He eyed the clothes piles in the hallway and covered his mouth to muffle the laughter.

From the studio doorway, they listened intently to some baffling sounds.

"What the heck was that?" Mason whispered.

"It sounds like...little kids giggling. Those must be happy mice."

"Those aren't mice," Mason contended confidently, "but more like cockroaches." He chuckled, amusing only himself.

"Shhhh!"

They strained their ears, trying to pinpoint the exact location of the emanating noises. They had difficulty detecting the location because another, all too familiar sound interfered with the investigation.

"Will you stop wheezing for a minute?" Liam whispered, jokingly.

Mason snorted as he tried to restrain himself.

"Quiet!"

Mason covered his mouth. "Then quit making me laugh."

"The sounds are coming from the easel." Liam reached for the switch. "Keep your eyes in that direction."

"Wait!" Mason tugged on Liam's arm. "We need a weapon." Before Liam responded, Mason hurried into the kitchen and blindly grabbed a utensil from one of the cabinet drawers. He returned with a long, wooden cooking spoon.

"Mom taught you well." Liam alluded to their childhood when, after misbehaving, their bottoms often came in contact with the notorious implement.

"What?" Mason understood Liam's comment when he held up the utensil. He buried his mouth in his hand to muffle his outburst. Mason regained his composure and readied himself by the doorway.

Again, came the giggling sounds.

"On three. One-two-three." Liam flipped the switch, illuminating the studio.

They heard the little creatures scurrying for a hiding place.

"Do cockroaches run that fast?" Mason kept up with the jocular theme.

"Never timed one."

They searched the studio, but found no immediate trace of the intruders.

"This is bizarre, Liam."

"Not as bizarre as that." Liam pointed at the wall where the airbrush spattered. "Do you see anything?"

Mason examined the wall. "Nothing except my doodles."

"Exactly! The droplets are gone!"

"Holy cow. I only washed off the table. Liam, what's happening here?"

"No clue, but you better clean soon. Maybe dirty apartments are the feeding grounds of these creatures," Liam teased.

"I have the easy part."

"What is more cumbersome than cleaning your apartment?"

"If the liquid has anything to do with the noises we heard and the paint falling off the wall, you better solve this puzzle fast. That's all we need is to have my murals disappear."

"Believe me, I will solve this mystery. Check the carpet under the doodles." Liam was desperate for answers. "Maybe the spatters dried and fell to the floor."

Mason knelt, rubbed his hand near the baseboard, but only felt the carpet. "This is where the droplets would have fallen and nothing's here." Mason showed Liam his dust-covered hand.

Liam gently shook his head.

"What?" Mason inspected his palm. "I'm definitely cleaning tomorrow."

"There's something on your desk." Liam cautiously inched closer.

Mason jerked up his head, banging it on the easel support. "Ow!"

They heard giggling, only more prominent that time. Mason rose from the floor, rubbing his head with one hand and assisting Liam with the other. Again, they uncovered nothing.

"They are neither mice nor cockroaches," Liam stated the obvious.

"What are they?"

"Sly little devils with a keen sense of humor."

Mason raised his brow. "Kind of like you, huh?"

"Exactly," Liam responded proudly. After clearing the entire desk and finding no traces, he was in no mood to play hide-and-seek. Liam thrust his hands in the air. "I'm outta here."

"Wait…you can't leave."

"I'm exhausted and can hardly think straight. And I still have to drive home. We'll finish our meeting tomorrow."

Mason followed Liam out of the studio and switched off the lights. "What about those bugs or whatever they are?"

"Did you sleep all right last night?"

"Yeah, why?"

Liam organized the papers on the dining table. "They were probably here, and you slept fine."

"Yeah, but I didn't know they were here."

"For someone who, as a kid, used to sleep in a dingy crawl space fort, you're a bit squeamish in your old age." Liam inserted the papers in his briefcase and the T-shirts in the vase box.

Mason shut the double doors, thinking it would keep the creatures from visiting the rest of the apartment. "What time are you coming over tomorrow?"

"I'll call you before I do."

"On second thought, I better call you after Pockets and I load the supply box."

"Works for me." Liam carefully avoided the scattered piles on the way to the door. "Sleep tight and don't let the bedbugs bite."

"Thanks a lot. Later."

The little fiasco in his studio actually motivated Mason to clean. He switched off his cell phone to avoid distractions and meticulously tidied the front rooms and tended to the dishes. His apartment appeared livable again.

On his way to the bedroom, he listened outside the studio doors. He heard more rustling sounds. *Great idea, Mason. I should sleep real well tonight.* Mason switched off the lights in the main living area and flipped on the hall light to avoid tripping over the clothes piles. "Tomorrow is definitely laundry day."

Setting The Trap

The next morning Mason awoke and rolled out of bed, yawning as he dragged himself to the bathroom for a shower. On the way, he verified that the studio doors were still closed. A slight chill ran down his spine as he imagined a million bugs crawling over his paintings and art supplies.

Mason's stomach growled in anticipation of breakfast. He quietly passed the studio doors on his way to the kitchen. Smiling at his newly cleaned living space, he listened to a new voice message from Pockets.

"Hey, Mason. I sealed the mural and the supply box is ready to load tomorrow. I'll meet you at ten, but call me if that doesn't work. Hope you arrived at the airport on time. Later."

"Of course, I was on time," Mason muttered.

It was 9:10 a.m. and Pockets would be arriving soon. Mason heard a muffled thud from the studio as if something had fallen. He had no more patience for his new residents. "That's it! You bugs are dead!" Mason dashed to the studio and swung open the doors.

"All right you little—" His jaw dropped. "What...the...heck?"

His painting had been altered. Initially, he grew angry, convinced someone had played a joke on him. *Who could have come in after Liam left, and why would they break into the apartment to change my painting?*

Mason closely examined the artwork. "This is cool."

The top right corner of the canvas drooped, having been detached, and there was a long tear across the middle. Visible through both openings, but actually painted on the wall behind the easel, was outer space with nebulas and a moon. However, from his angle, it gave the illusion that it was part of the artwork. The painting also exhibited a border resembling granite around all four edges.

Inspired, his mind swarmed with new ideas and he instantly resolved to incorporate them in future murals. Mason also noticed most of his paint brushes missing from a small storage can. Brush handle sections had been partially cut off and scattered across the carpet. He picked up one remaining modified brush from the floor. Everything else appeared to be in place and the windows were locked shut. He exited the studio to call Liam, wondering what made the noise he initially heard. Mason waited for Liam to answer while he observed the studio, clueless as to what was in there.

"Hey, what's up?"

"Get over here right away," Mason insisted as he twirled the brush between his thumb and forefinger before setting it on the counter.

"Aren't you meeting Pockets at ten?"

"Picking up the supply box can wait. Stranger things occurred last night after you went home. I'll explain it when you get here."

"I'll be right over."

On the drive to Mason's apartment, Liam reflected on his experience with Demitrius, the importance of the vase, and the missing drops from the wall. The meaning of it all still eluded him.

Pockets and Liam arrived simultaneously. Liam hurried out of his truck and Pockets casually stepped out of his car.

"Hi, Liam. Where's the fire?" Pockets asked light-heartedly.

"Mason's apartment."

"Oh, no!"

"Wait!" Liam grabbed Pockets' sleeve, realizing Pockets had taken him literally. "Pockets! There's no fire!"

"Huh?"

Liam released Pockets' shirt. "You have no idea what this is about, do you?"

"Not at all. Mason and I are picking up the supply box today."

"Hurry up!" Mason beckoned impatiently from the screen door.

They followed Mason into the studio. Standing just inside the doorway, Liam and Pockets reacted similarly. "You finished it," they complimented him.

"Very creative, Mason," Pockets added.

"I didn't do it."

"Who did?"

"I have no idea." Mason approached the painting. "It was like this when I came in here, just before I called Liam."

"Perhaps it's a matter of what rather than who," Liam conjectured.

"Will someone apprise me of the situation?" Pockets inquired innocently.

Liam briefly explained what he shared with Mason the previous night.

"Interesting," Pockets responded definitively. Nearing the studio doorframe, he neglected to see a baseball lying on the floor in his path. "Whoooa!"

Up in the air he went. Liam and Mason instinctively attempted to brace Pockets' fall, but they were thwarted by a ladder sliding out of his shirt pocket. He crashed to the floor with a loud thud. More items emerged from the inscrutable pouch. In all, the ladder, six airbrushes, a ten-foot air hose, a rolled-up extension cord, a bucket of rags, a six-pack of pop, and a Stumpf Fiddle had scattered onto the floor. Liam and Mason knelt beside Pockets.

"Are you all right?" Mason asked.

"Give me a minute," Pockets replied, dazed.

Liam handed the items to Pockets who returned them to his shirt pocket. "How do you—never mind."

From the beginning, Liam and Mason noticed nothing outwardly strange about Pockets' enigmatic shirt pocket. It didn't bulge, as one would expect, with everything he accumulated. Although intrigued by the physical impossibility, they grew to accept his uncanny ability of storing things. For personal reasons, Pockets simply didn't like discussing it, and he usually responded tersely when asked questions about it. Respecting his privacy, Liam and Mason promised him they wouldn't pursue the mystery.

"Wait a second. Is this Dad's Stumpf Fiddle?"

"The one and only," Mason replied. "Sometimes I share stories with the students about him playing this obnoxious noisemaker. Of course, they never heard of the instrument. I have Pockets carry it so I can show them."

"I haven't seen that thing in years."

"I came upon it in an old chest after Dad's passing." Mason held up the baseball. "This…is what fell off the top of the cabinet."

A chorus of child-like giggles emanated from around the studio.

"Was me tripping on that funny?" Pockets asked, somewhat annoyed.

"We weren't laughing," Liam and Mason replied defensively.

"Who was?"

"It shouldn't be hard to find them. I found a partially-cut brush on the carpet when I came in here earlier." Mason eyed the kitchen counter from the doorway. "No way! Where is it?"

"What's wrong?" Liam inquired.

"I don't believe it. They must have swiped the paint brush off the counter when I waited for you guys at the door." Mason scanned the studio. "Smart little buggers. That's the only time I took my eyes off this room."

More giggles were heard. Further evidence that their jocular sense of humor was more like Liam's.

"Clearly they're very intelligent," Liam concluded. "We need to beat them at their own game and I have an idea how to do it."

"Which is what?" Mason asked.

"Not here. I bet they understand what we're saying." Liam assisted Pockets to his feet. "Let's go to the dining table."

Mason closed the studio doors. To further prevent the critters from listening to the conversation, Liam texted Pockets and Mason instructions describing how to capture the unseen invaders. Pockets' task was to pick up a critical supply.

"I'll be back in a flash." Pockets proceeded to his car.

Mason read and understood his role as the one who would ultimately set the trap. "Seems easy enough."

"Perfect. I have to run some errands. Call me when something happens."

"Will do." Mason kept his eyes focused on the studio doors as he waited for the key component.

Pockets hadn't been gone long before he returned. "It was the last one." He handed a can of ultra-sticky adhesive to Mason.

"This should be more than sufficient." Mason removed the label, presuming the critters could read too.

"Pick up the supply box tomorrow?"

"Definitely."

"See you then," Pockets said as he left. "Good luck."

"Thanks."

Mason selected his favorite painting music. He set the spray adhesive can on his art supply cart next to the easel. From under the table, he withdrew a new canvas to replace the painted one. Mason mixed the necessary colors and airbrushed the border first. He purposely created a modest design—a painting fit for a trap, not a gallery—that included a broken wall with a blue sky and clouds. Mason heard faint "ooohhhs" and "aaahhhs" reminiscent of a fireworks show, but resisted the urge to peek over his shoulder.

It was a quarter past twelve when Mason stepped back from the canvas, pleased with the end product. He grabbed the adhesive can and removed the cap. Simple as it was, he wanted to enhance the painting, as his hesitation demonstrated. Remembering the objective, he added the final touch.

The canvas completely saturated, Mason chuckled at the faint coughing sounds. The creatures apparently didn't like the odor or the over-spray.

Mason replaced the cap on the can. He had fulfilled his role in the plan and could do nothing more than wait. Leaving the studio, he tightly secured the doors closed. His pinging stomach reminded him that he needed to eat lunch and buy groceries. That would help pass the time rather than idly sitting in his apartment awaiting the capture. He grabbed his keys and wallet from the dining table and out the door he went.

Mason would have returned home sooner, but he stopped after lunch at a nearby park, shot a few nature photos, and spent the afternoon talking with local children. They recognized him because he had painted a mural in their school that spring. He wanted to visit longer, but curiosity about the trap overcame him, and he still had to shop for groceries.

He arrived at his apartment at a quarter of seven, unloaded the van, and carried the bags into the kitchen. Eager to see if the intruders had taken the bait, he quietly opened one studio door just enough to get a glimpse of the canvas. He closed the door when he noticed nothing different.

Mason put away the groceries, except what he needed for dinner. While eating, he listened to his music and thumbed through an old art journal, shaking his head at a piece of art he didn't like or quietly expressing his appreciation for another. Periodically, he glanced at the studio doors, wondering if the trap had been successful.

After dinner, he rinsed the dishes and set them in the sink, demonstrating how his apartment soon reached its former state of disarray. The growing piles would eventually take over his living space.

Mason switched off the music. The silence gave way to a chorus of indistinct noises and more distressed than what he previously heard. He proudly smiled at the possibility of a victorious capture.

His palms sweating, Mason cautiously approached the studio, unsure what to do next. *Did we catch them? What will we do with them? Should I call Liam? Pockets? No, the critters might escape if I do.*

By the time Mason had reached the doors, the creatures' voices expressed panic. He wanted to believe they were stuck to the canvas but he needed to confirm it. He opted not to open the doors to avoid the possibility of scaring them away if they weren't trapped. Instead, he peeked through the narrow gap between the doors. Only darkness stared back at him.

He considered his options. *The windows.*

Mason slowly slid open the screen door, preventing any loud, startling noises. Once outside, he lowered himself to his belly and stealthily crawled to the studio windows. His heart pounded and his chest tightened as he heard himself wheezing. Upon reaching the first pane of glass, he slowly raised his head up to the window sill.

"Mason?" a voice called from behind him.

"Ahh!" Mason nearly wet his pants as he collapsed on the ground. His heart pounded faster as adrenaline raced through his body.

"Mason, is that you?"

"Yes, it's me." Mason calmed himself, rose to his feet, and recognized his short, silhouetted neighbor. "Hey, Paul."

"Why are you peeking through your own window?"

Mason chose not to reveal the truth. "I stepped out for a bit of fresh air and forgot my key card to the building. I was hoping I had left a window open."

To say that perception was not one of Paul's strengths was a severe understatement. Had it been, he would have noticed Mason's open screen door.

"Come on. I'll let you in through the main lobby."

"Thanks, Paul."

Mason intentionally positioned himself between Paul and the screen door, blocking his neighbor's view. They both walked in silence—Paul inept at idle conversation and Mason preoccupied with his uninvited guests. Arriving at the vestibule door, Paul unlocked it with his key card.

Inside, Paul retrieved his mail, and they both entered the hallway leading to the apartments. Reaching his door first, Mason inconspicuously turned the knob, hoping it was unlocked. It wasn't. He waited for Paul, who lived directly across the hall from Mason, to enter his apartment.

"Well?" Paul asked.

"Well, what?"

"Are you going inside?"

"Not yet." Mason folded his arms and tilted his head upward. "I'm getting an inspiration and I don't want to lose it."

"Can I watch?"

"Paul, you can't watch inspirations."

"Why not?"

"Paul, if you keep talking, I'll lose this one."

"Oh, yeah, uh, sorry, Mason." Paul opened his door. "Good night."

"Later, Paul, and thanks for letting me in."

"No problem."

The door to Paul's apartment closed. Mason held his position, remembering Paul's strange admission once that he always looked out the peep hole after entering his apartment. After a ten-second count, Mason bolted out the exit.

Seconds later, he returned to the spot where Paul discovered him. He lowered himself on his hands and knees, crawled to the window, and raised his head to the window sill. He hoped the creatures were trapped and the moonlight shone bright enough to get a glimpse inside the studio. As he scanned the room through the glass, his heart rapidly pounded and his wheezing intensified. Sweat drops trickled down his forehead and his palms moistened. His eyes focused on the easel.

"Mason?"

"Ahhhh!" Mason nearly jumped out of his shorts this time.

"Is that you again?"

Mason knelt as he composed himself. "Yes, Paul, it's me, and will you stop sneaking up on me?"

"Sorry. Did you lock yourself out again?"

"No, I lost something from the first time I was out here." Mason decided to ask the questions to squelch Paul's nosiness. "Why are you out here, Paul?"

"I forgot to bring the shopping bags into my apartment."

"Is that all?"

"That's it. Do you need help, Mason?"

"No, I found what I lost. Thanks anyway."

Mason's rapid heart rate subsided. He darted into his apartment before Paul could follow him. Peeking from behind the closed blinds, Mason watched his neighbor back away from the passenger side of his car with arms full of bags.

"Mason, you should—" Paul said before noticing Mason was no longer there. "Boy, I can never keep up with that guy."

Mason waited for the vestibule door to slam shut and used the sound as his cue to resume his investigation. Back on his hands and knees, he crawled over to the window, glancing over his shoulder to make sure Paul wasn't behind him. Raising himself a little higher, he cupped his hands around his eyes and peered inside the studio. The moonlight provided minimal illumination as Mason shifted his eyes to the side of the canvas facing the window. His eyes adjusted and immediately focused on movement in the upper right-hand corner.

"What is that?"

The Dropas

Mason was awestruck at the unidentifiable creature, the only one visible from his position. To distinguish the features of the tiny life form, more than the scant moonlight was necessary. He detected the figure was stuck to the canvas, empathizing with it as it struggled to free itself. Mason searched for others before observing movement on the top edge.

"Bingo." Mason needed to get closer to see more detail, which meant entering his studio and viewing them in the light. After briefly laying eyes on the unanticipated visitors, his feeling of attachment grew immensely. He felt compelled to free the captured one, if it would allow him to get close enough.

Forgetting where he was, Mason jumped up and away from the window. His body veered from its intended path as he flipped over the bushes bordering the apartment. Instinctively, he braced for impact. Accompanied by another adrenaline rush, flashbacks of his dancing days filled his mind. Only his experience saved his face from reconstructive surgery because the walkway awaited him on the other side of the foliage. His hands met the concrete first, absorbing the initial force. Arms bent, but only far enough that his thin, straight hair barely touched the unforgiving surface. With his face only inches away from kissing the sidewalk, his arms pushed up in spring-like action as his torso and legs thrust upward into a familiar handstand. Mason steadied himself while his hands maneuvered along the pavement.

"Mason?" A man called from the darkness.

The unexpected, yet familiar voice caused Mason's arms to buckle, but he skillfully maintained his balance. The man inched closer, and Mason recognized the distinctive red sneakers.

"Yes, Paul, it's me."

Paul knelt, lowering his face near Mason's. "Why are you walking on your hands?"

"I was—"

"Don't tell me. You had another inspiration and wanted all the blood in your head to help you remember it, right?"

Mason let his feet drop to the ground and established an upright position, his head throbbing as he felt the blood flow out of it. Both that and the accompanying lightheadedness subsided.

Mason played along. "That's very perceptive of you, Paul."

"You're an artist, and artists are strange, uh, unique individuals."

"Is that right?" Mason scraped away stony fragments embedded in his palms as he and Paul strolled to Mason's apartment. He had to get rid of Paul and assist the tiny captives.

Paul attempted to impress Mason with his art knowledge. "Did you ever read about Van Goff cutting off one of his fingers?"

"It was Van Gogh, and he cut off his ear."

"Van Goff, Van Goof, the name's not important. What matters is, cutting off your foot is abnormal behavior."

Mason resisted correcting Paul a second time. He slid the screen door, careful not to open it too wide, and entered his apartment with Paul right at his heels. "I'd like to chat about artists all night with you, Paul, but I need to get my work done." Mason glided the screen door closed.

Expecting to follow Mason inside, Paul's face pressed up against the wire mesh. "That's okay. After living next to you all this time, I recognize when you get an inspiration and understand you prefer to paint it pronto."

"Later, Paul."

Paul withdrew his face. "Good night, Mason."

Mason felt bad ditching Paul. He was a nice guy, despite rarely making sense, but Mason had to tend to the urgent matter at hand. He secured the glass door shut to prevent Paul from disturbing him again. The last time he left it unlocked, Paul entered the apartment, stealthily walked up behind Mason, and watched him cut frisket film. Paul commented on the artistry, resulting in a six-inch slit in the canvas. That incident prompted Mason to always secure his doors when engaged in anything requiring concentration.

Mason darkened the apartment and waited for his eyes to adjust before entering the studio. Slowly he turned the knob on the left door, careful not to startle the creatures. He sensed panic in their voices and felt remorse with his involvement in their capture, wondering if he had hurt the little guys. He gently pushed open the door. The miniature silhouettes scurrying across the top of the canvas caught his eye first, but they paid no attention to his entrance.

Mason flipped the switch. Even with the lights on, the life forms remained oblivious to his presence. Able to distinguish one from the other, he stared in awe at the painting.

Five creatures adhered to the canvas, each a bright, solid color: red, black, blue, white, and yellow. Each one's head and torso were proportionately sized—the latter larger than the former—and shaped like two water drops connected at the points. Their smooth, shiny bodies measured one and one-quarter inch tall with arms and legs each the width of a toothpick. They lacked fingers and toes, but when open, their hands resembled mittens capable of grasping as two of the five creatures held paintbrushes. Mason was unable to distinguish eyes, ears, a nose, and a mouth, yet they possessed human-like senses as speculated earlier.

He shifted his concentration to four additional creatures jumping up and down on the top edge, all different colors than the ones stuck to the artwork: orange, green, indigo, and violet. He associated the nine pigments with the spectrum plus black and white.

Mason inched closer to the canvas. The creatures showed no interest in him. The life forms atop the painting lined up in a peculiar fashion. The green and orange ones stood side by side, but the violet and indigo ones maintained a greater distance away from the other two. Mason detected another tiny figure, but it appeared to be suspended in the air without arms or legs. Craning his neck to bring his face within a foot of the "floating" body, he discovered why. The light reflected off a tenth, virtually transparent creature. That one seemed much calmer than the others, possibly the leader.

The transparent one waved its arms, motioning for others to hurry and confirming Mason's leadership assumption. To his left, a silver and a gold creature dashed across his desk carrying paintbrushes. They approached from the can of mineral spirits, intending to wash away the adhesive from the feet of the ones stuck to the canvas.

Rather than calling Liam, Mason elected to watch the gold and silver ones scurry to the edge. Without slowing down, they leapt from the desk and attached themselves to the left side of the canvas. They tended to the blue creature first, one of the two others holding a paintbrush. As the life forms executed the elaborate escape plan, they disregarded the lone onlooker. With precise and deliberate actions, they performed the next step. The blue creature raised its brush to the canvas top and extended it to the green, orange, indigo, and violet critters. They in turn grabbed the free brush end while the transparent one monitored the rescue. Simultaneously, the silver and gold rescuers, with bristles loaded with mineral spirits, carefully brushed around the blue creature's feet, whereby the others lifted it off the canvas. Next, they raised the white one to the top in the same manner. The creatures then lowered brushes down to the yellow and black ones as the silver and gold life forms acquired more solvent.

Paint streaked down the canvas from where the thinner had been brushed. Mason ignored it and instead focused on the intricate escape act. The silver and gold ones positioned themselves on the drawing table just to the right of the canvas, executed deft brush strokes, and freed the yellow and black creatures. One to go: the red one.

The silver and gold creatures ran for a final load of mineral spirits, while the others performed an incredible acrobatic feat. The life forms at the top lowered each other close to the red one attached to the middle. Each held onto the other's feet while the bottom one extended a brush. The black one, holding yet another brush, climbed down the other four until it dangled from the brushless end of the first brush with one hand and extended the second brush with its other hand. Preparing for the next step, the yellow, green, and white creatures had run down to the canvas support bar and climbed on each other's shoulders. The silver and gold creatures scaled the bottom three creatures where they intended to perform their brushing assignment.

Short of reaching the red one, Mason decided to assist the little guys. He lifted a brush from the holding can, dipped it into the mineral spirits behind him, and carefully stroked around the red one's feet. Oblivious to Mason's presence, the escape team at the top didn't expect the red creature's premature release as they tugged vigorously on the brush handle. The black and red life forms catapulted over the others. Losing their grip, they emitted high-pitched noises as they splattered against the wall behind the canvas. The creatures on the top and bottom of the canvas all giggled at their companions' misfortune. Soon after they splattered, the red and black ones reformed into their original shapes. Seconds later, they all reunited atop the canvas around the transparent one, dancing and jubilantly flailing their arms in the air. Refraining from the celebration, the transparent one focused on Mason.

Aware of Mason's presence, the violet creature gibbered a munchkin-like "uh-oh" that abruptly halted the celebration. As if they had snapped out of a trance, the others instantly became cognizant of everything around them. The colored life forms scattered themselves throughout the studio. Undaunted, the transparent one offered its right arm as if either greeting Mason or thanking him for his assistance. Mason extended his forefinger, barely feeling the tiny hand as if touching the head of a straight pin. Inexplicably, he understood the creature. It beckoned the others to emerge from hiding and greet their new friend. The miniature visitors bowed in unison.

Mason stepped away from the canvas. The last sound he heard resembled a warning cry. He planted his foot on the same baseball Pockets slipped on, sending him airborne and parallel to the carpeted floor. Everything went dark as Mason landed more on his head than his back. The creatures scurried down the easel to where Mason lay motionless. They reconvened on his chest. Joining hands in a circle, they chanted and danced in a prolonged healing ritual. Unconscious, Mason was unaware of this extraordinary ability.

When finished, and before Mason awoke, the curious critters investigated his face, oozing in and out of his nose and ears and jumping on his lips. Mason slowly regained consciousness and felt weird, tickling sensations in his nostrils. The creatures were too focused on the harmless game of facial hide-and-seek to notice what was happening. Mason sneezed, somersaulting the indigo creature peeking in his nose across his chest and launching the yellow and orange life forms trampolining on his lips straight into the air. The force splattered the latter ones against the ceiling. They instantly reformed and scurried down the walls, rejoining the others who were on their backs giggling uncontrollably with legs kicking in the air and arms wrapped around their bellies.

Mason propped himself against the desk and the twelve creatures ascended his legs to his knee caps. Mason offered his thanks as he flattened his palm, inviting them to climb aboard. He slowly rose to his feet. To prevent further mishaps, he returned the baseball to its original location.

The creatures scurried up his arm and spread out across his head. They swung from his hair or played around his nose and ears.

Amused at the tiny, frolicking guests, Mason phoned Liam. "Mission accomplished."

"We caught them?"

"Yes, but it's not what you think."

"What's that strange noise coming from your phone?"

"No idea." Mason played innocent as the creatures slid down the phone, jubilantly cheering. "I can't explain it. You have to see it to believe it."

"I'm on my way."

Mason texted Pockets to invite him over for the grand introduction.

Twenty minutes later, Liam and Pockets sat at the dining table, eagerly awaiting the event. The studio doors swung open and out strutted Mason carrying a covered cake plate. Attachment to his tiny friends was evident from the meticulously planned spectacle. Mason set the plate in the middle of the table.

"Liam and Pockets, I present to you, uh, the creatures," Mason stumbled, unsure of what to call them, and lifted the cover.

"Wow!" Liam leaned forward. "They resemble the vase images."

Pockets subtly nodded. "Remarkable little creatures."

Mason instructed the miniature guests of honor to form a single line, side by side, with half facing Liam and the other half facing Pockets. The creatures offered their mitten-shaped hands to welcome Liam and Pockets who acknowledged the greeting. Liam enjoyed the pageantry. Pockets seemed oddly at ease. Mason rotated the plate and they repeated the reception.

"No offense, Pockets, but they seem friendlier toward me."

Pockets merely smiled.

"I told them you brought the vase home," Mason said.

"How did they respond?" Liam inquired.

"They were ecstatic." Mason tapped the yellow one on the head with his finger. "I also taught them this welcome ceremony."

"We need to name them something other than creatures." Liam gently pushed his fingertip into the blue one's belly, eliciting a small giggle. "Sounds similar to the Pillsbury Doughboy, but they're obviously not made of dough. It's more like wet paint." Liam examined his index finger. "Although after touching the blue one, I didn't get any on my finger."

"They have the consistency of paint…and resemble paint drips or drops."

"That they do, but calling them drips has a negative connotation, as if they're wimps or weaklings. I do like drops, but we need a more whimsical variation."

Pockets and Mason agreed. The creatures perceived the introduction had ended and engaged in playful activity. Liam twirled two around his forefinger. The miniature circus performers thoroughly enjoyed it.

"Mason, watch this." Liam carefully spun them faster so they didn't lose their grip, and placed them on the table.

The two acrobats struggled to maintain their balance. The other creatures momentarily halted their activities, giggled at their companions, and scaled Pockets' arm. All joined in the laughter as the two disoriented critters sat staring at each other until the dizziness subsided.

"Let's name them the Dropas, with a long 'o' sound," Liam suggested.

"I like it," Mason acknowledged. "What do you think, Pockets?"

"There could be no other name," Pockets declared with strange assurance.

Mason flipped the red one off his forefinger. "That's a cool name."

"Henceforth, we'll call them Dropas," Liam announced formally.

"What about individual names?" Mason asked.

Pockets leaned forward in his chair, but before he spoke, Liam offered a suggestion. "We should call them by their colors."

Pockets sat back with a grin on his face. "An excellent idea."

"I agree." Mason lined up the Dropas. As he called out the names, each one stepped forward and bowed. "Blue–Orange–Red–Yellow–Green–Gold–Black–Silver–White–Indigo–Violet and, uh—"

"Clearcoat," Pockets insisted.

"Of course. And last but not least, Clearcoat."

The three-member audience applauded. The Dropas responded by bowing and then resumed their playfulness. Violet lifted the flap of Pockets' shirt pocket and peeked inside it.

"I'd keep that closed if I were you," Liam cautioned. "Our little friends might fall in and never get out."

Smiling enigmatically, Pockets buttoned the pocket flap. He playfully flicked Violet onto the table with his index finger.

"Can humans go in that thing?" Liam asked half-jokingly.

"No one has yet, but it's possible. Would you like to try?"

"Someday I might take you up on that."

Mason apprised Liam and Pockets of how he encountered the Dropas, highlighting their intriguing fascination with his face and hair. That became more evident as the majority headed for Liam's wavy locks. Red and Yellow opted to take turns using Mason's forefinger as a springboard. Their acrobatic twists evoked cheers from the small, captivated audience.

Red stepped up next. Yellow stealthily followed, making a loud noise just before Red leapt off Mason's finger. The unsuspecting Dropa performed a cock-eyed jump and fell head first onto the table, although not hard enough to splatter. The other Dropas erupted in laughter. Red arose and gently smacked its head, making sure all its "marbles" remained intact.

Six months had passed since the formal introduction. Liam, Mason, and Pockets deliberately kept the Dropas out of the public eye, inconspicuously introducing them to close friends and a select number of students. Because of their inability to explain from where the Dropas originated, they deemed it essential to isolate the tiny foreigners, especially from scientific communities and the GGB who both might consider them interesting specimens to study.

In two weeks, the Dropas would soon enjoy their first Christmas. Like every other aspect of their time on Earth, they had a ball with the yuletide activities. They enjoyed swinging from ornament to ornament on decorated trees, careful not to dislodge them from the branches. They also delighted in running around and playing inside the little porcelain villages. In fact, they loved the Christmas merriment so much, that one night, Liam and Mason brought them to the mall to experience the holiday festivities while picking up their favorite spiced cider.

Indoor malls after the war differed immensely from those before it. Prior to the conflict, they accommodated fifty plus stores, a centralized food court, and were always packed with frantic shoppers overspending hard-earned money. Postwar malls evolved into social meccas, analogous to the forums of Ancient Rome, only the socialization occurred all under one roof. The holidays accentuated these new communal hubs. Decorated for the season, they featured dedicated rooms for various musicians, bands, and choirs who performed befitting music. Food was seasonal and abundant, usually served from small kiosks spread throughout the building.

Liam and Mason strolled into the mall with the Dropas under their coats. They immersed themselves in the crowd and the plethora of Christmas activities, momentarily losing track of the Dropas which was not a good thing. They never knew what kind of mischief their tiny friends might create, but they always discovered it soon enough. Passing by center court, Liam and Mason observed the children anticipating a visit and photograph with Santa Claus.

A blur of movement around Santa's face caught Liam's attention. "They seem captivated with his long white hair and beard."

"That doesn't surprise me. Should we get them?"

"Not yet. Let's see what they're up to with ole St. Nick."

They leaned against a brick planter box, eagerly awaiting the latest episode of *The Dropas Show*. The lightweight Dropas are adept at concealing themselves, usually by blending in with colors in close proximity. A mother placed her little girl on Santa's lap. Expecting an antic, only Liam and Mason witnessed what happened next. A fraction of a second before the photographer snapped the picture, the Dropas yanked down Santa's artificial beard, exposing his face to the camera. Briskly, yet gently, they executed the prank, keeping Mr. Claus and the onlookers unaware of what had occurred. Initially amused, Liam and Mason had to end it before parents received pictures of Santa without facial hair.

"I'll cut in line and retrieve them," Liam said.

"These parents won't be very happy. Most of them have probably been waiting for hours."

"It's better than the alternative. Follow me."

Liam and Mason stepped over the short picket fence near the photographer's booth. They quickened the pace because one of the alert elves pursued with the intent to intercept the perceived troublemakers.

"Hey, you guys can't do that!" the elf commanded.

Liam and Mason had unwittingly stripped Santa of the spotlight. The elf closed the gap to forty feet when they reached the photographer.

"Mason, stall this guy."

"Stall him? How?"

"Any way you can."

Alert to the ruckus, Black and Silver scurried down from Santa's belt. They positioned themselves between Mason and the elf, painted a ten-foot high iron fence, and promptly fastened it to the floor just as the elf arrived. Moving in a blur, the two Dropas painted three adjacent sides, trapping the elf.

"Where did this come from?" The bewildered elf pressed his face against the iron bars of the small cage and unsuccessfully grabbed at Mason.

"Sit tight and make yourself comfortable. We have business to tend to." Mason gave a thumbs up to Black and Silver.

The elf detained, Liam conversed with the photographer. "I must visit Santa."

"Tell that to the hundreds of little kids waiting in line. Aren't you a bit old to be sitting on Santa's lap?"

"Perhaps."

"End of the line is over there." The photographer pointed behind Liam.

"If Santa's face was exposed in the images, would you change your mind?"

"Impossible." Standing in silence and mouth agape, the photographer examined the display on his camera. Mesmerized, he fumbled for the latch and opened the gate to Santa's house.

Liam hurried to the guest of honor, ignoring jeers from the perplexed crowd. "It will only take a second, folks," Liam announced calmly. "Sorry for the interruption." Hearing the Dropas giggling, Liam inspected Santa's beard. "Ignore everything I say, because I'm not talking to you."

"Who will you be talking to?" Santa asked, confused.

"Tiny friends of mine." Liam extended his hand. "I need to grab your beard."

"Hey, wait a minute!" Santa jerked away. "Why?"

"Because you have something in it."

Santa ran his fingers through his long facial hair. "I don't feel anything."

"Do you truly believe I would have gone to all this trouble just for the sake of tugging on your whiskers?"

"Probably not."

"Trust me. It will be quick and painless."

"Yeah, sure, knock yourself out."

Liam heard the familiar "uh-oh." He grabbed the long, white beard and shook it like a dust rag. The Dropas catapulted in the air, somersaulting and twisting. Santa's eyes, as well as those of the spectators, popped wide open as they caught a glimpse of the Dropas for the first time. Liam intercepted two in his hand, but the others landed on the floor or on Santa's suit.

"You guys get up here," Liam ordered.

The Dropas gathered themselves and swiftly ascended the outside of Liam's pants, up his coat, and onto his shoulders. Upon seeing that, Mason released the mental image, which kept the iron confinement real. The cage reverted to paint, covering the elf's face, hands, and clothes. The crowd erupted in laughter as the dismayed assistant contemplated his brief incarceration.

Liam and Mason zigzagged through the crowd who cheered as if they had been entertained by an impromptu magic act. The Dropas also relished the attention, waving to the spectators as if riding in a parade.

"We've had enough excitement for one day. Let's get out of here," Liam said.

* * * * *

Mason first discovered the Dropas' unique talent shortly after meeting them. While painting a mural, the Dropas occupied themselves in and around the supply box. Deep in concentration, contemplating the vanishing point location and forgetting Pockets had left to get lunch, Mason stretched out his arm and requested a level. The tool materialized in his hand.

Moments after drawing the perspective lines, Pockets arrived and asked Mason who lent him the level as he retrieved the original one from his shirt pocket. Confused, Mason lost concentration, resulting in the tool transforming to paint and splattering on the floor. Mason asked the Dropas for another level. Black and White obliged. He forced himself to believe it wasn't real, producing the same result. Essentially, the Dropas could paint whatever they wanted, whenever they wanted, and as fast as they wanted. The painted article converted into a tangible, physical object if the person using it, or the Dropas, completely believed it was real. And the Dropas' ability to preserve the existence of an object superseded any human's mental image. They also demonstrated an ability to clean up paint spills, either with their paint brushes or by absorbing the splattered paint into their bodies like sponges.

* * * * *

Large, falling snowflakes greeted Liam and Mason as they left the mall. Snow riding was the Dropas' favorite winter activity. They'd climb to a high perch, a roof or a tree, and hop onto a snowflake. Some liked riding a single ice crystal all the way to the ground. Others preferred a good slalom, either jumping or swinging from flake to flake. No matter the preference, they had a blast. And Liam and Mason enjoyed watching them, covetous they couldn't participate.

Liam typically limited the Dropas' riding time. Comparable to normal paint, prolonged exposure to cold temperatures adversely affected the Dropas. No matter the period allowed, they welcomed the opportunity to snow ride whenever possible. The Dropas utilized the nearest light post as the launch point. It also afforded ample light for Liam and Mason to view the performance.

Off Liam and Mason's shoulders they sprang and up the post they scurried. Once on top, they'd catch a flake. The absence of any sort of breeze kept them close to the take-off point. Ten minutes later, Liam advised them of one last ride. As each Dropa landed, it immediately ran up to Liam or Mason's shoulders, finding warm shelter underneath the heavy coats.

While waiting for Blue's descent, Liam spotted a car whose driver searched for a parking spot. Blue was in no danger until a small wind gust carried it into the path of the vehicle. Emerging from the coats, the other Dropas blurted out a customary "uh-oh" followed by a chorus of giggles. Liam expected the Dropas to save Blue by painting something, a road barrier perhaps, but they merely giggled. Unable to save Blue, Liam and Mason helplessly watched and hoped the vehicle pulled into a vacant spot before intercepting the descending Dropa. Unfortunately, the row was full, positioning Blue and the car on a collision course. The other Dropas covered their faces. Blue landed and the left, front tire rolled over it, followed by the rear one.

Liam and Mason's hearts sank as they rushed to aid their tiny friend. Upon reaching it, they knelt over the flattened Dropa and fell backwards when Blue suddenly popped up. The other Dropas tumbled onto the slushy pavement, giggling hysterically. It didn't matter how many times an unfortunate event happened to a companion, the others found it hilarious. Liam and Mason partook in the mirth. Blue was paper-thin, three times its normal width and height, and embossed with tread marks.

Anyone watching probably presumed the two men to be a bit crazy, sitting on the wet, snowy asphalt laughing their heads off, but they didn't care. Blue reshaped and waggled its body, drying itself like a wet dog. The Dropas returned to the warmth of the coats. Shivering from the cold, they huddled together and benefited from the body heat.

Inside the van, waiting for it to warm, Liam and Mason reminisced about memorable childhood Christmases.

* * * * *

Throughout the years, Liam and Mason's parents struggled to make ends meet. Their dad worked seven days a week hoping to earn enough income to pay bills and furnish the family with life necessities. Their mom kept everything in order at the house, especially Liam and Mason. No matter the financial burden, Christmases were always special. The boys never saw a house as festively decorated like theirs, many times taking multiple weekends to complete. And Christmas music always played in the background, usually starting when the decorations came down from the attic the day after Thanksgiving.

On Christmas morning, the boys arose early, discovering Santa had arrived while they slept. After quietly sorting the presents into appropriate piles, snacking on goodies left in the stockings, and running out of patience, they awoke their parents for the gift-opening festivity. A large, homemade breakfast followed, consisting of a breakfast casserole, sausage, muffins, and juice. The topic of conversation always revolved around the gifts. Afterward, Liam and Mason dressed in one of their new outfits before riding to their grandparents' house, where a similar ritual took place. And for them, it truly was "over the river and through the woods."

As Liam grew older, the true appreciation of giving embedded in his mind. He cared little about receiving gifts. His true happiness stemmed from celebrating Christmas with family and friends. Liam enjoyed watching each person open the gifts he gave them, whether it was something they wanted or something they needed.

Over the years, commercialization dominated the true Christmas spirit with promotions and advertisements starting in many stores before Halloween or even

Labor Day. Seldom were children taught the meaning of giving, but rather that of receiving, asking for everything and throwing tantrums when they didn't get what they wanted. Until after the war, the true meaning of giving was lost.

* * * * *

Before Mason shifted into reverse, Liam grabbed his arm. "Wait! We forgot the spiced cider."

"Right." Mason released the gearshift.

Returning to the mall would undoubtedly create another adventure with their whimsical friends.

"Do you want me to stay in the van with them?" Liam asked.

"No. I'm certain they learned their lesson. Maybe they'll be too cold from snow riding to get into any trouble."

"Let's go before they warm up completely."

Near the cider kiosk inside the mall, Liam peeked under his coat to check on the Dropas. "Learned a lesson?"

Mason rolled his eyes and opened his coat. "Not again."

"Let's hurry and get the cider. I don't want to come in here a third time."

They each acquired a gallon and retraced their path from the mall entrance.

"Where did they go this time?" Mason inquired.

"I have a pretty good idea." Liam located a small group of food kiosks. "Follow me."

"Where?"

"Think about it." Liam picked up the pace. "They were cold when we came back in here, right?"

"Yes."

"Recall passing anything that would have quickly warmed them?"

"No, not—wait a minute." Mason lifted his nose in the air as he caught the scent of freshly popped popcorn.

Liam and Mason ran to the popcorn kiosk. The Dropas loved sitting on the edge of Liam's popcorn maker, waiting for the kernels to burst. They would catch a freshly popped projectile in mid-flight and soar through the air. However, there was one major difference, Liam's was an air popper. The one in the mall had kernels falling out of a hot, oily pan and was encased with plastic sides. The Dropas would be unable to withstand the heat in that machine. After reaching the intended destination, they saw no signs of the Dropas.

Accompanying a woman's shriek from two kiosks away was an airborne cotton candy ball. They darted in and out of people toward the falling sphere of sweet delight. Liam lifted the candy before anyone else and Mason calmed the woman who had encountered the Dropas. Spinning the stick of cotton candy, Liam discovered what triggered the woman's reaction. Red and Orange were entangled in the sugary strands like flies in a spider web.

"Come on, we have to retrieve the rest of them!" Liam exclaimed.

"Right behind you."

"Hey, my candy!" the woman yelled.

"Follow us, and we'll get you another one," Mason promised.

At the cotton candy kiosk, Liam twirled a paper stick inside the machine. Numerous passes were required to retrieve every Dropa. It was by far their stickiest antic and even Clearcoat engaged in the escapade. Mason explained the situation to the attendant and, true to his word, ordered another treat for the woman.

"This is one way to keep them out of trouble," Liam said.

The Dropas had intertwined themselves such that movement was totally restricted. Mason texted Pockets to meet him at Liam's apartment.

Liam, Mason, and Pockets needed more than an hour to remove the candy threads from the Dropas, but each newly cleaned one assisted with the others. The Dropas apologized repeatedly for the trouble they had caused and vowed to stay away from cotton candy. Liam allowed the Dropas to revel in what they had originally intended to do during the second visit inside the mall. Liam filled the air popper with seeds and switched it on. Lined up along the top edge, the Dropas enthusiastically waited to board a fluffy aircraft. Liam, Mason, and Pockets watched the air show, drinking hot apple cider and listening to holiday music. The evening was filled with Christmas spirit.

Darkened Skies

Winter had come and gone, and spring would surrender to summer in a few weeks. The Dropas had easily acclimated to their new world and formed a strong connection with Liam, Mason, and Pockets. Because they spent the majority of their time with Mason, the bond with him was the strongest. Their mutual love of art played a major role. It was incredible to watch them collaborate. Mason's artwork had progressed to a magnificent blend of color, beauty, and surrealism—revealing his inner soul and visibly reflecting the Dropas' influence.

The Dropas' attachment to Liam and Mason differed from that of Pockets. Liam couldn't substantiate his intuition, but he detected Pockets and the Dropas already had an established relationship. He never questioned Pockets regarding the matter, but he kept his eyes open for more clues. Liam and Mason also desired more information regarding the Dropas—from where they came and their purpose on Earth. Although the two became proficient at understanding Dropa gibberish, the Dropas kept their origin and purpose exclusive.

In addition to his friendship with the Dropas, Mason had acquired a large global following over the past year. Art enthusiasts traveled from around the world to view his murals. As countries rebuilt their infrastructures, they frequently requested his services for the finishing touch in, and around, newly-constructed buildings.

Throughout the first half of the year, Mason's art seemed to be one of the few things fostering optimism. The return of gloom and negativity began while Liam toured Greece, although it likely started before then. That affected a meaningful portion of the population, including some of Liam and Mason's closest friends—the greatest fear was that it could reach pre-war levels. Rumors also spread about the re-emergence of ForLords. If true, it would pose a formidable threat to the GGB and the general population. Frequent, unexplained, and indiscriminate deaths occurred around the world but lacked meaningful correlation with areas where attitudes had changed for the worse.

Over that same six-month period, concerns arose regarding the increased levels of pollutants entering the atmosphere. In recent weeks, a cloud blanket formed around the planet, less than a mile above the ground. Meteorologists ambiguously described the anomaly as an abnormal phenomenon of an unidentifiable impurity and of unknown origin. The covering obstructed the sunlight, adversely affecting the amount of warmth, brightness, and energy that normally reached the surface. Fortunately, the vapor barrier still allowed the penetration of life-supporting rays, although at a reduced level. The gloominess, however, persisted.

Liam arranged a meeting with his best friend and GGB regional liaison, William "Willie" Thompson, to discuss the unusual occurrence. Willie possessed a stature resembling a pro linebacker, making even Liam feel small at times. His intimidating physique oftentimes masked his inherent kindness and loyalty.

They opted for Saturday morning to minimize Willie's typical weekday interruptions. Liam entered through the main vestibule of the GGB building and briefly chatted with the attendant. Overhearing the conversation, Willie awaited Liam just inside his office doorway.

"Good to see you." Willie shook Liam's hand. "Come on in."

"It's been almost a month, hasn't it?" Liam sat in front of Willie's desk.

"At least. May and I have been meaning to have you over for dinner, but I've been swamped with meetings regarding this global cloud cover, among other things."

"Dinner sounds great whenever time permits, but the other things are what we need to discuss."

"Absolutely. I'm glad you stayed on as a GGB special advisor so we can openly address issues like these recent events."

"And be privy to their responses. I never once considered relinquishing the position. I always want to be available if the GGB needs me because I strongly believe in the Treaty." Liam briefly looked out the window. "By the way, what is the latest on this cloud cover?"

"GGB scientists believe it's a result of postwar nuclear fallout," Willie stated dubiously. "Are you kidding me? It's been ten years since the war ended."

"I counter their tenuous hypothesis with one of my own, that maybe it's related to the increased pessimism."

"Perhaps, but how do we prove it?"

"Not sure if we can."

"Here's something that will interest you. Are you familiar with Barrow's Ridge in the Rocky Mountains?"

"Never been there, but I've heard of the area."

"There's been suspected ForLord activity west of the ridge."

"Then the rumors are true."

Emerging evidence showed that ForLords still existed, avoiding apprehension after the war. How many and where they hid remained a mystery. Recent news had spread stating that a ForLord contingent had initiated a movement to recapture the power they acquired during the early stages of the global conflict.

"Appears they're back," Willie asserted. "Based on intelligence information, the ForLords are growing in masses and Barrow's Ridge may be a primary cell. The GGB classified it as a possible central location when large amounts of toxic and ozone-damaging chemicals began disappearing from the inventory of a nearby disposal facility."

"Hmm, mounting pessimism…increased ForLords. Perhaps a brainwashing weapon?"

"That's an intriguing theory."

"There must be a way to fight it, otherwise we would all be brainwashed."

"Most likely, and maybe a finite quantity of weapons." Willie sifted through a stack of papers on his desk. "Here it is." He skimmed through his notes. "The GGB caught a group of ForLords stealing similar chemicals used in the war."

Throughout the conflict, ForLords armed bombs with highly destructive substances. The explosives detonated on impact, dispersing chemical spray and slowly disintegrating everything it contacted. Although effective over a lengthy period, the bombs were less viable weapons in the war because they required too much time to destroy the intended targets. Instead, they were utilized for non-critical structures that didn't necessitate immediate obliteration.

"Any ForLords talk?"

"One named Sam revealed the final destination of the chemicals. Unaware of any operating facility, the GGB dispatched a fifty-man recon team to verify the ForLord's story."

* * * * *

Anticipating a trap, the recon team equipped themselves with immobilizers, the only weapon allowed after the war. Its primary use aided the capture of Survival

Treaty obstructers, mostly ForLord outliers. Immobilizers shot an energy beam that temporarily paralyzed any organic substance it struck. Changing the setting and firing at an immobilized victim reversed the paralysis.

At the site, the investigators encountered a gorge, three hundred feet across and a thousand feet deep, with a shallow chemical-laced stream flowing along the bottom—exactly as Sam had described it. The ravine was not intended to be traversed and conventional methods made it nearly impossible, but the GGB investigators arrived prepared with special equipment to cross it.

The contingent pinpointed a large facade, presumably the front of the facility, two miles from their current position. Using binoculars, they observed no pollutants entering the atmosphere from behind the wall, but heat sensors did reveal gaseous emissions. The pollutants were invisible to the naked eye at normal temperatures, making their origin virtually undetectable.

The seemingly well-prepared investigators separated into four groups of twelve. The last two investigators set up an observation base on the west, or near side of the gorge. They were ordered to assist the other investigators, monitor the events taking place, and report mission details to the GGB.

One lead investigator retrieved a launching gun with a silencer and a box of carbide stakes from his vehicle. Attached to each blunt end of the stake was a long cable. He fired the first stake into the far wall, and anchored the cable to the ground on the near side. He repeated that procedure three times, each cable spaced ten feet apart. Because of the incline from the current position to the far wall, the teams needed motorized trolleys to travel across the cables but could disengage the motor and freely glide back in the event they required an emergency retreat.

Ten members from each team had crossed the chasm when one investigator spotted a squadron of drones flying at them. Sam, the captured ForLord, deliberately omitted those details, and it became obvious why he willingly divulged the location of the facility. He intentionally led them into a trap. The investigators scrambled for cover behind several boulders. Limited by the fixed speed of the trolleys, the eight individuals traversing the gorge were easy targets. The autonomous drones rapidly approached, and the two investigators standing guard had a clear view of the ensuing events. Their report described the drones as having a long, narrow, cylindrical shape, ranging in length from approximately four to twelve feet and no more than two feet in diameter. Each self-guided drone had an aft wing, additional wings on each side, and a dorsal propulsion system. The nose had the appearance of an airbrush nozzle, and the underside carried a multitude of missiles. The seven drones flew in a distinct formation: four four-footers in the front, a six-footer in the middle, and two twelve-footers in the rear.

The drones drew within range of the recon team. Forty immobilizers fired. Composed of inorganic materials, the unaffected aircraft homed in on the defenseless trespassers. The four lead drones zeroed in on the members traversing the gorge. In unison, each aircraft fired a chemical stream at the cable ends and released from formation. They avoided flying beyond the rim, disregarding the two observers. The cables detached, slamming the eight investigators into the near wall. Upon impact, six investigators lost grip of the trolleys and plummeted into the chemical stream. The two who survived the impact shattered every bone in their legs. The excruciating pain ultimately drained the strength from their hands and they slid down the rock face. Momentary screams echoed throughout the chasm as the bodies vanished into the unforgiving waterway.

On the far side, the six-foot drone led the assault, releasing four missiles from underneath its fuselage. The missiles exploded on impact, emitting a deadly chemical spray. Noticeably different than those originally designed for the war, the modified explosives disintegrated targets almost instantly. Unlike the eight who perished in the gorge, the other investigators died a painless death. Those who escaped the first onslaught were met by the twelve-foot drones. Each released six missiles on the initial pass, wiping out the lingering recon members hiding behind the boulders. Other investigators fled from cover in a futile escape attempt, only to be overtaken by the tetrad of four-footers. The pursuing aircraft unleashed a chemical stream shower on the targets, wiping out the fleeing intruders. The six-foot drone made a second pass, releasing another barrage of chemical bombs. In less than a minute, the forty-eight investigators had disintegrated. The drones regrouped and retreated from the battleground, intentionally overlooking the investigators on the near side.

The two survivors helplessly watched in shock. Their colleagues perished before their eyes, yet they were left unharmed. In the report to the GGB, the observation team hypothesized the drones were limited to the boundary of the ravine. Not anticipating an assault of such magnitude, the GGB was stunned when they heard the horrifying details recounted in the debriefing.

* * * * *

Liam was distracted by his cell phone as Willie disclosed the story of the ambush at Barrow's Ridge.

Willie snapped his fingers. "Are you listening to me?"

"I heard every—what's up with this phone? I can't get a decent connection anywhere."

"I've had cell phone problems too."

"Come to think of it...my connectivity issues started around the same time this cloud cover appeared."

"That makes sense, especially since the problem is widespread and worsening. Currently, the interference is only affecting lower frequencies. What are you searching for anyway?"

Frustrated, Liam returned the phone to his pocket. "You previously mentioned ozone-damaging chemicals."

"Yes, the chemicals the ForLords stole."

"This might be unrelated, but search your computer for Leonard von Zonek. That's what I was trying to find."

"Why Leonard von Zonek?"

"Near the end of school last spring, a group of students vandalized a mural where Mason was working. It reminded Mason and me of an artist whose paintings had been sabotaged by chemicals years before the onset of the war. He suffered severe injuries at the event."

Willie entered the name on his computer. "I vaguely remember you telling me about that incident. Here's the event article and a bio. I'll print it off for you." Willie handed Liam the printed copy. "Here you go. I'll read it on my screen."

Liam grabbed a pencil off Willie's desk. "Did you get to the section highlighting his threat to humanity...witnessing pure evil...worse than you can possibly imagine...and to remember his name?"

"Yep. Listen to this. Aside from his fame as an artist, his bio states he was adept with computers and had significant training in...get this...chemistry."

Willie resumed reading as Liam crossed off various letters in Leonard von Zonek's name, revealing an alarming alias.

"Lord Ozone!" Liam shouted.

"The Human Virus!"

"He started the war," Liam deduced.

"You honestly believe they're one and the same? Wasn't he reported dead?"

"Consider the situation. What sensible person presumes, from those threatening statements von Zonek made at his art show, that he will instigate a reign of terror on all humanity because of his destroyed paintings and injuries to himself? The empty threat is exacerbated as nothing happens for years and no one ever hears of him. Along comes the Human Virus, a man with no identity, who acquires access to clandestine information and releases it worldwide. Citizens are outraged. He capitalizes on a public already hostile by the world's current state for which they blame their own politicians. Each nation's government attempts to bring calm to the situation by broadcasting around the world that the Human Virus is no longer a threat, but it's too late, because a tipping point has already been reached. The general populace takes matters into their own hands which leads to the war—von Zonek's depiction of evil. Chemicals ruin his art and seriously injure him. His desire for revenge. Hacking of government computer systems. Dissemination of top-secret information—"

"Chemicals used in the war. Incident at Barrow's Ridge. Emissions from the structure on the other side of the gorge—"

"Increased number of ForLords. Willie...he's alive!"

Willie reached for his desk phone.

Liam grabbed the receiver first. "Not just yet."

Willie peeled Liam's fingers off the phone receiver with his other hand. "Liam, I'm obligated to inform the GGB."

Liam depressed the phone button. "We must be absolutely positive about this before you mention anything to them."

"You're right." Willie returned the phone to its base and resumed reading. "Here's something that may offer more insight."

"What is it?"

"It's an old newspaper article about Leonard when he was a baby."

* * * * *

...was killed in a car accident on the way to the hospital. Leonard never met his father. His mother, Josephine, devastated by her husband's death, attempted a homicide-suicide. She allegedly smothered her infant child, Leonard, with a pillow but only forced him into unconsciousness before taking her own life. When Leonard awoke, he started crying. The von Zoneks' neighbor and good friend, Jennifer Jurgens, heard the prolonged bawling from her garden.

It wasn't like Josephine to let Leonard cry for a sustained period of time. Jennifer dropped her hand weeder and rushed to the von Zonek home to determine what was wrong. No one answered when she knocked on the screen door. She let herself in, followed the sounds of Leonard's cry, and called out her friend's name. When she reached Josephine's bedroom, the distressed infant lay on the bed. She lifted him off the bedspread and held him close to her bosom. Although frightened by the attempted suffocation, Leonard showed no signs of physical harm. Jennifer's recollection of the event follows:

"Where's your mother, Leonard?" she asked, not expecting the infant to reply.
"Josephine! Where are you?"

While comforting Leonard, Jennifer noticed condensation on the dresser mirror due to the vapor flowing out from behind the partially-open bathroom door. "Josephine? Are you all right?"

No answer. She pushed open the door. Steam billowed outward. Protecting Leonard's face with her free hand, she momentarily closed her eyes and tilted her head to avoid the dense cloud. When Jennifer opened her eyes, she saw Josephine lying face down in the bathtub. Water overflowed onto the floor from the running faucet. Jennifer nearly dropped Leonard from her arms as she shrieked in horror.

Startled by Jennifer's scream, Leonard resumed crying. Jennifer laid the infant on the bed and darted into the bathroom, nearly slipping on the wet floor. She raised Josephine's head out of the water with her right hand and switched off the faucet with her left before desperately searching for the chain attached to the rubber stopper. Water cascaded over the side due to the bobbing of Josephine's body. Jennifer yanked on the chain, releasing the plug. As the water drained and eliminated the buoyancy, Jennifer failed to lift Josephine out of the tub.

Jennifer vigorously shook her friend. "Wake up, Josephine, wake up! Come on, Josephine, you can't die on me! Please! Please wake up!"

Unable to medically assist, Jennifer scrambled to her feet and rushed for the phone on the nightstand. Nearly falling, she caught herself on the vanity, but tipped over an empty prescription bottle attempting to regain her balance. She frantically dialed for help.

Hearing a voice, Jennifer shouted, "This is an emergency! My best friend tried to commit suicide! Send help immediately!"

"I'll send assistance as soon as possible, but I need some information first."

"Hurry! I can't do anything to help her!"

"Please tell me the address."

Jennifer tried to compose herself. "Uh. I'm at twenty-four, no, two-forty West Maple Street."

"Two-forty West Maple Street. Is your friend conscious?"

"No! She's not conscious! She's not moving! And she's not breathing!"

"I'll dispatch a medical team, but—"

Jennifer dropped the phone and ran into the bathroom. She leaned over the side of the tub and brought Josephine's hand to her face. Tears flowed down Jennifer's cheeks as she wept over her dear friend. She could do nothing more than wait for the ambulance to arrive...

* * * * *

"What a tragedy," Willie said after reading the article.

"I'll say. Is Jennifer Jurgens still alive?"

"Let me check our database. Jordan...Jurbana. Ah, Jurgens, Jennifer. She is...and she lives an hour from here."

"I say we pay her a visit."

An urgent email opened on Willie's screen. He sighed loudly at the content, shut down the computer, and grabbed his keys.

"What's wrong?"

"The GGB sent a second team to investigate the facility. This time from the south, through a dense forest. They lost all but one member. Guards used chemical weapons from atop the walls. The notification also mentioned tall towers armed with chemical artillery."

"Sounds more like a fortress. Twice now, a compelling message of strength and capability has been sent. I hope the GGB is convinced that the ForLords pose a major threat."

"Come on." Willie closed his office door. "It's time to meet Ms. Jurgens."

Willie parked in Jennifer Jurgens' driveway. The open front door led them to believe that someone was present. Liam suggested that Willie convey his association with the GGB. The majority of residents in each region recognize the name of their liaison, and it wouldn't seem like strangers barging in on her, which is what they were actually doing. Willie knocked on the screen door.

"Anyone home?" Willie inquired when no one answered.

"Maybe she's in the backyard."

Liam and Willie strolled around the side of the house. Jennifer, now an elderly lady with long silver hair in a ponytail, pulled weeds in her garden. She lifted her head as the two men neared. Jennifer slowly rose, dirt clinging to her slacks where her knees rested in the soil. Partially hunched over and clenching a trowel, she greeted them.

"I'm Willie Thompson, your GGB liaison." He presented his identification.

"Oh, yes, I'm familiar with you. Hello, Mr. Thompson."

"Please, call me Willie."

"Okay, Willie, how may I help you?"

"This is Liam Street. He's a special advisor to the GGB."

"Nice to meet you, Ms. Jurgens."

"Oh, this is much too formal. My name is Jennifer." She wiped her sweaty brow with the back of her hand. "What brings you out this way?"

"We'd like to ask you some questions regarding the von Zonek family," Liam replied.

"Oh, I don't discuss the von Zoneks. I'm afraid you've wasted your time driving out here."

"We're trying to establish—"

"If you don't mind, I have more weeding to do," she insisted.

Willie loosely grabbed Liam's elbow, but Liam wasn't through yet. He yanked his arm away and followed Jennifer to the garden.

"Here we go," Willie muttered.

"Leonard von Zonek may be alive," Liam blurted.

Jennifer pivoted abruptly. "How dare you!" She raised her trowel to Liam's face and gave him an old-fashioned tongue lashing. "How dare you come here and tell someone you don't even know that a close friend of hers, who was murdered many years ago by ruthless saboteurs, is alive! Have you no respect for the dead or even their friends or relatives? Please leave me be!"

Jennifer marched to her garden and resumed weeding. Although Liam had more to say, Willie opted to end the visit. His large hand enveloped Liam's mouth before Liam could utter a word.

"You've said enough for one day," Willie declared sternly as he tightened his grip. "Sorry to bother you, Ms. Jurgens."

Willie wheeled Liam around in the direction of the house. It was pointless to attempt to break free because Willie was much stronger than Liam. Willie withdrew his hand from Liam's mouth when they reached the front yard.

"Real subtle, Liam. Why did you tell her von Zonek is alive?"

"I want her to think about it."

Willie released Liam. "You want her to think about what?"

"We know, and she knows, he didn't die at that art show. It won't be long before she talks."

"What makes you so sure?"

"I have a feeling."

"I hate it when you get those feelings."

"They're usually right," Liam reminded Willie.

"I'm all too aware."

They entered Willie's car.

"Well, that didn't go as planned." Willie changed the subject. "Are you attending the Bubble Festival tonight?"

"Wouldn't miss it." Liam fastened his seat belt.

"Do you want to join May and me for that long-overdue dinner?"

"What time?"

"We usually eat around six and we'll head downtown around eight."

"Terrific. I'll be at your house around five-thirty."

"May and the kids will be happy to see you." Willie started the car. "Will Mason be at the festival?"

"Not until later. He's taking the Dropas to a school where he painted one of his first murals."

"Why?" Willie backed out of the driveway.

"He discovered the Dropas have been leaving the apartment every night for weeks. He's curious about what they've been doing." Liam snapped his fingers. "That reminds me, we're out of airbrush needles again. I have to leave a box in his van this afternoon."

Willie switched on the radio to listen to the latest GNS update.

"...countless individuals are missing and at least three dozen more individuals have died from undetermined causes. Presently, there are no explanations for what some believe to be a pandemic. The cumulative number of mysterious deaths has surpassed eighty-one hundred in the United States alone. Experts have no clues as to why..."

Spheres of Influence

Mason arrived home after running a quick errand and parked facing his sliding door. Through the open blinds, he noticed the chandelier swinging over the dining table. Intent to catch the Dropas in the act of their newest shenanigans, Mason entered his apartment from inside the building. In rapid succession, he unlocked the door, turned the knob, and flung open the door.

"Caught you!" Mason ensured they heard him over the loud, Greek music.

Yellow enthusiastically swung on the light fixture when Mason exploded through the door, forcing it to release prematurely. It missed the intended target and splattered against the side of the counter. The other Dropas bent over in laughter as Yellow dripped down the support wall onto the carpet. They regained their composure and aided their companion, playfully throwing the spatters into its body. Clearcoat jumped onto the remote to turn off the music.

In the kitchen, Mason deduced the Dropas' latest game. They had filled both sinks with paint and were diving from the ceiling light. Paint covered the countertops, linoleum flooring, and the surrounding carpet.

Mason directed the culprits to clean the mess. Dropas on the floor painted a large shop vacuum and sucked up the blotches from the linoleum and carpet. The others created squeegees and pushed the paint covering the counters into the two sinks. Upon completion of the clean-up duties, Mason lifted the vacuum off the floor and washed it down the drain along with the squeegees.

Mason heated some leftovers for dinner. He brought his plate and glass to the living room table, sat on the couch, and switched on *his* favorite music station.

The Dropas gathered around Mason's plate, either sitting on the edge or lying on the table with legs crossed and hands clasped behind their heads. Relaxing and watching Mason consume his meals evolved into a ritual for them. They were intrigued by the concept of eating because they never ate. It really didn't matter what Mason did, they enjoyed his company. The only time they were separated was when they ventured off on the recent, nightly excursions.

It was unimaginable how Mason would react if the Dropas returned to their home. He had a tendency to become extremely attached emotionally to certain people, keepsakes, etc. Liam witnessed prior occurrences and hoped to never witness another one. He could hardly bear the feeling of helplessness that nothing he said or did could ease Mason's heartbreak.

After dinner, Mason kicked off his shoes and stretched out on the couch. He asked the Dropas to wake him before the departure time. Not requiring sleep either, they scurried to the studio for playtime. Mason fell into a deep slumber and began dreaming intensely.

...a faraway place where two suns shone in the blue sky. Inside his small, rubber raft, Mason lazily floated down a river, enjoying the sounds of the water swirling around him. The serenity was hypnotic, and the warmth from the suns on his bare chest soothed him. He intermittently dipped his hand into the cool water and splashed it on his skin, resulting in goose bumps and shivers throughout his body, refreshing nonetheless. As he drifted along, he leaned his head back and listened to the birdsong and the wind rustling through the leaves. It was so peaceful. So euphoric.

The sound of rushing water snapped him out of his tranquil state. He had heard that sound many times before on other dream-related rivers, but not on this particular one. As he floated around a bend, the rapid revealed its swirling face. The raft swiftly carried him straight for the white water. He had no oar to row himself ashore, for he never needed one on this river. Using his hands, he desperately tried to paddle to safety but the daunting current forbade it. He clutched the sides, hoping to survive the unforgiving rapid awaiting him.

It was difficult to ascertain the direction at which the water crashed against the rocks. The foam surged over them and calmness was nowhere in sight. He tightened his grip and balanced himself in the raft. The merciless rapid tossed him around like a mechanical bull rider and the cold water drenched him from head to toe.

His watercraft caromed off a rock, jerking his body backward and nearly flipping him into the river. The water splashed against his face, and he painfully tried to open his eyes, certain he'd be catapulted into the jagged protrusions if he let go to wipe them. Another wave slapped his face, catching him with an open mouth. Coughing to expel the water from his lungs, he vanished into the raging foam, virtually blinded and hanging on for dear life. The river temporarily disappeared from underneath him as the rapid hurled him over a small waterfall. The raft crashed on the surface, jolting his slender frame...

Taking advantage of Mason's dream state, the Dropas enjoyed their latest prank. His hands clutched the seat cushions as his body twitched uncontrollably. Red, Black, and Blue giggled hysterically, causing them to lose their balance and roll onto his pillow. White, Yellow, Indigo, and Orange relentlessly flicked water onto Mason's face as he flopped around in his sleep. The Dropas had no idea what he was dreaming about, but the pelting water drops are what propelled Mason into the rapids in the first place. In his dream, he fought for his life—in reality, he fell victim to another practical joke courtesy of the Dropas.

Black and Blue climbed onto Mason's nose to wake him. Instead, he awoke abruptly as the raft impacted the surface water in his dream. His body jerked upwardly and he opened his eyes. Partially incoherent, he swatted Black and Blue off his nose with his right hand, splattering them against the wall. The other Dropas, already laughing as they watched Mason dream, somersaulted onto the lower cushions in hysterics. He lay motionless for a few seconds before he recognized the giggling sounds, his face and hair dripping wet from the droplets the Dropas had thrown on him.

Black and Blue popped themselves off the wall and gathered their remnants. They joined their companions on the coffee table. Mason glanced at the clock. It was seven-thirty. The Dropas awoke him at the time he requested.

"You guys are always creating something new." Mason wiped the residual water from his face. He arose from the couch with a big yawn and retreated to the bathroom to dry his hair.

The Dropas darted into the studio to retrieve paintbrushes. From the hallway, Mason heard them rummaging amongst his supplies as if searching for something.

"Aha, mystery solved. You're the ones taking my airbrush needles. They've been disappearing faster than Liam can replenish them."

The Dropas, heads hanging in shame, felt guilty about not telling Mason. Clearcoat explained that they needed them to shoot bubbles. He nodded in agreement, thinking they had designed another game specifically for the Bubble Festival. Eager to visit the school, Mason didn't think twice about the needle-carrying quivers the Dropas had painted themselves.

Mason felt his pockets. "Where are my keys?"

Customarily, the Dropas dispersed throughout the apartment and within seconds, Orange and Yellow brought Mason his keys.

"It's a good thing I have you here to help me." Mason patted them each on the head with his forefinger.

Orange and Yellow stepped back, bowed, and followed the other Dropas, all assuming their usual position on Mason's shoulders as he slipped out through the sliding glass door.

"Hey, Mason," Paul called from the shadows.

"Get under my shirt," Mason whispered to the Dropas. "What's up, Paul?"

"I'm heading down to the Bubble Festival."

"Didn't you hear? The GGB requested residents travel in groups for this event."

"That stuff doesn't scare me." Paul assumed an unorthodox martial arts position. "After all, I have a black ribbon in ka-ra-taaay."

"In that case, you have no reason to worry."

Paul uncoiled from his stance, uncharacteristically observant. "What are those lumps on your shoulders?"

Mason opted not to introduce the Dropas, for Paul was purposely not made aware of their existence. "It's a bad case of acne. I'm a bit embarrassed."

"I totally understand and won't ask any more questions."

"Well, I have errands to run."

"No problem. Hope your condition improves."

"Thanks, Paul."

Mason hopped into the van and drove north, chuckling at the silly story he told Paul.

After dinner, Liam, Willie, and May strolled a dozen blocks to the historic section of town, the location of their regional Bubble Festival.

It was a jubilant event. The annual celebration reminded nations of the hard work they had contributed to making the world a wonderful place again and for generations to come. The bubbles symbolized childhood—the innocence, yet the fragility. Scientists had engineered the synchronous, global event after watching their children play with simple, bubble-making devices at a Sunday afternoon picnic. From those devices, the scientists created larger replicas and demonstrated them to the GGB. Captivated by the machines, one member recommended a Bubble Festival be conducted annually to celebrate the global accomplishments. Her colleagues unanimously approved. Each subsequent festival is anticipated more than the previous one. Spectators eagerly await the plethora of bubbles varying in shape, size, color, and clarity—a result of the scientists' machine modifications. It is magnificent to watch, not only the bubbles but also the spectators.

Despite the warnings to stay at home until they uncovered the reason for the mysterious deaths, the GGB lifted the restriction for that special event. GGB officers were visible throughout the area, alert for potential assaults on the crowd. A draped banner above the main stage depicted the latest achievements resulting from the implementation of the Survival Treaty. Below the banner, the featured band played festive music.

"What a wonderful gesture by the GGB to sponsor this annually," May commented. "It's such a joyous occasion."

Willie did not share her enthusiasm. "I don't think it's a good idea this year."

"Don't be a party pooper," May urged.

"I agree with Willie. Considering all the recent deaths, it's risky having this many attendees gathered in concentrated areas around the world."

"Do you think you two can cheer up for a couple of hours?"

"Sure," Liam and Willie replied apprehensively.

"Wonderful. Let's go celebrate."

They immersed themselves in the crowd and inched closer to the main stage, hoping for a prime listening spot.

Mason drove into the empty parking lot of a junior high school he painted murals in many years ago. The poled lights supplied the only source of illumination due to the cloud cover blocking the moonlight. Wondering how much his style had evolved, he wanted to revisit all the murals in that school. Mason neared the gymnasium with no access to the building. The Dropas conveniently painted him a key to unlock the outside door.

"Will the alarm sound?"

Clearcoat gibbered in Mason's ear.

"No alarm? Good enough for me."

Mason inserted the key and opened the door. He didn't worry about someone spotting him because no one was present, not even a night custodian. He flipped on the light switches. The Dropas scurried down Mason's arms as the vapor lights hummed in the empty gym. On the floor, under the mural, were paint cans, roller trays, rags, and a pan of mineral spirits with soaking paint brushes. Mason presumed that the summer staff was touching up the walls. As the lights brightened, the visibility improved and revealed the mural details. The mascot was a dragon, and that school housed the only artwork he had painted depicting that animal.

Mason cringed. "Boy, has my work changed."

The Dropas wasted no time getting started. All but two ascended the wall. Silver and Gold kept Mason company.

Mason called to the Dropas. "Why are you painting over my murals?"

Silver assured him that the Dropas were not changing the original design. It divulged that they had been repainting his murals because there wasn't enough time for him to do it. Mason presumed they were using the liquid Liam had brought back from Greece.

"In time for what?"

Silver and Gold didn't respond and scampered to the paint containers. They slid a quart can next to a gallon can. Silver laid its paint brush across the lid of the smaller cylinder and balanced itself on the bristles. Gold climbed to the top edge of the gallon can, jumped off it, and landed on the blunt end of the brush, catapulting Silver. They repeated the acrobatic feat, each taking turns before Mason opted to participate in the fun. Disregarding the activities below, the painting Dropas concentrated on the mural.

Silver stepped onto the brush and Mason replaced Gold as the launcher. He hit the blunt end, propelling Silver three feet in a vertical ascent. Mason caught the flying Dropa and situated both it and the brush on the can. Silver and Gold performed somersaults and twists as they flew through the air. Comfortable with each new height, Mason whacked the brush a little harder and launched the Dropas higher.

Silver repositioned itself on the inadvertently misaligned brush. Consumed with the game, Mason failed to realize what would ensue. Instead of a vertical trajectory, Silver launched at an angle over the can. Mason stretched out to catch the misguided Dropa, but it was too far out of his reach. Silver's flight path terminated in the pan containing mineral spirits.

Silver let out a shrill scream, one Mason had never heard from any Dropa. Responding to the distressed cry, the other Dropas darted down the wall to aid their companion. Silver's body dispersed in the solvent. Mason spread out a rag. Rapidly dissipating, Silver failed to grab the brush end that Gold had offered it. Mason cupped his hands, scooped Silver's drops out of the destructive liquid, and laid them on the cloth. The cotton material absorbed the mineral spirits along with Silver's droplets. Their heads hanging, the Dropas formed a circle around the helpless Silver. They tightened the formation, careful not to step in the damp areas of the rag.

Mason instructed the Dropas to paint a strainer. They didn't respond, deeply involved in reviving Silver. Replicating the ritual they performed in Mason's studio when he lay unconscious, the intense concentration transcended their awareness of anything around them, especially when a Dropa was in danger. Mason raced outside to his van. He had a fine mesh strainer he could use to scoop any lingering parts of Silver from the pan of mineral spirits.

Mason searched frantically for the implement. He threw aside old sweatshirts, paper bags, and other miscellaneous items—burying the box of needles Liam had dropped off earlier. Tears rolled down his cheeks. He was truly distraught by the potential loss of his little friend and felt badly for the other Dropas.

"Here it is!" Mason sprinted to the gym door. His rapid heartbeat and tightened lungs instigated a wheezing spell. "Darn it! I left the key inside."

He banged on the door, hoping a Dropa would let him in the gym. Mason pounded louder. Again it went unnoticed. He leaned against the door, sliding down until his rear end rested on the cement entryway. He threw the strainer on the ground and buried his head in his palms.

Pulling his hands away from his face, Mason noticed the clouds brightening above the school. He rose to his feet and backed away from the door.

Inside the gym, a magnificent spectacle occurred. While the Dropas danced and chanted, an opening in the ceiling formed above where the Dropas encircled Silver. A second one formed through the pollution cover. And lastly, the hidden clouds parted, allowing a brilliant beam of light to descend upon Silver. While the

Dropas chanted and danced, Silver's glowing remnants rose a foot above the rag and out of the pan of mineral spirits.

A six-inch image of Athena descended the light source until she hovered alongside the afflicted Dropa. Raising her arms, she flattened her palms and repeatedly passed them slightly above Silver's dissipated body. The spattered droplets slowly consolidated with the larger, intact portion of its body.

On the floor, the other Dropas maintained the healing ritual. Athena passed her hands over Silver's body one last time. She raised both arms to the sky and lifted herself upward while lowering Silver's body to the gym floor. As she ascended through the ceiling, the hole closed and the light faded. The gap in the pollution cover coalesced below her as she vanished into the night sky.

The Dropas' chanting halted as they huddled around their companion. Silver kneaded its body, shifting the once spattered segments to their rightful positions. Convinced of its wholeness, Silver and the other Dropas scanned the gym for Mason.

Outside, Mason watched the light beam fade into the closing cloud cover. Appearing to morph from the beam, an oddly-colored sphere drifted toward him.

"That is cool." He examined the intricate details within the distorted reflection of the school. He took two steps before the greenish-brown bubble completely engulfed his body. Struggling to free himself, he yelled for help—doubting that anyone could hear him.

Beautiful images flowed through his mind: childhood experiences, swimming in the lake, painting, sunshine, blue skies. He relived everything that made him feel good. However, the memories didn't flow through his mind but rather outwardly rushed. Following the stream of wonderful memories, appeared images of poverty, hunger, rioting, and war. He fought diligently to release the mental pictures. The bubble collapsed further, exhausting more air from inside it. With suffocation imminent, he desperately shouted for help. His heart rate nearly ceased as he inhaled his last breath. The bubble adhered to him like cellophane as he fell unconscious onto the asphalt surface.

In his mind, he ambled through a prairie of grass nearly reaching his height. Mason admired the colorful birds flying overhead. He felt the florets brush across his cheeks, the sensation bringing him joy. He opened his eyes.

"Ahh!" Mason yelled as Blue and Red tickled his face with their paintbrushes. "When did you get here?"

Silver jumped out from behind Blue and Red, holding its archery bow high above its head.

"You survived!"

Silver bowed and then danced on the pavement. The other Dropas joined the abbreviated celebration.

"You guys are incredible," Mason complimented them. "How did you know I was in trouble?"

Clearcoat stepped to the front and explained that after reviving Silver he was nowhere in sight. Yellow spotted the door key on the gym floor and the Dropas decided to search the parking lot, deducing he couldn't re-enter the gym without assistance. Once outside, they found him trapped in the collapsed bubble. From its quiver, Silver drew a needle covered in its own paint and shot the overlay, popping it on impact.

"Is that the only way to stop them?"

Clearcoat nodded.

Mason patted Silver on the head and thanked the other Dropas for saving his life. As he recovered from his bubble encounter, he watched outlines of more bubbles floating far off in the distance.

"The Festival! It will be difficult to tell the difference between the bubbles. We must intercept them before they engulf others," Mason insisted, discerning the true reason why the Dropas had been depleting his needle supply.

Without divulging intricate details, Clearcoat defended the importance of completing the mission inside the school and that they only required minimal time.

"Then off you go. I'll wait for you in the van."

Mason contemplated the mental imagery resulting from his brief incarceration in the bubble. *Is that what Ozone is using to transform individuals?* He cringed at the possibility of becoming a ForLord had he not fought off the negativity or his imminent death if the Dropas had not popped the bubble in time. He sympathized with victims who were converted or died while ceasing to surrender. Sapped of energy from his own encounter, he almost drifted off to sleep when the Dropas returned. Although they accomplished the mission at the school, they had more work ahead of them.

"Let's go! It's time for a bubble hunt!"

The Dropas spread out across the open windows on both sides of the van. Clearcoat positioned itself on the dashboard ready to instruct the other Dropas. As they neared the celebration—within viewing distance of the crowd—the festive sounds resonated through the streets.

Citizens of the regions took full advantage of the GGB's exception for the special event. Experiencing cabin fever due to the recent restriction, more people showed up than expected. The streets and alleys overflowed with attendees eating, dancing, and thoroughly enjoying themselves. Mason searched for a parking spot, but the throng of people disrupted his effort.

Needles loaded in bows, the Dropas were ready to fire into the sky. Mason observed a small group of unsuspecting individuals simply watch the bubbles drifting over the building rooftops and down upon them. Others celebrated and cheered the arrival of the main attraction. Mason jumped out of the van, pushed his way to the stage, and snatched the microphone from the lead singer's hand. The music stopped abruptly.

"Take cover! Those aren't festival bubbles! Take cover!"

Confused by the unexpected announcement, the audience failed to respond. Mason repeated the warning. Finally, the majority heeded the danger and ran for shelter, throwing food and drinks to the ground. They pushed and shoved each other, attempting to return to their vehicles or find other means of protection. Those who fell were trampled by the mass exodus from the streets and those who stayed watched the bubbles descend upon them.

The Dropas climbed onto the van rooftop to attain a better vantage point. They released the first wave of needles, each intercepting a different bubble with the accuracy of a master archer and showering polluted residue onto the crowd. Another onslaught of bubbles descended from the sky, and another flurry of projectiles pierced through the air with the same precision. The streets cleared except for those individuals who ignored the warnings. More bubbles floated over buildings, more than the Dropas had needles. The Dropas consistently struck the targets, although four spheres escaped untouched and enveloped their prey. Those standing next to them tried desperately, yet unsuccessfully, to free the victims from the impenetrable globes.

Clearcoat directed four Dropas to vacate their current positions and assist the victims. The other Dropas reloaded the last set of needles and readied themselves for another round of bubbles.

Helpless, Mason had no means of fending off the evil spheres. Only the Dropas' needles could eradicate them. He brainstormed ways to help the Dropas, recalling his request of Liam to drop off the latest shipment of airbrush needles. Mason scrambled to the cargo area in search of the box. Finding it covered with sweatshirts from when he needed the strainer, he ripped open the carton and positioned it on the rooftop. Silver and Gold coated the new needles and the other Dropas immediately reloaded for another strike.

On the pavement, Yellow, Red, Orange, and Green had reached the first two casualties. The suffocating victims fought frantically to fend off the evil power of the bubbles. Green and Red propelled their needles into the spheres, spraying particles into the air. Yellow and Orange raced to find the other two victims. Another stream of needles launched, again hitting the intended targets, but two bubbles eluded that attack and were free to prey on defenseless onlookers. Fortunately, the majority of the crowd had safely retreated to shelter.

The two descending orbs zeroed in on a pair of unsuspecting individuals. Green and Red followed the trajectories and intercepted the bubbles before they engulfed the fleeing targets. Arriving too late at their destination, Yellow and Orange discovered a pair of casualties. The female victim lay dead on the sidewalk. Her husband had succumbed to the mind-altering forces, allowing the bubble to burst as his inner negativity prevailed. Devoid of positive emotions, he abandoned his wife and disappeared into the darkness.

Yellow and Orange hung their heads next to the woman, saddened by her death. After eradicating the lingering bubbles, the other Dropas joined their mournful companions with Mason on their heels.

Ducking in and out of the sparser crowd that rapidly filled the streets again, Liam, May, and Willie met up with Mason.

"When did you get here?" Liam asked.

"Right before jumping on stage. I wanted to arrive before the event started and it's fortunate I made it here when I did." Mason acknowledged the ten Dropas that returned to his shoulders. "Willie and May, do you remember Clearcoat and its companions?"

May knelt on one knee, offering her flattened hand to the returning Green and Red. She rose and held them in front of Willie. "How can anyone forget the Dropas?" May touched Green with her finger. "They're the cutest little things."

Green and Red waved as Mason leaned forward to allow the other Dropas to join them. Liam, Mason, and Willie stepped to the side.

"What can you tell us about these bubbles?" Willie asked.

"I believe they are responsible for the attitude changes and mysterious deaths." Paranoid, Mason searched skyward. "One swallowed me at the school."

Mason recounted his bubble encounter. He detailed how it attempts to remove all positivity from the mind, collapsing and suffocating its victim the more he or she resists the negative forces and influences. They concluded that the woman lying dead on the sidewalk fought it until the end and her husband gave in to its effects. Sadly, he would likely convert to a ForLord.

"Hence, the mysterious deaths," Willie added.

"We now have a tangible explanation as to why attitudes have changed," Liam offered. "I presume many of those victims have retained bad personal experiences from before and during the war."

Willie rubbed his chin. "That certainly makes sense."

"I imagine that others who succumb to a bubble assault are not in total agreement with the provisions set forth in the Survival Treaty." Mason handed Liam an airbrush needle. "It gets worse. This is the only way to counteract the bubbles. And they must be coated with paint from the Dropas' bodies."

Liam inspected the needle. "This explains our increased demand for needles."

"We'll ramp up production and make sure they are distributed across the globe," Willie announced confidently.

"Lack of supply is only part of the problem." Liam held the needle in front of Willie and ran his opposite index finger along the tip. "First, they must all be coated with the Dropas' paint."

"Okay, what do we do next?"

"I'm not sure yet."

Once the ambulance arrived, Liam and Willie concentrated on the responders, unaware that Mason had stepped away from them.

Two blocks away, Mason sighted a silhouetted figure wearing a beret and a leather duster. He deemed it unusual for someone to be dressed that way on such a warm evening. As Mason approached, the figure strode away, occasionally peeking over his shoulder to see if Mason followed. Intrigued by the individual's persistent evasion, Mason quickened his pace, gradually decreasing the distance separating them.

The figure darted into an alley. Mason remembered that alley led to a dead end and cautiously rounded the corner. The silhouetted figure waited in front of the brick wall. Without seeing any physical features, Mason had an eerie feeling he already knew the person. As the individual approached, the alley light revealed the figure's mask-covered head, concealing his identity. Mason stepped forward and felt a sharp pain in the back of his neck, almost instantly becoming lightheaded. Attempting to focus, Mason perceived two, then four, then too many images to count. He felt his legs wobble just before collapsing to the ground. Everything went black as he lay motionless on the alley pavement.

Ozone Alert

The recent bubble assault warranted a public communication from the GGB. As a first-hand witness, Willie would ensure the message was clear and accurate regarding what had happened at the festival.

Alert for ForLords, GGB officers cleared the lingering stragglers off the streets except for those who awaited questioning. After the ambulance drove off with the deceased woman, Willie strayed away to meet with two of his men.

Liam rejoined May who was occupied with the Dropas. Clearcoat, in its usual observatory position, watched over the others from her shoulder.

"May, have you seen Mason?"

"When you and Willie were with the medical responders, Mason mentioned he had to check out something. Is anything wrong?"

"Possibly." Liam scanned the area. *Why would he leave the Dropas, especially after what happened tonight?*

Liam neared Mason's parked van as a black sedan drove past him. It had a familiar sound, one he hadn't heard in years. Liam didn't give it much consideration since many GGB transportation services had similar-looking vehicles, but after it sped by, he recognized a distinct odor—exhaust from a fuel-burning car.

"Ozone." Liam waved his hands and shouted in Willie's direction. "Willie! Ozone has Mason!"

"You two, come with me!"

Willie and the two officers hurried to the van. Liam and Willie jumped in the front and the patrolmen hopped in the cargo area.

"Un...believable." Liam leaned back in the driver seat.

"What's wrong?" Willie asked.

"Mason always misplaces his keys or leaves them in the ignition, and the one time someone needs them, they're not here."

They stepped out of the van and slammed the doors shut.

"Now what?" Willie inquired.

Liam turned to the officers. "Do either of you have a vehicle here?"

"No, we're on foot patrol tonight," one officer explained.

"What makes you think that Ozone has Mason?" Willie asked.

"Call it a gut feeling." Aggravated, Liam scoped the area for anything drivable. "Does anyone have a car we can use?"

"Another gut feeling? We need facts, Liam."

"I don't have any at the moment. Willie, the questions can wait. We need transportation!"

Willie sternly addressed the officers. "Why are you two standing here? Find us a car."

The officers separated in search of a vehicle.

"Maybe you've just been lucky thus far. How can you be certain that was Ozone's car?"

"It was a fuel-burning car."

"Are you crazy? Those haven't been around in—"

"In years…but only one person is bold enough to drive one."

"Why would Ozone be here?"

"Maybe he decided to pay a personal visit to Mason."

"What would he want with your brother?"

"I don't have an answer! When I do—"

Willie stepped back. "All right. Take it easy."

"Willie! While we stand here twiddling our thumbs, Ozone is driving off with my brother!"

Tires squealed as a car approached from around the corner. It made a bee-line for Willie and Liam.

"It's about time!" Liam exclaimed.

The two officers, who had returned without a vehicle, drew their immobilizers and aimed at the driver in case it was Ozone returning. The car screeched to a halt next to the van and Pockets stuck his head out the window.

"Don't shoot!" Liam thrust out his hand. "He's a friend of mine. Pockets, I expected you here earlier."

"I would have been, but someone ransacked Mason's apartment," Pockets replied, "and they cleaned out his studio."

"Tell us about it in the car. I'll ride shotgun."

Willie sat in the back seat with the two officers.

"Pockets, head to the old transportation depot," Liam instructed. "If it is Ozone, he likely flew in with a small cargo plane. I'm sure he didn't drive all the way from Barrow's Ridge."

Hoping to gain ground on Ozone's significant head start, Pockets drove through the backroads.

"Why were you at Mason's apartment?"

"We had planned an early start tomorrow. I decided to prep the box before coming down here."

"Take a left at the next corner. What happened in the apartment?"

"I was rinsing airbrushes in the bathroom sink. After turning off the water, I heard a strange sound coming from the living room, as if someone was cutting glass. When I peeked around the hallway corner, a trio of men had pushed through the sliding door window. I didn't dare confront all three, so I retreated to the bathroom and hid behind the shower curtain. I heard them walk into the bedroom. Convinced Mason wasn't home, they went into the studio. When it was safe to come out, I discovered the missing supplies and equipment."

"Why would somebody steal art supplies?" Willie asked.

"Ozone was a famous artist," Liam reminded Willie. "I wonder if he wants Mason to paint for him. Remember, Ozone suffered severe wounds to his hands at his final showing."

"That seems pretty far-fetched for a man wanting to terminate human existence."

Liam braced himself as Pockets turned suddenly. "Do you have any other explanations?"

"No, but it must be more than just wanting Mason to paint for him."

"I agree. There it is!"

The abandoned depot comprised remnants of old neglected structures in the midst of being razed. The cracked runway and pavement around the buildings were pockmarked with pot holes and overtaken by weeds, making it improbable for any conventional plane to land or take flight. Pockets switched off the headlights and drove to the rear corner of the closest building.

The back end of Ozone's vehicle disappeared as the underside of the aircraft closed. From the tree line, three drones zipped overhead past Pockets' car.

"Replicas of the drones seen by investigators at Barrow's Ridge?" Liam asked.

"Yep," Willie replied, "two four-footers and one six-footer."

The onlookers helplessly watched, having no substantial fire power to combat the unmanned aircraft. As long as they didn't pose a threat to Ozone, the three armed drones paid no attention to them.

"How did he land on that airstrip?" Willie inquired.

"That's how." Pockets commented.

The small cargo plane rose vertically and flew westward. The drones maneuvered into formation in front of the larger aircraft, the six-footer flanked by the smaller ones.

Liam was frustrated. They all were frustrated. Not only had Ozone abducted Mason but he gained momentum in his effort to carry out his evil plot. He grew stronger as the size of his ForLord army increased. The majority who didn't convert to his ways were in more danger than ever.

Pockets switched on the lights and drove to the festival area. "Now what?"

"I'll set up an emergency GGB meeting, if they haven't called one already," Willie replied. "Liam, I want you there with me. We'll meet at my office and connect via the emergency land line since the cloud cover is interfering with the satellite signal."

"Perfect." Liam rubbed his chin. "I'll pay another visit to our friend before hooking up with you."

"Our friend?" Willie asked hesitantly.

"Jennifer Jurgens. She can't maintain this façade forever. She's hiding something, and I plan on uncovering it."

"It must be eating her up. Just go easy on her."

"I will," Liam replied empathetically. "Speaking from experience, reliving old, tragic memories can be tremendously painful."

Liam left for Jennifer's house at 6:00 a.m. He awoke a bit sluggish due to the activities of the previous night and only three hours of sleep, but he had to allocate enough time to question Jennifer and make it to the GGB meeting. Liam didn't want to arrive late, especially since he was an invited guest.

The bubble attacks occurred at every festival around the world. The GNS detailed the events and reported hourly updates on casualties. It also highlighted the public's amplified anger, especially since the GGB had not initiated a measurable response following the recent deaths or disappearance of loved ones. One veteran journalist summed up the situation by saying it reminded her of events prior to the war and past politicians' failure to handle critical issues.

Liam parked in the driveway. Jennifer sat on a porch swing sipping tea. As he set foot on the top step, she adjusted the cushion on the empty chair next to her.

"I expected a return visit from you," Jennifer said, unfazed. "Please sit down. Forgive me, what was your name?"

"Liam Street, but Liam will suffice."

"After the latest reports, Liam, I've decided to disclose all I know."

"I appreciate you changing your mind."

Jennifer organized her thoughts. "You and the GGB are dealing with a vengeful individual. What makes Leonard exceedingly dangerous is that he is an emotionally disturbed misanthrope but extremely intelligent. I lied yesterday when I told you he was murdered. I just couldn't deal with it at that moment." She set down her tea cup. "After hearing the morning news, I was convinced the recent chain of events, especially the abduction of your brother, could only be committed by Leonard. It would be just like him to kidnap a talented artist like himself, but I don't believe he did it to kill your brother…not just yet. Strangely, your brother's art likely hinders Leonard's plan for human annihilation."

"In what way?"

"Understanding Leonard's behavior as I do, I would surmise that he is jealous of Mason's work but admires it as he would his own. Mason's art touches many hearts and fosters kindness."

"Could it be as simple as just removing another positive aspect from our lives?"

"Perhaps, but Leonard may also be using your brother to somehow rekindle his own creativity. No matter the reason, it appears Leonard intends to make good on the promise he made on the Art Center steps, the promise the war did not fulfill, and the promise in which I played a role."

"You assisted Ozone?" Liam was taken aback. "His plan spanned the entire globe not just those who attacked him and his art."

"Yes, but I witnessed his pain first hand at the unveiling, in the emergency room, and in the days and months that followed. No one deserved such suffering. I felt sorry for Leonard and was enraged at what those awful vandals did to his art and to him. And I didn't care what happened to them. To make matters worse, he had no insurance and lacked the money for reconstructive surgery. I had none...and his friends turned their backs on him. We both agree it was a terrible time to be alive prior to the war. Humanity reached a tipping point and I had nothing in my life worth living for. I chose to help Leonard carry out his vengeful plot." Jennifer paused momentarily. "Liam, I granted him access to all the government files. I helped create the computer program that spread the classified information across the globe." No longer able to suppress her emotions, Jennifer's eyes welled with tears as she gazed into the morning sky.

Stunned by the vital information, Liam was moved by her expression of immense regret for her actions. "You realize you've admitted your guilt of serving as an accomplice to almost wiping out humanity."

Jennifer's voice trembled, "I understand by saying all this, I have essentially confessed to a heinous crime, one that is mentally replayed day after day. When you visited yesterday, all those memories of iniquity rushed through my mind. Because I enjoy the renewed life the Survival Treaty has offered, I can no longer withhold information from those wanting to stop Leonard from carrying out his evil plot." She could no longer refrain from crying.

Liam scooted forward in his chair and offered his hands. She tightly squeezed them, and glared into his eyes with rage.

"As much as I once admired Leonard, what he has done is unforgivable. It is imperative that you find a way to prevent him from attempting it again, or this time he *will* wipe out human civilization. And remember, he doesn't care if he dies in the process, as long as everyone perishes with him. Leonard will do everything in his power to make sure it happens. Your firsthand accounts should tell you that."

"We'll do everything we can, but the Treaty did not consider someone of Leonard's capacity and willfulness to eliminate the human race."

"I guarantee that you won't be successful with conventional means. You must find another way." Jennifer released Liam's hands.

"What can you tell me about his fortress near Barrow's Ridge?"

"Very little," Jennifer admitted, wiping the tears from her face with a tissue tucked under her sleeve. "Leonard and I haven't communicated since he started renovating that facility shortly after the war. All I can remember him saying is no one would be able to penetrate his walls."

"Both literally and figuratively."

"What do you mean?"

"Are you familiar with my brother's art, particularly the broken walls he incorporates in them?"

"Yes, it's beautiful work. Ah, I think I understand. No one will break through his fortress walls nor the walls he has built around himself."

"Exactly, the ones preventing goodness from penetrating and evil from leaving. His walls are exceedingly thick from the tragedy he suffered at his final exhibit. He is unwilling to forgive or reach out to anyone. Leonard is a remnant of what societies were like before the war. Caught up in their own acquisitions, accomplishments, and sole-survival, they forgot why they were given the gift of life. All greed-related problems. They lost sight of their true existence: mind, heart, soul, and the innate ability to make life enjoyable for all humanity."

"I couldn't have said it better. I assure you, my walls have been broken through, and I credit those who created the Survival Treaty and our new way of life for making it happen."

"You're not alone." Liam checked the time. "I must be on my way. We have plenty to do."

She patted Liam's hand. "If I can be of assistance, please call me."

"You have already been most helpful."

They both rose from their seats and walked to the porch steps.

"Should I be expecting a visit from the GGB for my arrest?"

"Waking up each and every day ruing your involvement in a plot to wipe out humanity is, in itself, punishment enough. Unfortunately, it is not for me to decide how the GGB will respond."

"I understand." Jennifer was visibly anxious, but not about her fate with the GGB. "Please stop him," she pleaded.

"We intend to." Liam gently shook her hand.

Jennifer released her grip and stepped inside the house. "Good luck, Liam."

"Thank you, Jennifer."

During Liam's drive to Willie's office, he contemplated the information Jennifer revealed, vacillating between extreme emotions of anger, fear, sadness, and helplessness. They had to put an end to Ozone, and Liam had to save Mason from Ozone's evil grip.

Mason awoke to a soft knock on the door. He felt a sharp pain where the needle had penetrated his neck and massaged the area with his fingertips. He rubbed his dry eyes and attempted to orient himself to the unfamiliar, yet lavish suite. Ten-foot high ceilings were precisely trimmed in the corners and on the surface with beautiful wood molding, and decorated with paintings within the waffle configuration. Also adorned with elaborate woodwork, the walls were covered with floral wallpaper in a most elegant pattern. Fit for royalty, the furniture accented the bedroom: intricate designs carved in the wood, velvet-upholstered cushions, and marble-topped tables, dressers, and vanities. Fresh flowers filled the room with an incredible aroma and sounds of melodic birds entered the room from the windows left ajar. The bed in which Mason slept had a high, hand-carved headboard and was piled with plenty of fluffy pillows and a down-filled duvet.

Mason heard a second knock. Memories of the previous night filled his head. Suddenly, it occurred to him that he may be in Lord Ozone's clutches.

"Come in," he responded, his mouth parched, an aftereffect from the substance injected in his body.

The door opened and in sauntered a petite, plainly dressed, Mediterranean woman. Complementing her medium-tanned skin, she wore her deep-black hair in a bun. Towels were draped across one arm and she carried a large, painted bowl with a matching ewer.

"Good morning, Mason." She situated the items on the vanity.

"Good morning, um—"

"My name is Shar."

"Good morning, Shar."

"I brought clean towels, washcloths, and hot water for you to freshen up. Lord Ozone has requested your presence for breakfast in the courtyard."

"The nightmare continues." Mason lay motionless. "If I refuse?"

"Lord Ozone would not take kindly to that," Shar calmly advised.

"Didn't suppose he would."

"I am making you new clothes and will deliver them when they are ready. Until then, you must wear what you wore last night."

"Lucky me, a one-stop hostage shop."

"You don't have much time. Breakfast will be served in twenty minutes and Lord Ozone doesn't like to be kept waiting."

"Of course, he doesn't. I presume he confiscated my cell phone."

"You won't need it here. Is there anything else?"

"It wasn't working anyway with this cloud cover. I do have one more question. How do I get to the courtyard?"

"Forgive me. When you leave the bedroom, take a right down the hall. Turn left at the bottom of the stairs. Walk behind the staircase and head straight out the double-glass doors. Lord Ozone will be waiting for you."

"Easy enough," Mason confirmed.

"Very well, I will leave you to freshen up. A pleasant day to you, Mason." Shar closed the bedroom door.

"Not too sure about that."

Consistent with his propensity to be late, Mason made no exception for Ozone. He deliberately washed and dressed himself. From his room, he made a right down the long, wood-trimmed hallway. Ozone's paintings lined the walls, each with a dedicated light shining on it. Mason wanted to admire each one but he was already tardy. He followed Shar's directions exactly. Outside, he was drawn to the courtyard's diverse array of trees and flowers, accented with an occasional statue placed in its own dedicated location. Cobblestone arranged in a circular pattern covered the ground. In the center, a large, magnificent fountain spurted water from its numerous spouts. Lord Ozone sat at a table beside the fountain, dressed in a black cloak with a hood over his head. A chill coursed down Mason's spine.

Mason strolled through the courtyard, relishing the fresh air across his face. A medley of birdsong and a variety of refreshing scents from the garden accentuated the scenery. Missing from that beautiful setting was the warm sunlight and the bright, blue sky. Mason cautiously approached the table. The pain in his neck intensified as he neared the cloaked stranger, stirring the anger Mason had for the man he hadn't officially met. He pulled out the chair across from Ozone.

"You're late," Ozone slurred slightly and refused to look up from his plate.

"No different from any other day," Mason snapped.

Ozone pointed at Mason's plate with his fork. "Please eat, the food is outstanding."

Mason removed the cover, revealing a generous portion of omelet, bacon, and toast. Accompanying the food were glasses of orange juice and ice water, and in the middle of the table was a large bowl of fresh fruit and a pitcher of hot tea.

"This looks delicious," Mason admitted, though somewhat suspicious. "I assume the food isn't poisoned since you could have disposed of me last night."

Ozone ate without commenting. Bits of food dropped from his mouth onto his plate. Mason's hunger had momentarily suppressed his ire, and he dove into the food as if he hadn't eaten for days. Periodically, he glanced at Ozone whose face remained hidden. Subtle blowing and pumping noises emanated from underneath the hood, analogous to those Mason heard from his compressor and airbrush, but much less prominent. After a period of eating without conversation, Mason broke the silence.

"Pull back your hood," Mason said boldly.

"Why?" Ozone kept his head down.

"Because I like to make eye contact when I talk to someone."

"I am certain you don't want to make eye contact with me."

"Listen, Leonard—"

Ozone slammed his fist on the table at what he perceived as Mason's disrespect. Pieces of fallen silverware clanged on the cobblestone, and Ozone's glass of water spilled onto the tablecloth. He pointed his gloved finger at Mason who sat straight in his chair trying to keep from choking on his last bite of toast.

"Don't ever call me Leonard!" Ozone's words were less distinct the louder he talked. "You will address me as Lord Ozone!"

"All right, all right. What do you want from me anyway?" Mason couldn't suppress his anger any longer. "You have your henchmen shoot me up with sleeping potion, drag me to this fortress, away from my family and friends, and then you're not even man enough to show me your face when you talk to me! I don't care what you look like! There's much more to a person than appearance! It's what exists under the surface that truly makes up an individual!"

"Don't bore me with your philosophical beliefs. You want to see my face so badly? Here it is." Ozone flipped his hood off his head with a dramatic flourish.

Ozone's face was hideous, his nose and eyelids completely consumed by the chemicals. His cheek bones, near his nose, were partially exposed where the scar tissue failed to cover them. Lacking lips allowed food and liquid to frequently drip out of his mouth and explained his slurred speech pattern.

Ozone wore a partial mask over the top half of his face, held on by straps stretching around and across the crown of his bald head. It featured a frontal, air-intake filter over his nasal cavity. The covering was screwed directly to his facial bones, securing it to prevent unwanted particles from entering his sinus passages under the seal. A thin, tinted visor protected his eyes, seemingly ready to roll out of their sockets at any time. Four tubes, two on each side, protruded from holes near, but under the ends of the visor. The tubes bridged to a pair of oblong compressors, one screwed to each side of his head, slightly above the ears. Two additional tubes projected from holes above the visor and connected with the top of the compressors. Sensitive to Ozone's condition, Mason refused to express any disgust or even avert his gaze regarding the pronounced disfigurement. He wanted to reach out to the man not because of his appearance but because of how and why it happened to him.

"Thank you," Mason simply stated. Nothing he said would improve the situation, but he was intrigued with the complexity of the facial apparatus. "Are those airbrush parts on the side of your head?"

"Yes, they are," Ozone replied, surprised at Mason's nonreaction to his appearance. "I designed this system myself."

"Very impressive. Tell me more."

"I couldn't afford reconstructive surgery, and I grew tired of wearing the inadequate facial mask the medical professionals provided to assist my breathing and keep particles out of my eyes and nose. The mask failed to moisten my eyes. They periodically stuck to my sockets. I also had problems with mucous draining out of my nasal cavity."

Mason maintained a stoic expression, but inwardly cringed as he vividly pictured Ozone's description.

"I designed the Inverted Transfer System or I-T-S. That, in turn, is made up of the Air Transfer Apparatus or A-T-A, and the M-R-T-A or Mucous Recycling Transfer Apparatus." Ozone paused for a moment, allowing Mason to process the acronyms. "Here, let me show you how it works."

Mason sipped his juice. "I'm listening."

Ozone used his index fingers to trace the system path as he explained its functionality. "A portion of air I breathe funnels through the top tubes under my eyes and into the small compressor up here, the ATA. This air is then filtered and discharged through these tubes to the Particle Deflector, up here above my eyes."

Mason leaned forward, closer to Ozone's visor.

Ozone afforded Mason time to examine it. "The Particle Deflector expels a constant stream of air in front of my eyes which keeps any minute, foreign particles from reaching them. The air flows out through these vents here." He positioned his fingers in front of the tubes—under the visor—that originated from his nose piece and traced the next path. "These tubes funnel mucous to the MRTA which recycles it and sends it to the moisturizing outlets in the Particle Deflector. This moistens my eyes and prevents them from sticking in the sockets. The nose piece—that's obvious what it does. And that's pretty much it."

Mason studied Ozone's face and mask. "How is your vision at night?"

"Ah, yes. I omitted that part." He ran his finger over a small slot, slightly above the visor. "This is a light sensor. When my surroundings are too dark, it automatically activates the night vision on the visor."

"The apparatus is amazing. How long did it take to design and build it?"

Ozone sipped his tea, barely keeping the liquid inside his mouth, and set his cup on the saucer. "Two weeks, at most."

"Wow! Do you have any problems with it?"

"Not anymore," Ozone replied proudly.

"The batteries must be tiny." Mason assumed the mask was operated by an external source.

"Unnecessary," Ozone responded smugly. "I have it feeding directly off neural impulses from my brain."

"No way!"

"That was one of many kinks I rectified. Always changing batteries was problematic, so I designed the system to connect directly to my brain." He pointed to the compressors with his index fingers. "These compressors are snapped onto the outlets coming out of my head."

"Do you ever take it off?"

Ozone meticulously sipped his orange juice. "No, it's very dang—" Ozone caught himself and changed the subject. "You're the only one who has looked at me without becoming repulsed. Why is that?"

Forgetting his original question, Mason instead responded to Ozone's. "I told you, I don't care what you look like. I don't care if you're black, white, or yellow. Nor do I care if your face is smashed into the back of your head. Don't you understand? It doesn't matter."

"I told you not to bore me."

"Not to bore you," Mason said simultaneously. "Fine. I'll change the subject. Why did you start the war and kill all those people?"

"They killed themselves," Ozone replied, emotionless.

"You started the fire."

"Perhaps, but the fuel was already in place. Leading up to the war, societies had a tremendous amount of hatred for their governments and each other." Ozone flicked a stray blueberry off the table. "I simply gave them a small nudge over the edge."

"I agree with your view of pre-war societies. They no longer allotted time to understand or accept each other's culture, heritage, and differences. Everyone wanted others to be like themselves. Once the governments collapsed, no distinct sides existed. Total chaos broke out and you used that to your advantage."

"Exactly! Humans are innately selfish and greedy."

"No, they are taught those traits," Mason argued.

Ozone sipped his tea instead of responding.

"Do you feel any remorse about being responsible for the death of billions?"

Ozone set his cup down and filled it with tea. "Why should I after the pain and disgrace they caused me?"

"As much as you refuse to believe it, only a small faction destroyed your art and brought you harm."

"Regardless, they all deserved to die, every last one of them."

"Why didn't you kill me?"

"Because you're the one person who can help restore the passion I once possessed and released through my hands."

"You could have easily admired my work outside your fortress."

"True, but your art is fueling positive attitudes. I had to remove that aspect of human life. Furthermore, I dearly miss the emotions I feel when painting. I want to experience those sensations again…watching the art come alive in front of me. You are here to paint my fortress."

Mason arose, stepped away from his chair, and collected his thoughts. "My art isn't the only thing keeping people positive." He again faced Ozone. "The Treaty allows us to discover our identity and true purpose. We're learning the ways of others by sharing experiences, beliefs, and peacefully solving problems. Governments always solved problems with war. And while leaders hid behind closed doors, brave soldiers sacrificed their lives because of the hateful, selfish, and greedy principles of world leaders. Over the course of centuries, the hatred governments directed at one another eventually permeated all societies, resulting in discrimination. Individuals despised one another because they lived in a different country, had different color skin, worshipped a different god, or just did things differently." Mason raised his finger. "We are here once, and only once. Why go through life hating each other? Our existence is more fulfilling if we make time to learn, share, and laugh with each other." Thinking he had made an impression, Mason misinterpreted Ozone's silence.

When Ozone spoke, he addressed only the last comment. "I used to laugh. I laughed often, but no more. I decided those who stole my mirth and dignity no longer deserve to live. It is exactly why I brought you here. The laughter and happiness must be removed from the world for my plan to succeed."

Mason leaned forward over the table and glared through Ozone's visor. "I feel sorry for you."

"I don't need, or want your pity for my appearance!"

"You misunderstand. I don't feel sorry because of your looks. I feel sorry for what you've become, because of your looks. You're worse than those who did this horrible thing to you. And today you intend to eliminate not only them but all humanity."

"They ruined my art and my life!" Ozone slurred.

"Then start over. You can have more than one dream or passion in life. That's where the beauty lies, you can always begin anew."

Ozone pushed his chair away from the table. "Believe me, I will accomplish my other dream." He replaced the hood over his head and retreated to his mansion.

"Ozone! You better find another artist to paint your fortress! I have no intention of applying one drop on those walls!"

Ozone whirled around. "Maybe not at the moment, but you will eventually paint my fortress." He disappeared through the doorway.

Mason sank onto his chair, having no idea how to escape from his current predicament. He leaned his head back, physically exhausted from his abduction and mentally drained from his conversation with Ozone. "We must stop him."

Later that morning in his communication room, Ozone flipped switches on a large panel covered with various types of instruments and gauges. The panel controlled small monitors lining the walls and a large one straight across from his chair. The small displays relayed images from security cameras positioned near the gorge and around the fortress. Ozone adjusted the panel controls that operated his personal satellites—equipped with instrumentation to penetrate his pollution cloud. Zeroed in on the correct position and frequency to intercept the GGB's broadcast, Ozone's likeness morphed over Willie's image. Willie had just concluded his update.

The GGB chamber resembled a congressional hall with a large screen located behind the main podium. Members already present in Athens populated the sparsely-filled room. Other representatives around the world attended via an emergency connection.

"Good afternoon. For those of you who don't recognize me, I am Lord Ozone, but you may remember me as the Human Virus."

Stunned at the image of Ozone on the large screen, members conversed amongst themselves trying to determine how this villain had infiltrated the closed session and perhaps others.

"I will be brief. Go home to your families. My plan remains on schedule. Your utopian system has left you defenseless. Human annihilation is imminent, so make the most of your abbreviated time on Earth."

Ozone ended the transmission. The members were silent. Due to the security breach, resuming the discussion there was no longer an option, even though Ozone had no interest in it. They immediately initiated their secondary meeting protocol and left the premises.

Waiting for the GGB to convene, formalize a strategy, and execute it did not match Liam's personal time schedule. Even the GGB had flaws, the most critical was the lack of preparedness for a crisis of that magnitude. The Survival Treaty creators severely discounted the need for threat management and other alarmist what-if scenarios, overly optimistic that survivors had learned from the catastrophic war. Instead, they chose to allocate resources for positive, uplifting programs. That, combined with Ozone already several steps ahead of anyone who challenged him, drove Liam to exploit his experience as a revolutionary and take matters into his own hands. Although he had no plan and no army to speak of, something had to be done sooner rather than later.

Liam left the GGB regional building before Willie could intercept him. Meanwhile, disheartened by Mason's kidnapping, the Dropas patiently waited for Liam's return—Clearcoat on the steering wheel and the other Dropas spread across the dashboard. Liam slid into the front seat of his truck.

"Clearcoat, Ozone disrupted the session. He will execute his plan very soon and I can't wait any longer for the GGB to act."

Clearcoat inquired regarding Willie's position on the matter.

"I'll get him on board later. First, we must establish our next step."

Clearcoat gibbered.

"Everything's ready? You want to show Pockets and me Mason's latest mural? Hold on. What do you mean everything's ready?"

The other Dropas lined up directly behind Clearcoat as it relayed additional information.

"Of course, I trust you guys...tonight will paint a brighter picture." Liam smiled, wondering what the Dropas had in store.

Welcome To Our World

Later that evening, Liam, Pockets, and the Dropas waited inside the outer gym doors of the school where Mason completed his latest mural. The emergency lights provided the only illumination as they gazed at the artwork.

Above the interior doors was painted a thick outline of a giant, red letter "N", encompassing a blue sky and clouds. A large, metallic hawk, or Robohawk as the students had aptly named it, appeared to be flying at an angle out of the letter with open mouth, spread wings, and outstretched talons.

"What's happening up there?" Liam pointed at the rafters.

The Dropas' excitement intensified as they stood on Liam's shoulders and watched a hole form in the ceiling above the mural. They scurried down his body, joined hands, and danced in a circle between him and Pockets. They chanted as a light beam, reminiscent of the one Liam witnessed with Demitrius, gleamed through the opening onto the gym floor.

The image of Athena descended the light ray. Unlike the smaller form maintained when she saved Silver, Athena's present life-size body was clad in her battle gear. Equipped with a spear in her right hand and a shield strapped across her left arm, she ended her descent three feet in front of Robohawk. Athena pulled back her spear, thrust the tip through the heart of the painted bird, and withdrew it. The Dropas chanted louder as she ascended through the ceiling and out of sight. Once the light beam faded the Dropas bowed after concluding their dance. Mesmerized, Liam and Pockets fixated on the mural as the two-dimensional Robohawk exhibited initial signs of life.

Its lone discernible eyelid blinked before scanning the premises. Next, its unrestrained head moved from side to side, revealing the other eye that was not visible from outside the mural. The hawk emitted an ear-piercing screech as life traveled through the rest of its body, from head to talons and out across the massive metallic wings. Aware of its freedom, the giant bird emerged from the wall, without resistance or fear, in full three-dimensional grandeur.

As it initiated its inaugural flight, its armored feathers reflected the emergency lights. Surprisingly, the wall stayed intact as the mighty hawk entered a new world, its size increasing upon its departure from the cinder block wall. Flaunting its fifty-foot wingspan, it landed on the floor, shaking the entire gym. Unable to withstand the creature's tremendous weight, the wooden panels buckled underneath it. Sounds of popping boards releasing from the floor echoed throughout the gym. Standing thirty feet high, Robohawk pierced its talons into the slats. It lowered its head just in front of Liam and screeched. Not even flinching, Liam gazed at the astounding living mascot.

The Dropas celebrated their accomplishment between Liam and a grinning Pockets. Unexpectedly, three additional hawks flew out from the painted blue sky and alit near center court, popping more boards loose. Non-metallic and two-thirds the size of Robohawk, Liam wondered from where they originated since Mason had only painted the one.

"There must be more to their world than what the mural depicts."

"More than you can fathom," Pockets whispered.

A half dozen exuberant Dropas returned to Liam's shoulders and the other six to Pockets' palm.

"Clearcoat, is this happening to all of Mason's murals? The Tigers? Panthers? Eagles? Dragons? Every one of them?"

Clearcoat excitedly gibbered in his ear, assuring Liam that it was.

"Yes, the picture is much brighter, my little friend. How will they leave the gym without destroying it?"

Clearcoat apprised Liam of the creatures' ability to liquify. This altered state allows them to inconspicuously ooze into and across surfaces.

"Interesting. Where will we hide these enormous life forms without bringing widespread attention to them?"

"Indigo indicated to me that each mascot is equipped with an internal guidance system, activated when Athena arrived," Pockets explained. "It is unnecessary for us to transport them."

"Very clever. Where is the guidance system leading them?"

"Through the old underground drainage system connecting each town. Final destination is the abandoned Huckabee warehouse by the defunct water plant."

"Well done, Dropas," Liam commended as they bowed. "I just hope the creatures travel stealthily and go undetected by any ForLords in the area."

After witnessing Robohawk and visualizing the multitude of distinct mascots coming alive, Liam's confidence in thwarting Ozone and the ForLords grew. Liam deemed it possible to rid the world of Ozone, his followers, and demolish the fortress, but he couldn't accomplish it alone. He needed assistance from like-minded community members who strongly believed in the power of good. From information Willie shared about Barrow's Ridge, Ozone had undeniably built an outwardly impenetrable fortress. In the little time available, Liam had to devise a plan and assemble an army to end Ozone's reign of terror.

Across town, two senior students, Cooper and Ti, snuck into their high school through the loading dock doors and crept through the corridor that led to the gym. Painted on the wall was a floor-to-ceiling mural depicting several tigers in a rocky, zoo-like setting. From the parking lot, their two friends, Brian and Lauren, spotted the moving silhouettes through the glass windows and doors of the hallway. Somehow, Cooper and Ti had eluded the motion-sensor lights. The light beam that had descended through the gym roof, and initially aroused their curiosity, ascended into the cloud cover.

Just past the mural, Cooper carefully opened the first gym door. He stood behind Ti, arms protectively wrapped around her, as they stared at the mural on the far wall past the basketball court. A painted broken wall with a blue-sky background and marble-framed 'W' comprised the backdrop. Positioned on the border at the top of the letter, a giant tiger, Stripes, appeared to be stepping onto the floating cinder blocks within the blue sky.

Emergency lights barely lit the gym. Hearts racing, they watched the tiger's oscillating head survey the uncharted territory. Ti gasped and Cooper quickly covered her mouth to silence her, but not fast enough. Stripes' sensitive ears heard the faint noise and peered in their direction. Its eyes reflected the dim light directly at Cooper and Ti. They both wanted to reunite with Brian and Lauren, but knew if they flinched, it could lead to their demise.

"Don't move," Cooper whispered into Ti's ear, "or make another sound."

Ti nodded slightly as they watched Stripes watch them, their muscles cramping as they waited motionless for an opportunity to escape.

Uninterested, Stripes scanned the floor below it. The cat's flaring nostrils attempted to distinguish the unfamiliar scents in the air. Stripes' rear leg muscles tensed, and with one swift movement, it leapt off the marble and floating blocks. It glided out of the mural with front paws outstretched, bracing for impact on the gym floor. Stripes mimicked Robohawk's entrance into the new world, increasing in size as it emerged. The front paws landed on the floor with a loud thud, followed by the rear ones, buckling the wood strips. Positioned on the far free throw line, the twenty-five-foot tiger surveyed the unfamiliar environment and announced its presence with a deafening roar that resonated throughout the empty gym.

Cooper and Ti had hung around long enough. Ti released the door, causing it to slam shut, and they rushed to the exit. Stripes responded to the sound, its footsteps thundering across the basketball court. Out the doors they sprinted, not once looking back to see if the giant cat was tailing them. Stripes burst through the gym doors and into the empty corridor. It attempted to pick up the scent of the elusive prey.

Outside, Brian and Lauren watched their two friends' hasty exit, this time activating the sensor lights. Only then did they catch a glimpse of the pursuing tiger. Choosing not to follow, Stripes waited in front of the hallway mural.

"Run!" Cooper yelled at Brian and Lauren.

The four teenagers raced through the parking lot and across the street where they stopped to catch their breath.

"What happened to you guys?" Lauren inquired.

Out of breath and visibly frightened, Cooper and Ti disregarded the question.

"There are more tigers staring out the window," Brian declared.

"Must be...from the other...wall," a panting Ti replied, "outside the gym."

"Where are they going?" Cooper questioned as the smaller tigers trailed Stripes to the loading dock.

"C'mon. Let's see where they're headed," Brian suggested.

"No way," Ti replied, averse to the idea.

"I'm with Brian," Cooper responded. "Ti, if they wanted to hurt us, they would have chased us out of the school."

The huge felines leapt off the loading dock, strolled across the school grounds, and navigated through the vegetation that bordered the property. The four teenagers cautiously pursued. When the tigers reached a grate leading to the underground drainage system, they liquified and disappeared below the street.

The next morning, in unusual fashion, Mason awoke early to the melodic birds in the courtyard. He couldn't resist the peaceful sounds serenading him from outside his window. Mason donned his new apparel. Practicality and comfort overshadowed the prison-looking attire. The solid blue overalls, made of light-weight material, had a multitude of pockets to hold a wide array of art supplies.

Outside, the birds sounded more spectacular. If not for the cloud covering, the joyful chirping almost made Mason forget where he was. Rather than feeling dejected, Mason immersed himself in the courtyard mystique, ambling on the cobblestone path and marveling at the marble statues standing amongst the tall trees. Consumed by the ambience, he failed to hear approaching footsteps.

"You like it?" Ozone asked.

"Jeez, don't do that," Mason admonished, his heart racing. "You scared the heck out of me!"

Ozone merely shrugged.

Mason studied the sculpture in front of him. "I'm admiring the statues. Who's the artist?"

"I am. I created these early in my career, decided that no one else was worthy of owning them, and opted not to sell a single piece."

"They're incredible."

"Yes, they are. Believe it or not, we have a lot of similarities."

"Do we?" Mason strolled to the next statue. "Enlighten me."

"For instance, you didn't hear me walk up behind you because you were absorbed in the sculpture. I, too, become one with the art."

"We have a lot of differences," Mason reminded Ozone, unimpressed. "I can't believe you've chosen to obstruct everyone's view of the sun and blue sky. It's a calming aspect of life, enjoying the brightness and soaking up the energy."

Ozone clasped his hands behind his back as he moseyed to the next statue. "Humans don't fully appreciate things until they're gone. We both know that."

Mason glared at Ozone. "Get out of your cocoon, forget what humanity has done in the past, and enjoy the present."

"Even if they have altered their ways, it required billions of deaths to convince them Earth is the only place they have. And presently, they can't enjoy parts of it because they devastated those areas during the war."

"We have you to thank for that," Mason countered.

"It's all irrelevant. No matter how people think, how they get along with each other, or even if they do appreciate nature, it won't erase what they did to me."

"Quit feeling sorry for yourself. People are enjoying life and each other, that is, until you started interfering." Mason marched away in disgust.

Ozone followed, unmoved by Mason's statements. "You're the one who's not seeing the big picture. Humans will never change. They will always remain the same greedy, selfish beings they've always been—failing to co-exist since setting foot on this planet. One would surmise that a species possessing the highest intelligence should be able to make things work, yet they continue to screw up, time and time again."

"The majority of the population has already progressed." Mason shook his head, frustrated with the conversation. "It's hopeless trying to convince you to see the positive in the world. Changing topics, I've reconsidered your demand of painting the fortress…however, I have two conditions."

"I can't guarantee they will be met, but I'm listening."

"I choose the wall where I begin."

"Done. Just tell me where. And your second condition?"

"I need my own art supplies," Mason added, confident he had outsmarted Ozone and potentially delayed the inevitable.

"Delivered from my studio within the hour," Ozone replied smugly.

"What?" Mason was flummoxed, caught off guard by Ozone's response. "My supplies are here?"

"We transported everything when we brought you."

"You broke into my apartment?"

Ozone shrugged. "Didn't want to make two trips."

"You have no consideration for anything." A furious Mason clenched his fists as he approached Ozone. "Is nothing sacred to you?"

"At this point, not really." Ozone extended his hand to prevent Mason from getting closer. "Relax, they only pilfered your supplies."

"Are you sure?"

"They wouldn't disobey my orders."

"You said yourself that humans will always be selfish and greedy. Don't lend too much credence to your ForLords' allegiance."

Ozone paused momentarily, impressed by Mason's clever attempt to throw his own words back in his face. "My loyal ForLords wouldn't dare betray me, for the consequences would be fatal."

"You will not win, Ozone."

"Enough of your babble!" Ozone grew annoyed at his captive's persistence. "Face it. Human life is coming to an end."

"Don't underestimate the people on the other side of your walls, Ozone, the ones you have so easily dismissed."

"Funny you should mention the other side of my walls. My spy network tells me your brother is up to something."

Mason pointed his finger inches from Ozone's face. "You better not touch—"

"Don't threaten me." Ozone calmly pushed Mason's hand aside. "Remember, I can dispose of you anytime I want. I like your art and have decided to keep you around for now. Just don't cross me, or I'll get rid of you like that." He attempted to snap his fingers, but only a soft, muffled sound came from his gloved hand.

Inside the mansion, Ozone led Mason underneath the main level into his studio at the end of the long corridor. Sculptures and paintings, in various stages of completion, populated the studio. It was also stocked with more supplies and equipment than an artist could ever dream of possessing. Everything escaped damage from the war. Mason's supply box and equipment was positioned in the corner. Free of dust and cobwebs, they visibly stuck out from everything else.

"As you can see, I don't spend much time here."

Detecting despair in Ozone's voice, but not in the mood to hear his sob story again, Mason walked to his supply box. "Appears everything is here and undamaged."

"Just like I told you. You should start believing me."

"Believing you isn't the problem. I just don't believe what you stand for."

"So be it. Where would you like your equipment delivered?"

Mason considered the locations he had inspected. "Take it to that hideous-looking west entrance. I will also need scaffolding set up before I begin."

"I have that too."

"Doesn't surprise me." Mason inserted his hands in his pockets and chuckled.

"Is that funny?" Ozone asked defensively.

"The scaffolding isn't, but I'm always searching for my keys or forgetting them altogether. Now that I don't need them, here they are." He withdrew the keys from the overalls and dangled them in front of Ozone. "Shar must have transferred them from my old clothes."

Ozone expressed no interest. "You have a strange sense of humor."

"I didn't expect you to be amused."

That same morning, Liam drove to Willie's office and summarized the arrival of Robohawk and the other mural creatures. Willie expressed disappointment with the slow pace at which the GGB was addressing the current crisis, but presently offered no commitment to support Liam's effort.

"That brings you up to speed on the events of last night. The next step is to engineer a way for the Dropas to deliver a message to Mason."

Willie mulled over the situation.

"Getting them there isn't the problem. Ozone's defenses essentially disregard what happens on the other side of the gorge. The question is…how do we get them across undetected? They absolutely cannot travel through the chemical stream running along the bottom."

Willie intently observed the Dropas playing on his desk. "I have an idea."

"What is it?"

"They're small enough that when launched, they should elude Ozone's security system."

The Dropas danced excitedly on the desk upon hearing the word "launched."

Liam consulted the Dropas. "Will that work?"

Clearcoat gave Liam an enthusiastic thumbs up.

"Silver and Gold, you will stay with me. I have a special mission for you."

Clearcoat gibbered a small concern about separating the Dropas.

"It won't be for very long," Liam assured. "I need Silver and Gold to help me get the creatures to the fortress."

Clearcoat consented.

"Willie, how do you intend on propelling the Dropas over the gorge?"

Willie nodded, impressed with his own idea. "We'll utilize stake-shooting guns, the ones the investigators used to fire the cables into the far walls."

The Dropas grew more excited. Liam conferred with Clearcoat regarding their ability to withstand being shot out of a gun. The lead Dropa indicated that it wouldn't be a problem as long as they were encased in a protective cylinder.

"They can carry their brushes with them in the tubes," Liam added. "Wait a minute, what about the patrolling drones?"

"With their miniscule size, they should go unnoticed."

"You keep saying should."

"I can't guarantee anything, but I'm confident in our odds."

Clearcoat and the other Dropas flashed Liam the thumbs up sign. They longed to reunite with Mason, and Liam greatly needed them inside the fortress.

"Let's do it," Liam approved.

"I'll notify Pete and relay the logistics. He's the head of the regional office in that area."

"How will we transport them?"

"Jim, a co-worker here, will escort them via maglev bullet train. The speedy trip will ensure that the Dropas meet up with Pete who will discharge them over the gorge. From there, it's up to the Dropas to get your instructions to Mason."

"Sounds good."

Liam held out his hand, allowing the Dropas to return to his shoulders. Willie stared at Liam with arms folded. They were best friends and Willie's body language sent a definitive message.

"You're going to make me ask, aren't you?" Liam concluded.

"You bet I am, and you better hurry up before I change my mind."

"Do you want to be a part of this?"

"Heck yes! I knew when you left the GGB meeting yesterday that you would take matters into your own hands. I want Ozone as much as anybody."

"There isn't another man I'd want by my side."

"Same goes for me." Willie bear hugged Liam.

Willie and Liam had experienced a lot together, especially as revolutionaries. It was an extremely dangerous mission, but if they waited for the GGB to act, it may be too late.

"How will you explain this to May and your kids?"

"I'll tell them the truth and I guarantee you that May will request inclusion. She can spearhead the needle prepping and packaging for distribution."

"Perfect. There is a huge supply to coat. Pockets and I will meet you and May back here to review my plan, assuming I formulate one by then." Liam winked. "I'll need the most recent satellite image of Barrow's Ridge."

"I'll have an interactive holographic map ready when you return."

"Great. All but the astros are at the Huckabee warehouse."

"Why not the astros? Oh, I know what you're up to, but how will they get to Ozone's satellites?"

Clearcoat gibbered in Liam's ear.

"The Dropas will equip the astros with specialized jet packs and release them at the airport. In a liquid state, they can form themselves around the plane fuselage. Once the aircraft reaches peak altitude, the astros will reshape and rocket themselves into orbit."

"You're joking, right?"

"C'mon, Willie. It's the Dropas."

The Dropas playfully folded their arms as they tapped their feet.

"Right, sorry guys," Willie apologized.

"The school where the astros are located isn't far from here. The Dropas and I will transport the astros to the airport and I'll pick up Pockets on my return trip to your office. The Dropas can assist May with the needles as we discuss our strategy."

"That'll give me time to explain to May what's happening."

"Let's roll."

Willie laughed nervously as he switched off the light and closed the door. "You do realize I could lose my liaison position circumventing the GGB like this," Willie remarked.

"That you can replace." Liam placed his hand on Willie's shoulder as they strolled to the front vestibule. "You can't replace your life."

The Assembly

While Liam escorted the Dropas to the school with the astro murals, he envisioned various ways to utilize the mascots during the incursion of Ozone's fortress. As if his own anxiety wasn't enough, Liam was subjected to the Dropas' parody of angst as they paced on the dashboard, once again mocking human behavior. Mason had only been gone a short time and the Dropas missed him dearly. Before the reunion could take place, Liam and his tiny allies needed to prepare the mural creatures for the upcoming journey.

It's one thing to transport a normal-sized bird or cat, but it's another to discreetly relocate a twenty-five-foot tiger or thirty-foot astro. Complicating matters, the entire effort involved transferring over two hundred large living mascots. Clearcoat assured Liam that the Dropas would properly prepare the creatures and his team for the trip.

Liam's task force had much to do. They needed to act fast and as inconspicuously as possible for fear of alerting any ForLords potentially lurking in the area. Ozone's surveillance capabilities and covert spy network increased the probability that Ozone had already acquired information regarding the recent activities. In any event, the sooner the response, the better chance Liam's group had of maintaining the element of surprise.

At the school, Liam waited for the Dropas as they assisted the liquified astros. He compiled a list on his phone of all the mural mascots and considered various combinations that would leverage each one's capabilities alone and teamed with other creatures. As he strategized, four sizable blobs oozed out from the gym doorway followed by one substantially larger one. They flattened on the asphalt and flowed across the parking lot. The masses molded themselves around Liam's truck and inside the bed, blending in with the vehicle colors.

"Well done," Liam commended the Dropas.

The Dropas bowed and Clearcoat instructed Liam to transport the cargo to the airport. To avoid detection and minimize the distance the astros had to cover, Liam had to park alongside the plane on which the astros would be flying.

"I'll use my GGB badge to gain access to the appropriate gate."

At the airport, the Dropas equipped the astros with customized jet packs and stealthily guided them to the designated aircraft. The outside crew loaded luggage as the passengers boarded. It wouldn't be long before the astros orbited with Ozone's satellites.

Liam and Pockets arrived at Willie's office in midafternoon. Willie and May had efficiently arranged the cartons of needles. The Dropas initiated the coating process and May prepared the packages for shipment to the regions with the highest bubble activity.

"GGB personnel are ready to assist with distribution," Willie advised. "If necessary, Silver and Gold can take care of any bubbles in the area tonight."

"Excellent. Thanks for helping us, May."

"My pleasure, Liam," she replied with a smile.

Liam, Willie, and Pockets retreated to the conference room to discuss Liam's plan. As promised, Willie had the most recent satellite image and a schematic of Ozone's fortress displayed holographically. They carefully examined the visuals.

To the north and south, dense forests bordered the fortification and to the west, a desert-like terrain with a scattering of large boulders and fir trees comprised the area between the gorge and the fortress entrance. The mountainous base of Barrow's Ridge protected the east walls. The Winding River flowed underneath the fortress and furnished Ozone's chemical-producing facility with a constant supply of water. The north, south, and west ramparts formed a semicircle with the eastern walls taking the shape of a wedge, conforming to the mountain base. Located on each side of the west entrance were two towers with three more each constructed at the vertices of the wedged section. The surviving investigator from the GGB's second recon team reported that the towers were equipped with chemical-emitting artillery, more powerful than the guns on Ozone's drones.

Inside the ramparts, the fortress was comprised of four distinguishable areas. The first was Ozone's chemical-producing facility, an L-shaped building located on the north side. Just to the south of that, the circular-shaped courtyard. Further south and adjacent to the courtyard was Ozone's mansion. The final structure, located in the eastern portion, contained housing for the ForLords. All other fortress ground area comprised the barren terrain similar to that outside the western wall.

Willie pointed to the inner edge of the southern forest. "This area is only guarded along the inside perimeter with cameras located on the outside wall. The last group of investigators didn't encounter any resistance until just before reaching the fortress."

"Why isn't it heavily guarded?" Liam asked.

"Perhaps Ozone feels no one can successfully mount a formidable attack from within the dense forest. Thus, he has grossly underestimated our capabilities."

"What kind of resistance did they encounter once they reached the fortress?" Pockets asked.

"According to the last mission report, ForLords line the walkway of the wall and operate the southern tower artillery. You also have the perimeter guards I mentioned."

"And the northern forest?"

"I'm not sure." Willie rubbed his chin. "I assume it's guarded the same way."

"That's a dangerous assumption," Liam commented.

Willie examined the north wall image. "It might be less guarded because the river acts as another deterrent for penetration."

"Or it is more heavily guarded because they need the water supply and it provides underground access," Pockets surmised.

"Excellent points, Pockets, and we best make that supposition. In any case, we'll leave the northern forest alone for the moment." Liam inspected the holographic map. "Something is missing here."

"Shouldn't be." Willie scratched his head. "These images are current."

"No, that's not what I mean." Liam passed his hand over the area.

"What don't you see?"

"Where's the airstrip?" Liam traced possible locations with his finger.

Willie examined the holographic satellite image and schematic representation. "That's a good question."

Pockets enlarged the area of interest. "It has to be located here somewhere."

"Agreed, but where?" Liam asked. "Neither the image nor the schematic show any sign of an airstrip."

"Seeing the cargo plane take off and those drones fly the other night, they probably don't require a conventional airstrip," Willie postulated, "but they do need room to take off and land."

"It must be between the gorge and the fortress," Pockets conjectured.

"That's a sizeable area to cover," Willie argued. "And where do they house the drones?"

"My guess is that Ozone stores them underground, beneath a camouflaged opening," Liam said.

"Granted, but it can't be anywhere else," Willie contended. "There's no room in the fortress, the forests are too dense, and the mountains are too jagged."

"Who gets to find out where it is?" Pockets inquired.

"I'll get to our assignments in a minute," Liam advised. "Aside from capturing Ozone and freeing Mason, our primary objective is to level the fortress, but limit the number of ForLords killed."

"According to what, the Geneva Convention?" Willie challenged. "Let's go kick—"

"Hold on, G.I. Willie. Listen up for a second."

"Sorry, I'm a little pumped right now."

Liam pulled out his phone. "What I have here is a list of mascots assisting us on this mission." He transferred the information to the computer displaying the fortress layout.

The software converted the data into mascot holograms.

Willie considered their new allies. "That's impressive."

"The astros are already on a mission. Soon they'll be orbiting Earth with the purpose of dismantling Ozone's three satellites." Liam opened up a projection of a satellite above the fortress and positioned the astro holograms next to it. "It won't be easy. Ozone likely has security and defense systems protecting them."

"This guy seems to have every angle covered," Willie concluded.

"To complicate matters, we have no way of communicating with our spacemen. However, the Dropas and I calculated the approximate time required for the astros to disengage the satellite flying over America. We will depart the warehouse at a specific time, with the assumption that Ozone will be unaware of any movement."

Willie sighed deeply. "That's another risky assumption."

"Yes, it is, but our hands are tied."

"This gets more interesting by the minute," Pockets commented.

Liam moved the first set of mascot holograms into place. "Once the astros dismantle the satellites and we're in position, we'll send the pioneers, tigers, panthers, wildcats, and lions through the southern forest. They're more accustomed to that sort of terrain than the other creatures. The hornets will accompany that group. Pockets, the southern group is yours."

A huge smile lit up Pockets' face as he burst with gratitude over his leadership role.

"Why are the hornets in that group?" Willie asked.

"We'll utilize their nest-making ability. They'll construct structures large enough to detain the captured ForLords. The hornets can also attack the ForLords lining the top of the fortress and fly over the walls if we can't penetrate them."

"Understood. Are we setting up nests in the northern forest?"

"It's too dicey. We don't have recon information regarding that area. Besides, we have another group traveling down the Winding River from the north." Liam positioned the next two groups of mascots. "The Vikings, Indians, Warriors, and gators will be responsible for deactivating the chemical-producing facility. We'll send the largest contingent, that is, the Spartans, Trojans, raiders, knights, chargers, huskies, bulldogs, dragons, and cardinals in from the west. They'll be the most exposed in the effort to locate the hidden hangar. The question is—"

"Go ahead, ask me," Willie exhorted.

"Which do you want, the western attack or the river attack?"

"I'll lead the western attack," Willie responded emphatically.

"You sure?" Liam questioned, surprised by Willie's answer.

"Positive! Who wouldn't want to command dragons?"

"So be it. The western contingent is all yours."

Willie's eagerness buoyed Liam's spirits. "The dragons and cardinals will carry your group across the gorge and assist with the air attack. The huskies and bulldogs will locate the underground hangar. Direct the remaining creatures to penetrate the fortress after neutralizing the fleet of drones. Let's hope, by the time you arrive, Pockets' group will have accomplished its task to allow your contingent entry into the fortress. The final unit will furnish the blitzkrieg."

"Final unit?" Willie questioned.

"Yes. A squadron of hawks, eagles, and falcons." Liam arranged the bird holograms over the mountains bordering the fortress. "They'll arrive from the backside of Barrow's Ridge and strike from the east. Silver, Gold, and Robohawk will lead that assault."

"Wait a second," Willie contended, not believing what he heard. "You're letting two Dropas and a painted creature lead a critical air raid?"

"After all that you've seen, you still underestimate the Dropas," Liam chided.

"They'll do it," Pockets assured Willie.

"Silly me. Tell me more about this Robohawk."

"That's right, you haven't met Robohawk." Pockets nodded confidently. "I will personally acquaint you two when we meet at the warehouse."

The three battalion leaders spent another two hours strategizing the incursion. It was all the time available before they had to dispatch the Dropas to the gorge. As the details materialized, they were increasingly optimistic about successfully ending Ozone's reign of terror. Their concern for rescuing Mason persisted, but even if he wasn't alive, the main objective was to stop Ozone. Liam wrote instructions on a small piece of paper for the Dropas to deliver to his brother. He rolled the note into a miniature tube, easily carried by the tiny messengers.

"What questions do you have?" Liam asked.

"Seems straightforward to me," Willie answered. "It's time to cancel the Ozone Alert."

Liam slapped Willie on the back. "Let's check in on the others."

"You think Mason is still alive, Liam?" Pockets inquired.

"We can only hope he is."

"I truly miss him," Pockets said sadly.

"We all do."

The three men reconvened with May and the Dropas who had completed the needle-coating process and prepared all shipment packages for distribution. Liam conveyed the plan, evoking memories of the war. May broke down in tears and clung to Willie. Although unhappy with the decision to carry out the mission themselves, especially without sanctioned support from the GGB, she understood the likely outcome if nothing transpired. Silver and Gold, however, expressed elation at the opportunity to pilot Robohawk. It always amazed Liam how the Dropas viewed situations differently from humans. Although aware of the importance and the danger associated with the upcoming endeavor, it didn't interfere with their excitement.

Liam, Pockets, and the Dropas comforted May as Willie contacted Jim to arrange the Dropas' transportation. After Willie ended his call, he sat next to his wife and pulled her close to his chest.

It wasn't long before Jim arrived. Liam gave Clearcoat the note for Mason before wishing the ten Dropas good luck. They bid farewell to Silver and Gold, mocking human good-bye gestures by hugging each other, pretending to cry, and carrying on like goofballs. Based on Clearcoat's earlier apprehension about separating the Dropas, Liam expected a solemn parting from the little fellows, but as usual, they found humor in the situation. They appeared confident that a reunion would happen shortly, and believed everything would return to normal.

According to Liam's plan, the Dropas would arrive at the fortress in early afternoon the next day. Attack on Ozone's fortress would commence the following morning. It wouldn't afford Mason and the Dropas much time to carry out Liam's instructions, but time was not their ally. Liam counted on the astros' prompt dismantling of the satellites and that the execution of his strategy was ahead of Ozone's schedule for human annihilation.

Silver and Gold loaded up their quivers with needles for an abbreviated bubble hunt later that evening and then rested on Liam's shoulders. Willie phoned his GGB contacts to initiate the needle disbursement. He accompanied May home where he spent precious time with her and their two children. Liam dropped off Pockets at his place before returning home. Liam, Willie, and Pockets would meet at the Huckabee warehouse early the next morning

Upon arrival at the warehouse, Liam was astonished at what awaited him. Thirty teenagers had gathered around Pockets outside the building. They pelted him with questions regarding Mason and the events happening the previous nights. The assemblage of creatures was no longer a secret. Not to the kids anyway. And perhaps, not to Ozone either. Pockets and the curious youths exhibited relief at the sight of Liam approaching.

"Good luck!" Pockets bellowed.

"Thanks!" Liam shouted, bracing himself for a barrage of inquiries.

Silver and Gold willingly welcomed the excited teens who surrounded Liam.

"Silver! Gold!" two girls squealed, plainly sidetracked by the Dropas on Liam's shoulders.

The other teenagers expressed concerns about more important matters: the current situation, Mason's well-being, and entry into the warehouse. In the distance, Pockets broadly smiled, openly amused by the whole ordeal.

"Easy, easy. One at a time." Liam couldn't distinguish who asked what question and gestured to quiet the rambunctious crowd. "Lauren, I'm designating you as the spokesperson."

Preoccupied with the Dropas, Lauren redirected her attention at Liam. "Excellent. I have some things to say, on behalf of everyone here, of course."

"Certainly, but first, why are you all here?" Liam asked.

"Two nights ago, Ti, Cooper, Brian and I were hanging out in the parking lot of Cooper's school when this light beam penetrated the cloud cover onto the gym roof. Ti and Cooper entered the building to investigate. That mural has the profile of Stripes stepping onto the suspended blocks."

"Yes, I remember it."

"Long story short, Stripes and the other tigers emerged from the walls. We followed them—after they vacated the school—until they liquified down a drainage grate. Brian is familiar with the old pipeline system because he occasionally shadowed his father who once managed the maintenance crew. When our friends said they observed similar occurrences near their schools, Brian concluded the mascots may be gathering here."

"It won't be long before others have similar suspicions," Liam conjectured.

"We didn't tell anyone because we wanted to verify this was real."

"It's not every day you run into larger-than-life jungle cats and Indians," Ti added. "No way would our parents believe us."

"Are you absolutely certain you told no one else?"

"Positive," all but one student replied.

"Well, maybe one other person," Bob remarked from amidst the crowd. "Tony knows, but we haven't spoken since this all took place. It's odd because we see each other almost every day."

"That could pose a problem. He might have fallen victim to one of Ozone's bubbles. If he's in the ForLords' hands, then it's only a matter of time before Ozone discovers we're up to something." Liam changed the subject. "Lauren, what was it you wanted to tell me?"

"Pockets also mentioned this Ozone guy. We're pretty upset about Mason's kidnapping."

Liam glanced at Pockets who innocently shrugged.

"What else did Pockets tell you?"

"He informed us of Ozone's desire to eliminate humanity. We're all wondering...who's going to stop him?"

"Great question, Lauren." Liam briefly assessed the teenagers. "Hold that thought."

Liam walked away to consult Pockets. "Now that they are aware of Ozone's plot and Mason's abduction, tell me about this group of teens."

"From observations and interactions with them at schools, I would categorize most, if not all, as upstanding young men and women," Pockets replied confidently. "They are smart, energetic, and dependable. Why do you ask?"

"Bear with me for a second. I know most of these kids' parents from fighting alongside them in the war. From what I've perceived through previous interactions and what you just shared, many of them take after their parents." Liam subtly shook his head. "However, I can guarantee you that the majority of those parents who fought in the war want nothing to do with another conflict."

"Are you thinking what I think you are thinking?"

"Probably. Pockets, this may be crazy, and extremely risky, but I want them on this mission."

"Yes, most would find it crazy, arguing that these teenagers are too young to take on such responsibility. I, on the other hand, am not one of them. I consider it a rather sensible decision."

"You're not the one that needs convincing. I'm asking them to be part of a potentially fatal undertaking, but given that time is not our ally, I feel we have no other options."

"You are making the right choice."

Liam had to act quickly. If Ozone caught wind of the planned attack before they arrived, the element of surprise would vanish and Ozone would regain the advantage. He shifted his concentration to what had to be done.

Liam drew the kids closer. "Please listen up, everyone. You all have a general understanding about what's happening here. Because of that, I want you to discuss something among yourselves. Your answer, however, must be united. Understood?"

"Yes," they replied in unison.

"Tony is the only other person privy to the mascots coming to life, correct?"

"Yes," the group reassured Liam.

Inquisitive looks abounded. Observing the conversation, Pockets gently smiled off in the distance.

"Lauren, you inquired about who was going to stop Ozone. I'm asking each one of you to be part of a team to defeat him."

Not expecting such a request, the group kept silent with the exception of Roberto and his visibly excited friends. As they all contemplated Liam's request, Willie's car approached the warehouse.

"You don't have much time to decide. I need to talk to Willie for a moment. Remember, all in...or all out."

That was an enormous responsibility to ask teenagers to bear, but Liam needed reinforcements immediately. He knew they could help and deep down he hoped they would agree to his request. Pockets listened in on Liam and Willie's conversation regarding the current situation.

Lauren led the discussion with the intent of reaching a unanimous decision. They all remembered at least a small part of the war, the older ones more than the younger ones. Many lost friends and family in it, and the memories lingered, but Liam was unsure of their willingness to risk their own lives for the cause at hand. They openly conversed with one another as Liam, Willie, and Pockets reviewed options regarding Tony, concluding that they didn't have enough time nor resources to track him down.

Liam reconvened with his pending recruits. "What did you decide?"

"Count us in," Lauren replied enthusiastically.

"All of you?"

"All of us!"

"Even though you could lose your life?"

"We could also die if we don't help," Roberto answered. "We would rather take the risk and try making something good happen rather than just sit around and hope for something good to happen."

"Besides," Brian added, "our parents willingly fought in the war for their beliefs and a better life. The world we presently live in is a great place. We want to keep it that way, don't we?"

"Yeah!" the group shouted.

"Fantastic. Welcome to the team." Liam quieted them as they cheered excitedly. "In order to carry out the plan and return you all home safely, you must follow my instructions precisely, understood?"

They stood at attention and saluted. "Yes, sir!"

"Follow me, my eager, young soldiers. I want to introduce you to your comrades."

The kids playfully marched in step behind Liam. Although ecstatic with their inclusion, he questioned whether they completely understood the danger involved. As they approached the entrance, Liam concluded that he had the right assembly to bring down Ozone and rescue Mason, a team possessing a tremendous amount of energy and desire to accomplish the same objective, and an unconventional army of mural mascots.

Before entering, Liam assured the kids that he, Willie, and Pockets would do everything in their power to protect them. They believed him and, in turn, promised Liam they wouldn't disappoint the team. Above all, they expressed sincere concern for Mason. Sadly, Liam had no new information to communicate regarding his brother's well-being. He made the kids vow that until they had substantiated evidence, they would preserve the hope that he was alive, and they would free him and all humanity from Lord Ozone's grip.

Nobody expected what awaited them inside the warehouse. Mason's painted mascots were gigantic and barely fit in the overcrowded building. The most captivating sight was the determination in their eyes, like hungry challengers seeking to overthrow the champions. The sole purpose for stepping out of their world was to assist against Lord Ozone.

Silver and Gold directed Liam to pet the first mascot, a twenty-foot black panther. Unexpectedly, the panther's fur absorbed his hand. He likened the sensation to immersing it into a gallon of paint. Upon retraction, Liam's unblemished hand appeared as if he never inserted it. The Dropas explained to Liam that, because of each creature's size and presence on Earth, they use vast amounts of energy and periodically need to re-energize to restore their strength.

When they do, they are most vulnerable to Ozone's chemicals, such that one strike could obliterate them. The Dropas expounded that, when active, the clearcoat shells can withstand a substantial amount of Ozone's firepower, but they will ultimately wear down and be as vulnerable as when they are inert. This also results in them re-energizing in a motionless state. Because the infrequent process can occur at any time, the Dropas advised Liam, Willie, and Pockets to constantly be aware of this phenomenon in their respective groups and ensure the re-energizing mascots receive protection. Pockets translated these details for the others.

Afterward, the kids ventured off, seeking a close-up view of their allies. They all fearlessly searched for the mascots from their schools. Once found, they treated them like personal pets and as though they belonged on Earth. As the recruits made the rounds, Silver and Gold apprised Liam, Willie, and Pockets that the creatures could comprehend human language. Although they couldn't verbally communicate back, understanding commands, gestures, and directions were vital elements needed to lead and mobilize the mural mascots.

Pockets tugged on Willie's elbow. "Let me introduce you to a special friend."

"Oh, yeah, the one you call Rambohawk."

"That's a new one," Pockets chuckled.

The group gathered at the far corner of the warehouse. Many of the onlookers hadn't seen Robohawk up close either. Awaiting its assignment, the giant bird isolated itself from the other mascots.

"What's so special—" Willie's jaw dropped as he gazed at the mighty bird lifting its head for all to view. "Say no more."

"Incredible!" Brian exclaimed.

"Awesome!" another declared.

Robohawk's head protruded forward with a laser stare. The light reflected brilliantly off the armor plates as it pushed its breast high into the air. It flapped its wings, creating a whirlwind of dust from the warehouse floor. The air movement forced the team members back six feet before they regained their balance, and it blew Roberto's beret off his head. Robohawk screeched, alerting the other mascots. Awakening from a trance, the mural allies focused on their recognized leader.

"I'm glad that bird is on our side," Willie whispered to Liam.

"We're fortunate they're all on our side."

Robohawk lowered its neck and Liam climbed aboard, situating himself as it raised him above the others. It was time to brief the team. Speaking from that height allowed everyone to hear Liam, but he personally wanted to experience what it was like aboard that magnificent creature. Only then did he understand Silver and Gold's excitement about piloting the armored bird.

During the quickly waning time left before departing the warehouse, they reviewed the strategy. Confident in their individual and collective roles, Liam divided the youths among Willie, Pockets, and himself. The three accompanied the teens home where they had a difficult conversation ahead of them and little time to convince their parents. Understandably, most parents were saddened and others initially angered. No mother or father wanted a child involved in a battle, knowing he or she may never return. In every instance, the teens reminded their parents of the war they had fought and that the young recruits would be fighting for related reasons—the principal one, the end of humanity if they didn't. Distraught over the decision, the parents respected and supported their children. Tears flowed freely and, as expected, most parents feared the worst. They could only be reassured so many times that Liam, Willie, and Pockets would do their best to bring the loved ones home safely.

Later that afternoon, Willie's GGB officers would transport the contingent to a central location near Barrow's Ridge. The officers were familiar with the area and Willie trusted them not to inform the GGB of the mission. From the central location, the organized teams would travel separately to their strike positions, and carry out the overall objective.

Doorstep Of Fate

Mason painted from dawn to dusk, effectively passing the time. Additionally, the concentration needed to run Ozone's equipment diverted his attention from family and friends back home, especially Pockets and the Dropas who were usually with him on a daily basis.

Ozone provided Mason with a sophisticated hydraulic lift. He invented the machine himself, hoping to use it if he ever painted again. It delivered superior efficiency over regular scissor lifts, eliminating the need for task interruption to vertically or horizontally reposition it. A specially-designed helmet utilized guided sight information received from the user's mental impulses, maneuvering the lift to wherever the user wanted. Once he learned the intricacies of the helmet, Mason rapidly covered a large area of the fortress wall.

Mason broke twice a day for meals. Shar brought his food around noon and six. Although he asked for her company each time, she denied his requests, citing Ozone's disapproval. Instead, Mason ate alone and yearned for the warmth of the sun, but mostly he contemplated Ozone's desire for human extinction. That thought upset his stomach and he returned to painting.

This day marked a significant change in Mason's outlook. While eating his noon meal, Mason's stomach knotted at the thought of Ozone's horrible plan. He threw his partially-eaten sandwich on the tray and climbed aboard the lift.

Mason raised the platform to the position where he quit working prior to lunch. He locked the platform into place and filled his spray gun can with paint. He flipped on the compressor switch and aimed the gun at his supply box in order to check the pressure. The whir of the small motor, comparable to a vacuum cleaner, resonated off the semi-enclosed section of the fortress wall. Noticing a slight clog, he tilted the nozzle and examined it. He unwittingly squeezed the trigger, only to receive a face full of spattered paint.

"Jeeezz!" Mason yelled.

As Mason wiped his cheeks, he heard faint giggling sounds. He assumed it was the ForLord who regularly harassed him from atop the rampart, but he saw no one when he glanced over his shoulder.

He switched off the compressor to determine what made the noise and from where it originated. Emanating from inside the top drawer of his supply box, the giggling grew louder as the sound of the humming motor diminished. Mason's hope mushroomed as he slowly opened the drawer to peek inside, placing his eyes just over the top edge. When he slid the drawer far enough, the Dropas showered him with more paint from miniature squirt guns.

"Darn you guys!" Mason wiped his brow with his fingers and intentionally slammed the drawer shut.

The Dropas tumbled over the supply trays.

"Who you talkin' to, painterboy?" a ForLord barked from above, his chemical weapon aimed at Mason.

"Myself. It's a sign of genius," Mason retorted, squinting at the ForLord to avoid getting paint in his eyes.

"I'm no expert, *genius*," the ForLord smirked, "but aren't you supposed to be painting the wall instead of yourself?"

"Oh, thank goodness I have you to mentor me," Mason replied sarcastically.

The Dropas giggled louder.

The ForLord raised his weapon. "Think it's funny?"

"Not really." Mason brushed his fingertips across his eyelid. "You're right, I must look silly with paint dripping down my face."

"You look like a fool. Get to work."

Noticing the residual paint on his fingers, Mason saluted the ForLord, deliberately flicking droplets onto the ForLord's uniform.

The ForLord raised his weapon at Mason. "Watch it, painterboy, or I'll spray you with more than paint."

"I doubt it," Mason replied, confident that no ForLord would touch him without Ozone's order.

Back at the watch tower, two comrades mocked the ForLord sporting his newly decorated uniform. The three tussled a bit before the on-duty commander intervened and ordered them back to their posts. Mason used a towel to remove the remaining splotches from his hands and face, leaving faint streaks where he had wiped. He opened the top drawer where the Dropas had lined up side by side. Clearcoat stepped forward and offered Liam's instructions. Verifying no one watched, Mason accepted the tube, removed the note, and read it:

M – We're throwing Ozone a surprise party at dawn tomorrow. You and the Dropas need to paint a blue sky, a ledge, and cracks on a fortress wall near main gate. Once party starts, head to the river under fortress. We'll be there. – L

"You want a blue sky?" Mason whispered. He passed his hand in front of the wall. "There it is. We're on the same page."

At his core, Mason believed Liam would devise an escape plan to release him from Ozone's grip. Clearcoat advised him to destroy the message. The Dropas giggled as Mason crumpled the note and swallowed it.

"Shh," Mason whispered as he gagged on the paper. "You guys need to stay quiet. I'm happy to see you, too, but we can't let anyone discover you."

Clearcoat settled down the other Dropas as only it could. Excited about reuniting with their human companion, they eagerly wanted to play, but understood the mission took precedence. Mason felt the adrenaline rush after reading Liam's note, but stifled his elation to avoid raising any suspicion with the nearby ForLords, or worse, Ozone.

"Okay, guys, the band's back together. We need to add more clouds and cracks to this blue sky."

The Dropas acknowledged Mason's directions and scattered themselves on the wall. He restored the clogged spray gun, donned his helmet, and resumed painting. Unlike before, he worked with an intended purpose, dispersing the colored liquid and only pausing to refill the empty can. To avoid any suspicion, the Dropas located themselves near the paint stream, ensuring the illusion that the discharge came from Mason's spray gun. As he and the other Dropas painted, Clearcoat hid itself underneath Mason's helmet and briefed him on Liam's plan. Together, Mason and the Dropas transformed the dull fortress wall into a huge blue sky, with billowy clouds, and strategically-located cracks. More cracks would come later. They next concentrated on painting the ledge.

Ozone operated three satellites to view the world from his fortress, one each over Europe, Asia, and America. The latter satellite relayed communications from the other two and provided air security for the fortress. Ozone had equipped the orbiters with instruments capable of acquiring reconnaissance information through the pollution layer blanketing the globe. It was crucial that the astros dismantle the one over America first, otherwise it would alert Ozone of the ground attack and pose a major threat to any airborne intruders, namely the birds. Disabling the first two satellites would be the easiest.

Late in the afternoon, the five astros reached the first satellite. It was heavily armed with Ozone's exclusive chemical weapons. The four smaller astros cautiously approached the America-hovering orbiter while the giant astro morphed into a weather satellite, furnishing hidden protection for the others, if needed. The astros effectively jammed the security system and disabled the defense systems.

They disconnected the satellite communication switches and cameras, but not before an emergency, function-lost message was relayed to the Asia-hovering satellite which propelled itself to the astros' location. Forced to act more quickly, the astros reprogrammed the defense systems. The goal was to eliminate the advancing Asia-hovering satellite while sustaining minimal damage to the reconfigured one. This was imperative because when the orbiter over Europe arrived to replace the newly destroyed one, it would have already received information pertaining to the destruction of a sister satellite and be prepared for battle. The astros relied on the reconfigured satellite to distract the third satellite long enough for them to destroy it.

While en route, the Asia-hovering satellite transmitted a message to Ozone, updating him of a malfunction with the one hovering over America and that it initiated its repositioning protocol to replace the damaged orbiter. Liam counted on Mason and the astros to successfully complete their respective operations. In order to maintain the element of surprise, Ozone must interpret the satellite malfunction to be accidental.

Adhering to the timetable Liam allotted for the astros to disengage the America-hovering satellite, his task force initiated their departure strategy. Each group carefully carried their liquified creatures in special holding tanks to underground rail cars. The containers resembled scuba tanks, could easily be strapped to one's back, and were labeled with the mascot names and accompanying equipment loaded inside them. Silver and Gold condensed three, sometimes four creatures into each tank. Any more than that and an undesirable amalgamation would occur. Compressed inside the cylinders, the mascots were incapable of assisting in the event of an unforeseen attack. Upon release at the intended destinations, the creatures needed approximately four hours to restore themselves to their normal state. Silver and Gold also cautioned Liam that the tanks could only be used once, explaining that the density of the compressed creatures in his world would severely diminish the integrity of the cylinders. New ones would be required to bring the creatures home.

The task force drove to the bullet train station, transferred the tanks and gear to the storage car, and traveled to the designated GGB regional office. Thus far, resistance from Ozone's ForLords was nonexistent—too easy and too good to be true.

Silver and Gold's fleet of birds departed for the eastern slope of Barrow's Ridge. Upon arrival, they would wait until just before sunrise to intercept Ozone's drones. From the regional office, Liam's group was transferred to a remote site ten miles from the fortress. They hiked through the forest, reaching a location within three miles of the north wall. Willie's group established a position at the regional office where they unloaded their creatures, allowing them to re-energize prior to departing for the gorge. Using multiple vehicles, GGB officers transported Pockets' group to the edge of the southern forest. If Ozone's satellites had been destroyed, each contingent would arrive at their destination undetected and, again, without resistance.

Mason stopped painting when an increased number of ForLords gathered atop the walls. He also observed Ozone's drones practicing maneuvers in the distance. The sudden uptick in activity troubled him. From the base of the lift, Ozone ordered Mason to lower the platform to the ground.

"No more painting!" Ozone commanded loudly with a slur.

Mason squinted, somewhat bewildered. "Why? It won't be dark for another few hours."

"Blame your brother. He's more daring than I expected, especially with you as my hostage."

Mason lowered the lift to its final resting position. "He probably thinks I'm dead." He stepped off the platform, preventing Ozone from espying the Dropas' retreat to the supply box.

"In due time. Whether you're dead or alive, you two will never lay eyes on each other."

"That remains to be seen." Mason briefly glanced skyward over his shoulder. "Is that the reason for the flyovers and increased ForLords on guard?"

"Very perceptive. It's time to carry out my promise, but first I must deal with your brother and whoever is helping him."

"You would be wise not to mess with my brother," Mason warned.

"Save your empty threats for someone who cares. Pack up your equipment. My men will transport everything to my studio. Then return directly to your quarters. You will remain there until I decide what to do with you."

"Oh, am I grounded?" Mason snickered mockingly.

Ozone ignored the comment and retreated to his war room. Mason examined the wall, admiring how much more he and the Dropas had accomplished under such time pressure. *I have to get one of these lifts.* The painted ledge that Liam requested in the delivered note included a sill four feet above the ground.

Liam hopped up onto the platform and ensured no one was watching. He opened the supply box drawer, nearly scaring the daylights out of the Dropas, but not as much as they frightened him. "What the heck are you doing?"

As disgusting as it seemed from a human perspective, the Dropas' new game was harmless to them. They had interchanged their noggins, each Dropa sporting a different colored one from that of its body.

"All right you guys," Mason instructed as he wielded his finger at them, "get your heads on straight." He chortled at his pun.

The Dropas removed the heads from their bodies, tossing them to their companions like a circus juggling act. Finding a match, each Dropa replaced its noggin on its own body and fell into a straight line, still giggling over their twisted humor.

"Listen closely, I have a job for you," Mason whispered. "When it gets dark, and throughout the night, we need more cracks in various locations of the wall, including the section I wasn't able to paint." Mason paused. "What's so funny?"

Clearcoat softly gibbered into Mason's ear, telling him they didn't need the entire night to paint cracks, rather they would achieve the goal in five to ten minutes.

"Sorry. Minor brain cramp." Mason backed away from Clearcoat. "Remember, wait until it's dark."

The Dropas saluted.

As he cleaned his supplies, Mason grew concerned with Ozone's anticipation of an attack. "What would Liam tell me in this situation?" he murmured before chuckling. "Mason, you worry too much. Yep, that's exactly what he'd say."

The second satellite arrived from Asia as predicted. The four spacemen retreated for cover around the giant astro that had morphed into a weather satellite. When the second satellite came in range, the first opened fire with three chemical streams. All three streams hit the oncoming spacecraft with pinpoint accuracy, completely disintegrating it. The second satellite did fire one successful shot, damaging the shield of the first satellite and rendering it useless. It also transmitted a signal to the Europe-hovering satellite which received the message and reprogrammed its coordinates before vacating its position. It utilized its thrusters and emergency fuel to reach the America-hovering satellite as quickly as possible and geared up its defense systems and shield for the anticipated conflict.

Waiting for the third satellite to appear, the astros tried diligently, but unsuccessfully, to repair the damaged shield. They only improved the maneuvering capabilities of the spacecraft that might buy them some time to destroy the third and final orbiter.

One astro spotted the approaching satellite and motioned for the others to shove off from the one they were repairing. The three astros barely dodged an oncoming stream of chemicals as they propelled themselves out of harm's way. Both satellites exchanged fire, with the America-hovering one striking first and weakening its enemy's shield. The Europe-hovering satellite continuously missed as it anticipated the other's movement. But each time it fired, the streams zeroed in on the target as it learned the maneuvering pattern. The four astros watched, waiting for the Europe-hovering satellite shield to wear down before it pinpointed subsequent shots. After a prolonged barrage, time finally expired for the first satellite. The Europe-hovering satellite homed in on its mark and discharged three chemical streams, intercepting and obliterating the America-hovering satellite.

Having addressed the first enemy, the third satellite pursued the four defenseless astros. They needed to elude its firing range, but failed to assess the safe distance. The satellite realigned its weapons and fired at the fleeing astros, the trajectories of the streams on a direct course to strike three of the four unknowing enemies.

A huge fireball erupted where the satellite once existed. The four astros, oblivious to what transpired behind them, traveled further through space. The light from the fireball reflected off orbiting metal debris. The astros turned to investigate, still unaware of the pursuing chemical streams. They could do nothing but wait to be vaporized. As the chemical streams neared, the enemy fire merely dispersed into space having reached a maximum range, which had been set for the distance between it and the America-hovering satellite.

The astros directed their attention to the origin of the enemy fire. Floating in place of the attacking satellite was the fifth astro, and a gigantic one it was, measuring nearly thirty feet tall and eight feet wide.

With the two satellites engaged in chemical fire, the fifth astro morphed into its original form. Once the Europe-hovering satellite destroyed the other, the newly reverted astro demolished the satellite from behind, compressing it between its gigantic hands until it exploded. Seeing the fifth astro drifting alone, the others headed for it. They successfully fulfilled their mission requirements and re-energized before the return trip to Earth.

Greeted By Adversity

By the time Liam's team encamped, they were exhausted. Liam hardly slept the past few nights and his recruits, Cooper, Brian, Ti, and Lauren were weary from staying up late the previous night coupled with the rigorous journey. The agenda did not call for rest, just yet. They had to discharge the creatures from the tanks to allow re-energizing time for the battle less than eight hours away.

They emptied the tanks, releasing the liquid mascots near camp but hidden from any lurking ForLord scouts. They marveled at the reshaping creatures, growing from a small puddle to fifteen or twenty feet in height. Taking advantage of their inert state, Liam opted to touch a gator, keenly aware that he'd never get that close to a live one. He was enthralled with the idea of immersing his hand inside an animal, real or not. Entranced in his own amazement, he suddenly heard a distressed voice amidst the forest.

Unsure of what had happened, Cooper's friends rushed to his aid. Clarity of the situation presented itself as the huge Viking ship returned to its normal size seventy-five feet from the water, making it impossible for the five of them to transport it down to the riverbank.

"Nice job, ace," Brian admonished.

"Now we'll never get to the fortress on time," Ti added.

"That's enough negativity." The four teens jumped at the sound of Liam's voice, oblivious he was behind them. "Cooper feels bad enough on his own."

"I'm so sorry," Cooper apologized, dejected. "I didn't see a label on this tank."

"You're right," Liam confirmed as he lifted the empty cylinder. Unbeknownst to the others, he discreetly removed the partially-detached identifier from the underside of the canister and slipped it into his pocket. "It's not your fault, Cooper. The label must have fallen off in transit."

Cooper was partially relieved at the discovery. Although the delay could significantly alter the schedule, Liam chose to free Cooper from the burden of fault. After all, he and his friends had enough to worry about on the mission.

As the boat reshaped, the situation worsened. The vessel merged with every tree trunk in its path. Removing it would leave gaping holes in the hull.

"How will we transport it to the river?" Ti asked. "It's not even close to the water, and it has trees growing out of it."

"We are all aware of the situation," Liam said. "Let's focus our energy on a solution."

"You're right," Ti answered empathetically. She hugged her boyfriend. "I'm sorry, Cooper. I'm just crabby from lack of sleep."

"Me too. I apologize for snapping at you." Brian fist-bumped Cooper.

"Can we reload the tank and empty it by the river?" Lauren suggested.

"Under different circumstances, yes, but each cylinder is only good for one cycle. We don't have any unused ones with us."

"I forgot about the single-use restriction," Lauren acknowledged, dispirited.

"Let's at least finish what we started and call it a night. We'll have two or three hours to devise a plan after the creatures fully re-energize."

They unloaded the remaining tanks and laid out the sleeping bags. It was a chilly night near the mountains, and they couldn't wait to feel the warmth of the down cocoons for the brief rest. Building a fire was out of the question for fear that they would be discovered.

Liam lay awake, listening to the night sounds: a choir of crickets, pine limbs dancing in the wind, and the current massaging the river rocks. Although exhausted, sleep eluded him as he mentally reviewed the mission details.

"Liam?" Brian whispered. "Are you up?"

"Yes, Brian," Liam replied plainly.

"Something's bothering me." Brian rolled over to face Liam.

"What's on your mind?"

"I was wondering…have you ever killed another human?"

Liam didn't expect such a profound question, but given the situation, it was certainly appropriate. "Sadly, I have, but not because I wanted to."

"Why then?"

"It was a matter of survival during the war. If I didn't, they would have killed my family, my comrades, or me."

"You killed more than one?"

"More than I care to remember."

"How did you feel?"

"Awful. I killed my own kind."

"Didn't they deserve it?"

"No one deserves to have their life taken by another."

"What about murderers?"

"Not even murderers. The desire to commit such an act is what needs to be terminated."

"I'm not following you."

"Take for instance Bob's friend, Tony."

"Shouldn't he be killed? He's likely one of Ozone's ForLords."

Liam sat up and draped the sleeping bag around himself. "Absolutely not. Tony is a wonderful person. He's a ForLord because of what Ozone has done to him, similar to how drugs affect an individual. Drugs often make users evolve into something they're not and behave in ways they don't normally act. In many cases, the addiction causes them to perform wrong or horrible deeds. Drugs also alter the way users treat others, as well as themselves. Ozone's bubbles have affected Tony in a similar manner. What needs to be killed is the element inside Tony that changed him. Does that make sense?"

Brian rested his head on his hand. "You're saying that we all enter this world as good people, but things in our life can transform us into someone we're not."

"In simple terms, yes. Remember, those triggers making a person greedy, inconsiderate, or even malevolent are a result of adverse experiences and influences. They impact a person in a negative way, but we are also shaped by the positive ones. However, both embody an individual's uniqueness."

"I think I understand."

"We can't always control what influences or experiences affect us. Although it can happen throughout our lives, it usually occurs when we're most vulnerable and most impressionable, during our childhood. The responsibility of molding us falls in the hands of those closest to us, primarily our family and friends, who are affected by their family and friends."

Brian clasped his hands behind his head. "It's all interrelated, isn't it?"

"Yes, and very complicated if you think about it. The bottom line is, children must grow up with as many positive influences as possible and be taught how to navigate through the negative ones, understanding that the latter are always present. The Survival Treaty provisions aim to maximize this philosophy while highlighting common goals, such as coexistence and enriching all lives."

"That makes sense."

Liam adjusted the position of his sleeping bag. "Negativity was a major contributor to instigating the war. Already-overwhelmed societies were unable to deal with all the gloom and distrust."

"I like the way the world is evolving, at least until Ozone interfered."

"As do I."

Brian contemplated everything Liam shared. "I don't want to kill any ForLords."

"Neither do I. Our objective is to capture the ForLords in order to restore the goodness in them, but prepare yourself, Brian. When the thought of not wanting to kill enters your mind during the battle, and it will, remember one thing. Ozone and his men want to kill you. And if you think about it too long, it will be your last thought. Do you understand?"

"Yes."

"My intention isn't to frighten you, but that's the reality of our situation."

Brian hesitated. "Are you scared, Liam?"

"Darn right I'm scared. If we fail, none of us will survive, but at least we have a chance to do something about it."

"Thanks for the talk, Liam." Brian tucked his arms in his sleeping bag.

"Anytime." Liam rested his head on the pillow. "Get some rest, Brian."

"Good night, Liam."

Willie and the GGB officers who had accompanied the task force on the bullet train busily emptied the tanks in a vast, underground storage facility located six miles west of the gorge. Prior to their arrival, Willie's associates scrambled to empty the building in order to accommodate the transient guests. Over the next hour, the associates were amazed each time they released a creature.

Exceptionally proud of the mascot army he would lead, Willie strutted from end to end of the facility. Head held high, he admired each one. As he neared the dragons, he eyed something peculiar. Remembering the Dropas' explanation, that the creatures did not move when re-energizing, he was intrigued by the small traces of smoke emitting from the dragons' nostrils.

Bob, one of the young recruits, walked up next to Willie. "Something wrong?"

"Not at all. I'm picturing what these dragons will do to Ozone's drones."

"Ozone has no idea what's coming for him."

An exceedingly witty character, Bob used that as a perfect opportunity to play a joke on Willie's associates. They had just arrived with the other students and were also fascinated by the wafting smoke.

Bob winked at his friends. "Everything seems to be all right with this one. Let's have a peek inside." He inhaled deeply and thrust his head into the closest dragon's midsection, trusting his noggin would be attached when he withdrew it as he had seen Liam's hand do at the warehouse.

Willie played along with the harmless prank. "Holy mackerel, the dragon swallowed his head!"

"Pull him out!" one associate commanded.

Bob's friends also partook in the hoax, yelling and screaming frantically. Bob flailed his arms as three officers yanked him out of the dragon's body.

"What…took you…so long?" Bob gasped.

The associates were dumbfounded. The teenager had no traces of dragon innards on him. Bob, Willie, and the others relished the tomfoolery.

"You should have seen your sorry faces." Willie doubled over in hysterics.

"Not funny," Pete chided, unamused. "This is no time to be goofing around."

The other associates joined in the mirth.

"Get back to work!" Pete ordered.

They took two steps before releasing another outburst of snickers.

"Sorry, Pete, but I couldn't resist the opportunity," Bob extended his hand.

Pete glared at the prankster. "Don't let it happen again."

"Yes, sir. By the way, Willie, everything is functioning inside the dragon."

The associates could no longer contain themselves. Even Pete chuckled.

"Come on," Willie called to the kids, "we have work to do."

They followed Willie and Pete into a conference room. Repeatedly, Willie reviewed every detail of their role in the mission. The plan had to be executed precisely and the group welcomed the repetition. Following the review session, the kids briefly napped to recharge before the upcoming conflict.

Acclimating to his new role, Pockets found himself leading the majority of teenagers. The largest contingent's main objective involved capturing the ForLords and detaining them in the hornets' nests. Pockets' ability to relate with students proved to be a huge asset in that situation and the rationale Liam used to assign him to that operation. And Pockets needed to channel every bit of his charismatic nature.

The group hiked through two-thirds of the forest and exhibited signs of tiring from the long journey. Pockets chose to empty the tanks at the current location, hidden by the dense forest and far enough from the fortress to minimize detection by the ForLords.

As the tanks discharged, Pockets laid out the sleeping bags for the abbreviated rest. He unrolled the last one as everyone assembled behind him.

"We're done here, Pockets," Roberto announced.

"Excellent."

"Hey, wait a minute." Roberto considered Pockets' method of encampment extraordinary. "Where did you get these sleeping bags? None of us carried any, and come to think of it, you didn't have anything on your back."

Pockets shrugged modestly.

"There's no way you hauled all that in your pocket!"

Pockets intentionally avoided the interrogation pertaining to his enigmatic cache. "Let's review our mission responsibility one more time." He unfurled an area map onto a fallen log, and the kids gathered around it. Never had they observed the seriousness in Pockets' eyes. "Before I start, I want to commend you all for having the courage to be here."

The students solemnly nodded.

"Let me remind you of our purpose." He gestured in the direction of the fortress. "Beyond those trees, and beyond the walls past those trees, an evil man exists. A man wanting to eliminate you, your family, your friends…everyone. He harnesses so much selfishness, loathing, and self-pity that he feels no human deserves to live. Tomorrow you will see this hatred up-close, the same hatred evident before and during the war. Although many of you have heard, read, or even witnessed firsthand what occurred in that conflict, you now have the opportunity to rid this world of his evilness and write your own history."

The harsh reality of what lies ahead had set in. Students locked arms, held hands, or others, less unnerved, stood tall. Pockets' intention wasn't to scare them but rather prepare them for the upcoming confrontation.

"If this scenario I'm describing is too frightening, please let me know." Pockets waited for someone to speak or even walk away.

The teens eyed each other. Even if fearful, they were more afraid of abandoning their friends. No one left. Pockets lifted his hand over the map and the others followed suit.

"Good," Pockets spoke softly, "we are all in this together until the end."

"Together until the end," they all whispered loudly.

"Please focus on the map."

Pockets extracted three flashlights from his pocket and handed them to those standing closest to him. The kids watched, dumbfounded.

"Once the creatures are re-energized, we will hike to an area near the fortress. One by one, each hornet will separate from the group to construct a huge nest." He referred to the marked locations.

"How do we get them into the nests, especially the ones farthest away from the fortress?" Roberto asked.

"Good question. The hornets will transport the captured ForLords to those nests. The pioneers will position themselves at the forest edge and assist your effort to fill up the closest ones. I will lead the cats into the fortress for the initial encounter with the ForLords." Pockets pointed to the appropriate areas on the map. "You guys will seek cover among the trees and wait for the captives. Although I do not anticipate much resistance once we get them to, and inside the nests, I want you all to prepare for potential opposition." From his pocket, he withdrew enough weapons for the entire group.

"What's this?" Kelly examined the firearm.

"An immobilizer. Hold it in your hand like this, wrapping your fingers around it with your thumb on the black button."

They followed Pockets' instructions.

"If a ForLord charges you or attempts to escape, aim the immobilizer and press the black button. The emitted pulsed beam will paralyze the ForLord."

Pockets fired at a lightning bug. The insect dropped to the ground.

"Cool!" Roberto exclaimed.

"Once immobilized, drag the ForLord into a nest where the tending hornet will position the detainee. Effects of immobilization vary among individuals—ranging from thirty minutes to three hours. Err on the side of caution and act swiftly. If you need to mobilize the person, change the setting like this."

Pockets made the adjustment and shot a second beam at the paralyzed insect. Moments later, the lightning bug returned to flight.

"It will all be clearer when the creatures awaken and we position ourselves. I'm designating Roberto as the prison warden. Can you handle it?"

"Yes, sir, I can handle it."

"Excellent. Before calling it a night, what other questions do you have?"

A long pause indicated they all understood their role.

"Wonderful. Let's get some sleep."

"Good night," they responded.

The kids dispersed to the campsite, whispering about the upcoming conflict. Pockets inserted the rolled map into the tube, unaware that Kelly silently waited.

"Pockets?"

Startled, Pockets released the cylinder upward and instinctively caught the falling object in his pocket.

"I'm sorry. I didn't mean to frighten you."

"No harm." Pockets leaned up against a tree. "What troubles you?"

"I can't picture this world without us in it. Can we truly defeat Ozone?"

"If we stay positive and believe in ourselves, otherwise defeat is inevitable."

"I mean no human beings at all." She lowered her head.

"It is difficult to fathom, but that is what Ozone is trying to do. He is attempting to bring out the greed and hatred instilled upon us over the generations. The same greed and hatred we have tried to abolish since the war. We are here to give humanity another chance. That is a great task to have bestowed upon us." Pockets lifted Kelly's chin. "We cannot let Ozone, or anyone else, prey on the undesirable attributes humans possess within their self-made walls. Those walls must come down and stay down. We must realize the importance of life and all the intangibles it has to offer."

Kelly detected anger, resentment, and yet sadness in Pockets' voice. "I do cherish my life and I want to live it to the fullest. That's why I'm scared, Pockets. What if we aren't successful?"

"We are all scared, but we will get through this. Together."

Pockets and Kelly strolled toward camp, admiring the awe-inspiring mascots.

"It must be a full moon tonight or close to it." Pockets surveyed the campsite. "A faint light penetrates the cloud cover, enough to view the giant silhouettes."

"You're right. They're magnificent, even in the dark." Kelly's mind briefly wandered. "Do you think Mason is alive?"

"I believe he is, but no one knows for certain."

They stopped at Kelly's sleeping bag. Although most of the team had taken Pockets' advice and gone right to sleep, he heard a few lingering whispers.

"I miss him."

"We all do, Kelly. Please, try to get some rest."

"Good night, Pockets."

Silver and Gold's uneventful journey with the birds took a turn for the worse. Halfway up the eastern side of Barrow's Ridge, a rare, summer snow storm greeted them. The infamous Western Winds swirled with gusts over seventy miles per hour. The birds would not have enough energy to fly through the storm and fight Ozone's drones upon arrival. In addition, the sub-freezing temperatures complicated matters by hindering the birds' flying abilities and posing a threat to the Dropas.

Silver pinpointed a location on the mountainside suitable for a temporary shelter to house the squadron. Gold directed the other birds to follow Robohawk to that area. The avian leader screeched often, helping guide them in the low visibility to the desired destination.

After landing, Silver and Gold worked in tandem to paint an enclosure big enough for the entire contingent. Time was of the essence as the frigid temperatures hindered their progress. Silver created a door to close off the entrance and Gold painted a camp fire. As the hollow warmed, the birds re-energized side by side, gearing up for the morning battle with Ozone's air force.

Silver and Gold could do nothing more but wait out the tempest. Taking advantage of the lull, the Dropas created two grand prix cars and a miniature track. They raced around the cavern, painting obstacles for the other to overcome. Understanding the criticality of their mission role, the squadron leaders needed to compensate for lost time—once the storm subsided—in order to arrive at the fortress as planned.

A chair shattered against the doorframe, barely missing the two most senior ForLords, Alpha and Bravo, as they entered Ozone's war room. Alpha was first commander and chief strategist. Bravo was second in command and chief tactician.

"What the—" Bravo exclaimed.

"Silence!" A furious Ozone kicked a second chair that smashed into the wall. "I want every man double-shifted and every weapon in this fortress checked and rechecked to ensure they are in top working order."

"Yes, sir!" Alpha and Bravo acknowledged.

"I also want every drone battle-ready by tomorrow morning. Understood?"

"Yes, sir!" They pivoted to leave.

"Alpha, you stay here."

The commander stopped short of the door as Bravo exited. Ozone glared out the window into the darkness. The sufficient brightness in the room prevented the night vision on the visor from activating, otherwise he might have noticed the Dropas painting cracks on the dimly-lit walls.

"We must delay our plan to terminate human existence."

"But everything is in place?" Alpha contested.

"Circumstances have altered our schedule."

"And what would those be, sir?"

"They destroyed my three satellites."

"What?" Alpha questioned, shocked as he approached Ozone.

"You heard me. My satellites are gone!"

"Who did it?"

"I'm not exactly sure, but I have a good idea."

The war room door flew open again.

Restrained on both sides, Mason struggled to free himself. "Let me go!"

Ozone signaled the ForLords to release Mason and stand by the door.

Mason straightened his shirt. "Why did you drag me in here?"

"What's your brother up to?"

"How should I know? Even if I did, why would I tell you?"

An angered Ozone raised his index finger close to Mason's face. "I'll cut your throat right here if you don't tell me what he's planning."

"Why wait?" Mason challenged. "You're going to do it anyway."

Ozone walked away. Anticipating Mason's urge to follow, Alpha stepped between the two men.

"Tell me what your brother is up to!"

"Really? You've had me under constant surveillance since my abduction."

Ozone pivoted and Alpha stepped back. "How do you explain my missing satellites?"

Mason leaned forward, inches from Ozone. "Let me say it this way. Good!"

Pain radiated across Mason's face after the back of Ozone's hand struck it. Unwilling to submit, he clenched his fists, ready to strike the evil man.

"Save your anger for another day. For the moment, you're worth more alive than you are dead. Take him to the bubble."

As Mason resisted the two ForLords, he felt a cool rush through his veins. Ozone sedated Mason from behind with a needle concealed in his glove. Mason stepped forward and fell limply into the ForLords' arms. They each clutched Mason and carried him away, his feet dragging across the floor. They brought him down into the fortress bowels and left him in Ozone's specialized bubble.

Alpha stayed behind to help modify Ozone's strategy at the conference table. Ozone sank into the chair closest to him. The chair and Ozone crashed to the floor. A faint giggle emanated from under the table.

"Is it funny?" Ozone asked, furious.

"I'm not laughing."

Ozone raised his right hand. "Help me up!"

Alpha assisted Ozone to his feet. Ozone examined the chair remnants. Every support brace that connected the legs was missing.

"You must have broken the chair during your outrage."

"I didn't touch this chair. Get me another one," Ozone demanded.

Ozone and Alpha combed through the detailed plan of human elimination. With satellites absent from his arsenal and the strong possibility of an imminent attack, they spent the next several hours making adjustments. Underneath the table, Blue and Red lay outstretched on two leaves of a Corinthian column supporting the table, listening to every word spoken.

Unable to sleep anymore, Liam opened his eyes at ten past midnight and stared through the treetops at the cloud cover, wondering if he would ever see the twinkling stars. He ambled down to the river, rehashing the mission objective in his mind.

"Good morning…I think."

The soft voice startled Liam, resulting in him losing his balance and almost falling in the river. He shined the flashlight on the person standing behind him. It was Lauren. Her long, blond hair tousled in all directions, her face was somewhat pale from lack of any makeup, and she had sleep lines on her cheeks. She knelt to Liam's left, grabbed a stick, and stirred the water. Liam shined the light at the edge of the river.

"How was your nap?"

"I could have slept longer," Lauren replied, rubbing her eyes. She lost interest in the sleep deprivation conversation. "Have you seen any creatures move?"

"No, Cooper and Brian are sound asleep," Liam joked.

She giggled. "Seriously."

"None have stirred yet. The Dropas estimated four hours, but it will probably be sooner. They expended very little energy before we loaded them into the tanks."

As Liam spoke his last sentence, a faint reflection of two horns appeared on the surface water. He followed the horns with the light beam as the reflection stretched across the river. "Your wish is my command." Liam directed the light onto the Viking standing behind him.

Liam and Lauren were again awed by the detail Mason had given each mascot, especially the determined eyes. Lauren returned her interest to the river. She suddenly shrieked, delivering a piercing audio bullet into Liam's ear. In her attempt to escape, Lauren knocked Liam to the ground and frantically crawled over him. Scrambling to his feet, Liam had to calm Lauren and prevent her from potentially alerting any ForLords.

Lauren screamed again. This time the Viking covered her entire face with its mammoth hand, effectively muffling the sound. Liam drew his immobilizer and shined the flashlight at the bulging eyes and large nostrils visible above the surface water. A thirty-foot gator had re-energized in time for a late-night swim.

Cooper, Brian, and Ti soon joined the excitement at the riverbank. Lauren calmed herself enough for the Viking to release its grip.

"What's all the noise? It's only a giant alligator," Brian commented.

Lauren clutched Brian. "Yeah, well that gator almost swallowed my head."

"I highly doubt it," Cooper commented.

"I'm going back to sleep," Ti announced.

"Nice try, Ti," Liam said. "The creatures are stirring. It's time to get started. You kids clean up camp and have a quick bite to eat. I'll discuss the boat situation with our friends."

All the mascots had awoken and the first order of business focused on relocating the ship. Liam communicated with the Vikings, Indians, and Warriors regarding what to do with the immovable watercraft. Two viable options existed, both of which could cause an unwanted delay. Liam contemplated the pair of possibilities and opted to have the creatures dismantle the boat, board by board, and rebuild it in the clearing by the river. Unfortunately, the time estimate for task completion was rough at best. Because they would be working at extremely high speeds to dismantle and rebuild the ship, they would need time to sufficiently re-energize prior to the ensuing battle.

Liam explained the situation to the kids. "Relax for a bit. We're not leaving any time soon."

"How long will this delay us?" Cooper was visibly discouraged.

"Rebuilding and repairing the boat won't take long, but they must re-energize afterward. Cooper, I need your help with something."

Cooper accompanied Liam. "This is my fault."

"Cooper, please don't blame yourself. The tank didn't—"

"Thanks for defending me, but I found the label in your sleeping bag when we cleaned up camp." Cooper dejectedly withdrew the identifier from his pocket, crumpled it up, and cast it to the ground.

Liam gently grabbed Cooper's shoulders. "Everything will work out. There's probably a good reason why this happened."

"Yeah, a good reason for Ozone."

Liam tightened his grip, surprising Cooper. "This is exactly what Ozone wants from us, to work against each other. You promised me at the warehouse you wouldn't disappoint the team, right?"

"Yeah, but—"

"But, nothing! I need you as much as I need every person on this mission, but I want somebody who won't wither when times get tough. People in this world are counting on us to defeat Ozone. We'll overcome this, Cooper, but only if we're working together. Are you with me? If not, I'm feeding you to the gator." Liam smiled, attempting to lessen Cooper's anxiety.

Cooper chuckled. "Yeah, I'm with you. All the way."

"That's the Cooper I know. Come on, let's help rebuild the boat."

Pockets' group arose shortly after one in the morning. The sleepy-eyed troops downed their breakfast meals, promptly cleaned the campsite, and attempted to sleep a bit more—sitting on the ground with backs against one another. Pockets wanted to let them rest longer, but that wasn't an option. His mascots also re-energized before the full four-hour period. After instructing them individually, Pockets gathered the gear and placed it all in his pocket.

Only Roberto and his friends awoke ready to go. Pockets motioned to him to organize the teenagers. They arose, many rubbing their eyes or displaying exaggerated yawns and stretches as they huddled around their leader. Maintaining silence, Pockets beckoned the contingent deeper into the dimly-lit forest.

Pockets led the way with a rope tied around his waist and each kid gripping a section. The tigers, panthers, and wildcats stealthily moved a fair distance in front of the others, scouting for any undesirable ForLords. The majority of pioneers blazed a path while the lions and remaining pioneers trailed in the rear, affording additional protection. Periodically, on Pockets' command, a few hornets veered away to construct nests for the detainees.

At one point, Pockets paused to observe some hornets, fascinated at the way they intricately constructed the large, ovoid shells among the trees. And due to the size, the nests they built had room for hundreds of ForLords. The superficially hollow shells were all but that, having layers and layers of interconnected cylinders. And the wind the hornets' wings generated delivered much needed relief in the dense forest where little breeze existed.

Pockets imagined the different forms of entertainment the Dropas would have created using the nests. *A good game of hide-and-seek would probably have kept them occupied for hours*. He gazed at nothing in particular, wondering if Clearcoat and the other Dropas had reached Mason and if Silver and Gold had successfully landed in the treacherous terrain of the mountains. Pockets snapped out of his trance when he felt a tap on his shoulder.

"Are you okay, Pockets?" Kelly asked.

"Yes." Pockets waved everyone onward, otherwise he might have stayed there indefinitely, preoccupied with the safety of all involved.

Time quickly passed as they hiked through the trees, stopping intermittently to listen for ForLords. Reaching the designated positions, the cats scattered themselves out across the forest floor and amongst the tree limbs, keeping a watchful eye out for the enemy. Pockets and the kids caught up to the felines ten minutes later. The last three hornets constructed the final detention cells. After re-energizing, they flew to the closest nest, waited inside until the attack commenced, and protected the curious teens investigating the creation. Meanwhile, the cats and pioneers guarded the perimeter.

Roberto huddled his comrades together for one last review. Pockets spared no details. Everyone understood the importance of the confrontation, reassured Pockets they would handle their responsibilities, and dispersed to their positions.

Noticeably bothered by something, Pockets paced among the trees. He couldn't understand why they hadn't encountered a single ForLord. Not one. Although relieved the kids had been momentarily spared from fighting, he felt uneasy about the situation. He tried convincing himself it was the result of the astros' success in space, but it was difficult to fathom, with such close proximity to the fortress walls, that no ForLords patrolled the forest.

"Something is wrong," Pockets murmured as he noted the time on his watch.

It was 3:10 a.m. They would begin in less than an hour.

Willie's group arrived at the gorge earlier than planned. His creatures also required less than the estimated time to re-energize. They had the easiest travel schedule, but an extremely dangerous part of the mission. Once they crossed the gorge, they would be completely exposed to Ozone's drones. It was crucial that Silver and Gold guide the birds over the mountains before Willie's team made it to the far side. Willie was confident the huskies and bulldogs would locate the underground hangar, although he would have preferred hound dogs.

Using his infrared binoculars, Willie scoped the area near the fortress. As he scanned the structure, something passed through his line of sight. He peered in the glasses a second time but saw nothing. Recalling what the GGB officers encountered when attempting to cross the gorge, Willie presumed the objects to be Ozone's aircraft. Raising the binoculars, he confirmed his presumption as he identified two drones landing in an area midway between the fortress and his present location. He informed the creatures of his discovery.

This will be a piece of cake...wait a second. Why are they flying maneuvers in the middle of the night? Something's not right. Willie located the drones again. "Ozone knows we're coming." *Does he know when? This is not good, not good at all.*

Another drone flew into view. Overcome by helplessness, he knew sneaking over there was suicidal. His mind raced as he inserted the glasses in the case. *It won't be long until we know the outcome.* His watch displayed 3:10 a.m. Onset of the world's fate would commence in less than an hour.

The creatures had finished rebuilding the boat around 1:30 a.m. and, as expected, assumed a stationary position. Liam had no idea how long they would remain dormant and he could do nothing to expedite the process. Unable to depart without them, his group simply waited. They would leave for the fortress once his mural allies re-energized.

Liam rested, propped against a tree near the campsite. The kids sat silent and deep in their own thoughts. Liam sensed his young companions were equally nervous and scared, understanding they were responsible not only for their future but for the future of the entire human population. It was a lot of pressure for kids that age—preserving the existence of mankind. It was a lot of pressure for anyone, but never had Liam seen a more courageous group of teenagers than what he assembled for the journey. Regardless of their fear and anxiety, they demonstrated a great amount of certainty with the decision to be part of the mission. They were ready and, no matter the outcome, Liam was proud of them.

Liam closed his eyes, listened to the sound of the river, and reflected on his life. The past. The present. And, the future. He eventually drifted off to sleep.

...Apollo barked furiously as two men crashed through the door. In one swift motion, the canine leapt at the first intruder and bit into his arm, forcing him to release his weapon. Unsympathetically, the second intruder shot at Apollo, aware

that if the bullets reached its target they would also take out his comrade. Apollo yelped. It was the last sound Liam heard from his loyal, furry companion. If Liam survived, he would always be grateful to Apollo for saving his life. Liam fired a barrage of bullets into the torso of the second intruder who stumbled backward before collapsing on the floor. Liam shot another round into the hallway, hoping to scare off any other enemies. His effort to reload in time was unsuccessful.

In walked the third intruder, a stocky man with a rifle aimed at Liam's head. "Drop the weapon and get on your knees."

At that stage of the war, Liam wasn't sure what was better: dying or hoping the conflict would end. He dropped his weapon. The man pressed the gun barrel between Liam's eyes. Beads of perspiration rolled down Liam's face as he knelt on the floor, gun to his head, looking up at the individual prepared to decide his fate. Liam detected confusion in the man's eyes, but if he flinched, those eyes would be the last thing he ever saw. The man slowly drew back the gun hammer with his thumb. Numb to the sweat stinging his eyes, Liam matched the stare of his apparent assassin. Liam was a proud man and refused to look away. The hammer clicked into its final firing position, and the man's forefinger tensed on the trigger.

"What have we become?" Liam wondered aloud...

"Willie!" Liam leaned forward from the tree, drenched in sweat and staring at nothing. That nighttime memory replayed many times—it had been suppressed for years—and he often awoke in similar fashion. His loud cry startled the kids.

Lauren arrived first. "Liam, are you all right?" She gazed into his glassy eyes and gently shook him.

Temporarily catatonic, Liam's stare still fixated on nothing.

"Liam, are you okay?"

Liam finally blinked. "Yeah, I'm okay."

The others arrived and huddled around him.

"What happened, Liam?" Lauren inquired.

"Just a recurring nightmare. One that keeps the memory of the war alive."

"Will you share the story with us?" Ti pleaded.

Liam wiped the perspiration from his face with his sleeve. The kids listened intently as he described the haunting details.

"You're obviously alive," Brian stated.

"Indeed. The man pondered my question, lifted his finger off the trigger, repositioned the hammer, and lowered his weapon."

"Did you then kick his butt?" Cooper asked.

"Not at all." Liam smiled. "He's now my best friend."

"What?" they responded in shock.

"You befriended the person who almost killed…wait…that was Willie?" Ti asked. "And you two are best friends?"

"In the truest sense."

"How?"

"We talked. We talked for a very long time about the current state of the world and what could be done to halt the uncontrollable killing. We were two independent revolutionaries who united our supporters with the sole purpose of ending the war. Together, we progressively gained a trusted following until the fighting ultimately ceased."

"The war ended a decade ago. Why do you keep having that nightmare?" Lauren inquired.

"Before, it was a constant reminder of what happened. Since I haven't had it for years, it's likely a warning that Ozone is alive, and as long as he is, we're not safe."

"It's up to us to stop him," Brian interjected.

"That's right," Lauren added.

"Your chance will be here soon enough." Liam checked the time. "We have less than an hour before it all starts." He caught a glimpse of an approaching Warrior. "It's time to roll. The creatures are ready."

They jumped to their feet and rushed down to the river.

In the bowels of the fortress, Ozone checked on Mason's progress. The bubble in which Mason was imprisoned transformed victims differently than the ones Ozone unleashed on the public. It required more time but conformed them to Ozone's exact specifications. However, the process contained the same flaw as the others. If prematurely interrupted, the victim's mind reverted to its original state. Ozone stepped up to the sphere, surprised at Mason's persistence. Mason had been resisting it for several hours. The bubble would either change him or ultimately kill him. Unsure as to how much more he could withstand, a weakened Mason approached Ozone.

"I expected this to be over by now. I'd like to stay for the grand finale, but I must prepare for your brother."

Mason pressed his hands against the inside wall. "What about my brother?" he asked half-heartedly, his eyes partially open.

Ozone backed away. "My informants tell me he hasn't been seen lately. I believe he is paying me a visit very soon."

"You better hope he doesn't."

"I'm ready for the little maggot. Once I dispose of him, I can rid my eyes and my conscience of the entire human race."

"Your plan will fail, Ozone."

"I doubt that. I'm abreast of the military tactics your brother used as a revolutionary. The next time we meet, you'll either join me or I'll have your dead body tossed into the river."

The pressure inside Mason's head increased and his knees buckled, but he refused to let Ozone believe he would succumb to the bubble. "I'd rather die than join you."

"Have it your way. I must deal with more important matters."

"Remember, Ozone, things aren't always what they appear to be."

Ozone ignored Mason and ascended the stairs. Once Ozone disappeared from sight, Mason collapsed, unable to fight the mind-altering effects any longer. He reached feebly for the inside wall, his hand sliding down it. Mason barely had enough energy to breathe let alone attempt an escape. His vision blurred and unconsciousness overtook him.

No Turning Back

Dawn was awakening. Had the creatures taken any longer to re-energize, the delay would have jeopardized the entire mission. The majority of creatures gathered by the shoreline, and the gators lingered in the water. Adrenaline flowed through everyone's veins, prevailing over their fatigue. Events prior to their departure were insignificant. What truly mattered was the looming conflict. One way or another, the fate of the human race would soon be determined. Would it exist and continue to evolve, or would it join the likes of the dinosaurs?

The foursome gathered around Liam. He raised his binoculars and searched skyward above the fortress, near the gorge, and in the direction of Barrow's Ridge. Peering through the glasses a second time, Liam grew a bit concerned not seeing the birds, but trusted that Silver, Gold, and the avian air force would arrive on time.

Liam handed the binoculars to Cooper. "See anything?"

Cooper peered through the glasses. "No," he whispered, "not a thing." He returned the binoculars to Liam. "Willie is about to cross the gorge without any air support. He'll never find the hangar before they discover—"

"Don't worry, they'll be here," Liam calmly interrupted. "Are you all clear on what to do once inside the fortress?"

"We're ready," Brian responded for his friends.

"Great. Let's get this boat in the water," Liam commanded.

Lauren and Ti grabbed the noosed end of each rope connected to the bow and passed them to the gators. With the first encounter fresh in her mind, Lauren threw her rope into the water ten feet from her targeted reptile. The gators inserted their closed mouths inside the loops. The Indians and Warriors positioned themselves along the sides and rear, ready to push. The Vikings established a position near the bow.

In a concerted effort, the creatures dragged the vessel with ease. The gators rapidly propelled their massive tails in the water and the Vikings tugged on the ropes, leaving behind large footprints in the dirt. The Indians and Warriors moved easily and silently along the ground, and unlike the Vikings, they left no trace of where they had stepped. Everyone watched the entire event in amazement. As

Liam marveled at the size and strength of those magnificent creatures, he felt more confident with each passing moment.

Liam requested silence until they reached the transfer point and, if necessary, only talk in a whisper. Prematurely revealing themselves would be detrimental, especially since the tower guards were not yet distracted by Pockets' ground attack or Silver and Gold's air assault.

After everyone boarded, the Indians and Warriors dispersed along the riverbank, searching for ForLords potentially patrolling the area. Four gators flanked the watercraft, allowing the Vikings to navigate. Pulling the looped ropes, the two lead gators propelled the boat with powerful tail swishes. The rapidly-cruising vessel ensured arrival at the fortress before sunrise.

Liam kept an eye out for the winged fleet, but they were nowhere in sight. His trepidation for Willie's group grew stronger. He searched until the vessel reached the penultimate destination. The gators slowed the boat a mile from the fortress, the Vikings steered it onto shore, and the team disembarked.

The young tetrad sought words of wisdom Liam could not provide. Instead, their leader extended an arm and they followed suit, each grasping one another's hand.

"I'm very proud of you and I'm bringing you all home with me," Liam said confidently.

Their hands gripped tightly. They were ready. They had to be because there was no turning back.

The cloud cover brightened ever so slightly and soon the assault would commence. They situated themselves inside their assigned gator, Lauren included—having overcome her herpetophobia. It was a snug fit and luckily no one was claustrophobic. The gators' mouths closed, but not completely, leaving enough space for fresh air to reach the passengers. One by one, the giant reptiles sprawled into the water. Liam eerily felt like a torpedo waiting to be fired.

Forceful tail strokes and the aid of the river current expeditiously glided the passengers to the fortress. The Vikings steered the boat behind their reptilian allies, armed and ready for battle. The Warriors and Indians traveled along the riverbank, ready to overpower anyone who confronted them.

During that brief trip, Liam experienced flashes of his late wife, his close friendships, the war, and the progress humans had made to better their world.

Then Ozone's image appeared. His capacity to hate and his desire for human extinction mystified Liam. That abruptly ended the train of pleasant thoughts.

"Fire!" the commanding ForLord shouted from atop the north wall. As the gators' mouths closed completely, engulfing the passengers in darkness, the ForLords bombarded the Vikings with chemical streams.

The gators submerged and travelled underneath the fortress walls. Once inside, Liam's group had no idea what awaited them when the mouths reopened. They all readied their immobilizers for the grand entrance.

Swoosh! Thump! The lion's paw struck the ForLord's head like a large frying pan. The last sentry outside the fortress fell quietly to the ground. A pioneer stepped out from behind a nearby tree and carried the prisoner to the closest hornet's nest. In much the same manner, the other cats had stealthily neutralized the ForLords lining the forest edge and standing guard outside the stone walls.

It was time for Stripes, Pockets, and the other tigers to make their furtive entrance. As Pockets leaned over, Stripes' companions effortlessly leapt into the unknown abyss of his open pocket. After the last one disappeared, he climbed aboard Stripes and exited the safety of the forest while avoiding the perimeter cameras. Once inside the fortress, the hornets would begin the assault outside the walls, expecting to draw fire away from Pockets and Stripes.

Stripes crept low alongside the walls with Pockets straddled on its back, tightly gripping its scruff. Each stride covered a large amount of ground—the huge tiger reached the fortress doors in very little time and unnoticed. Pockets dismounted, staying close to the wall, and Stripes oozed into one of the huge doors. Its head liquified into the thick, wooden panels, followed by its paws.

Osmosing its body through the cellular fibers, Stripes' head surfaced on the opposite side. The giant cat surveyed the area. Three ForLords, with weapons slung over their shoulders, faced away from the furry invader, momentarily unaware of what was happening behind them. Stripes pulled its backside into the door, filling every crack possible until its tail disappeared from outside the fortress.

Detecting movement in his peripheral vision, one ForLord approached the entrance. Stripes retracted its head, concealing it in the wood pores.

"Did you guys see that?"

"See what?" a second ForLord inquired.

"I swear I saw a tiger's head on the door." He brushed his hand over the area.

"A tiger? Seriously?" the third ForLord responded. "You're hallucinating from working a double shift."

"It's just a door," the second ForLord assured his comrade.

"Yeah, you're probably right."

Stripes resurfaced after the soldiers pivoted away from it. Hearing a slow oozing sound, the inquisitive ForLord slid his weapon off his shoulder as Stripes' faint image appeared. Convinced the others didn't believe him, he investigated the strange phenomenon himself. He slowly approached the entry, weapon raised in anticipation of a confrontation. Standing three feet from the door, the ForLord craned his neck, mesmerized by the tiger's brightly glowing eyes. When he blinked, Stripes' massive paw emerged, immediately solidified, and swatted the ForLord. He crashed into the stone wall, instantly rendered unconscious.

The other two ForLords rushed to aid their fallen comrade. As they neared the door, Stripes' front paws struck them down before they could react, the force of the cat's powerful blow smashing them together. Two more ForLords dashed to investigate the commotion as Stripes ran along Mason's painted ledge to intercept them. It leapt onto the approaching soldiers, driving them helplessly to the ground. Safely inside the walls, Stripes dislodged the wood beam that secured the doors shut, allowing Pockets to enter.

The commanding ForLord shouted from atop the north wall, "Fire!"

Upon Pockets' disappearance, the hornets took flight. The rapid movement of their wings emulated the sound of a squadron of single-engine planes. ForLords atop the walls scanned the forest perimeter, in the presumed direction of the loud humming noises, but saw nothing. They raised their chemical weapons and directed the tower lights into the trees. The hornets rose from the base of the walls and snatched the curious sentries from their positions. Chemical streams wildly filled the air as the ForLords alerted others in the vicinity. Loud sirens echoed throughout the fortress. Additional lights from the towers illuminated the ground and the tower artillery fired at the tree line.

The spirited cats had already vacated the forest and entered the fortress walls through the sky Mason had painted, much the same way Stripes entered through the doors. The assault of the devastating chemical streams emitted from the artillery abruptly ended when the hornets captured the operators and sealed off the tower entrances.

Dozens of ForLords charged Pockets. He knelt, leaned over, and opened his pocket flap, narrowly allowing the ambush of tigers to exit. As the last feline emerged, Pockets rolled on the ground, avoiding a barrage of enemy fire. He repositioned himself, drew his immobilizer, and shot at the attackers.

ForLords peppered the tigers with chemical streams, but the protective coats resisted the onslaught. The tigers gallantly held their ground during the prolonged assault. An alert Pockets watched for re-energizing creatures.

Pockets felt a sense of doom as the number of ForLords dramatically increased. At a minimum, thousands existed within those fortress walls, maybe even tens of thousands. As he ran for cover, firing his weapon along the way, the lions, panthers, and wildcats leapt out of the walls. The opposing army became less intimidating.

Pockets watched the huge cats effortlessly paralyze the attacking ForLords. Over the ramparts, and through the doors, swarmed the hornets. Each grabbed five, sometimes ten ForLords at a time and carried them to the nests where Roberto's unit executed their duties with deft efficiency. Pockets wanted to assist, but he and Stripes had another objective: finding Mason.

From behind a cluster of empty barrels, Pockets searched the crowded battlefield, trying to locate Stripes. Among the cats fighting the relentless ForLords, he saw no sign of his furry companion. Looking to his left, a circle of felines battled the enemy with heads facing away from what they surrounded.

The cats suddenly broke formation. They had been protecting Stripes during its brief re-energizing state—a shining example of others sacrificing their lives for the life of one of their own.

Stripes charged at Pockets, increasing its speed as it did. He held out his hands, signaling Stripes to slow. The oncoming cat drew within yards of Pockets who had ducked and closed his eyes, cringing at the notion of what the force of the giant beast would do to him. Stripes' powerful hind legs catapulted it up and over Pockets and the barrels, taking out a dozen ForLords who had been sneaking up behind Pockets. With one blow from the gigantic tiger, the unsuccessful assailants lay unconscious on the ground.

Pockets squinted one eye open, bracing for the impact, which was not to be. Stripes was no longer in front of him.

"Stripes?" Pockets called.

The huge tiger ferociously roared. A startled Pockets pivoted, only to have his face licked by a large, sandpapered tongue.

Pockets rubbed Stripes head. "Come on, save the bath for Mason."

Stripes jumped into Pockets' shirt pocket, smacking him in the face with its tail. Pockets dragged one unconscious ForLord behind a barrier and out of sight. He removed the ForLord's jacket and pulled it on over his shirt, feeling very strange in the enemy's garb. He hoped that no one noticed the non-regulation pants as he searched for Mason. Picking up a chemical weapon, he passed through the courtyard, leaving the cats and the hornets to battle the ForLords within the fortress walls.

The last creatures had crossed the gorge and the huskies and bulldogs began sniffing out the underground hangar. Based on the GGB's recon data, Willie expected the drones at any moment.

Bob pointed in the direction of the fortress. "Here come the birds!"

Willie raised his binoculars and gazed at the approaching objects. The teens cheered the arrival of their flying allies.

"No! No!" Willie yelled. "Take cover! Take cover immediately!"

Large squadrons of Ozone's drones flew straight at them.

"Take flight!" Willie ordered the dragons and cardinals. "Oh, no! Not now!"

The dragons and cardinals all remained dormant, briefly re-energizing after carrying Willie, the kids, the land creatures, and the equipment over the gorge. Willie's contingent was completely defenseless. Dozens of drones closed in on them, first unleashing an assault on the dogs. Facing more powerful streams than the ForLords' hand-held weapons emitted, the canines absorbed only a few rounds before disintegrating. And, worse yet, it would take only one stream to destroy any re-energizing creature.

Firing torrent after torrent, the drones pelted the dogs as they tried to outmaneuver the chemical assault. The more agile huskies avoided the bombardment better than the stouter bulldogs. Many of the latter had already disappeared. Unless the birds arrived soon, Willie's battalion would succumb to a similar fate. The boulders where they hid wouldn't protect them for long.

"Head for the gorge!" Willie commanded.

"We'll be shot!" Bob responded.

"It's our only chance." Willie waved at them to leave.

Instantly, the creatures and all the teens followed Willie's command and boarded the newly re-energized dragons and cardinals. The drones stayed focused on the dogs, affording just enough time for the group to cross the expanse. Numerous dogs escaped into a small cavern after eluding the attacking aircraft. The squadron changed course en route to the gorge.

The last set of passengers landed on the other side. Willie needed to position himself at the edge of the rocky cavity, minimizing the travel distance of the creature retrieving him. He ran toward the intended destination, periodically glancing over his shoulder at the approaching drones.

"Faster, Willie!" the kids shouted.

Neither a dragon nor a cardinal had taken flight. His leg muscles tightened, preventing him from running any faster. The drones closed the gap as he peeked over his shoulder near the rim. The powered-up guns aimed directly at Willie.

"Willie!" the kids yelled. "Stop!"

The ground vanished from beneath his feet and he descended into the chasm. Simultaneously, the six lead drones fired, missing Willie and hitting the far wall.

A loud screech rang across the sky. Holding the steel neck feathers of Robohawk with one hand, and raising paintbrushes in the air with the other, were Silver and Gold. Robohawk had plucked the firing drones out of the air with its mighty talons, three drones in each one. And with its powerful grip, it crushed the steel aircraft like aluminum cans in a vise and released them to plummet helplessly to the ground. Robohawk retracted its massive wings and dove straight for the plunging Willie. Its speed was awesome, rocketing into the gorge like a guided missile. The talons reached forward to retrieve its prey and the wings opened to redirect the bird's flight path. Unlike the drones, the claws gingerly grasped Willie ten feet above the chemical-laced current. Robohawk veered away from the water and flapped its steel wings. Seconds later, Willie was gently placed on solid ground, legs wobbling and head spinning.

The kids surrounded their rescued leader. Silver and Gold saluted as Robohawk took flight, joining the other birds battling Ozone's air force. The elusive eagles, hawks, and falcons avoided the brunt of the chemical offensive.

The dragons and cardinals carried the rest of the group to the dogs' location, outside the protective cavern. The canines resumed the search for the underground hangar, and Willie directed the Spartans, Trojans, and knights to proceed to the fortress. They mounted their horses and chariots, and rode straight for the structure, leaving nothing behind but a trail of dust. The cardinals took flight to assist the hornets and the dragons joined the air assault.

The fire-breathers demonstrated a blitz against the drones even more impressive than the birds' attack. The scorching flames shot from their mouths and melted the defenseless drones in mid-flight, igniting the chemicals into fireballs and raining metal fragments across the terrain. The winged creatures incessantly battled Arton's air force with minimal resistance, but it would take considerable time before they completely wiped out the entire fleet.

The raiders and chargers assisted Willie with any ForLords they may encounter at the underground hangar. Squadrons of drones departed the open entrance. Peeking inside, Willie's jaw dropped as thousands of drones readied for takeoff. Although many were capable of flying, others had been disfigured in various, humorous ways: square tires, water guns instead of chemical weapons, wings pointed in unorthodox positions, or reshaped like bananas.

"Hah! The Dropas strike again," Willie proclaimed.

"Look at those drones!" one kid yelled from behind Willie.

The reconfigured aircraft fired popcorn at the eagles. Everyone laughed at the fluffy kernels falling from the sky. The amusement halted abruptly as a thousand ForLords, who found no humor in the situation, emerged from the underground facility. The raiders and chargers immediately stepped to the front to intercept the enemy while Willie and the kids fired immobilizers.

Hours passed before Ozone's entire air force had been obliterated and the small ForLord battalion had been captured. The birds and dragons re-energized on the ground and would rejoin their comrades at the fortress upon completion.

The gators resurfaced and sprawled onto the concrete dock of the dimly lit fortress bowels. Liam and his young companions crawled out of the reptiles.

"Everyone all right?" Liam asked.

"Just fine," Ti replied.

"That was awesome!" Cooper exclaimed.

"How long before the Vikings arrive?" Lauren inquired.

"I'm not sure." Liam searched for ForLords. "It depends on how much resistance they encounter outside. Get down!"

Liam barely ducked in time as chemical streams passed overhead. Assaulted by the ForLords standing guard, there was no more time for small talk. Scattering behind whatever protection was available, the pentad raised their weapons and returned fire. The young gunslingers, who were quick studies, adeptly demonstrated their proficiency with the immobilizers, paralyzing a large number of ForLords as if seasoned marksmen.

Engaged in the battle from the river, the gators propelled ForLords into the walls with their powerful tails. Their protective coats endured the enemy fire. Liam and the four teens maintained their ground as long as possible, but their means of protection kept disappearing. They even repositioned themselves behind paralyzed ForLords piling up on the floor, but those bodies also vanished from the constant barrage of chemical streams.

The enemy seemed to have an infinite number of personnel, but the invasion improved immensely as the Vikings finally emerged from the fortress wall. Soldiers redirected the assault onto the giant intruders who had shields raised and hand weapons drawn. The Norse mascots counter-attacked, rendering numerous ForLords unconscious from each massive blow. Confident the Vikings and gators controlled the situation, Liam and his four comrades retreated in search of Ozone's chemical-producing equipment.

Above ground, it wouldn't be long before the weary cats needed to re-energize. Had that happened any sooner, the enemy would have scored a major victory. The ForLords outnumbered the cats a hundred to one, but the felines valiantly held their own. The interior soldiers drove the furry mascots away from the entrance and barricaded the doors shut, preventing penetration of any large reinforcements. The guns on the far walls were useless, also sabotaged by the Dropas—they shot harmless gelatin cubes instead of deadly chemicals. Gunners vacated the ramparts, mostly from the west, to join the fight inside the fortress.

The ForLords gained more confidence with each assault. Prepared to apply the final wave, demise of the cats imminent, the western fortification crashed to the ground. The sky with the added cracks came into play. The painted fissures transformed into real ones and the Spartans, Trojans, and knights barreled effortlessly through the structure. The walls collapsed and the relief squad exuded tremendous amounts of energy. The Indians and Warriors, who had successfully scaled the north wall, neutralized the ForLords lining the northern and eastern walkways and descended from the towers to assist in the primary battle. Confused by the new invaders, the ForLords unexpectedly abandoned the attack on the cats and focused their efforts on the Warriors and Indians.

ForLords fired wildly. Most missed their targets, but several struck their own men. The cats used the brief amount of time they had to re-energize before combatting the enemy from the rear. Moments later, the revitalized birds and dragons overpowered Ozone's army from the air. Each creature accounted for ten or fifteen ForLords at a time, but the soldiers refused to surrender.

The birds veered off to assist the hornets that were rapidly filling the nests. Roberto's group, including the pioneers, barely kept up with the incoming prisoners. Soon, the ForLords conceded their impending defeat and initiated a mass exodus, only to be apprehended from the ground by the cats or from the air by the birds, dragons, and hornets. Willie's troops, approaching the fortress from the underground hangar, intercepted the deserters heading for the gorge. The ForLords had no means of escape. By nightfall, the majority of ForLords had been detained, allowing the winged creatures to re-energize near the riverbank by the southern part of the fortress.

A stunned Ozone surveyed the darkened battlefield from the war room window. His relentless desire for human extinction endured, but his plan had crumbled right before his eyes. He refused to let himself be captured. Allowing the GGB the opportunity to change his conduct and accepting the new way of life were not options for him. Fighting until the end to fulfill his objective was.

He closed the blinds and sat at his desk, holding his head in his hands. "I will not be defeated!" He slammed his fist on the desktop.

Ozone momentarily assessed the current situation. From underneath the middle drawer, he slid out a control console. It was time to execute his escape plan. He fumbled around under his garment and withdrew a chain necklace holding a key that activated the fortress auto-destruct mechanism. He angrily yanked the chain off his neck and inserted the key into a slot on the console. "You haven't seen the last of me," he slurred. Ozone turned the key to the right and punched in the code sequence.

As he entered the last digit, Pockets and Stripes crashed through the door. Navigating the fortress maze, the duo had confronted hundreds of ForLords during the search for their abducted companion. Although they were unsuccessful locating Mason, they found the next best thing.

"You're finished, Ozone!" Pockets shouted.

"No, I believe you are." Ozone stared at Pockets as if they had met before, and then refocused. "In less than fifteen minutes, this place will blow sky high and disintegrate everything around it, including your pathetic zoo animals."

"Not if I can help it," Pockets countered. "Stripes!"

The tiger took one giant stride and leapt into the air. Simultaneously, Ozone pushed a blue button on the console and the floor below him opened, swallowing him and his chair. By the time Stripes landed, the floor had closed and Ozone had vanished.

"Thanks for saving me from the bubble...again." Awaiting Ozone, Mason peeked into his shirt pocket at the Dropas. "You guys stay out of sight. Something's going on above us."

The ceiling opened suddenly. Ozone and his chair landed in a safety net, six feet from Mason.

Mason jumped back, wondering if others may be dropping in on him. "Nice entrance, Ozone. Any desire to audition for the circus?"

Ozone rolled off the net and landed feet first on the floor. "We have less than fifteen minutes to escape before this place blows," Ozone instructed, believing Mason's survival from the bubble meant he had successfully become Ozone's ally. "Follow me."

Ozone led Mason through several corridors to the river that flowed out under the south wall. Two dozen armed loyalists awaited his arrival. Together, they all raced for the submarine-like vessels that would aid their escape.

Several ForLords unlocked the hatches. Abandoning the Vikings to prevent the attempted escape via the river, the gators intercepted the deserters with open mouths. The ForLords lost their balance and splashed into the water, swimming for their lives, unaware the gators had no intention of devouring them.

After successfully disengaging the chemical-producing equipment, Liam's group retraced their path to the river—shocked at what awaited them. Teamed with Ozone, Mason had his weapon drawn, ready to fire on his brother and friends. Liam refused to believe it, but any hope he had was rapidly diminishing.

"Mason, you're alive!" Lauren emerged from around the corner.

"Don't take another step, you spoiled brat!" Mason ordered. "All of you, drop your weapons and get out into the open!"

Lauren regarded Mason as a friend, always visiting him wherever he painted. Stunned, tears filled her eyes as she retreated. Her friends surrounded her at once, consoling her to no avail.

Almost convinced Mason had allied with Ozone, Liam saw two colored heads rise from Mason's shirt pocket. Mason failed to notice Red and Black investigating the ruckus, and before he could, they descended to avoid detection.

Liam discerned that Mason was only following Ozone's lead, and for a very good reason. If he didn't, they wouldn't have been enjoying that delightful reunion. Liam opted to play along with the charade until he devised a plan to get Mason out of Ozone's clutches.

"He's no longer one of us, Lauren. Ozone converted him. Do what he says."

"Everyone, move away except you, *Liam*!" Ozone ordered. "I've been waiting to get my hands on you."

"Why are you doing this, Ozone? The world has changed."

"Another idealist, just like your brother, except your life will end right here, right now. Mason, he's all yours. Shoot him."

Not expecting such a command, Mason hesitated, then conceived an alternate method of dispatching Liam, perhaps more appealing to Ozone. It would also afford Mason additional time to somehow signal he wasn't a ForLord.

"I don't need a weapon. I've wanted to do this since childhood."

"Ah, a little sibling rivalry. Make it quick. Time is running out."

Mason set his chemical gun on the ground.

"Time for what?" Liam inquired.

"This place is set to blow!" Mason warned before Ozone said anything to the contrary.

"Eruption will commence in less than ten minutes," Ozone confirmed.

"Whoops," Liam remarked.

"What do you mean, whoops?" Lauren inquired.

"Didn't account for that." Liam approached Mason.

Mason glanced at Liam then at his own pocket as a black-handled knife with a red blade materialized. He re-established eye contact with Liam.

Liam had to alert Mason, indicating that he was aware Mason wasn't a ForLord. Liam shouted the first thing that came to mind, "Holy Stumpf Fiddle!"

Ozone and the ForLords exchanged confused expressions. The kids reacted similarly, unfamiliar with the story of the instrument to which Liam referred.

Mason rushed at Liam like a fullback at the goal line. Liam absorbed the initial blow, purposely pulling them both to the ground. Liam withdrew the knife from Mason's pocket. The ForLords raised their guns. Ozone gestured to the soldiers who lowered their weapons and allowed Liam to carry out his deed.

Lauren and Ti screamed in disbelief as they watched Liam thrust the knife into Mason. Upon contact with Mason's midsection, the dagger transformed into paint, covering his shirt and hands in red and creating a crimson puddle. Holding his abdomen, Mason rolled over on his side, facing away from Ozone and hiding the fact that the knife no longer existed.

The ForLords charged Liam but tripped and tumbled over each other like dominoes, unaware the other Dropas had painted shackles around their ankles. Hiding around the corner, the onlooking Vikings patiently waited for an opportunity to appear. They rushed from their position and seized the weapons from the fallen ForLords. Ozone used that diversion to make his escape in a vacant vessel. He successfully eluded the gators and submerged into the water.

Liam motioned the gators to pursue. "Mason, it's safe to get up."

Mason opened his eyes. That astonished the kids, especially Lauren and Ti.

Liam assisted Mason to his feet. "Glad you're not one of them."

"That makes two of us." Mason chuckled, "Holy Stumpf Fiddle?"

"I wanted you to know we were on the same page. Only you would understand that."

"Good thing." Mason sighed. "If we weren't on the same page, we would both be dead. I appreciate you guys coming to my aid."

"Spoiled brat?" Lauren inquired, squinting at Mason.

"Sorry, Lauren. It was all part of convincing Ozone I was on his side."

Lauren smiled. "I understand, but don't let it happen again."

"Never." Mason feebly attempted to wipe the paint off his shirt.

"Ahem, gentlemen, we have to get out of here," Cooper reminded Liam and Mason, interrupting the family reunion.

They all hopped into an available vessel. The Vikings boarded their ship, steering it into the south wall. Ready to close the hatch, Liam heard a shout from the corridor.

"Wait for us!"

Pockets and Stripes used Ozone's escape hatch to get below ground. Because he was wearing a ForLord jacket, Brian and Cooper didn't recognize Pockets and raised their immobilizers.

"Don't shoot!" Liam alerted them. "It's Pockets!"

The two teens finally detected their ally, and that Stripes was following Pockets like a pet rather than pursuing him like prey.

"Ozone is blowing up the fortress!" Pockets yelled.

"I know!" Liam shouted. "Get those legs moving!"

Stripes leapt onto the Viking ship as it entered the wall. The boat needed more time to osmose through the stones than Liam's contingent required to steer under the obstruction. Pockets climbed aboard the vessel, slammed the hatch shut, and sealed it as they submerged. Time was running out before the fortress, everything in it, and everything around it would be obliterated.

One gator caught up with Ozone's vessel and pierced holes in it with its large, sharp teeth. Water began filling the inside of the watercraft. Realizing he had to escape by land, Ozone surfaced just past the fortress walls, quickly opened the hatch, and jumped ashore. He disappeared around the corner leading to the front of the fortress. The pursuing reptile lost sight of Ozone and high walked past the re-energizing creatures.

Liam's vessel emerged next and the passengers hastily exited; however, the Viking ship needed more time, only three-quarters was visible. From its position at the bow, Stripes leapt onto the riverbank.

"Mason, get the kids and any creatures that can't fly onto those that can!"

"Will do!"

The birds and dragons had just finished re-energizing in front of the fortress when Mason arrived. Pockets directed the hornets into the forest to retrieve Roberto's group. Willie's contingent and the creatures inside the fortress joined the others and boarded the birds and dragons.

When the Norse watercraft completely solidified, one Viking signaled Liam to retrieve it, the crew members, and the gators downstream. The boat and the reptiles cruised down the river to maximize their distance from the impending explosions.

The lingering ForLords pleaded with Liam to take them, but there wasn't enough room. Liam wanted to help rid them of their evil ways, but his choice had been made for him as the birds and hornets had already departed. Liam and Mason boarded Robohawk last for it didn't need much time to safely whisk them to the gorge. Liam scanned the area. He had accounted for everyone, at least he felt confident he did.

"The Dropas!" Mason yelled. "Where are the Dropas?"

"I haven't seen them since they tripped up the ForLords."

"We have to find them!" Mason attempted to slide down Robohawk.

Liam latched onto Mason's arm. "We don't have time!"

Robohawk took flight, nearly knocking the two off its backside. Liam tightly held the bird's armor with one hand. The grip of his other hand was the only thing keeping Mason from plummeting to the ground.

"We need to save the Dropas!" Mason shouted.

"It's too late!"

Unsure if Mason was situating himself on board or fighting to free himself, Liam refused to let go regardless of his brother's intent.

In a matter of moments, the entire task force had reached the gorge. Just after landing, the fortress erupted in a massive explosion. Chemicals spewed hundreds of feet in all directions, destroying everything in their path. The fallen structure illuminated like a baseball stadium. Subsequent explosions dispersed fire and chemicals, but the last, monumental eruption was by far the most gratifying. It hurled a tremendous fireball into the pollution cover, igniting it and discharging a fire blanket around the globe. Everyone felt the blazing heat as it passed overhead—leaving behind wispy smoke and the cool night air. The kids jubilantly cheered. For the first time in weeks, the moon and stars visibly lit up the ebony canvas and, by daybreak, the blue sky, billowy clouds, and the bright sun would again cast their subtle beauty on the planet. Definitely another day beyond that turning page, a symbol often depicted in Mason's murals.

"There it is." Lauren pointed at an area over the southern forest.

Streaking south above the forest trees was a spectacular shooting star. They all gazed at the spectacle as it zipped across the night sky.

"Make a wish before it disappears," Liam suggested as the glowing tail faded into the darkness.

Many GGB staff members from the nearest regional office enthusiastically greeted Liam's contingent. One officer reported that victory had been declared around the world, but it was likely nations already perceived it after witnessing the burning cloud cover.

Although the objective had been realized and humanity would live to experience another day, Mason refrained from the celebration, for he was devastated by the loss of his miniature friends. The Dropas had played a major role in his life, influencing his artwork and making each day a joyous time to live and to paint. He would miss them dearly. All who came in contact with the Dropas would miss them.

Liam empathized with Mason's sorrow about leaving the Dropas behind, but had they stayed to search for them, Liam, Mason, and likely Robohawk would not have survived. Liam sensed the Dropas controlled their own destiny, whatever it was, but he couldn't convince himself that even they could have survived the final series of explosions. He wanted to console Mason at the time, but much work needed to be done. Instead, they would sit down one night and reflect on the entire series of events.

Liam joined Willie who was conversing with Pete and two GGB officers. Pete and the officers eagerly shook Liam's hand.

"Phenomenal job, Liam," Pete commended. "That was an exceptional mission you engineered."

"Thanks. I never expected to be in another conflict of this magnitude, but it was definitely a team effort."

"Before Willie led his kids to the gorge, he asked me to bring a supply of new holding tanks after the battle to safely transport the creatures home."

"Positive thinking." Liam winked at Willie.

"I never doubted our inevitable triumph for a minute," Willie replied confidently as he reciprocated the wink.

"Right. Willie, I need you to retrieve the Vikings and gators just south of the fortress. Once in flight, we'll meet up with you."

"I'm on it."

"Pete, you'll find thousands of detained ForLords among the hornets' nests in the southern forest. They're all yours." Before rejoining his group, Liam remembered one last detail. "Please instruct our regional office that we'll arrive at the forest preserve and to rope off part of the grassland area for the creatures."

"Yes, to both requests," Pete acknowledged.

Pete and the two officers left to assemble personnel needed to gather the ForLords. Willie and his kids each grabbed an empty tank, boarded their birds, and departed for the river.

Liam, Mason, Pockets, and the remaining teenagers loaded the land creatures into the metal cylinders, minimizing the shipment size that the other birds, dragons, and hornets would be required to carry.

Once everything was prepared, they journeyed home. The passengers exchanged stories from their segment of the mission, including Mason's experience with Ozone. As they shared their accounts, it was difficult not to think about the Dropas. They all wanted to believe the Dropas survived and, after helping save humanity, possibly traveled back to their world. They simply couldn't fathom how the Dropas endured the explosions, or if they did, why they didn't say good-bye. Those sad feelings lingered, but the immediate excitement of returning home made the trip a little more joyous.

Nature's Paradox

It was midafternoon the next day when the returning fleet neared the open field within the forest preserve boundaries. Thousands of exuberant onlookers erupted in cheers when they espied Robohawk leading the way. What a wonderful experience it was aboard the soaring mascots. The task force viewed the blue sky, relished the warmth of the sun, and witnessed the assembly on the ground. They could have stayed airborne indefinitely, but they were all eager to reunite with loved ones.

The winged mascots landed in the roped off area. The passengers slid off their respective transports and readied themselves for the jubilant celebration.

Parents of the young heroes gently pushed through the crowd. Liam was thrilled that the teens survived the journey and all reunited safely with their families. They played a major role in the mission, and he was proud of every one of them. The energy flowing around embracing loved ones left him breathless.

Willie searched for May and his children. His son and daughter spotted Willie first and made a bee line for him. Unable to contain her excitement, May leapt into Willie's arms and wrapped her legs around his waist—what a joyous reunion.

Liam imagined how wonderful it would have been if Ashley was alive to greet him. Admittedly, a very small part of Liam's void created from losing her in the war had been filled with defeating Ozone and stifling his goal for human extinction.

Elation replaced Liam's temporary sorrow as the crowd engulfed him and Mason, clamoring to hear the details. How fitting was the reception. Most attendees surrounding Mason were teenagers and young children from schools where he had painted murals. Those interested in Liam's stories were adult friends or individuals who fought alongside him in the war. Overwhelmed with inquiries, they both did their best to answer each one.

After spending time acknowledging congratulations, shaking hands, and responding to questions, Liam moseyed through the crowd to the re-energizing creatures. Standing next to Robohawk, Liam gazed westward in the direction of Barrow's Ridge. He reflected on the overall success and wondered about the Dropas.

Given all their magical abilities, Liam struggled with believing the Dropas didn't somehow survive, but he had no way of proving it. Nonetheless, the Dropas left a huge impression on all who met them—most notably, to cherish every single day. Mason's art reached a new level, one which certainly would not have been achieved without the Dropas' influence.

Liam and Mason would surely miss their dear little friends. They had lost the Dropas, but achieved the main objective. Ozone was gone, and humanity was preserved, having broken through the last walls that kept individuals separated. Those same walls keeping love, unity, and peace outside, while holding hatred, dissension, and war inside, stood no longer. Liam felt a deep assurance that humankind would survive, and their lives would be serene and enjoyable again. They would learn to co-exist and love each other, creating a wonderful world to live in for everyone, not just for one's own self.

A re-energized Robohawk raised its head and, unlike any time Liam heard before, it screeched somewhat distraughtly.

Liam curiously looked up at Robohawk. "What troubles you, my friend?"

The journey continues...

TRANSCENDENTAL

JOURNEY

BOOK II

The mind has a unique way of protecting us from emotional pain. It creates barriers that harness memories of negative events. Although beneficial at times, its persistence is often unwarranted. At some point, the walls the mind erects must fall. For beyond those walls exists a wonderful force of nature. It is more than an organ that nourishes our body and keeps us alive, but a magical enigma for sharing a powerful energy. It provides a source of appreciation and an ability to intertwine that vitality with other living organisms.

Many people often struggle with the question, should I listen to my heart or my mind? Both have a solution, yet more often than not they are not in harmony. When should one be followed over the other? Some spend a lifetime searching for the answer. Those who discover it are the fortunate ones, but so are those who do not. For it is not the destination, but the journey that determines our identity and where we are headed. It is a journey like no other...

It is a transcendental journey.

Phantasm in the Sky

Sporadic raindrops periodically disrupted Liam's reflection in the puddle. His drifting mind returned to the present as he heard the precipitation pattering the leaves. The scent of rain reminded him of sailing on the Great Lakes—one of many wonderful memories associated with his grandfather.

Liam stared at the headstone. "I miss you, Grandpa."

His grandfather, who had died prior to the onset of the recent war, played a major role in sculpting Liam's character. He also offered Liam valuable insight pertaining to events leading up to the global conflict.

Liam rose from a crouched position and resumed his usual routine, meandering through the cemetery gravestones and down a barren hill. The lower half of his legs disappeared in the fog-covered valley and reappeared as he ascended another knoll.

Much like the space Liam saved in his heart, the top of that prominence was a special place for those closest to him and he purposely selected it for its isolation from the rest of the crowded graveyard. It also reflected his peaceful solitude.

Liam calmly whispered a few words in front of the first headstone. Buried there was Apollo, his faithful dog that saved his life during the war. To the right, a much more conspicuous monument where Ashley rested. He recalled memories of when he first lost her.

* * * * *

Liam exhibited the same grieving ritual every time he visited. Wiping away tears, he knelt, smelled a single rose, and situated the fresh flower at the base atop the dozen wilted ones he had left during prior visits.

The first six weeks after losing Ashley passed by slowly as Liam's inner wounds began to heal. He visited frequently, at least once a day. Liam tried to keep himself busy, hoping to occupy his mind as he dealt with the heart-wrenching pain of losing his beloved wife and closest friend.

Unfortunately, time waits for no one. As the months passed, Liam visited less often. He had to. It wasn't to forget her, but because he needed to move forward.

Ashley would want that as well.

"It's time to carry on with my life." Liam leaned closer to the well-manicured gravesite and repositioned the flower next to Ashley's stone. "Other people need me to be strong." Liam placed his left hand on his chest and caressed the engraved granite with his right. "You will always be in my heart." Tears streamed down his cheeks as he kissed the top of the monolith. "I will search for you when my time on Earth expires."

* * * * *

Liam felt a strong desire to visit today. Perhaps it was the memories of the events leading up to the war, the conflict itself, or the recent battle against Ozone. He wiped his eyes upon arriving at the third site where he and Mason had memorialized the Dropas. The marble holder—attached to the face of the headstone—held new paintbrushes. *Mason must have been here recently.*

Mason had sculpted the dedicated marker himself, chiseling twelve Dropas with each of their names. Positioned near the top, Clearcoat watched over its eleven companions. Mason depicted those Dropas performing various antics he and Liam were accustomed to seeing. He carved a peel in the upper right-hand corner. It appeared as if the stone was constructed of paper, turning to the next page and revealing Mason's customary shooting star trademark.

"I miss you guys, and I hope wherever you are, you bring more joy than you brought me." Liam's eyes welled up when he backed away and collectively viewed all three sites. As if on cue, anger replaced the sadness in his heart and he could do nothing more than curse Ozone one more time.

* * * * *

...ForLords charged Liam but tripped and tumbled over each other like dominoes, unaware the other Dropas had painted shackles around all their ankles...

The Dropas completed their assignment of helping eradicate Ozone and focused on rescuing Shar. There wasn't much time before the fortress would erupt and they had to get her, as well as themselves, out before it did. They scurried through the darkened corridor where they encountered two small beacons approaching. Stripes' eyes emitted a glowing indicator to assist the Dropas in locating it and Pockets.

The Dropas recognized Stripes, but deemed it odd that their furry ally accompanied a ForLord—Pockets still wore the enemy's uniform jacket. Clearcoat ordered the Dropas to apprehend the perceived adversary and free Stripes from its apparent abductor. The Dropas readied their paintbrushes, initiating *Operation Capture ForLord*. Before Pockets uttered a word, the Dropas painted duct tape and sealed him up like a shipping package. Two Dropas rushed to his face and taped his mouth shut. Three more tightly secured his ankles together. Pockets lost his balance and fell to the ground where the other assailants finished the encasement, leaving only his nose, eyes, and forehead exposed. Superseded by the Dropas ability to maintain tangibility of the tape, Pockets failed to transform it into paint.

Stripes unleashed a deafening roar of disapproval at Pockets' untimely predicament. With one swipe of its giant paw, the massive tiger cast four Dropas into the side wall.

Excited about capturing another ForLord, the others triumphantly celebrated with brushes held high above their heads. The splattered victims reformed and joined their companions on the captive's chest. Proud of the victory, Clearcoat studied the enemy only to realize they had made a grave mistake. It ordered the other Dropas to do away with the adhesive binding. Clearcoat opted for a humanistic method, swiftly peeling the tape from Pockets' mouth.

"Ow!" Pockets howled. "What happened to removing it like paint, my little friend?"

Clearcoat apologized for its oversight and brushed soothing lotion on the area to ease the pain.

"Shar is waiting for your assistance," Pockets alerted the lead Dropa. "Give me a second to pinpoint her location." Eyes closed, he anticipated a message from Shar regarding her whereabouts. Pockets had never exhibited this ability before, at least not in the presence of Liam or Mason. He received a faint signal and opened his eyes. "She is in Ozone's studio. Do you know where it is?"

Clearcoat nodded.

"Then go and safely bring her home."

The Dropas dashed to save Shar. Pockets and Stripes raced in the opposite direction to escape from the activated time bomb.

It didn't take long for the Dropas to reach Shar inside Ozone's filthy workshop. Unlike their encounter with Pockets, the Dropas immediately recognized her, scurried up the outside of her clothing, and perched themselves on her shoulders.

"What a welcome sight," Shar said with a warm smile. "I've missed you all."

Clearcoat reminded the other Dropas of the limited time. The Dropas dashed down Shar's sides with paintbrushes drawn. They swiftly painted a curved, transparent skeleton that would ultimately evolve into a spherical aircraft. However, the manner in which they created it was unusual compared to their normal method of painting objects. This time, they repeatedly dipped their brushes into Clearcoat's body, masterfully producing several distinct modules.

After finalizing the bottom portion, Shar placed it on top of a large, sloped platform. The support structure that Silver and Gold built was designed to launch them at a precise angle away from the fortress.

Shar sat inside the unfinished section to give the Dropas the necessary reference information for sizing the pod. In a blur, they wielded their brushes around Shar and themselves. Outside the capsule, Black painted a large engine, much like the ones rocket hobbyists use, but considerably larger and powerful enough to carry them a safe distance from the demolition—Yellow added a long fuse.

Black and White hurried to the ceiling, rapidly painted a hole to allow the airship to inconceivably exit the studio, and reunited with the others inside the spheroid airship. Running out of time, the Dropas worked furiously. Only connection of the top portion remained.

The Dropas ignored the loud blasts from deep within the fortress bowels. As they enclosed themselves inside the sphere, numerous smaller explosions ensued. After capping off the escape vehicle, they patiently waited to be launched out of harm's way.

Light from the sustained eruptions flashed through the gaps around the door. The powerful blasts eventually blew away the wooden barrier. The strobing effect surrendered to a constant light stream as the blaze from the hallway penetrated the studio. The launch sequence commenced.

The inner pod warmed dramatically, but the temperature was much greater outside. Withstanding the fiery assault, the aircraft survived a critical test, keeping the intense heat from incinerating Shar and the Dropas. The flames engulfed Ozone's tables, easels, and artwork as they roared through the workspace closer to the bubble. Some Dropas gathered on Shar's shoulders and others hid under her long hair or inside her blouse pocket. At last, the fuse lit, and they braced themselves for the launch into the night sky.

The large engine ignited, rocketing the bubble through the ceiling opening. As the airship propelled itself away from the building, Shar and the Dropas caught a glimpse of the fallen fortress—illuminated like a baseball stadium. The bubble ascended to the cloud cover above the forest where the engine flame set ablaze Ozone's temporary shield, rapidly burning away the shroud of pollution.

...kids jubilantly cheered. For the first time in weeks, the moon and stars visibly lit up the ebony canvas and, by daybreak, the blue sky, billowy clouds, and the bright sun would again cast their subtle beauty on the planet. Definitely another day beyond that turning page, a symbol often depicted in Mason's murals.

"There it is." Lauren pointed at an area over the southern forest.

Streaking south above the forest trees was a spectacular shooting star. They all gazed at the spectacle as it zipped across the night sky.

"Make a wish before it disappears," Liam suggested as the shooting star faded into the darkness...

The flame consumed the remaining fuel and faded from the ebony sky. The Dropas disengaged the spent engine from the craft, allowing momentum to carry the still-airborne sphere away from peril.

Confident they were safe, the Dropas catapulted themselves off Shar's body and bounced off the inner walls. Giggles and gibbers abounded as they enjoyed the aerial circus ride, again exhibiting their fascination with flying.

Leading the winged fleet against Ozone's drones allowed Silver and Gold to fly aboard Robohawk. Escaping from the fortress gave the two Dropas the opportunity to share similar exhilaration with their companions as they all soared through the darkness inside the spherical glider.

Shar did not revel in the same excitement. Her concern transcended soaring at such a tremendous speed. She sat quietly with chin resting on her knees and arms wrapped around her legs, worrying more about whether the bubble would land safely or burst on impact.

Clearcoat, as usual, refrained from the Dropas' playtime, instead calming her during the ride. As she watched the childlike Dropas, her skepticism waned. Elated to be reunited with her miniature friends, a smile lit up her face. The Dropas always had that effect on people, and she was no exception.

The bubble slowed and the stars no longer passed by them in the same direction. The pod started its descent and Shar's trepidation returned.

Sensing her anxiety, Clearcoat assured her everything would be all right before instructing the other Dropas to prepare for touchdown. They halted the playful activity and readied their paintbrushes for action. Running along the wall, they covered the inner lining with painted cushions, leaving a small opening to view the outside terrain. The padded protection would provide a gentle, safe landing for all passengers.

Shar appreciated the reassurance. "I've been away from you too long."

The aircraft speed increased as gravity pulled it toward the ground. Had only the Dropas been encased in the bubble, it would have landed softly on its own, but because of Shar's additional weight, the buoyancy could not be maintained.

Shar clenched the cushions as the time of impact neared. The moonlit treetops disappeared from view moments before the bubble completed its descent. Darkness dominated the interior with the initial touchdown. Shar and the Dropas tossed around after she lost her grip. The bubble launched into the air again, and the light reappeared. After final impact, the sphere stabilized on the liquid landing strip but failed to come to a rest as it floated down the river.

The brief loss of concentration by the Dropas caused the cushions to disappear. The moonlight illuminated the interior of the bubble. They had definitely landed, miles downstream from Ozone's fortress.

The rapid current worsened the situation. The rushing sound intensified as they neared a waterfall. Complicating matters, the residual chemicals in the river had weakened the outer coating, allowing water to seep into the pod.

Reacting quickly, the Dropas dipped their brushes into Clearcoat and painted a protective shield around Shar as the lining deteriorated further. The current thrust the sphere into a tailspin over the edge of the forty-foot cascade, bursting the bubble on impact at the base of the fall.

The lightweight Dropas catapulted in all directions toward the riverbanks. Shar, on the other hand, submerged. She prepared to inhale once her body buoyed to the surface, anticipating she would be swallowed again. Her head emerged, and the relentless water slammed her into the side of a protruding stone formation. Her head snapped back as her forehead caromed off the unforgiving protrusion, cutting her forehead and rendering her unconscious.

The rushing river receded and the current slowed as it carried her away from the turbulence. Shar lay face down, her lungs filling with water. She floated downstream for a short time before a large fishing net snared her.

The Dropas had scurried down both riverbanks. Upon arriving at desirable positions, they painted a net that stretched across the water and a winch to reel it ashore. The Dropas from the east bank darted across the outstretched net to the west bank after successfully catching Shar. There they engaged the winch and reeled her toward dry land. The other Dropas prepped for the ensuing recovery procedures, painting critical pieces of equipment to revive the incoming patient and surgical scrubs for themselves.

Aided by four other Dropas, Silver and Gold led the water rescue mission. The winch dragged the entangled Shar out of the river, across a tarp, and onto a dry ground cloth next to a tree.

The first piece of machinery the Dropas utilized was a pedal-powered water pump. Indigo and Yellow inserted one end of the pump hose into Shar's mouth. Wearing a mining light on its forehead, Indigo guided the conduit into her throat and further down into her lungs. Blue and Violet transported another forked tube from a second pump—an air pump. They inserted each flared end into Shar's nostrils and plugged up any gaps to prevent air from escaping. After verifying the placement of the hoses and that Indigo had resurfaced from inside Shar's lungs, Clearcoat nodded at Green, Black, and White.

The three Dropas pedaled vigorously as the water pump siphoned the liquid from Shar's lungs and sprayed it away from her body. In an orchestrated manner, Red and Orange similarly operated the air pump, distributing fresh air into her lungs to replace the water. With the pumps in full operation, "Dr. Silver" and "Dr. Gold" rhythmically lowered and raised a net full of rocks onto Shar's chest, made possible by the pulley system they had constructed. Dropas were pumping.

Dropas were compressing. Perfectly harmonized, the one-of-a-kind CPR system proved to be just as effective as any human method.

Shar coughed up water, barely missing Indigo and Yellow as they extracted the hose from her mouth. Blue and Violet removed the tube from her nose, allowing her to breathe normally. They pushed the netted rocks away and down from Shar's chest. Unexpectedly, the stones collided with the ground. Silver and Gold launched into the air and landed in some nearby ferns. They scurried out of the foliage to celebrate with their friends.

Shar coughed a few more times, expelling the residual water from her lungs. Her eyes remained closed as she moaned in pain. Silver, Gold, Indigo, and Yellow tended to the cut on her forehead. Although she didn't squarely strike the rock formation, the impact resulted in a serious wound nonetheless. Hitting it straight on would have surely ended her life. Clearcoat directed the other Dropas to paint thick blankets to insulate her.

Red and Orange also built a fire to provide additional warmth. While Shar rested, the Dropas encircled the flames, imitating humans singing campfire songs in their own Dropa gibberish. It wasn't long before they stopped, each resting— head on hands—and thinking about Shar. They no longer desired to play games until their companion recovered. Clearcoat seemed to be the most concerned because Shar didn't open her eyes during the entire time they tended to her. For the remainder of the night, the Dropas watched her sleep.

Although the Dropas hadn't seen the blue sky in some time, they were subdued when the sun shone the following morning. Shar's condition had worsened. Perched on her forehead, Clearcoat concluded from the burning sensation in its feet that she had a high fever. Her body shivered as the blankets and fire failed to keep her warm. Clearcoat didn't understand her prolonged suffering—her head wound showed small signs of healing.

Clearcoat ordered the Dropas to paint a fresh set of dry clothes as it hurried down to uncover her. It pushed the blankets aside and removed the damp outer garments from her body. At first, the long horizontal cicatrix below Shar's collarbone went unnoticed. Clearcoat withdrew the final garment layer and called for the other Dropas. Undressing her exposed the five-inch scar that stretched from her left armpit to her sternum, revealing why Shar's condition had not improved. She was feverish more from her sealed pocket than the blow to her forehead, the former likely caused by Ozone.

Shar could only live a short period of time with this part of her body closed, and Clearcoat had no idea how long it had been in this condition. Clearcoat extended the blunt end of its paintbrush near Silver. Understanding what Clearcoat needed, Silver promptly painted a scalpel at the end of it. The Dropas held hands, formed a circle, and chanted as they often did in times of crisis.

Clearcoat gently inserted the tip into the scar near her armpit and meticulously guided the blade along the length of it. The fresh incision did not bleed as one would expect, but rather emitted a bright light from within Shar's body and out through the opening.

The Dropas kept their heads bowed as the incision expanded and more light escaped. Unlike the times when she descended from the sky to assist the Dropas, Athena's image rose from within Shar's pocket.

Athena used the blunt end of her spear to lift the surgeon's tiny head. "Clearcoat, you and the other Dropas have done well. My time for keeping her alive was running out, but I can always count on you. She will require an extended period to heal before you reunite her with Bandor. Let her rest."

Clearcoat gibbered to Athena.

"You will be coming home soon," she assured the curious Dropa.

Clearcoat bowed one last time as Athena descended into Shar's chest. The incision reverted to its normal width as the small image of Athena receded, taking the bright light with her.

Heads raised, the Dropas released their grips from one another. They were confident Shar would survive and that made them extremely happy. Since she needed time to recuperate, they decided to enjoy a well-deserved vacation.

Clearcoat opted not to engage in the playtime. While the lead Dropa stayed behind to observe the recovering patient, the others scurried down to the riverbank where the sun shone brightly. Some Dropas painted themselves palm trees, attached canvas hammocks, and enjoyed some relaxation. Others painted beach chairs and umbrellas, shading themselves from the sun. When boredom arose from lying around, they painted a net and used blueberries from a nearby bush as volleyballs. By the time Clearcoat visited, every Dropa was spattered with juice.

Clearcoat beckoned the Dropas to visit Shar who had stirred and asked about them. Elated to hear she had awoken, the "two-legged blueberries" abruptly ended the volleyball game and rushed to her side. A resting Shar ate an apple Clearcoat had freshly picked for her.

"How are my little rescuers doing?" Shar asked weakly.

They dragged their feet in the dirt and lowered their heads, all pretending to be bashful.

Shar scooped up half the Dropas and opened her hand in front of her face. "Have we been picking berries?"

The guilty Dropas giggled.

Shar set them on the ground. "Clearcoat told me everything you did to save my life. I am so grateful."

They giggled and bowed.

Shar consumed the last bite, core and all, and flicked the stem into the trees. "Now that my pocket is accessible, I have a little something for you all to enjoy."

The Dropas' heads lifted in anticipation. The more activities in which they could partake the more enjoyable the vacation. Shar retrieved twelve customized garments from her pocket. The Dropas jumped up and down with excitement.

She always carried them with her for times when they went to the beach together. The Dropas loved the water, but because of their composition, could spend limited time exposed to it. One rainy day, when the Dropas yearned to play in the puddles, Shar crafted them all waterproof bodysuits. Each colored outfit matched the color of a Dropa. She intentionally created a transparent headpiece, allowing the Dropas clear visibility.

The eager Dropas huddled in front of Shar to receive the coverings. Without hesitation, they donned the protection, thanked Shar, and scampered down to the riverbank. She indicated to Clearcoat to play with the others. As much as Shar wanted to join them, she acknowledged the need for more rest. After making herself comfortable, it didn't take long before she drifted off to sleep.

The other Dropas wasted no time engaging in various water sports. Black, White, Indigo, and Yellow painted jet skis and raced each other from one side of the river to the other, occasionally losing their balance and falling off the equipment. Amused by a companion's misfortune usually resulted in one or more Dropas ceasing self-control and splashing into the water too.

Silver and Gold chose a more relaxed approach. They painted rubber inner tubes and pretended to sip tropical drinks while floating. The remaining Dropas engaged themselves in waterskiing, having painted two speed boats and the necessary gear. Ever the responsible leader, Clearcoat mimicked Silver and Gold, in case Shar awoke and needed assistance.

* * * * *

Months had passed since Shar's escape from the fortress and her unfortunate encounter with the waterfall. Her head wound had fully healed within the first couple of weeks, but regaining her strength from having her pocket sealed required more time than expected. Nonetheless, she was as spirited as ever, especially since the release from Ozone's evil clutches. Shar dreaded the entire time she spent with him, but kept reminding herself it was necessary in order to carry out the mission Athena had requested of her.

That evening, Shar received a message from Pockets. Ignoring the telepathic communication, the Dropas played in her hair as she quietly slipped into a trance.

"Are you there?" Pockets called.

"I am here," Shar replied.

"I have not heard from you in some time. Is everything all right?"

"A mere setback that hindered my communication abilities. All is good."

"What happened?"

"During our escape from the fortress...well, it is a long story, but basically, I whacked my head on a rock that blocked my telepathy." Shar paused. "Actually, it was...my pocket...well, it does not matter. I am healing."

"You had me worried. I have been trying to contact you since we arrived home."

"You are home?" Shar replied excitedly. "Oh, I want to be—"

"Not our home. My Earth home."

Shar said nothing.

"When will you be well enough to travel?"

"I am improving every day."

"Good, because I am sensing something is not right here."

"What do you mean?"

"I will explain the situation when you return."

"I need directions to the nearest GGB regional office," Shar insisted.

"Head up the river to the fortress. I will have some officers meet you there."

Shar felt a chill course down her spine. "Must I return to that horrid place?"

"I am sorry, but it is the easiest way. Besides, not much is left."

"Not physically, but many bad memories linger."

"This will be the last time."

"All right, Bandor."

"If you have any delays, please contact me."

"I will."

"Safe travels." Pockets cut off the transmission.

Shar emerged from her trance and updated her twelve little friends—they would be heading back in a few days—not at all surprised by their ecstatic reaction to the news. The Dropas were vacationed out and ready to reunite with Pockets, Mason, and Liam.

Unforeseen Shadow

Mason and Pockets required several months to return all the creatures to the mural world. This included the astros that safely arrived home shortly after Liam's group. The undertaking elicited another sad moment, especially for the teens who played a role in the adventure. They had taken a liking to the painted mascots and established a strong connection with the "living" entities when they existed on Earth. Every mural entailed some degree of work over the long process: surviving creatures that acquired battle scars needed touching up and those lost during the conflict had to be completely repainted.

They progressed rapidly through each school, utilizing a newly constructed supply box furnished with the latest equipment and a high-tech lift that engineers replicated from Mason's description of Ozone's hydraulic machine. Coupled with Pockets' tremendous emotional support, uninspired painting might have been the best therapy for Mason during that period. The loss of the Dropas occupied his mind for the majority of each day as he was unmotivated to create anything new.

The GGB had assembled the captured ForLords hundreds of miles away from Ozone's fortress. Removed from their traumatizing environment, the detainees resided in a more comfortable compound. There, the GGB initiated a long rehabilitation process, bringing in renowned experts to assist with the healing.

In addition, the GGB's ongoing apprehension of the stray cadres of ForLords spread across the globe. In most cases, the outliers surrendered on their own. It was unclear if the effects of Ozone's bubbles weakened over time or if the detainees realized a better life awaited them. Nonetheless, ForLord capitulation made the GGB's job substantially easier, yet innumerable holdouts, averse to global unity, avoided capture.

Most encouraging was the perpetual transformation of civilization. Diverse pockets of people resistant to co-existing before the war discovered ways of unified interaction. The execution of the Survival Treaty policies was yielding the expected dividends, and individuals sought to change their old ways and beliefs, replacing them with a more harmonized manner of living. It was a wonderful spectacle to behold what no one had ever deemed possible. Societies strived for equality and all performed as one, recognizing similarities while embracing and celebrating differences. They had broken down their walls, opened their minds, and enjoyed the wonderful second chance they had all been given—life itself—and they did it together.

Liam and Willie attended a GGB briefing regarding the status of the ForLord holdouts, as well as the rehabilitation progress of those in detention. The briefing flowed smoothly, as each report was read, until a lead board member raised an intriguing question, one that neither Liam nor Willie could definitively answer.

"How is Ozone's rehabilitation progressing?" the member asked.

"He wasn't among the men in our custody," another verified.

The board member turned to Liam and Willie. "Did either one of you witness his death?"

Willie answered confidently, "We did not, sir. No one survived those explosions except the ForLords detained in the Hornets' nests and the individuals on the mission task force."

"Yes, I do recall you mentioned the intensity of the destruction during the debriefing. The account of his demise must have been overlooked due to the excitement at the time, but it occurred to me that his actual death was never officially documented." The board member shuffled through a small stack of reports. "I guess we have no other choice but to assume he indeed lost his life during the fortress obliteration."

Everyone except Liam and Willie refocused on the meeting.

Liam whispered in Willie's ear, "I didn't see him die." His eyes wandered as he replayed the events following their departure from inside the fortress. "After our sub surfaced, I was preoccupied with evacuating everyone. Ozone's vessel sank into the river and I thought nothing more of it."

"I never saw him when I vacated the fortress, nor when I returned to retrieve the Vikings and gators. In fact, I've never seen that man."

"He certainly wouldn't have been able to survive those explosions."

Both men listened to the remainder of the briefing, but not without difficulty concentrating. Liam contemplated the evil Lord Ozone's purported death.

That same day, Mason and Pockets were touching up Robohawk and the wall on which it was painted. Its wings had been slightly damaged by a number of chemical streams. In honor of the bird's prominence during the battle, they intentionally left this as the last restoration mural before painting new ones.

High up on the platform, Mason airbrushed the bird's talon. Down below, Pockets mixed additional colors at the supply box located near the base of the lift. Something disrupted Mason's concentration. He raised his index finger off the airbrush and peered down at Pockets whose eyes fixated on the mural. They had witnessed the same anomaly.

"Am I crazy or did I see movement inside the mural?"

Pockets crinkled his brow. "Perhaps it was a shadow."

They scanned the empty gym, including the rafters, perceiving nothing peculiar that could have made a shadow traveling in front of the wall.

Mason braced himself on the railing. "Please explain this to me, Pockets."

"Sorry, but I have no explanation."

"Neither do I." Mason surveyed the gym a second time.

"Maybe a bird is loose," Pockets suggested weakly.

"As much as I'd like to believe that, I'd bet my art career that a bird did not cause the shadow. Besides, I heard no flapping wings." Mason's half smile disappeared when he noticed Pockets' expression of horror. He slowly pivoted. "Holy cow!" Mason's airbrush flew out of his hand. His body fell backward over the railing as if he had seen a ghost. He wished he had instead of the distinct image in its place.

It was Ozone. He had mysteriously survived the massive explosions. Quick to react, Pockets instinctively withdrew a mini-trampoline from his pocket and threw it precisely in the path where Mason would land. Eyes closed, Mason braced himself for impact with the gym floor and the subsequent shattering of his leg bones. Instead, his feet squarely contacted the jumping mat that catapulted him above the lift.

"Grab on!" Pockets instructed.

Mason opened his eyes and thrust his hands forward, unaware of what had propelled him to where his fall originated. He grasped the railing bars.

"Well done! Nine point seven from the Russian judge!"

"Where did that—never mind?" Mason adjusted his grip. "You're amazing."

Pockets bowed graciously. "Why, thank you, but not as amazing at what we saw in the mural."

"Do you believe he's still there?"

"One way to find out." Pockets stepped to the side of the lift.

Mason pulled himself up and onto the platform, hesitating momentarily before investigating the mural. There stood Lord Ozone, leaning with his back against the painted side wall and behind Robohawk's tail, but definitely inside the artwork. He appeared somewhat smaller than in real life due to the perspective laid out in the painting. The man thought to be eliminated unequivocally existed. Dressed in his black cloak, he proudly wore the hood down around his neck, exposing his unmasked, chemically damaged face.

"Bravo! Bravo!" Ozone slowly clapped his hands. "Encore! Encore!"

Mason and Pockets stared in disbelief.

"Seriously…no hi, how ya doin' from either one of you?" Ozone asked sarcastically, his customary slurred speech had all but disappeared.

An enraged Mason hurled a quart can at Ozone. Upon impact with the wall, the lid dislodged, splattering paint across that section of the mural and a good portion of the cinder blocks below it. Ozone didn't flinch.

"Tsk, tsk." Ozone calmly walked behind Robohawk to the bird's frontside, showing no signs of being struck by the container or the paint.

Mason searched frantically for something else to throw.

"You are wasting your time, Mason," Pockets advised.

"Listen to your friend, my fellow artist," Ozone added.

"No one's talking to you, Leonard," Mason replied, remembering Ozone's abhorrence toward that name.

"Come a little closer and say that," Ozone dared.

"Keep your distance, Mason!" Pockets warned as he scaled the lift, anticipating some kind of retaliation.

"Not to worry, I can handle this guy." Mason inched closer to the evil man.

"Mason!" Pockets stepped onto the platform. "Let it go!"

Mason clenched both fists, ready to strike. Ozone crouched and glared directly into Mason's eyes. Mason swung at Ozone's face. Before contact with the wall, Ozone snatched Mason's wrist. He yanked it and part of Mason's body into the mural. Pockets exhibited an uncharacteristic lightning-quick reflex as he grabbed Mason's other arm while bracing himself on the platform. Mason felt pain in the arm that Pockets tugged but not in the one Ozone gripped. That arm numbed as it entered the mural. Mason felt like a rope in a tug-o-war match, having his head and shoulders repeatedly pulled into the artwork by Ozone and yanked out by Pockets.

"Release him, Bandor, he's mine!" Ozone shouted.

"No way, Arton!" Pockets contended.

Failing to hear Ozone and Pockets call each other different names, Mason's arm was yanked into the mural one more time before suddenly being released. This time, both Mason and Pockets flew across the lift railing as Ozone fell off the painted ledge.

Pockets grabbed onto the crossbar with one hand and clutched Mason with the other. Mason, who had flown over the top of Pockets, was dangling fifteen feet above the gym floor. He grasped a lower crossbar with his right hand, released Pockets' arm with his left, and secured a hold on the next crossbar. After situating himself onto the platform, he assisted Pockets.

"What happened? I only heard a screech."

"You missed the best part," Pockets chuckled. "Robohawk gave Ozone a quick jab with one of its talons and sent him sprawling off the edge of the wall."

Mason raised his eyebrows. "Is he gone for good?"

"Not on your life," Ozone bellowed as he climbed onto the painted ledge.

"You're like a bad rash that has no cure." Mason clenched his fists again. "Answer this before I get rid of you for good."

Ozone brought his hands against his chest. "You want something from me?"

"How did you survive those explosions and get inside the mural?"

Ozone pointed at Robohawk. "Your generous friend gave me a lift."

"What? No way would Robohawk help you," Mason insisted.

"Perhaps not intentionally." Ozone recalled the chain of events.

* * * * *

...gator caught up with Ozone's vessel and pierced holes in it with its large, sharp teeth. Water began filling the inside of the watercraft. Realizing he had to escape by land, Ozone surfaced just past the fortress walls, quickly opened the hatch, and jumped ashore. He disappeared around the corner leading to the front of the fortress. The pursuing reptile lost sight of Ozone and high walked past the re-energizing creatures...

Ozone desperately searched for a hiding place. Certain he was being hunted by the gator, he espied Willie and some cats approaching from the front. Robohawk unwittingly shielded Ozone as it re-energized alongside the other birds and dragons.

The fugitive leaned against Robohawk's metallic breast to avoid being seen by Willie and the felines. The liquid armor absorbed Ozone's shoulder. He deduced this would be a perfect hiding place until the gator, Willie, and the giant cats terminated the search. He inhaled deeply and stepped inside Robohawk, barely disappearing before Willie's group passed in front of the massive hawk's body.

Ozone had no idea how long he could survive inside the avian refuge with limited air. Eventually, he required another breath, but also wanted to assess the situation. He attempted to extend his face outward, but Robohawk's body had solidified, preventing Ozone from moving. He was trapped.

Robohawk and the other re-energized birds prepared for evacuation. Absent a viable escape strategy, a frantic Ozone exhaled and instinctively inhaled, expecting a mouthful of whatever made up the insides of the bird. Nothing entered his lungs. Ozone's brain essentially disengaged his respiratory system. He ceased breathing altogether, no longer requiring oxygen to survive.

Robohawk's metallic body shifted with Liam and Mason astride. Unbeknownst to them, the winged transportation departed with a third passenger. At that moment, Ozone realized he was regaining the form he once possessed, that of Arton.

Although unsure if he would ever escape from inside Robohawk, Ozone began plotting his next devious undertaking during the flight home. This time, the objective did not involve the people on Earth, but rather those who existed in the world from which he was exiled.

* * * * *

"Impressive story, isn't it?" Ozone extended his hands, expecting recognition.

"Don't flatter yourself." Mason's rage had subsided—replaced with disappointment and tremendous consternation. "This world that you mentioned…where is it? Another planet?"

"No, I'm not an alien from some other galaxy, if that's what you think."

"Then where?" Mason asked, unamused with the guessing game.

"I hate to spoil this party, but I have much to do. I already shared one story." Ozone smiled smugly at Pockets. "Maybe Bandor will tell you from where I originated and where my current journey will take me. I have an old debt to pay. It was nice seeing you again, Mason." He winked at Pockets. "Tough luck, ol' friend." Ozone jumped off the painted ledge and fled deeper inside the mural.

Mason contemplated Ozone's comments. "Bandor?" Mason turned to Pockets. "Why did he call you Bandor?"

Although somewhat ashamed that he had deceived Mason, Pockets knew his deception was justified. "Because that is my name."

"This is getting weirder by the minute. Your name isn't Pockets?"

"It is in this world."

"Okay, I can handle the name change. People change names, but why do you and Ozone keeping mentioning another world?"

"I hoped it would not come to this, but it is time I tell you and Liam the entire story," Pockets confided.

"That's a wonderful idea." Mason furrowed his brow. "What guarantee do we have that you won't mislead us this time?"

"Because when I share the whole story, you will understand why I changed my name, among other things."

"Oh, there is more deception than your name?" Mason folded his arms in disgust. "I can't even trust my best friend. Deception was a primary cause of the war, remember?"

Pockets squarely eyed Mason. "You and Liam must choose whether or not to believe the information I impart. Please allow me the chance to explain. You know I would not intentionally deceive you guys."

Mason sighed deeply and nodded in agreement.

"Phone Liam and select a meeting location. Ask him to invite Willie."

"Okay," Mason unfolded his arms. "Pockets?"

"Yes, Mason."

"Whatever you tell us, I already believe you."

"Thank you. While you call your brother, I will clean up the paint."

Mason lowered the lift to floor level. He jumped off the platform, sat on the first row of bleachers, and contacted Liam.

"Hey, what's up?" Liam was about to depart with Willie from the GGB meeting.

"Guess who's alive."

Based on the discussion at the recent GGB meeting, Liam considered only one person, as much as it pained him to admit it. "Ozone."

Willie's face expressed disbelief.

Mason pulled the phone away from his face. "How did you know?"

"The tone in your voice and the fact that a GGB member questioned the progress of Ozone's rehabilitation." Liam let the call transfer to the truck speakers. "Willie and I told the members that we presumed he had perished in the explosions, although we had no physical proof."

"Well, he's alive and all too well," Mason assured, "and Pockets and I do have physical proof."

"Where did you spot him?"

"Inside the Robohawk mural."

"How is that possible?"

"Remember telling me how you inserted your hand into the re-energizing panther?"

"No way!"

"He essentially melded with Robohawk and survived in there. He indicated he was regaining the form he previously possessed. What do you make of that?"

Liam had no viable explanation. "We could be in serious trouble again."

"I disagree." Mason rose from the bleachers. "Ozone spoke about an old debt to pay before disappearing into the mural."

"What does that mean?"

"I haven't a clue, but that's also why I'm calling. Bandor, I mean Pockets, has something to tell us."

"Bandor? Who the heck is Bandor?"

"Pockets will explain. He wants to meet with you, Willie, and me."

"Let's meet at my place." Liam glanced at Willie for confirmation.

"Yeah, sure," Willie replied. "I'll call May after we're done here and tell her I'll be a little late."

"Great."

"Pockets and I need to pack up. We'll be there in an hour."

"See you then." Liam disconnected the call.

"Man," Willie sighed, "I thought we were rid of Ozone for good."

"I did too."

While Willie phoned May, Liam pondered two questions. *Who the heck is Bandor and what debt is Ozone repaying?*

Waiting at his apartment, Liam engaged in a discussion with Willie about Ozone's survival and how it could potentially impact humanity again. They also considered Ozone's debt repayment. Their presumptions made little sense.

"Hello," Liam answered his ringing phone.

"Hey, we're downstairs." Mason's voice echoed from inside the vestibule.

"Come on in." Liam entered the access code on the number pad of his phone to unlock the main door.

Minutes later Mason and Pockets entered the apartment and sat with Liam and Willie at the dining table. Mason offered further details pertaining to Ozone's escape from the fortress. Liam listened to Mason but concentrated on Pockets. Pockets' face expressed considerable worry, more intense than when Ozone wreaked havoc on Earth, and that deeply concerned Liam.

"…and that's it in a nutshell," Mason concluded.

"I can't believe he's alive," Willie commented.

"He is, and we have work to do!" Pockets exclaimed.

Liam and Mason jerked their heads back. Neither one had ever seen Pockets boldly react like that, and they were unsure how to interpret it.

Pockets folded his hands on the table. "Since Arton, or Lord Ozone as you call him, has revealed my true identity, I ask that you call me Bandor. First and foremost, please accept my apologies for misleading you about my name and purpose for being here. My explanation will justify the secrecy." Bandor cleared his throat. "I am certain you have many questions, but please hold them until the end."

They all nodded in agreement.

"Do not expect me to pull my face off and reveal an alien organism. This is my true form, but I am not human—well, not completely. Arton recognized me through my eyes."

"If you're not human—" Mason inquired.

Bandor held his hand in front of Mason. "Please, do not ask any questions until I have shared all the details."

Bandor's gesture reminded Liam of Demitrius, the old man he met in Greece. For a moment, he supposed that the two men may have some connection.

"I am Bandor, and I come from Dropa. This makes me a Dropian, but do not confuse us with our little friends, the Dropas. Although we share the same existence, we are clearly different life forms. Dropians bear resemblance to humans more than anything else, but there are many distinct types of Dropians just as there are humans. However, unlike humans' perception of each other before the war, we exist harmoniously in Dropa and treat each other as equals."

Bandor opened his left hand. "We have Dropians," he proceeded as he opened his right hand, "and we have Dropas. Then there is Athena—she oversees Dropa. I am one of her messengers and one of two messengers dispatched to Earth to help rid your world of Arton. The other is Lindor, or Shar in your world. Mason, you have already met her. She was responsible for communicating to me vital details pertaining to Arton's activities and location. And Willie, among other things, we both assisted the GGB by exposing the ForLords that revealed Arton's fortress. Both Lindor and I had to conceal our identity. Had Arton known we were here, his preparation would have been more thorough, and humanity's demise inevitable. When Dropians arrive in your world, we are not allowed to directly interfere, but we can furnish information and tools to help you. If you had not adequately exploited the mascots, the human race would have been eliminated, and Dropa would have ultimately vanished. I hope you understand why I concealed my identity and kept our purpose secret."

The enrapt trio were lost for words.

"You are probably wondering how Arton fits into the grand scheme of things. I will address that in a minute, but first I will offer a brief history of Dropa." Bandor folded his hands on the table. "Dropa was created from the place humans refer to as Atlantis, the lost continent. It is lost to you, and you will never find it using conventional means. During the time it flourished on Earth, Atlantis was regarded as the most beautiful and most highly evolved place to live. Its advancement of culture and civilization far surpassed that of the rest of the world. It was envied by everyone. Atlantis, which was cherished by its creator, Zeus, bestowed a wonderland for its residents. However, as evidence shows repeatedly with humans, Atlanteans underappreciated the small continent and their material possessions. They transgressed into a greedy civilization and amassed a large army to conquer and rule the world. Outraged at seeing this, Zeus used them as an example for other civilizations. He orchestrated severe storms and earthquakes throughout the continent. Volcanoes erupted and tidal waves swept across the once magnificent terrain. Athena, Zeus' daughter, could not bear watching the mass destruction of her beloved paradise. Atlantis was her escape, a place where she played music or immersed herself in her art. Before Zeus totally obliterated the continent, Athena persuaded her father to let her keep and oversee the remains of the "lost continent." Zeus agreed, but emphasized two strict conditions: the continent would never be *physically* seen and she could never leave it. Athena, being the lone individual who knew the Dropas existed, instructed them to encase the continent in a protective bubble, preserving its survival as it receded into the sea. During the creation of the defensive shield, many Dropas perished from the effects of the ocean salt water, among other things, but a fair number survived."

Bandor ensured he kept everyone's attention. Their eyes were fixated on him.

"Atlantis, presently Dropa, was preserved, and Athena had devised a way for the continent to avoid being discovered. However, with no other survivors, Athena grew lonely. Unable to leave, she relied on the Dropas to assist her with one final transformation. When they completed the work, Dropa had morphed from a physical place into an existence. You cannot get there using a map or any conventional means of transportation. It is an ethereal sanctuary for souls, if you will. Many of you refer to heaven and hell as places where your soul resides after death, depending on how your life on Earth has been judged. Dropa is most comparable to the former. However, one can arrive before dying. Because of Athena's love of art, many artists have unknowingly created portals, or gateways. I am sure you have heard the expression, 'gateway to the soul.' These are gateways for the soul. A handful of artists have discovered their presence, and even less have learned how to use them. I will need your assistance to intercept Arton before he reaches a gateway. You see, he is on his way to wipe out Dropa—it was once his world as well."

Astounded at Bandor's story, the three sat paralyzed. Liam and Mason were overjoyed at the prospect of traveling to Dropa. After all, that's what many hoped for, that chance to deliver their soul to the heavens. The difference here was that it was no longer driven by faith, but rather by a matter of certainty. Souls truly transcended to another existence, the body merely provided a host as individuals discovered the important things during their brief time on Earth. Liam was overcome with peace, elation, and contentment. The feeling, however, was short-lived.

Bandor rubbed his hands over his face. "This brings me to why Arton wants to abolish Dropa. Arton grew furious hearing about Zeus destroying Atlantis. Even more so when he discovered the Dropas, and their assistance during Athena's preservation of her paradise. Determined to prevent them from finishing the bubble before the continent disappeared, he began eradicating the Dropas in any way possible. Once Athena located Arton, she banished him from her beloved paradise. Upon his exile, Athena had him followed by various messengers to observe his activities. Arton is a demigod, a mortal that exhibits powers of a god. He is also the last Atlantean Existor."

Wondering how this amazing story would end, Liam, Willie, and Mason attempted to process what Bandor had shared with them.

Bandor paused and refocused, but this time with greater concern. "As I mentioned, he possesses certain powers of a god, but he lost many of those abilities during his banishment. They will likely return as he nears Dropa. His biological constitution is that of a human, but being an Existor has allowed him to survive in your world for thousands of years by body jumping. That is, before the host body physically dies, he leaps into an unborn child. He plans on returning to Dropa to terminate its existence and we must intercept him before he does!" Bandor rechanneled his consternation. "I have shared much with you. You may now ask questions." He had certainly piqued the three's curiosity.

"Why did Ozone, or Arton, decide to kill everyone instead of simply jumping to another body?" Liam inquired.

"I am unsure, but surmise that Arton grew tired of migrating from body to body. Remember, he has been jumping from the time he was exiled from Atlantis. I sense Arton wanted to vacate Ozone's body after his partial disfigurement resulting from the art show tragedy. He could not handle his hideous appearance and was enraged by the fact that he could not make the leap. Again, he was from Atlantis, and those people were consumed with vanity."

"Why didn't Arton take his own life?" Willie asked.

"Simply put, Existors cannot kill themselves. When they reside in a body, they cannot leave it until just before it physically dies. Because of their vanity, Existors struggle internally if they are unhappy with the physical traits of the host. Their training includes learning how to love and believe in themselves no matter their appearance. However, not all Existors fully absorb that lesson. Much like humans, Existors refer to others as being normal or abnormal. Of course, to them, they are the normal ones. We all understand that normalcy is subjective, thereby making everyone unique."

"I have one," Mason said before Willie or Liam asked another question, "one that we all have pondered the answer to for a long time. Will you please, please tell us how you fit all of that stuff in your pocket?"

"I fully expected that question. The ultimate power must remain a mystery at present, but I will say it is part of being a messenger. Dropians chosen for this role are given a pocket, as you call it, before leaving Dropa. We learn about the world we are visiting and carry items to accommodate our stay. If we do not have everything, we collect it as we go. That is all I can tell you at this point."

"Bandor, how will Arton get to Dropa?" Liam asked.

"By traveling through the murals."

Liam and Mason exchanged quizzical looks.

Willie buried his head in his hands. "You can count me out."

"No one has asked you to go," Bandor asserted. "Besides, I will need you to stay outside as our guide. If they choose, Liam and Mason will accompany me into the murals."

"Seriously?" they both exclaimed. "Of course, we will."

On many occasions, Liam and Mason fantasized about traveling inside Mason's artwork. They imagined discovering new creatures and coalescing with the surreal art, but never believed the fantasy would become reality.

"Liam, you had asked about Arton's route to Dropa. We must find an existing portal that leads there...and arrive before Arton does."

"Which mural contains a portal?" Mason asked. "Because I certainly don't remember painting one."

"We will discover it soon enough. As will Ozone. That is why we need to enter the murals. Arton becomes more dangerous the deeper he penetrates and will be increasingly more difficult to stop. However, we have three things working in our favor. One, we have the mural creatures to assist us. They have already demonstrated their loyalty to us and Athena. Two, the body that Arton is using will not last much longer. And third, we have Lindor and the Dropas."

Liam, Mason, and Willie exchanged looks, questioning Bandor's perceived delusional state.

"Bandor, the Dropas didn't survive," Mason reminded him.

"You do not give those little guys much credit, do you?" Bandor chuckled. "They are very much alive."

"How?" Mason asked joyfully in anticipation of reuniting with his tiny friends.

"Did you see them?" Liam inquired.

Bandor shook his head, playfully shaming them for doubting him.

"Tell us how they skirted death," Liam implored enthusiastically.

"A story for another time. Lindor and the Dropas are alive, and they are enjoying a well-deserved vacation. However, I have already asked them to return home."

"Vacation?" Mason asked.

"Oh, yes, the Dropas and Dropians love vacations, as you call them." Bandor closed his eyes and deeply sighed. "We call them cleansings. The time and activities are used to refresh the soul. That is exceedingly important in preserving the creativity of Dropas, as well as Dropians."

Antithetical Reunions

Lindor awoke to the giggling Dropas dispersed on her face. Lying on her side, she opened her eyes to find Clearcoat standing with its hands clasped behind its back, waiting patiently for her to surface from a deep sleep. Detecting Lindor's alertness, Clearcoat informed her the Dropas were prepared to leave whenever she was ready.

"First, I need to freshen up a bit." Lindor rubbed her eyes.

The Dropas leapt off her face onto the ground cloth and Lindor threw off the blankets. Rising to her feet, she yawned, stretched, and meandered down to the river. She retrieved from her pocket a fresh set of clothes and a pair of hiking boots appropriate for the trip. Lindor shed her sleeping attire and waded the chilling water. The sun emerging above the treetops provided her with a trace of warmth.

Although nippy, the river felt rather refreshing. From her pocket, Lindor withdrew a bar of soap and a soft sponge. As she bathed, she sang a popular Dropian song—her beautiful voice reaching every note perfectly. After cleaning up camp, four Dropas painted themselves harps and flutes to accompany Lindor's ethereal melodies. The other Dropas immersed themselves in the performance.

Lindor vividly imagined herself in Dropa. She was eager to return, especially after spending more than five years on Earth—the majority with Arton. Dropa afforded tranquility and beauty unlike any other place, and she truly missed being there.

She inserted the sponge and soap into her pocket, and submerged one last time to rinse. Lindor stepped ashore where Orange had painted a plush rug on which to stand. The miniscule Violet attempted to politely hand her a large, fluffy towel to dry herself. As the others played instruments, she resumed her vocal performance.

Lindor wasted no time dressing in the brisk, morning air. As she did, Clearcoat set an apple and a hearty portion of blueberries on the rug. She stuffed the old clothes and towel into her pocket, tied her hair in a ponytail, and enjoyed her breakfast. The Dropas serenaded her as she ate.

Although happy to be free from Arton's evil grasp, Lindor couldn't stop thinking about returning to the fortress. She assured herself that he was no longer there and that Bandor had simply guided her that way because it was, indeed, the easiest way to meet the GGB officers.

After breakfast, Lindor laced up her boots, ready for the journey that would reunite her with Bandor. "Come on, my little friends."

The Dropas did away with the instruments and the rug before comfortably positioning themselves on her shoulders for the long hike. They giggled in excitement, ecstatic about returning home.

Lindor surveyed the grounds, making sure they had everything. "Let us be on our way."

The hot sun beat down on Lindor's dark hair. She lifted her ponytail off her nape and tied it in a bun. Some Dropas promptly relaxed on the crown of her head. Sensing Lindor's warmth, Silver painted a small fan and aimed it at the base of her neck. The thoughtful Dropa reclined against her shirt collar, enjoying the artificial breeze as well.

"Thank you, Silver. That is refreshing."

Lindor entertained the Dropas with Dropian songs while hiking along the riverbank. It was late morning when she noticed the faster moving current and the sound of rushing water in the distance.

"We must be getting close to the waterfall."

The Dropas gibbered to Clearcoat, although not loud enough for Lindor to understand. Clearcoat imparted the Dropas' desire to take a break at the cascade.

"That sounds delightful." Lindor wiped the sweat off her forehead.

The Dropas cheered and Lindor speculated about what new game they had in mind. Listening to the roar of the rushing water, Lindor maintained her course along the embankment until the waterfall came into view. The water tumbled and spewed over the jutting rock formations and down into the river below, cooling the air as it did. The one recollection she had of her horrifying encounter with those same protrusions was from what Clearcoat had described.

Turning away from the river, Lindor spotted a desirable shaded area. "That will make a fine picnic spot."

The Dropas darted to the location, created a soft ground cloth, and painted themselves metallic surfboards for the benefit of Lindor's viewing pleasure.

"Here are your suits." Lindor redistributed the waterproof protection.

In no time at all, the Dropas, Clearcoat included, slipped on their garments and ascended the near side of the waterfall with boards in hand. Lindor pulled off her boots and spread out her food for lunch. Before she bit into her apple, the Dropas had already reached the top of the fall where they initiated the surfing activity. They caromed off the divergent water streams as they flowed over the ledge, becoming extremely efficient at choosing their course, like a surfer methodically selecting the perfect wave. Lindor zeroed in on the shimmering boards to view the Dropas' initial descent. From her vantage point, they surfed in an arc-like direction from midway down the fall and out beyond the main turbulence at the bottom. Each Dropa followed the same path. Lindor had difficulty understanding how they changed directions mid-course, descending vertically before unexpectedly traveling mostly horizontal.

Lindor investigated the peculiar trajectory from the riverbank. Only then did she discover the new game. The sunshine beating down on the water created a rainbow extending from the middle of the cascade out past the turbulence. Her seated position had obscured her view of the adept rainbow surfers.

Oh, to be a Dropa and have that much fun. Lindor enjoyed another bite of her apple as she watched them glide down the colorful arc before splashing into the water. They paddled to shore and scampered to the top of the fall. Not all the Dropas surfed down the same rainbow. Others had formed and Lindor edged up the river until she saw the additional spectral arches from the new position. Smiling at her little friends, she returned to the clearing to finish her lunch, covetous of the things they could do.

Aware they needed to leave soon, Lindor desired a bit more rest. She had grown tired from the morning hike, still lacking full strength from her pocket being sealed. The hypnotic sound of the waterfall faded as she drifted off to sleep, lulled by its harmless spell.

...butterflies flitted in the air above the greenery. Lindor visited Butterfly Meadow every chance she could to observe the winged creatures' courtship—a magnificent sight, especially during a sunny day. Individually, the crystal butterflies exuded radiance in their own way, but they all shared a common trait. An onlooker could peer through the transparent bodies to view the distorted blue sky or green grass. Their singular beauty was magnified when they united to produce their offspring. As the two butterflies attached

themselves to one another, they emitted a multitude of spectrums that glittered
in the daylight. Each spectrum lasted for a brief moment, but the impression
was unforgettable.

After witnessing the wonderful exhibition, Lindor normally located a clearing
amidst the tall blades, lay on her back, and hoped a crystal butterfly landed on
her face. She had performed this ritual often with no success, but this time
yielded a different outcome. A female fluttered in the wind, landed on a nearby
flower, and drew some sweet nectar before leaving its perch. Lindor waited
patiently and quietly. She closed her eyes, thinking that maybe her open eyes
might have deterred them from landing. Feeling a tickle on her nose, she tried
not to twitch, but the sensation overcame her. Surprisingly, the butterfly
lingered, slowly flapping its crystal wings to balance itself in the wind. Desiring
to view the beautiful creature at close range, Lindor slowly opened her eyes...

A startled Lindor shrieked. Indigo, perched on Lindor's nose watching her nap,
somersaulted backward into her open mouth. She gagged briefly before coughing
the unsuspecting Dropa into the air. The Dropas had returned from surfing and
waited for her to awaken.

"You scared me, Indigo," Lindor laughed.

The Dropa giggled, proud of the accomplishment.

"I was dreaming about the crystal butterflies back home and one had landed on
my nose. When I opened my eyes, I expected a butterfly, not you, Indigo."

The Dropas displayed a great deal of pleasure hearing the details of Lindor's
dream. They, too, enjoyed the crystal butterflies, but for a different reason. The
Dropas liked riding the butterflies and the winged insects relished the passengers.

Lindor offered her hand. "If you will return your suits, we can be on our way."
Lindor inserted them in her pocket.

The Dropas disposed of the ground cloth and dashed up to her shoulders. She
furled her sleeves and pant legs to help stay cool. Silver already had the fan
blowing and some Dropas lounged alongside Lindor's neck.

"All aboard."

Lindor climbed the rocks that bordered the waterfall. The cool mist kept her
comfortable until she reached the top. Given her weakened condition, the rocky
terrain, and that they were still a fair distance from the fortress, it would require

most of the afternoon to reach the desired destination. She let the river guide her rather than risk getting lost in the dense forest. Although cooler among the trees, following the waterway was her safest path.

Mason and Bandor unloaded the last piece of equipment for the next mural, a painting for a company that manufactured X-ray tubes. They had completed touching up Robohawk the preceding day. Painting a mural in its entirety—the first one since returning from the fortress—was a refreshing energy boost.

This artwork differed slightly from school murals. Although it incorporated his usual trademarks, the design paid tribute to the discoverer of the X-ray, Wilhelm Roentgen, the company co-founders, and the engineered products.

Their enthusiasm to paint a full mural was apparent as they drew the outline and taped it off before lunchtime. Bandor loaded the spray gun canisters with various shades of blue for the sky background. He experienced an emotional roller coaster, awaiting the return of Lindor and the Dropas while battling the anxiety of saving Dropa from Arton.

"Hey, guys," a soft voice came from behind Bandor.

"Goodness!" Bandor's hand twitched, spilling a third of the contents before he set the canister on the box.

The blue paint splattered across the floor. Bandor whirled around to identify the culprit. Mason, who had been silently watching the perpetrator from the lift, chuckled at Bandor's mishap.

"Sorry, Pockets," Lauren apologized, "let me help wipe it up."

"No need." Bandor grabbed some clean rags. "How are you?"

"Fantastic."

Mason lowered the lift and swung off the platform. "It's been a couple months since we last saw each other."

"I've been away at college, but I'm on break this week. I saw your van here this morning while out with my mom." Lauren presented a brown paper bag to Mason. "I brought you and Pockets some lunch."

"That was thoughtful," Bandor said.

"Thanks," Mason replied. "By the way, Pockets' real name is Bandor."

"What?" Lauren responded, bemused.

"Pockets' real name is Bandor. I'll explain it outside. Bandor, you coming?"

Bandor glanced up at Mason. "Right after I finish addressing this mishap."

"We'll be out front at one of the picnic tables."

"Be there in a minute."

Sitting across from Mason, Lauren listened intently as he shared a portion of Bandor's story.

"It may take a little time getting used to calling him by another name, especially since Pockets suits him," Lauren admitted.

"Yes, it does." Mason emptied out the lunch bag and arranged the contents on the table. "I catch myself sometimes too."

"Catch yourself doing what?" Bandor sat next to Mason.

"Calling you Pockets." Mason slid Bandor's food and drink to him. "Lauren and I were discussing the adjustment to calling you by your real name."

"I understand. I went through the same thing when I first arrived here and was given that nickname. Oftentimes, I unintentionally ignored people who called me Pockets." Bandor unwrapped his sandwich and opened his juice container. "Until I grew accustomed to the name, I told people I had a hearing deficiency. I will answer if you call me Pockets, but I prefer my chosen name."

"Fair enough. I will spread the word."

"Thank you, Lauren. I appreciate that."

"Great." Lauren arose from her seat. "I hate to deliver and run but I must finish my errands."

"Thanks again for lunch," Mason said with a mouthful of sandwich.

"Yes, thank you, Lauren," Bandor added.

"My pleasure." Lauren waved to them. "I'll catch you guys later."

"Oh, before you go, I almost forgot to tell you." Mason swallowed one more time. "We're having a welcome home party at Liam's place tomorrow night. You're invited. And tell Brian, Cooper, and Ti."

"A party? For whom?"

"Holy cow. I can't believe I left out that part. The Dropas are coming home."

"That's not funny, Mason. The Dropas didn't escape from Ozone's fortress."

"He is serious, Lauren," Bandor confirmed casually. "The Dropas survived."

"Honestly?" Elated at the news, Lauren rushed back with a grin. "How could you forget to tell me?"

"Sorry, Lauren," Mason chuckled.

"How are they getting here?"

"A very dear friend of mine is escorting them as we speak," Bandor replied. "They should be here sometime tomorrow evening."

"Omigosh, I love those little guys." Lauren hugged Mason, followed by one for Bandor, smashing part of his sandwich into his cheek.

"Easy, girl." Bandor wiped the peanut butter and jelly from his face.

"What a wonderful day. You bet I'll be there. I can't wait to tell the others."

"I'm texting you Liam's address," Mason said.

"Great." Lauren danced away from the table. "The Dropas are alive!"

Mason and Bandor laughed at her effervescence as she rode off on her bike.

"She is an excitable one," Bandor commented.

"Yes, she is. It's refreshing to observe that kind of enthusiasm and happiness in people again, although she has always had that for as long as I've known her."

"On another note, the cans are ready for you to paint the blue sky. After lunch, we should be able to complete the background and Wilhelm Roentgen's portrait before the end of the day."

"That's doable."

Lindor had hiked ten miles beyond the waterfall. Sweat rolled off her arms, dripped down her face, and dampened her clothes. Even the coolness from the water could not offset the heat from the sweltering sun, but she wasn't far from the fortress, or rather, from where it once existed. Also feeling the warmth and receiving no relief from the fan, the Dropas sought shelter under Lindor's shirt.

She leaned against a large pine tree to have a drink and cool down a bit before the final leg. Kept cold inside her pocket, the bottled water was a welcome refreshment. The Dropas revealed themselves a few seconds later. The shade furnished relief, but they understood it was temporary.

With the remains of Arton's fortress less than a mile away, an eerie feeling overcame her. She pushed aside the horrible memories of her experience with Arton, sealed her water bottle, and inserted it into her pocket. She wanted to get to, and away from, the scene of her extended stay as quickly as possible.

Lindor resumed her hike and the Dropas returned to their shaded positions. Further up the river, she detected two charred Hornets' nests, intact nonetheless. Around the nests were scorched pines, purportedly lifeless, with needles burned off and bark blackened from the intense flames of the fortress fire. The barren trees became more abundant as she struggled to make her way up the river to the once evil palace. She could no longer block out her wicked flashback…

* * * * *

"Shar, I have been a lonely man since my accident. No one will cast their eyes on my hideous face."

"I am sorry that you have been lonely." Shar's muscles tightened and she intentionally avoided making eye contact with Ozone, fearing he may recognize her and from where she originated.

Ozone reached out to Shar. Her entire body cringed as she cautiously inched away from him. It wasn't at all due to his hideous appearance, but because of what he had done to the people on Earth. Shar's tremendous disdain for the man prevented her from clearly formulating an escape plan that wouldn't blow her cover. Her stomach knotted as Ozone carried out his evil desires.

"It doesn't have to be that way." Ozone grabbed her shoulders.

Utterly repulsed by Ozone's intentions, Shar attempted to free herself. Ozone's fingers snagged her ruffled collar. A faint light emanated from underneath the material.

"Well, well, well. What do we have here?" Ozone asked in a stern voice.

"What do we have where?" Shar replied innocently with her eyes closed. She winced in pain after the back of Ozone's hand struck her cheek.

"Don't play coy with me. There's only one place where this is possible. Who are you, and who sent you here?" He definitively realized the answer. "Of course! Athena!" Ozone clutched Shar's nape and yanked her face close to his. "Why did she send you?"

Shar refused to reveal the information.

"All right! If you won't tell me, you will pay for your deception!" Ozone tightened his grip. "Let's go!"

Shar struggled to break free, to no avail. The more she resisted, the harder Ozone squeezed. She had no idea what Ozone had in mind for her, but she anticipated an unpleasant and severe punishment. Arriving at his studio, he kicked open the door and hauled her inside to a table where he strapped her down—first her arms, next her legs, and lastly her chest.

Ozone plugged in a soldering gun he had used many times on steel sculptures. In desperation, she transmitted a cry for help to Bandor. Shar couldn't understand why he didn't respond. Athena assured them their ability to communicate with each other would never be hindered.

"It is time to seal you up for good, my little Dropian spy, but first I will give you one more chance to explain why you are here."

Shar broke out of her trance. "I would rather die before I tell you anything."

"So be it, but I hope your reason is worth your life."

"What are you waiting for, you sadistic maniac?"

Ozone positioned the soldering gun above Shar's chest. She already felt the intense heat and braced herself for the ensuing pain. Using the forefinger and thumb of his left hand, Ozone pinched the two sides of the opening and cauterized the first inch together. Shar's deafening screams resonated throughout the studio as she briefly endured the agony of her sealing pocket. Tears flowed from her eyes until she went into shock from the unbearable trauma. Ozone persisted, fusing the pocket shut until the last stream of dim light vanished from her chest.

* * * * *

Lindor spotted the remains of the fortress. One partially-standing wall was visible. The others had collapsed, either from the charging creatures or from the massive explosions. The southern forest was sparser near the perimeter. She observed additional vacated Hornets' nests among the barren trees. The dreary sight brought a smile to her face. The fortress had been demolished and the air and water had been rid of Arton's destructive chemicals. Her smile vanished at the notion of Bandor's unsettling feeling during their last communication.

Lindor followed the river to where the forest ended. At what was once the main gate, she carefully negotiated the rubble, unsure of what she was searching for or why she was doing it.

Lindor navigated through the debris to where Arton's courtyard once flourished. Several statues surprisingly persevered, although heavily marred and blackened from soot and smoke. She passed by each figure before stopping in front of the sculpture of Arton. This is where she realized why she had forced herself to walk through the fortress ruins.

"Clearcoat, I need a sledgehammer!"

Before Clearcoat gibbered the full request, the other Dropas scurried to the ground. Seconds later, Lindor accepted the three-foot sledgehammer as if it had no weight. The sudden release of rage she had harbored from being in Arton's clutches more than compensated for the lack of strength within her slender arms.

"Your evil destruction of civilization has ended, Arton!" Lindor hoisted the hammer and struck the left leg, breaking it off at the knee and causing the statue to lean precipitously. She watched the marble replica slowly fall to the ground and shatter into a thousand pieces. "Good riddance, Arton!"

Lindor had never exhibited uncontrollable rage in Dropa. Athena had apprised her and Bandor that during their lengthy stay on Earth, they would transmute and acquire many mortal characteristics—including negative emotions and physical sensations not present in Dropa.

Lindor dropped the hammer by her feet and fell to her knees, her eyes welling with tears as the Dropas hid themselves in her clothing. Although she wished it had been Arton himself, striking down the statue brought some respite. A sobbing Lindor buried her face in her hands, yearning to reunite with Bandor.

Lindor felt a hand on her shoulder, scaring her. Squinting toward the sunlight, she saw a silhouetted, uniformed man. A tremendous chill rushed down her spine.

"Are you Lindor?" the man asked.

Lindor backed away and scrambled to pick herself up and run.

"I'm sorry. I didn't mean to frighten you," the man said calmly to allay her fear. "I'm Officer McCleary with the GGB..."

"Impressions?" Mason stepped away from the portrait of Wilhelm Roentgen.

"Incredible," Bandor replied. "Your art would be most appreciated in Dropa."

"That would be awesome to paint there one day. Can you arrange it?"

"Perhaps, but contain your excitement. We must deal with Arton before you do any painting in my world."

"Did you have to mention him?" Mason selected another airbrush and made a small addition to the portrait.

"Sorry, but until we dispose of him for good, he poses a great threat to us all," Bandor advised.

Mason checked his phone. "I can't believe how late it is. We accomplished a lot today."

"Agreed."

Mason cleaned out his airbrush with water. "It feels good working on a full mural rather than doing touch-ups."

"It does, but you cannot discount the gratification felt from restoring the mascots to their original states."

"Without their help, we wouldn't have leveled Arton's fortress."

"Not in your wildest dreams." Bandor gathered the supplies. "And we will likely need their help on this mission as well."

"What do you say we call it a day?"

"That works for me. I will finish packing up the box."

Mason lowered the lift platform to the ground, allowing Bandor to jump off it. Mason returned to where he had been painting and admired his work. The image faded ever so slightly. He rubbed his eyes and examined it.

It's a good thing I'm finished with you, I'm starting to get blurry-eyed. He peeled away the excess contact paper from the wall, crumpled it into a ball, and cast it down to the floor. "Until tomorrow, Wilhelm." Mason lowered the lift, tossed the key from the controller to Bandor, and stepped off the platform.

Bandor latched the last lock on the supply box. "Lead the way."

The following afternoon, Willie and May volunteered to help Liam prepare for the Dropas' homecoming. May made a cake and a Jell-O mold and Willie helped Liam decorate the apartment with streamers and balloons. Liam had fastened the last one when his phone rang, displaying Mason's caller ID.

"What's up?" Liam answered.

"Are you busy?"

"Willie, May, and I are decorating for the party."

"Can you break away for a bit and check out this mural?"

"You guys done already?" Liam joked.

"Funny," Mason laughed. "No, something weird is happening."

"The last time weird things happened, we ended up battling ForLords."

"History may be repeating itself," Mason remarked.

"I'll be there in fifteen minutes." Liam ended the call. "That was Mason." He attempted to touch the Jell-O mold but May lightly smacked his hand. "Something strange is occurring."

"Now what?" Willie asked.

"I'm not sure, but Mason wants me to check out his latest mural and you should come with me."

"Any problem with that, dear?" Willie asked May.

"No. Having you guys gone," she teased, "I'll be able to finish the food preparation without you two sampling it."

"Great." Willie kissed her on the cheek. "You're a sweetheart."

"We won't be long," Liam said.

"Bye, guys."

Bandor greeted Liam and Willie at the main entrance of the mural site.

"What's the latest?" Liam asked, hoping for some positive news.

"I am afraid it is not good," Bandor replied, troubled. "It is imperative we enter the murals shortly after the Dropas return. Arton is progressing much faster than I anticipated."

"What evidence do you have?"

"Let me show you."

Liam and Willie followed Bandor into the building and wound their way through the hallways. Mason was on the lift staring at the faded portrait.

"Mason!" Bandor shouted. "Liam and Willie are here!"

"Hey, Liam." Mason lowered the lift, allowing them all to climb aboard. "How are you doing, Willie?"

"Fine until you called us over here," Willie admitted.

"Tell me about it." Mason raised the lift to a position in front of the portrait. "What do you make of this?"

A faint outline of Arton's hideous face had replaced the portrait.

"Did you paint that ugly thing, Mason?" Willie asked semi-jokingly.

"Yeah, right, Willie."

"I'd like you to meet Arton," Liam quipped.

"That's what the man looks like." Willie scrunched his face. "Lord have mercy."

"What's the implication of this, Bandor?" Liam asked.

"First, I believe Arton has taken on the identity of Wilhelm Roentgen. How much? I am unsure."

"What do you mean by that?"

"Most definitely, he has the man's appearance." Bandor rubbed his chin. "He might have also attained some of Roentgen's other qualities, like his intelligence, not that Arton needs anymore."

"From a painting?" Willie questioned.

"Yes, from a painting," Bandor confirmed emphatically. "This could be good and bad. At first, I presumed Arton was in a single mural. It is evident the murals are interconnected and he is able to go wherever he wants."

"Then we could feasibly enter a different mural other than the Robohawk mural or this one," Liam hypothesized.

"And head him off," Willie added.

"Exactly," Bandor concurred.

"Which mural should we enter?" Liam inquired.

"I have not determined that yet." Bandor lowered the platform. "It will not be long before he discovers the portal to Dropa."

"When do you suggest we enter the murals?" Liam asked.

"Around daybreak." Bandor jumped off the lift, followed by the others. "Lindor may have additional information for us, but we need a plan before her arrival. And perhaps extra help."

"Lauren's bringing Brian, Cooper, and Ti to the party tonight," Mason reminded Bandor. "I bet they would be more than willing to help us on another mission."

"I hate endangering the kids' lives a second time, but we may have no choice," Bandor advised. "On the upside, we will just need a few this time."

"I'm all for those four accompanying us," Liam declared. "They did a great job the last time we asked for their assistance."

"I cannot argue with you," Bandor said.

"Why don't you pack up and come to my place? We can discuss this further before the Dropas and Lindor arrive."

It was almost eight o'clock when Lindor was dropped off at Liam's apartment entrance and less exhausted than anticipated. Napping on the maglev train and the excitement of reuniting with her friend, Bandor, invigorated her. Following his instructions, she climbed the stairs, entered the vestibule, and paged through the electronic directory.

"Here it is." She punched in the numeric sequence.

"Hello," Bandor answered Liam's phone.

"Bandor?" Lindor asked happily. "I am here."

"Lindor! You made it!" Bandor gave her directions to Liam's apartment before keying in the access code.

She and the Dropas were moments away from seeing their friends. The Dropas couldn't contain their elation.

"Quick! Turn off the lights and everyone take your positions," Bandor instructed after making some final preparations in the kitchen. "Lindor is coming down the hall."

Bumping into one another, everyone hastily scampered to get out of sight as Liam switched off the lights except for the one in the entryway. There he waited for Lindor and the Dropas to arrive.

Liam barely heard the quiet knock. Adrenaline exploded through his body in anticipation of seeing the Dropas. Liam slowly opened the door. A long-forgotten emotion replaced his exhilaration. Captivated by the aura of the petite woman standing in the doorway, Liam didn't hear the animated Dropas' gibbering on his shoulders. He simply gazed into Lindor's green eyes as she stared into his.

"Why isn't he letting her in?" Willie whispered.

"I don't recall ever seeing him like that," Mason replied.

"I hope he does something fast," Ti said softly. "My legs are cramping."

"Shh," Bandor peeked over the dining table.

The captivating guest broke the silence. "Hello, my name is Lindor." She offered her hand as Liam snapped out of his hypnotic state.

"Hi, I-I-I'm Liam." Liam gently shook her hand, almost forgetting to release it. "Please, come in."

"Thank you."

"Oh, man! You guys scared the heck out of me."

Liam finally acknowledged the Dropas' presence. They were jumping up and down, pulling on his earlobes, and creating a stir at his expense. Liam raised his left hand. Violet dashed down his arm and perched itself on his palm. Liam withdrew a party blower from his shirt pocket and blew in Violet's direction, startling both the Dropas and Lindor. The unfurling end smacked Violet and spattered the Dropa into the coat closet door. The other Dropas tried to keep themselves from falling off Liam's shoulders, laughing their little heads off as Violet dripped to the floor. Liam flipped on the lights.

"Surprise!" Everyone sprang from their hiding spots.

No one had never seen the Dropas startled before, but witnessing it firsthand was priceless. The only obstructions preventing each and every Dropa from launching themselves into space were the walls and ceiling that abruptly halted their flight paths. They splattered everywhere. Violet giggled at its companions after returning to its original form. The elated welcome committee roared with laughter and waited for their miniature friends to gather themselves. When they did, they all scampered to Mason whose face lit up as bright as a shooting star. The Dropas had returned.

Heart Over Matter

As the Dropas celebrated with the others, Bandor and Lindor reunited with hugs in the living room. Liam respected their desire to spend some private time together after a lengthy separation. The others stayed in the dining area and introduced the Dropas to games Liam created specifically for them.

"Line up in a straight line," Liam instructed the Dropas. "We want to greet you in a language similar to yours."

Emulating human behavior, the bewildered Dropas scratched their heads and rubbed their undefined chins. The reception committee twisted their bodies away from the Dropas and filled their lungs with harmless gas from helium-inflated balloons. They presented the guests of honor with a munchkin-tainted salutation for all to remember.

"Welcome home! We missed you guys!"

The Dropas pondered the peculiar greeting and then burst into knee-slapping mirth. They rolled around in laughter on the dining table in familiar fashion. Silver and Gold gathered themselves long enough to gesture for an encore.

The Dropas giggled uncontrollably each time they heard the altered voices and only calmed down after the helium was depleted. Had the entire tank been brought home, they would've wanted the unique conversation to last all night. Another reminder that joy is abundant and often exists in the simplest form.

Lindor and Bandor sat on the couch facing each other, paying little attention to the party games.

"It has been such a long time." Bandor held Lindor's hands in his.

Lindor squeezed them. "Much too long."

"How is your wound healing?"

"It is doing fine," Lindor replied modestly. "The Dropas did a wonderful job re-opening my pocket. I dearly missed them."

Bandor glanced at the Dropas. "It is amazing the effect they have on everyone who comes in contact with them."

"With one exception."

"Speaking of him—"

"Oh, Bandor, you do not realize what a horrible experience I went through with that nefarious man." Emotionally scarred from serving as Arton's personal assistant, Lindor nestled against Bandor's chest.

"I am so sorry you had to suffer through that." Bandor tried to comfort her. "Had you not the courage and strength to sustain that facade, we would have never been successful at ridding Earth of his evil ways."

"I do not regret my mission, but it was a tremendous ordeal."

"Remember, Lindor, the pain will disappear once we return to Dropa."

"Being partially human for that long, I almost forgot my heart and soul will no longer conflict with my mind." Lindor sat up and composed herself. "That has been the hardest thing to endure since I arrived."

"For me as well."

"Thank you, Bandor."

"For what?" he asked with a quizzical expression.

"For being such a good friend and being here when I returned."

"I will always be your friend."

"Enough of this mushy stuff." Lindor wiped the lingering tears from her cheeks. "You interrupted our vacation for a reason. What have you discovered?"

"Unfortunately, there is no way to sugarcoat this. Arton circumvented the explosions. He is returning to Dropa to terminate our existence."

"How is that possible?" Lindor whispered. The same sick feeling she experienced at the fortress overcame her at the revelation of Arton eluding death.

"He has made his way into Mason's murals."

"How did he escape...and get into the artwork?"

"When a mural creature enters this world, it must periodically re-energize because of the effort expended to exist here. Its body becomes penetrable in that state. Arton inadvertently discovered this vulnerability and hid inside one of the birds. His innate powers allowed him to survive. He escaped into the mural after we returned the mascot to the wall."

Lindor grew more concerned. "How do we stop him?"

"We are entering the murals tomorrow morning." Bandor glanced at Liam and Mason. "We must find him before he locates the portal to Dropa."

"Have you warned Athena?"

"I have attempted to contact her since I learned of Arton's intentions, but my telepathy is unable to reach Dropa." Bandor furrowed his brow. "It confuses me. I was able to communicate with her up until...a few months ago. Maybe Arton is interfering with the transmission."

"Possibly." Lindor changed subjects. "How do you intend to find the portal?"

"I hope the mural mascots can guide us to it, unless you have a better idea."

"I do not. Ever since Arton closed my pocket, it has been difficult to concentrate. I have been doing everything in my power to heal myself in hope of making a full recovery. I am sorry, Bandor." Lindor clutched his hands. "We must find another way to warn Athena and the Dropians."

"Once inside the murals, we may have to use my pocket for transportation."

Lindor yanked away her hands, shaking her head emphatically. "That is out of the question, Bandor. You are well aware of the danger."

"I am."

"Promise me we will do it only if we exhaust all other options."

"You have my word. We will let the success of conventional means dictate the need."

Peering out the window, Lindor contemplated Bandor's suggestion. They both understood that allowing a non-Dropian to travel through his pocket could kill him. If Bandor died during the transport, whatever was inside would perish along with him. Without either person, saving Dropa would be impossible.

"It's time for the flying Dropa contest!" Liam knew he had the Dropas' attention when they heard their name and "flying" in the same sentence. "Willie and May, you both stand by the dining table. You are the catchers." Liam stood a few feet from Lindor and Bandor, disregarding their conversation. "The rest of us are the launchers, and we'll stand at this end of the living room."

Liam resided in a standard apartment where the dining area transitioned into the living room. He, Mason, and the four teens positioned themselves by the window and readied their party blowers. Liam summoned the Dropas to choose a launcher—two Dropas per person. They obliged, eager to take flight.

The launchers exhaled to fully extend the party blowers, and each Dropa lay sideways near the tip. Relaxing the blowers rolled the Dropa "bullets" into place. After firing the first six, the launchers would load the others.

"Only two at a time," Liam called out the final directions. "Willie and May are limited to how many they can catch. Mason and I will go first when Willie gives the signal. Ready when you are, Willie."

The others missed the last set of instructions and readied for launch.

"Blast off!" Willie yelled.

In unison, a half dozen Dropas propelled through the air. Willie and May scrambled to catch all six projectiles.

May caught Silver and Violet landed softly in her thick hair. Willie snared Green, but Yellow smacked him square in the nose, splattering on his face. Red and Orange landed in the Jell-O and chocolate cake, respectively.

Liam and Mason hurried to rescue the two food additives. Mason dug out the squirming Red with minimal disfigurement to the mold. Retrieving Orange from the chocolate cake was less tedious because the dense chocolate frosting prevented the Dropa from penetrating any further.

"Mason, watch this." Liam lowered Orange head first into his mouth, gently wrapping his lips around its body. He lifted it out, having removed the majority of frosting from its tiny frame. "One more time ought to do it."

"Quit eating the Dropas," Mason laughed at Liam's humorous cleansing.

Orange enjoyed the unusual bath, giggling as it neared Liam's mouth. Down it went and up it came, clean as a whistle. Liam was fortunate enough to sample the frosting at the same time. He set Orange on the table with its companions.

"I hate being the party pooper, but it is time we talk," Bandor interjected.

"Already?" Ti asked disappointedly.

"You will understand why very soon," Bandor replied in a serious tone.

Reluctantly, the teens pulled up chairs around the table. The older adults spread amongst them. Bandor's concerned expression said it all. He worried about the fate of his world, much the same as the others had about theirs. Presently, the opportunity arose to repay Bandor and Lindor for helping save humanity. Liam was confident that everyone would take part.

Liam's eyes were drawn to Lindor, as they had been many times when she sat beside Bandor on the couch. This time, however, their eyes met. They were both unaware Mason was watching the exchange of glances. Bandor detailed the situation to the kids who were, up to that point, oblivious to what had transpired. They could barely fathom what Bandor had told them.

"…and we welcome your help, if you are willing." Bandor clasped his hands on the table.

"Willing? Are you kidding?" Lauren replied. "After all the help you gave us, darn right we're willing. Aren't we?"

"Yeah!" her friends replied.

"Does this mean we get to go inside Mason's murals?" Brian asked, beaming.

"That is exactly what it means," Bandor replied.

"Awesome!" Brian high-fived Cooper.

"This will be more exciting than our first adventure," Ti added.

"I hate to squelch your enthusiasm, but it will be riskier than the first one," Bandor assured. "Arton is more formidable than he was in your world. And the closer he gets to Dropa, the more powerful he becomes."

"How much more?" Cooper inquired.

"Perhaps stronger than Athena." Bandor sighed. "If he catches Athena by surprise, it will be the end of her."

"Isn't Athena a goddess?" Cooper questioned.

"She is, but in Dropa, Arton is a demigod."

"I don't understand, Bandor," Ti remarked.

"Arton was a student of Proteus, a shape-shifting god."

"He may have been Proteus' finest student," Lindor offered.

"It was rare for a god to mentor a partial mortal, but Proteus treated Arton like the son he never had." Bandor snapped his fingers. "Of course, Atlantis is where Arton completed most of his training. I believe that is the reason for his outrage when Athena received the continent from Zeus."

"That's plausible," Lindor surmised.

"We have already seen that he has regained some of his shape-shifting ability by assuming the body and image of Wilhelm Roentgen. Imagine what surprises we will encounter once inside the murals. Undeniably, this will be more dangerous than the first mission, and you have the same freedom of choice."

"I'm in," Lauren confirmed without hesitation.

"Me too," Brian added.

Ti and Cooper grasped each other's hand. "Count us in," they chimed.

"You guys know the drill with your parents," Liam reminded them.

Brian sighed deeply and rolled his eyes. "Yeah, all too well."

"Can we call them from here, Liam?" Cooper asked cowardly.

"You could, Cooper, but they will want to spend what little time there is with you before you leave. Willie!"

"Huh?" Willie grunted after having stuffed a piece of cake in his mouth.

Liam handed Willie a napkin. "If you can stop eating for a minute, I need you to contact the GGB to supply us with rations for our journey."

"No problem." Cake crumbs fell from Willie's lips.

"You will not require food or water," Bandor advised. "Only two things are required when we arrive in the murals: your heart and a positive state of mind. Once inside, you eventually become one with the art."

"Those two reasons are why we want you on this mission," Liam said to the teens. "We're confident you can maintain that state better than anyone else and you each have a good heart."

The four best friends eyed one another and nodded at Liam.

"It sounds easy, but your attitudes will be challenged greatly by Arton. He grows stronger the deeper he penetrates and you will face many more temptations than you presently encounter." Bandor held out his hands, palms an inch apart from each other. "And there may be a time when you come face to face with him and no one else is around to help guide you." Bandor definitely had a captive audience. "Your mind will become confused." Bandor touched his index finger to his temple and made a fist over his chest. "And that is when you must rely on your heart to guide you."

From the kids' expressions, Liam perceived slightly more trepidation than when Bandor initially invited them to join the adventure. Liam especially sensed it from Cooper, but they responded as expected.

"Yeah, we can do it," Lauren spoke first.

"Absolutely," Ti added.

Cooper and Brian fist bumped. "We're in."

"Excellent," Bandor responded. "Go home to your families, rest up, and meet us at Lauren's former elementary school. Tomorrow morning at seven sharp."

"Do *not* be late, or you will be left behind," Liam warned.

"Nine o'clock, no problem," Cooper changed his jocular demeanor after detecting seriousness among the others. "I'm kidding. Don't worry, I'll be there."

Bandor's true leadership abilities impressed Liam, but not as much as his acting skills, having convinced countless people, including Liam and Mason, that he was a mild-mannered, risk-averse person. Regardless, this was Bandor's mission and Liam had no problem deferring to his guidance. After all, he knew Arton better than anyone. Liam hoped that assisting him would result in the same success they achieved at Barrow's Ridge.

The door closed behind Cooper. Liam, Bandor, and Mason expressed a shared feeling of uneasiness.

"Cooper concerns me," Mason said, breaking the silence.

"You and me both," Liam replied.

"He will be all right, but we need to keep an eye on him, more than the others," Bandor advised.

"Agreed," Liam and Mason responded.

"Willie." Liam shook his head at his friend's eating exhibition. "Care to share your insights?"

Willie packed another piece of cake into his mouth. "Yeah, sure."

"How many have you eaten?" Mason inquired.

"It's good cake." Willie licked frosting off his fingers. "You should try some."

"Is there any left?" May laughed.

"Have you absorbed anything we've said tonight?" Liam asked.

"Everything." Willie smacked his lips. "Perhaps you have forgotten. I'm staying on this side of the murals."

"It doesn't mean you can't participate in the discussion," Liam reminded him.

Willie wiped his hands with a napkin. "You want my opinion?"

"Yes, if you can keep that cake out of your mouth long enough to tell us," Mason remarked.

Willie ignored Mason's ribbing and swallowed the last remnants before sharing his long-awaited opinion. "This is how I see it. After fighting alongside you guys as we ended Arton's reign of terror on Earth, demolished his fortress, and captured the ForLords, I have the utmost confidence in your abilities and determination, especially working together as a team. And no matter the conceived plan, you will execute it and ultimately rid all worlds, wherever they may be, of this Arton dude. Period. End of opinion. Now, if you'll excuse me, I'd like one last piece before driving my lovely wife home."

Laughter ensued as Indigo and Violet swept away the lingering crumbs from Willie's goatee with their paintbrushes.

Willie devoured the last mouthful. "Well, that's it. I'm done. What do you say we hit the road, my sweet young thing? It's my duty to wake up early and get these little scouts off to mural camp tomorrow."

"Ready when you are, my gluttonous husband," May responded playfully.

"I'll be there before seven. Do I need to bring anything?"

"Just yourself," Bandor replied.

"Try to eat before you get there." Liam elicited chuckles out of everyone. "Thanks for helping with the party."

"Goodnight, all," Willie and May said as they left the apartment.

"Goodnight," the others replied.

"Speaking of everyone, where's Lindor?" Liam asked.

"Asleep on the couch," Bandor replied. "She had an exhausting journey."

"You have a thing for her, don't you?" Mason teased.

"What makes you say that?" Liam responded defensively, aware that Mason was toying with him.

"You've been staring at her all night, beginning when you first opened the door." Mason winked at a grinning Bandor. "If you could have seen your face."

"Was it that obvious?"

Indigo and Violet poked Liam with their brushes. He light-heartedly flicked them with his first two fingers, somersaulting them backward until they collided with the cake pan. They both stared at each other until the dizziness subsided.

Bandor rose from his chair and stretched. Liam and Mason were preoccupied watching the other Dropas climb to the top of the ceiling fan light and slide down the crepe paper attached to the counter. Most landed on the countertop. Others were less fortunate, either veering off the paper or getting nudged off by a companion. When that happened, they splattered against the wall.

Liam decided to make the game more interesting. He peeled off a strip of crepe paper and untwisted it. Although simple, the Dropas would enjoy another welcome home gift.

"What are you doing?" Mason asked.

"Creating something that will keep the Dropas from splattering."

"What is it?"

"Watch."

"Excuse me, Liam, do you have a blanket?" Bandor inquired.

"Sure, it's in the linen closet on your way to my bedroom," Liam replied without lifting his head. "Are you done for the night too?"

"Not yet, but I want to make sure Lindor stays warm." Bandor patted Liam's back. "I would have asked you to cover her, but you seem a little preoccupied."

Mason and Bandor chuckled.

"Keep it up, you two, and I may stay home tomorrow." Liam knew it would be a long time before he lived down being attracted to Lindor.

She was wholesomely beautiful and her eyes and smile were an invitation to her soul. Liam imagined her heart being as true as Bandor's.

"Yeah, right! You wouldn't miss this opportunity for the world," Mason said.

"What?" Liam responded as he drifted back into reality.

Mason snapped his fingers. "Snap out of it, lover boy. I said you wouldn't miss this opportunity for the world."

Liam ignored Mason, staying focused on converting the crepe paper into a carnival ride. Piquing the Dropas' interest, they gathered along the edge of the countertop, waiting patiently for the enhanced entertainment.

"All right, one half twist and connect the ends."

"Will you please tell me what you're making?"

"Patience, I'm almost done." Liam secured the connected ends with tape and attached the loop to a streamer hanging from one of the ceiling fan blades. He offered his flattened palm to Yellow, the first Dropa in line.

"Oh, big deal, you made a loop."

"More specifically, it's a Möbius loop." Liam positioned Yellow.

"A Möbius loop?"

"Correct." Liam watched Yellow successfully circumnavigate the entire path.

"Wait a second." Mason was intrigued. "How did Yellow do that?"

Liam followed Yellow with his forefinger as it completed another lap. "By twisting an end one-half turn before connecting it to the other end, the Dropas can cover both sides of the loop, in this case, both sides of the crepe paper."

"What good is that?"

"In this instance, the Dropas have a connected trail that is a bit more challenging to stay on than a standard loop." Liam switched on the fan.

The Möbius loop followed the circular pattern of the blades.

"And now they can glide as they spin." Liam switched off the fan, attached two additional loops to dangling streamers, and assisted Red and Orange to the expanded ride.

"Do you stay up nights thinking of this stuff?"

"No, I stay up thinking of—" Liam was interrupted by a knock on the door.

Mason checked the stove clock. "It's almost eleven. Who's visiting at this time of night?"

"I have no—yes, I do."

"That's right," Mason laughed. "I forgot he relocated to this complex."

Liam opened the door. "Hello, Paul."

"Hey, Liam." Paul pushed his glasses up on his nose as he noticed the streamers. "Am I too late for the party?"

"Only three hours," Liam replied playfully.

Paul gently forced his way past Liam into the dining area. "Hey, Mason!" Paul rubbed Mason's head like a dog. "Long time, no see."

"Shh!" Mason pointed at Lindor lying on the couch.

"Sorry," Paul whispered. "Where are the Drips? I heard they were returning."

"They're Dropas, Paul," Mason corrected him, "and how did you learn of their return?"

"Yeah, right, Droopas." Paul didn't realize that Yellow, Red, and Orange were circling on Möbius loops in front of his face. "I overheard some kids talking about them in the hallway." Mesmerized, yet ignorant to the Dropas' presence, his eyes followed the circular path. "Liam, your apartment makes me woozy." Paul snapped out of his hypnotic trance. "Oh, there they are, and they're skiing on dubious loops. I remember those from grade school."

Liam rolled his eyes as Bandor chuckled from the couch.

"Paul, I have a favor to ask." Liam gently grabbed Paul by the elbow.

"Sure thing." Paul winked at Mason as if Liam considered Paul to be more important.

"Bye, Paul." Mason lowered his head onto the table to muffle his laughter. He knew Liam was getting rid of Paul for the night.

Liam escorted Paul to the door. "We're having a business meeting. Would you mind visiting another day?"

"No problem."

"Thanks for understanding," Liam said politely.

Paul strolled down the hallway as Liam ducked inside his apartment and locked the door.

The next morning, Liam and Mason waited for the kids on a bench near the front entrance of the school. They watched the gorgeous sunrise that morning, both wondering if they would return to view another. Vibrant oranges painted the eastern sky as the sunlight illuminated the large patch of clouds spanning the horizon. Bandor had taken Lindor inside to show her the mural.

Liam ate the last donut hole and checked the time. "They have fifteen minutes."

"You don't think they'll chicken out, do you?" Mason asked.

"It's not a matter of chickening out," Liam replied sternly, "rather a matter of punctuality."

"They'll show." Mason rose from the bench as Bandor burst out of the entrance. "Bandor, what's wrong?"

Bandor quickened his pace. "The situation has worsened." He checked the parking lot. "No kids yet?"

"No, but here comes Willie." Mason followed Bandor to the van.

"We're leaving once they arrive."

"Why?" Mason grasped Bandor's arm.

"It is completely colorless!" Lindor dashed out of the building with the Dropas clinging to whatever they could to keep from falling off her.

"Leave at once? Colorless? Bandor, please explain what is happening."

Bandor broke away from Mason's grip. "We cannot go through this mural!"

"Why?" Liam asked.

"Arton has already discolored it," Lindor interjected.

"Discolored it?" Liam inquired. "How?"

"It is comprised of gray tones," Lindor explained. "All color has been removed from it."

"What's wrong with it being colorless?"

"Lack of color means that the mural, or those that enter it, could possess the influences of Arton," Bandor answered. "If we enter into a tainted mural, we have essentially surrendered to him."

"Can the Dropas restore the color?" Mason suggested.

"I never considered that," Bandor responded. "How about you, Lindor?"

"It is worth a try."

"Come on." Bandor led everyone into the building.

"Hey!" Willie shouted as he stepped out of his car. "Wait for me!"

"Hurry up!" Liam directed.

The Dropas worked furiously on the bottom right corner of the mural, but as fast as they painted, the mural reverted to gray tones.

"Curse you, Arton!" Bandor raised his fist in the air. "I will not be defeated by you! Come on!"

"Now where?" Mason trailed Bandor down the hallway.

"We need to get to the closest school fast."

"I'm right behind you," Liam said. "What about the kids, Bandor?"

"If they are not in the parking lot when we get there, we are leaving without them."

They all darted past Willie and out the doors.

"Wait a second, where—"

"This way!" Liam yelled. "We don't have any time to waste."

"I wish you guys would make up your mind where you want me!" Willie hastily caught up with them.

They arrived at the vehicles as two cars parked next to Mason's van.

"Get in!" Bandor yelled.

"Love you, Mom." Lauren shut her mother's car door. "Where are we going?"

"To another mural," Mason replied.

"What's wrong with this one?" Ti asked.

"I will explain it on the way." Bandor hopped into the cargo bay.

Willie slid into Liam's truck. The others piled into Mason's van. Liam and Mason sped to the nearest school, hoping Arton hadn't de-colorized that mural. In transit, Bandor explained to the kids the chain of events that had transpired prior to their arrival. Liam and Mason steered into the drop-off lane. They all hurried out of the vehicles to the entrance.

"Keys?" Mason felt his pants pockets. "Where's my school key ring?"

"Oh, not again," Bandor moaned.

"I just had them." Mason rechecked his pockets.

"You might have had them." Liam jingled the keys. "I grabbed them off the bench where you set them." Liam tossed the keys to Mason.

"Wait a second, this school has a security system." He inserted the key into the lock. "When I open it, the alarm will trip."

"Forget the alarm," Bandor contended. "We will be in the murals and long gone before anyone arrives. Besides, Willie can explain what happened."

Willie shook his head. "Really? I can just picture it. Nothing to see here, officers, my friends simply disappeared inside a mural. They will haul me away if I tell the GGB officers that."

"It's a good thing you have trusted connections within the organization who might pardon you," Liam quipped.

"I'm not laughing, Liam. I'm not laughing one bit."

"Perhaps you would like to reconsider going with us."

"Nope, I'm good. I'll contrive something."

"I hate to break up this little conversation, but we need to get inside this building," Bandor instructed.

Mason turned the key, opened the door, and as expected, the alarm sounded. He led everyone to the mural located in the multipurpose room. Upon entering, the artwork was intact, unscathed by Arton's touch. The brilliant colors filled the room without any sign of lost coloration.

This mural differed from Mason's typical style. Instead of his usual broken wall effect, Mason had painted a vertical rip through it. In the background of the ripped section was a gradated blue sky filled with cumulonimbus clouds. Floating across the sky was a postcard image of a forest with trees and ferns lining a forked path. In the upper right-hand corner of the postcard, the corner was peeled downward, exposing a night sky with a shooting star—a peek at tomorrow, and a reminder to follow one's dreams. Located underneath the postcard image were individual windows depicting the four seasons. The same beautiful, yellow-orange sunset carried across each one. The spring window displayed a rainbow, a butterfly, and raindrops dispersed on the window ledge. The summer window highlighted a tall sunflower with bubbles floating in the air. The iridescent spheres drifted behind the painted wall and reappeared in the autumn window, which had colored leaves gliding into it and resting on its windowsill. Finally, a snowdrift blanketed the winter window ledge and icicles hung from the top of the frame.

Liam's anticipation heightened, as did everyone's. Reality set in as they would soon enter Mason's artwork.

"I need you all to line up by the windows, two each in front of spring, summer, and autumn," Bandor ordered. "You will enter the mural through your designated opening."

They clumsily formed a line like untrained soldiers on the first day of boot camp.

"Listen carefully, there is only enough time to explain this once. After the Dropas paint your entire bodies, you will feel a slight tickling sensation and possibly goose bumps. However, as they paint your head, you will temporarily lose all senses. In addition, breathing will be impossible. It is important that you inhale deeply before they cover your face or you will suffocate underneath the paint. Lindor and I will lead you into the windows before we enter the winter scene. Your brain will resist, informing your body that it is physically impossible to walk into the wall. Remember, you have limited amount of air. Relax and allow your heart to guide you into the murals." Bandor motioned for the Dropas to position themselves. "Three Dropas will follow you through your respective windows, and we will all meet behind the summer window. Cooper and Ti, you are already standing in front of that opening and merely have to wait for us. Once in the walls, your senses will be restored and you will breathe normally. However, you do not need air inside the murals. The sensation is present to help you relax once you go beyond these walls." Bandor allowed a few seconds for everyone to process the instructions. "Questions?"

"How long must we hold our breath?" Ti asked, concerned.

"Roughly forty-five seconds at most. Can you do that?"

"Yes," Ti replied confidently.

Bandor checked with the others. "Any more questions?"

They all exchanged glances and indicated their readiness to Bandor. As the Dropas painted, Willie left for his post to intercept the anticipated officers.

Liam and Mason were entering through the spring window. Liam let Mason go first since he was the artist. Mason inhaled one final breath as the Dropas coated his head. Lindor led him to the wall. His face pressed flush against the painted cinder blocks before reshaping. Mason's head penetrated the surface until it melded with the art. After the mural swallowed the rest of him, the Dropas followed Mason and removed the paint from his body. Liam was next.

Liam felt goosebumps on his scalp and inhaled one last time. Once the Dropas overlaid his head, the tickling feeling subsided and his senses disengaged, making him unaware of Lindor's presence as she escorted him to the spring window.

Fighting his heart and winning, Liam's mind prevented him from penetrating the artwork. Mason grabbed Liam's hand, but could not pull him through the wall. His lungs burning, Liam needed to get inside the mural to stave off impending suffocation.

"Liam," a soothing voice called to him telepathically. *"It is me, Lindor."*

"Lindor! I can't breathe!"

"You are all right. Listen to me. I will guide you through the wall."

"My mind won't let me pass."

"Liam, do not say another word. Clear those thoughts."

Ninety seconds elapsed. Yearning for oxygen, Liam's brain relinquished control of his body. All senses were lost, but not in the way Bandor explained it.

Lindor's voice faded, "Follow your heart..."

Liam collapsed in a heap outside the mural. Upon Lindor's command, the Dropas removed the overlay from Liam. He barely survived the incident. Clearcoat gibbered an alternate solution in Lindor's ear.

"That could work. Willie! We need your help!"

Willie hurried from his post at the front entrance. "What happened?"

"No time to explain, but we must get Liam to the Warrior school." Lindor examined the wall. Everyone else had safely arrived in the artwork.

Willie lifted Liam to his feet and threw him over his shoulder. "Let's get rolling before the officers arrive."

Willie, Lindor, and Liam's three designated Dropas hurried to Liam's truck. Lindor and the Dropas waited in the cab. Willie set Liam inside the bed and removed from his pocket the keys Liam had previously given him. He slid into the driver's seat, destined for the Warrior school.

"I hope Arton has not been there," Lindor said.

"You and me both." Willie exited the parking lot as two GGB vehicles entered. "Phew, that was close."

Parked next to the main entrance, they hurried out of the truck and Willie hefted Liam onto his shoulder. Using a key Silver created, Willie unlocked the door and led Lindor to the atrium. By the time they arrived, the Dropas had already painted a scaffold.

Clearcoat's idea involved transporting Liam to a mural where Mason had used Liam as a human model. The school was in close proximity to the one from where they came. The mural border consisted of a steelcrete (gradation of steel and concrete) entrance and an Enter button in the lower right-hand corner. Two large, steelcrete doors opened to a desert scene. Mason used Liam's likeness to depict a Warrior sitting cross-legged on the large doorway ledge. The Warrior faced a sunset that had a dream catcher opening into outer space at the top. In the sky, he had painted smaller doorways leading to alternate dimensions and following the vanishing point of the sunset. Silhouettes of fellow Warriors ambled across the desert sand in the direction of the doorways.

Willie carried Liam to the top level of the scaffold. Liam remained unconscious but breathed normally.

"This has to happen fast," Lindor instructed. "He cannot take a deep breath this time."

"Tell me what to do, Lindor."

"Hold him against his image in the mural."

Silver, Indigo, and Red painted Liam's body.

"Ready?" Lindor asked.

Willie and the Dropas nodded.

Lindor examined Liam's breathing pattern. "One-two-three-go!"

The Dropas covered Liam's head and Willie pressed him against the Warrior image. Nothing happened.

"Press Enter!" Willie shouted, desperate for a solution.

Lindor pushed the painted button. Again, nothing happened.

"Time is running out," Lindor reminded Willie and the Dropas.

"Someone is calling us." Willie attempted to locate the voice.

Directly across from them was another mural. A Warrior chief stood with outstretched arms, facing away from another sunset and praying to the sky. On his left arm was a shield, scarred from battle, with three feathers hanging from it. The Warrior clutched a hand-crafted tomahawk in its right hand. As it did when it left the mural to fight the ForLords, the Warrior came to life. It had no intention of leaving, but instead readied itself for something almost as spectacular—this time without a light show or an appearance by Athena.

"Arton!" Willie presumed the Warrior had succumbed to the demigod's power. "Get out of the way, Lindor!"

The Warrior repositioned its body and hurled the tomahawk. Lindor ducked before the deadly weapon hit the target, sticking in the middle of the Enter button. Before Willie spun around, the painted Warrior image of Liam absorbed the real Liam into the mural.

"Thanks for your help, Willie." Lindor morphed into the artwork.

Willie made eye contact with the Warrior chief. Partially smiling, it twitched its fingers, signaling Willie to return its tomahawk.

"I can't even get respect from a mascot."

Willie mumbled additional comments as he freed the tomahawk from the Enter button. He hurled the weapon to its owner. The Warrior chief snatched the tomahawk in its right hand and reverted to its original position.

"Unbelievable." Willie climbed down the scaffold.

From an outsider's vantage point, Liam osmosed into the pores of the block wall with the mere existence of himself. Once Liam's head entered the painting, the Dropas didn't wait for the rest of him to pass through the wall. They effortlessly removed the special coating as each body part entered the artwork.

Lindor and the Dropas assisted Liam across the desert and through one of the entrances. Applying uncanny intuition, the doorway they selected led directly to the mural where everyone else had entered.

As some of Liam's senses returned, the multipurpose room came into view. Peering out through the window, he felt dampness on his pant legs from kneeling on the wet ledge. The raindrops that dotted the bottom of the window frame dripped down the inside of the mural. Everything seemed real.

"What happened?" Mason asked. "I was concerned you wouldn't make it."

"I'm not exactly sure," Liam replied, confused. "Perhaps my mind refused to let go." Liam tried recalling the chain of events. "I perceived Lindor's voice. I don't understand how, because Bandor said we wouldn't be able to hear anything. That's all I remember."

"You didn't enter this mural."

"Of course, I came through this wall."

"No, Lindor and the Dropas guided you in from behind me."

Liam crinkled his brow. "Seriously?"

Mason raised his right hand. "I swear to you. I watched as you struggled to get into this mural. Willie came and carried you off on his shoulder."

"Willie carried me off? Wow, I have no idea what happened."

"Glad you made it." Mason offered a hand to help Liam stand on the ledge.

Liam changed the subject. "How surreal is this?"

"Nothing else compares to it. We always dreamed of doing this," Mason grinned. "Liam! Can you believe we are inside my art? This is incredible!"

"Shh!" Liam raised his hand. "Listen."

"Not this again." Mason froze. "I don't hear anything."

"Exactly. You're not wheezing in here."

Mason inhaled deeply and exhaled emptiness with a smile. "Totally mindboggling. Come on, let's get down from here."

"How far up are we?"

"It doesn't matter," Mason answered. "That rainbow there is our chute."

"Should be fun. Let's do it." Liam followed Mason's lead.

They leapt off the ledge and stretched for the rainbow. Grasping it at first touch, they slid down the spectral arch, leaving behind a colored dust trail. The cloud impaired Liam's vision and he ended up landing on top of Mason who crashed to the ground first.

"What a rush!" Liam yelled.

"Incoming!" Mason warned.

Liam wheeled around in time to get splattered in the face by three Dropas. Silver, Indigo, and Red had followed Liam down the rainbow. Liam and Mason waited a few seconds for the little guys to collect themselves before strolling to the summer window.

They admired the sunset—no longer a painted image on the wall, but instead, a realistic projection of vibrant pinks and oranges across the sky. It reminded Liam of a sunset that follows an early evening, spring shower. The dark gray cloud bottoms contrasted magnificently with the sunset colors and blue sky. An overwhelming sensation of calmness and peacefulness had overtaken them, making it difficult to determine their present location. Was it a physical place or perhaps another existence? Or merely another state of mind? No matter, it was definitely somewhere other than Earth.

Threshold of Existence

Brad and Ti dangled from the summer window ledge. How they ended up in that position is a mystery since they had entered in the same manner as Brian, Lauren, and Mason.

"I'm slipping!" Ti exclaimed.

"Hold on a little longer until I figure out something," Cooper encouraged her.

Ti tried using her feet to climb the inside wall. "Hurry, Cooper."

Cooper peeked over his shoulder. "Can you reach that sunflower?"

Ti estimated the distance between her and the stalk. "I think so."

"Go for it." Cooper also struggled to keep a firm grip on the wall.

Ti pushed off from the window ledge, opening her hands in anticipation of grabbing the sunflower stalk. Misjudging the required force of propulsion, she flew past the towering plant as her hands failed to grasp it. "Ohhh, no—" Ti face-planted the soil-covered ground. "Ptooey." She wiped the powdery dirt from her mouth.

"Are you okay?" Cooper managed to maneuver himself to Ti's vacated spot.

Ti tilted her head upward to determine the reason for her abbreviated shriek. "Cooper," she laughed. "Cooper!"

"Hold on. I'm getting ready to jump."

"Let go," Ti said bluntly as she dusted off her clothes.

"Are you nuts?"

"Trust me. You're only three feet above the ground."

Cooper's awkward position prevented him from seeing anything below his shoulders. "This is no time to be clowning around, Ti."

"Cooper, look at me."

Cooper cocked his head to the left, straining to get a glimpse of Ti whose chin was barely above his knee.

Ti smiled at Cooper. "Let go, you fool."

Cooper released his grip. "Don't I feel silly."

"It's no big deal. We had no clue how high up we were."

Gold, Yellow, and Orange opted for a different method of getting down from the ledge. They launched themselves, one by one, into the middle of a sunflower.

The subsequent catapulting action propelled them into the air. If their aim was accurate, they would reach the next targeted floret. The Dropas sunflower-hopped until they landed on the ground. Gold and Yellow flawlessly executed the feat. Orange's endeavor proved to be less fortunate. It missed the center of the third sunflower. The minor miscalculation hurled Orange twenty feet past the fourth plant, much to the amusement of the onlookers.

Shortly after Orange's mishap, the rest of the group met up with Cooper and Ti in the sunflower garden. Everyone had arrived safely in the mural. Liam and Mason listened to the kids chatter regarding how cool it was inside the walls. The sentiment was shared collectively.

Bandor and Lindor led the others to the forest edge, inside the floating postcard above them. Captivated by the new world, the adventurers strolled silently into the sunset toward the towering trees. Everyone enjoyed the serenity of the surroundings. On occasion, if anyone took notice, they would have seen Liam and Lindor surreptitiously exchanging glances.

The mural travelers reached the near forest perimeter at nightfall. The well-defined trail carved through the enormous trees was more prominent inside the artwork. They would follow the forked path to the right once morning broke. Bandor issued a stern warning, with no explanation, about venturing to the left.

Bandor, Mason, and the teens each selected a place to sleep along the tree line. The wooden monoliths provided more than adequate cover.

Arrival in that new world prompted many questions. Liam sought answers from Lindor who propped herself up against a tree and gazed at the night sky. The Dropas occupied themselves with her long hair.

"Do you have a moment, Lindor?"

"Sure, have a seat." Lindor patted the dirt. "What is on your mind?"

"I am overcome by curiosity."

"Not surprising. Bandor and I anticipated many questions."

Liam inhaled deeply. "I'm confused as to why we don't need to breathe in this world, yet we must sleep."

"Your bewilderment is to be expected." Lindor adjusted herself against the trunk. "I will explain it as best I can."

Silver and Gold dashed down Lindor's arm to Liam's lowered palm.

"Mason's murals represent many different ideas and philosophies, correct?"

"Yes." Liam smiled as Silver tickled his ear.

"Most notably, his painted walls depict the barriers people on Earth tend to build around themselves for various reasons. Often it is done to protect themselves from recurring, traumatic experiences or against concepts or beliefs they do not comprehend." Lindor raised two index fingers to her temples. "Those walls are built, or created, by the mind. For the mind is what holds those memories and maintains the capacity to feel pain. Picture us in the heart of the walls that your brother symbolically breaks through in his mural art."

Thus far, Liam followed her explanation.

"You have already entered this mural and will voyage through dozens more. Each mural represents a different part of the heart, closely related to the positivity, goodness, and energy that centers you and guides your emotions. The mind holds the negative imprints you encounter through the course of life. Bad experiences and temptations are embedded there. Arton acts as the control center for this aspect of the mind, and we will encounter his efforts more than once on our journey. That is why it is critical to keep your heart on the right track to fend off his enticements. Life support systems are no longer needed here because you are not living in the murals as you do in your world. The heart is required to guide you, and replenishing the full capabilities of it is the single most important thing needed to exist here and fight against Arton. You will rarely need the decision capacity of your mind. As you make that transition, because it does not happen all at once, the mind will no longer require sleep, which allows it to function properly on Earth. Sleep requirement is temporary. As it diminishes, the mind will relinquish control and the heart will guide you."

Liam processed her thorough explanation. "That makes sense. Do you and Bandor require sleep?"

"Originating from Dropa negates our sleep need. However, due to the lengthy stay on Earth, our physical and emotional sensations require an indefinite period to return to the former state prior to arriving in your world."

Liam changed the subject. "What can you tell me about Arton?"

"Not much." Lindor relished the twinkling stars through the treetops. "I acquired most of my knowledge of Arton's destructive capabilities on Earth. Our history scrolls also detail what he did to my world, but it will not compare to what he has in store this time. No matter his plan, Arton is a highly intelligent being with a vengeance like I have never seen. I expect the worst."

"As do I."

Lindor brought her legs to her chest, wrapped her arms around her shins, and rested her chin on her knees. "What I fear most is that he will find his way to Dropa before we can stop him."

"Had we not successfully entered the murals, I would have agreed with you."

"Your words of encouragement are sincere, but Arton is a powerful being and gaining strength as he nears Dropa. He must be stopped."

"We will finish the job this time, Lindor," Liam assured.

Lindor extended her legs and leaned against the trunk. "I enjoyed our conversation, but I must rest and you should too."

"I thought you don't require sleep," Liam said, somewhat confused.

"That is correct, but I need to rest in my own way to help heal my wound." She closed her eyes.

"Thank you for answering my questions."

"My pleasure," Lindor whispered with a smile. "We will talk again, yes?"

"It will be *my* pleasure. Goodnight, Lindor."

"Sleep well, Liam."

Liam returned to his designated tree for the night, fidgeting to get comfortable against the bark, and investigated the phenomenon of the hovering tree roots. Adding to the perplexity, the roots gained nourishment from the air rather than from the minerals and nutrients in the soil. He discerned the same peculiarity with the other trees. Their root tips also protruded upward. He accepted their method of sustenance, thinking it had something to do with his discussion with Lindor. Existing in a surreal world, as Mason had painted it, Liam opened his mind to accept anything different from his world. After the bombardment of random thoughts subsided, he fell into a deep sleep.

Struggling to reposition himself, Liam opened his eyes. At some point during the night he had slid down the tree trunk into a prone position on the forest floor—perfectly sensible. The problem, the same for everyone in the small entourage, was that he was pinned underneath the tree. Liam appreciated that the wooded entity demonstrated considerate restraint by not resting itself on him, for had it, he would have certainly been an additional sediment layer. Struggling was futile. Consequently, Liam lay there and talked with the others.

"Hey, Mason," Liam called.

"Yo," Mason responded.

"I'm trying to get to the root of our problem here," Liam quipped.

Mason rolled his eyes. "Very funny."

"Mason, are you stuck under your tree?" Lauren inquired.

"I believe we all are." Mason attempted to free himself.

"Brian, are you here?" Liam asked.

"Present," Brian replied light-heartedly, "and not leaving anytime soon, sir."

"Cooper."

There was no answer.

"Cooper? Ti?"

Again, no answer.

"They were next to me last night," Lauren offered, "but definitely not now."

"Bandor? Lindor?" Liam lifted his head and scanned the area.

Nothing but silence. "This is your fault, Mason."

"Why is it my fault?" Mason asked defensively.

"Simple. Had you painted these trees rooted in the dirt, they wouldn't be pinning unsuspecting visitors to the ground."

Mason chuckled at Liam's needling. "Have you seen the Dropas?"

"No. I honestly haven't seen much of anything but the bottom of this tree."

The tree took exception to Liam's comment by lowering itself onto his chest.

Realizing he had offended it, Liam apologized, "I'm sorry!"

The tree released the pressure.

"Sorry for what?" Mason questioned.

"I was apologizing to the tree."

"Why?"

"Trust me, don't say anything to offend the trees," Liam advised everyone. "They are very sensitive."

"Mason! Liam!" Bandor had returned from the right fork of the path with Lindor and the Dropas trailing him. "Where are you?"

Liam raised his brow. "Right where you left us, Bandor."

Bandor telepathically communicated to the trees to free the mural guests.

"You were responsible for this restraint?" Liam brushed the dirt off his pants.

"It was for your own safety."

"Bandor, I haven't fallen out of my bed since I was four," Liam remarked.

"That is not why we did it," Bandor said.

"Has anyone seen Cooper or Ti?" Mason inquired.

* * * * *

A nudge at Cooper's shoulder stirred him from a sound sleep. He quietly moaned before rolling onto his side. He felt a second prod, harder this time.

"Ti, is that you?" he whispered groggily.

She didn't answer. A third nudge came and he emerged from his sleepiness. The forest was dimly lit from the first quarter moon, and he needed a few seconds to focus on the four-legged equine—a solid white unicorn.

"For real?" Cooper jerked away from it, but the suspended tree roots inhibited his movement. "No way."

"Ti," Cooper whispered, hoping not to startle the animal. "Ti."

Ti squirmed. "Yes, mother, I fed the dog."

"Get up, Ti." Cooper tugged on her arm as he chuckled at her disorientation. "You have to see this."

"I already took out the trash." A semi-conscious Ti retracted her arm.

Cooper shook her. "Wake up, Ti."

She reluctantly rolled over to face Cooper. Her half-opened eyes widened at the sight of the magical beast. "Is that a—I love unicorns." Ti reached out to touch its horn. "Where did it come from?"

The magnificent creature prodded Cooper and stepped onto the path.

"I have no clue, but I think it wants to take us somewhere."

"No way. Bandor told us to stick together."

"Shh. You'll wake the others."

Ti lowered her voice to a whisper. "I'm staying here, Cooper."

"Come on, Ti. It's a unicorn. How dangerous can it be?"

"I'm not disobeying Bandor."

Cooper waited a few seconds for Ti to change her mind. When she didn't, he followed the unicorn. "Fine. I'll go myself."

"Cooper," Ti called softly, ensuring she didn't alarm the others. "Wait." She laced up her shoes and mumbled, "I hate when he guilts me into doing things."

"Hurry up," Cooper murmured.

"I'm coming. Hold your pants on." Ti gently grabbed Cooper's elbow. "Should we wake Lauren and Brian?"

"No," he replied definitively. "Let's go."

"What's the big hurry?"

"It must be exciting. Hey, it wants to give us a ride."

"Seriously? As a child, I always dreamed of riding one."

"Here's your chance." Cooper assisted Ti before climbing aboard and gripping the animal's mane.

Ti wrapped her arms around Cooper's waist. He gently kicked his heels into the unicorn's sides. Captivated with their fairy tale transportation galloping down the path, they failed to realize they had veered down the left side of the fork, the side Bandor warned them not to use.

"Cooper, this is amazing." Ti nuzzled her cheek into Cooper's back.

"Aren't you glad you came with me?"

"Yes, but we shouldn't be doing this."

"There's nothing to be nervous about," Cooper guaranteed.

Cooper and Ti rode throughout the night. They reached a canyon rim as the sun peeked above the horizon. Ti, half asleep, barely held onto Cooper. He pressed her hands against his waist as the unicorn traversed down the steep slope. The sudden shift in direction alerted Ti who tightened her arms around Cooper and her legs against the animal's flank.

"Where are we, Cooper?"

Cooper adjusted his grip on the mane. "I'm not exactly sure what mural we're in, but geologically speaking, we're in a canyon."

Ti peeked around Cooper's shoulder. "What's down there?"

"I don't know, Ti," Cooper replied briskly, "I'm on the same ride you are."

"I'm scared." Ti firmed her grip around Cooper. "Take me back."

He tried to ease her anxiety. "This is likely our destination."

"I don't care." She stretched for the mane. "I want to be with the others."

Cooper deflected her hand away, becoming agitated. "Quit whining!"

"Cooper!" Ti reached again for the mane.

"It's too late." Cooper pushed her arm away a second time and pointed at the wall ahead of them. "We have arrived!"

Cooper squinted, attempting to focus on the figures imprinted on the stone walls. The heavily shadowed canyon prevented him from identifying the painted images on the rock faces. The unicorn navigated through the terrain on the rocky floor before reaching its final destination. Cooper and Ti dismounted and investigated the surrounding walls, cringing in disgust. Upon the walls were mutations of original mural mascots that Mason ultimately repainted. Arton had made a feeble attempt at filling in the missing parts.

"Cooper, do you recognize this one?"

"Oh, yeah. From my cousin's school. It was the first time Mason painted there and most parents and staff were opposed to the mural. The same teachers visited constantly, asking why the school needed such artwork. He struggled with that Trojan for days until he painted over it." Cooper scrutinized the image. "It's more sickly now. And those sagging shoulders look worse after the mutation."

"I remember when you showed it to me. Mason was constantly bummed."

"Until some students cheered him up him one day. The next time I visited, he had created a noble, muscular Trojan in place of that pathetic-looking thing."

"This is like a cemetery for mutants," Ti concluded. "Check this one out."

Indeed it was a graveyard for all the mascots and scenes Mason had repainted. Occasionally, he was not warmly welcomed in schools. Before the war, many people associated his art solely with cost instead of the intangible benefits to the students. His murals touched more than people's pocketbooks. The artwork lifted school spirit and instilled unity among staff and students. It encouraged a passerby to pause and expand his or her mind and imagination, if only for a moment. It also inspired thoughtful consideration of the pursuit of one's dreams no matter how crazy they might seem or realization that personal problems weren't as bad as perceived. For many, viewing an energetic blue sky or a peaceful sunset temporarily washed away their troubles and carried them through the rest of the day. If the paintings touched people in a positive way, his time and occasionally his frustration were worth it.

Cooper and Ti investigated the canyon walls of mutated creatures. They observed Warriors with protruding tentacles instead of arms, horses with wart-like armor instead of well-groomed, shiny coats, and wildcats with exaggerated teeth and nails. It was a hideous sight.

"I've seen enough, Cooper," Ti said, breaking the silence as she grasped Cooper's arm. "This place gives me the creeps."

"I'm with you. Let's get out of here."

A silhouetted person appeared behind them. "What's your hurry?"

Startled, Ti shrieked and pivoted to view the ominous figure. "Who are you?"

"We can skip the formal introductions," the person calmly replied.

"What do you want with us, Arton?" Cooper asked with sudden recognition.

"I want what you're willing to give me," Arton responded cordially.

"You'll get nothing from us," Ti snapped.

Arton shrugged. "If that is your choice, then I will simply dispose of you."

"Go ahead and try."

"In due time." Arton emerged from the shadows, exposing his new physical features, those of Wilhelm Roentgen.

"We'll be on our way," Cooper said politely, trying not to upset Arton.

Arton folded his hands in front of him. "Very well, Cooper, but it's hard for me to believe you want to return to the two men who murdered your brother."

Cooper momentarily dismissed Arton's mind game of wrongful blame. He loved his brother dearly, idolizing him like no other.

"Come on, Cooper," Ti whispered, "he's messing with your head."

"Wait a second, Ti. Arton, how did you know about my brother?"

Ti tilted her head closer to Cooper. "Remember what Bandor—"

"Because of the two people that murdered him."

Cooper kindly pushed away his girlfriend. "Arton, are you telling me Liam and Mason killed Carl?"

"That's exactly what I'm saying," Arton replied matter-of-factly.

"I don't believe you."

"Recall what happened, Cooper." Arton placed his hand on Cooper's shoulder. "You were there."

Cooper felt a strange sensation course through his body from Arton's touch. He stepped away and offered his hand to Ti. "Let's go."

"Don't you remember, Cooper?" Arton's voice grew louder and more hypnotic as Cooper and Ti distanced themselves from him. "Replay it in your mind. That rainy night. You were a young boy asleep in your bed…"

...clap of thunder ripped through the sky. Cooper awoke, trembling underneath the covers. Another lightning bolt flashed in the darkness, immediately followed by a booming sound. His parents away for the weekend and afraid to stay alone any longer, he threw the covers off his body and darted out of his room and down the hall. Noticing the door ajar, he stopped short of his brother's bedroom. Although extremely frightened, Cooper was attentive enough to realize that Carl always slept with his door closed. He cautiously crept to the doorway where he heard muffled voices. Cooper feared the worst as he peeked through the narrow opening. His eyes focused on two figures dressed in black clothes and wearing ski masks. Cooper froze as he watched the two men pounding his older brother. With relentless fury, they pulverized Carl and cursed him for not joining the revolution. Cooper desperately wanted to help, but he was paralyzed with fear. Powerless, he watched the fatal beating until Carl lay there motionless on the bed. The two men neared the door, unaware of the child's presence. Their movement in his direction ignited a response from Cooper. He quietly inched away from the door and hurriedly tiptoed to his room. From his window, he watched the assailants rush to their car parked in the driveway below his bedroom. Cooper hoped that the men who committed the heinous act would reveal their identities. The men obliged, removing their masks before entering the vehicle. As they did, a streak of lightning illuminated the sky and the driveway below him. Cooper recognized the faces of both men...

"You're right." Cooper wiped the tears from his face. "It *was* them. How could they do that to my brother and act like they're my friends?"

"Cooper, you're not making sense. Arton is playing tricks with your mind. Mason and Liam didn't murder your brother."

"I can't believe that anymore." Cooper clutched Ti's arms. "Unquestionably, it was them. They will pay the price."

"One down, one to go," Arton murmured.

"It doesn't add up." Ti gently held Cooper's face and tried to convince him otherwise. "Their car swerved off the wet pavement and crashed into a tree a mile from your house. You identified the two men that the police arrested."

"No, Ti. Mason and Liam did it. I want revenge, Arton."

Ti charged at Arton with her fists clenched. "What have you done to him?"

Arton smacked her with the back of his hand, sending her sprawling across the canyon floor.

Cooper intentionally ignored Ti who wept on the ground, her lip already swollen from the blow. With Arton's cunning assistance, Cooper had let negative thoughts fill his mind, allowing it to regain full control of his feelings. He marched down the canyon trail.

"Cooper!" Arton called.

Cooper pivoted as if still entranced under Arton's spell. "Yes, Arton."

"Would you like some assistance?"

"If you feel it's essential, Arton, I will accept it with gratitude."

Arton gestured to the mutated creatures. One by one, they emerged from the stone walls and lined up behind Cooper who overlooked their peculiar, two-dimensional appearance.

The creatures' lack of wholeness was a direct result of Arton initially struggling to recall his long-forgotten shapeshifting abilities. His success with the unicorn demonstrated that his skill had significantly improved.

Astride the unicorn and his mind in disarray, Cooper set out on a mission of revenge. He left Ti behind, not caring what happened to her, and embarked on a path to intercept Liam and the others to avenge his brother's murder.

"Get up!" Arton ordered as he grabbed Ti's hair and lifted her off the ground.

Ti struggled briefly before realizing her effort to fight him was fruitless. "What do you want with me?"

"Patience, my child." Arton pulled harder on her hair. "As long as we are dealing with mortals, you are always more valuable to me alive." Arton smiled smugly as he watched Cooper and the mutated soldiers ascend the rocky trail. He tightened his grip on Ti, and the two of them morphed into the canyon wall.

* * * * *

"Nobody has seen Cooper or Ti since last night," Lindor admitted. "We were searching for them when you awoke."

"Why didn't you wake us to help?" Mason inquired.

"You needed sleep, and that is why we had the trees cover you. To prevent all of you from wandering off and separating yourselves from us."

"Exactly how long have you been searching for them?"

"Since shortly after your brother went to sleep," Bandor responded.

"Do you have any clues, Bandor?" Liam asked.

"Only one, and it is an unpleasant one," Bandor answered, distracted. "There are hoof prints that lead down the path and to the left."

"Before we went to bed last night, you advised us not to use that side of the fork," Lauren contended. "Ti and Cooper would not have disobeyed your warning, Bandor."

"Not on their own." Bandor expressed dismay as he stared down the path. "I presume they had some assistance."

"Why didn't you or Lindor hear them?" Brian wondered aloud.

"It must have been when we attempted to contact Athena," Lindor offered.

"It had to be," Bandor agreed. "We were aware of everything else."

"Where were the Dropas during this time?" Lauren asked.

"Scouting the right fork," Bandor answered.

Clearcoat nodded in agreement.

"Is this the type of trickery we can expect from Arton?" Liam inquired.

"It is only the beginning," Bandor concurred, "and it will definitely worsen."

"Let's not waste any more time," Mason insisted. "We must find them."

"I am afraid we cannot."

"Why not, Bandor?"

"It is imperative we stay on our own path to intercept Arton. Following Cooper and Ti is exactly what Arton intended. It will delay us in finding him."

"We can't leave them," Brian argued.

"Yes, we can," Bandor answered firmly. "Before we entered the murals, I cautioned all of you regarding the things Arton might do. This is a mere taste of what lies ahead. We have no choice but to leave them."

"Can we search for them on our way back?" Lauren asked dejectedly.

"Possibly," Bandor replied, "but I cannot promise."

Lauren wept in fear for her best friend, Ti. Brian tried to console her as he drew her close to his chest. Also saddened, Brian had grown close to Ti as well and Cooper was like a brother.

Bandor would have none of it. Similar to their mission on Earth, the ultimate goal focused on stopping Arton. The risks had been outlined before the adventure commenced. Liam understood Bandor's position, but hoped they would have the opportunity to find the missing teenagers on the return trip. Until that time, they had to proceed without them.

Liam also felt a void as a result of Cooper and Ti's disappearance, for he was accustomed to having them by his side. After all, they accompanied him during the last adventure.

Lauren walked alongside Liam down the path. "I'm sorry, Liam."

"For what, Lauren?"

"For being soft," she answered, somewhat ashamed.

"No worries. You are extremely close with Ti. It's totally understandable."

"I want to be strong on this trip like I was on the last one."

"I'm confident you'll be resolute when we need you to be. Besides, waking up on the wrong side of your tree this morning likely had something to do with it."

Lauren chuckled. "You enjoy making people laugh, don't you?"

"As often as they'll let me. And besides, I'm funny."

"Liam!" Bandor yelled. "Mason!"

"Keep your chin up, my young warrior. We'll need your strength and courage later."

"I will. Thank you, Liam."

Liam and Mason met Bandor and Lindor at the fork.

"These are the hoof prints I mentioned. I have informed our wooded friends of this position. Upon your return they will assist you in your search for Cooper and Ti should Arton alter the path." Bandor beckoned everyone. "We must continue."

"This means a lot to all of us, Bandor," Mason said.

"Please understand I would like to show more compassion for their disappearance, but we must—"

"Bandor, you don't need to explain."

"Thanks, Mason."

They all followed Bandor down the right side of the fork. The Dropas scattered themselves among the group and everyone welcomed their company. Lauren and Brian walked backward until the left path disappeared from view.

Primordial Shift

It was pleasantly cool among the vibrant green vegetation. Healthy ferns and flowering plants blanketed the forest floor bordering the path. Occasionally, a tree cordially waved a limb at the visitors. The mural travelers quickly acclimated to the new surroundings, but at times needed an explanation pertaining to plants and animals exhibiting human characteristics or peculiar behavior. Periodically, a squirrel scampered amidst the foliage or a woodpecker jackhammered the tree bark with its beak.

"Lindor," Liam called, puzzled.

"Yes, Liam." She fell back from the front of the line.

"Why do animals here gather food, yet we don't need to eat?"

"They are not accumulating resources for consumption," Lindor countered, grinning at the anticipated bewilderment.

"I saw a squirrel carrying acorns," Lauren added.

"Did the squirrel eat the acorns?"

"No, but that doesn't mean it won't eat them later."

"In your world you would be correct."

"What are they doing?" Mason asked.

The conversation had all but Bandor interested, but he subtly displayed his amusement at the curiosity of his bemused friends.

"If you closely observe the squirrels, they are not eating the acorns, nor are they storing them for future consumption." Lindor passed her hands above the ground. "Their purpose is purely for cultivation. They are considered the forest farmers. Unlike on Earth, the trees do not allow their acorns to fall for fear that one could injure a ground-dwelling animal. Instead, they signal to the squirrels when acorns are ready for planting, and the bushy-tailed farmers promptly gather the seeds from the branches."

"Aren't the woodpeckers searching for insects?" Lauren asked.

Lindor resumed walking. "On the contrary, they are relieving the trees of unwanted itches."

"Get out of here," Brian contended in disbelief. "You mean they're back scratchers?"

"Bark scratchers to be more precise."

"Would they scratch mine?" Lauren wondered aloud.

"Sure, if you do not mind holes in your back," Lindor laughed.

"How did these critters get here?" Mason inquired. "I didn't paint them."

"It is what you would refer to as spontaneous generation. You created the environment and the critters naturally followed. A significant difference is that their roles have been altered from what they would be in your world, for example the woodpecker and the squirrel."

"Isn't overpopulation a concern since no animals feed on each other?" Liam inquired.

"The number of animals fulfilling each role is predetermined. And please do not ask me how it is done because I do not have the answer."

"Do they produce offspring?" Brian asked.

"Sometimes," Lindor replied, "but once the offspring become adults, the same number of other adults will cease to exist."

"Does this happen with every creature in this world?" Lauren maneuvered in front of Brian.

Lindor lifted a praying mantis to her eyes. "Every one of them."

"Incredible. I may stay here forever," Lauren admitted. "I love the serenity, and the animals have unique personalities."

Lindor returned the insect to its original location on a fern frond. "If you are amazed with the mural world, Dropa will astound you."

"Tell us about it, Lindor. Pleeeease," Lauren insisted.

"I would love to, but my description, or anyone else's for that matter, would not do it justice." Lindor strolled down the path.

"Will we experience Dropa?" Brian asked.

"I cannot definitively answer that question." Lindor caught up with Bandor.

The diminishing shade indicated the nearing of the forest edge. The tree density had thinned out, and the travelers felt the warmth of the sunshine from outside the perimeter. Bandor gazed across the grassland that extended beyond the trees. Although interested in what Bandor was contemplating, Liam and Mason considered their own wonderment.

Liam studied the scenery. "Is this the mustang mural?"

"Yes, but something is missing," Mason replied.

"What else did you paint besides the prairie grass and the buttes?"

Mason snapped his fingers. "The curled paper ripping through the sky."

"I bet it's here," Brian said confidently.

"I'm not seeing it."

"Consider where we are," Lauren reminded Mason.

"Right," he concurred.

"We could create any one of your trademarks," Liam added. "If we wanted to rip through that sky, we could. And it might lead us to a different painting."

"This is awesome, Mason," Brian said. "We are *inside* your murals."

The four grinned, astonished at what they were witnessing. As for Liam, the short journey had already surpassed what he had imagined when he often lost himself in Mason's artwork.

"What is it, Bandor?" Liam asked.

Bandor didn't answer while in a temporary catatonic state.

"He is contacting the mustangs to serve as our transportation," Lindor explained. She beckoned the group away from Bandor. "They will carry us across the prairie to the forest on the other side."

"What mustangs?" Brian squinted. "And what forest?"

"They will be here shortly, and the forest is a great distance from here." Lindor tapped Brian's nose with her forefinger. "That is why we will be riding mustangs instead of walking."

"Check this out!" Lauren had wandered away from Brian.

They all abandoned Bandor and his telepathic phone call to share Lauren's excitement. She had discovered an animal community under investigation by mutual friends. Bored waiting for transportation, the Dropas instead visited a village of affable prairie dogs. An inspection crew, led by none other than Silver and Gold, explored the underground condos. They wore hard hats and masqueraded as building superintendents.

The prairie dogs played along with the two inspectors that darted down one entrance and reappeared from another, twenty or thirty feet away. Not wanting to participate with the "professional" Dropas, the "leisurely" Dropas rounded up willing dogs and rode them like a band of wild cowboys. The spectator rodents enjoyed the performance, standing on their hind legs and barking in sync.

Lauren befriended another dog and cuddled it against her cheek. Taking advantage of his nonexistent allergies in the murals, Mason uncharacteristically partook in the festivities. He knelt and welcomed a prairie dog of his own. It was the first time Liam had seen Mason willingly handle a furry critter—other than a stuffed animal on his childhood bed. Mason was wholly caught in the moment.

"Time to go!" Bandor shouted. "The mustangs are here!"

The brief reprieve ended abruptly with the arrival of the transportation. Mason and Lauren returned the prairie dogs to the village. The Dropas exchanged good-byes with their transient friends before scurrying to their usual positions upon various shoulders.

"Two of you must double up," Bandor advised, managing to only round up four horses—all stunning nonetheless.

"I'll go with Brian," Lauren said.

"I'll ride with Liam," Lindor added.

Lindor's response pleasantly surprised Liam. He purposely avoided making eye contact with Mason and Bandor. Liam felt their stare, but he chose not to confirm it. He merely smiled and asked the Dropas to paint him a western saddle, preferring that to riding bareback. Mason and Brian requested the same for their horses, but Bandor opted to demonstrate how to properly ride without a leather seat. Liam assisted Lindor onto his horse before climbing aboard himself.

Liam again observed Mason's joyous interaction with an animal. Like his handling of the prairie dog, this was the first time he had ridden a horse without fear of allergies igniting an asthma attack. As Mason relished the new experience, Liam enjoyed his own pleasantries with Lindor's arms enfolded around his abdomen.

The riders ostensibly traveled for hours. Unsure of the time concept inside the murals, Liam compared it to his world. And thus far, the sun had set and risen once, and it was ready to set again. Lindor barely spoke on the journey across the prairie, but intermittently highlighted various landmarks and animals along the way. Liam oftentimes felt her snuggle her face against his shoulder. And each time she did, her grip tightened around him. Liam savored the perceived affection, a sensation he had coveted for some time, and one he enjoyed throughout the long ride.

As the sun descended, Bandor slowed his mustang, indicating it was time to sleep. Weary from the journey, the travelers welcomed the interlude. It had been years since any of them had ridden a horse, but the burning sensation throughout their legs and rear ends provided an instant reminder. Liam walked gingerly as his inner thighs quivered relentlessly. Humored by the unorthodox manner of walking, the Dropas seized the opportunity to imitate him.

"The pain will fade over time," Bandor assured, noticing their discomfort. "The longer you are in the murals, and as your mind relinquishes control, the sooner the physical sensations will disappear. Your emotions will wane as well."

"And this tunnel vision I have?" Liam asked.

"Does anyone else have restricted sight?"

"No," they replied, except for Brian.

"Mine has been improving," Brian answered.

"You will probably have normal vision by sunrise." Bandor gently led Liam away from the group. "You must let go, Liam. Although you are both creative and analytical, the latter is dominating the former. You are the most logical one here, but it is essential that you let your heart guide you inside the murals."

"I'm trying, Bandor."

"We are weak against Arton if we let our minds steer us. It worked well on Earth, but we will not achieve the same outcome inside this world."

"I understand that." Liam lifted his right shoulder and moved his head in a circular motion to relieve the tension.

"Relax, my friend. You will make it."

"I have no reason to believe otherwise, Bandor."

Once everyone regained the circulation and strength in their legs, they bedded down for the night in sleeping bags the Dropas had generously supplied.

It was a picturesque evening. Brilliant stars twinkled against the ebony sky and the distant, howling wolves serenaded the visitors. The rising super moon cast a night-light upon the grassland. And occasionally, a shooting star streaked across the darkened canvas.

Liam tilted his head to the left and admired the moonlight glimmering off Lindor's face. Surprisingly, she exuded more beauty inside the murals. Lindor opened her eyes to find Liam gazing at her. Without saying a word, she held his hand for the duration of the evening as she rested. Liam slept soundly that night.

The majority of the team quietly awoke to the stirring mustangs. Liam's unique alarm clock was not as subtle, a sharp object prodding his kidneys and ribs. He rolled onto his back in an attempt to rid himself of the rude awakening. The four-legged wake-up call was not to be denied. The black rhinoceros wedged its horn underneath Liam and with one swift and powerful motion, log-rolled him across the grass. He opened his eyes to the encircling sky, ground, and animals while discerning two distinct sounds: the rough-skinned lumberjack's snorting and laughter from the entertained audience.

After the dizziness subsided, Liam discovered the Dropas had made sport of his situation. The strange tickling sensations he felt across his head were the Dropas' feet scampering to stay aboard as they participated in a birling contest. Liam counted ten miniature woodsmen, but heard muffled gibbers among the giggles and laughter. He rolled off the victims, revealing flattened Orange and Yellow in his vacated spot. Using Silver and Gold as stretchers, Black, White, Blue, and Green rushed to aid their squashed friends, scraped them off the ground, and carried them to a mock medical unit set up by the other Dropas.

Liam observed other visitors besides the aforementioned rhino. A pride of lions surrounded the campsite: one male, a dozen females, and their cubs. Beyond the pride, Liam sighted large herds of zebras and wildebeests in the foreground, and gazelles roaming the vast plain behind them.

"Did somebody relocate us?" Liam ran his fingers through his hair.

"Yes and no," replied Bandor. "We did not physically change position, but when a disturbance exists within the murals, sometimes a shift occurs to avoid any further disruption, in this case, Arton." Bandor helped Liam to his feet.

"Are we presently amidst the Serengeti ecosystem?"

"Not entirely. No murals are exact replicas of locations in your world, but that is a close approximation."

"What does this mean to us, Bandor?" Mason joined the conversation.

"Judging from the new scenery, we will be delayed in reaching the forest."

"How long of a delay?" Liam inquired.

"It depends on the severity of the shift we encountered."

"Any way of determining that?" Mason asked.

"I am afraid not." Bandor knelt and passed his hand over the grass. "We must stay on our chosen path and hope for the best."

"That raises an interesting question regarding this shift. How do you get us to where we want to go when we're not sure where we are?" Liam furrowed his brow at Mason. "Did that make any sense?"

"Because Arton has already disrupted multiple murals, I am communicating with mascots across the artwork. They are guiding us through the unaffected ones. This will eventually lead us to the creatures in the sky where we will learn the portal location."

"Look what's coming!" Brian alerted everyone.

Seven adult giraffes galloped in the onlookers' direction. They glided gracefully and effortlessly across the plain to their next destination.

Liam offered his hand as a welcome gesture to the male lion, remembering as a child always wanting one as a pet, most likely from watching too much *Tarzan*. Purring loudly and deeply, the friendly feline nuzzled its head into Liam's midsection as he stroked its coarse mane. Mason and Lauren engaged with two lion cubs while Lindor and Brian played with the lionesses. Bandor was busy making more telepathic phone calls.

The Dropas were not to be alienated from the activities. They partook in a game of mousetrap, or in this case Dropatrap, with three lionesses. The Dropas circled in front of the felines, darting back and forth in an effort to avoid being smothered. Unsuccessful Dropas were splattered on the ground. After one lioness lifted its large paw to view its captured prey, the solid Dropas had virtually dematerialized, confusing the furry predator. It became more bewildered as the Dropas' drops reformed to their original shape.

"Time to saddle up." Bandor led the mustangs near the cats. "We have some distance to make up today."

Everyone mounted their equine transports—Lindor seated behind Liam—and prepared to ride. They bid farewell to the pride as Liam guided his horse to the front alongside Bandor.

"What have you been doing, Bandor?" Liam asked.

"I was transmitting messages to all the creatures we encounter as we journey through the murals. I want them alert and ready."

"Alert and ready for what? Your answers are a bit cryptic lately."

"My apologies," Bandor replied, plainly preoccupied.

"Bandor, I realize how vital defeating Arton is to you and Lindor. It is critical for humanity as well. We will succeed, like we did the first time."

Lindor tightened her arms around Liam's waist.

"He is growing more powerful."

"No matter how insurmountable it seems presently, Arton will not succeed. Please don't feel like you must bear the entire burden of this mission. We are a team, as we were when we brought down the fortress. For us to effectively function and succeed as a team, I'm asking that you share with us what you're thinking and provide details in your answers."

"You are absolutely right, Liam. Thank you for reminding me that I am not alone on this expedition. To answer your question, the creatures need to be alert for anything peculiar associated with Arton, like color removal and shifts…and ready themselves for the next battle."

"You anticipate a confrontation like that at Barrow's Ridge?"

"Much worse. Many mural creatures will not endure the conflict as easily as they did in the first one. Arton and his mutated beasts will be stronger."

"Mutated beasts?" Liam pulled on the reins to halt his mustang.

Bandor stopped his horse. "From my communications. These mutations have been spotted roaming through the murals."

Liam steadied his horse. "Do they all have the same destination in mind?"

"Most likely."

"Why aren't we pursuing them?"

"Because our army is not strong enough yet and we must surprise Arton like we did at the fortress," Bandor affirmed.

"Are you sure we will arrive in time?"

"If all goes well." Bandor gently kicked his heels into his horse.

The ride across the endless sea of grass displayed spectacular views. Among the knee-high, flexible stalks gracefully dancing in the wind were stately *kopje*, island hills beautifully accented with small trees and grass. At first glance, the decorated rocky formations seemed out of place as they did in the Serengeti, but in the mural world, everything belonged.

This plain was noticeably greener than the parallel sanctuary Liam visited on Earth. And in this world, hippos and elephants shared small marshes, indicating that the former exposed pachyderms did not require protection from the sun, rather they safely frolicked with their trunked playmates in the open.

Recalling Lindor's explanation of the farming squirrels, Liam dismissed the elephants stuffing their mouths with reeds protruding from the water. Instead, he accepted the behavior and let the captivating scenery wash over him.

The description would not be complete without mentioning the vast array of unusual thornless acacias that dotted the grassland. Their flat tops furnished shade like huge umbrellas on a tropical beach. For the monkeys and baboons that populated this mural, the trees presented outdoor jungle gyms.

Liam eyed something peculiar. "Lindor, does that seem strange to you?"

She focused on a cheetah engaged in full-out pursuit of an adult eland. "It appears to be preying on the antelope, but observe the upcoming sequence."

Liam shook his head in amazement, his concern unwarranted. The cheetah customarily leapt onto the eland's back. Rather than clenching its powerful jaws into its prey's neck, it steadied itself as if on a hooved surf board, reminding Liam that the food chain to which he was accustomed did not exist in this world.

"It is quite different here," Lindor commented.

"I keep telling myself that, but I am getting better."

"Your complete acceptance of this world will happen soon enough."

They rode a bit longer before Lindor tugged on Liam's left arm to redirect their horse. "Bandor!"

"What is it, Lindor?" Bandor slowed.

She pointed in the direction they were heading. "Another mural shift."

Bandor considered the shift characteristics. Preoccupied with the conversation, the current sparseness of the high grasses and acacias went unnoticed before suddenly vanishing, only to be replaced by desert sand. And if it didn't feel hot enough on the pseudo-African plain, the temperature superficially increased by ten or twenty degrees.

The arid conditions generated another oddity within the artwork. Although the travelers felt the heat of the sun and observed the rising vapors from the sand, they did not perspire nor yearn for water. Their bodies did not respond as they would have on Earth, and as a result, they remained entirely comfortable.

Bandor kicked his heels into the mustang.

"Hold on, Lindor," Liam said. "Yyaah!"

The monotonous desert crossing was a lengthy one. Again, Liam contemplated the concept of time during the journey, estimating travel segments relative to his knowledge and experience from home. He spotted a distant oasis, but it lacked any signs of civilization or ancient structures as anticipated. Away from that, plant life and water didn't exist. Only sand, lots and lots of sand.

Liam felt like a miniature army man—the plastic figures he used to play with as a kid—alone in the backyard sandbox. He hoped a giant firecracker didn't explode underneath him. With nothing more to appreciate other than the endless granular dunes, Liam intentionally fell behind the others to have a private conversation with his riding companion. "Lindor?"

"Yes, Liam."

"Are you in a relationship?"

"Relationship? Can you be more specific?"

Liam tilted his head, allowing her to hear him better. "Let's see," he said softly, uncertain of what he had started, "someone with whom you share yourself." That didn't reflect his intention, but they had considerable time to trudge through the conversation.

"I share myself with Bandor." She rested her chin on his shoulder.

Liam's heart sank. "You truly share yourself with Bandor?" Liam inquired, not really wanting confirmation.

"Yes," Lindor answered plainly, "we are Dropa messengers. That is how we communicate."

"Messengers, right." Liam desperately tried to overcome his foolishness.

"Does that mean he and I are in a relationship?"

"Yes, but not in the sense I'm speaking." Liam attempted to recover from his emotional thrill ride. "Let me say it another way. Generally speaking, you and Bandor are in a relationship. To clarify my definition, I meant one with whom you share experiences, feelings, and strong affection, stronger affection than you would show for any other friend of yours. In essence, a boyfriend or girlfriend." Liam felt a bit more comfortable with his explanation.

Lindor tightened her grip around his waist. "You mean like the affection I have been showing you?"

Liam's face turned beet red. "Yes, exactly like that."

"No," Lindor said softly.

"No, what?" Liam had forgotten his original question.

Lindor spoke a little louder. "No, I am not in a relationship."

"That's good," Liam said with relief in his voice.

"Forgive me for my initial naiveté to your intended meaning of relationship. In Dropa, we do not have boyfriend or girlfriend connections the way you do on Earth. And spending all my time with Arton certainly did not expose me to that type of human behavior."

Liam's heart sank. "Now you are confusing me."

"Dropa is a tranquil sanctuary. Although many Dropians exist there, we all interact with one another, but share no distinct feelings or emotions other than a common love. Dropa is wholly different from your world."

Liam pondered her response. "How is it possible to lack emotions and feelings?"

"There may be distinct emotions and feelings. Because Dropians lack negativity, we do not single them out like you do on Earth. The best way I can explain it is to say they are all part of the communal fondness. To iterate, Dropa cannot be depicted in words. It would be a great injustice and a feeble attempt on my part to describe it. You must immerse yourself in it to understand it."

A contented smile brightened Liam's face. "I look forward to it."

"You should. And you should feel honored to have the opportunity to visit Dropa before your time."

"Before my time?" Liam peeked at Lindor over his shoulder.

She raised her hand and gently pushed Liam's face forward, reminding him to watch where he was headed. "You will understand when you arrive."

"What do you—" Liam craved more information.

She covered his mouth with the same hand. "Ask questions related to me or my people, but please do not ask any more about Dropa."

"Fair enough."

"Thank you."

"Back to the original topic. How are you able to show me affection?"

"I previously mentioned my horrid experience with Arton at his fortress where my positive emotions were suppressed. Free from his stranglehold, I am able to reciprocate the positive emotions of others, especially the affection with you. They are present within me, but when we reach Dropa, they may disappear. Please understand this because I do not want you to misconstrue that I have lost my feelings for you. It is impossible to know exactly what will happen when we arrive in my world. This was my first time visiting Earth."

Lindor tightened her hold around Liam. He felt a warm sensation course through his body, predominantly in his chest. He had difficulty grasping the concept of not sharing earthly emotions or feelings with someone, especially under the current set of circumstances. Glancing at Mason and thinking of people close to him back home, Liam couldn't imagine what it would be like to lack those sensations, those feelings. For this instant, he relished the moment.

"Bandor, what are those buildings ahead of us?" Lauren asked.

"The one appears to be some kind of pyramid," Mason suggested.

"Possibly, but it could also be a mirage." Bandor slowed his mustang, allowing Liam to ride alongside. "We have been in the sun for some time."

"It is not a mirage, Bandor," Lauren countered confidently.

"Perhaps you are right."

Upon their arrival, the enormous pyramid dwarfed the onlookers. It reminded Liam of the Great Pyramid of Giza but with smooth, impeccable faces. Another structure of considerably less magnitude, but enormous in its own right, had been built to the right of the colossal pyramid. Unlike its taller counterpart, this shorter structure consumed a tremendous amount of area. Although shaped much like the Sphinx, it lacked a pharaoh's face or a lion's physique. Instead, the body shape resembled a smaller pyramid. A crystal clear pool, approximately half the size of a football field, extended beyond the entrance of the smaller structure.

Bandor signaled the others to stop as he rode onward.

"Follow him, Liam," Lindor insisted, "something is not right here."

"Will do. Mason, stay here with Brian and Lauren."

Liam and Lindor rode to where Bandor had stopped. At first, Liam presumed Bandor was communicating with more creatures. Instead, he simply stared at the horizon.

"What's wrong, Bandor?" Liam asked.

"You see those trees in the distance?"

Liam squinted, his eyes battling the glare. "Barely."

"My exact point. Those trees should be slightly past these pyramids."

"Do we need to ride further than you estimated?"

"No, they should be a short distance from here."

"Did we go through another shift?" Lindor inquired.

"I do not think we did," Bandor replied. "The shifts usually result in an entirely different landscape, not one we have already seen."

"What else could it be?"

"Unsure. I am positive those trees should be close to these structures."

"Perhaps the answer will present itself in the morning," Liam offered. "It will be dark soon."

"You are right. The sun sets fast here in the desert. We will sleep inside the smaller pyramid tonight and leave at sunrise."

"I'll tell the others," Liam said.

"Thank you." Bandor slid down the side of his horse. "Lindor, will you stay with me? I need help communicating with the creatures in this region."

"Of course, Bandor." Lindor dismounted the mustang, keeping her eyes on Liam. "I will be with you shortly."

Liam rode back to update the others that they had finished riding for the day. Although present, Liam felt less discomfort and soreness in his legs, precisely as Bandor had predicted.

"With whom do we need to communicate, Bandor?"

"Each other."

"What do you mean?" Lindor expressed confusion.

"Lindor, you are taking a major risk getting involved with Liam."

"I am aware of that."

"And you are willing to go through with it?"

"I spent almost my entire time on Earth with Arton and was only exposed to pain and negativity," Lindor reminded him. "For the first time since leaving Dropa, I am experiencing positive emotions—most notably ones of affection. So, yes, I am willing to go through with it."

"He will not stay in Dropa," Bandor asserted boldly.

"How do you know?"

"I have spent the last few years with him."

"What have you learned that convinces you he will not stay?"

"Dropians' emotions and feelings for one another are different."

"I realize that."

"The love is universal with everyone. If he resides in Dropa prematurely, he may yearn for those feelings familiar to him on Earth, and you may be unable to share them with him."

"I disagree, Bandor."

"You are entitled to your opinion."

"I am willing to take the risk."

"Yes, Lindor, but is he?"

"I do not understand."

"Have you asked him if he is willing to take the risk? You will not feel pain if he does not stay. He will." Bandor gently clutched Lindor's arms. "And you will not feel his pain if he stays."

"What kind of pain?"

"The pain of loss. Loss of feelings, affection, and the connection of people especially close to him. Liam will be separated from his loved ones on Earth. It is the same pain that has been erased from Dropians, a feeling we no longer experience in our world. No matter what happens, we will not sense it. Remember, you and I are in a transitional phase. Negative emotions that recurred during our time on Earth will disappear after we return to Dropa."

Lindor's eyes filled with tears. "I do not want to cause him any pain, Bandor."

"Then end it, Lindor." Bandor wiped the rivulets from her cheeks. "If you let it persist, you may hurt him whether he stays or returns home."

Lindor momentarily considered the advice. "I cannot." Lindor hugged Bandor, burying her face in his shirt. "My feelings for him are too strong."

Bandor gently pushed her away, still holding her arms. "You are being selfish, Lindor. You know what the likely outcome will be and you will hurt him. I do not want my friend hurt like that again."

"What do you mean, again?"

"Liam lost his wife during the war. He grieved for a long, long time, and honestly, I believe he is still healing."

"In that case, I am not being selfish," Lindor replied justifiably.

"What makes you say that?" Bandor inquired, puzzled.

"I will help heal his wounds."

"In the process, you may create new ones."

"Perhaps, but all I can do is try. My intentions are no longer for me, but for him."

"I cannot convince you otherwise, can I?"

"No, Bandor."

"Please be careful, Lindor. And please do not hurt my friend."

"I promise you, I will not cause him any pain."

"Your promises are always good with me."

"As are yours with me."

"Go to him." Bandor kissed Lindor on the forehead. "I will catch up with you later. I have some work to finish here."

Lindor broke away from him. On her way back, she peered briefly at Bandor who nodded and gently smiled. He refocused on his objective as Lindor returned to the pyramid.

Lindor sat poolside where Lauren and Brian were splashing water on their faces. The sun descended close to the western horizon, cooling the desert air and transforming the light blue eastern sky into a much darker shade.

"Liam," Mason called, admiring the sand dunes.

"What's up?"

"What do you make of this?"

At first, Liam couldn't identify the objects by the distant dunes. They emerged from and dove into the sand with tremendous speed, rhythm, and synchronization. They covered a vast amount of distance in the brief time Liam and Mason watched and were headed straight for the two observers.

"Desert dolphins."

"Desert dolphins?" Mason examined the life forms more closely. "You may be right. What the heck are dolphins doing in the desert?"

"You tell me. These are your murals."

"Lauren!" Mason called. "Brian! Lindor! Come see this!"

They rushed to investigate Mason and Liam's discovery.

"Dolphins!" Lauren exclaimed. "I love dolphins!"

"No way! Those can't be dolphins," Brian contended, "can they?"

"They're dolphins all right," Mason confirmed.

They all watched in a mild state of disbelief. The porpoises rhythmically advanced with orchestrated arching leaps in and out of the sand. They resembled bottle-nosed dolphins, but assumed the same color as their surroundings. Periodically, they released plumes of sand from their blowholes before disappearing below the surface. In total, twenty neared the pyramid.

As the sun dipped below the horizon, the Dropas positioned painted torches around the pyramid entrance to provide adequate lighting. The dolphins dove one last time into the sand, approximately fifty feet from the onlookers.

"Watch out!" Brian alerted everyone.

They all ducked in the nick of time as five dolphins emerged in front of the sandstone edge bordering the pool. Five more followed, then another pentad, and finally the last five. They leapt over the observers' heads and splashed into the water. The sand granules disappeared from their skin, so did their transparency. The Dropas rushed to Lindor. She redirected them into the pool, for they didn't need the protective suits inside the murals. Liam, Mason, Lauren, and Brian all had the same idea.

"Last one in the pool is a rotten egg!" Brian shouted.

They playfully shoved and elbowed each other like a band of little kids jockeying for position to jump in the pool first. One after another they dove, splashing water onto the sandstone. The dolphins had already engaged in familiar activities. Some propelled themselves backward through the water on their tails while others leapt high in the air and completed the descent with a thunderous splash. The light from the flames and glimmering stars reflected off and shone through their crystal-like bodies. Lindor chose not to partake in the playfulness, but instead relaxed at the edge of the pool.

The dolphins acquainted themselves with the Dropas, balancing them on their noses and flipping the giggling acrobats in the air to another nearby dolphin. In that moment, Liam smiled at how much aspects of the Dropas' giggling and gibbering resembled sounds of dolphins as they communicated with each other.

Lauren and Brian befriended another pair and requested the dolphins tow them around the pool. Mason played ball with two finned companions.

Liam chose a more daring activity. He beckoned two dolphins to meet him at the bottom where they positioned their noses under the soles of his feet and thrust him to the surface using their powerful tails. They launched him fifteen feet into the air like a missile from a submarine. Mason, Lauren, and Brian instantly craved the same thrill. Lauren outshined her companions. She utilized her gymnastics training by performing twists, flips, and gainers. The small, rapt audience admired her grace and beauty as she carried out her routines.

"You wasted little time acquainting yourselves with the desert dolphins," Bandor acknowledged from poolside.

"How did you know they were coming?" Mason asked.

Bandor smiled modestly. "I invited them."

"You invited—"

Lauren dunked Mason in the water.

"Yes, I invited them," Bandor replied after Mason resurfaced. "You guys could use a little fun before we continue our journey."

Liam winked at Bandor. "This is exactly what we all needed to relieve some tension."

Although his preoccupation with the matter at hand persisted, Bandor responded with another smile.

"Do you want to play with us?" Liam asked in a child-like tone.

"I pass."

Liam raised himself out of the water and sat on the sandstone. "You sure?"

"Positive. You guys should probably call it quits anyway. I have a strange feeling we will encounter some interesting challenges tomorrow, and the four of you will need to be well-rested."

"Understood." Liam cupped his hands around his mouth and yelled out to the others, "It's time to say good night to our new friends!"

Everyone bid farewell to the dolphins before exiting the pool. The dolphins re-established a four-row formation, met at one end, and accelerated to a speed where they gracefully completed their leaps into the desert sand. Within seconds they faded into the darkness.

Although Liam and the others felt every bit like they had been immersed in water, it was unnecessary to dry themselves after the swim. The day's journey and last bit of exercise had exhausted the visiting nomads. Because it was such a beautiful night, they slept under the starlit desert sky in the sleeping bags the Dropas had created. Bandor extinguished all but one torch. With the exception of Bandor and Lindor, they all fell into a deep sleep.

Unorthodox Migration

Bandor woke the mural travelers early the next morning. Their need for sleep diminished further. Utilizing those extra hours, Liam envisioned enhanced productivity of himself and others back home. Present in the murals for several mural days, he also appreciated the convenience of forfeiting meals, especially since his taste for certain foods or flavors was nonexistent inside the artwork. He felt more effective not wasting two or three hours a day preparing, eating, and cleaning up. The group broke camp and mounted the rounded-up mustangs.

"It will not take long for us to reach the next mural." Bandor checked everyone's readiness to ride.

"Then what?" Mason asked.

"We will change our mode of transportation to the eagles."

Right on cue, the Dropas danced and gibbered with excitement. The brief celebration halted after Bandor beckoned everyone to leave behind the desert inn and begin another day through the surreal world.

Judging from the low position of the sun, Bandor's prediction of a short ride that morning didn't disappoint. As he had speculated the previous day, the next mural that awaited entry seemed different. It appeared farther off in the distance. Liam and Lindor dismounted their mustang and joined Bandor who studied the intended destination with a puzzled expression.

"Is there a problem, Bandor?" Liam inquired.

"Off in the distance, do you see that?"

"Yes, that's the next mural we're entering."

"Exactly, but we are currently traveling away from it. If we stay on this path, we will return to the point where we originated this morning." Bandor stepped away from Liam and Lindor.

"How is that possible?" Lindor pivoted. "Bandor? Bandor!"

Bandor mysteriously vanished.

"Where is he?" Liam asked.

"I have no idea. He was here a second ago. Bandor!"

Liam knelt and investigated the sand in front of him. "Here are his footprints. One. Two. Three. And they disappear."

Lindor followed the indentations.

"Lindor!" Liam reached out for her arm. "Don't go any—"

Lindor virtually evaporated, crossing an invisible threshold. Liam called to the others who were preoccupied with the Dropas.

Mason detected consternation in Liam's voice. "Where are Bandor and Lindor?"

Liam pointed straight ahead at nothing.

"I don't see them." Lauren inched closer.

Liam straightened his right arm, preventing her from taking another step. "No, you don't, but they are there, somewhere."

"What happened?" Mason asked.

"Lindor and Bandor disappeared into some kind of void." Liam gently pushed the others away from the footprints. "And we will, too, if we're not careful where we walk."

Everyone except Liam thought they had reached the entrance to Dropa. Liam paid close attention to the Dropas whose lack of enthusiasm was not apparent to the others.

"Aren't you excited, Liam?" Mason inquired.

Liam detected no relevant clues. "It's not as it seems."

"Are you sure?" Mason's elation spilled over to the others. "This must be the portal to Dropa."

"The Dropas' reaction indicates otherwise. If we were only steps away from Dropa, they wouldn't be sitting quietly on our shoulders."

Mason's eagerness dissipated. Exhibiting no concern regarding the matter, Clearcoat leaned closer to Liam's ear and gibbered some instructions. He unmistakably received the message.

Liam sighed deeply. "We're going in."

"Without knowing what's on the other side?" Lauren asked, apprehensive.

"It will be all right, Lauren," Mason confided. "If the Dropas felt it wasn't safe, we wouldn't do it. Have faith in them."

Lauren smiled after Indigo gibbered to her in a comforting tone.

"Who's first?" Brian inquired hesitantly.

"We're entering together." Liam extended his arms.

They all tightly clasped hands. Liam and Mason nodded at each other and then at Lauren and Brian.

"Let's do it," Liam directed.

They each took one step forward, followed by another, and another. On the fourth step, they entered the invisible doorway. Strobing light among the predominant darkness replaced the bright desert sky. Unharmed, Lindor and Bandor awaited their arrival.

"At last, you made it."

"Happy we could oblige, Bandor," Liam offered, "wherever we are."

"Lindor and I have not established our location yet. From what I can tell, it appears we have entered a gap or perhaps a discontinuity within the mural system. Get down!" Bandor tackled Brian to the ground.

A light flash bolted over Brian's head, triggering a chorus of giggles at his new hairdo.

"What's so funny?"

"Those light flashes are electrically charged," Bandor explained. "It passed above you, causing your hair to stick out straight."

"They're more like miniature lightning bolts," Mason conjectured.

"Exactly." Bandor assisted Brian to his feet. "Individually, they do not seem to have a deadly charge, but I suggest avoiding them. The voltage increases when flashes combine or if you come in contact with them often enough."

"Speaking from experience, Bandor?" Liam inquired, half-jokingly.

"I am. As we awaited your arrival, I retrieved a lantern from my pocket and lit it. For some reason that intensified the flashes until they struck me and extinguished the flame. This place does not like fire or any additional light."

"Have you observed anything else?" Mason watched the periodic light emissions.

"During your entrance, and as we converse, the frequency of flashes around us has escalated," Lindor said softly. "We are a disturbance and the light bursts act as a defense mechanism. The amount of liquid flowing around us has also increased with your presence."

"What kind of liquid is it?"

"Honestly, Lauren, I have no idea," Lindor admitted. "There seems to be an intricate grid of pipes in here, but I do not understand the purpose."

"The light discharges originate from a separate network, much smaller than those carrying the liquid." Bandor waited for another set of flashes. "The light seems to be jumping across the conduits."

"I noticed the same thing," Mason confirmed.

Bandor led the group through the complex pipe system. Liam and Mason didn't recognize the mysterious place as a section of a mural Mason had painted nor did they associate it with any other art he had created—another painting or drawing perhaps—hoping it would tie in somehow. They navigated through the maze, confident they would make it through unscathed. Most of their effort focused on negotiating the numerous obstacles and dodging sporadic light flashes.

Water pipes were abundant in some areas, but scarce in others. Their sizes varied as well, the majority ranging from one to eight inches in diameter with others much larger. The latter ones were intricately designed to follow a path above and alongside steel girders and duct work. The network of smaller conduits extended along the walls and disappeared in the distance, but strangely, they produced the light flashes that jumped across the pipes and directly at the intruders.

Unlike the other artwork in which they had traveled, there wasn't much scenery—not that could be viewed anyway. The brilliant colors in Mason's murals had been replaced by grays and blacks when they could see, and darkness the rest of the time. It was difficult to recognize anything. Thinking about the unintended location, an escape plan, and the mission suppressed the dullness in that leg of the journey. The frequency of flashes tapered off the longer the intruders lingered—almost as if the place had become accustomed to them.

They traveled through the mysterious network for nearly three segments, briefly napping twice. Liam had no basis for estimating time in the new surroundings and the diminished necessity to sleep made it virtually impossible.

Despite the concentration needed to navigate the dark and unfamiliar environment, Liam's mind wandered. He reflected on friends, family, and the progression of the new global society. Liam chuckled at a non-related thought.

Mason interrupted Liam's daydream. "What's so funny?"

"I'm wondering about the excuse Willie offered the GGB officers who arrived to investigate the school alarm."

Mason laughed. "I'm sure he concocted a good one."

They had both inadvertently fallen back from the others. Mason propped himself up against a lower pipe and Liam sat on a large one.

"Any clue where we are?"

"Not at all, but since we're here, I want to investigate something." Mason gently plucked Gold off his shoulder. "Stay where you are, Liam, and hold steady. I'll create a disturbance to generate some additional light. Drop your head below the lowest pipe."

After Liam crouched to avoid getting zapped, Mason asked Gold to paint a torch. As expected, it attracted a fair amount of light flashes. That, combined with the actual light from the flame, was sufficient illumination for Mason to distinguish what puzzled him. Seconds later, Mason extinguished the torch, avoiding a similar hairstyling encounter to what Brian experienced.

"Notice anything?" Liam asked.

"Aside from the pipes, there's a wall behind you…with mortar seeping out of the joints."

"Did you say mortar?"

"We are behind the mural walls," they both concluded.

"When the light flashed in front of your face, the pipes faded," Mason added.

"Did they disappear?" Liam repositioned himself next to Mason.

"Not entirely, but rather phased in and out. This is wild." Mason whispered, "Where's your light source?"

Liam craned his neck. "What did you say?"

Mason jumped up from his seat. "The light source is wrong here. That's why he has us in darkness."

"He, meaning Arton?"

"Who else? Jeez, I should have realized this earlier. When I was inside Arton's studio, a number of his paintings seemed strange to me. I didn't say anything at the time because of the circumstances. In those paintings, the light source was wrong. Liam, when the light flashed, not only did the pipes phase, but your shadow was in front of you. In order to be correct, your shadow should have been cast upon the wall and the pipes behind you."

"We're not trapped behind the walls," Liam deduced. "If we were, our need to breathe would have returned."

"Where are we?"

Liam retraced the journey in his mind. The forest. The plain. The "Serengeti."

The desert. And this place. Liam drew a blank until the joyful gibbering of the preoccupied Dropas jolted his memory.

"Of course!" Liam yelled. "That's it!"

Mason jumped back, startled by Liam's outburst. "What's it?"

"We're missing one piece to this puzzle."

"Oh good, another puzzle."

"How do you get to the rear of something when in front of it?"

"Walk behind it," Mason replied confidently.

"Yes, but what if the obvious path prohibited you from doing that?"

Mason had no answer. Liam asked the Dropas to estimate the distance traveled "behind" the murals.

"The Dropas believe the distance covered here is almost equal to what was traversed inside the murals. If they are correct, we should be near the end."

Mason furrowed his brow. "This place or the murals as a whole?"

"This place."

"How are you able to verify this as the end?"

"I'm getting to that." Liam maneuvered over a conduit. He rested his hand on Mason's shoulder as one Dropa squeezed its way out between his two fingers. "If we're trapped in what I think we are, we should reach the forest soon. That Arton is a clever one."

"We're in a Möbius loop, like the one you made for the Dropas the night before we left."

"More precisely, it's a Möbius mural loop." Liam raised his hands in front of his face, careful not to whack his head on any overhanging pipes. "Arton didn't merely create a regular loop because it wouldn't detour us for as long, but—"

"The Möbius mural loop would take at least twice as long."

"At a minimum. If we failed to discover the anomaly the first time, we would wander through this loop until we did."

"Liam!" Lindor called from ahead. "Mason! Check this out!"

Liam knew what Lindor wanted to show them. They followed the light flashes and caught up with the others, minus Bandor.

"Bandor is gone!"

"Follow him!" Liam instructed emphatically.

Lindor ducked as the frequency of the electrical discharges increased. "Follow him?"

"Go!" Liam guided everyone forward. "We've wasted enough time!" He was the last to vacate the darkness.

And there they were, standing in the sunflower garden—the place where they had first arrived in the murals.

A dejected Bandor propped against a sturdy stalk. "We have traveled in a circle for three suns plus who knows how long in the darkness." Bandor rubbed his hands over his disheartened face.

Lindor attempted to console him. Unseen by the others, Bandor tugged at his pocket and whispered something to Lindor. She shook her head in disagreement.

Mason approached his dear friend. "It will be all right, Bandor."

"Easier said than done. We have gone nowhere and further distanced ourselves from Arton."

"No time to sulk." Liam clutched Lindor's hand and led her through the garden. "Follow me!"

"Where?" Bandor questioned.

"We need to find our footprints! Will you contact the forest trees?" Liam conveyed to Bandor what message he needed communicated.

Without hesitating, Bandor transmitted the request to their wooded friends. He informed Liam when the trees were ready. "What about the footprints?"

"Lauren and Brian, you two are unaware of the game I created for the Dropas because you had already left. Do you know what a Möbius loop is?"

"Yes," they replied.

"Good. Bandor, do you recall me making the Möbius loops for the Dropas?"

"Out of streamers, right?"

"Yes, and we have just traveled through a Möbius mural loop. What we exited was a virtual backside of the murals created by Arton."

"Of course," Brian agreed, "all those pipes. That makes sense, but whose footprints do we need to find?"

"Our own."

"We've been through a lot of murals. Our footprints are all over the place," Lauren contended.

"No, not all of our footprints," Liam clarified, "only those in the desert sand where we went from the front of the murals to the back."

"I am beginning to understand," Bandor acknowledged. "We need to find the spot where the loop is attached."

"Precisely." Liam resumed his quickened pace to the forest. "Once there, we can sever the connection. That should launch us to the next mural."

"It is a good thing we only went through once," Lindor commented.

"We're not in the clear yet," Liam reminded everyone. "We must disconnect the loop, careful not to cross over to the backside. If we do, we'll have to repeat the process—Arton's intention all along—due to its one-directional nature."

They reached the forest edge where the trees awaited their arrival. The six closest trees each lowered a long limb. Everyone climbed aboard and braced themselves for another carnival ride. To make up for lost time, this was the most viable means to rapidly get them through the woodland. Liam briefly explained that they would be passed from limb to limb until reaching the grassland on the opposite side of the forest.

The trees initiated the unique mode of transportation. Although somewhat daunted at first by the ground passing underneath them, they gained confidence that the trees wouldn't err during the progression. Occasionally, Lauren exuberantly screamed as if riding on a roller coaster. Everyone enjoyed the unique excursion. Nearing the perimeter, the trees launched the passengers into the air because the distance was too great to simply pass them between branches. Those exchanges provided the most exhilarating transitions. As for the Dropas, they delighted in yet another flying experience.

They reached the far side of the forest in considerably less time than it had taken to hike through it during the initial trip. Bandor summoned the fastest mustangs for the next leg of the journey. The friendly prairie dogs greeted the travelers, but everyone regretfully declined the invitation to play with their furry companions. However, Liam requested that a dozen dogs accompany him. They graciously thanked their wooded comrades and mounted the mustangs. The trees felt honored that they assisted in the mission to stop Arton.

Unlike the first trip through the grassland, everybody rode solo and raced much faster than the slower mustangs they had previously ridden. The Dropas' decision to sit near each horse's mane instantly resulted in a comical adventure.

The Dropas had created small saddles and secured them to the mustangs' necks. The tiny riders exhibited a whole new appearance as the horses blazed through the tall grass. The heads of the Dropas stretched far behind their bodies, resembling thin brush strokes. Seeing them splatter on countless occasions, Liam expected their heads to detach and be lost forever. Even Bandor enjoyed the unusual form of entertainment the Dropas had unintentionally performed.

There was no time for sightseeing during the second ride. Due to the rapidly passing scenery, Liam and the others barely recognized what they had witnessed the first time. They needed less than half as long to reach the desert oasis. Accustomed to the lengthy time in the saddles, the riders' legs no longer wriggled like loose Jell-O molds after dismounting.

The Dropas expended a great deal of effort preventing their noggins from blowing off their bodies which resulted in them locking into an unconventional position. The Dropas resembled a dozen pieces of stretched, inedible taffy. Consequently, they required time to reposition and reshape their heads. Liam, Mason, Lauren, and Brian used that opportunity to take a short nap as their sleep requirement was almost nonexistent.

Bandor led them to the intended destination. "Here we are. I hope your theory is correct, Liam."

"As do I. Allow me to commend you on our speedy arrival, Bandor."

"Give the credit where it belongs." Bandor stroked his horse's mane. "To the trees and the mustangs."

"Bandor! Liam!" Mason knelt near the invisible seam. "Here are the footprints where we disappeared behind the walls!"

Liam reached for Lindor's hand, but Bandor had already escorted her in the opposite direction. "Careful, don't go too far, Brian."

"Liam, what are Bandor and Lindor doing?" Mason asked.

"They'll be back shortly. Bandor commented to Lindor about contacting the desert dolphins."

While waiting for the porpoises' arrival, Liam instructed the Dropas to disperse themselves astride the prairie dogs and await his signal. Once in position, Liam indicated to the miniature excavators to commence digging.

"What are they searching for, Liam?" Lauren asked.

"They're locating the seam where the two ends of the murals are attached." Liam pointed in the general vicinity of the junction. "Once they locate it, they will implant a marker, and the dolphins will sever the connection."

Brian tenderly wrapped his arm around Lauren. "What happens to us?"

"If all goes well, we will end up at the eagle mural as originally planned."

"And if it doesn't go as planned?" Lauren asked.

"Your guess is as good as mine, but let's stay positive."

"The dolphins should be here in no time," Lindor affirmed. "Have the Dropas located the seam?"

"Not yet," Mason replied, alert for any sign of success.

"What's that?" Brian shouted.

Two hundred feet away, a marker popped up six feet above the sand. Followed by another one. And another. Every hundred feet the Dropas discharged a white flag attached to a pole to help indicate the path of the seam. And consistent with their usual playfulness, a picture of twelve Dropas decorated each banner. Again, they made light of a dire situation.

"Whew! That was close," Mason said as Liam prevented his brother from falling over to the other side.

The sudden appearance of the nearest marker—inches from where he knelt—startled Mason. Had he crossed the seam, he would have entered the mural backside. The others would have had to either follow Mason or wait for him to complete the loop again. In either case, it would have prolonged the expedition.

The prairie dogs emerged from the depths of the sand, waggling the residual grains from their furry bodies. The Dropas exulted over their latest accomplishment, waving arms and nearly falling off their respective rodents.

"The dolphins are here," Lindor announced joyfully.

Bandor transmitted detailed orders. Without hesitation, the dolphins submerged into the sand and positioned themselves along the markers. Seconds later, one dolphin surfaced and communicated with Bandor. His expression indicated a slight problem had arisen.

"What's wrong, Bandor?" Liam asked.

"Call it a minor setback. The dolphins cannot properly position their teeth to sever the tightly-connected seam. They are assembling reinforcements comprised of marlin and lobsters. The marlin will use their bills to cut into the seam and the lobsters will ride the dolphins and snip any remaining threads. In the meantime, let me explain what will happen to us." Bandor positioned everyone with their backs along the seam. "When the ends detach, we will launch in the direction of the eagle mural. The loop is under extreme tension and the force will be powerful as it restores itself to its original state. Tightly lock arms with the person next to you. We must end up in the same location, whether or not it is our planned destination. If we lose anyone, we cannot go back for you."

The Dropas playfully imitated the procedure, interlocking arms across Liam and Mason's shoulders. Bandor snapped his fingers and the Dropas dispersed into the closest shirt pockets. He positioned himself at the opposite end of Lindor. They acted as stabilizers for the human airship.

"The lobsters and marlin are here. As they sever the seam, the tension will increase beneath our feet. Brace yourself as that happens, because you will only feel it for an instant. Hold on tight, everyone. I am giving the signal."

Liam tilted his head forward, catching a glimpse of Mason and the kids before making eye contact with Lindor. He felt her arm tighten around his as she reciprocated his smile. As he spoke, words he never expected to utter again, the ends disconnected beneath his feet.

"Woo hoo!" Lauren and Brian yelled.

The passengers were airborne. And what an exhilarating ride it was, flying and tumbling without nausea. It was impossible to identify the exact murals they entered and exited. Liam saw mountains, then water, then desert, then forest. The sporadic screams persisted on that mural thrill ride as Liam tried to gauge their location.

The sky transitioned from a panoramic sunset to bright blue and revealed one of Mason's "turning pages." They were destined for outer space through the exposed area behind the drooping corner. Because of Liam's height, the toe of his hiking boot clipped the peeling paper, changing their trajectory.

"Hold on tight!" Bandor yelled.

Upon entering the outer space behind the peel, a shooting star intersected them and whisked away the human flyers. The slightest probability they had of reaching the eagle mural vanished. The shooting star faded, and they were free-flying in space. Seeing their dilemma, the ghosted Warrior in an adjacent mural pulled back a portion of its sunset sky, allowing them to enter its mural. Their speed tapered off as they traveled through a series of Indian reservations. Unfortunately, their current flight path would lead them directly into a huge bonfire amidst three large teepees.

"Save us, Warrior Spirit!" Lauren yelled.

They traveled through the mural of her school—a female Warrior Spirit with its sky cloak spread wide, exposing a celestial reservation. Instantly, the spirit draped the cloak closed, shielding them from entering the towering flames of the cosmic bonfire. Unsure if they would have been affected by the intense heat, but greatly relieved the question went unanswered, the group entered yet another blue sky.

"This is awesome!" Mason yelled in Liam's ear.

"What's the next destination?"

"I have no—"

They plunged to the ground and tumbled in the high grass.

Bandor arose first. "Is everyone all right?"

"We're okay down here," Mason replied with a muffled tone from underneath Brian and Lauren.

"We're good." Liam and Lindor confirmed.

Internal Struggle

Liam examined the present mural. "Recognize where we are?"

"Not yet," Mason replied. "It's a fairly simple one though."

"Nothing more than another one of your blue skies," Lauren commented.

"That's the confusing thing. You have the sky and this ground, but there's no theme here. Any thoughts, Bandor?"

"No, it seems like the basic background of most of your murals." Bandor raised his arm to silence everyone. "Did you hear that?"

Weak, high-pitched sounds emanated from a distant location.

"Where are the Dropas?" Liam questioned, noticing his empty shirt pocket. "I wonder if something happened to them on the landing."

"They're not in my pocket either," Mason confirmed.

Bandor gestured broadly with his arms. "Spread out and head in the direction of those faint noises."

During the search, the sounds grew more distressful. They neared a canyon in the next mural where the screeches echoed off the stone walls.

"There they are." Lindor noticed the Dropas first.

The Dropas darted at her, frantically waving their arms and gibbering so fast that no one could understand the message. The search party closed the gap.

"Clearcoat, what is wrong?" Lindor asked calmly.

The lead Dropa jumped onto her palm and explained the situation.

"Oh no!" Lindor hurried into a cave carved in the canyon wall. "Follow me! Robohawk is in here!"

That particular cave differed slightly from others lining the canyon. No boulders or trees obscured the entrance—simply a prominent hole within the rocky chasm.

Jaws dropped upon arriving. The powerful Robohawk lay helplessly on the ground, crumpled up in a ball with its massive wings limp on the cave floor and its head wedged between two small boulders. It barely had the strength to screech because corrosion had consumed its metallic structure. Small puffs of dust periodically rose from the dirt floor as the corroded material fell off the hawk's body.

Lauren rushed to the wounded bird. "Who did this to you?"

"If Robohawk's condition is any indication of what has happened to other mascots, it explains my inability to contact them," Bandor concluded.

"Arton's evil is propagating throughout the murals with his renewed strength," Lindor added.

Suddenly, everyone shared the burden Bandor had been carrying.

"We must act fast," Liam advised. "Clearcoat, seal the entrance."

Clearcoat and the other Dropas swiftly responded before engaging in a short conversation with Mason.

"We have work to do." Mason assumed control of the situation.

Up close, Robohawk's condition was more gruesome. Deteriorated sections detached from the rest of its body, ready to slide off like ice sheets from a glacial face. The Dropas swiftly painted a neutralizing liquid across Robohawk's body to halt the escalation of further damage and created wire brushes for Bandor and the others to remove the corrosion. They worked furiously together, hoping to revive their companion. Lauren concentrated on the area around Robohawk's face, soothing the massive creature with her soft voice. The hawk's distraught sounds slowly diminished as everyone tended to the broken mass.

After the initial preparation, a magnificent, almost miraculous set of events occurred. Bandor handed Mason two airbrushes from his pocket. Red and Blue made some modifications, creating two compressorless devices. They retrieved a pair of hoses from Bandor, connecting one set of ends to the airbrushes and the other ends to Silver and Gold—a direct supply of paint to the implements. Together, Mason and his tiny assistants initiated Robohawk's resurrection.

Meanwhile, Liam huddled the others and requested they do whatever they could to infuse exuberance within the cave. All responded admirably, grasping hands and directing positive energy at Mason and the Dropas: Bandor and Lindor projected a Dropian aura as only they could, Liam visualized Robohawk in its most majestic form, and Brian and Lauren offered encouraging words throughout the restoration process.

Working in unison, the Dropas rapidly reconnected the detached parts and Mason repainted the damaged and missing areas. Delicately, but in earnest, they revitalized Robohawk to its original splendor. Absorbed in their own artistry, Mason and the Dropas were oblivious to the others who closely observed the magic unfold. Optimism supplanted trepidation.

At last, Mason stepped to the side. "Give Robohawk some room."

Mason popped the air hose ends from the torsi of Silver and Gold, their bodies wriggling like gelatin. They each massaged their bellies after the disconnection.

The other Dropas removed the temporary barrier, allowing all to leave and wait in anticipation. Robohawk emerged from the cave into the brightness of the canyon. The sunlight, still visible above the canyon walls, reflected dramatically off the massive bird's newly-created, golden body, forcing the observers to squint and shield their eyes. And then, as if on cue, the customary, ear-piercing screech of their beloved friend echoed throughout the canyon.

"Gold-plated titanium," Mason affirmed, beaming with satisfaction.

"That is one awesome-looking bird," Brian proclaimed.

"Robohawk will lead the other mural creatures once more." Lauren hugged the glimmering mascot.

"You did a wonderful job, Mason," Bandor commended. "We will need every bit of its restored power."

"Thanks, Bandor." Mason lifted the Dropas onto Robohawk.

Before anyone batted an eye, they gibbered joyously as they glided down the bird. Locating a curve in its armor, they completed their slide across the outstretched wing and into Mason's chest.

"Don't you wish you were a Dropa?" Lauren clutched Brian's arm.

"That would be awesome."

Shadows lengthened as the setting sun would soon disappear behind the canyon walls.

"You guys need to sleep," Bandor instructed.

"A bit early for that, isn't it, Bandor?" Lauren questioned.

"Yes, but based on your reduced requirements, it will be the last time."

They all retreated into Robohawk's lair. The newly refurbished bird and the Dropas stayed outside on guard duty. The miniature sentries entertained themselves by periodically executing a changing of the guard ritual.

Inside the cave, those who needed sleep unrolled a personal sleeping bag the Dropas had supplied before taking their posts. Bandor settled on the cave floor next to the single lit torch. He closed his eyes and rested his head on the stone wall, contemplating the next series of events. The dull whispers between Brian,

Lauren, and Mason faded as they each drifted off to sleep. The cave felt chilly, but like the heat in the desert, the temperature had no adverse effect.

Lindor snuggled next to Liam after removing her shoes. "What were you about to say to me just before we launched?"

"I have fallen in love with you," Liam replied softly.

A huge smile lit up Lindor's face. Liam grew warm as the two lay together, a warmth unlike any other he had felt. From the first time their eyes met, a shared energy flowed between them. A euphoric sensation passed through his midsection—beginning with a slight tickle that rapidly intensified. The source? His heart. The uncontrollable energy and sensation traveled into his arms and legs. His eyes closed tighter and a single teardrop seeped out from underneath each of his eyelids. Lindor experienced similar sensations. Liam's energy traveled through her and hers through him, gently massaging his heart. His limbs tingled from the out-of-body experience. Although he physically remained in one piece, his soul had traveled inside Lindor. Their bodies quivered as the sensation escalated to yet another level. He didn't want it to end, convinced their hearts and souls had coalesced.

When the sensation subsided, both souls returned to their own bodies. Lindor tightened her grip on Liam's hand and listened to his slowing heartbeat.

"Did you feel—" Liam whispered.

"Of course, I did." Lindor brought Liam's hand to her lips and gently kissed the top of it.

"I'm glad we experienced it together," Liam whispered.

"Something as wonderful as that can only be shared by two people totally in love." Lindor nestled her head into his chest. "Go to sleep, my precious one. Bandor will be waking you soon."

Liam kissed her forehead.

"Wake up." Bandor nudged Mason's body. "Wake up, Mason."

Unlike Mason's usual resentful morning greeting to consciousness, his eyes opened immediately. "I'm wide awake, Bandor."

"Not used to that, are you?" Bandor knelt between Brian and Lauren and gently shook them. "Rise and shine."

Brian and Lauren also awoke energized.

"How long did we sleep, Bandor?" Lauren asked.

"Only a short time."

"From now on, sleep is unnecessary?" Brian stretched out his arms and waited for a yawn to follow, but nothing happened.

"Not one wink," Bandor assured.

Liam felt a soft kiss on his lips and his eyes opened instantly, not yet grasping the unusual phenomenon of awakening devoid the residual effects of slumber.

"Did you sleep well?" Lindor whispered.

"Exceptionally well, and you?" Liam chuckled at his momentary memory loss. "Forget I asked."

"Liam! Lindor!" Bandor called from the cave entrance.

"Come on." Lindor arose first. "Something is troubling Bandor."

"What's wrong, Bandor?" Liam asked.

"Notice anything peculiar?"

Liam surveyed the canyon without initially finding anything. However, an abnormality in the sky caught his eye. Darkness was prevalent.

"Shouldn't the morning sun be rising in the east?" Liam inquired.

"It is not rising." Bandor pointed to the west. "When we retired to the cave, the sun was dipping behind those walls, yet well above the horizon. You barely slept. It should not be this dark."

"What's causing it?" Mason flicked his ear as Blue tickled it.

"My guess is that Arton continues blackening the murals."

"That's not surprising, especially with the amount of corrosion on Robohawk," Liam said.

"He is sealing the murals to prevent anyone from entering," Lindor affirmed.

"Or exiting," Mason added.

"Follow me," a distracted Bandor beckoned the others. "A shadow is moving across the canyon rim. There it is again. Come on." He picked up the pace.

Before anyone covered much ground, the dirt swirled behind them. Unexpectedly, Robohawk's talons grasped all six bodies in one swoop. Four quick flaps of its wings and they arrived at the top of the wall. The giant bird released its grip, gently setting them on the plateau. Robohawk veered skyward, gracefully gliding above the canyon as they inspected the mysterious shadow.

"That's odd," Mason commented. "It's like looking through a filthy window."

"There's the shadow," Brian whispered, "and it's darker."

"We must be getting closer to it," Lindor acknowledged.

"What do you suppose it is?" Lauren refused to take any more steps.

"Nothing's creating it...as if it has a life of its own," Liam conjectured.

Bandor motioned to the Dropas. "Whatever it is, we will soon find out."

The Dropas darted at the shadow. The onlookers waited quietly, captivated by what transpired next. Each Dropa created a rope for itself with spikes attached on one end. They positioned themselves in front of the shadow, anticipating its next move. The animated darkness inched closer. The Dropas instantly dispersed and collectively lassoed the figure: two ropes around each arm, two around each leg, and four around its head. Within seconds, they had captured the anomaly and anchored the spikes to the inside wall of the mural. The Dropas proudly exhibited their catch, each wearing a ten-gallon hat.

The silhouette became clearer, and the face more familiar, as Liam closely examined it. "Willie?"

* * * * *

The custodian led Willie and Roberto into the school, navigating through the hallways to the gym. He unlocked the door and entered with the visitors. "I'll show you what the kids discovered this afternoon." His jaw dropped after switching on the lights. "Where is it?"

Willie and Roberto approached the Robohawk mural. Not only had the giant metallic bird disappeared, but the mural was darkening as well.

"Where's Robohawk? It was bad enough this afternoon when the students said the bird was corroding, but it's completely gone."

"Do you have a hydraulic lift?" Willie wanted to inspect the mural up-close.

"Yeah, I'll drive it over to you."

"What do you make of this?" Roberto inquired.

"I'm not sure." Willie scratched his chin. "I presume this is Arton's work. Liam and the others had to enter a mural that hadn't lost its colors yet. I don't know what he hopes to achieve by blackening the murals, unless—"

"Unless what?"

"What if this prevents them from leaving? They would be stuck inside the artwork with no means of escape."

"Can we do anything to counteract the effect?"

Before Willie answered, the custodian arrived with the requested machinery and jumped off. Willie boarded, positioned the lift below the mural, and raised the platform to where Robohawk used to be. He extended the platform and examined the painting, pacing as he searched for clues.

"What the heck are those shadows?" Willie murmured.

"What did you say, Willie?" Roberto yelled.

"There are shadows moving inside the mural." Willie positioned his eyes close to the wall. "Ahh!"

"Willie!" Roberto rapidly scaled the lift. When he reached the platform, he laughed uncontrollably.

Willie's arms and legs were tied to the mural with two ropes apiece. Four additional ropes tightly secured his head against the wall.

"Is it funny?" Willie questioned in a muffled voice, struggling to talk with his mouth smashed against the cinder blocks.

"Willie?" A voice came from inside the mural…

*　*　*　*　*

Willie stared into the mural, even more surprised by the voices emanating from the walls. He recognized Liam inching closer. "I should have known you were behind this little escapade."

Barely able to understand him because of the restraint, Liam had the Dropas remove the spikes from the inside face of the wall, freeing Willie from capture.

Willie massaged his cheeks, restoring the circulation. "What just happened?"

Liam detailed to Willie and Roberto the current events and then briefly described the journey through the artwork.

"Arton has disturbed numerous murals already," Willie updated Liam.

"We need a favor from you, Willie," Bandor requested.

"No problem." Willie backed away and braced himself against the railing. "As long as I'm not required to enter any mural."

"I want to go inside the wall," Roberto said enthusiastically.

"Be my guest." Willie motioned for Roberto to step inside the painting.

278 The Dropas: Transcendental Journey

The eager teen face-planted the wall. "Ow!" He vigorously rubbed his head in an attempt to relieve the pain.

"Sorry, Roberto," Mason said, "maybe another time."

"Roberto, we will need you to assist Willie," Bandor instructed.

"Yeah, sure, no problem," Roberto grimaced, still massaging his noggin.

Bandor retrieved a container out of his pocket and the Dropas loaded it with torches. He slowly pushed the container through the outside of the mural.

Willie accepted it. "What do you want me to do with these?"

Bandor retracted his arm. "Those are special torches that will light up the murals. You and Roberto must distribute them among the blackened ones."

Willie furrowed his brow. "How do we light them?"

"Throw two torches directly at the mural, hard enough to penetrate the wall. The force will ignite them."

"Are two enough?" Willie asked.

"It should be. They will burn brightly and serve as beacons for locating the murals." Bandor tilted his head to the left. "They will also allow us to exit."

"What is it, Bandor?" Lindor questioned.

"I spotted a silhouetted figure heading down into the canyon," Bandor replied. "One more thing, Willie."

"I'm listening." Willie already had his hand on the control box.

"I need you to go to the mural with the Thinker painted in it." The movement in the canyon again diverted Bandor's attention.

"There it is. I'm on it." Mason pursued the figure.

"We need to be on our way, Willie," Bandor declared. "Find the Thinker and instruct it to visit this mural. We have strayed off course, and it will furnish directions to the portal. Be swift, Willie. Dispatch the Thinker first before distributing the other torches."

"Until we meet again, my friend." Liam pushed his hand out of the artwork, although not as far as Bandor could, and struggled to hold it in that position.

Willie grasped Liam's hand and gave it a hard squeeze. "Yeah, we better meet again." He released his grip and lowered the lift. "Good luck."

Liam's hand snapped back inside the mural. Gazing out at his best friend, he questioned for the first time whether he would return. Willie and Roberto reached the gym floor, jumped off the lift, and thanked the custodian.

Willie and his young assistant hurried through the corridors and out to the parking lot. He said nothing en route to the school where the Thinker resided. Roberto's attempt to converse was stilted before he finally gave up, letting Willie mentally wallow in silence. Upon reaching the school, they had no problem entering, but encountered one minor distraction once inside the building.

"Paul's the name. Custodial engineering is my game. May I help you, gentlemen?"

"I'm Willie Thompson and this is Roberto." Willie flashed his badge. "I'm with the GGB and we're here to inspect the mural with the Thinker in it."

"No identification necessary." Paul enjoyed his newfound, but dubious position of power, such that he could be of important assistance to the GGB. "How could anyone forget your face? Wow, the head of the GGB, live and in person. Come on in."

Willie and Roberto chuckled at Paul's customary misconception. As they followed their guide, Willie handed his radio to Roberto and whispered some instructions.

"No matter what I clean that mural with, I can't seem to remove the blackness in the one section." Paul led them down the next corridor. "The other paint seems to come off, but not the black stuff."

"The other paint?" Willie expected the worst had happened.

"I better call Mason to come touch up the artwork. I accidentally removed a naked man throwing a frisbee before realizing I used the wrong cleaner."

Willie and Roberto exchanged dismayed expressions. Roberto veered off by himself and zeroed in on the correct frequency. Paul received a call on his radio as he let Willie into the cafeteria.

"Paul," Roberto's voice crackled over the speaker.

Paul pressed the talk button. "Roger that," he replied, lifting his thumb to hear the response.

"Can you come down to the boiler room A-S-A-P?"

Paul neglected to depress the button. "That's a 10-98 here. Sounds like a Code 8-High." Paul reconnected the radio to his belt with a flourish. "Willie, can you handle this situation without me?"

"Oh, I'd prefer it that way, Paul." Willie rolled his eyes at Paul's bungled use of police codes. "Thanks for your help."

Paul sauntered down the hallway, failing to notice Roberto standing around the corner. When Paul reached the boiler room to assist the "co-worker" who radioed him, he remembered being the only person on duty. And due to his absent-mindedness, he had already forgotten the visitors in the building.

Willie and Roberto entered the cafeteria, pleasantly surprised by what awaited them. Paul had wiped away the Ancient Olympic discus thrower on the left side of the mural. However, the Thinker, with its body formed by nebulas and constellations from its head to below its kneecap, remained intact and unaffected by the impending darkness.

"This should be interesting, Roberto. How do I talk to a painting?" Willie approached the wall. "Yo, Thinker. Wake up, man."

No response.

"Hey, Thinker! Can you hear me? I have a message for you." Willie shrugged at the lack of response. "Any ideas, Roberto?"

Roberto cupped his hands around his mouth. "Dude! Get up! My friend here has something to tell you!"

"Well done," Willie said jokingly. "Wait a second." He set down the container of torches. "This will wake it up."

"If it doesn't, I'm not sure what will."

"Throw one at its feet, Roberto."

Roberto wound up like a major league pitcher and hurled a strike at the Thinker's blueprint-looking lower legs. The torch penetrated the wall, lighting on impact underneath the Thinker's left foot. From its resting position, the huge foot lifted slightly and extinguished the flame.

"Perfect. Someone else to stamp out forest fires."

Roberto grabbed Willie's arm. The Thinker raised its head off its right hand and made eye contact with Willie and Roberto.

"Why did you choose to burn me?" the Thinker bellowed in a galactic voice.

"To get your attention," Willie replied. "You were ignoring us."

"I was thinking. That is what I do."

"Please stop thinking for a minute and listen."

"Speak."

"My friends need your assistance. It's urgent. They are trapped in the Robohawk mural. Bandor says you can help them find some kind of portal."

"Yes, I can assist them. They are with the mighty Robohawk?"

"That's what I said," Willie answered.

"I will go to them."

Before Willie or Roberto spoke, the Thinker rose from its perch and disappeared into the postcard of outer space painted behind it.

"Come on, let's distribute these." Willie handed Roberto two torches. "We have our work cut out for us. This is one of many murals."

Roberto hurled the torches at the wall, igniting them on contact.

Bandor and the others caught up with Mason who was hiding behind a large boulder. Without saying a word, Mason pointed at a location halfway down the canyon, his eyes fixated on the silhouette. Bandor communicated to the circling Robohawk. Bandor exploited the bird's superior visual capabilities, especially as the canyon darkened. Utilizing its keen eyesight and silent flying ability, Robohawk retracted its wings and torpedoed at its prey. The onlookers watched in astonishment as the mighty bird displayed its prowess. Gaining speed as it descended, it waited until the last second to extend its talons at the interloper.

"Let go of me!" the individual cried out as Robohawk screeched in triumph.

The Dropas arranged a dozen flares to mark a circular landing strip. Seconds later, Robohawk released its prey in the center.

"Look who it is!" Lauren recognized Cooper lying on the ground.

His face full of rage and revenge, Cooper rose to his feet. "Where are the murderers?" Frantically his head swung from side to side, ready to attack anything that came near him. "There you are! You two killed my brother!"

"Killed your brother?" Liam responded, dumbfounded. "Where did that brainchild originate?"

"Arton, no doubt," Mason presumed.

Cooper reached into his pocket. Bandor snapped his fingers and within seconds, the Dropas enveloped Cooper in a cocoon of duct tape, leaving only his head exposed. Liam couldn't wait to hear the ridiculous story Arton implanted into his young companion's mind.

"Welcome back, Cooper," Lauren said hesitantly. "Is Ti with you?"

"You two are so stupid," Cooper admonished, avoiding Lauren's question. "Mason and Liam murdered Carl before the war. Arton told me the whole story, and I pictured their faces as I recalled the events."

"Cooper," Brian calmly spoke as he knelt beside his best friend, "you always told me I reminded you of Carl, right?"

"What's your point?" Cooper barked.

Bandor gently held back Liam and Mason whose urge to intervene was evident. "Let Brian talk to him first," Bandor whispered.

Liam and Mason deferred to Bandor's suggestion.

Brian slowly peeled off a strip of tape. "Do you trust me, Cooper?"

Cooper squirmed for a moment. "Of course, I do."

"Do you trust Lauren?"

"Yes."

Brian removed the tape one strip at a time. "Cooper, remember the story about Arton that Bandor told us in Liam's apartment?"

Cooper quizzically glanced at Brian. Lauren nodded in agreement with Brian.

"Do you remember?"

Cooper, unwilling to admit that he did, freed his left arm from the tape.

"Listen to me, Cooper." Brian recaptured his friend's attention. "Bandor told us that Arton is a shape-shifting demigod. He penetrated your mind, filled it with negative thoughts, and turned you against Liam and Mason."

Lauren assisted Brian by removing the last strips. "Cooper, Liam and Mason are like family to you. Remember how Liam watched out for us on our last adventure? They would have never harmed Carl. Besides, the police apprehended the men who killed your brother down the street from your house."

Cooper sat up and, with fear and confusion in his eyes, glanced at Liam and Mason. "Are you sure they didn't murder my brother?"

"Yes," Brian and Lauren both replied with absolute conviction.

Cooper focused on the Dropas standing between his knees. "Are you guys certain?"

The Dropas nodded solemnly.

His face covered in dirt and his eyes open wide, Cooper rose to his feet. Sorrow replaced his disorientation and misdirected anger. Tears streamed down his face, leaving clean trails through the dirt on his cheeks.

"I am sorry." Cooper hugged Mason.

"It's all right."

Cooper embraced Liam next. "Liam, will you ever forgive me?"

"I already have, Cooper."

Bandor called to Robohawk. The winged transport swooped down, picked up the passengers in its talons, and carried everyone to the canyon floor.

"Omigosh, Ti! What have I done?"

"Is she alive, Cooper?" Lauren inquired excitedly.

"I can't believe I abandoned her, and with Arton no less."

"Was she alive when you left?" Lindor asked.

"Yes, but she could be dead by now."

"Knowing Arton, she is worth more to him alive," Bandor answered vehemently. "Arton is counting on us to come after her."

Bandor was ready to step into the cave when Robohawk's warning screech alerted him. The Dropas scattered among the rocks.

"Watch out, Liam!" Mason yelled.

Before Liam could react, a mutated Warrior from Cooper's army tightly secured its tentacles around him. As he struggled to free himself, the Warrior sealed the rest of his body like cellophane. It shifted its torso to the top of Liam's head and repeated the same maneuver. It couldn't suffocate Liam because he no longer needed to breathe, but it wasn't doing that at all. Much like the discolored bubble Mason encountered the evening of the Bubble Festival, the two-dimensional creature attempted to alter its victim's attitude. It pushed its tentacles into Liam's ears, preparing itself to inject his mind with negative impressions. Concealed in the cocoon, Liam could do nothing to remove the creature from his head. Its tentacles penetrated deep inside his inner ears, making their way toward his brain.

Everyone else was preoccupied with their own two-dimensional adversary. Bandor managed to peel the long-tooth wildcat from his body before it sank its exaggerated claws into his head. He crumpled the creature in a ball and threw it against a rocky projection. The wildcat rolled to the ground, unfurled into its original shape, and relentlessly pursued Bandor.

The Dropas, donned in swashbuckling outfits and scimitars drawn, sliced away at the countless beasts that attacked the three teens. Unaffected by the myriad slices through their bodies, the two-dimensional creatures sustained a relentless onslaught on their enemies. Unaware their severed body parts dangled freely, they were determined to reshape their victims' minds.

Spiked horses trapped Mason and Lindor inside the cave. Each horse tried ramming its armor into their bodies, hoping to pin them against the walls. Red, Orange, and Yellow did away with the swords and replaced them with flame-throwers. Silver and Gold came to Liam's rescue, meticulously slicing the tentacled Warrior away from him. As it limped across the ground, Red and Orange discharged a barrage of flames at the fallen creature, disintegrating it instantly. Next, they assisted Yellow, blasting away at the armored-spiked horses. They too vaporized.

The other Dropas continued carving up the enduring Warriors and wildcats. The creatures appeared as though they had been inserted into a paper shredder. Nonetheless, they protracted their pursuit of Bandor and the kids. Red, Orange, and Yellow steadied their flame-throwers and incinerated the last two-dimensional life forms.

Visibly shaken by the surprise attack, they all followed Bandor into the cave. Inside, the Dropas, having rid themselves of weapons, sported leaf blowers on their backs and cleared out the smoke.

"We cannot do anything else until I speak with the Thinker," Bandor explained. "Robohawk will inform us when it arrives."

Liam and the others sat and talked, listening mostly to Cooper who detailed his encounter with Arton, and Arton's increased strength and greater shape-shifting ability.

Passages to the Nexus

Awaiting the Thinker's arrival, the Dropas set up a three-ring circus. All but Bandor and Lindor formed a semi-circle to watch the impromptu performance.

Clearcoat played ringmaster, donned in top hat and tails. In the center ring, Blue, Red, Indigo, and Yellow masqueraded as clowns, complete with eyes, mouths, and red spherical noses. Accustomed to their simple features, the audience was amused by the Dropas with faces. The mirthful act consisted of riding unicycles, juggling balls or pins, and walking on stilts.

To the left, Silver and Gold portrayed the tiger tamers. Orange, White, and Black played the cats, accurately painting each other and morphing their bodies into the circus felines.

The third ring showcased Green and Violet in the cannonball act. Violet curled into a sphere and Green painted a plunger to stuff Violet deep inside the barrel. Green retreated to the other end, lit a torch, and counted down from ten. A net opposite the cats' cage served as the intended target.

Green reached two when Robohawk screeched loudly. As the bird landed in front of the entrance, the dust-filled air swirled into the cave. The other Dropas disposed of the circus equipment, including the net. Green lit the cannon and finished the countdown. A small explosion fired Violet out of the barrel with nothing to catch it but the rear wall. It splattered against the unforgiving rock face, resulting in a roar of laughter.

"The Thinker is here," Bandor declared.

The spectators' silliness subsided as they followed Bandor into the canyon. Once outside, Liam and Lindor leaned against a large boulder to the right of the cave entrance. Bothered, Lindor squeezed Liam's arm rather tightly.

Liam heeded her troubled state. "What is it, Lindor?"

"Just a weird feeling." Lindor shook her head. "It is nothing."

Everyone's head movement mimicked Bandor's as he examined the colossal Thinker. Lack of solid form made it difficult to distinctly view the enormous creature. Mostly comprised of nebulas and constellations, the onlookers focused on the Thinker's motions to distinguish the location of its legs, arms, and head.

"We are searching for the portal to Dropa," Bandor informed the Thinker. "Can you help us find it?"

A chill rushed through Liam's body. Due to the anomalies inside the murals, the feeling differed from chills experienced back home. Nonetheless, the impact was the same as he pictured the next destination, the entrance where only souls are allowed to pass.

"Yes, I can assist you," the Thinker's galactic voice resonated. "Access to the portal is located in the Nexus." The Thinker's body constantly shifted. "It is where all the murals intersect. A map exists that guides you through the artwork, but that route will take too long. I will offer a more direct path. Getting there is easy. Staying there will be more difficult."

Bandor approached the massive entity. "Why is that?"

"Realizing its significance, Arton has contrived a vortex." The Thinker lowered its colossal body down into the canyon, settling its posterior on the rim and resting its feet on the dirt floor. It assumed its customary sitting position.

"I do not understand."

The Thinker lifted its chin from its hand. "The vortex is a four-dimensional zone, with time being the fourth dimension. It swirls like a tornado, although those inside the center are left unaffected. One mural will appear around you, followed by another, and another. They constantly change over time, unlike the static vortex center."

"You said we would be unaffected."

The Thinker offered its left arm. Robohawk, dwarfed by the living statue's sheer size, perched itself on the Thinker's forearm.

"Unaffected in the sense that you will not spin around with it." The Thinker gently caressed the crown of Robohawk's head. "Do not get trapped in the swirling wall of murals or you will likely be doomed to reside there forever."

"How will we recognize the portal?"

The Thinker calmly lifted its arm and Robohawk promptly departed. "A mural with a Spartan standing guard between two columns will materialize. Behind the sentinel is a rip through the blue sky, revealing a sunset with a silhouetted landscape of Greece. In the vortex, it will appear as if many Spartans are present." The Thinker shifted. "Choose the one clenching a spear in its left hand. All others will hold a weapon in the right hand. Do not delay, for it will not stay long and you will be required to wait indefinitely before it reappears."

"How do we enter the portal?"

"Rotate that Spartan's shield to the right one-half turn. This will reveal the concealed entrance. It is a circular opening with steel-looking doors that open vertically. Use the combination I have already inserted in your pocket, Bandor. Enter this portal and make your way to Dropa." The Thinker rose from its sitting position. "Anyone left behind must wait for the next opportunity, if there is one."

"What do you mean, if there is one?" Lindor asked.

"Some murals cycle more frequently than others. The one with the portal appears far less often. Others may never be visible if they have been blackened by Arton. You have instructions to share with your friends. When you are ready to depart, I will be here waiting." The Thinker reverted to its customary pose.

A troubled Bandor led the group into the cave. "Have a seat, everyone."

They formed a semi-circle around Bandor. Lindor grasped his hand.

"Time is of the essence so I will be succinct." Bandor assessed his small entourage of courageous companions. "Whatever happens from this point, Lindor and I are extremely proud and grateful for your assistance. For us. For humankind. And for Dropa."

Everyone anticipated the next bit of news would be unpleasant. Liam considered the teens, their families, and their futures. He also thought of Ti and how much he wanted to bring her and her friends home safely.

Bandor interrupted Liam's temporary trance. "It is time for us to separate."

Liam eyed Lindor. Mason glanced at the kids. They exchanged looks among themselves. Then Mason's eyes locked onto Liam's.

"We've already been split up once," Cooper protested.

Bandor calmly gestured to silence the teen. "Mason, we need you and the Dropas to repair the mural mascots. Much like Robohawk, they need mending to give us even the slightest chance against Arton's power."

Liam and Mason each recalled being apart when Arton kidnapped Mason. This time, the associated, unsettling feeling was not present in the artwork. They refocused on the vital purpose for being inside the murals, preserving the existence of souls.

"Mason?" Bandor rested his hand on Mason's shoulder. "Are you listening?"

Liam and Mason nodded at one another, accepting the fact that they must do whatever Bandor and Lindor required of them.

Mason broke his concentration from Liam and rose from his seat. "Yes, Bandor, where do we need to go?"

Bandor handed Mason a list of mascots. "The Thinker has already imparted a map of the murals to Robohawk." From his pocket, he retrieved ten intricately redesigned airbrushes, one each for Mason's fingers. "I have been saving these for a special occasion." Bandor handed them to Mason. "These will drastically increase the speed at which you paint. Together, with the Dropas at your side, you should complete your assignment expeditiously."

"Then what?" Mason examined the new implements.

"Direct each set of newly restored creatures to the vortex. After the final group, Robohawk and the Dropas will lead you to us."

Mason firmly embraced Liam. "See you at the vortex."

"You can count on it."

From Liam's shoulders, Clearcoat wished Liam good luck and requested he care for Silver and Gold. The ten other Dropas hopped onto Mason's palm.

"Silver and Gold are coming with us?" Liam inquired surprisingly.

"We can always use a couple of Dropas," Bandor reminded him.

Robohawk emitted a series of condensed screeches. Three hawks landed on the canyon floor to transport the others. Mason boarded the golden Robohawk and the Dropas strapped themselves into painted seats behind the bird's neck.

Mason saluted with two fingers. "Let's bring down Arton for good this time."

Robohawk vanished into the night sky. The others boarded their respective birds: Bandor, Silver, and Gold on one, Liam and Lindor on another, and the three teens on the third.

"Your birds will fly into my chest and be implanted with directions to the vortex." The Thinker beckoned the hawks to enter its nebula body.

The birds took flight. One by one, the giant hawks departed through the Thinker's midsection. After the final bird penetrated, the Thinker's body spread outward before drawing itself into the same void the hawks entered. The colossal statue returned to its original mural, its role as a conduit for Bandor fulfilled.

The large boulder next to the entrance of Robohawk's cave had vanished. In its place was a wickedly smiling Arton, fully aware of Bandor's plan.

"See you at the vortex," he said sardonically, "for the last time."

Robohawk rocketed through the murals at speeds Mason deemed absurd. Everything passed by in a blur. He grinned at the Dropas as they raised their hands high above their heads, screaming and gibbering. It was another theme park ride to them. Learning from the speedy mustang adventure, they created seats with high backs for this voyage to keep their noggins in place.

Only when Robohawk slowed did Mason ascertain how dark it had become. Yellow unhitched a paintbrush from the side of its seat and painted headlights on the crown of the bird's head and its wings. The Dropa completed the task in mere seconds and returned to its seat. The bright lights improved the short-range visibility, but the ostensible endless darkness persisted well beyond the beams.

At last, two dim lights appeared in the distance. Willie and Roberto had preceded Mason's arrival and successfully implanted two torches, marking the location of his first destination.

From his pocket, Mason retrieved the mascot list Bandor had given him. "Oh no! Our first mascot is Stripes."

The silent Dropas erupted in cheers.

"Why so happy?" Mason asked, surprised at the reaction.

Clearcoat suggested giving Stripes a special coating similar to Robohawk's.

"Always the optimist."

Robohawk prepared to land. The headlights and pair of torches Willie had left provided adequate lighting for touchdown. The giant bird stretched out its talons, flapped its wings, and lowered its passengers gently to the ground.

Mason and the Dropas wasted little time unstrapping themselves and sliding down Robohawk's body. As Mason's feet contacted the ground, he felt the Dropas strike his back. They grasped onto his shirt and scampered to his shoulders.

"Everyone aboard?"

Clearcoat gibbered affirmatively.

"Let's find Stripes." Mason unfastened a light from Robohawk's wing and hurried to the rocky formations in front of them. "We have a good deal of work ahead of us and not a whole lot of time."

Mason expected to find Stripes, but instead encountered other tigers. He recognized the current mural to be the artwork outside Stripes' gym. Painted in the same building, the close proximity made sense.

To the right, four extremely weakened tigers lay helplessly on a large, stone slab. They could barely open their eyes, let alone raise their heads. Mason knelt beside the nearest one, unfazed by six pairs of eyes peering out from a cave. He gently stroked the tiger's head and noticed the stripes coming off on his hand.

"Let's do it." Mason extended his arm, giving the Dropas a ramp to reach the vanishing tiger.

Orange, Yellow, Black, and White stayed with Mason. The other Dropas left to prep the additional tigers. Unhooking the airbrushes and hoses from around his waist, Mason felt a strange adrenalin rush throughout his body. Similar to the "chill" Liam felt outside the cave, the altered physical feelings experienced inside the murals produced unique sensations, more intense than those on Earth but without the emotional attachment.

After connecting the hoses to ten containers of colors the Dropas assembled, Mason inserted his fingers into the airbrushes, manipulating them until they fit comfortably. "Let the transformation begin."

Mason and the Dropas painted. And painted. And painted. By the time they reached the second tiger, Mason's fingers danced like a virtuoso pianist. Paint flowed from the airbrushes and the Dropas refilled the containers without missing a beat. The miniature artists exhibited similar efficiency. They effortlessly dashed and darted, while their brushes made quick, precise strokes over the designated sections.

They revived the second tiger. And the third. Unlike painting outside the walls, fatigue was nonexistent. After repainting the fourth feline, Mason and the Dropas relocated the operation, restoring the tigers in the cave one by one.

"Done!" Mason had revitalized the tenth and final tiger. "Let's find Stripes."

Yellow and Orange had positioned beacons indicating the location of the feline leader.

"Up there!" Mason sprinted to the lights with the resurrected tigers loping alongside. His sudden burst surprised the Dropas and they hung on tightly.

Mason stopped abruptly, swinging his passengers from side to side. Twenty feet above the ground, a nearly colorless Stripes lay motionless, supported by numerous floating cinder blocks—the surreal effect Mason incorporated in the mural back home. A lone beacon was visible through Stripes' semi-transparent body. Its head and front paws dangled helplessly off the front blocks. Its hind legs draped over the sides of the rear blocks. Any sudden movement would bring the once-powerful cat crashing to the ground.

Mason communicated a plan to Robohawk and the other Dropas. Clearcoat, Red, Green, and Black gripped the bird's huge talons. Robohawk took flight, initially veering away from Stripes to prevent the air movement from dislodging the cat. Robohawk circled twice before flying over the fading mascot. The Dropas released their grip and landed on the motionless patient.

Within seconds they created a body harness, attached it to Stripes, and waited for Robohawk's next approach. The hawk swooped down with open talons, snatched the loop from the Dropas, and lifted its furry ally off the floating blocks.

Robohawk cautiously alit near Mason and the other Dropas, airbrushes and paintbrushes armed and ready. This time, every Dropa involved itself in the restoration process. They zigged and zagged over, under, and through Stripes in a continuous blur. Mason's fingers maneuvered almost as fast, manipulating the brushes as the cat's brilliant colors re-appeared.

The other tigers surrounded the artists and the feline canvas, lying on the ground with heads between their front paws. Only their eyes followed the Dropas' movements.

Stripes' restoration required the same amount of time as the ten other tigers combined, but Mason and the Dropas persevered. Mason smiled at the revitalized creature, satisfied with what he and the Dropas had accomplished. Incredibly, he wasn't the least bit tired.

"I wish I could bottle this unlimited energy for painting murals back home."

Indigo proudly volunteered to awaken the sleeping cat. The captivated audience watched in anticipation. From in front of Stripes' right eye, Indigo gently stroked the cat's nose with a paintbrush. Detecting no movement, it repeated the action, slightly sweeping the brush hairs inside Stripes' nostrils.

Stripes' left eye gradually opened and the other tigers instantaneously lifted their heads. Green softly cried out a familiar "uh-oh." As Indigo glanced at Green, Stripes pancaked Indigo with its huge paw. The feline tilted its head back and roared loudly. The other cats followed suit. Stripes raised its paw and Indigo reverted to its original form. While the Dropas and cats reunited with Stripes, Mason reviewed the list of damaged murals. The rhinos came next.

Mason's jubilation abruptly ended. "Party's over. Let's roll." He rubbed behind Stripes' ear. "Glad to have you back."

Stripes purred loudly and licked Mason's cheek. Mason lowered his palm, allowing the Dropas to climb aboard.

"Clearcoat, Stripes and the other cats need to head for the vortex. Bandor said you'd pass along instructions."

The Dropa relayed an okay sign that resembled an "O" because of its mitten-like hand.

Mason chuckled, "I understand, Clearcoat."

Clearcoat darted to Stripes. The transparent Dropa delivered animated directions, repeatedly making hand gestures and gibbering as it danced in place. Stripes lowered its head to improve its view. The cat's nostrils flared, attempting to detect the scent of something it could hear, but not distinctly see.

Unable to wait for this mural to randomly appear in the spinning wall and due to the instability of the vortex, the mascots were not guaranteed entry. Accounting for these obstacles, the Thinker's route included short-cuts to secret passages where a guide would safely lead the revitalized creatures to the intended destination.

Stripes acknowledged Clearcoat's instructions by licking the Dropa with its pink, oversized tongue. The duration coupled with the roughness of the surface, doubled the transparent leader's height and left vertical ridges in its body. Enamored with its temporary physical appearance, Clearcoat patted Stripes on the nose and staggered to Mason's hand. The other Dropas giggled at Clearcoat's non-vogue appearance. Taking the hint, Clearcoat reshaped its body.

Mason rubbed the bridge of Stripes' nose. "Meet you at the vortex."

Stripes offered its enormous right paw and Mason grasped it with both hands. The rejuvenated cat roared at the other tigers to initiate the journey. Mason boarded Robohawk, ensuring the Dropas secured themselves in their seats.

"Let's go find the rhinos!" Mason commanded.

Robohawk took flight and gracefully negotiated the floating blocks. From above, Mason watched the ambush disappear into the darkness. He examined his hands, twitching his fingers as if he had the new airbrushes attached. Although they had many mascots to restore, Mason felt confident he and the Dropas would accomplish their assignment in time.

"You're in my neighborhood now, Arton."

The flight thus far had been uneventful. An encounter with Arton was inevitable, but Bandor had no idea when it might occur. Liam and Bandor were in a much more precarious situation than the confrontation at Barrow's Ridge. On Earth, they pinpointed Arton's location with certainty and held the element of surprise. Inside the murals, Arton maintained that strategic advantage.

"Lindor." Liam called without a response. "Lindor?" He presumed she was communicating to mural mascots in tandem with Bandor. His thoughts shifted to the journey on which they had embarked. *The unstable vortex will be another unique, unpredictable adventure.* He felt Lindor's arms tighten around his abdomen. "Welcome back."

"Back from where?" Lindor asked, confused.

Liam rested his free hand on top of hers. "Your trance."

"Sorry," Lindor chuckled, realizing what Liam meant, "I have not been very talkative. Bandor needed help as we near our next transition. In fact, there it is."

Lindor spotted one of Mason's peeled corners, revealing a bright blue sky scattered with wispy clouds. The exposed sky contrasted brilliantly with the blackened outer space through which the hawks currently soared.

"Liam!" Cooper yelled. "One of the astros is greeting us."

This guide was the same thirty-foot astro that had crushed Arton's final satellite between its hands. The three hawks tightened their formation as they neared the weightless creature.

"What is that bright light reflecting in the astro's face shield?" Lindor asked.

No sooner did she get the words out of her mouth when the astro fired its jet pack, directing itself into the peel. Curious as to what pursued them, Liam heard Silver and Gold gibber a distraught "uh-oh." This one was quite different than a response to a mischievous companion. Approaching Liam's hawk from the rear, and visibly in attack mode, raced a Gravalo—an enormous, bright white torus, or donut-shaped entity with a powerful gravitational field.

"Head into the peel!" Bandor commanded.

The hawks furiously flapped their wings. The sudden acceleration thrust Brian off his bird's back.

"We lost Brian!" Lauren shouted.

Overhearing Lauren's cry for help, Lindor communicated to her hawk to retrieve the drifting passenger. She also relayed a message to Bandor for him to forge ahead. Liam's bird reversed course, flying toward Brian, but also at the Gravalo. The hawk made a semicircular path and swooped by the floating teen.

"Gotcha!" Lindor grabbed Brian's arm and helped situate him onto the bird.

"Hurry!" Brian bellowed. "It's getting closer!"

The vertical Gravalo closed to within a thousand feet. The high-speed gases spinning around the eighty-foot-diameter entity created a gravitational field that pulled Liam's hawk toward it. Now within five hundred feet, two more Gravalos emerged from behind the larger one and shot past Liam's hawk straight for the other birds.

The pursuing Gravalo trapped Liam's bird in its center. The diameter of the gaseous tube forming its shape decreased to forty feet. The tremendous inward force resulted in the hawk's wings collapsing against its own body and compressing the passengers against each other. Satisfied with a successful capture, the Gravalo constricted around its prey like a huge boa. As the diameter across the entity decreased further, the gaseous torus morphed into a sphere. The passengers' bodies compacted in the sustained death grip. Compression into a single ball of mass was imminent.

Ahead of the larger predator, the two smaller Gravalos drew closer to the other hawks. The astro, appearing to have deserted the victims for its own safety, maneuvered behind the peel and into the next mural—one with two giant sabres pierced through a floating shield. Both sabres had etchings, one with a learning tree and the other with the symbol of an atom. The black and gold hilts protruded above and behind the golden shield, whereas the silver blades had been thrust through the open midsection. The bottom third of the giant blades extended out to the sides opposite the handles but in front of the shield.

The huge spaceman gripped the hilt of the sabre depicting the atom. Tugging mightily, the astro freed the sword and rocketed out of the peel. As it returned to outer space, the two Gravalos had reached the targeted prey and drew the defenseless hawks into their gravitational fields. Positioned between the pair of entities, the astro wielded the glimmering blade above its head, and cleanly sliced each Gravalo, severing their gaseous tubes. Their ends instantly separated, propelling the Gravalos into a spiraling frenzy. Uncoiling like a detached garage door spring, the gases dispersed harmlessly throughout the vast outer space.

Bandor, the Dropas, Cooper, and Lauren helplessly watched, hoping the astro would reach their companions in time. The diameter of the Gravalo sphere collapsed to half its original size and engulfed them with its white gases. Suddenly, it expanded. Then contracted. Then expanded. Rather than crushing its victims, it attempted to rip them apart bone by bone, cell by cell, atom by atom before mashing its four victims together. Fortunately, they felt no pain.

As the gaseous mass expanded, the astro's sabre sliced through the Gravalo. Instantly, the gravitational force reversed and hurled Liam's hawk out of the gigantic stomach-like sphere. Unlike the smaller Gravalos, this one exhibited tremendously more power in its spherical form. The gravitational force reversed a second time and engulfed the giant astro.

Liam directed the hawk to join the others before the lifeform pulled the bird in again. At a minimum, the astro would disrupt the Gravalo's pursuit long enough for Liam's hawk to escape into the next mural. However, the astro had no intention of simply delaying the destructive entity. Timing the expansions perfectly, it sliced apart the gases until the sphere opened completely. With the sudden disconnection, the severed gas strands uncoiled and dispersed like the two smaller Gravalos.

"You all right, Brian?" Liam asked as his hawk arrived next to Bandor's bird.

"Yeah." Brian kneaded his belly. "I feel like a Dropa."

Liam shifted parts of his body back into place. "You will for a bit, until your body has a chance to settle into its original form."

"Everybody okay?" Bandor inquired.

"Yes, we're fine," Liam replied. "And you guys?"

"We survived unscathed," Bandor answered.

"Was that one of Arton's beasts?" Brian slid onto the hawk with his friends.

"Anything evil in these murals is because Arton created it," Bandor sharply replied as he scanned the vicinity for other Gravalos.

"That was scary." Lauren emphatically hugged Brian.

The astro returned and led the three hawks into the bright daylight of the peel. The birds glided in front of the floating shield.

The astro propelled itself to a point behind the shield, but away from the three hawks. It examined its position carefully before proceeding to the upper right-hand portion of the mural. In that corner, as well as in the lower right-hand corner, were screws holding the blue sky "in place." Mason occasionally used that surreal effect, giving the impression that he had attached the sky to something in the mural, the wall in this instance. However, it wouldn't be long before discovering what in fact existed behind that particular blue sky. Liam found it interesting that the hawks had already come from behind the mural and would travel somewhere between the front and rear of the same mural.

The giant spaceman inserted the sabre tip in the screw and rotated it counterclockwise until it popped free. After repeating the same procedure in the lower right-hand corner, the astro wedged the sabre into the far, right edge of the sky and pried it free. Demonstrating keen agility, the galactic handyman avoided being trapped as the sky recoiled like an extended party blower. Expecting more, Liam was unimpressed at the virtually identical blue sky.

Given the travelers' urgency, the astro led the hawks into the next mural where a cast of circling falcons awaited. Those birds led the group to the main section of the artwork where they met additional falcons, all soaring in front of the subsequent gateway.

That entrance consisted of a rip through a blue sky that exposed another section of outer space, different from where the travelers had originated. A round stone medallion purportedly held the rip together. As they neared the gateway, Liam realized the large medallion was positioned in front of the sky, like the shield had been in the previous mural. The astro entered the gateway into outer space. With the recent Gravalo encounter fresh in his mind, Liam hesitated. The astro emphatically beckoned the hawks. They, along with the falcons, flew into another quadrant of space.

"We are almost there," Lindor whispered into Liam's ear. "I overheard Bandor communicating with the astro." She rested her chin on Liam's shoulder. "We have one more gateway to go through before reaching the vortex entrance."

"This is weird," Liam insisted.

"What is?"

"At the very least, I should feel a little fear, but I don't." Liam glanced at the young trio and they showed no signs of being scared either.

"It is because of where you are."

"Yes, but it's strange nonetheless." Liam briefly observed the three teens sitting on their hawk with arms outstretched. "My actual emotions don't align with my expected ones. Does that make sense?"

"Of course, it does. Remember, your heart is guiding you. It is unnecessary to concern yourself with the constant hurdles your mind creates or the terrible feelings and memories it holds."

"Honestly, I wish this would end. I want to be with you, and only you."

"As do I." Lindor kissed his cheek. "One way or another, it will end soon."

"What is that?"

Lindor peeked over Liam's shoulder. "Appears to be a space station. This means we are close to the vortex."

The hawks veered away from the large satellite where they were greeted by two additional astros conducting a spacewalk near the gateways—six space windows Mason had painted in the original mural. In one opening, a space shuttle. In another, a nighttime lightning storm. The last four contained sunsets: one in Greece, another in Egypt, the third on a tropical beach, and the final one in a forest-covered mountain range.

"Which window would you select, Lindor?"

"If I had a choice—"

"If you had a choice?"

"Yes, if it was up to me. I would opt for the Greek sunset. And you?"

"It's a toss-up between that one and the tropical sunset."

"That is a good one too."

"Why don't we have a say in the matter?"

"We must go into the one that will lead us to the vortex entrance."

"Bandor is waving at us to follow him and the astro." Liam chuckled at the least desirable selection. "We get to fly into the lightning storm."

The hawks circled in front of the gateway. Bandor briefly communicated with the astro before it returned to the space station.

"Aren't the astros coming with us?" Brian asked.

"Their role is to guide the other creatures into the vortex," Bandor replied.

"You mean everyone is required to travel through the storm?" Lauren inquired.

"No, the gateway to the vortex changes. If a single gateway existed, discovering it would be absolute for inadvertent travelers. We have six choices."

Before entering, Bandor explained what to expect after passing through the window. Silver and Gold stayed with Bandor, and the six passengers joined hands. Bandor bowed his head and everyone else closed their eyes. They drifted to the opening as a wolf howled in the background, relying on the passengers' hearts to interpret the encrypted map within the music. The entire group floated into the gateway, mesmerized by the musical soliloquy. The long, beautiful notes charted the path to the vortex entrance.

Upon entering the disturbance, a constant array of lightning bolts illuminated the inside of their eyelids. The energy created would shield them from Arton, should he happen to appear. Mostly horizontal, they penetrated the magnificent storm, drawn into it by the hypnotic music. During the short voyage, Liam lost all sense of where and why he and the others were there. Energy flowed through him, not from the storm, but rather from those next to him. Gliding along effortlessly, they shifted to a vertical ascent above the clouds. The music grew louder and clearer as the lightning and thunder abated below them.

"Open your eyes," Bandor instructed.

"Is this the vortex, Bandor?" Brian inquired.

Bandor released his grip from Lindor. "No, but we are almost at the entry point."

Liam surveyed his present position. Under his feet, the lightning storm reflected off the clouds. A golden harvest moon, in three-quarter phase, shone in the distance. Behind the moon, appearing as if it rested atop the clouds, loomed planet Earth. Beyond the planet existed a silhouetted forest of enormous pine trees with a shooting star streaking above it. Another peel exposed a blue sky.

The soothing music was no longer guiding the travelers but welcoming them. The musician? A beautiful wolf, magnificently painted with gradated patches of white, black, gray, and beige, stood with its nose facing its tail.

Lindor tapped Liam on the shoulder. "Here comes our next guide."

Liam's jaw dropped. Everyone but Bandor and Lindor reacted in the same manner. Enormous fingers and a thumb emerged. The helping hand had arrived. As the fingers ascended above the clouds, another set of fingers came into view. A much smaller hand pressed up against the larger one. One hand of an infant and one of an adult would lead them into the vortex. The murals are synonymous with the heart, a precious organ that sustains life in living animals and nourishes an infant as it evolves into an adult.

The infant hand drifted to the group. Accompanied by the wolf pack, the travelers strolled across the clouds to meet the oncoming transport.

"Climb aboard." Bandor assisted Lauren.

Liam and Lindor followed the two boys, stepping onto the gigantic, yet smooth, soft fingers. Bandor and the wolves jumped on last. They all huddled in the palm as the infant hand gently carried them to the larger adult hand.

Lauren tugged on Bandor's arm. "What happens next?"

"The adult hand will form a cup over the infant hand and both will safely lower us into the vortex."

The hands, escorted by the hawks and falcons, drifted into the clouds and entered the vortex. The travelers sat quietly in total darkness, everyone except Silver and Gold. The two Dropas could no longer contain their excitement, gibbering and giggling as if part of a surprise party.

"We are no longer moving," Lindor whispered.

"Are we here?" Brian comforted Lauren tightly in his arms.

Light replaced darkness as the adult hand lifted. Astonished by the visual spectacle before them, Liam and the others slowly slid off the infant hand. Arriving in the vortex center, they had been set down on the white sand of a tropical beach. Small, foamy waves from Vortex Sea rolled ashore. Although mesmerized by the overall beauty, Liam perceived the prominent integrated landscapes. Tropics, deserts, forests, mountains, grasslands, and the like had all been interconnected: palm trees standing next to cacti, beaches on mountain slopes, and prairie grass growing on the surface water.

The animals also exhibited this fascinating aberration. Liam likened it to what he observed in the "Serengeti" mural with the cheetah's pursuit of the antelope. Carnivores mingled joyfully with herbivores, sharing the same source of water and playing with each other. The elephants splashed water at the lions and the zebras playfully chased the jaguars. The serenity was powerful in the vortex, reminding him that despite human differences, all could live peacefully together. As they embraced the magnificence, the hands slowly ascended out of sight.

Liam wrapped his arm around Lindor. "The skies are overlapping."

"Beautiful, is it not?"

Sunsets magically blended both day and night skies. The unpredictable patterns constantly changed. Clouds transformed from brilliant oranges, yellows, and reds to silhouettes, then whites, and back to colors as if peering into a huge kaleidoscope. Lindor affectionately kissed Liam. They had arrived at the doorstep of paradise, at least for the moment.

"Hey, lovebirds." Brian positioned his face next to Lindor and Liam's cheeks.

Still kissing Lindor, Liam carefully opened his left eye and peeked at Brian.

"I hate to break up this little smooching session," Brian urged, "but Bandor is requesting our presence."

Liam pulled away from Lindor. "You have your own sweetheart." He playfully pushed Brian's face away from his.

"Come on, Bandor has discovered something."

Liam and Lindor followed Brian to where Bandor and the others gazed at one section of the vortex.

"What do you make of this, Liam?" Bandor inquired.

Precisely as the Thinker had described, the murals transitioned within the inner wall of the vortex, some visible for no more than thirty seconds and others a bit longer.

"It appears that, except for the ground, everything surrounding the center is unstable," Liam surmised.

"What's that coming out of the mural?" Lauren asked.

"And there," Cooper added.

As each mural phased in and out, mascots existing in their respective murals, as well as those that didn't, entered the vortex center to form Bandor's army. Liam glanced at Bandor who had a faint smile on his face. The teens rushed to greet the creatures and waded the water with the elephants and rhinos.

"Your communications must have been successful, Bandor," Lindor commended him.

Bandor's smile grew a little bigger. "Keep your eyes open for the mural with the portal. Do you notice any sequence, Liam?"

"No, but the murals seem to be staying in phase longer, and—"

"And what?" Bandor asked.

"We have already seen this one," Liam asserted.

"You are right. I wonder how long we must wait."

Another mural materialized, and out of it leapt two dozen dolphins. The majority landed in the water, but others plummeted onto the beach, missing the intended entry point. Brian, Cooper, and Lauren aided the less fortunate ones, safely returning the marine animals to their natural environment.

"You could not have picked a better group of kids," Bandor congratulated Liam.

"Thanks, Bandor, but one remains missing."

"We will find her."

Images of Ti rushed through Liam's head. It had been some time since he considered her well-being. Lindor reminded Liam that it wasn't because he had forgotten her, but it was the effects of being inside the murals. His mind had released control of his thoughts. Although present, they no longer influenced his emotions and decisions.

As Lauren and Brian returned the last dolphin to the water, Lauren espied a familiar ally. "Look who's here!" Lauren sloshed ashore toward the vortex wall.

Brian echoed her excitement. "Stripes!"

Wrestling with the gators in the water, Cooper heard Brian's call and peeked at the newest arrival. "Ahh!"

Unaware that Cooper had quit playing, one gator tail-whipped him, undercutting his legs.

Cooper splashed into the water, swallowing a fair amount as he did. He emerged, expecting to expel liquid. "You guys win!" Cooper coughed and spit a few more times, but nothing came out of his mouth. Shaking his head at the abnormality, he ran to Stripes.

Lauren arrived first and enfolded Stripes' fluffy neck in her arms. The energized cat welcomed Brian with a playful right paw to the temple, knocking him to the ground where Stripes gave him a huge, coarse lick across the face.

"Hey, Stripes, I missed you too."

Lauren helped Brian to his feet and they both climbed aboard the furry transport. The other tigers charged at Cooper who dodged as many as he could before they bowled over him. As he spun around on his knees, Stripes strutted by and swatted him in the face with its tail.

"That's it, I surrender." Cooper raised his hands above his head.

Liam, Lindor, and Bandor reconvened with the others on the beach, welcoming Stripes and the tigers to the vortex. Silver and Gold busily entertained themselves as usual. The two gibbered a greeting to Stripes after being sprayed high into the air from an elephant's trunk. The Dropas each intended to land on water plumes erupting from two different orcas. Silver successfully accomplished the feat. Gold did not.

One killer whale smacked the misguided Gold with its bent dorsal fin, hurling the Dropa toward the opposite shoreline. Another participant waited under water for the golden projectile. With impeccable timing, the dolphin emerged, caught Gold in its blow hole, discharged it, and swatted it to shore with its tail as it flipped into the water. Gold flew over Lindor's head and splattered against a palm tree behind her. Before its remnants dripped down the tree trunk, Gold gathered itself. Both Silver and Gold scurried to give Stripes a warm Dropa greeting.

The kids continued playing with the animals, both on the beach and in the water. Bandor's separation from the others piqued Lindor's interest.

She gazed across the water. "Something is wrong, Liam." Lindor led him to Bandor. "Bandor's thoughts are overflowing into mine."

"Doesn't that usually happen between you two?"

"Not this way. They are usually organized. These are random and free flowing. Bandor has discovered something extraordinarily bad."

Liam and Lindor reached Bandor who had fixated on the center of Vortex Sea.

"What is it, Bandor?" Lindor waited for a response. "Bandor!"

Bandor did not respond from his trance.

Lindor gently placed her hand on his back. "Talk to me, Bandor."

Bandor finally spoke, "This…was the calm, and here…comes the storm."

Existential Pocket

Bandor nodded at Lindor. "I will gather the creatures. It is time for you to brief Liam on your next mission."

"Next mission?" Liam inquired, unaware of the altered plans.

"Lindor will impart the details of the destination," Bandor replied bluntly as he walked away from Liam.

"Wait a second!" Liam followed Bandor. "If we are in such grave danger, you will need at least one of us here."

"No!" Bandor abruptly pivoted, fully expecting Liam's persistent reasoning. "It is critical that you and Lindor leave us!" Bandor's stern voice reverted to his customary easygoing tone. "Your next journey is vital to defeating Arton. Lindor will prepare you for it." He briefly embraced Liam. "You are like a brother to me. I will never forget you."

Confronted with overwhelming consternation and bewilderment, Liam said nothing in return.

"Good luck, my friend. Be swift in your quest for the answer." Bandor left to address the mascots.

Liam remained stationary until Lindor rested her hand on him. "Quest for the answer?" He brought her near his chest. "Where do I find this answer, Lindor?"

"In Dropa, where else?"

"The plan intended for us all to arrive together," Liam reminded her, confused about the present situation. "Why only you and me?"

"Because you hold the map that will uncover the secret."

"Map? Secret? I don't hold any—"

Lindor gently covered Liam's mouth with her fingers. "The map will lead you to the secret that will help save our existence."

"Why do I possess the map…which I am certain I don't?"

Lindor confirmed that Bandor was communicating with the creatures. "Because we do not have much time, I will be brief."

"I'm listening."

"Remember, we are not allowed to interfere—"

"We are no longer on Earth," Liam countered.

"Please, let me finish."

"I'm sorry. Go on."

"We can only assist. The Dropa scrolls revealed that if Arton threatened the existence of Dropa, a chosen mortal from Earth would be given the sacred map and escorted to Dropa. As part of Athena's agreement with Zeus, neither the Dropas nor Dropians could serve that role. Uncovering the secret is the key to preserving our survival."

"I understand the rationale behind selecting a human, but are you suggesting I'm that chosen mortal?"

"Not suggesting…you are the one."

Liam patted his empty pockets. "Given the circumstances, I won't dispute it, but I don't have this map of which you speak."

"It does not reside in a pocket, Liam." Lindor placed her palm on Liam's chest. "Instead, it is here."

Liam's attempted conceptualization of the internal map gave rise to another revelation. "Do you remember our experience in the cave?"

"Of course, I do. It was the most loving connection I have ever shared. How is that related to our current situation?"

"Before you woke me," Liam recalled, "I had a strange dream. I've had weird dreams before, so I didn't think much of it. Oftentimes, they don't make sense until an event triggers the meaning later. Anyway, in that dream, someone was present, someone unfamiliar to me. His name was—Ette—Ettepious—Ettepox. Do any of those names sound familiar?"

"Not at all."

Liam reached into the depth of his subconscious to evoke the name. "Ettepo. Exott Ettepo. That's it!"

"I am sorry, Liam. I have never heard of Exott Ettepo."

"Nor have I. Maybe Ettepo, the map, and Dropa are interrelated."

"Perhaps Athena has heard of this Ettepo. She knows every soul who exists in Dropa. What else?"

"Nothing else. You woke me and that's all I remember."

"You have not dreamt about him since?"

"Our bodies no longer required sleep after that. There must be a correlation." Liam blankly stared at Lindor. "If the map and Ettepo are indeed linked, how will I find him? I've never been to Dropa!"

Lindor grasped Liam's hands and smiled. "That is why I am escorting you. As you read the map, I will guide you. I am familiar with many areas of Dropa."

"And how exactly do I read this map?"

"From within." Lindor knew he didn't understand entirely. "It will become clearer if we get to Dropa."

"If…we get to Dropa?"

Lindor untwisted the other kink in the plan. "We must travel through Bandor's pocket. It is harmless when a Dropian voyages inside a messenger's pocket, but it will be exceedingly dangerous with you present. Because you are a physical being, unlike my transcendent form, it could be a perilous journey."

"Perilous to what degree?"

"It could bring death to us all," Lindor replied assuredly.

"In essence, sealing our fate. Then why are we doing it?"

"Because we have exhausted all other possibilities."

"Let's not waste any more time."

"Why are you smiling?"

"I'm contemplating the irony of a conversation I had with Bandor. When we first met the Dropas, I asked him if people could go in his pocket. Although no person had at the time, he didn't see it as a problem. He asked if I'd like to try."

"And your response?"

"I told him that someday I might take him up on that, although I envisioned it would be under different circumstances. Perhaps merely a peek inside, but not as part of a transcendental journey." Liam glanced at his good friend, Bandor. "I never imagined traveling through his pocket would threaten his life…or mine."

Liam and Lindor caught up with Bandor who had directed every creature present to disperse throughout the vortex. Stripes stayed with Bandor. Silver and Gold, paintbrushes by their sides, positioned themselves on Stripes' forehead. Something was about to transpire, and Bandor feared the worst.

"I want you three by the vortex wall. When you see the Spartan mural, alert me immediately," Bandor instructed Brian, Lauren, and Cooper.

Without saying a word, they dashed to their posts.

"Bandor, why didn't you tell them that Lindor and I are leaving?"

"We cannot afford more delays," Bandor answered firmly.

Liam wondered if he would ever see those kids of whom he had become so fond. "They have a right to know."

"I am sorry, Liam, but we do not have time for long good-byes." Bandor verified that the creatures had reached their positions.

Before Liam spoke regarding his departure, Bandor shifted his concentration to the middle of Vortex Sea. Numerous orcas, sparking from electrical charges, floated to the surface—followed by an enormous surge of bubbles.

"He has arrived!" Bandor announced. "Duck behind that boulder!"

Bandor peered around the left side while Lindor and Liam peeked around the right. Protected by a force field, Arton's platform rose above the bubbles. After coming to rest, Arton deactivated the semi-transparent shield and revealed his new version of ForLords.

Arton no longer had the appearance of Roentgen, but rather of himself when he existed in Dropa. Standing six-and-a-half feet tall, the shape-shifting protégé was clad in gold armor, exposing only his bearded face, neck, muscular arms, and knees. His chest plate boasted an embossed profile of his mentor, Proteus. In his right hand, Arton carried a six-foot scepter topped with a crystal orb.

Two new generals flanked Arton, Feri to his right and Eci to his left. Feri commanded the Pyrotons, human-shaped masses of fire and heat. Besides burning whatever crossed their path, they were capable of extracting fireballs from their bodies and hurling them at the enemy. Eci led the Icics, also humanoid and composed of liquid coolants. Much like the Pyrotons, the Icics hurled liquid ice balls, instantaneously encasing the target in a block of frozen matter. They were also capable of emitting freezing winds and leaving ice trails wherever they traveled.

The other formidable members of Arton's army, human-shaped Dartons and Cyclotons, assembled behind the Pyrotons and Icics. The Dartons followed their leader, Tradon. Like porcupines, the Dartons launched varying-length spears from their bodies. Dwin controlled the Cyclotons. The fierce creatures blew away anything near them and spawned smaller destructive cyclones.

The final force in Arton's land army consisted of Electromorphs, under the direct command of Ectorel. Appearing as giant gaseous masses with orbiting charged particles, the Electromorphs emitted deadly, high-voltage electrical bombs. The explosives caused damage similar to lightning strikes, but also converted positive energy into negative energy.

Arton's strength did not stop on land. Protecting him in the water swam the Medusamorphs, cousins of the Electromorphs. Resembling the lion's mane jellyfish, the large, translucent creatures were difficult to spot and also used numerous tentacles to emit high voltage currents into their prey. Seduma commanded these deadly water beasts.

"From where did these entities come?" Liam questioned, stunned. "I know Mason didn't paint them in his murals."

"He has unmistakably regained his shape-shifting prowess," Lindor concluded. "I remember reading in the Dropa scrolls that the full extent of this power allows the bearer the capacity to not only transform himself, but transmute harmless organisms into ones with unimaginable, destructive abilities, and also create ones from mere nothingness."

"I warned you all of the surprises Arton would present as he drew closer to Dropa," Bandor advised, discouraged. "We do not stand a chance against his superior army."

"That was our stance the last time we confronted him."

"These are not the ForLords on Earth. They are powerful and have weapons our creatures cannot defend."

"Don't underestimate the mascots," Liam assured.

"Your optimism is admirable." Bandor sat against the boulder. "They might hold them off for a short period, but it is time you and Lindor travel to Dropa."

Liam and Lindor nodded in agreement.

"Bandor!" Arton's voice rang throughout the vortex. "Come out and play, little Dropian."

Hearing this, Cooper redirected his attention to the nefarious man. Standing in front of Arton was Ti who was dressed like an Ancient Greek princess. Gold necklaces hung from her neck and sparkling jewels were woven in her hair.

"Ti!" Cooper attempted to run to the shoreline.

Instinctively, Brian grabbed his friend, fearful of Arton's murderous intent.

"That's right," Arton bellowed, "I have Ti, Cooper. You left your girl for me."

"Let her go, Arton!" Cooper attempted to break free.

"You had your chance." Arton creepily stroked Ti's hair. "You could have been standing here with me, but you decided to ally with your pathetic friends. She is now mine."

Although repulsed, Ti could do nothing more than succumb to Arton's desires lest she seal her fate and never reunite with her loved ones.

Cooper broke free and sloshed in the water up to his knees. "Ti, I'm so sorry!"

"Enough of this!" Arton aimed his scepter at the beach. "Find the cowards!"

Responding to his command, Dwin and the Cyclotons proceeded to shore. Their wind speed exceeded a hundred and fifty miles per hour. The hippos emerged first from under the water to create a barrier between the Cyclotons and the intended targets. The forceful winds lifted the two-ton beasts out of Vortex Sea and strew them across the beach as if they were stuffed animals. Additional cyclones emerged from Dwin's body and pursued Brian, Cooper, and Lauren. The three separated, running in different directions at the outer edge of the vortex. The Cyclotons pursued relentlessly. They leveled trees, swirled sand, and propelled mural mascots into the air. The Cyclotons capped off the initial offensive by launching the three helpless teens into the spinning vortex wall, where they would remain forever.

Arton relished the ease that he and his army would overtake Bandor's. Ti's eyes welled with tears. Her sense of doom was apparent.

Arton raised his scepter. "Destroy this place!"

Eci and the Icics led the onslaught, forming an ice bridge from Arton's platform to the shore. Next came the Electromorphs, followed by the Dartons, and then the Pyrotons. Already on land, the Cyclotons carved a destructive path in search of Liam, Bandor, and Lindor. The rhinos made a gallant charge at the powerful wind entities. Lowering their horns, they successfully neutralized the first half dozen they encountered. Although outnumbered, the Cyclotons eluded the slower pachyderms and catapulted them into the vortex wall.

As the Pyrotons marched onto the icewalk, the elephants emerged next, spraying water on the fire monsters. The liquid streams forced a number of them off the bridge and extinguished their combusting bodies. The dolphins and remaining killer whales initiated an auxiliary attack against the flaming entities. Some leapt out and back into the water, producing large waves in the enemy's direction. Others conducted a full assault on the fire demons, attempting to knock them off the ice bridge. Plumes of steam billowed from the surface water, remnants of the unfortunate Pyrotons.

Protecting their own troops, the Dartons and Electromorphs, already at the beach, mounted a counterattack on the surging mammals. Lightning bolts and spears filled the air against the dolphins, orcas, and other creatures that opposed them. The Medusamorphs assisted Arton's troops from Vortex Sea. The jellyfish encountered little resistance as they injected the defenseless marine creatures with high voltage current from their tentacles.

The elephants charged the Dartons, their tough skin resisting the initial barrage of spears. Again, the land creatures had early success, but over time the combatants outmaneuvered and overpowered the mural mascots with weaponry they had never before encountered.

Even the agility of the giant cats was no match for the savage soldiers. The felines swatted away fire and ice balls, only to be bombarded with spears or electrical bombs from the other evil beings. Debris from the wind storms flew everywhere. The beauty and serenity of the vortex center transformed into a mascot graveyard. Fire erupted throughout the land mass and flushed out the fleeing or hiding animals. Their escape from the flames, spears, and electrical bombs would only lead them to another form of expiration.

Bandor lay on the ground by the boulder. Due to the importance of initiating Liam and Lindor's escape, Silver and Gold refrained from combat. Instead, they assisted Bandor by stretching open his pocket to its maximum width.

"Hurry!" Bandor whispered loudly. "Get in!"

Without hesitating, Liam and Lindor dove into the pocket. Liam didn't know what to expect once inside it—Lindor barely had time to tell him that the pocket was their passageway to Dropa. The Dropas focused on Bandor who was grimacing in pain from Liam's entrance. They let loose of the opening, allowing it to close to its original size. Bandor transmitted a last-ditch message…

The final dragon had been revitalized when Robohawk alerted Mason with a loud screech. Clearcoat hurried to the hawk. The golden bird lowered its head near the Dropa and relayed Bandor's communication. Clearcoat updated Mason on the current situation. Bandor called for immediate assistance, but warned of Arton's formidable army and the exceptional weaponry they carried.

"I know it is essential we leave, Clearcoat, but we must make some crucial preparations." Mason further explained the details.

The Dropas painted alongside Mason according to his instructions.

"Time to battle," Mason warned, as if relaying a message of his own to Arton.

Silver and Gold scurried across the sand to assist Stripes. Their powerful friend lay buzzing and twitching, riddled with electrical currents and pierced with spears throughout its hind quarters and midsection. Silver gibbered into Stripes' ear, encouraging the cat to lie as still as possible.

Bandor opened his eyes, expecting Silver and Gold. Instead, the demigod wanting to terminate the existence of the souls stood over him.

"Well, well, well," Arton said smugly, "deserted by your friends."

Ti did everything in her power to resist the overwhelming urge to help Bandor. If she followed her heart and assisted him, Arton would surely end both her and Bandor's life.

"You made a grave error, Arton." Bandor exhibited discomfort.

"And how is that, Bandor the Feeble?"

"You blew the three kids into the vortex walls," Bandor stated. "They will inevitably find the portal."

"On the contrary." Arton knelt and leaned closer to his victim. "This here is all an illusion."

Bandor winced, his discomfort intensifying from Liam's presence in his pocket.

"That's right." Arton waved his scepter above his head. "I fabricated this little paradise that my army is destroying and created the rotating vortex wall."

Bandor's expression transformed from that of pain to one of greater trepidation.

Arton slowly twirled his left forefinger. "Your friends will never escape to another mural, but will instead spin around and around. The real portal to Dropa is under water. That's what happens when you arrive first…and what's possible when you have my powers."

"You will not succeed, Arton," Bandor insisted half-heartedly.

Arton assessed the devastated mural creatures strewn across the vortex. "I genuinely want to believe you, Bandor," he replied sarcastically. Arton motioned to Eci. "He's all yours."

Arton loosely grabbed Ti's arm, about to escort her away from Bandor. She desperately reached for Bandor's pocket. Bandor opened his eyes one last time, long enough to watch Ti wriggle from Arton's grip and observe Arton's expression of surprise.

Arton felt his empty hand. "You're coming with me." He pivoted, discovering Ti had vanished. "Eci, where did she go?"

Eci finished encasing Bandor in an ice tomb. Bandor lay frozen with a partial smile of content.

"No idea," Eci replied in a cold voice. "She was here, then she wasn't."

"I have no more use for her anyway." Arton flicked his hand in disgust. "Onward to the portal."

Their destruction complete, the Cyclotons and Pyrotons stabilized to their pseudo-human form. The region Arton had attacked was decimated. He smiled with satisfaction at the ravaged area. The plant life was obliterated. Only sparse boulders and palm trees endured his wrath within the quasi-center he had created. Annihilated mural mascots blanketed the area or floated in the water. Those spared lay weakened and severely wounded. Although the mascots outnumbered the group that attacked Arton's fortress, Arton's god-like strength overpowered them, drawing him one step closer to his ultimate goal. Arton evaluated his army. Despite suffering casualties, it retained a high number of soldiers.

"Lindor!" Liam called, from underneath a tarp.

"Over here!"

"Where?" Liam struggled to remove the canvas cover.

"I am on my way." She crawled over a number of boxes, ladders, and paint cans before tripping on a folding table that collapsed underneath her feet. Her momentum carried her onto the tarp.

"Ooph!"

Lindor removed her knee from Liam's abdomen by bracing her arms against his chest. "Liam, are you okay?"

"Agggghhh." Starting to feel claustrophobic, Liam frantically fought to get the tarp and Lindor off of him.

Lindor steadied herself on a section of scaffolding and removed the covering. "There you are."

"Where's there? Or here?" Liam noticed his paint-splattered pants and the punctured paint can next to him. "What a mess."

"Here, happens to be the beginning of Bandor's pocket."

Liam arose with Lindor's assistance. "Bandor's pocket? This reminds me of the basement in my childhood house."

"Your basement?"

"Basement. Garage. Crawlspace. Take your pick."

Lindor examined the cluttered pile. "Yes, this is Bandor's pocket, at least the beginning, or end, depending on the direction you travel."

"Wow, this brings back memories."

"This is merely the beginning of your memories," Lindor promised.

"What does that mean?" Liam wiped the paint off his pants with a corner of the tarp.

"You will recall innumerable memories on your way to Dropa."

"How is that possible?" Liam dropped the tarp. "I thought my mind was relinquishing control as I traveled through the murals."

"You have not lost your memory," Lindor reminded him, "rather you have detached the majority of the emotions tied to those memories."

"I guess that explains the claustrophobic feeling under the tarp."

Liam and Lindor navigated down the pile of equipment and supplies Mason used on murals and the necessities Bandor had amassed during his extended time on Earth.

The usual, now even more prominent question entered Liam's mind. *How does he get all this in here?*

"Someday I will explain it to you."

"Explain what…how I'm able to feel emotions in here?"

"That, I will explain to you now. I was referring to how Bandor gets all this stuff in here."

"I didn't ask you that."

"Not aloud."

"Wait a minute. That's not fair."

"I am only reading your mind in here," Lindor advised.

"Why are you doing it at all?" Liam asked defensively.

"I will be monitoring your emotions on our journey. Traveling through Bandor's pocket will reignite your sentiments. And some, maybe all, of your senses will return as well." Lindor held both Liam's hands to calm him. "You will ride an intense, emotional roller coaster. You may feel pain. Then happiness. Then remorse. Then solitude. The pattern is unpredictable but it will persist until we reach Dropa. You will feel everything as if you were dying."

Liam withdrew his hands from Lindor. "As if I was dying?"

"Have you ever spent time with someone whose life was ending?"

"Yes," Liam replied, thinking of his grandfather.

"Were you with him often enough to observe the different emotions he went through during that time?"

"Yes, I remember instances of hopelessness when he suffered great pain. The cancer had progressed into his bones. Other times, he displayed his typical sense of humor. The last day I spent with him, we talked—about many different things. He found peace that day, like he had his bags packed, ready to go home. Shortly after that, he slipped into a coma and passed a day later."

"His soul had been purified," Lindor confirmed.

"Does it always end with a peaceful emotion?"

"No, there is a randomness to the process. It is different for everyone, depending on the strength of each emotion in that person."

"Will I die?"

"Sort of, but not really."

Liam sighed deeply. "Lindor, please help me understand this."

"In order for you to enter Dropa, your soul must be purified. It is essential that all emotional baggage is eliminated before you can enter. Everything must be left behind."

"Including this pile?" Liam joked.

Lindor laughed and gave him a warm hug. "I love you too."

"That's not fair, Lindor."

"Come on, we must start our journey." Lindor gave Liam a quick kiss and led him by his hand away from the massive heap.

They entered an endless array of colors. It was spectacular, almost like traveling through a rainbow. Lindor forewarned Liam it would be painful at times, yet euphoric during other times. Repeatedly, she emphasized that he should never release her hand. If he did, he would be lost in Bandor's pocket forever. Although Lindor had provided a thorough explanation regarding what Liam would potentially experience, no amount of preparation was enough for his upcoming transcendental journey.

Liam encountered Arton's image first. Both he and Lindor were surprised by Arton's appearance, although Lindor had guaranteed Liam that the meeting was inevitable.

"I do not understand. Why is he here this soon?"

"Lindor, Arton is standing alongside Ti."

"Why is that unusual?"

"You said I would relive memories." Liam shook his head at Lindor. "This never happened to me."

"You are right."

"Arton is turning away."

"Bandor is conveying a message." Lindor guided Liam in Ti's direction. "This could be our lone chance to rescue her."

"Noooo!" Burdened with immeasurable pain and sorrow, Liam closed his eyes and collapsed to his knees, causing Lindor to fall backward. The flashbacks commenced. Overwhelmed by the first memory, Liam realized it wasn't one of which he was directly involved, but rather one that affected a person close to him.

Lindor longed to comfort Liam, but she had to capitalize on the opportunity to save Ti. She tugged desperately on Liam's arm, slowly dragging him, but still a fair distance from the pile. Liam's cries of pain, anger, and struggle persisted. Hearing those faint noises, Ti reached for Bandor's pocket. Lindor closed her eyes. Instantly, the distance between her and Bandor's opening became negligible. Lindor grabbed Ti's extended hand, pulling her away from Arton and into the pocket.

"Hang on!" Liam yelled. "Stay with me!" An image of his late wife, Ashley, appeared. She was assisting a small group of revolutionaries tend to the needs of orphaned children when they were ambushed by a band of ForLord holdouts who refused to surrender after the war ended. Writhing on the ground, Liam shared Ashley's excruciating pain and agony resulting from her multiple gunshot wounds. The physical suffering transmuted into mental anguish. He experienced Ashley's emotions associated with the global conflict, her physical trauma, and ultimately her struggle to survive. His lungs tightened as Ashley exhaled her last breath.

"Lindor!" Ti called, distraught. "What's wrong with Liam?"

Her eyes fixated on him, Lindor released her grip on Ti and lifted her hand to silence Ti's concern. "Hold on to me, Liam."

"Ashley, is that you?" Liam questioned.

"No, Liam, it is me, Lindor."

"Lindor, I've lost her." Tears filled Liam's eyes. His pain from loss and abandonment heightened. "Ashley's gone forever."

"She is not gone forever. She is in a better place, but I am here for you."

Curled in a fetal position, Liam trembled in fear. "Is your love for me strong?"

"Stronger than you will ever know." Lindor gripped Liam's hand and tightened her other arm around him.

"Do you intend on leaving me?" Liam couldn't stop shaking.

Lindor recalled the conversation with Bandor—in the desert mural—regarding her feelings for Liam. "I will never leave your side."

"I love you, Lindor."

"And I love you, Liam."

Lindor gently brushed her fingertips across Liam's face. At last she made eye contact with Ti. "Welcome back," she whispered.

Ti bowed her head, happy to be free from Arton's grip, but worried about Liam. She had no clue what was happening.

Liam's eyes opened. Dazed, he caught a glimpse of Ti. After reorienting himself, he realized Lindor had freed her from Arton's control. Liam extended his free hand and Ti gently squeezed it. "Are you all right?"

"Me?" Ti was astonished at the question. "What about you?"

"A mild flashback," Liam deadpanned. "I enjoyed that immensely and can't wait for the next one."

"Are you ready to stand?" Lindor asked.

He uncurled. Lindor and Ti assisted him to his feet.

Liam hugged the teen with his free arm. "I'm glad you're safe."

"We need to push ahead," Lindor instructed.

"What about Ti?" Liam inquired.

"Yeah, what about me?" she chimed. "Do I get to go with you?"

"I am sorry, Ti. You must return from where you came."

"No way, Lindor!" Ti retreated, vigorously shaking her head. "I'm not going back with Arton."

"We are not asking you to return to Arton. Believe it or not, we are in Bandor's pocket."

"Seriously?" Ti responded with amazement.

"Lindor, why aren't you holding Ti's hand?"

"Because she is heading in a different direction and is not undergoing the transformation you are."

"Where exactly are you sending me?" Ti wondered aloud.

"Bandor's junkyard," Liam teased.

"What?" Beyond the colors, Ti identified Bandor's silhouetted mound. "What do I do when I get there?"

"Find a way to the opening," Lindor explained.

"You mean I have to climb Mount Clutter?"

"At least get close enough to call for Bandor's help. Otherwise, he will be unable to hear you."

Ti shook her head at the pile. "Where are you two headed?"

"To intercept Arton," Lindor answered.

"Be careful. He's immensely stronger than he used to be." Ti embraced Liam and Lindor. "I'll see you guys later, right?"

"Yes," Liam and Lindor assured.

Ti stepped back and gave them one last wave before setting off for Bandor's heap. Liam and Lindor resumed the journey to Dropa. After the last experience, Liam wasn't especially thrilled with the forthcoming evocations. He didn't want to feel any more pain, hardship, or discomfort. However, two things motivated him to endure the suffering: Lindor at his side and the hope that something magnificent awaited him at the end.

"Everything all right, Liam?"

"I feel chilled. Are you cold?"

"I cannot sense temperature. I do not understand why the temperature would change in here." Lindor expressed sudden realization and concern. "I hope Bandor is not dying."

"If he dies?" Liam whispered.

Lindor nodded, imagining the worst possible outcome. "Come on. We need to stay positive." She pulled Liam's hand.

The mosaic of colors shifted—darkness replaced the brilliancy followed by random swirls of light. The flashbacks resumed. This time Liam revisited early childhood memories—some good and some less pleasant. Pain became comfort. Satisfaction became disappointment. Love became hate. Sadness became joy.

Again, Liam collapsed, but Lindor stayed right with him. The light swirls disappeared as his eyes closed, but the emotional frenzy endured. He felt his insides constrict as his heart rate increased and then returned to normal. His breathing was erratic. Liam opened his eyes. A disjointed, holographic montage of memories, accompanied with the attached emotions, encapsulated him.

A soothing warmth replaced the chill in his body. Liam floated in space. No, not space at all, but liquid. He was suspended in a warm, pacifying fluid. Hypnotized by a calm, rhythmic beat, he drifted effortlessly in this liquid world. It was peaceful. He was content. It was steady. He was euphoric. It was precisely as Lindor said it might be.

Suddenly, the peacefulness transitioned into chaos. The liquid rushed away from Liam. No longer content and now positioned upside down, his head and body were forced into a confined cavity. He was being compressed. The pressure was extreme. The steady beat intensified—now rapid and urgent. Why was his body being pushed out of its sanctuary? Liam was happy there. He didn't want to leave. Restriction replaced his freedom of movement. He was trapped in a small chamber with no way of escape.

Then light appeared. Dim at first, it quickly brightened. The pressure around Liam's head eased. As did the restriction of his shoulders. Once his shoulders freed themselves, the rest of his body followed. The warmth transformed into extreme cold. Liam's state of confinement disappeared, replaced instead with total freedom. The warmth returned. And then the familiar heartbeat, although different this time. Rapid, yet steady, and not as loud. It belonged to Liam. His own heartbeat. He was breathing. Liam had been given the greatest gift of all, that of life.

Lindor witnessed and felt Liam's entire experience. Lying beside him, she gently caressed his arms and chest. Liam smiled. She reciprocated. He didn't want this memory to end, but it did. His eyes opened and met Lindor's. Their smiles widened.

"How are you?"

"I'm alive, Lindor. I'm alive."

Lindor rubbed her hand through his hair. "Are you ready?"

"I believe I am, but I'm getting colder, and tired."

"You will become weaker. After your soul is entirely purified, you will initially lack the strength to stand on your own."

"What about this chill?"

"It concerns me too. Stay close to me and I will keep you as warm as possible." Lindor helped Liam to his feet.

Initially, he had trouble standing on his trembling legs, but eventually regained his balance. Maintaining a firm grip on Liam's hand, Lindor wedged herself under his arm to support him. At least he felt warmth on his left side.

The memories persisted, unpredictable and sporadic. The negative ones attacked Liam and the positive ones uplifted him. They remained intertwined, making each subsequent session more exhausting.

After each series of flashbacks, Liam shared his experiences with Lindor until the next set began. Although she concurrently felt them, she wanted to know more about them. More about Liam. She was so comforting. So caring. So loving.

Portals to Dropa

Despite being seriously injured, Stripes inched near Bandor. Silver and Gold tended to its wounds as best they could, wishing the other Dropas were there to help. Unable to lift its head off the ground, Stripes licked the ice tomb encasing Bandor. The strokes were slow and methodical, and the wounded cat used every bit of energy it had left to try to free its companion. Silver and Gold built small fires around Bandor, but the heat sources had little effect on the thick, dense ice. Stripes licked one last time. Exhausted, it had no strength to retract its tongue. Instead, it fell limply onto the dirt and the weary feline closed its eyes.

Silver and Gold emerged side by side from behind the boulder, superficially exhibiting uncharacteristic signs of discouragement. They exchanged gibberish remarks and helplessly watched Arton's army return to the platform. The two Dropas assessed the casualties of the creatures strewn across the beach as well as those spinning in the vortex wall. Unable to free them or their three teenage friends, the captives would remain imprisoned forever. And if Bandor died, Liam and Lindor would perish with him.

As Silver and Gold examined the wall more closely, they raised their paintbrushes in anticipation. Suddenly, a large opening formed and Robohawk rocketed into the vortex. In customary fashion, the bird's signature screech announced its presence. Many severely injured creatures mustered enough strength to lift their heads and witness the golden hawk. Even Stripes' eyes opened momentarily upon hearing the welcome sound.

More prominent than its shimmering new color were the special weapons Mason and the Dropas armed Robohawk with to fight Arton's military. Astride the well-armed bird rode Mason and the 101st Airborne Dropas.

Stationed in the driver's seat, Mason manned the missile command. Five Dropas were positioned on each wing to ensure that he didn't exhaust the ammunition. Each missile they created had a special purpose: fire missiles for the Icics, water missiles for the Pyrotons, positively-charged neutralizing missiles for the Electromorphs, explosive missiles for the Dartons, and clockwise typhoon missiles for the Cyclotons.

Robohawk led its winged allies directly at the enemy. The close-trailing dragons exhibited the same intensity as their squadron leader. They stoked their internal arsenal, ready to aid the assault. Silver and Gold danced in the sand, cheering for their comrades.

Arton sought out the origin of the screech. Before he could relay an order, Mason unleashed a barrage of armed projectiles at the enemy. The first wave blew four Dartons into the air. A half dozen Pyrotons lost their balance from the explosive force and tumbled off the ice bridge into the water, immediately quenching their flames. Arton summoned as many of his soldiers as possible. They boarded the platform, where he engaged the force field.

As Arton's protected sphere submerged into the water, his forsaken troops initiated an onslaught on the reinforcements. They returned to shore and launched a battery of fire, ice, and electrical bombs, striking two dragons. The winged fire-breathers that evaded the attack returned a shower of fire bombs at the enduring Icics. Ice fragments scattered across the beach. The Icics retaliated. Two ice spreads intercepted the intended targets, sending the frozen dragon blocks splashing deep into the water before buoying to the surface. Two other dragons unleashed fire streams at the huge ice cubes, immediately thawing their comrades. Free from temporary incarceration, the dragons returned to flight.

Robohawk circled the vortex again while Mason aligned the crosshairs on the desired targets. He unleashed another flurry of missiles, striking the enemy with utmost precision and obliterating three Electromorphs. Their demise resembled the sound of a bug zapper frying a swarm of mosquitoes. Arton's soldiers refused to surrender. They prolonged their defense, hurling ice at the dragons and launching electrical bombs at Robohawk. Mason summoned six dragons. Flanked by the firebreathers, Robohawk changed course. He reviewed his arsenal and locked onto the targets. Together, the heroic squadron dove at the opponents on shore. The aerial team discharged what would be the final volley against the enemy. Arton's abandoned soldiers had been eradicated.

Mason twirled his finger, signaling the dragons to take one more pass. With the mission aboard Robohawk complete, the focus shifted to Arton's sphere. The Dropas dashed from the top of Robohawk's wings to its underside. Awaiting each of them was a miniature, shark-shaped submarine, armed with weapons similar to Robohawk's. Mason glanced to his left and received five thumbs-up. He received five more from the right wing. He called to Robohawk. The golden bird passed by the shore and glided over the surface water. Mason released the submarines once Robohawk neared Arton's entry point.

Indigo, Red, and Orange followed Clearcoat in pursuit of the enemy watercraft. Violet, Green, and Yellow broke off to the right. Black, White, and Blue veered to the left. Upon entry, four Medusamorphs challenged the latter trio. The three Dropas steered their subs into a coral valley and maneuvered through a series of fissures. The first Medusamorph gave chase into the narrow chasm, only to be torn apart by the sharp coral reef. Polyps retracted like falling dominoes as the other three Medusamorphs swam overhead seeking to intercept the Dropas on the other side.

The Dropas rocketed out of the fissures. Not expecting to meet their adversaries, they instantly reversed course. Negative-charged projectiles filled the water, but again, the Dropas successfully evaded the ambush. This time, Black, White, and Blue split up, each luring a Medusamorph.

Black darted into a school of Caesar grunts, but the pursuing jellyfish wasted little time eliminating the Dropa's cover. A few hundred fish disintegrated in the wake of the devastating electrical charges, leaving Black exposed. The Medusamorph aimed its long tentacles at the lone Dropa and released streams of electric current. Black ducked into a coral cave. The voltage missed the intended target and filled the reef instead, ejecting shrimp, crabs, sea horses, anemones, and various other colorful victims from the crevices. As the enemy drifted by, Black unleashed two positive-charged torpedoes. The current zigzagged through the Medusamorph's bell and out into its tentacles before ultimately blowing the beast apart into tiny jelly fragments.

White and Blue reunited and sought cover behind a garden of mirror sea fans. The two trailing Medusamorphs believed they had doubled their own forces. As the deceived creatures neared their reflections, White and Blue launched torpedoes into the jellyfish bells while Black attacked from the rear. After disintegrating the Medusamorphs, the Dropas vacated the coral valley in search of their comrades.

Away from the chasm, Violet, Green, and Yellow initiated a discrete tactic against the four tenacious jelly beasts in pursuit. The Dropas lowered their submarines into the sea floor. The flanked Medusamorphs followed their agile enemies. Hovering above them, they inserted their tentacles into the underwater sand and slowly lowered their bells, preparing to release a collective electrical blast that would leave the Dropas charged for a hundred years.

Instead, thirty barbed tails emerged from the seabed, stunning the four Medusamorphs. Violet, Green, and Yellow rose from their hiding spots and torpedoed the paralyzed predators. Black, White, and Blue put an exclamation point on the attack as they fired from above. Jelly-like globules floated to the surface from the obliterated enemy.

The six Dropas relocated Clearcoat's squadron. Together with the fever of stingrays, the relief corps found Clearcoat, Indigo, Orange, and Red engaged in a full-fledged battle with a bloom of Medusamorphs protecting Arton's watercraft.

Arton's vessel drew closer to its destination—the portal to Dropa. The steep wall played like an outdoor movie screen. The murals came and went, some staying longer than others. The giant jellyfish prevented the Dropas from advancing as they filled the water with an electrical shield.

Unaware of reinforcements, the Medusamorphs maintained focus on Clearcoat's squadron. The other six Dropas launched a surprise attack at the unsuspecting opponents. The onslaught of fire power disintegrated the suspended jellyfish outside Arton's vessel.

The ten Dropas aligned their subs, expecting to have an unobstructed shot at Arton. They had each saved two specialized torpedoes, relying on a combined attack to break through the force field and allow the stingrays to apply the final blow. Instead, they discovered yet one more barrier. Eci and the Icics had created a huge iceberg behind the electrical shield in case it failed.

Arton waited impatiently for the portal to appear. The Electromorphs held their position, aligned and ready to emit an electrical charge through the crystal on Arton's scepter. The powerful, synchronized emission would override the combination and open the portal to Dropa.

The Dropas watched helplessly. They had to save the last missiles for Arton. If they blew away the iceberg, they would have nothing left to torpedo his sphere. Indigo motioned to Clearcoat. It spotted fifty bright, blue marlin swimming at them. Silver and Gold piloted the two lead fish, safely encased in see-through, protective compartments. The onlooking Dropas waved their arms in excitement.

The fifty marlin swam to the iceberg. Using their snouts as ice picks, the fish coordinated the approach and made the first penetration. Repeating this technique, the fish chipped away at the massive ice barrier. Pieces broke away and fissures formed within the block itself, further weakening the frozen obstruction. Arton would soon be unprotected.

As the armed Dropas waited, the Spartan mural appeared. Eci vacated the watercraft. It rotated the left-handed Spartan's shield, exposing the portal. Once Eci safely re-boarded the vessel, the Electromorphs released electrical charges that refracted through the scepter crystal. The focused power opened the portal, bringing Arton closer to his final destination.

A huge light flashed through the ice block. The fissures penetrated most of the iceberg, but the Dropas were running out of time. Arton steered his watercraft into the portal. Utilizing his shape-shifting prowess, he slowly morphed the large vessel into the much smaller gateway. He and his evil soldiers disappeared into the secret passageway, on their way to meet Arton's final adversary.

Unexpectedly, an enormous sperm whale emerged from the depths of Vortex Sea. The marlin, stingrays, and Dropas willingly gave way as the whale propelled itself at the ice barrier.

Its massive tail pushed aside the water, forcing the huge battering ram into the ice blockade. The whale's blunt end shattered the frozen target into pieces. The Dropas immediately maneuvered through the debris. Re-aligning their submarines, they fired every torpedo they had at Arton's watercraft as it vanished into the portal. It was too late. The portal had closed and the mural transformed into another one. Suspended in the transition, the torpedoes failed to detonate. The Dropas changed direction and resurfaced.

Momentum carried the tiny vessels onto shore where Mason anticipated news of victory. The Dropas set foot on the sand and briefly waited for the marlin to return Silver and Gold. The reunited Dropas scurried to Mason who reached down and lifted them close to his face. Clearcoat detailed Arton's escape, further explaining how close they had come to destroying his vessel.

"It gets worse," Mason said. "I haven't seen Liam, Bandor, or anyone else."

Silver and Gold revealed Bandor's location. Before hearing everyone's current position, Mason hurried to the frozen tomb, stunned at his friend's icy predicament. The Dropas darted up Mason's arm and onto his shoulders.

"Is he alive?" Mason knelt beside the ice block.

Gold gibbered what had happened.

"If he's alive, we need to get him out of this ice."

Clearcoat assured Mason that Bandor would be okay and that they needed to rescue the others first.

"Where's Liam? And Lindor?"

Silver informed Mason that Liam and Lindor were traveling through Bandor's pocket with the purpose of reaching Dropa before Arton.

"Well, his wish of wanting to go in Bandor's pocket came true. I hope they make it." He flattened his palms against the ice block and stared inside at Bandor. "That's all we have, isn't it?"

The Dropas gibbered quietly in agreement.

"Let's focus on what we can control. Time to set up shop again."

The Dropas immediately donned surgical attire, including masks, and assembled Mason's mobile hospital.

"This is becoming a habit with you, Stripes." Mason stroked the cat behind its ear. "We'll have you back to normal in no time."

Mason unhooked the airbrushes from his waist and tossed the hose ends to the Dropas. He attached the brushes to his fingertips and sat on a stool that Silver and Black created for him.

"Give me paint," Mason ordered.

Mason and the Dropas performed their magical surgery. They started with Stripes' head and rapidly traversed its body. Unlike his previous revitalization of mascots, these wounds were different. Arton's recent attack produced more realistic lacerations. As he manipulated his fingers, the airbrushes sprayed paint that not only coated the injured areas, but healed them as well. After surgically repairing the wounded tiger, Stripes purred with appreciation.

"Your strength will return shortly," Mason assured. "Lie there and rest a bit. Clearcoat, we need to find every *living* creature."

Silver and Gold interrupted Mason's healing endeavor, informing him about the teens and mascots trapped in the vortex wall. Mason rushed to the beach. Leaning against Robohawk, he scrutinized the wall as it swirled around him. Mason suggested various ideas to the Dropas, but each came with slight flaws. Robohawk screeched as it dipped its head.

Mason patted Robohawk and focused on a point in the wall. "It's spinning counterclockwise." He tilted his cheek toward the Dropas on his right shoulder. "What are you guys waiting for? Find a dragon and follow me."

In their haste and excitement, the Dropas bumped into each other like the Keystone Kops. When they regained their composure, the tiny aviators scampered down Mason's leg and each boarded a dragon. Mason climbed aboard Robohawk, strapped himself in the pilot seat, and gave a thumbs-up to the Dropas. They reciprocated.

"Let's go, Robohawk!" Mason commanded.

Robohawk returned to the air first, followed by the fire breathers. The dragons formed a single vertical line above and below the giant bird. They all flew clockwise next to the wall, picking up speed each time they circled.

Mason reveled in the fact that he didn't feel the slightest bit dizzy. "All right, Robohawk, ramp it up."

As the flying squadron elevated their speed, the clockwise force applied to the counterclockwise rotation exhibited signs of success. The rate of the spinning vortex wall slowed.

"A little faster, Robohawk."

The wall finally stabilized. Mason heard welcome screams from the teenagers as they plummeted from the wall. A slew of creatures tumbled right behind the human captives, including the rhinos. Everything the Cyclotons had propelled into the wall escaped imprisonment. Mason and the Dropas made two more passes before they slowed. Aside from the abrupt and unpleasant fall, the vortex prisoners embraced their freedom.

Robohawk guided itself and Mason to shore. The dragons landed safely right behind their squadron leader. Brian, Lauren, and Cooper joyfully greeted everyone. They were covered in ashes, having fallen in the burnt remnants of Arton's destruction. Mason and the three kids hugged each other, engulfed in a dense cloud.

"When did you get here?" Lauren chimed first.

"I've been here awhile." Mason dusted the soot off himself.

"Thanks for freeing us," Brian acknowledged.

"No problem."

Lauren focused on the Dropas running at her. "There you are." She lowered her palms and the Dropas climbed aboard.

"Where are Liam and Lindor?" Cooper asked.

"They're on their way to Dropa," Mason answered.

"I'm jealous," Cooper admitted.

"It's not as glamorous as it sounds. Arton's on his way too. We can only hope that Liam and Lindor arrive first."

"Is there anything we can do?" Brian inquired.

"We can revitalize the creatures." Mason hesitated. "And Bandor."

"Bandor?" Lauren inquired, concerned.

"Yes, Bandor. He's encased in ice behind that rock formation."

Lauren hurried to him with the others tailing her. "Stripes!" She enveloped the giant cat's head and examined its body. "You're okay."

Stripes roared loudly in response.

Her jubilation disappeared at the sight of the huge ice block. "Bandor." Distraught, Lauren knelt by Bandor's left side as Stripes licked the ice tomb.

"Why is he smiling?" Cooper asked.

"I wouldn't be smiling if I was encased in ice." Lauren positioned her face near the frozen mass. "Do you hear that?"

Brian brought his ear closer. "It sounds like a woman calling for help. Listen."

Cooper listened intently to the faint voice. "That woman is Ti!"

"Are you sure?" Brian questioned.

"Am I sure? Don't you think I recognize my girlfriend's voice?"

"It is Ti," Lauren confirmed. "She's inside...Bandor's pocket?"

"How the heck did she get in there?" Brian wondered aloud.

"It doesn't matter at this point." Mason gestured to the Dropas. "Let's melt this ice and get her out."

The Dropas were a step ahead of him. Already equipped with their own, they distributed newly created welding torches. Mason and the teens began melting the ice block. Because of its density, the Dropas abandoned the time-consuming thawing effort. They extinguished the torches and replaced them with jackhammers. Chunks of ice flew everywhere as the Dropas penetrated the icy slab. When they neared Bandor's body, the Dropas exchanged the miniature power tools for ice picks. As they carefully chiseled away at the remaining chunks to free Bandor, Ti's calls grew louder...

* * * * *

Ti arrived at the base of Bandor's pile. "Where did all this junk come from?" She investigated the pocket opening, estimating it to be forty feet above her head. "How am I supposed to get up there?"

Bandor's pile barely reached ten feet. Complicating the situation, the pocket remained frozen shut and long icicles hung from the opening. Ti diligently searched the mound for items that would allow her to escape. She cleared out a small area directly underneath the opening. Three sections of scaffolding comprised the foundation of her tower. Once Ti understood how to assemble the first section, she wasted no time piecing the others together.

The view is much better from up here. I have roughly twenty feet to go. From there, Ti eyed four planks leaning against the heap opposite her. She descended, dragged the boards to the scaffolding, and hoisted them to the top section. Ti spotted a ten-foot aluminum ladder, the light weight making it less cumbersome to carry to the highest level.

Ti opened the ladder and tested its stability. She climbed to the second to last rung—six feet short—and called for help. "Hello! Can anyone hear me! Bandor!"

She repeated her calls numerous times before descending the ladder. As she set foot on the plank, an icicle dropped from the opening and shattered on the top support. Startled from the noise, Ti lost her balance and fell off the scaffolding. Fortunately, a queen size mattress cushioned the impact. Unfortunately, Ti catapulted off the mattress, bounced off a miniature trampoline, and landed on a stack of bulk food items Bandor had saved from his days working at the grocery store. As she rolled down the clutter, the lid of a five-gallon bucket containing marshmallow fluff popped open and the bucket landed on her head. Besides covering her hair and face, it oozed onto her shoulders and midsection as she tumbled down the pile. Adding to her misfortune, the bucket of fluff dislodged the lid off another five-gallon bucket filled with dill pickles.

Ti lifted the fluff bucket off her head, desperately wiping the sticky marshmallow mixture off her face and out of her hair.

"You are kidding me. This is disgusting." She lifted her chin and raised a fist in the air. "You best let me out of here, Bandor!"

As Ti methodically cleaned herself, additional icicles dislodged. Ignoring the falling ice spears, Ti stuck her tongue out and made a series of smacking sounds. More peculiar than the ice melting above her, she could taste the marshmallow fluff. *Why are my senses returning?* Smelling something more distinct than the unwelcome substance, she raised her nose before finding two pickles rooted in the sticky goo on her left shoulder.

"Will somebody please wake me up?" Ti laughed aloud at her predicament. "Out of the way, Dough Boy, Pickle Fluff has arrived."

Preoccupied with building her means of escape, Ti hadn't perceived the initial temperature change inside Bandor's pocket. She soon realized it had warmed considerably. Ti re-ascended the scaffolding and climbed the ladder, making sure to steady herself this time.

"Hello, can anyone hear me?" Hearing no response, Ti yelled louder, "Anybody there?"

* * * * *

...the Dropas chiseled the last ice fragments covering Bandor's pocket. Sadly, Bandor still lay unconscious.

"We hear you, Ti!" Lauren shouted into the pocket.

"Oh, thank goodness!"

"Are you okay?" Mason inquired.

Ti laughed at her pickle fluff body. "I could be worse, I guess."

"I'm trying to determine how to use Bandor's pocket," Mason said.

"Please work faster," Ti pleaded. "I'm less than six feet from the opening."

Confused, her three friends questioned the estimate, "Six feet?"

"How do I get her out of here?" Mason asked no one in particular.

"Stick your hand in," Bandor whispered weakly, "and pull her out."

Everyone focused on Bandor.

"Bandor!" Lauren exclaimed. "You're okay!"

"I'm alive, but I do not know for how much longer."

"What can we do to help?"

"First, you can get that screaming girl out of my pocket."

"Right away," Mason acknowledged.

Ti waited on the ladder as the Dropas stretched open Bandor's pocket. Expecting a hand the size of hers, Ti momentarily lost her balance as Mason's fingers passed through the opening. She was smaller than his pinky finger nail.

"Thanks for telling me I didn't need to build this tower!" Ti yelled as she jumped into Mason's palm. "How will I explain to my mom that her daughter has transformed into Thimble Girl."

"I have her."

"Gently withdraw your hand," Bandor instructed.

Mason's wrist emerged from the pocket first, then his palm, and finally his fingers. As Ti's body slowly passed through the opening, she instantly reverted to normal size. Brian, Cooper, and Lauren assisted Mason with lifting her out of Bandor.

Elated to hug his girlfriend, Cooper abruptly backed away from her. "What the heck happened to you?"

"And what's that smell?" Lauren crinkled her nose.

"You may call me, Pickle Fluff," Ti replied proudly with arms outstretched. "C'mon, who wants to hug me first?"

"Pickle Fluff?" the kids and Mason asked in unison.

The Dropas erupted in laughter, amused by Ti's new appearance.

"Real funny, isn't it?" Ti flicked Indigo off Bandor's shirt, somersaulting it across the dirt.

That added fuel to the Dropas' giggling fire. Everyone else partook in the amusement except Bandor. Mason placed his hand on Bandor's forehead. When the others saw this, the laughter ceased.

Stripes gave Ti a long lick and walked away in disgust.

"I missed you too," she said.

The Dropas, carrying tanks resembling fire extinguishers, sprayed Ti with a harmless, sweet-smelling dissolvent that removed the fluff and vinegar from her body. After finishing, they cleaned the others. Everyone huddled closely around Bandor.

"What can we do to help you, Bandor?" Mason inquired.

"It is extremely difficult to hold on."

"You will make it," Mason promised his dear friend.

"Did it help to get me out, Bandor?" Ti asked.

"Yes, but I am," he murmured, "rapidly losing my strength."

Lauren gently rubbed Bandor's forehead. "You're so cold."

"Yes," Bandor whispered, "I believe Arton did us a favor."

"How?" Mason inquired.

"By freezing me, he essentially slowed the dying process."

"Dying process?" Lauren asked sadly.

"If they do not reach Dropa soon, I will not survive," Bandor replied weakly as he failed to open his eyes.

"What happens to Liam and Lindor?" Mason inquired.

"If I do not make it—" Bandor struggled swallowing. "They will die with me."

Mason and the kids eyed each other with extreme trepidation.

"Bandor, how can we help you?" Mason asked a second time.

"Keep talking to me."

Mason noticed the tears rolling down the kids' cheeks. His eyes filled as well. He refocused on Bandor, wiping his eyes with his fingers. "Bandor, why are we," Mason inquired as he rubbed the tear drops between his thumb and fingertips, "experiencing emotions?"

"And our senses are returning," Lauren added. "I could smell the vinegar on Ti."

"Arton's power is increasing," Bandor whispered. "He is leaving behind the elements of mortality. It is only a matter of time before you will require oxygen to breathe. If this happens, you will certainly perish in your paintings. I will not answer you anymore." Bandor struggled to get the words out of his mouth. "I must...concentrate."

"Do what is necessary." Mason gently rubbed Bandor's forehead. "We're not leaving you."

"I'm not sure how much more I can handle, Lindor."

"Purification of your soul is almost finished, Liam," Lindor said confidently.

Lindor helped Liam to his feet. Barely able to stand, she supported the majority of his weight and kept him upright. The memories had severely weakened him but the numbing of his body from the cold would not relent.

The intervals between sessions had grown much closer together. After four short steps, Liam collapsed. This being the shortest interval of all and he hoped it was his last.

From a kneeling position, Liam stared at the barrel of Willie's gun with the hammer already in the firing position. This time, however, Willie ignored Liam's question. Everything went into slow motion as the hammer struck the firing pin. Liam heard the loud bang and watched the projectile near his brow. It was over. Just like that. He had no control of when his time ended back home. The feelings of hate, greed, and selfishness of people on Earth plunged through his body. Those same traits constructed the walls that prevented them from realizing the importance of life. They built the foundation of the war, and terminated billions.

The bullet tip penetrated Liam's forehead. Guilt and anger replaced the hate, greed, and selfishness. Guilt for not having told people how he truly felt about them. Anger for all the people who failed to realize their dreams and for not assisting those he could have helped. Torn apart inside, Liam questioned whether he would survive that session. The tears spilled from his eyes. Lindor embraced him tightly in her lap as the lingering negative emotions left his soul.

Liam devoted every bit of positivity he had to his final memory. Innocence prevailed over exhaustion with the appearance of a young woman—Liam's first love. The energy. The attention. The devotion. They explicitly focused on each other and nothing else mattered. It's a sensation many never forget, and oftentimes won't ever be replaced. For the first time in one's life, the heart is opened and shared with another in a way it had never before been shared. Being wholly in love with someone and having that love unequivocally reciprocated is the greatest emotion one can experience. It is one that should be cherished and held forever. It is the closest thing to what one will feel when they arrive in Dropa.

Lindor brought her lips to Liam's and closed her eyes. When she pulled away, they opened their eyes together and smiled at each other. The brilliance of her projection was indescribable. Still holding Liam in her lap, the energy cloud around them lifted slightly. Focused on her eyes, Liam failed to realize the brightness beginning to surround them. The exhaustion and chill had subsided. He felt only peace and love.

"We made it."

"Yes, we did," Liam whispered.

"How do you feel?"

"Words cannot describe how I feel. And you?"

"I am home, Liam." Lindor made a gesture for them to stand. "And you are here with me."

They helped each other to their feet. Liam tested his balance. He no longer needed Lindor's assistance. The slow-lifting cloud delayed Liam's long-anticipated view of Dropa. He relinquished all expectations, thrilled to view that new world for the first time.

"This indescribable feeling you mentioned is present in every Dropian."

"Now that we are here, Lindor, has our relationship ended?"

"On the contrary, we have arrived together."

"Will I meet Ashley?"

"Eventually, but she will likely be with someone else. When people arrive in Dropa, it does not take long for one to discover their soul mate."

"That means we are truly—"

"Yes, we are truly soul mates. Not everyone finds a soul mate on Earth. Those that do are fortunate. There are also rare instances like ours when soul mates arrive in Dropa together."

"And those that don't find each other on Earth?"

"They make up the majority. They are regarded as guardians of the souls. Guardians share different feelings and expressions of love. They help each other through their duration on Earth until it is time for them to exist in Dropa. Some may find their soul mate already here. Others must wait for their soul mate to arrive at a later time."

Liam and Lindor strolled hand in hand through the encompassing cloud.

"Is it true that we may live out our life on Earth without ever identifying our soul mate?"

"Yes, but it is very unlikely that a person completes their journey on Earth without ever encountering one's soul mate."

"You mean talking to them?"

"More subtle than that. It may be as simple as being in the same location concurrently, but eye contact will be made at least once."

"Why is that important?"

Lindor paused for a moment, placed her hands on Liam's face, and gently kissed him. She tilted back her head and gazed into his eyes. "Because…the eyes are the window to the soul."

Freeing Ti from his pocket afforded Bandor a little more strength, but he was fading fast. With eyes closed, he lay in silence.

Everyone was crying. The Dropas, feeling as helpless as the others, gathered on Bandor's chest. Their chanting was ineffective now. Blue and Yellow gently stroked his chin. The other Dropas followed suit. When each Dropa had taken its turn, they joined hands in a circle, like they did many times before, and chanted anyway. It was difficult to perceive any sadness among the Dropas as they held their heads high. At the very least, it elicited a brief smile from Mason and the four teenagers. The tears no longer flowed as they watched the Dropas perform their ritual.

"Please don't leave us, Bandor." Ti kissed Bandor on the forehead. "He's not getting any warmer."

"Now what, Mason?" Brian asked.

"I don't know," Mason replied helplessly.

"They made—" Bandor whispered.

The Dropas halted their dancing and everyone leaned closer to hear Bandor's words.

"What did you say, Bandor?" Lauren inquired.

Bandor slowly opened his eyes and whispered a little louder. "They made it."

"They made it?" Cooper sought confirmation.

"Yes, Lindor and Liam have arrived in Dropa."

The journey continues...

FATE OF ETERNITY

BOOK III

The mind is a complicated organ: capable of handling millions of computations, storing a vast amount of information, and creating images from transmissions of sight, sound, smell, taste, and touch. Yet, its ability to form barriers from one's experiences is mystifying; barriers that ultimately connect to emotions.

On the other hand, the heart is less complicated in its truest sense. It continuously nourishes the body. For many, this remarkable organ can do so for nearly a hundred years. Still, it remains an enigma in the perception of guiding, holding, and experiencing one's emotions. And often times, the heart finds itself in a constant struggle with the mind.

But the most mysterious "organ" humans possess, is not one that can be seen. It is not one that can be held. It cannot be heard, tasted, or smelled. Instead, it reaches far beyond the normal senses and the physical nature that surrounds us. This organ is the essence of who one is, and where one will ultimately exist. For the soul holds the key as to why one is here and unlocks the door to the infinite destination. And each key is necessary to determine the fate of eternity…

Many only search for happiness on the surface,

but digging deeper within oneself,

can often reveal an existential map to a treasure of

eternal love and tranquility.

What a Wonderful World

Liam no longer felt the emotions he did back home, but something unmistakably flooded his body. Beaming from ear to ear, he had arrived in Dropa, an analogous destination to those worshipped in various religions on Earth. Heavenly? Unequivocally. Spiritual? Definitely. Magical? Undeniably.

Lindor gently stroked Liam's cheek as they exchanged smiles. They said nothing, for there was no need. The hovering cloud dissipated and Liam shifted his focus from his soul mate to behold the mystical beauty before him. Never had he seen such a landscape, for it was beyond his imagination.

The Prism Alps spanned the horizon, refracting the light from the three radiant suns. The brilliant, scattered rays intersected with those from the other mountains and created a multitude of vibrant rainbows. As Liam's eyes panned across the various peaks, the kaleidoscopic view changed with it.

Billowy clouds drifted from the mountain tops. Unlike a steady rain on Earth, these bursting crystal formations spilled water into an endless sea. Distinct from the Prism Alps, sparkling rainbows arched from the waterfalls and traveled to another enchanted place in Dropa.

At first glance, a typical forest of oak and maple trees blanketed the terrain, yet the similarity ended there. Musing Woodland exhibited a perpetual metamorphosis of alternating autumn hues and spring greens. Leaves glistened and reflected the sunlight as the wind weaved its way through the branches.

Liam followed Lindor's lead after she kicked off her shoes. The soles of his feet pressed firmly against the grass, yielding another pleasurable sensation. The soft, silky blades tickled his skin, yet soothingly massaged his arches.

They strolled to the city as he absorbed the fairy-tale surroundings. Beyond the city was Mystic Sea. Like a bird feeding its young, the waterfalls from the clouds filled the hungry mouth of the vast expanse. The faint sound of the rumbling cascade resonated through Liam's head. Islands of pyramids were dispersed amidst the body of water. Several transparent ones distorted the scenery behind them, yet others exhibited a reflective quality that mirrored the captivating beauty. And one lone Pyramidic Island was encased in a bubble.

"Do Dropians live on those islands?"

Lindor gently laughed. "Dropians live everywhere in Dropa, well, almost everywhere."

"I imagine those islands are more picturesque up-close."

"You could say that about virtually everything here."

"As it should be." Liam realized his silly statement. "If this is any indication, I want to explore all of Dropa."

"Unfortunately, the current circumstances do not allow us to immerse ourselves in Dropa as you desire. Your tour will have to wait until after we complete our mission."

"I almost forgot why we came." Liam plucked a flower amongst the grass—its yellow petals blended into a magnificent turquoise near the tips. "The beauty is hypnotic." Liam admired the flower's contrast against the blue sky and the dynamic variegation of the trees. He situated the flower behind Lindor's left ear. "For my soul mate."

Lindor tightly embraced Liam. "Thank you." She gently held his hand on their way to the city entrance.

"You said Dropians lived almost everywhere. Where don't they live?"

"We have vowed to circumnavigate certain places sacred to the Dropas."

"The Dropas we left in the vortex?"

"Yes, but others exist here."

Liam raised his eyebrows. "There are more?"

"Oh, yes. They created this glorious place for our souls to eternally exist."

Liam considered the landscape and marveled at the Dropas' artistry. Still physically recovering from the emotional roller coaster of his purification, Liam ambled with Lindor down the cobblestone. The smooth stones, both transparent and colorful, reminded him of the those he polished in a rock tumbler as a child. The surface also soothed his feet.

The road led to the city gateway where pillars of water supported the marble entrance. Although Ionic in style and vertically grooved, the columns did not contain water as one would expect, but consisted of it. The liquid swirled upward on the left and downward on the right. Nearing the gateway, Liam noticed the hovering entry.

"Lindor, how do we get up to the gateway?"

"The stairs," Lindor replied plainly.

He failed to perceive any steps leading to the columns. "And where are those stairs?"

"Exactly where they should be." Lindor realized his dilemma. "I am sorry, Liam. I forget that this is all new to you."

Comprised mostly of water, the steps merged with a pool leading to the gateway. Lindor ascended the stairway. Accepting the fact that it actually existed, Liam cautiously followed. He stabilized his footing on both the surface water and on each individual transparent step. Lindor awaited his ascension between the two pillars.

The Dropas' surrealism was evident in every element of Dropa. Additional columns of water, mist, and light inconceivably sustained the load of stone and marble. Many marble columns lacked middle sections or possessed a multitude of broken segments, also defying the concept of structurally supporting monuments of any size or mass—impossible, except in Dropa.

Fountains were plentiful throughout the city. The architectural masterpieces spilled, splashed, spurted, and sprayed. Others emitted spectral arches from one source to another. To Liam's right, a fountain of bubbles. He stopped to view the artistic splendor. The orbs magnificently reflected the buildings, the blue sky, and incredibly, the multicolored Musing Woodland surrounding the city. The latter was a peculiarity in itself as the forest was not viewable from that location. Anticipating the globes to float away, Liam contemplated the unexpected. He watched the iridescent spheres roll over the edge of the highest tier and gradually drift to the pool below, gently bouncing on the bubbles that had broken their fall. They danced along each other until settling in a new position. The sequence repeated in the same manner with the subsequent lower pools. Occasionally, a bubble popped, dispersing remnants of colors into the air. Lindor cherished Liam's early admiration of Dropa.

Liam released Lindor's hand at the next fountain, constructed of blue-green granite speckled with turquoise and black. She purposely chose not to follow. Water slowly dripped from each level—the elusive droplets were consumed by puddles or deflected off the stone-laden ground.

The fountain triggered a recent memory. Liam drew a parallel with the last visit to his grandfather's grave. Sporadic raindrops splashed off the top of the headstone during the gentle shower that day. He stared into the bottom pool where his reflection rippled in the water. Another reflection appeared next to his. Memories of conversing with his grandfather on his grandparents' patio swirled through Liam's head.

For an instant, the descent of the droplets mysteriously paused long enough for the ripples to disappear. The facial features in the reflection were unrecognizable, however the eyes were not. "Grandpa?" Liam quickly pivoted.

"What do ya know, fella?"

Liam's mouth dropped, for he had heard that question every time he visited as a child. "Grandpa!" Liam tightly hugged the man.

Standing behind Liam with her hands covering her mouth, Lindor treasured his reconnection. Liam speculated that this was a daily occurrence as new arrivals in Dropa reunited with loved ones from Earth.

"Please call me Krolic. That is my name here."

"Very well…Krolic."

"It is good to see you."

"It's wonderful to see you, but your appearance is different."

Krolic dismissed Liam's observation with a shrug as he spoke over Liam's shoulder. "Welcome home, Lindor."

"I am elated to be back."

"Lindor, this is, or was my grandfather."

"Yes, we have already met." Lindor surveyed the premises.

"Is something the matter, Lindor?" Krolic asked.

"Have you seen Athena?"

"She is listening to a harp recital in the courtyard."

"You two can visit while I find her."

Lindor's search for Athena again brought the mission to the forefront. Because of the beauty and wonderful sensations, it was easy to lose sight of the real purpose in Dropa. Krolic led Liam to a nearby table.

Liam sat across from Krolic and revisited his initial observation. "Why do you look different here?"

"I have no definitive explanation for you."

"There has to be something to it," Liam insisted.

"Thank you." Krolic accepted a bowl of fruit and a paring knife from another Dropian. "I never considered it. A tenuous explanation is that if our soul had a form, this is what mine looks like."

"My appearance has not changed," Liam countered.

"Of course not, you arrived as a visitor." Krolic picked through the fruit. "Our bodies on Earth are mere shells for our souls to take up residence. Rest stops, if you will."

Liam's curiosity regarding appearance was diverted as he watched Krolic examine the individual fruit. "I thought it wasn't necessary to eat in Dropa."

"Technically, that is correct." Krolic selected a nectarine from the bowl. "Here in Dropa we can partake in activities we enjoyed on Earth." Krolic sliced a section of the nectarine and placed it into his mouth. He held the knife and dripping fruit in front of him. "For many of us, eating is—"

Liam's chin dropped. "You were the old man in the shop!"

Krolic simply smiled and sliced another section from the succulent nectarine.

"Why didn't you say anything to me?"

"I was forbidden." Krolic wiped away the juice trickling down his chin. "We are not allowed to interfere, we can only assist people on Earth."

"It would have been nice to reminisce."

"I agree. A good amount of time had passed since we last spoke."

Liam selected a portion of grapes from the bowl and popped them into his mouth one at a time. "It was in your hospital room."

"Correct." Krolic removed the last section of nectarine and placed the pit on an empty dish beside the bowl.

"Why did they send you?"

"It gave me an opportunity to visit you."

A smile lit up Liam's face.

"Besides, they needed someone you could trust."

"Wouldn't that have been the case with any Dropian?"

"Hmm, probably."

"We selected him because you trusted him when he resided on Earth," an unfamiliar voice spoke from behind Liam.

Approaching the table alongside Lindor was Athena. She was absolutely stunning, yet intimidating at six feet tall. Her beauty radiated in a bold sort of way even more than the light of the three suns reflecting off her gold battle armor. Her green eyes contrasted elegantly against her smooth, tawny skin. Extending from underneath her helmet was a long, blonde braid that dangled down to the middle of her back. Accented with gold, the intertwined lacing of her leather sandals ended just below her knee.

"Liam, this is our beloved Athena," Lindor announced.

Liam pushed away his chair and knelt before Athena.

She gently guided him to his feet. "There is no need to bow before me."

"You are a goddess."

"Thanks for noticing," Athena replied with a wink, "but we are all equal in Dropa. I was a goddess among mortals. Dropa is much different than Earth." Athena further assessed Liam. "So, you are the one who carries the map."

"According to Lindor. But why me?"

"Please sit down," Athena requested.

Liam joined Lindor and Athena lowered herself next to Krolic.

"Where should I start?"

Liam detected concern, but also regret in Athena's voice as he waited to hear her story. He eyed Lindor and Krolic. Both shared the same sentiment as Athena.

"Liam, what can you tell me about this beloved paradise?"

"Let's see, Bandor depicted the transformation of Atlantis to Dropa, but furnished little detail regarding Arton's expulsion. He did explain, however, that after his exile, Arton attempted to destroy Dropa as the Dropas created the protective bubble around it."

"I permanently exiled him from the continent," Athena said emphatically.

Lindor's grip tightened around Liam's arm. Krolic sat up tall in his chair.

"Through the teachings of Proteus, Arton intended to use his new powers to help his mentor overthrow my father as ruler of the gods. Upon hearing this, I banished him. When Zeus granted me the continent and Arton heard of our agreement, he became outraged—for Atlantis, now Dropa, was his favorite place. It is where he conducted his training. During our last conversation, Arton promised he would devote his life to destroying Dropa, and me. Because Dropa transmuted from a physical place to an existence, I erroneously deemed it impossible for him to return. As a precautionary measure, I periodically dispatched messengers to Earth to observe him, hoping that one day the reported news would include his death."

Liam listened to Athena's story as she ostensibly blamed herself for what was happening. "His death never came to fruition, did it?"

"If it did, you would not be here. Instead, talented, passionate artists unknowingly created portals to Dropa. When I discovered this, I knew it would only be a matter of time before Arton would find a way here."

"You are not only the goddess of art, but of war."

Athena rose from the table and stared into the bubble fountain. "I shed the latter designation, preferring the former along with my other desirable epithet, goddess of wisdom. I grew weary of wars and fighting in general. When I asked my father for Dropa, I envisioned a place absent of conflict—a paradise for souls to exist and share with one another. I simply wanted to be."

"Unfortunately, the fighting persisted," Liam responded, "whether you were a part of it or not."

"Yes. Arton is true to his word, and he becomes stronger the closer he gets."

Liam could offer no words of consolation. "Why was I chosen to receive the map?"

Athena rejoined them at the table. "Bandor transmitted a message before you left for Athens…"

* * * * *

Standing near the shore of Mystic Sea, Athena watched the water cascade from the clouds, awaiting the arrival of two elder Dropians, Psiloh and Sherop.

"You have called for us, Athena?" Psiloh inquired.

"I appreciate your promptness."

"Of course."

"Why have you summoned us?" Sherop asked.

"This morning I received a troubling message from Bandor. The situation on Earth has darkened once again."

"What has transpired?" Psiloh inquired.

"Arton has re-acquired significant power, and he will resume his objective of wiping out humanity."

"We cannot let that happen, Athena," Psiloh affirmed.

"If he destroys Earth, that is the end of Dropa," Sherop added.

They contemplated the situation in silence.

"The map!" Sherop abruptly declared.

"Yes, the map," Psiloh confirmed.

"Are you two referring to the Dropas' sacred map?"

"There could be no other," Psiloh answered with certainty.

"Who will be the recipient?" Sherop inquired.

"In Bandor's message, he notified me of a unique man traveling to Greece. He is a true survivor and was instrumental in ending the last war on Earth."

"Is he the right one?"

"Bandor has a close relationship with him." Athena strolled along the shoreline. "Consistent with the Dropas' scrolls, he is the one who will receive the sacred map. His natural curiosity will lead him to the designated location."

"Which one of us will deliver it?" Psiloh eyed Sherop, smiling with confidence as they awaited Athena's decision.

"Krolic," Athena replied after considering possible candidates.

"Krolic?" they responded, dumbfounded.

"Yes. Krolic will deliver the map."

"Why Krolic?" Psiloh questioned.

"He was this man's grandfather. His trust on Earth will be unquestioned by the recipient."

Sherop removed his sandals as they reached a grassy area. "When do you anticipate Krolic's departure?"

"He will leave Dropa upon the individual's arrival in Greece."

Psiloh also walked barefoot. "Is it not ironic that preservation of the souls' existence is left to mere mortals?"

"Indeed, it is, my friend," Sherop replied. "And we can do nothing more than wait for the outcome."

Athena squinted at the three suns. "Let us hope these mortals are worthy of the role..."

* * * * *

"Where will this sacred map lead me, Athena?" Liam asked.

"To the answers that will help save humanity and our souls."

"Where have I heard that profound statement before?" Liam inquired, prompting a wink from Krolic. "Who conceived this map?"

"Presumably, the most recent generation of Dropas."

"They must have considered Arton an enduring threat," Lindor concluded.

"Apparently."

Liam was puzzled by Athena's ambiguous responses. "You don't seem very familiar with the Dropas."

"No one is. I consider myself to be the closest to them, and even I have much to learn. The Dropas are magical as you are aware. Their personalities are incomparable and their passion for the arts is unequaled, bestowing upon our souls this magnificent existence. Yet, their most incredible attribute is the desire to protect themselves, their friends, and Dropa if any or all are ever threatened."

"In my abbreviated time with them, I have witnessed all those things. Athena, how were you made aware of this map?"

"The Dropas apprised me of it shortly after Atlantis submerged into the ocean. Recall my promise to Zeus about not interfering with the fate of Earth—I could only offer guidance."

"As you have already demonstrated."

"Under this premise, the Dropas assured me that we could assist humanity if Arton, or any other force, threatened Dropa."

Liam processed the information. "How did I acquire the map?"

"I will defer to Krolic since he partook in the delivery."

Krolic shifted in his seat. "Do you remember our visit to the chamber?"

"As if it happened yesterday. I had numerous bumps on my head from whacking the ceiling beams on the way there."

They all chuckled.

"That chamber contained the map."

"I don't recall seeing one in that room."

"It was not one to which you are accustomed. Instead, the details were encrypted on the walls. As the lights emitted from the vase mesmerized you, light rays behind you absorbed the coded etchings and directed them into your body.

Once the transmission ended, you hosted the map that would lead to the key and unlock Arton's demise. Do you remember kneeling on one knee?"

"Yes, my shoulders cramped from the prolonged hunching."

"The energy from the rays triggered that sensation as the map entered your body. The intensity must have been overwhelming."

"That's an understatement. What about the liquid in the vase?"

"A decoy," Athena affirmed.

"A decoy? Please enlighten me."

"We utilized the vase to help deliver the map to you. Look around at the splendor of Dropa, all that they have created here is proof the Dropas do not require special liquid, rather the paint and artistry from within themselves."

"I wholeheartedly agree. How did the Dropas arrive on Earth?"

"How did we get here?" Lindor questioned.

"Naturally...Bandor."

"They arrived the morning he met Mason at his apartment—the day you returned home. They entered Mason's studio from Bandor's pocket."

"I suspected there was more to Bandor than his mild-mannered personality—the pocket for one, and his peculiar demeanor after the Dropas arrived."

"If you will excuse me," Krolic said as he rose from his chair, "I promised my companions that we would visit the islands."

Liam met Krolic behind Athena. "I'd like to spend more time with you."

Krolic offered Liam a quick embrace. "Perhaps we will have an opportunity after your mission."

"Enjoy your visit, Krolic," Lindor said.

Krolic waved and ventured to the islands.

Liam settled in his chair. "How do I read this map I possess?"

"From within," Athena replied in a matter-of-fact manner.

"I remember Lindor saying that exact thing."

"Yes, Liam, from within," Lindor repeated. "You have already started doing it. Remember the dream you told me you had."

"Yes, the dream. Athena, are you aware of a man named Ettepo?"

"Ettepo?"

"Exott Ettepo is his full name."

"Do you believe Ettepo is here?"

"He must be. Lindor, do you still not recognize the name?"

Lindor shook her head.

"I know every soul here in Dropa," Athena affirmed. "I have never heard that name spoken or seen it written."

Liam surveyed the city. "These surroundings also seem familiar."

"This information must be coming from the map," Lindor conjectured. "Athena, his soul was purified before he arrived."

"He resides at the top of Bubble Mountain," Liam added.

"No one has ever visited Bubble Mountain," Athena assured. "It is one of the Dropas' sacred grounds."

"Maybe that is why you never heard of Ettepo."

"We have talked long enough." Athena arose from her seat. "Lindor, please accompany Liam to the base of Bubble Mountain."

"Yes, Athena."

"Why no further than the base?" Liam asked.

"Because Dropians will keep their promise to the Dropas and not tread on their sacred land. You must go. Time is not our ally." Athena scooped a bubble from the fountain and held it in front of Liam. "This is the beginning of your journey. Discover Dropa yourself, for it is different to each of us." She blew the iridescent sphere high into the air. "As you travel, the souls of Dropa and the mortals of Earth wish you good fortune in your quest for the answers that will free us all from Arton's evil intentions."

Liam bowed his head. "Thank you, Athena."

Athena placed her hands on the sides of Liam's face and gently kissed his forehead. "Remember, the map must be read from within. If you lose your way, search deeper to reveal the path. I will be here when you return."

Lindor enthusiastically grabbed Liam's hand. They hurried down the road and out of the city.

Journey to Bubble Mountain

Liam didn't have time to admire the city's grandeur or bask in its ambiance, yet he was in a state of tranquility from passing Dropians. As a visitor, with restoration of his prior physical and emotional senses imminent upon his return to Earth, he wanted to harness the splendor of Dropa. The answer to whether he possessed the ability to retain it—for the purpose of conveying the feeling to friends and family—eluded him.

The mission called for a journey straight to Bubble Mountain, yet Liam marveled at the extraordinary scenery. The array of vibrant colors highlighted the landscape, and the surrealistic setting was idyllic.

Liam and Lindor traveled along a route that cut through Musing Woodland. The kaleidoscope of colors emanating from the leaves he had initially observed from the portal was even more spectacular. And mystical music resonated amidst the charming forest. The wind weaved in and out of the treetops and around the branches, emulating an orchestra of small wind chimes impeccably striking each note. The music transected his body, intertwining him with the trees and the ethereal melody. Liam was enthralled by his surroundings. Had Lindor not reacted to his mesmerized state, he might have never departed.

"Liam." Lindor received no response. "Liam!"

"Huh? Sorry, Lindor."

"Stay focused or you will never reach your destination."

"It is difficult, Lindor. Listen to that exquisite music."

"I hear it, but this is not the time to drift away."

"You're right, but I'm captivated by...everything."

"I understand." Lindor grasped Liam's arm and rested her head on his shoulder. "I truly want to explore Dropa with you. And we will, but you must keep your purpose at the forefront. It is critical."

"You have my word."

Still transfixed on the music, they traversed the path until reaching a small opening near the outer tree line. There the forest floor transitioned into much taller silky grass than that outside the city gateway. The florets tickled his hands and forearms.

Just beyond that, a gemstone beach of Mystic Sea—home to the Pyramidic Islands. Jeweled sand blanketed the coast for as far as he could see. Carried down from the Prism Alps and across the expanse, the minute, precious fragments of Dropa sparkled along the water's edge. The foamy waves rolled upon the shore and washed over their feet.

"This doesn't seem right, Lindor."

"Bubble Mountain is over there," she advised. "You must read your map, Liam."

"I'm trying, Lindor, I really am." Liam resisted her intention of leading him into the water. "You don't expect me to swim across to the other side, do you?"

"Of course not," Lindor laughed, "we will travel by water taxi."

Liam played along, perceiving nothing that resembled marine transportation. "Do we have reservations?"

"Yes, I arranged our rides myself."

As if on cue, two bottle-nosed dolphins—comprised of the foamy water—surfaced with their skin in perpetual motion.

"Tightly grip the dorsal fin," Lindor instructed.

Liam complied and was instantly swept below the surface. Instinctively, he wanted to close his eyes and hold his breath, but his recent presence in the murals prevented that innate urge. And he would have missed another spectacular part of Dropa.

Although flanked next to Liam, Lindor's dolphin gave the illusion that she was swimming alone. He detected the same phenomenon with his finned transport. The outline of the porpoise was barely visible. Once immersed, its foamy skin became one with the water.

Underneath them was Fluorescent Valley. It was an extensive reef decorated with a palette of vivid colors. The coral exhibited a plethora of shapes and sizes interwoven across the sea floor. Unlike reefs on Earth, the brilliance was preserved no matter the depth of the observer. Large sea fans, plants, and arcane formations populated the coral structure. Complementing the underwater intensity were the fish and other marine life—exuding hues rarely seen on Earth.

Liam spotted hundreds of multicolored sea horses measuring two inches high. Their speed and agility initially prevented him from close examination. However, they grew curious, abruptly changing direction and swimming alongside him. One brave sea horse came within an inch of Liam's nose, demonstrating its uncanny ability to swim backward and match the rapid pace. Its head bobbed and weaved as it inspected the interesting visitor in front of it.

The intrigued critter swam to Liam's right ear and dipped its nose in and out, emulating the Dropas' fascination with human facial features. Before Liam blinked, six marine equines partook in the inspection. Another half dozen investigated his left ear and he hoped they were unable to communicate through the middle. Lindor joyfully watched the underwater entertainment. Bored with the treasure hunt, the sea horses reunited with the herd and zipped out of sight.

A light flashed off to the right and Lindor had already fixated on the source. Six giant manta rays, teal in color yet translucent, glided through the water. Their brightness fluctuated as the majestic sea birds flapped their wings.

Tempted by the opportunity, Liam directed his unresponsive dolphin at the flying carpets. Opting for a solo adventure, he released his grip to intersect the manta rays, swimming with the ease of the other marine life. Lindor and the two dolphins pursued. The manta rays warmly welcomed Liam's visit. Flaunting their twenty-foot wing spans, they swam around and over the top of him.

Admiration of his new friends unexpectedly halted as Lindor clamped onto Liam's ankle while his dolphin maneuvered underneath him. On course again, they soon arrived at the opposite shoreline. Lindor surfaced first. She thanked her aquatic companions for the ride and set foot ashore.

"At this rate, you will never meet Ettepo." Lindor grew concerned with Liam's ease of distraction. "You must resist the temptations."

"I'm improving," Liam joked. "I was sidetracked only once."

Lindor briefly chuckled before regaining her seriousness. "Liam, you understand the importance of your journey. *Please* stay focused."

"I will fulfill my purpose here," Liam reassured.

Unlike on Earth, Liam's mind lacked considerably less control of his actions, making it difficult to stay on track. The magnetic beauty of Dropa constantly lured him away from his objective.

"You already gave me your word," Lindor reminded him.

"This time I promise. I will make it to Bubble Mountain."

The beach was narrower than the one from where they came. The small amount of sand also comprised the fragmented gemstones, but transitioned into rock and grass not far from where they stood. The Prism Alps were more fascinating up close, further accentuating the vibrant colors Liam admired when he first set eyes on them. His eyes shifted as he heard an extraordinary sound. Off to the left, billowy clouds released thundering cascades into the sea. Larger cumulus-like clusters spewed enormous waterfalls and dwarfed the smaller formations producing less grandiose streams. Although not as powerful, the latter provided a pristine magic all their own.

"We are nearing the boundary of the Dropas' sacred land."

"Why is it considered sacred?" Liam inquired.

"It is one of their many sanctuaries and, per our agreement with them, off limits to Dropians."

"What happens if a Dropian visits there?"

"That is one of many differences that separates Dropians from mortals. We respect the Dropas' wishes and honor them."

"Another admirable trait."

"You should consider yourself lucky."

"Why is that?"

"Because you are the single person who will enter one of the sanctuaries."

Liam pondered the opportunity. "I'm honored."

Lindor winked. "I expect a comprehensive report."

"I won't leave out a single detail." Liam gave her a small kiss.

They both chortled.

"It's a good thing we don't lose our sense of humor in Dropa."

"Never. It is part of the happiness." Lindor navigated through the changing landscape. "I want to share with you one of my favorite places to visit."

"I'm sorry Lindor, but I'm on a mission," Liam said wryly.

"It is on the way."

Liam and Lindor climbed over the rocky formations along the waning shoreline before veering away from the sea, eventually exposing a vast grassland.

"This is Butterfly Meadow. Is it not beautiful?"

"It's gorgeous." Liam relished the sight of an exuberant Lindor skipping amidst the tall blades of grass. He had never seen that jovial side of her.

"Wait until you meet the butterflies, Liam!"

"Uh, Lindor," Liam called rather softly at first. "Lindor!"

"What is it, Liam?"

"You mean these butterflies here."

Lindor pivoted and gasped at the sight of five transparent butterflies quietly resting on Liam's nose, ears, and shoulders. The winged insects partially reflected the colors of the sky and meadow.

"Oh my, Liam," Lindor whispered loudly, "do not move." She inched closer. "They are magnificent." Lindor meticulously examined each butterfly, starting with the one on Liam's nose. "I do not believe this."

"What's wrong?"

"Nothing is wrong." Lindor circled Liam. "Do you have any idea how many times I have visited this pasture yearning for a butterfly to land on my nose, or any part of me?"

"I haven't a clue."

"Neither do I." Lindor swooshed the butterflies off Liam. "Because it is too many to count!" She tackled him, pinning him to the ground. "I cannot believe that on your first visit, you not only have one, but five butterflies land on you."

"What can I say?" Liam beamed with false machismo. "Critters find me irresistible."

"I also find you irresistible," Lindor affirmed as she gazed into his eyes.

"As do I with you. It is one of many reasons why I love you."

"And I...love you."

Before succumbing to the moment, Liam playfully threw Lindor off himself. "I promised to stay focused. Remember?" He assisted Lindor to her feet.

"That is not fair."

"I didn't make the rules."

"Come on, Mr. Focused," Lindor said begrudgingly.

The winged escorts flitted alongside the two guests ambling through the tall grass. Lindor delighted Liam with stories of her visits to the meadow during the magical courtship of the butterflies. Recalling the recent view of the Prism Alps, he imagined a scintillating picture of the event.

"The sky is darkening over the mountain tops," Liam stated, somewhat confused. "I didn't expect rain here in Dropa."

"Why not?"

"Does Dropa need rain?"

"We do not *need* any of this. This was bestowed on us by the Dropas. It is a mere reminder of when it rained on Earth and another splendor to enjoy. When a downpour occurs, the blue sky is never completely hidden. "And that means—"

"Rainbows!"

"Yes. That cluster of clouds up there is ready to empty. Observe the beauty, but keep walking, Mr. Focused."

As they strolled through the meadow, the billowy masses released crystalline raindrops. From the suns behind Liam and Lindor, the light refracted into miniature spectrums. A more spectacular event transpired when the droplets contacted the rocks leading up the mountainside. Tiny rainbows briefly formed from the water pelting the hard surface. They intently viewed the display before she spun him around to embrace another unforgettable moment. Unique from those on Earth, dozens of animated rainbows did more than appear and fade from sight. The giant, multi-hued Slinkies danced across the sky, arcing down to the ground and up again. Heavy rain, that invariably brought destruction on Earth, presented another medium to paint the Dropa canvas. The brief shower surrendered to the blue sky, taking with it the clouds and rainbows.

"That was amazing!"

"I knew you would like it."

"How often does it rain here?"

"Occasionally, but when it does, rest assured that every Dropian stops what they are doing to participate in the spectacle."

"Really?"

"It is undeniably a merry event when it rains over the city."

"Why is that?"

"When those crystal drops pitter-patter on the streets, the Dropians enjoy dancing with the miniature rainbows."

Liam considered everything he had already seen in his brief visit. "Lindor, tell me more about the city."

"Think of it as the forum or capital of Dropa. It is quite large, filled with a variety of art galleries and theaters. We hold the majority of concerts in the coliseum located at the outer edge."

"Have you seen all of Dropa?"

"A fraction of it at best."

"I didn't realize Atlantis was as big a continent as what you portray it to be."

"Remember, this is no longer a continent, rather an existence of endless boundaries. It can expand forever and we all hope it will."

"It will."

"It must. There is no better place to exist than here in Dropa."

Liam felt a strange tingling at the edge of the meadow.

"Any luck contacting Bandor?"

"None. Arton has completely blocked our communication."

"Can you tell if he survived our trip through his pocket?"

"Not at all. Nor can I establish if Ti made it out safely."

They both wondered about the well-being and condition of Mason, Bandor, the kids, and the mural mascots, but the usual accompanying anxiety didn't exist. His presence in Dropa filled Liam exclusively with positive images. The vibrant colors and magnificent scenery soothed him with warmth and comfort. Everything was new. Everything was good. Everything was pure.

"Lindor...what is this sensation?"

"It is the energy from the Eternal River."

"River?" Liam observed no such thing from a short embankment. "Where's the water?"

"It is not a river of water, but one of eternal energy."

Liam raised his eyebrows, intrigued.

"It is Dropa's lone river of this kind and runs through the entire existence."

"Only one?"

"That is all we need."

Liam recollected the waterless riverbeds in Tanzania at the end of the dry season. Following the path of the visible gully in either direction, the banks and depths exhibited signs of erosion. To his right, the river disappeared into the Prism Alps. And to his left, it vanished within the unseen landscape.

"Come on, we must cross."

"That should be easy enough," Liam said confidently.

"It is easy, but you will feel something entirely new." Lindor knelt beside the edge. "Insert your hand."

Liam's fingertips tingled. Lindor gently wrapped her fingers around his wrist and lowered his hand into the energy field. The sensation intensified around the submerged area, but diminished near his wrist and completely faded across his forearm.

"What you are feeling is the essence of the Eternal River. It is the energy that nourishes the soul."

"Fascinating," Liam whispered.

Lindor inserted Liam's arm up to his elbow. The energy danced around his entire limb and the circumference of the field expanded the longer his arm was submerged. The pleasant tingling traversed his shoulder and into his neck.

"Is it dangerous to immerse your whole body?"

"You keep forgetting where you are." Lindor withdrew his arm. "It is exhilarating."

Liam attempted to discern the enduring energy around his forearm. Although not present, the sensation lingered. Lindor gestured for Liam to enter. He dipped in his right foot and experienced similar results. In went his leg—slowly absorbing the feeling—next his left leg. The encircling energy reached his knees. The energy bubble expanded as it had around his arm.

"Keep going, Liam," Lindor instructed.

"Are you coming with me?"

"Soon. When a Dropian resides here long enough, it is possible to perceive the energy."

"What does it look like?"

"It closely resembles the heat vapor you see rising from asphalt on a hot day."

Liam further waded the invisible phenomenon—up to his waist. "Is that it?"

"Color is present too."

"And what color do you see?"

Lindor examined his bubble. "I am unsure. Go in a little deeper."

The energy field consumed his chest and the euphoria passed through him. "Is it visible yet?"

"Definitely," Lindor answered. "It is a faint teal blue."

"One of my favorite colors."

"You wear it well."

Lindor patiently waited as the height of the river reached Liam's neck, making it difficult to ascertain the size of his energy bubble. An enchanted Lindor observed from the riverbank. Liam submerged his entire body. He became one with it, bathing his entire soul and allowing the current to slowly carry him downstream.

Lindor sauntered along the edge. Although reluctant to relinquish the experience, Liam elevated his head above the surface. Then his shoulders, chest, and waist. He lacked the knowledge of how to control the energy flow, resulting in Lindor joining him. Smiling from ear to ear, she initially kept her distance.

He submerged his entire body, but this time accompanied by Lindor. Liam glowed as she shared his peace and serenity. The two embraced. They resurfaced together, encased in a sphere of combined energy. Liam lost total awareness that he was with another person as she guided him to the opposite bank.

"The residual energy will stay with us as long as we are touching one another," Lindor explained.

"Then don't let go."

"I would love to hold on, but your weakness will persist if I do."

Lindor led Liam to a nearby tree, gently propped him against the trunk, and waited for the sensation to subside.

"That was unbelievable."

"Everything here is unbelievable, even after residing here for as long as I have. It is further enhanced when you can harness the river energy and completely absorb the beauty and aura of Dropa."

"It gets better?"

"Much better," Lindor replied confidently. "You have merely skimmed the surface."

Liam closed his eyes and leaned his head against the tree.

"How do you feel?" She brushed her fingers over his forehead.

"Mesmerized."

"Are you ready to continue?"

He opened his eyes to Lindor's smile. "Yes."

"We are almost at the base of the mountain." Lindor rose first and assisted Liam to his feet. "Just over this hill is a canyon. On the far side of it, we will pass by the most sacred part of Dropa."

"And what would that be?"

"The Dropas' procreation ground."

Near full strength, Liam no longer needed Lindor's assistance. "Have you ever been close enough to see it?" Liam peered into the distance, more in amazement than attempting to view something.

"No, the Eternal River is as far as I have come."

"You mentioned a canyon?"

"Yes, there it is," Lindor declared from the hill crest, "Fog Canyon."

"Holy cow! How do we get across that?"

Describing the canyon as huge is as foolhardy as calling the Atlantic Ocean a puddle. It spanned at least twice the width of the Grand Canyon. Monoliths towered from the base and glimmering clusters of Dropa metals lined the walls. Waterfalls flowed from openings spread throughout the canyon face. From the rim, the couple observed the seemingly endless depth. The water spewing from the walls never contacted the bottom. It dissipated before ever striking a single stone on the floor of the rocky abyss.

"Lindor, do you see an oddity with the waterfalls?"

"Astounding, is it not?"

Randomly, a number of spouts "turned off" from the present locations, but burst out of another section of the wall. This peculiar occurrence perpetuated throughout the vast hollow expanse.

"Repeating my original question. How do we get across?"

Lindor discerned movement to her right. "Here comes our ride."

An enormous fog mass bowled through the canyon. Before long, it would pass in front of them.

"Are we walking across it?" Liam asked incredulously.

"Not exactly. We will let it roll us over to the other side."

"This should be interesting."

"Interesting? Thrilling is a more appropriate description."

"I'm up for it."

"Good." Lindor leaned over the edge, awaiting the fog. "Are you scared?"

"Scared? C'mon. I'm in Dropa."

"You are catching on. Ready?"

"Say the word."

"Now!"

Tightly holding each other's hand, they jumped into the rolling fog with nothing to break their fall.

"Lindor! We're not rolling!"

"Patience."

Freefalling two-thirds into the canyon, they reached the base of the fog and rolled with it to the top. Once there, they tumbled to the bottom of the next cloud and spun up to its peak. The routine repeated. Like articles of clothing in a colossal dryer, Liam and Lindor tossed, rotated, dropped, and twisted until the last wave catapulted them onto the far side. Lindor somersaulted across the grass before coming to a rest.

"Was that exciting, or what?" Lindor inquired.

"It was a blast."

Lindor searched for Liam. "Where are you?"

"Up here." Liam dropped from a tree. "You let go prematurely. Since you were below me, you fell to the ground and I landed between two branches."

"The good news is we did not get separated."

"And the bad news?"

Lindor scanned the area. "The bad news is, it is not such bad news after all."

"Okay, what is the mediocre news?"

"We did not end up far from our desired landing site." Lindor oriented herself. "Our destination is that way."

Lindor and Liam headed for the base of Bubble Mountain. Along the way they joked about their experience in the Dropa "laundromat." Because Lindor was unfamiliar with the exact boundaries of the Dropas' procreation ground, she plotted a course primarily by the canyon rim.

"How do you recognize this part of Dropa if you have never been here?" Liam questioned.

"When Athena finalized the agreement with the Dropas, she requested details of the forbidden lands. In order to clarify specific boundaries, the Dropas imparted a dynamic map of Dropa inclusive of comprehensive descriptions of various terrains, canyons, mountain ranges, water masses, etc. Each sanctuary is carefully marked, allowing us to determine if our proximity is too close to it."

"How did you acquire this knowledge about the landscape?"

"After Athena bestowed upon me the responsibility of a messenger, I had to quickly learn the geography of Earth. As a result, I acquired an interest in reading maps altogether."

"You can probably navigate around the globe better than me."

"I assure you I can, and probably better than anyone else on Earth. As a messenger, we had to know Arton's location at all times and how to get there."

"Soooo, how did you learn—"

"Right. Prior to leaving for Earth, I studied the maps along with legends of the Dropas themselves. I have always loved exploration. Possessing knowledge of the landscape when I venture out on my frequent journeys, I no longer have to carry a physical map."

"That is fascinating, especially the Dropas' legends."

"The legends must wait I am afraid. See that area to the left of the mountain range. It is the procreation ground. We will veer right to the base of Bubble Mountain."

"Aw, please share the legends with me," Liam pleaded playfully.

"Sorry, junior," Lindor quipped, "it is almost time to send you off to camp."

The skies grew darker with nightfall—Liam's "first full day" in Dropa—and they had arrived at the base of Bubble Mountain. Lindor climbed to the top of a boulder and viewed the Dropas' procreation ground with an expression of wonderment.

"Take a look at this." Lindor studied the terrain.

Liam joined her to improve his view. "What is it?"

"Do you notice anything strange out there?"

Liam examined the sacred area. "Yes, the color is missing. It is nothing but gray tones."

Hearing confirmation, Lindor jumped up and down and nearly fell off the boulder.

"Does this mean—" Liam wondered aloud.

"Yes, that is exactly what it means."

A jubilant Lindor embraced Liam, knocking them both off the boulder. Interlocked, they rolled across the ground. Lindor joyfully kissed Liam all over his face.

Lindor jumped to her feet. "This is so exciting!"

Liam extended his hand for assistance, but Lindor had already returned to her perch. "Doesn't this happen all the time?"

"No, no, no! This happens every twenty-five hundred to five thousand years."

"What?" Liam rejoined Lindor.

"Twenty-five hundred to five thousand years when they lived on Atlantis. Since the creation of Dropa, no one can predict when this spectacular event will occur. This would be my first time to witness it." An elated Lindor knocked them to the ground a second time.

"That's it, I'm staying off the boulder."

"This is good and bad."

"Not the good news–bad news."

"Liam, this makes your mission more crucial!"

His eyes fixated on hers. He opened his mouth to speak, but Lindor refused to let him interrupt.

"The Dropas will be unable to offer us assistance. None of them. Do you understand?"

Liam nodded.

"If Arton and his army wipe out Dropa or this sanctuary alone, it is over! All over! Dropa is gone and so is Earth! The soul will have nowhere to evolve and nowhere to exist!"

"I realize this, Lindor. Arton will not succeed. Do *you* understand?"

This time Lindor nodded.

A New Beginning

The night sky had blackened, yet two moons lit a path for Liam's initial ascent of Bubble Mountain.

Lindor led Liam to a small clearing. "Have you ever seen a moonset?"

"You know we don't have them on Earth."

"Nonetheless, they are extraordinary." Lindor stared at the two glowing orbs. "It is a rare occurrence, but when a moon here in Dropa sets before the suns rise, the clouds are lit with different shades of whites, yellows, and blues. Sometimes other colors are present."

"It does sound extraordinary."

"It gets better. When the moons set in tandem against an ebony sky, the colors are as brilliant as they can possibly be at night."

"I cannot wait to view one."

"Prepare yourself, my dear soul mate." Lindor located a level spot in the clearing. "Stand here."

Liam eagerly obliged. Of the Dropa experiences thus far, he had difficulty choosing a favorite. They each offered something new and uniquely special.

Lindor slid behind Liam, set her hands on his shoulders, and gently pointed him in the direction of the smaller moon. "Take a good look."

"All right."

Lindor returned to Liam's frontside and gently closed his eyes with her fingertips. She positioned his right hand above his left, palms facing each other and eight inches apart. "Do you have a vivid image in your mind?"

"As if my eyes were open."

"Perfect." Lindor stepped to the side and guided Liam's hands toward the smaller, celestial sphere until his arms were fully extended. "Slowly pull your arms in and open your eyes."

Liam did as Lindor instructed. His eyes widened. Between his palms was the tiny moon. "How is—" He glanced at the larger moon orbiting alone.

"Shhhh," Lindor whispered, "enjoy the moment."

Liam carefully rotated the glowing ball as he inspected the craters. "This is mindboggling, but how is—"

"You are in Dropa and you should let the colors, the places, and everything else travel through you. Savor the magic and splendor for it no longer matters how, but instead, that it can."

As he rotated it, the energy of the moon swept through him. Closing his eyes accentuated the euphoria.

"When you finish, extend your arms and let it go."

Liam released the moon, opened his eyes, and separated his hands—his eyes fixated on the cratered orb drifting to its skyward home. Lindor slid her cheeks between Liam's palms. They gazed at each other. The moonlight of Dropa illuminated her skin more than when they lay in the desert mural—her beauty ever so radiant. Liam gently drew her face to his much like he did with the moon from the sky. They shared their last kiss.

Lindor withdrew her lips. "You must go, Liam."

"I wish you were accompanying me."

"As do I, but it is forbidden. Besides, the Dropas have solely given you the map for a reason. Travel to your destination and uncover what you must."

"I will return to you."

"And I will be here waiting." Lindor gently pushed his shoulder, guiding him to the mountains. "Until then." She placed both hands over her heart.

A surefooted Liam initiated his journey to the peak of Bubble Mountain, maneuvering effortlessly through the first stretch of the sloped terrain. Hiking at a steady pace under the moonlight, he expected to cover significantly more ground once the suns rose.

Liam capitalized on an opportunity to acquire a better view of Dropa from a small ledge. Gazing from the perch, he observed Fog Canyon. The rolling clouds filled the abyss and magnificently reflected the moonlight. To his left were glimpses of the Pyramidic Islands. His night view of the city would come later as it was obstructed by the islands and the dense Musing Woodland. Distant mountain ranges completed his panoramic investigation and he wondered what other brilliant landscapes surrounded them.

Peering down near the base, Liam's eyes zeroed in on a silhouetted boulder. The moonlight glimmered off the formation ever so slightly. Lindor sat against the rock formation, knees against her chest and her arms wrapped around them.

Liam reflected on their short time together. She sated him with a great deal of happiness and peacefulness, and he hoped he had reciprocated in his own way. How fortunate he was to find his soul mate before arriving in Dropa. Wants and needs of life on Earth had faded, a concern or barrier that once divided many people. Absent of those obstacles, he and Lindor could devote themselves to one another, sharing the energy and love that comes from within each of them. It was truly a treasure. Humanity strived for that existence on Earth. Liam believed that one day, with guidance from the new Treaty and the strong desire of individuals, humankind might come extraordinarily close to achieving it.

Liam savored one waning moment of the awe-inspiring spectacle before him. He sought a great deal: learn more about Dropa and the Dropians, engage in profound conversations with Athena and Krolic, and reconnect with Ashley and perhaps meet her soul mate. He yearned to find others, including close friends who perished during the war. All that paled in comparison to his desire to grasp the mystique of the Dropas. He coveted far more than the introduction to it on Earth. From what he had already witnessed that day, he imagined a plethora of magical attributes associated only with the nonpareil life forms. Until he spent more time in Dropa, his desires had to wait.

Liam bid farewell to the setting moons. The sky brightened slightly which meant daylight would soon be upon him. Experiencing a moonset would have to wait, for the sky was too light for that enchanting phenomenon. His pace increased as the suns hurdled the horizon, exposing more of the mountainside. Liam had not yet identified the exact location of Ettepo but maintained confidence that once he explored deep inside himself, the map would reveal the essential information.

The suns rose rapidly as Liam ascended the mountain. Without any reason, he opted to observe. As the glowing orbs arced above Dropa, they exhibited different moon-like phases. Unlike the last time he saw them, one achieved full phase, another exhibited quarter phase, and the third sun was merely a sliver against the blue sky. Liam no longer considered anything to be an aberration in Dropa, fully expecting the unexpected.

As he skillfully negotiated the rocky terrain, he wondered why this land mass was called Bubble Mountain. The brightened sky unveiled the answer at a short switchback.

Wedged in the crevices of the mountainside were bubbles of various sizes. Liam estimated that the largest diameter measured no more than four inches and the smallest no less than an inch. At first sight, the bubbles appeared normal, but presented a uniqueness all their own. Superficially transparent, Liam could not see completely through them. Encased in each one was a discrete Dropa scene.

Liam carefully lifted a bubble from its resting place and recognized the dynamic landscape of Butterfly Meadow through the spherical window. Unlike a static replica of a setting displayed in a globe figurine at a gift shop, this spectacle exhibited life. Grass swayed in the encapsulated wind and butterflies superficially fed on florets or flitted in the gentle breeze of the enclosure.

Liam gingerly placed the near-weightless bubble in its crevice and selected another one. That unique one contained a moonset. *It is extraordinary, as Lindor had indicated.* Although a single moon in that scene, the highlighted clouds and bluish tones painting the sky displayed magnificence nonetheless.

"Remarkable, is it not?" A munchkin-like voice asked from in front of Liam.

Startled, Liam fell backward and his arms flew outward, causing him to lose grip of the sphere. Amongst a chorus of giggles, he dropped ten feet before softly landing on a conveniently located bed of bubbles, bobbing up and down as if on a water mattress. Lacking a sturdy base, Liam briefly struggled before steadying himself enough to grab a small tree growing out of the mountainside. Attempting to elevate himself, the sapling uprooted and cast him onto the welcome mattress. He heard more enthusiastic laughter. His body caromed across the bubbles until he rolled onto firm ground. Liam climbed near his original location where he was greeted with cheers and applause.

"Who's there? Is that you, Lindor?"

"We are here, and no, we are not Lindor," a second voice replied.

"Where's here?" Liam attempted to zero in on the origin.

"On the rock."

Liam revisited the spot where he had admired the moonset bubble. "Isn't that interesting? Different Dropas."

"Yes, a slight variation from the ones sent to Earth," another munchkin-like voice replied. "And who are you?"

"My name is Liam, and you?"

"I am Granite."

Comparable to the dozen Dropas he had met back home, eleven additional Dropas welcomed Liam. They exhibited similar physical appearance with one distinct exception. These Dropas had textured surfaces.

"Nice to meet you, Granite." Liam crinkled his brow. "Wait a minute. We're speaking the same language."

"Of course, we are—"

"In Dropa," Liam interjected.

"Everyone speaks the same language here," Granite affirmed.

"What a novel idea."

"Novel idea?"

"That everyone uses the same means of communication. I wish it was possible on Earth. There are many gaps...or there used to be. People of different cultures and backgrounds had difficulty understanding one another, though it has remarkably improved."

"How do you like Dropa?" Granite inquired.

"I'm honored to be here. Dropa is such an idyllic place."

"Thank you," chimed the twelve Dropas before bowing.

Liam examined the others. "And who are the rest of your friends?"

They individually introduced themselves, each name consistent with their texture. Their method of introduction ignited Liam's memory of when he first met the other Dropas in Mason's apartment.

"I am Marble, master of architecture and statues."

"I am Slate."

"They call me Mica."

"Coal."

"Sandstone."

"Shale."

"Address me as Lemonstone," one formally announced with a giggle.

Shale playfully elbowed the Dropa.

"All right," the Dropa laughed. "My name is actually Limestone."

"I am Quartz."

"My name is Lava."

"I am Clay."

"And I am Diamond, the hardest, but most beautiful Dropa."

"Maybe the hardest head," Mica intoned.

"A witty gibe from the flakiest Dropa has little value," Diamond retorted.

"That is all well and good, but you cannot ignore the fact that you are nothing without me," Coal bellowed.

Liam was amused by the giggling Dropas' quips. "What are you carrying?"

"Some of us have picks and others are equipped with appropriate tools such as a hammer and chisel," Granite replied.

"Are you miners?"

Four Dropas hoisted tools over their heads. Mildly offended at Liam's assumption, Clay scooped a wad from its belly and light-heartedly threw it at Liam, splatting it on his forehead.

"Miners?" Granite chimed. "We are artists. Sculptors of Dropa, to be more precise." Granite gibbered to Clay, words Liam did not understand.

Clay stepped forward. "My apologies for throwing myself at you."

"No, I'm sorry. That was a silly presumption." Liam peeled the clay off his brow and rubbed it across Clay's belly. "I hope I didn't hurt your feelings."

Clay giggled from the tickling sensation.

"I met a group of Dropas on Earth, perhaps friends of yours."

"Yes," Granite acknowledged, "you met one of our Palettes."

"Palettes?"

"Yes, Palettes of Dropas, or Paldropas, are in charge of painting."

"And what are you?"

Granite pivoted and gestured to his gang as they bowed. "We are one of many Quarries, or specifically referred to as Quadropas."

Liam lowered his open palm, inviting the Dropas to climb aboard. "How many Palettes and Quarries are there?"

Granite remained sitting crossed-legged on the rock. "There are hundreds of Dropas left, but that number will significantly increase."

"It's time for you to procreate, isn't it?"

"Yes," Granite replied proudly.

The other Dropas danced and cheered in Liam's hand, thrilled with the upcoming communal event. An overexcited Sandstone fell off backward and smashed onto the rock, shattering into pieces. Much like the Dropas on Earth, the others erupted in hysterics. Sandstone's remnants gravitated to the core of its body, restoring the Dropa to its original form. Lava almost fell, too, but Liam snared its hot legs between two of his fingers. Its body stretched like melted caramel before it escaped his grip, plopping safely on the ground. Like Sandstone, but more like the Paldropas, its body reshaped itself.

"In fact, that is where we were headed before greeting you," Granite said.

Liam recalled what Lindor had said regarding the Dropas' vulnerability during procreation. "Arton is on his way."

"We are aware of Arton returning to Dropa. We are privy to all that happens in Dropa and on Earth, including your summons."

"Do you know what I seek?"

Granite scratched its head. "Not specifically. That is why *you* have the map. And I am confident you will find the answers at the top of Bubble Mountain."

Liam set the Dropas on the rock. Coal and Sandstone dramatically returned their implements to their waist as if they were gunslingers.

"It is time for us to continue our journey and for you to resume yours."

"Good luck to all of you." Liam lacked the appropriate words to say to those about to procreate. "And enjoy your celebration."

"Thank you," Granite said.

The Dropas scurried down the mountain. Liam tracked the miniature dust trail for a bit, before reversing direction and resuming his trek. "A distinct set of Dropas. How cool is that?"

The suns had attained their apex. Liam estimated he had scaled a third of the elevation. He deeply examined the inner map. The answers resided just below the peak.

It was difficult to avoid the distraction of the scenic bubbles, but onward he pushed. Intermittently, he smiled broadly, visualizing the Quadropas he recently met. His mind wandered to the Dropas left inside the murals. The smile disappeared as he wondered about the others in the vortex. He had no idea where, when, or even if they would reunite. Liam had to focus on the lone task before him. All of humanity counted on him as did the Dropians and Dropas.

Liam investigated a solitary, vined tree growing in a small clearing. The tree itself didn't interest him, rather the cocoons dangling from the branches—hundreds of them spread throughout the limbs. Upon closer inspection, the cocoons were actually sizable water droplets, each encasing a butterfly seeking freedom. The distinction of their wings and bodies indicated arrival in Dropa drew near. And composed of the same material as the cocoon, Liam presumed them to be water butterflies.

"I'd love to stick around for your emergence, but I have an appointment," Liam offered as he gently touched one of them.

A muffled gurgle interrupted his departure. "Don't you have an important engagement?" Liam assumed the Quadropas had returned to play a trick on him. He pivoted to catch them off guard, his discovery disparate to his expectation.

Encased in an oblong bubble, partially exposed under giant leaves, lay a baby boy. The child's blue eyes glimmered in the light and the infant uncontrollably flailed his arms and legs against the protective shell.

Although the infant smiled from cheek to cheek, Liam inched closer, cautious not to alarm him. The baby's moist gums sparkled as his jaw opened wider, creating a mouthful of saliva bubbles.

"Hey there, little fella," Liam said softly with a smile.

Happy to greet Liam, the gurgles grew louder and the baby's arms and legs went spastic. Precious as the moment was, Liam searched for evidence of a guardian.

"Do you have a mother and father? Where are they?"

Liam retrieved the transparent cocoon from underneath the plant, but discerned no opening. Wondering how long the encased infant could survive, he had a strong desire to free the baby. He scanned the area in hope of finding a sign of someone returning. His effort came up empty. Left alone once, Liam struggled with the notion of deserting the boy. Refocusing on the child, Liam received the same greeting as he did the first time. The situation paralyzed him with helplessness.

The child didn't require food or water and a life form dying in Dropa—where souls flourished for eternity—was inconceivable. Would his premature popping of the bubble interfere with the natural process of creation?

The answer presented itself in the form of an emergent butterfly that landed on Liam's shoulder. Its wings spread slightly at first, moist from isolation. Gradually flapping in the new, unrestricted environment, the wings dried and the energy of life coursed through its body. Flight of this newborn creature was inevitable, likewise for the life of the infant Liam held in his arms.

368 The Dropas: Fate Of Eternity

Liam sliced open the gelatinous bubble, exposing the naked boy inside it. The butterfly took flight.

"Aren't you a happy little baby? You can hardly stand the freedom."

"Ghhgghhh." The infant kicked his legs and jerked his arms with excitement.

Liam gingerly removed the infant from the cocoon. His skin was smooth and soft as were the ringlets of hair on his head. The baby stopped flailing its arms and legs and gazed into Liam's eyes.

"You're welcome," Liam acknowledged. "And there's another smile. What should I do with you?"

Overjoyed with the lack of restriction, the infant gurgled as his limbs resumed their spasmodic movement.

"You haven't mastered control of those things, have you?" Liam teased. "You clearly can't walk, but it's never too early to start. Hmm, how would you like to skip the preliminary motor skills and jump right into mountain climbing?"

Another set of indecipherable sounds exuded from the infant's mouth, not to mention more saliva bubbles.

"Good. The first thing on the agenda is to create an apparatus to carry you without drastically delaying me."

Liam set the baby in its severed cocoon and searched the area for something strong enough to hold the child. The sliced bubble was unusable. "Where are the Dropas when you need them?" He eyeballed the tree and then the infant. "Could the solution be any closer?"

Liam detached a half dozen vines, gathered an armful of giant leaves, and weaved a small basket to hold the infant passenger. Proud of the tiny contraption, he coiled two longer vines like a rancher and tied them to his waist.

Liam had constructed a transportable carrier with an open top section and small holes for the baby's arms and legs to slip through, adequately providing unfettered movement. He lined the inside with the leaves and added straps to tote the carrier on his back. Practicality made up for lack of extravagance.

Situating the child, Liam tested the conveyor for comfortability and fit—too much space. It required more than leaves to keep the infant from shifting.

"Bubbles! Wait here...as if you're going anywhere."

Liam remembered passing a pool of bubbles like the one he had fallen into when Granite scared the bejesus out of him. A short distance from his current location, he removed his shirt and tied off the sleeves. Picking through the bubbles, he selected mostly smaller ones, packed his shirt to the top, and returned to the baby boy.

"This will be like riding in a luxury car." He lined the carrier bottom with a few large bubbles and placed the infant on top of them. "You're liking it already, aren't you?" Liam filled in the spaces around the baby's body. "Let's hope the straps are strong enough." He buttoned up his shirt, loaded the cargo, and tied the vines in front of him. "A few minor adjustments and we are on our way." Liam repositioned the carrier. "Perfect. Have baby, will travel. Here we go."

The three suns had passed overhead to Liam's right. He searched deep inside for guidance from the map, already adept at reading it on the go. Periodically, he reminded himself of his baby passenger. To pass the time, he considered names for his infant companion, ultimately settling on Connor.

"Connor, how do you like your new name?"

Liam contemplated the situation. *Yep. As if Connor would respond, and in complete sentences too. Possibly spit out math formulas that offer the precise and most efficient path to my destination.*

Liam confronted his first true obstacle, coming face-to-face with a fifteen-foot crag and neither the left nor right side provided a way to bypass it. More fascinating than the wall itself was Bubblefall, an endless supply of bubbles cascading down the mountainside.

"Holy cow! Take a gander at this, Connor. Oh, right, you can't see it from there." Liam pivoted to offer Connor a view.

"Ghghghghhhhh."

"Exactly." Liam lowered the carrier onto the ground. Referring to the internal map, he confirmed his original analysis.

Reaching the next level meant climbing the wall. Liam investigated the rocky formation. Fairly smooth and unscalable for the first ten feet, the wall transitioned to a rougher, more jagged surface with numerous openings.

"How do I get to the openings? Connor, any suggestions?"

Connor gurgled and kicked his legs, dislodging a small bubble that moderately bounced across its path, reminiscent of the city fountains.

"Connor, my boy, you are a genius."

Liam assessed the flight of the bubbles from the fall. They contacted the ground with a good amount of spring to them. "That's it!"

Equipped with a sharp-edged rock, Liam scraped away the dirt in front of the obstruction. He selected an area under the most openings, increasing his chances of grabbing on to something. Liam deepened the pit and formed a ramp in front with the excess dirt. Satisfied with the size, he removed his shirt again to transport the bubbles from the fall.

Once filled, Liam utilized the two furled vines from his waist, tying two ends to the carrier and the other two around his torso. He situated the contraption, with Connor in it, next to the wall and on one side of the bubble pit. Liam had plenty of slack in the vines to distance himself from the pit and afford sufficient running room.

"Ready, Connor?" Liam set himself. "Here goes!"

Liam sprinted up the ramp and launched himself into the pit, purposely landing in a sitting position with legs extended. This exposed the maximum area to contact the bubbles while controlling the trajectory of his body. On the initial attempt, Liam flew into the pit at a slight angle. He landed on the bubbles perfectly, but the minor discrepancy caused him to fly facing away from the wall and with a clear view of Connor.

"This can't be good! Ooooph!"

Liam's back squarely slammed against the unforgiving wall. He caromed away from the formation and descended into the pit. The trampoline effect catapulted him a second time and he collided with the lower section of the rock face before coming to rest on the bubbles.

Liam's eyes met Connor's. "I hope you're laughing at something else. Do you know why I don't care if I smash into the wall, Connor? Of course, you do, but you can't speak. I'm in Dropa and I feel no pain. I can repeat this as many times as it takes until I get it right." He detangled the vines. "So, this is what that ridiculous coyote feels like." Liam returned to his starting position for the next attempt. "Be afraid, Mr. Roadrunner, be very afraid. I have my Acme bubble pit and I'm coming for you."

On his second attempt he smacked the wall once. Similar encounters accompanied the next three trials before he achieved partial success on the sixth try—he made contact with his noggin. Although humorous, it was a small victory, because on his seventh attempt, Liam grabbed two openings. Struggling at first, Liam ultimately boosted himself high enough to wedge his feet into a pair of cavities before climbing to the top.

The next stage was the easiest. Liam slowly pulled on the two vines and gently hoisted his companion.

"We did it, Connor."

Connor's dimpled smile and spasmodic arms and legs expressed joy for Liam's accomplishment. He was one happy little baby. And Liam was one ecstatic rock climber.

"You lost a few bubbles, but nothing a little rearranging can't rectify. There you go. How does that feel?"

Connor blew saliva bubbles at Liam. Connor's tongue extended slightly, accentuating the extent of the little guy's response.

"I bet you'd react similarly if I tied a vine around your tummy and dragged you along the mountainside."

Liam was intrigued by the infant's reaction. Connor ceased smiling, presumably understanding Liam and displaying displeasure with the idea.

"Don't worry, I have no intention of doing that."

The happiness had been restored. Liam strapped Connor to his back and they resumed the journey.

Uncharted Mazes

Connor serenaded Liam with gurgled songs as he hiked up the mountainside. Liam came upon another unique formation. Large stones amalgamated with smaller ones, randomly drifting within a confined area. Although hard to the touch, when two rocks converged, they absorbed each other as if made of a viscous liquid—reminiscent of how the Dropas regrouped themselves.

"Connor, they have lava lamps in Dropa…sort of. A colored light source would complete the novelty."

Liam positioned himself sideways, allowing the infant to view the nostalgic delight. Connor's pleasant babbling indicated his enjoyment.

"All right little fella, it's time to press onward."

Liam climbed to the top of another plateau. This one spanned a quarter mile before angling near the mountain summit. Impeding his progress were four unrecognizable stone entrances—uncharted on his internal map.

Liam allowed his navigator to peruse the area. "Which one, Connor?"

"Hgggghhhggghh."

"You read my mind."

Both stacked and floating rocks comprised the entryways. Nearing the four openings, Liam selected the second one reflecting the number in his party. At the archway, he slipped his hand between two stones—one floating and the other attached. Had he not been attentive and withdrawn his hand, it would have been crushed as the floating stone dropped onto the attached one.

"Grrrggggrrr." Connor's palms flattened up against his cheeks.

Liam began to believe Connor was highly cognizant of his surroundings and the events taking place. Unprovable at that age back home, but in Dropa, anything was possible. Liam imagined Connor's potential verbal wisecracks had he the ability to speak.

Passing through the ingress, he encountered additional pathways bordered by tall walls. Liam chose the closest path. The walls themselves were rocky, mossy, or covered with a variety of foliage. When faced with a dead end, he backtracked and selected the next open route. Repeating the pattern, the two penetrated deep into the maze.

Initially, Liam enjoyed the challenge, but the longer they remained in the grasp of the puzzle, the more he grew concerned of not meeting Ettepo in time. Thoughts of the others swirled through his head, only to be replaced by an image of Arton's advancement. That impression faded as Liam confronted a maze traveler's unwelcome segment—a triple dead end.

"This is not good, Connor." Liam lowered the carrier by the wall and sat next to his infant companion. He closed his eyes and drew a mental picture of the recent path through the maze. When he opened them, a grinning, blue-eyed boy stood three feet in front of him.

No more than eight or nine years old, the boy's blonde, wavy hair was perfectly combed. "Are you lost?"

"You could say that." Liam eyed the child in a peculiar manner.

A smile of complete gratification lit up the boy's face. "Wonderful!" He clasped his hands and raised them to the sky.

"That we're lost?"

"No, that I stumped you."

"Silly me." Liam smiled, acknowledging the boy's achievement.

"Welcome to Maze Number Two. I designed and built it, along with the others." The lad broke into a dance, hopping on his left foot while punching his fists and kicking out the right foot. He switched feet and performed the same punching and kicking motions on the other side.

"What are you doing?"

"This is my happy dance."

Liam joined him, requiring little effort to learn the simple movements. And there he was, stuck in a maze on his way to find the answers that would reveal the fate of eternity. Doing what? The happy dance. Glancing down at Connor, Liam sensed the infant's enjoyment of the temporary sideshow. As did Liam's newest friend. Both the boy and Connor giggled as only children can, igniting laughter from Liam before he ended the celebration.

"You are the only person who has ever performed the happy dance with me."

"There's a first for everything." Liam rubbed the small boy's crown.

The child jerked his head away and tended to his hair.

"I used to make puzzles when I was your age."

The boy dragged his fingers across the foliage. "Did you enjoy it?"

"Without question. I also made word searches and designed obstacle courses, but mazes were by far my favorite."

"You are the first to try my maze."

"Another first." Liam shook the boy's hand. "I am honored."

The boy giggled loudly. "And the first to not make it out."

Liam chuckled, accepting minor defeat. He officially introduced himself, "I am Liam. What's your name?"

"They call me Dalnar," he said with a scowl.

"It sounds like you don't care for it. What name do you prefer?"

"Posaan."

"Why that name?"

"I like the way it sounds. Po-SAWN."

"Very well. Posaan it is. A pleasure to make your acquaintance."

Posaan disregarded the greeting and directed his interest at Connor. "What is your baby's name?"

Liam knelt next to Connor and brushed his forefinger over the infant's cheek. "This is not my child."

"Whose child is it?"

"I stumbled upon the baby in a cluster of leaves. I waited for one of the parents but could wait no longer."

"The baby was abandoned?"

"I doubt someone would abandon their child here in Dropa."

"Probably not." Posaan squatted next to Connor with his arms draped over his legs. "It does not have a name?"

"I'm sure it does, but I have no idea if it is a boy or a girl," Liam replied coyly.

"We must give it one," Posaan insisted.

Liam crinkled his brow. "We need to first determine its gender."

Posaan giggled, somewhat embarrassed. "That would help, but who will be the one to find out?"

"I can handle that." Liam rearranged the bubbles to have a look. He aimed a dumbfounded expression at Posaan. "There's nothing there."

"There has to be."

"Take a peek for yourself." Liam gingerly lifted Connor out of the carrier, exposing Connor to Posaan.

"There is something there."

Liam laughed loudly, proud of the joke he played on his new friend. Posaan chuckled in tandem, realizing Liam had tricked him.

"We are even." Liam resituated Connor in the carrier. "You had your fun with me and I with you."

"That is fair. What should we call him?"

"I have already named him Connor."

"I like it."

"Connor, Posaan has approved your name."

Connor smiled as drool trickled down his chin.

"Why did you choose that name?"

"Had I a boy of my own, I would have given him this name."

"It is a fine name." Posaan leaned over and gently stroked the baby's forehead. "Hello, Connor."

Liam let Posaan briefly engage with the infant. His vision of the internal map had grown cloudy. He attributed the temporary deterrent to his entrapment in the maze and anticipated it clearing once they reached the other side.

"No rest for the weary." He nestled Connor in a comfortable position and hoisted the carrier to his backside.

Posaan assisted by tightening the straps around Liam's waist.

"Thanks, Posaan."

"You are welcome."

Liam made one last adjustment. "Posaan, can you guide us back to the entrance?"

"You are kidding, right?" Posaan giggled. "This is my maze."

"Just checking."

"Follow me." Posaan darted in and out of the passageways and avoided all dead ends. True to his word, he navigated through his own creation and adeptly led them to the egress and over to Maze Number Four.

Liam tapped Posaan's shoulder. "Maze Number Two does not have an exit, does it?"

Posaan chortled and kept walking.

"You're a crafty little guy." Liam admired Posaan's cleverness, but did not necessarily approve of his tactics. "All mazes should have an exit."

"Why?"

"Because no one would attempt to go in if there was no way out."

Posaan escorted Liam deeper into Maze Number Four. "You did."

"I was unaware that it was a maze when I entered, let alone it had no exit." Liam suspected Posaan was leading him into a mental web.

"That is the difference between your mazes and mine." Posaan admirably patted the nearest wall. "Mine are real."

"What does that mean?"

Posaan directed his blue eyes at Liam. "When you created a maze, how did you make it?"

"I drew—" Liam answered before grasping Posaan's point.

"If an exit on your maze was not distinguishable, no one would attempt to go through it." Posaan resumed walking. "When they approach one of mine, the exit is not in view, but they go in anyway, assuming there is a way out."

"And that is the trick you like to play on them, isn't it?"

"Exactly. My intention is to make them realize that everything that begins, does not necessarily have a distinct end."

Liam contemplated his worthy counterpart's statement. "You're a smart little boy, Posaan."

"What else does it mean?"

"To me it symbolizes many of our life quests or dreams, when we realize later that the undertaking may not lead to the desired outcome. Perhaps numerous attempts are required before achieving success."

Liam recalled his aspiration to be a professional baseball player. Although the dream was not realized, he transferred skills such as leadership, teamwork, strategy, and preparation to other aspects of his life—most notably his success at helping end the war, leveling Ozone's fortress, and disbanding the ForLords. Posaan listened to Liam's recollection with unwavering attentiveness.

"Our pursuits do not always transpire the way we intended. In many cases, the lessons learned and the knowledge gained guide us when chasing other dreams. Essentially, success doesn't necessarily mean achieving a planned goal."

"You are a smart man," Posaan said, somewhat mockingly.

"Thanks, Posaan." Traveling with his young sidekick, Liam grew confident that he would find Ettepo in time and attain the answers he sought.

As expected, Posaan flawlessly guided them through Maze Number Four. The walls mimicked those in the previous structure, with one exception. The barriers would not prevent Liam from finding Ettepo. Intermittently, they passed by a hatchway embedded in the ground. Posaan paid no attention to the prior ones, but the next one piqued Liam's curiosity.

"Where do the hatches lead, Posaan?"

"To underground mazes."

"Impressive. Will you show me one?"

"When we come upon the right hatch. Each leads to another hatchway, but in a different part of the maze. The one we enter will keep us on course to the exit."

Liam smiled, appreciating Posaan's ingenuity.

"We are almost there."

Liam chuckled as he noticed Posaan's untied moccasins. He drew a parallel to his frequent disentangled laces as a boy. Liam considered Posaan's intellectual maturity to be beyond the boy's age. His actions and physical nature, however, contradicted that. Posaan was playful, energetic, and emotionally young, yet philosophical. It led Liam to believe that's how it was with all Dropian youths. Liam arrived at the same assessment of Connor. The one-way conversations with the infant and Connor's profound reactions supported his theory.

"Here it is." Posaan lifted the opening. "Please seal the hatch after you enter."

As the hatch closed, the inner maze illuminated. It sparkled and gleamed as colorful light beams radiated from the crystal walls. Liam's mouth was agape at yet another incredible spectacle.

"It is my favorite part of the maze."

"I can understand why."

"There is more to it."

"In what way?"

"You have not felt anything because you have been motionless. Wait until you start moving." Posaan led Liam and Connor through his crystal palace.

"I'm speechless, Posaan."

"You like it?"

"Like it?" Liam raised his arms overhead. "This is awesome!"

"If you do not mind, please follow me in silence. This will allow us to fully enjoy it."

"Silence it is."

Liam and Posaan allowed their arms to undulate effortlessly in front and by their sides. The colorful light rays perpetually penetrated and danced around their bodies, filling them with energy although not as intense as what Liam felt in the Eternal River. It was stimulating, nonetheless. Further enhancing the experience, ethereal music echoed throughout the cavern resulting from the light beams contacting the crystal walls. The beautiful crystalline tones touched their souls in yet another way. Together, the light and music mesmerized them completely, Connor included. Occasionally, Liam heard Posaan's gentle humming during the infrequent musical pauses.

Posaan frolicked in front of Liam. The music flowed through him as if he was part of the enchanting orchestra. His baby blues sparkled above his endless smile. Desiring the same sensation, Liam emulated Posaan's movements without caring about his technique or style. His fragmented reflection bounced off the crystal walls. The euphoria was different. It was exhilarating. It was childlike.

They danced and twirled. Twirled and danced. Posaan grasped Liam's hand as they pirouetted in unison and fluttered like butterflies in the wind. All three hummed in harmony as if familiar with the music. Without realizing where the unscripted ballet led them, they had arrived at their desired destination.

Posaan leaned against a crystal wall and observed Liam who was unaware that Posaan left his side. The young boy relished Liam's unabashed dance. Each time Connor came into view, Posaan waved as the infant passed.

Posaan tapped Liam on the shoulder. "Liam."

Liam stopped, as did the light shower and music.

"It is time to go," Posaan insisted.

Liam considered how pleasant it would be not to have to keep trudging forward. He longed to fully enjoy his brief existence in Dropa without needing to be somewhere else.

Posaan ascended the crystal stairs leading to the hatchway. "By the way, Liam, where are we going?"

"I am searching for a man named Ettepo."

Posaan pushed open the hatch. "Ettepo?"

"Yes, Ettepo. Have you heard of the man?"

"Nope."

"Never?"

"Never." Posaan assisted Liam out of the underground crystal maze.

"Thanks." Liam sealed the hatch shut. "Which way?"

"Follow me. What is special about this man you call Ettepo?"

"He supposedly holds the key to stopping Arton."

"Arton? Who are all these people?"

For fear of scaring the boy, Liam hesitated before telling Posaan about the nefarious man. He then considered where they were. "Arton is on his way to Dropa."

"People come to Dropa all the time."

"He is not coming to exist here."

"What other reason is there?"

Liam didn't answer.

"Why is he coming?" A persistent Posaan inquired.

"He wants to destroy Dropa." If not in Dropa, Liam would have sworn that Posaan was about to cry. "Let's rest for a moment and I'll explain the situation."

Liam untied Connor's carrier and set it on the ground. Posaan and Liam sat across from each other as Liam conveyed Arton's intentions. Not once did Posaan's eyes leave Liam. He explained the war on Earth and Arton's second attempt at wiping out humanity, emphasizing how Arton's evil plots were thwarted each time. He described Arton's escape into the murals and the inability to defeat his army in the vortex. Liam summarized the journey with Lindor to Dropa and expressed his concern for those left behind. An enrapt Posaan listened without interruption. Liam closed with the conversation he had with Athena, and his belief that Ettepo is the man who holds the key to stop Arton.

Posaan anticipated more, before realizing Liam had finished. "I will help you find this man you call Ettepo."

Liam peeked at Connor who was presently fascinated with his fingers and toes. Posaan assisted Liam, helping Liam adjust the carrier into a comfortable position. Without hesitating or saying a word, Posaan resumed leading them through Maze Number Four.

"I thought only Dropas were allowed up here, Posaan."

"Yes," he replied, "but I have an agreement with them."

"What kind of agreement?"

"I believed this to be a non-sacred ground because I had visited this part of the mountain many times without ever meeting any Dropas." Posaan knelt and finally tied his moccasins, having nearly tripped on one of the laces. "When asked why I was here, I told them that I was enjoying one of my favorite areas." Posaan resumed walking. "We talked and played together all day. When they learned of my interest in mazes, they made a deal with me."

"And what was that deal?"

"They said that if I built mazes on the mountainside that prevented travelers from reaching the sacred area at the summit, I could play here as often as I like."

"Why did you let me through?"

"It seemed like the right thing to do."

"That was nice of the Dropas." Liam abandoned that subject and draped his arm around Posaan. "How long have you been in Dropa?"

"How long?" Posaan questioned, somewhat confused.

"Yes, when did you arrive?"

"When my time on Earth ended," he answered directly.

"When was that?"

"I have no idea. How long have you been here?"

"A couple of days, perhaps. I've seen a moonset and the suns twice."

Posaan giggled.

"Is that funny?"

Posaan rolled his eyes. "Seeing the suns on two separate occasions does not mean you have been here two days."

"Fair enough. How long have I been here?"

"Time is irrelevant in Dropa," he answered curtly.

"The sunrises mean nothing?"

"Everything here is created by the Dropas."

"I understand that," Liam concurred.

"What you do not understand is that everything the Dropas create includes the moonsets and sunrises." Posaan giggled. "You could have been here a year in Earth time—or you could have been here for five seconds."

Liam's dismayed expression abruptly ended Posaan's laughter. "I wonder how much time we have left."

"Left for what?"

"Until Arton arrives."

"Yes, Arton. Onward we go."

Posaan's pace quickened as they made the last turn, bringing the egress into view. Because the concept of time was no longer essential—his arrival predestined—Liam refused to estimate how much time he had spent in Posaan's puzzles. Once outside the maze, Liam studied the map. He had scaled two-thirds of the mountain. The extensive crown of Bubble Mountain depicted another plateau rather than tapering to a point. An entrance slightly below the flattened summit would lead him to Exott Ettepo.

A Time of Innocence

Just past the exit of Maze Number Four, the mountainside steepened and the extremely rocky terrain was prevalent again. Liam stared at the motionless Posaan who waited for Liam to take the first step.

"Well," Liam said.

"Well, what?" Posaan inquired.

"Are you leading?"

"No." Posaan squinted.

"Why not?"

"I have never been on this side of my mazes. Besides, you have the map."

"Right. Then allow me to lead."

"Please do," Posaan giggled.

Liam drew a path in the dirt with his finger and briefly explained the course they would take up the final third of the mountain. Because of the sharp incline and the large weight discrepancy between the two, Liam advised Posaan to walk in front. If Posaan slipped, Liam would break his fall.

The secured jagged rocks made the ascent much easier, allowing the climbers to grasp and step on the formations without slipping. Occasionally, a fragment broke off, but not enough for them to lose their balance or slide down a level.

They came upon the first difficult segment, a small archway. The agile Posaan easily cleared the sides. Liam's larger body and extra payload meant he had to chart a new course to bypass the structure. If he wasn't carrying Connor, he might have squeezed through the narrow opening. Posaan shouted instructions as to which rocks to grab and which ones to avoid. Upon Liam's arrival, Posaan welcomed him with a celebratory hug.

Liam and Posaan had one more steep climb to conquer before the mountainside leveled out. They eagerly accepted the challenge, demonstrating a keen propensity to recognize and choose the ideal path to traverse.

Nearing the top of the ascent, they had to negotiate a formidable obstacle. A wide, but thin rocky mass jutted out from underneath a group of trees. Appearing unstable, Liam presumed it would not support Posaan's weight, let alone his. He opted for an alternate route, but Posaan had already chosen the course Liam intended to avoid.

"Posaan! That is not safe!"

Posaan clutched the protrusion. "It is strong enough."

Liam shimmied closer to Posaan who swung his legs in an effort to reach the top of the formation. On his last attempt, Liam's concern became a reality.

"Aaaahh!" Posaan screamed as a chunk dislodged.

Liam extended an arm over his head to break Posaan's fall. Instead, the descending rock struck Liam's elbow. Posaan's torso brushed the top of Liam's head and barely missed hitting Connor. Unable to grab Posaan and retain his position without all three tumbling down the mountainside, Liam instinctively gripped the rocks with both hands. As Posaan's body deflected away from Liam, Posaan desperately, but unsuccessfully grasped on to something to interrupt his descent. Liam's body suddenly jerked backward from the force of extra weight.

"Ugggghhh," Posaan groaned.

Liam presumed Posaan had wedged himself in Connor's carrier. "Posaan!" He struggled to re-establish a secure hold, but eventually stabilized his position.

"Liam!" Posaan yelled.

"I can't see you."

"I am right behind you."

"Are you holding on to me?"

"No, I assumed you caught me." Posaan peered upward. "Somehow, Connor snatched my left arm."

"Connor has you?" Liam asked, perplexed.

"Yes."

"Connor truly has hold of you?"

"That is what I said," Posaan replied, amazed at Connor's feat.

"Can you grab anything near you?"

Posaan extended his right hand. "Yes, but I cannot quite stretch far enough."

"I can't move without losing my grip." A discontented Liam felt the carrier teetering across his back.

"A little further, Connor," Posaan instructed. "Just a little—"

"Posaan, what's happening back there?"

"Connor is swinging me over to something I can grab."

Liam shook his head in disbelief.

"Perfect!" Posaan grasped the target, eliminating the extra weight. "Great job, Connor."

Connor clumsily clapped.

"Are you okay, Posaan?" Liam looked to his right where Posaan's face greeted him.

"Yes. How are you?"

"Much better now that you're safe." Liam's head movement suggested the path he originally meant Posaan to take. "Let's veer to your right."

After negotiating several more rocky formations, they reached the top of the rise. Liam assisted Posaan up over the ridge. There they admired the beauty of the Dropa landscape. Clouds were highlighted with brilliant oranges, yellows, and reds, as if part of a painted sunset, yet the suns shone high in the sky. They viewed Fog Canyon, the Eternal River, and further off in the distance, the city. Beyond the city protruded more mountains. An enchanting prairie bordered Bubble Mountain to the left. It oscillated in the wind, transforming into waves and swirls of water and back to grass. To no avail, Liam searched for Lindor near the base of the mountain in the location where he left her.

"It's breathtaking, isn't it, Posaan?" Liam chortled.

"Yes, it is, but why do you find it humorous?"

"I don't need to breathe in Dropa, thus my description doesn't apply here."

Posaan shrugged, unamused.

They viewed the canvas in silence. Wonderful sensations coursed through Liam's body as he absorbed the resplendent beauty and surrealism. An image of Arton abruptly ended his reverie.

"Come on, Posaan."

Posaan accompanied Liam down a path. "Where does this lead?"

"This will bring us to Bubble Bridge."

"Bubble Bridge?"

Liam raised his brow. "Your guess is as good as mine."

They covered a good distance on the winding trail. During that stretch, Posaan articulated question after question—most pertained to life on Earth and others relevant to Arton and the war. Liam patiently answered every one. He explained as best he could that societies were progressing. People had changed their ways,

leading to a much more positive and harmonious existence. On a global scale,
humanity had realized the importance of preserving life, not simply for oneself but
for everyone. Safeguarding one end of life's eternal spectrum had been achieved
and now it must be preserved at the other end.

"I am glad to hear that war no longer exists on Earth," Posaan said.

"Me too."

Posaan kicked a small stone into Liam's path. Liam countered but aimed for a
spot in front of Posaan. They played that simple game during their conversation.

"Do you recall much about your time on Earth?" Liam asked.

"I do remember playing baseball and watching games whenever possible."

"Hmmm, you liked baseball?"

"I used to play it all the time. Even in the dark, until my mom called for me."

"Sounds familiar."

"After this is all over, Liam, may we play catch?"

"I would like that, Posaan." Liam smiled. "What else do you remember?"

"I enjoyed learning in school, but especially looked forward to recess."

"Why is that?"

"Most days we played football or kickball."

"What did you do on the other days?"

"Sometimes," Posaan replied shyly, "I chased girls or they chased me."

"And what happened when you caught each other?" Liam already suspected
the answer.

Posaan kicked the stone off the edge of the path. "Um—"

"Did you kiss the girls, Posaan?"

Posaan buried his head into Liam's hip. "Yes, I kissed the girls."

"I did that too."

Connor gurgled loudly, triggering laughter from Liam and Posaan.

"Did you have a girlfriend at school?"

"Yes," Posaan responded bashfully. "She actually lived down the street in my
neighborhood."

Liam detected Posaan's embarrassment. "Would you rather not discuss it?"

"I prefer not to."

"All right, new subject." Liam considered possible questions. "How did you
arrive in Dropa?"

Posaan recollected the event that led to his arrival. "I was riding my bike one day during summer vacation…"

* * * * *

A light rain had fallen early that overcast morning. Dressed in a T-shirt, shorts, and a pair of gym shoes, Dylan—Posaan's earth name—rode his bike around the subdivision. He pedaled cautiously on the damp pavement as he purposely slowed into the turns, but churned his little legs as fast as possible through the straightaways. He repeated that pattern except for the final stretch. Dylan closed in on the ninety-degree curve in front of the creek—located at the bottom of the hill a quarter mile from his house.

From his vantage point, he mistakenly presumed a dry road surface. A quick glance up the hill confirmed no cars traveled down it. Dylan clicked the bike into the highest gear and pedaled harder. Throwing caution to the wind, he challenged the curve at full speed.

His body leaned to the right, tilting the bike frame closer to the road as he entered the curve. The narrow tires lost traction, slipping out from underneath him. Dylan's right leg skidded over the asphalt. The pain of his bare skin scraping across the pavement and loose pebbles was excruciating.

The single barrier preventing the bike from sliding into the running water was the metal grate where the water drained from the street into the creek. The front wheel wedged into one of the narrow slots, bringing the bike to a sudden halt. The jolt caused Dylan to lose his grip of the handle bars. His momentum carried him into the creek, ten feet from the curb. Dylan's head squarely impacted a jutting rock and his body came to rest in the chilling stream.

* * * * *

"…that is the last thing I remember." Posaan kicked the stone over a ledge.

Liam's childhood flashed before him. "You were so young. You had your whole life in front of you." He snapped his fingers. "Gone, in a heartbeat."

"You never know when your time is up, do you?"

"No, you don't. That's a perfect example of why people should make the most of their life."

"Besides playing baseball, I was nice to people and enjoyed helping them."

"That's important, isn't it?"

"I believed it to be." Posaan contemplated his arrival in Dropa. "Falling off my bike into the creek was not all bad."

"Why do you say that?"

"Because it brought me to Dropa."

"That is true."

"And I have a new friend."

Liam hugged Posaan. "I also have a new friend."

They resumed walking for a short distance.

"Here we are," Liam announced.

Bubble Bridge, a fifty-foot long expanse comprised of bubbles with seven-foot diameters, welcomed them. Each sphere reflected the colors from the sky and the surrounding landscape in a distorted, but impressive sort of way. The bridge platform was three bubbles wide and spanned a crevice that dropped hundreds of feet into the valley. The tops of the first set of bubbles were level with the rim from where Liam and Posaan viewed the bridge. Absent of handles or railings to hold onto would make the trip across extremely challenging.

Posaan peeked over the ledge. "It is a long way to the bottom."

"Yes, it is."

Posaan giggled. "Come look at this."

Staring into the same bubble as Posaan, Liam understood Posaan's reaction. Their reflections were half as tall and twice as wide as if in a House of Mirrors at an amusement park. Liam removed Connor from his back so the infant could view himself. He reacted similarly.

"Okay, Stumpy," Liam joked, "we must devise a safe way across this bridge."

"We can get a running start and bounce across the bubbles."

"I do not recommend that," an adolescent voice cracked from behind them.

Liam and Posaan wheeled around before chiming in unison. "Who are you?"

"I am Tesmar." He graciously shook Liam's hand.

Tesmar was a tall, lanky young man, approaching Liam's height. He, too, had blue eyes. His hair was dirty blonde, wavy, and medium length—bangs to his eye brows and the sides covering his ears. And, like Posaan, not a single strand was out of place.

"Nice to meet you, Tesmar. My name is Liam."

"I am Posaan." He glanced at Liam indicating his real name be kept a secret.

"And nice to meet you...Dalnar." Tesmar smiled crookedly.

"Hey, how did you know my real name?"

Tesmar winked. "Just say a little Dropa told me."

"I would prefer you call me Posaan."

"If that is your wish, then Posaan it is."

"Thank you," Posaan said politely.

"Any time. Liam, what brings you to this part of Bubble Mountain?"

"My exact question for you," Liam countered.

"I am hiking to my favorite spot on the mountain."

"Which is where?"

Tesmar pointed at the bridge. "Right here, of course."

"How did you get through my mazes?" Posaan asked curiously.

"I came through the last one," Tesmar replied boldly.

Posaan hung his head in disappointment. "Was it easy for you?"

"Are you kidding me?" Tesmar lifted Posaan's chin. "I have no idea how long I needed to solve that masterful design, let alone the first three. And it does not matter how many times I travel through them, they are as difficult as the first."

Posaan's face lit up. "Do you mean that?"

"Those are the most elaborate mazes I have ever navigated, although I question whether the first three have exits. No matter, they challenge me every time. I am honored to meet the creator. I also am a puzzle lover."

"I suppose you have an agreement with the Dropas too," Liam stated, a bit skeptical.

"In fact, I do. I am the guardian of this bridge," Tesmar replied.

"How did that evolve?"

"The first time I solved Posaan's maze, a dozen Dropas awaited my arrival on the other side. They advised me to return to the city because I was on sacred ground. After a lengthy conversation, they designated me the guardian of this bridge because of my love for Bubble Mountain. If Dropians are ever clever enough to make it past his mazes, it is my duty to prevent them from crossing the bridge in a *Billy Goat's Gruff* sort of way."

"We need to cross that bridge," Liam said sternly.

"That is why it is presently in place. It only materializes for permitted travelers. Those bubbles comprising the bridge are usually disconnected—floating freely in the crevice—for uninvited guests. Discouraged by an errant map, they would leave the mountain."

"Anything is possible here," Liam reminded Tesmar.

"You are correct. As much as they would like to cross, it is my responsibility to discourage them and send them home."

"How often have you done this?"

Tesmar laughed. "Not once." He approached the infant. "And what is your name, little one?"

"His name is Connor," Posaan answered, "named after the son Liam never had."

"Hello, Connor." Tesmar softly caressed Connor's cheek. "What a cutie."

Connor wriggled in his carrier, gurgling and smiling.

"They told me you were coming."

"Who's they?" Liam recalled hearing almost identical words from Krolic in the Greek shop.

The boys exchanged glances. "The Dropas, who else?"

"Hmm, very interesting."

"They did not tell me why," Tesmar added.

"I'm searching for a man named Exott Ettepo."

"Exott who?"

"Exott Ettepo," Posaan blurted out proudly.

"Excellent, Posaan," Liam commended his young sidekick for the correct pronunciation. "Have you heard of him, Tesmar?"

The adolescent scratched his temple. "I cannot say that I have."

Posaan expressed urgency as he tilted his head at the bridge.

"Yes, right," Liam acknowledged the gesture. "I don't have time to explain. I'm…rather, we're in a hurry to locate him."

"I understand, but I hate to disappoint you. Hurrying across that bridge is the last thing you should do."

"Why is that?" Liam asked impatiently.

Tesmar led them to the first stage of bubbles. "If you *hurry* across, inevitably you will fall off and plummet into the valley before reaching the other side."

"But anything—"

"Yes, anything is possible, but I created a bridge that requires a specific technique for safe passage."

"And that would be?"

"Slowly," Tesmar replied.

"How slowly?"

Tesmar pondered the question. "I will explain under one condition. You must take me with you."

"Who will guard the bridge?"

"No one has made it this far," Tesmar replied confidently and winked at Posaan, "and I doubt they will anytime soon."

"All right. You may go with us."

"There is one more thing."

"Yes, I'll tell you why I seek Ettepo."

Tesmar furrowed his brow, surprised Liam knew the second condition. "Thank you."

"You're welcome. May we please cross the bridge?"

"Yes…but not just yet." Tesmar winked at Liam and contemplated the situation. "We should probably test it first."

"It hasn't been tested?" Posaan asked with a puzzled expression.

"No one is supposed to cross the bridge, remember?" Tesmar considered his options. "Let me see…Connor is incapable…and Liam and I are too heavy. Yes, that should work. Posaan, I designate you as the tester."

"Why me?" Posaan inquired anxiously.

"Because you are the smallest and most agile."

"Liam, I prefer not to test it."

"This is Dropa, Posaan," Liam reminded Posaan. "What can happen? Besides, you will have to cross it sooner or later."

Posaan subtly shook his head and did not respond.

Liam nodded at Tesmar, effectively ending the brief charade.

"Posaan," Tesmar called.

He raised his chin.

"We are even now."

Posaan realized Tesmar had also played a joke on him for having to solve the mazes. Liam recalled how thrilled Posaan was having stumped him in the maze and purposely broke into Posaan's happy dance, prompting Posaan to celebrate too. After observing the movements, Tesmar joined in the fun, forming a trio of fools performing the happy dance on Bubble Mountain.

"Yes, we are even," Posaan admitted.

Liam affectionately rubbed the top of Posaan's head. "You're a good sport."

Posaan fixed his hair as everyone gathered at the crevice edge.

"Although we can safely make it across, we cannot transport the carrier through the bubbles," Tesmar advised.

"You're joking, right?" Liam questioned.

"I am afraid not."

"We need it on the other side," Liam insisted.

"No problem. We will secure the bubbles already in the carrier, tie it up nicely, and throw it across to the far side."

"It's fifty feet to the other rim."

Posaan and Tesmar glanced at each other. "Anything is possible here."

Liam chuckled as he and Tesmar prepared the carrier. They positioned themselves close to the ledge. As Liam considered various methods to catapult the carrier, Tesmar twirled like a discus thrower and hurled the homemade transport. They all tracked its trajectory to the other side of the crevice. It descended, short of its intended destination, and shattered against the rocky wall. They disappointedly watched the bubbles disperse.

"Liam was supposed to throw it, Tesmar," Posaan chided.

"I expected it to reach the other side," Tesmar responded sincerely.

"There's nothing we can do about it," Liam admitted. "Tesmar, how do we get across?"

"Piece of cake."

"I hope your method for us is more successful."

"It is. Remember, travel slowly to avoid falling out the bottom."

"We're not walking across?" Liam questioned.

"Without handrails? Let me explain. Slowly press your foot into the top of the bubble like this." Tesmar's foot penetrated the delicate surface. "Do this with the rest of your body and utilize this technique through each bubble. When you arrive on the other side, slowly pass your hands out the top and pull yourself up as if emerging from a cocoon."

"Cool." Posaan wasted no time stepping into his first bubble.

"There is a separate row of bubbles for each of us, and each row contains seven bubbles. Meet you on the other side." Tesmar gradually osmosed into the bubble. "This is why we had to discard the carrier because only people can pass through the sphered walls."

Posaan was already halfway inside the first bubble as Liam comfortably positioned Connor in his arms. In went Liam's left foot and then the right. After observing Tesmar, Liam expected something inside to prevent him from falling out the bottom, perhaps a liquid solution to keep him afloat. Completely encased in the first bubble, Liam detected nothing of the sort. Tesmar and Posaan had already penetrated their second bubble and neared their third one.

"They're racing, Connor. We cannot let them win. Remember...slowly."

The contest had commenced. Connor assisted Liam by stretching his arms to the next bubble as Liam transitioned through each one. By the fourth sphere, Liam and Connor had closed the gap with the two boys. And by the fifth, they all were tied. It would be a slow sprint to the finish.

On Liam's right, Posaan kept an eye on the competition. To Liam's left, Tesmar closely checked his adversaries. They simultaneously entered and exited their respective sixth bubbles. Nearing the side closest to the crevice wall of the seventh one, they all stretched for the finish line. Already having an advantage of longer arms over his competitors, Liam's reach spanned an additional two feet as he elevated Connor high above his head. Connor pushed his tiny hands through the bubble and onto the ledge, capturing victory for Team Liam.

After lifting themselves onto the ridge, two disgruntled participants refrained from applauding the winners.

"That is not fair," Posaan contested. "You had Connor."

"And you two started before I did," Liam countered.

"Yes, but we are shorter than you."

"He is right, Posaan," Tesmar conceded. "It was a fair race."

Posaan reluctantly agreed. "You win, Liam."

Liam nestled Connor into his chest as the two boys offered sincere congratulations. The bubbles separated and drifted down to the valley floor.

"How do we get back?" Posaan inquired.

"We will cross that bridge when we come to it," Tesmar chortled.

Both Liam and Posaan expressed disapproval and groaned at Tesmar's pun.

"Hey, there are Connor's bubbles!" Posaan shouted.

"How did that happen?" Liam asked.

"Anything is possible here," Tesmar replied. "As we raced across the bridge, the carrier bubbles floated above us and settled on this side."

"Did you see it happen?" Posaan asked politely.

Tesmar stood at attention. "No, but I am the guardian of the bridge. I know all that transpires here."

Posaan attempted to stump the bridge keeper. "Where is the carrier, Mr. Guardian?"

Unfazed by Posaan's inquiry, Tesmar surveyed the area. "It is over there, leaning against that tree."

The three gathered the bubbles and placed them in the intact carrier, despite it appearing to have shattered against the rock face. It inexplicably morphed into its original condition without any evidence of damage. The two boys helped secure Connor to Liam's back.

"Where do we go from here, Liam?" Posaan inquired.

Liam reviewed the map. "We don't have much further. A short climb to our left and we'll be underneath the plateau."

"Is that where Ettepo is located?" Tesmar asked.

"Yes, Ettepo is there," Liam answered confidently.

The four mountaineers began the final stretch. Liam was developing a strong bond with the three boys and reminisced about many wonderful childhood memories as they playfully forged ahead. Connor kept himself entertained, resuming concentration on his fingers and toes either with his eyes or his mouth, and chattered away with joy and contentment.

As promised, Liam explained to Tesmar the purpose of meeting Ettepo. Tesmar refrained from asking any Earth-related questions or discussing either one's arrival in Dropa. Satisfied with the information, he chose to lead, shadowed by

Posaan, Liam, and Liam's passenger, Connor. It was obvious Tesmar was familiar with the area, at least the terrain. He weaved in and out of the rocks and low-hanging branches with relative ease, clearing any obstructions for those following him.

"There should be a waterway ahead," Liam informed Posaan and Tesmar.

"Yes, the Suspended River," Tesmar specified, "slightly above this stretch of trees."

"You've heard of it?"

"From the maps I studied before coming up here."

"Do you see it?" Posaan asked.

"Not yet." Tesmar pointed at a distant opening. "There is a lake over there."

Trees surrounded the lake and thick vines dangled from the branches that stretched over the water. Peculiar were the droplets rolling off the leaves as if it was raining. The dry trunks and limbs they passed were evidence to dispute any precipitation. They couldn't understand from where the water originated.

"Last one in has to kiss my feet." Posaan sprinted to the lake.

Tesmar immediately pursued him. "It will not be me!"

"Connor, let's get wet!"

Posaan arrived first. In one fluid motion, he vaulted off a fallen tree, grabbed the nearest vine, and swung over the water. Releasing the dangling stem at his swinging apex, he splashed into the lake. The vine swung back to the tree and, without missing a beat, Tesmar imitated Posaan's entry. Liam timed his pace perfectly, caught the vine, and performed a cannonball. He landed right between Tesmar and Posaan, casting a wave over each of their heads.

Posaan spit out a mouthful of water. "That was awesome!"

Tesmar wiped his eyes and noticed the empty carrier. "Where is Connor?"

"Oh no! How could I have forgotten him?"

The trio frantically searched the lake for the infant. He was nowhere to be seen. Not needing to breathe meant there were no rising air bubbles to signify Connor's location.

"I'm going under!" Liam exclaimed.

"Wait!" Tesmar pointed at an emerging object. "What is that over there?"

Seconds later, Connor's head surfaced like a submerged cork. Instead of crying, he wore his customary smile. His flailing arms and legs made it appear as if he was attempting to tread water.

Liam swam to the location and cuddled the boy next to his body. "Connor, I'm sorry I forgot you."

Liam playfully hoisted Connor above his head. The infant promptly burped a short stream of water out of his mouth. It splashed in front of Liam and incited laughter from Tesmar and Posaan.

Liam lowered the infant's "weapon" before it could fire again. "I suppose I deserved that." Liam swung his free arm, delivering a wave at the vocal audience that hit Posaan.

Tesmar escaped the assault by swimming under water out of Liam's range.

"That was pretty funny, Liam," Posaan giggled.

"Yes, it was."

"Liam," Tesmar yelled from where he had surfaced, "I found the river!"

Liam secured Connor in the carrier and he and Posaan towed it over to Tesmar. Upon arrival, they observed a tiny waterfall originally hidden from their view. The water purportedly descended from the sky and over the top of the huge tree leaves—eight feet wide and ten feet long. Examining further, a river located behind the waterfall flowed over the treetops. The river was truly suspended.

"That explains the water drops in that part of the lake," Tesmar concluded.

"And why it is called the Suspended River," Posaan added.

"Tesmar, you weren't kidding when you stated it was above these trees," Liam said.

"Believe me, I did not mean it literally."

"Come on."

Posaan and Tesmar glanced at each other and shrugged before following Liam to shore.

"What is it, Liam?" Posaan asked.

"It's time for me to leave you guys," Liam replied.

"Why?"

"Because my internal map has instructed me to do so."

"Please stay," Posaan pleaded.

"May we wait here for you, Liam?" Tesmar inquired.

"That would be nice."

"Yes!" Posaan victoriously clenched his fists.

"You two will have to watch Connor," Liam reminded them.

"No problem," Tesmar assured.

"Have you pinpointed Ettepo's location?"

"Yes, Posaan." Liam spread his arms. "Give me a hug, my little puzzle maker."

Posaan squeezed Liam. "I hope you find what you seek." He released his grip.

Tesmar followed suit. "It has been fun during our abbreviated time together."

"Thanks for getting us across the bridge."

"That is my job."

"Watch the boys for me."

"I will."

Liam knelt beside Connor and wiped the drool from the infant's lower lip. "Take care of these guys."

Acknowledging Liam's request, Connor gurgled and clumsily clapped.

"See you all later." Liam waved good-bye to the trio. He climbed the nearest vine to the treetop.

Liam entered the Suspended River—the depth slightly above his knees. He needed only six steps to cross the narrow waterway. The plateau, approximately twenty feet above him, indicated the peak of Bubble Mountain. He hiked along the riverbank before locating the cave opening.

Ruminating on the adventure with his three young companions, Liam peeked over his shoulder. Part of him hoped they had tailed him and another part was glad they didn't. He refocused on what awaited him. Sighing deeply and releasing all expectations, Liam entered the cave.

Reflections

Liam presumed the cave to be the river's source, but the liquid's movement puzzled him. The water streamed out from a groove in the floor. Yet, ten feet away, water flowed in the opposite direction through another channel. He deduced that the Suspended River circulated around the mountaintop with it originating and terminating inside the cavern.

Liam drew a parallel between his journey *to* Dropa and that of his brief existence *in* Dropa. Both involved circular patterns. This river. The vortex. The Möbius mural loop. And, foremost, the cycle of life itself. Dropa needed Earth to exist as much as Earth needed Dropa. Without an ending, there would be no beginning. Although true of life on Earth, Dropa revealed a slight variance. An origination doesn't necessitate an ending. Posaan demonstrated that with his mazes. In Dropa, Liam discovered that beginnings and endings could be the same. Intrigued by this phenomenon, he wondered if the concept had anything to do with what he might learn from Ettepo.

Liam followed the two channels. Strolling deeper into the cave revealed another peculiarity. Subtly flickering and shimmering crystals from the walls, ceiling, and floor supplied a faint illumination of the inner cavity. The dim sparkles were easy on the eyes and, comparable to many occurrences he had encountered in Dropa, offered another wondrous and mystical experience.

The grooves drew closer with each step. Fog hovering over the water and rolling onto the floor added another charm to the cave. Scaling the sides of the walls, the reflective nature of the cloud distorted to create arches and arrays of soft, colorful luminescence.

Mesmerized by the light show, he recalled his presence in Krolic's chamber, observing the vibrant arches from the vase dance on the table.

Liam leapt over the channels to the nearest wall. A gentle current of energy tickled his fingers after entering the light arrays. His outstretched palm penetrated the fog until it pressed against the rocky surface. The energy flowed only as far as the light. It reminded him of the Eternal River. Because of the weaker energy, it felt more like Posaan's crystal palace below Maze Number Four.

To increase the positive sensation, Liam pivoted and inched backward until his posterior was flush with the wall. The glowing arches and arrays penetrated through his body, but retained the magical connections on the other side of him.

Liam nearly became one with the light. He gently closed his eyes and imagined himself as a single photon intersecting uncharted galaxies on an indeterminate path across the universe. The feeling calmed him. It freed him. It brought him peace.

Liam opened his eyes—no longer standing against the wall. He had embarked on an enigmatic journey. The fog had vanished and the grooves in the floor had merged. The single channel led Liam to a quiet waterfall in the rear of the cave, having reached the inner depth of the mountaintop. Yet, there existed no sign of Ettepo—no sign of anyone.

Liam sat on a boulder near the cascade. *They chose me, and are relying on me, to find the answers, but where is the man who can furnish them?* He contemplated the present set of circumstances.

"The answers will come forth in due time," a soft voice said encouragingly.

"Who's there?" He frantically searched the area, but found no one. Feasibly an internal voice initiated by his desire to find Ettepo.

Liam discerned his reflection in the waterfall. He inspected the cascade, realizing the splendor of it flowing out of thin air. Walking behind it removed any trace of doubt. Returning to the front, he stared at his likeness. The smooth flowing water provided a mirror-like image.

"I look different." His partially transparent body was perhaps an illusion created by the reflection. *Only Dropians appear different than they did on Earth.*

Liam perceived a definitive resemblance in his reflection's face, but the dissimilar clothing confused him. Liam wore the same clothes he had when he entered the murals—cargo pants, hiking boots, and a collared button-down shirt with rolled-up sleeves. Conversely, his reflection exhibited typical Dropian apparel—a soft, white tunic tied at the waist with a silk rope and leather sandals strapped in a crisscross pattern up to the knees. The most significant difference was the uncharacteristically simple gold medallion worn around his image's neck with a leather strap. Four compartments bordered the perimeter of the slightly concave face and surrounded a lone, engraved Dropa standing with a paintbrush in its left hand.

Liam inched closer and gazed into the eyes, deeper and deeper into the window of the reflection's soul. About to touch the waterfall with his fingertips, the reflection's hand suddenly seized Liam's wrist. Startled, he jumped backward, extracting the image out of the waterfall.

"Freedom at last," the man said, elated.

"Ettepo?"

"Exott Ettepo to be precise, but yours truly nonetheless. You may simply call me, Ettepo, if you wish."

"You look like me...sort of," Liam responded, dumbfounded.

"And here I was thinking...what a fine-looking man. Are you disappointed?"

"No, I guess not."

"Good. Do I get a handshake and an introduction or should we merely converse in anonymity?"

"You don't recognize me?" Liam offered his hand and Ettepo shook it briskly.

"Of course, I do. Come on, humor me."

"My name is Liam."

"Liam, huh? A peculiar name, but if that is what they call you. A pleasure to make your acquaintance, Liam."

"Nice to meet you, Ettepo."

"What brings you up my way?"

Liam studied Ettepo, mystified by his doppelgänger. Ettepo exhibited cat-like reflexes as he side-stepped Liam before Liam could touch Ettepo's body for confirmation.

Ettepo promptly addressed Liam's obvious fascination. "You cannot get over the fact that I resemble you?"

"Not really."

Liam attempted a second test on Ettepo's realness. Ettepo whirled around as Liam was about to touch his shoulder. Liam immediately withdrew his hand and nonchalantly expressed eagerness to hear Ettepo's explanation.

Ettepo glared suspiciously at Liam before enlightening him. "We appear the same because it is your reflection that emerged from the waterfall. If it would have been someone or something else, I would have resembled that person, animal, Dropa, or whatever looked into my eyes."

Liam peered into the cascade. "Why can't I see myself?"

"*Yourself* is over here. Remember? Hello. I am your reflection." Ettepo placed his index finger across his lips. "Hmmm, I already revealed that information."

"Yes, you did." Liam concentrated on Ettepo.

"Splendid. Back to my original line of questioning. What brings you up to the top of Bubble Mountain?"

"I'm supposed to find you."

"Here I am, in the—forget that part." Ettepo held out his arms. "How can I be of assistance?"

"I seek answers that will save humanity and the eternal souls."

"From me? You are not asking for much, are you?" Ettepo laughed before realizing Liam's seriousness. "I will do my best." Ettepo changed the subject. "How was your trip up the mountain?"

"Huh?" Liam expected Ettepo to impart the vital answers he sought. "Exhilarating."

"Wonderful boys, are they not?"

"You've met them?" Liam asked, caught off guard.

"All three are good kids. Creative. Playful. Energetic. Boys with big hearts. Introverted, but once you get to know them…they will do anything for you." A curious Ettepo tilted his head.

"What's that look for?"

Ettepo stroked his chin. "Those boys remind me of you."

"You just met me," Liam argued.

"I spoke with Lindor before you arrived."

"Is she here?"

"No, she is not here. She is right where you left her."

"You talked to her telepathically?"

"Yes, telepathically, of course."

Liam dismissed Ettepo's disjointed dialogue and refocused on the matter for which he came. "So, where is this secret I seek?"

"You told me it was here," Ettepo responded curtly. "Describe it for me."

"I have no idea what it is." Liam furrowed his brow. "I presumed you would help me find it."

"Search for yourself." Ettepo glided his hand from one side of the barren hollow to the other. "This is all that is here. Unless you specifically tell me what I am looking for, how will I recognize it?"

Disappointed, Liam sat on the boulder. The answers were more elusive than he had originally anticipated. Liam retraced his path, hoping to recall something he might have overlooked, a clue that would perhaps lead him to resolution of the enigma at hand. It was painfully obvious that Ettepo was of no assistance, merely offering an array of prattle and wisecracks.

"You seem concerned," Ettepo offered a glint of sensitivity. He propped against the cave wall across from Liam. "What is wrong?"

"I came here to find the answers that will save humanity. I honestly believed you were the one who would help me find them. Analogous to my life on Earth, I find myself on a path of solitude. Seeking the answers on my own…again."

Ettepo fluctuated between eyeing Liam and himself. "Correct me if I am wrong, but when more than one animate object are together, you cannot constitute that as *on your own.*"

"Not physically alone, but alone in search of answers."

"I will accept that. I am sorry you always find yourself alone."

"No!" Liam responded adamantly. "Don't feel sorry for me. I don't want anyone to pity me. This is who I am. And if my path calls for me to travel alone, I accept it. Maybe I've chosen this for myself. I'm just trying to understand why."

Ettepo nodded.

"Perhaps it was meant to be." Liam rose and faced the cave wall behind him. "Here I stand while my soul mate waits at the bottom of the mountain. After the war and learning my wife had been killed, I carried on by myself. I returned to solitude after leading the defeat of Arton on Earth." Liam looked at Ettepo. "And here I am with you, yet the boys who accompanied me up the mountainside wait for my return. Why am I always separated from the people closest to me?"

"I do not have that answer for you."

"My point, exactly. I must uncover it myself. I am the sole individual responsible for my feelings and actions." Liam visited the waterfall and pondered the empty reflection. "I always accepted the fact that people randomly came in and out of my life due to natural social behavior of humans. Contrarily, I believe I am intrinsically drawn to people who suffer from hardship, encounter an emotional void, or require spiritual support. I was present for many people, helping them overcome unexpected challenges, easing their pain, or offering guidance. And when they regained enough strength and fortitude to solely return to their customary way of life, I reverted back to my solitary journey."

Still as a statue, Ettepo tracked Liam's every move with his eyes as Liam paced the cave. "That may be true in many instances, but consider those who came into your life. They afforded similar succor, whether or not you were aware of your pain or emptiness at the time. When that happens, it is sometimes difficult to distinguish who is helping whom because the end result is always the same—you are alone."

"How do you know this?"

"That is how life is. The journey on Earth is part of the evolving soul. Feeding it with good and expelling the bad. It is what brings one to Dropa. Everyone is alone, because each soul is unique, but the souls on Earth must be nourished in order to assist others seeking nourishment. They are fed by the spirits of each other. The principal element is to bring the soul to a state of eternal existence. What happens on Earth is merely a stepping stone."

Again, Liam sat on the boulder. "On Earth one has to contemplate many questions, the answers they find, and the choices they make."

"Sure they do. It is part of the nourishing process. Each time you are alone is an opportunity to search deep inside yourself for resolutions only you can provide." Ettepo drew his hands close to his chest. "Some people need longer to find those resolutions. Thus, they must spend more time by themselves." Ettepo rose and visited the cascade. He filled his cupped hands with water and splashed the water onto his face. He repeated the process before returning to his vacated position. "By the way, how *are* things on Earth?"

"Things have changed considerably," Liam responded confidently, "and we're all progressing in a positive direction."

"Good to hear."

"If we are on Earth to nourish our souls in a positive way, why do people insistently explore darkness?"

Ettepo crinkled his brow. "I need a bit more information."

"I'm recounting behavior of humanity prior to the war. People tested the dark side of life—the negative temptations: drugs, greed, murder, etc. They sought resolution regarding how far they could push the envelope without negative consequences, seeking immediate self-gratification for something that could potentially hurt many people in the process." Liam rose from the boulder and looked in the direction of the cave entrance. "We're striving to eliminate those things from our world. We've removed many negative aspects and aspire every day to live in a positive environment. The war was the darkest of the dark."

"Will humanity succeed?"

"I hope so."

"That falls short of certitude. Do you, Liam, believe your new utopian world *will* preserve itself and sustain that state?"

"I am cautiously optimistic. The effects and results of the war are fresh in people's minds. However, history has shown that, over generations, humans tend to forget their mortality and seek immortality—always experimenting with the darker side."

"Why is that?"

"I'm not sure." Liam ambled around the cave. "Can we have virtue without evil? Is it possible to have love without hate? Laughter without tears? Happiness without sadness? Do we need one in order to wholly grasp the concept of the other? Must a person be hated or abused first to feel the true essence of love? Do we need to confront the trials and tribulations on Earth in order to appreciate our eternal time in Dropa? Why can't we simply value the goodness…preserve the goodness…and treasure the goodness? People on Earth are aware of both sides. Why can't we have benevolence without malignance? Always and forever."

"I wish I had the answers," Ettepo responded compassionately.

Ettepo and Liam exchanged dissimilar expressions: Liam's one of deep consternation and Ettepo's one of peace.

Liam broke the silence. "Is there hope for our species?"

"There is always hope. Sometimes hope is all one has." Ettepo addressed the current issues. "Two problems exist. First, Arton must be stopped from destroying Dropa."

Taken aback by Ettepo's knowledge of Arton's advancement, Liam surmised that it stemmed from Ettepo's contact with Lindor, but he was skeptical that the two actually communicated. He refrained from asking. Ettepo seemed to be offering vital information rather than useless innuendos.

404 The Dropas: Fate Of Eternity

"The second problem involves preserving the source of the soul."

"The source?"

"You!" Ettepo glared at Liam. "Humanity. You are all the source. You are a species who has polluted the water, the air, and the land needed to help maintain the body that hosts the soul on Earth. You bury your garbage, expel toxins into the air, water, and ground. Worst of all, you kill your own kind."

"I already told you it is different," Liam argued.

"Presently." Ettepo's voice softened. "It is imperative that it remains that way." He rested his palms on Liam's shoulders and penetrated Liam's eyes with his. "You said yourself that history tends to repeat itself. If it repeats itself one more time, your species will have ruined its last chance. And the evolution of the soul will end."

Ettepo stepped away from Liam who truly wanted to believe that humanity had learned its lesson and would choose survival over extinction.

"Your method of survival is by destruction," Ettepo affirmed as if reading Liam's mind. "In order to have, you subtract. In a matter of two or three hundred years, your species has consumed what Earth required eons to create. Humans must realize the true essence...of life. For with life comes the nourishment of the mind, the guidance and love of the heart, and—" Ettepo crossed his hands over his chest. "The evolution, and ultimately the preservation, of the soul."

"We have a new beginning, Ettepo," Liam assured. "We will evolve and preserve the soul."

Ettepo half-heartedly expressed his assent, wanting to believe it possible. Silence fell upon them, each deep in their own thoughts. Ettepo said nothing more regarding the matter.

"Let's address the other problem," Liam suggested.

"Yes, the first critical issue." Ettepo shifted focus to the immediate concern. "I want to help you find what you seek, and I may be able to assist you."

"Really?"

"No promises. The answer may indeed be here, but I do not have it. I will, however, do my best to help you extract it."

"I'm open to anything at this point."

"I need more info on this Arton character," Ettepo insisted.

Feeling closer to unveiling the answer, Liam presented a soliloquy about Arton and how negative energy saturated the world. Liam described how Arton instigated the war on Earth and detailed Arton's second attempt to rid the world of humanity.

Ettepo, who had resumed his sitting position against the cave wall, hung on Liam's every word—attempting to fit the pieces of the puzzle together. "Stop."

"Stop?"

"Yes, stop. This desire for global domination or destruction you speak of—has it ever happened on Earth prior to the events you just described?"

"Many times," Liam replied confidently, intent on understanding Ettepo's thought process.

"What can you tell me?"

Liam dug into his mental archive of global history. "Not in chronological order, an obvious one is Adolf Hitler."

"Start with him," Ettepo insisted.

"There were Caesar and Alexander the Great. Many rulers during the Egyptian and Persian empires. Napoleon also comes to mind." Liam drew a blank. "Forgive me, that's all I can recall at this time. I'm sure others exist. There's never a shortage of individuals trying to achieve world domination."

Ettepo twitched his finger back and forth in front of his chest, as if plotting something on an invisible sheet of paper.

"Something is missing," Ettepo asserted.

"What's missing?"

"From where did Arton originate?"

"He's coming from Earth." Liam approached Ettepo.

"No, not presently." Ettepo mentally stumbled upon something.

Liam attempted to coax Ettepo into verbalizing it. "You mean initially?"

"Yes."

Liam recalled Bandor's story after learning of Arton's presence inside the murals. "From Atlantis, but he was banished by Athena."

Ettepo furrowed his brow. "I once read a story pertaining to a unique group of individuals. Hmm, what were they called?"

"Are any alive?"

"Most died when Atlantis was demolished."

"Did they have any distinctive traits?"

"If memory correctly serves me, they had the ability to jump from body to body," Ettepo recalled.

"Existors!"

Ettepo snapped his fingers as he jumped to his feet. "Yes. They were Atlantean Existors."

"Arton is one of them. In fact, he is the lone survivor."

"Sounds logical. After Athena exiled Arton, he set out to eradicate her and Dropa. Failing to accomplish either one, he attempted to do it indirectly, concluding that if he erased humanity on Earth, Dropa would cease to exist."

"The river."

"What?" Ettepo asked, confused. "The river?"

"It transcends the river. Throughout my journey, I've discovered many circular or cyclical patterns. The last occurrence is the river leading into…and out of this cave. Arton set his sights on eliminating part of the cycle."

"Okay, I am with you."

"Each unsuccessful attempt—"

"Led Arton to body jump," Ettepo interjected. "He is each individual who tried to eliminate humanity."

"That makes perfect sense!"

"Hence, the perpetual existence of negativity on Earth. Arton permeated it throughout generations like a virus. Those infected acted as the conduit of propagation. Humans investigate the darkness because they are contaminated with negativity. And positive people are the ones who can provide the cure."

"Everyone is infected to a certain degree with this negativity, just as latent and asymptomatic viruses indefinitely reside in the body," Liam added. "Many survive by warding off its evil, yet others are not as fortunate."

"Exactly. And each time Arton jumped, he grew stronger because more people succumbed to the negativity. It fueled his fire."

Ettepo revisited the waterfall, filled his cupped hands, and splashed the water over his face. Liam again dismissed the peculiar ritual and Ettepo returned to his previous position.

"Liam, Arton is that negative part of humans, no matter how strong or weak it is. He is the anger, the hatred, the greed, the selfishness, and on and on. And if it is nourished properly, it strengthens inside individuals and propagates exponentially. Remember the maple tree in your front yard."

The reference to the maple tree growing outside Liam's childhood home surprised him, but not entirely. Liam recalled images from his youth when he relaxed against that tree. "I'll let you decide if this is relevant."

"What is it?" Ettepo inquired, interested in Liam's response.

"I'd sit in the shade of that tree and think about an older cousin of mine. Prior to my birth, he was stricken with a rare disease for which no cure existed. Periodically, I'd ask my mother if we could visit him. She responded the same each time, stating she knew nothing about this sick cousin to whom I referred."

"Did you ever verify what happened to him?"

"No. She became increasingly annoyed at my inquiries. I deemed her cold, uncaring nature strange. I was certain he existed, to the extent that I felt his emotional suffering. Between my mother's annoyance with this *imaginary cousin* and the passage of time, I had forgotten him…until now."

"What sort of disease did he have?"

"I don't remember. However, in my mind's eye, a cure was ultimately developed. Ettepo, does this have any significance?"

Ettepo contemplated Liam's story. "When did they discover the cure?"

"Around the time I was born."

Ettepo briefly paced as he assembled the puzzle pieces. Liam watched in silence and waited patiently until Ettepo spoke.

"Yes, I believe there is a viable connection here."

"I'm listening."

"It might sound a bit farfetched."

"That's questionable. I would contend that me searching in a cave for answers that will save humanity and the eternal souls with my doppelgänger is farfetched. Please, enlighten me."

"Nonetheless, your mother was probably right."

"About what?"

"That your sick cousin did not exist."

"Let's assume this cousin wasn't real. Don't most kids have an imaginary friend during childhood? How is this relevant?"

"I believe Arton was close to jumping into your body."

"What?" The progression and nature of events played rapidly through Liam's mind and the timing would have been right. "That's an interesting theory. I can't wait for the explanation."

"Have a seat on the boulder," Ettepo offered, pacing in front of Liam. "Arton's progression of jumping is not necessarily a fine art. In fact, it is most likely arbitrary as to whose body is next in line. It could be defined by proximity, appearance, or innumerable parameters, but that is irrelevant. More specifically, Arton's succession of jumps does not bring him into one world dominator after another. There are states of limbo, for lack of a better term. After Hitler died, he made one, possibly multiple jumps. My guess is...more than one."

"Leonard von Zonek being one of them."

"Yes." Ettepo stroked his chin. "Arton usually requires a trigger to set off his rage. In von Zonek's case, it was his final art show."

"What does this have to do with me?"

"When you spoke of your cousin, that was a superficial term. You could have easily chosen a friend or a brother, but you happened to select your cousin. I believe the reason you had these images was because Arton was beginning to make the transition into your body right before they developed the cure. Your recollections of your cousin are memories of Arton at the age his current host almost died. Once he was cured, the transition terminated, but the memory of a sick cousin had already been embedded. This artificial memory could have been created by Arton to prevent you from discovering his true existence."

Liam rose from the boulder. "Does this have anything to do with why I'm here?"

"Yes. Although Arton did not complete the transition to you, a part of him exists inside you."

"You said Arton was part of everyone," Liam reminded Ettepo.

"I did say that, but you hold a discrete part of him. A part that probably no one else has."

"And that is why I was selected, isn't it?"

"You undeniably hold the key that unlocks the secret to Arton's demise."

"The difficulty is determining not only the secret but how to utilize it."

"Precisely."

Liam considered the conundrum. His face lit up with excitement.

"Have you uncovered the key?" Ettepo asked eagerly.

"The key is in the soul."

"We have already established that."

"No," Liam insisted, as he elatedly grasped Ettepo by the shoulders, "you don't understand."

Startled by Liam's sudden jubilation, Ettepo attempted to back away. "You are right, I do not understand."

Liam released his grip. "What has been my lingering concern?"

Ettepo shrugged.

"Being alone—alone to search my soul for answers. I possess the key and the time has come to locate the souls who will unlock the secret. The souls are here in Dropa."

Ettepo raised his index finger. "I believe we were better off searching inside this cave. It is much smaller than the ever-expanding Dropa."

"It doesn't matter." Liam pondered various possible souls. *Were they people I already knew?* No one came to mind. "I guarantee you that I will ascertain the souls before reaching the city."

"I have the utmost confidence in you."

Ettepo had a sudden revelation, removed the medallion from around his neck, and displayed it in front of Liam. "You will need to find three."

"Three?"

"Yes, three souls."

Liam accepted the medallion. "What purpose does this serve?"

Ettepo touched each of three gold compartments surrounding the engraved Dropa. "This medallion will hold the souls needed to assist you."

"Why are there four compartments?"

"I am unsure, but the reason will become evident to you."

"How certain are you that no more than three souls are required?"

"You must trust me." Ettepo smiled.

Liam closely examined it. "Why can't I simply escort the souls in physical form?"

"Perhaps concealment is necessary until the appropriate time."

"When will that be?"

"Only you can determine that." Ettepo situated the leather strap of the medallion around Liam's neck. "It befits you."

Liam rubbed his fingertips over the etchings. His eyes met Ettepo's. Liam stared deeper and deeper into them, perceiving images of war: killing, brutality, gunfire, and chaos. He heard a woman's voice, calling out for someone, but he had difficulty understanding the name. Liam perceived a second woman's voice, and a third, all summoning for different individuals. He also struggled to decipher those names. The vision of war faded as did the voices—replaced with a clear view of Ettepo's pupils and blue irises.

Ettepo repeated his ritual at the cascade, piquing Liam's curiosity.

"Why do you do that, Ettepo?"

"It reminds me of a time during my childhood." Ettepo wiped away the excess water from his face, revealing an expression of peace and tranquility. "Never let go of the child in you."

Liam approached the waterfall and Ettepo positioned himself behind Liam. Liam captured the water in his cupped hands, closed his eyes, and slowly brought the water to his face. Absorbed in the moment, he felt the coolness against his skin as the liquid streamed past his mouth and rolled off his chin. Ettepo stepped into Liam's body. Liam opened his eyes to a reflection in the cascade—gone was the emptiness he witnessed earlier. His fingertips traced the path of the water across his mouth and chin. He examined the reflection, *his* reflection, wearing *his* clothes.

Liam touched the waterfall. "Ettepo?" he whispered. The water circumvented his finger, hand, and arm as he passed them through the cascade. "Ettepo?"

The reflection did not respond. Liam withdrew his hand and cupped it with the other one. Ettepo's last words echoed in his head. *Never let go of the child in you.* He filled his hands with one more dose of water, but this time splashed it against his face. "Wooooo!" It was exhilarating.

Convinced of Ettepo's departure, Liam retraced his steps to the Suspended River outside the cave. This time, instead of running alongside the grooves, he briefly splashed through the incoming stream then hopped over to the other one. The game became more challenging as the channels grew farther apart.

The entrance came into view. One last jump and Liam would have successfully accomplished every maneuver. He launched himself, but the grooves were too far apart. Liam landed on the flat, wet bank of the right groove and slid into the river, immersing the middle third of his body. The upper and lower thirds stayed above and below the water, respectively. The current had increased during his visit with Ettepo and swiftly swept him downstream, or "around stream" for this river.

"Tesmar! Posaan! Connor!"

The river carried him past the tree he had previously climbed.

"Liam?" Tesmar yelled as he and Posaan waded the lake. "We will meet you at the waterfall!"

Liam entered the final turn before the river relinquished him down the giant leaves. "Woo hoo!"

Over the top he glided, gushing downward to the lake. The force of entry plummeted him to the bottom. Seconds later, his head emerged, only to be dunked by Posaan and Tesmar. As the boys waited for him to resurface, he stealthily swam underneath them.

"Where did he go?" Posaan inquired.

"He has to be somewhere," replied Tesmar.

They scanned the lake as Liam clutched their ankles and submerged them both. Liam surfaced first and rapidly climbed a dangling vine. Positioned halfway up, he waited for his "enemies" to resurface. On shore, Connor giggled and clumsily applauded at Liam's feat.

His head now above the water, Posaan craned his neck in search of Liam. Tesmar emerged five feet from Posaan, leaving enough room for a human cannonball without landing on top of them.

"Is he under water, Posaan?"

"I did not see him down there."

"Bombs away!" Liam plunged into the lake, resulting in a giant wave engulfing both their heads.

When Liam resurfaced, Tesmar and Posaan bombarded him with a barrage of splashes. Unable to fend off the assault, Liam submerged and swam underwater.

"Hey, get over here!" Posaan yelled as Liam set foot ashore.

The two boys swam to greet him.

"Did you find Ettepo?" Tesmar asked.

"Hey there, Connor." Liam wiggled his fingers over Connor and let the water drip onto the infant's forehead. "Yes, I met Ettepo."

"What did he look like?" Posaan eagerly inquired.

"A lot like me."

"Like you? How boring is that?"

"We expected him to be a deity," Tesmar added.

"He is no deity," Liam confirmed with a partial smile and lifted Connor. "Before we head down the mountain, please know that I am grateful for all your help. You were instrumental in my search for Ettepo." Holding the baby in one arm, Liam drew the other boys close for a heartfelt embrace.

As Liam hugged his young companions, they slowly morphed into his body. First Tesmar. Then Posaan. And finally, Connor.

He raised his arms toward the cave. "Thank you, Ettepo!"

Liam initiated his return, darting in and out of the trees like a hunted deer and descended the last section of the mountain he had climbed with the boys after crossing Bubble Bridge. He sprinted to the crevice, opting not to wait for the bridge to reassemble. His momentum carried him away from the ledge. Liam's descent into the valley commenced. With arms overhead, he pointed his toes downward to steady himself. Liam bounced off the first platform, a suspended bubble in the chasm. His rear end caromed off the second one. Making his way down the spherical steps, he increasingly improved his proficiency at landing on one and gracefully transferring to the next target.

Liam detected unusual movements across the ground, comparable to hundreds of ants scurrying to build their next fortress. The colorful terrain transitioned as the bubbles floated out into the valley entrance. Liam hitched a ride on a bubble that ultimately carried him to a safe landing.

"This is unbelievable," Liam acknowledged.

The colors gradated into gray tones. Liam attained his bearings in reference to the open land outside the valley. He had arrived at the edge of the Dropas' procreation ground, and the color had completely receded. Unlike the occurrences of vanishing colors in the murals, this was a most welcome sight.

Hundreds of Dropas, outwardly oblivious to his presence, proceeded to the desired destination. Afraid to take a step for fear of crushing them, Liam patiently waited as the Dropas rushed past his feet to their precious sanctuary.

Liam's goal of locating the three vital souls overshadowed his desire to witness the remarkable event. Certain the Dropas had safely passed, Liam set out for the boulder where he left Lindor.

Lindor was nowhere in sight. Recalling his experience with Ettepo and the boys, he hoped the same phenomenon wasn't true with Lindor—that she was a part of him too?

Two hands gently covered Liam's eyes.

"Guess who," the familiar voice softly spoke, presenting him with the answer to his question.

Liam whirled around and emphatically embraced Lindor.

"What happened to you?" Lindor eyed Liam in a peculiar way and caressed his cheek. "You...appear younger."

"Lindor, I rediscovered the child in me."

She kissed Liam on the lips. "Yes, I perceive it in your face."

"Something else is happening. The Dropas are traveling to their sacred procreation ground." Liam pointed to the valley opening. "That's where they marched around me."

Lindor stepped toward the clearing. "A once-in-an-existence opportunity, Liam."

"We must stay focused, Lindor," Liam lightheartedly reminded her. "We have much work to do in order to save them."

"Touché." Lindor redirected her enthusiasm. "Did you find Ettepo?"

"Come on." Liam wrapped his arm around his soul mate. "I'll share everything with you on the way to the city."

Collective Souls

Liam recounted details of his ascent of Bubble Mountain, emphasizing his happenstance with the Quadropas and their anticipation of the sacred procreation ritual. His unforgettable awakening with Connor, Posaan, and Tesmar comprised the majority of the story. Liam's face lit up as he recalled his time with the three precocious boys. Lindor occasionally tugged on his arm as childhood memories displaced his recollection of recent events. He described the bubble launching pit Connor and he created, the mazes Posaan designed, and Bubble Bridge that Tesmar proudly guarded.

Realizing his oneness with them, Liam contemplated how they "persuaded" the Dropas to enter one of their sanctuaries. *That should have been my first clue regarding their anomalous existence.*

He concluded his magical tale with Ettepo and his own reflection inside the cave. Lindor showed rapt interest in every aspect of the story and asked many questions during his revelation.

"What did you do during my absence?"

"I did not have time to do much of anything," Lindor replied innocently. "You were not away for long."

Liam glanced at Bubble Mountain. All he encountered replayed in his head. "How is that possible? I climbed to the mountain peak and stopped numerous times along the way."

Lindor chuckled, "Time is—"

"Irrelevant here. I've been reminded of that." Liam recalled his conversation with Posaan. "What *did* you have time to do?"

"I admired the blossoming flowers and perched myself in a tree to view the Dropas."

"That's it?"

"Yes. When you returned, I snuck up on you."

"Amazing."

"The transition from Earth time to Dropa *non-time* does not happen overnight," Lindor giggled. "Remember, you did not arrive in Dropa the way most people do. You will eventually complete the change."

"I'll have to take your word for it. C'mon!"

"What are we doing?"

"I'll show you when we get there." Liam led Lindor to their previous landing spot on that side of Fog Canyon. He broke into a sprint as they neared the rim.

"Liam! The fog is not here yet!"

"We don't need the fog."

"How will we get across?"

"By flying, Lindor."

They tightly squeezed each other's hand and launched into the vast expanse.

"Woo hoo! Are we flying or falling?"

"Stretch out your right arm!" Liam countered with his left, allowing them to soar within the spaciousness of the enormous canyon.

"We are flying, Liam!"

"How does it feel?"

"It is more exhilarating than our flight through the murals."

"Here it comes." Liam adjusted his arm angle, steering them on a course to intercept the fog. "Let's try something."

"What are you up to?"

"An attempt to bounce off the fog."

"Copilot to pilot," she announced playfully, "all systems go."

Liam and Lindor passed over the front edge and dove onto the surface of the cloud. If it didn't go as anticipated, they would toss around to the other side like the first time they crossed the canyon. They exceeded Liam's expectations and ricocheted higher into the air. The second encounter with the rolling mass yielded similar results.

"One more time should do it!" Liam yelled.

"Where will we land?"

"Land?" Liam questioned on impact with the fog.

"Yes, land!"

"Oops...didn't consider the landing...or slowing for that matter."

"There's a clearing just past the canyon ridge. It may cushion our blow."

Liam and Lindor soared past the targeted area and over the Eternal River, descending feet first, but at a forty-five-degree angle into Butterfly Meadow. Upon impact, butterflies emerged from cover and flitted away from the unexpected visitors. The two aviators somersaulted several times before sliding to a stop.

Liam spit out blades of grass and wiped his tongue on his shirt. "Are you all right, Lindor?"

"Next time—"

"Learn how to land first." Liam removed the interlaced grass from Lindor's hair. "Wasn't that a blast?"

"Yes, it was, little boy."

Liam gently grasped Lindor's arm and whispered, "Don't move."

"What is it?" Lindor inquired softly as her eyes darted back and forth.

"Shh. You'll find out in a second." Liam's pupils reflected an image of the object above her head. "A little longer."

"Is it a—"

"Be still."

Lindor slightly tilted her head backward, enough to give the crystalline butterfly a landing pad. She refrained from smiling, afraid her cheek movement would startle the curious visitor.

Liam savored her elation. "There's your butterfly, my love."

Silently, they observed the movement of the butterfly's transparent wings on her forehead. Liam gazed into Lindor's eyes, but this time battle scenes appeared accompanied by three female voices.

"Lindor!" Liam whispered loudly. "Do you hear that?"

"Shh, you will frighten my new friend."

The voices grew louder.

"Tell me you can hear them."

The butterfly took flight.

"You scared it."

"I'm sorry, but I'm hearing voices again."

"I do not hear anything, Liam."

Liam examined the pendant for clues. "They're the same voices I heard when I accepted the medallion from Ettepo."

"What are they saying?"

"It's difficult to understand. Sounds like three women calling out for help."

"Do they need assistance or are they attempting to aid someone?"

Liam remained frozen for fear of losing his concentration. "Yes, they're definitely calling to someone, perhaps a child." Making that recognition, Liam assimilated the voices. Instead of listening to them collectively, he concentrated on one individual. "I can't make out the first name—sounds like Norolen."

"Norolen?"

He refocused on the fading images in Lindor's eyes. "No, not yet!"

"What is wrong?"

"They're disappearing," Liam replied disappointedly.

"I am sorry, Liam."

"Lindor, have you ever heard of someone named Norolen?"

"No." Lindor rubbed Liam's back. "What did you see in my eyes?"

"Images of war, like what I perceived in Ettepo's."

"What specifically comprised the images?" Lindor asked intently.

"Tanks firing on bunkers."

"Just tanks?"

"That's the confusing part. There were horsemen alongside the tanks."

Lindor persisted with the questioning, trying to help Liam solve the puzzle. "What kind of tanks?"

"World War II German Panzer tanks."

"Describe the uniforms of the soldiers riding horseback."

"Tight white pants with black, knee-high boots. They also carried swords."

"Is that it?"

"Yes. I focused more on the voices than the images."

"It is a good start." Lindor arose, eager to return to the city. "We will attempt to decipher the meaning on the way."

Liam dusted off his pants. *Why were the tanks and horses together?*

They briskly walked through the meadow to Mystic Sea. Liam paid little attention to the numerous fluttering butterflies this time, focused on why he kept perceiving battle images and hearing the same voices. Lindor questioned him on a different subject.

"Tell me more about your discussion with Ettepo."

"We covered a variety of issues."

"For example?"

"Solitude and searching for answers. Preserving souls."

"All sensible, but they likely will not provide us with any clues," Lindor supposed. "What else?"

Replaying the conversation in his head, Liam conveyed subsequent topics of interest. "We discussed the current state of Earth, the fascination people had with the darker side of life, and events that led up to the war."

"Keep going," Lindor urged, steadfast in her search for information that might reveal the souls Liam sought.

Liam stopped walking. "Negativity and history repeating itself. Our method of survival is that of destruction: among other things, consuming and destroying our resources and killing each other."

Lindor listened carefully as Liam revisited his encounter with Ettepo.

"I explained how Arton was exiled from Dropa." Liam offered a random recollection. "Arton—history repeating itself—human annihilation." Liam stared into Lindor's eyes as the war images reappeared. "Existor—Alexander the Great—Hitler." Liam heard the distressed women—louder and clearer. "Body jumping—world domination. Arton's evolution into leaders that aspired to achieve global supremacy or destruction." Liam concentrated on the voices, the volume increasing and the clarity sharpening. He repeated a name. "Noro—Norolen." Liam listened intently. "Napoleon!"

"One of the individuals was Napoleon?"

An enrapt Liam heard the second and third names. "That's it!"

"Please tell me what you heard," Lindor insisted.

"The names! The women were calling out to their sons."

"And what were the boys' names?"

"Napoleon…Adolf…and Leonard."

"Do you truly believe those three souls are here in Dropa?"

"Not at all. Arton was an Existor, correct?"

"Yes."

"Ettepo revealed that Arton is the negativity source on Earth."

"Arton alone?" Lindor inquired.

"No, but he is the primary one. Because of his body-jumping abilities, Arton was Napoleon. He was also Hitler."

"And Leonard," they said together.

"You are supposed to find the mothers of those three evil men?"

"Yes. Don't you understand?"

"No!" Lindor replied emphatically.

"You have three people who tried to rule the world."

"I am with you thus far," Lindor acknowledged unconvincingly.

"Why do we need their mothers?"

"My question exactly."

"Is there a special connection between a mother and her son?"

"Yes, the bond they form with each other on Earth."

"I'm aware of that, but there must be a transcendent relationship we don't comprehend," Liam surmised.

"Maybe there is, but I am not aware of it."

"Lindor, did you have kids when you were on Earth?"

"No."

"That's why this notion eludes us. Neither you nor I parented children. We must consult with those mothers who understand that bond."

Upon arrival on the far shore of Mystic Sea, Lindor telepathically contacted Athena, informing her of what Liam had uncovered and asking her to locate the souls of three women: Letizia Bonaparte, Karla Hitler, and Josephine von Zonek. After completing the communication, she transmitted a message to a pair of dolphins.

"What a coincidence that Arton assumed those men's identities," Lindor said.

"It is, and it isn't."

"What do you mean by that?"

Liam extended his fingers to emphasize his points. "One, all three men had an ambition to conquer the world. Two, they all exhibited strong leadership skills."

"Although morally questionable," Lindor added.

"Agreed. And three, each one loved and appreciated the arts in one way or another."

They waded up to their waist as the dolphins arrived.

Liam grasped his porpoise's dorsal fin. "How can these three ladies help us?"

The water taxis submerged and carried the passengers across Mystic Sea.

"Please don't leave us, Bandor." Ti kissed Bandor on the forehead. *"He's not getting any warmer."*

"Now what, Mason?" Brian asked.

"I don't know," Mason replied helplessly.

"They made—" Bandor whispered.

The Dropas halted their dancing, and everyone leaned closer to hear Bandor's words.

"What did you say, Bandor?" Lauren inquired.

Bandor slowly opened his eyes and whispered a little louder. "They made it."

"They made it?" Cooper sought confirmation.

"Yes, Lindor and Liam have arrived in Dropa."

"Are you sure?" Mason whispered.

Bandor assented with a weak smile. The Dropas and the kids danced in jubilation.

"They made it!" Lauren swung Brian's hands from side to side. "They arrived in Dropa!"

Contented to hear the news, Mason wore an expression of deep concern about the fate of his good friend. "Will you survive, Bandor?"

All ceased the celebration and waited for Bandor's response.

"Bandor." Mason gently nudged him.

"I am here," Bandor whispered.

"Why do I feel your coldness?"

Bandor slowly opened his eyes. "It is Arton's aftermath."

"How can we help warm you?" Ti inquired compassionately.

"Stripes," Bandor called weakly.

"Stripes," Mason echoed. He felt the warmth from Stripes' body, motioned the cat to lie down, and situated Bandor next to the four-legged bed warmer. "Help me position Bandor."

Mason and the four teens nestled Bandor into a comfortable resting place. Stripes curled his large, furry body around Bandor, leaving his face exposed.

"Let Bandor rest." Mason led the group to the beach.

Lauren felt helpless. "What can we do?"

Mason surveyed the area. "Clearcoat!"

Clearcoat gently yanked Mason's earlobe.

"Sorry, Clearcoat, I assumed you stayed with Bandor. "Lauren, you and the others round up all mascots that can walk. The Dropas and I will set up the infirmary."

"How do we assist those that can't move?" Ti asked.

"We'll relocate the mobile unit as necessary," Mason instructed. "All right, let's get started."

The four teens herded the wounded animals. Mason and the Dropas prepared the makeshift medical center and commenced mending the injured. Unaware of what might happen next, Mason wanted the maximum number of creatures available if Arton's army resurfaced.

As he and the Dropas performed their magic, Mason roughly estimated that less than a hundred mascots had survived Arton's onslaught. *I hope they are well-prepared for Arton and his army in Dropa.*

Liam and Lindor hurried through Musing Woodland, barely hearing the captivating music of the forest. Liam wondered if he would enjoy the angelic melodies or view the spectacular scenery of Dropa ever again.

They returned to the bubble fountain where Liam had spoken with Athena and Krolic before his search for Ettepo. Athena sat at the table with the three women Liam had identified. She rose from her seat.

"Hello, Athena," Liam and Lindor greeted her.

"Welcome back. I trust by Lindor's message you successfully located Ettepo."

"I did." Liam glanced at the three invited guests.

"Liam and Lindor, this is Vincora, Pricera, and Nima."

"Nice to meet all of you," Liam said politely.

They warmly smiled as Athena, Liam, and Lindor lowered themselves on the seats across from the three women. Both Pricera and Nima had long, dark hair to the middle of their backs. Pricera had green eyes and Nima's were brown. Vincora's blonde hair was tied back in a ponytail. Her eyes were light blue. Similar to all Dropians Liam had seen, they exuded a natural beauty with unblemished complexions.

"Athena, do they know why they're here?" Liam asked.

"I requested they embark on a mission for me. They all are curious about how they can assist. Please enlighten us on their roles in the next phase."

"First, I need clarification. Which of you was Napoleon's mother on Earth?"

"That would be me," Pricera answered softly.

Vincora spoke next, "I was Adolf's mother."

"You must be Leonard's."

"Yes," Nima replied, puzzled by Liam's expression. "Is something wrong?"

"Your picture…you look…never mind." Recalling his conversation with Krolic, Liam remembered that physical characteristics of Dropians are different than they are on Earth.

"Why have you summoned us?" Vincora wondered aloud.

"During my visit with Ettepo, we deduced that Arton's body jumping path on Earth included your sons…" Liam imparted additional details of his conversation with Ettepo. He felt compelled to reveal Arton's arbitrary selection process, believing it would remove any responsibility the three women might have carried with them concerning their sons' actions.

When Liam finished, the three women exchanged glances with one another, unfazed by the news.

"I sensed we had more in common," Nima revealed to Vincora and Pricera.

"You were right all along," Vincora confirmed. "Although three, we are almost one ourselves."

"How can we help, Liam?" Pricera politely offered.

"That's it?" Liam asked, somewhat taken aback by their willingness to assist.

"What did you expect?" Pricera inquired.

"A stranger comes to Dropa and—"

"There are no strangers here," Nima calmly interrupted.

Vincora eyed the others. "Dropians are all connected to one another."

"You've been told that you are each the mother of Arton and I get little or no reaction from any of you."

"This is Dropa," Pricera reminded Liam in her gentle voice. "If informed that we are Arton's mothers, we believe you. We recall much of our time on Earth as you do, are well read here, and aware of the lone Existor's banishment from Atlantis. Remember, all negative feelings and emotions are nonexistent in Dropa. We no longer carry any regret or remorse regarding our sons' behaviors on Earth. Our mutual reaction is that we intend to help you."

"From the time you left on your search for Ettepo, the Dropians have been discussing Arton's arrival," Nima said. "We understand he is a tremendous threat to Dropa and, to the fate of eternity."

"And if we can assist," Vincora added peacefully, "we will oblige. Please…impart what is required of us."

"You have made this much easier." Liam glanced at Athena who was humored by his naiveté.

Charmed by the love, purity, and sincerity in Dropa, Liam offered his open hands. The three women placed theirs in his.

"I'd like the three of you to accompany me."

"Where?" Nima inquired.

"We must confront Arton," Liam replied.

"You mean travel through the portal?" Lindor asked in disbelief.

Athena gently placed her palm on Lindor's arm.

Liam deferred to Athena to calm Lindor. "I believe you three hold the secret that can help transform Arton. Lindor and I surmised that there is a special relationship between mother and child. A powerful bond that is not always apparent, especially to those who are without children."

"You did not tell me we must face Arton," Lindor insisted.

"Lindor, my child," Athena spoke with a slightly firmer voice.

Liam anticipated Lindor's reaction because of her harrowing experience with Arton on Earth. Arton's negative power was likely responsible for the lingering effect on her, but that would inevitably disappear the longer she remained in Dropa.

Liam released the women's hands and wrapped his arm protectively around his soul mate. "It will be all right, Lindor."

Lindor rested her head on his shoulder. "Why must we confront him again?"

"It is our only hope." Liam caressed her back. "If you prefer to stay behind—"

Lindor lifted her head. "I will never leave your side."

"Nor will I leave yours." Liam kissed her on the brow. "You were my strength when you escorted me to Dropa. Now I will be yours."

"What do we do when we meet Arton?" Pricera asked.

"Connect with him. Get inside him. And remove the evil from his body."

"How do we do that?" Nima inquired.

"That is something I cannot answer."

Everyone's troubled expression told the story. The proposed solution didn't seem like a plausible one for combating the evil that loomed over Dropa, but it was all Liam had. He was confident Ettepo had guided him to the answer he sought and the time had come to execute it.

Athena rose first. "I will lead you to the portal."

"There's one more thing." Liam removed the medallion from around his neck and flipped up three lids. "I must transport the souls in these compartments."

Athena examined the medallion. "Why are there four?"

"I honestly don't know," Liam answered dejectedly.

"I am certain you will uncover its purpose in due time," Athena affirmed. "Onward to the portal. Arton is almost here."

Liam beckoned Arton's mothers who positioned themselves by the fountain. He crinkled his brow at the height of Pricera whose head came up to his chin. "You're much taller than I expected."

"His father was the short one," Pricera retorted with a wink.

Liam presented the medallion and the three women's bodies slowly transmuted into glimmering dust clouds—their physical features now a swirling state of existence. After all three bodies metamorphosed, the clouds vanished into the three compartments. Liam carefully sealed the lids and replaced the medallion around his neck.

"Lead us to the portal, Athena," Liam requested.

Lindor tugged on Liam's arm as she hesitated to follow.

"He will not hurt you," Liam consoled her. "You have my word."

Lindor tightly gripped Liam's hand as the two accompanied Athena to the portal.

The Lost Key

During the short walk to the portal, Liam paused to admire the heavenly scenery surrounding him. "What a wonderful world," he whispered.

Those were the last words spoken until they reached the gateway. Tension was palpable: Lindor detesting a reunion with Arton, Athena preoccupied with the preservation of Dropa, and Liam deliberating over the viability of his strategy. Reflecting on his spiritual transformation—struggling to enter the walls, relinquishing his mind in the murals, traveling through Bandor's pocket, and his unique awakening on Bubble Mountain—Liam truly believed it was.

Impressions of the journey to visit Ettepo were deeply embedded in his mind: the beautiful landscape, brilliance of Fluorescent Valley, and precious time with Lindor in the Eternal River. Two adventures across Fog Canyon, both meaningful in their own way. The butterfly on Lindor's forehead and the sight of the Dropas' sacred procreation ground each held a special place.

By far Liam's most prominent memory resulted from his encounter with Connor, Posaan, and Tesmar. Frolicking with the boys as they ascended Bubble Mountain was extraordinary. They restored the child in him that had been missing for a long time, most likely suppressed during the war. Analogous to a lost key, he found it and opened a most precious treasure.

"We are here," Athena announced.

"This isn't the same portal we came through, is it?" Liam questioned.

"No, you arrived through the portal used by messengers."

"Are Dropians free to travel through the gateways?"

"Not at all. Foremost, why would anyone want to leave Dropa unless absolutely necessary? And apart from me, only messengers utilize the portals. However, they do so with purpose and with my consent."

Liam examined the two-tiered area. The floor comprised of large marble tile bordered with various marble columns: either floating, fragmented, or aberrantly reinforced with water filling the apparent empty spaces. In the rear of the main floor, a stairway led up to the second level with several steps perceived to be missing, yet safe to climb like the liquid stairway entering the city. Beyond that towered two unadorned monoliths, each approximately twelve feet high.

"What type of structure was this on Atlantis?" Liam inquired.

"A temple...razed during the transformation," Athena replied.

Compared to the beauty and exquisite architecture in Dropa, the uncharacteristically plain pillars puzzled Liam. "Those monoliths seem rather simple to be present in a temple, or in Dropa for that matter."

"Simplicity has its place," Lindor countered softly.

"She is right," Athena confirmed. "Those *simple* monoliths are the pillars of the portal."

The physics of the portal functionality eluded him, but he refrained from asking questions. Distracted by a water-supported column, Liam inserted his hand into the liquid portion, astonished at the surrealism. "Incredible." Prepared to start the next critical leg of the mission, he gently pulled Lindor close and led her to the stairs. "Stay by my side, Lindor."

"I will, Liam."

Upon reaching the second tier, Liam absorbed the aura of Dropa, perhaps for the last time. He coveted a picture of the idyllic setting cemented in his mind before finishing his stay—for himself and to impart to people on Earth.

"Liam. Lindor. Are you two ready?"

"Will you assemble your army while we search for Arton?"

"There is no army here, Liam."

"How will you protect Dropa if Arton gets past us?"

"You *cannot* let him get past you, for there is no means of defense here," Athena explained solemnly. "This is Dropa. A place of love, beauty, and peace. You are the last barrier."

"I understand the marvel of Dropa, but it is yours to protect from those who intend to destroy it," Liam argued.

"The Dropians lack the means and the essence to fight. They are incapable of protecting their existence."

"Then we're wasting time discussing it." Liam led Lindor between the monoliths. "We have a mission to complete."

"Wait! I have not prepared you for what to expect when you go through this portal."

Liam and Lindor had already departed through the invisible entrance as they heard Athena's fading voice.

"Travel safely," Athena cautioned as she folded her arms across her heart.

Upon entering the gateway, the beauty and surrealism of Dropa vanished—replaced with simplicity similar to what they perceived in the messenger portal.

"Are you all right, Liam?"

"Yes. And you?"

"So far, so good." Lindor viewed the unexpected narrow passageway. "It is much darker than the other portal."

"I presume Arton's presence has something to do with it."

An anxious Lindor squeezed Liam's hand. They wandered away from the entrance, tentatively at first, but soon with greater purpose. The actual sensation of their feet contacting the surface eluded them. Adding to the eeriness, the dimly lit surroundings and a mysterious, swirling fog encircling them made it difficult to verify the boundaries.

"Is the medallion around your neck?" Lindor sought confirmation.

Liam checked with his free hand. "Yes, it's here."

"Do not lose it."

"I won't."

Liam and Lindor proceeded down the path of uncertainty. Visibility diminished to fifteen feet in front and to the sides. Liam estimated it had decreased to five feet in the rear. His intermittent attempts to touch a wall revealed nothing.

"Did you see that, Liam?"

"No, what is it?"

"I am unsure, but the fog whirled in a strange way."

"Keep your eyes peeled," Liam advised.

"Believe me, they are peeled."

Liam glanced at Lindor—her eyes open wider than usual. Visibility improved minimally as they ventured further into the unknown.

"There it is. To our right," Lindor whispered.

"I don't see it, Lindor."

Had Liam circulation in his body, Lindor's vise-like grip would have certainly cut it off. And if anyone had attempted to separate them, his hand might have remained lodged in hers.

"Over there—to the left."

"I saw it this time."

Their eyes tracked the fog's movement. Strangely, it had thickened, rapidly diminishing their visibility to ten feet. Then five. The swirls abruptly separated into small whirling clouds before coalescing and completely engulfing them.

"I feel strange," Lindor whispered.

"What is it?"

"I have the sensation of fear." Lindor's grip tightened further.

Liam grimaced. "And I have the sensation of pain."

"Are we getting closer to him?"

Two hands shot out of the fog and seized their necks. Liam and Lindor instantly released their grips from each other and clutched the wrists attached to the hands strangling them. They struggled vigorously to free themselves.

"Closer than you want," a harsh voice spoke.

Arton's face appeared first. His anaconda grip prevented Liam and Lindor from speaking. Clad in armor, Arton became fully visible. His wavy, dark brown hair dangled past his shoulders. He was more intimidating up close than when Liam observed him from afar, standing on the platform in the vortex.

"Well, well, well, what do we have here?" Arton elevated them like feathers, demonstrating his incredible strength. He had regained all of his original powers as Bandor had warned. Arton recognized his captives. "The woman who betrayed me and the pathetic man who tried to terminate my existence." Arton glared at each of them. "Sweet revenge has begun."

Arton's hands squeezed tighter, clearly not a good time for the earthly sensation of pain to reappear. Liam's head was ready to explode from the pressure building inside it. Instinctively, he released his right hand from Arton's wrist and desperately grasped the medallion. After fumbling for a moment, he managed to open a compartment. Nothing happened. He had unsealed the empty one. Straining more, he unlatched the second compartment. His eyes closed as a cloud rapidly whisked away from its secret concealment.

"Release them, Napoleon!" Pricera commanded.

Arton tilted his head toward the voice and inched Liam's face closer to his. "What is this sorcery you attempt before me?"

"Napoleon! Release them at once!"

Arton exposed a momentary lapse of identity. "Not until they are dead!"

Pricera's illuminating cloud swooped down and intertwined itself around Arton's fingers. His grips loosened, dropping Lindor and Liam at his feet.

"Who dares call me Napoleon? I am Arton."

Pricera's cloud swirled in front of the demigod. "I was Letizia Bonaparte, and to me, you will always be Napoleon."

Arton swung at the cloud. "I never heard of any Letizia Bonaparte."

"I am your mother, Napoleon."

"If you are my mother, show yourself," Arton insisted as he retrieved suppressed memories of the woman. "Or are you too cowardly, like you were when you often locked me in the cellar?"

Pricera's face formed in the spinning cloud. Shocked at the image before him, Arton jumped back from it.

Liam, his head pulsating, crawled to Lindor and dragged her away from Arton. She had survived, but was dazed from the assault. They both massaged their extremely sore necks.

"I did not lock you in the cellar, Napoleon," Pricera affirmed tenderly.

"Be that as it may, depart from me or I will destroy you too." Arton approached Liam and Lindor.

"Do not touch them, Arton!" Pricera gently warned.

"And who will stop me?" Arton menacingly eyed Lindor.

Liam sprang to his feet. "I will."

Arton struck Liam with his forearm. "Out of my way, mortal."

Liam's body cut through the dissipating fog and landed ten feet from Lindor. Arton leaned over Lindor who desperately scooted away from him.

"Your man is no match for my powers," Arton sneered, raising his fist to strike Lindor.

Pricera's cloud weaved around his arm like a spider entwining its prey and yanked it away from Lindor. Arton fell to the ground and rolled several times.

"I've had enough of you!" Arton bellowed.

Shapeshifting into a powerful cloud of his own, he darted at Pricera. Their whirling masses coalesced as the battle commenced. Pricera did everything she could to escape Arton's relentless vigor. Once freed, Arton swirled around and through her, dispersing her particles through the air and making it more difficult for them to reunite.

Liam unlatched the other two compartments. Nima and Vincora emerged, rapidly achieving tremendous speed and striking Arton. The force of the blow knocked him to the ground and he reverted to his original physical state.

Arton shook his head. "What was that?"

"We are your mothers too," Nima and Vincora answered.

Arton stared at the faces in the swirls. Pricera had gathered herself and rejoined her companions as Arton rose to his feet.

"This can't be happening," Arton insisted.

"It is truly happening, our troubled son," Vincora confirmed.

Arton's evil tone had diminished slightly as he gazed into their eyes. "You, I already know," he asserted, recognizing Pricera. "Who do you two claim to be?"

"I am Karla, Adolf."

"And, I am Josephine, Leonard."

Arton squinted his eyes as he tried to match names with the appropriate faces. "Napoleon...Adolf...Leonard...What is this black magic?"

"You are my son," they replied in a tranquil tone, each offering a hand from their dust clouds.

"I've had enough of this family reunion." Arton backed away and eyed Liam. "It's time you halt this wizardry."

Vincora flew in front of him, preventing him from advancing.

"Out of my way." Arton swung wildly and missed.

"My dear Adolf," Vincora whispered soothingly, "I gave you all the love I had when you were a child. What has become of you?"

"Why all the anger?" Nima asked quietly.

"I have an old debt to pay," Arton responded.

Pricera swooped in front of Arton. "A debt to whom?"

"To Athena." Arton stepped back from Pricera.

No matter where he repositioned himself, one mother pursued. Liam and Lindor watched closely as Arton's mothers slowly penetrated his "walls."

"I will obliterate her and Dropa," Arton added arrogantly, unwittingly succumbing to the mesmerizing effect of the three souls.

"Where did you acquire all this anger and hatred?" Vincora asked.

"Much of it came from the mothers of the sons into which I jumped."

"How were we responsible for the wrath and loathing you possess?" Nima inquired calmly.

"I'll start with you." Arton glared at Pricera. "You used to lock me in the cellar, where I would pound and yell for hours until someone released me."

"It was not me," Pricera reasoned. "Do you remember the faulty latch on that door?"

"Vaguely."

"And how oftentimes it automatically locked when the cellar door closed?"

Arton visualized the chain of events. "Yes."

"Do you recall the time when all of us sheltered there during a storm and were trapped until your aunt came to the house and freed us?"

Arton nodded.

"Those times you were locked in the cellar were either when you were hiding from us or when I passed by and closed the open door, unaware that you were inside there." She extended a hand to Arton who backed away from her. "I would never purposely confine anyone in the cellar, let alone my own child."

Unconvinced, Arton questioned Vincora. "And what's your story?"

"My story?"

"I'm referring to all the times you sent me into the orchard to pick apples…alone. Upon my return to the location of the truck, you had already left."

"That is not true," Vincora refuted.

"A forsaken child," Arton claimed, "left for the coyotes. When I found you, I was bawling—frightened to death. Scared that you abandoned me. Petrified that I would be eaten."

"I did not desert you. Nor did your father." Vincora's face continuously changed in the swirls during her explanation. "It was not revealed until later that you were directionally impaired."

Arton sneered at Vincora. "You expect me to believe that?"

"Do you remember when your teachers allowed you to use the bathroom or deliver a note to the office?"

Arton recalled those occurrences.

"Every time they did, a student was sent to locate you. It was not because you opted not to return, rather you could not find your way to the classroom. They eventually provided you with an escort."

Arton contemplated Vincora's explanation. She rested her palm on his shoulder. Arton unintentionally placed his right hand on hers. The connection jolted his body and he sprang away from her.

Arton raised his index finger. "Don't ever touch me!" His eyes shot daggers at Nima. "Care to give your two cents?"

"We did not spend much time together, did we?"

"No, we didn't," Arton replied angrily. "You were preoccupied with attempting to suffocate me before you killed yourself."

"Do you honestly believe I would murder my own son?" Nima asked innocently.

"That's what was reported," Arton said confidently, "and the story that stayed with me throughout my life."

"It was reported incorrectly to protect your father."

"He had nothing to do with this," Arton insisted. "He died in a car accident."

"Untrue. It was all part of a cover-up. Your father was a government agent."

"A spy? Don't be ridiculous! He worked in a factory."

"Yes, a spy. When I discovered his real occupation, the feds staged my murder for fear that I would reveal his true identity and jeopardize his current and future missions."

"How do you explain the empty prescription bottle?"

Nima rested her palms on Arton's shoulders. He jerked backward, unaware of Pricera and Vincora's presence behind him. When Nima removed her hands, they had replaced hers with theirs.

"Arton." Nima purposely used his current name. "I had epilepsy."

Nima's hands slowly danced in front of Arton, entrancing him. Liam and Lindor silently observed the hateful entity's transformation.

"Epilepsy?" Arton inquired. "So, what happened?"

"The day of my death I had set you on the bed before drawing your bath. I experienced a mild seizure after turning on the faucet and consumed my normal dose of medication." Nima retracted her hands into the dust cloud, leaving her face exposed. "The substituted placebos caused the minor seizure to escalate into a major one and I collapsed into the tub."

"The report stated attempted asphyxiation," Arton challenged as Vincora and Pricera penetrated his armor.

As Arton's conception of the reasons for his hatred changed, the positive energy from two of the three souls permeated throughout his body. His face morphed, cycling the images of the individuals he invaded. Arton's legs weakened, dropping him to a knee.

Nima placed her hands on his head as she finished her explanation. "The hitman hiding in the closet smothered you with a pillow until you were unconscious. Satisfied with my assassination, the individual left unnoticed. My friend, Jennifer, discovered the two of us after investigating your distressed cry."

Arton's head lowered as a black cloud emanated from his body—freeing particles of anger, hatred, and all the negative energy encapsulated in his core. Nima nodded at Pricera and Vincora. The three souls swirled vigorously and then darted into him, penetrating his body with tremendous force in search of his lost soul.

Arton grimaced with pain as he lifted his chin and thrust his arms outward. His voice resonated throughout the portal as his soul purged the negativity—the pain more excruciating than what Liam had encountered on his journey to Dropa. Arton's wrath and loathing was a thousand-fold, a result of retaining it as he jumped across bodies. The emanating particles grew thicker and darker as they escaped. The rapid facial metamorphosis made it difficult to identify all the people he had assumed. Liam and Lindor briefly distinguished one prominent individual, Leonard von Zonek. Both opted not to view the gruesomeness: his exposed flesh and bone, the missing eyelids, and the eaten-away nose and lips.

The screaming and agony ended abruptly. Arton's mothers left his body with the tail end of the negativity cloud trailing them. After releasing it, they swirled next to Arton and transmuted into solid forms.

Liam and Lindor cautiously approached the others, apprehensive about Arton's new state of existence. A hand clamped around one's neck like a steel vise can have that effect on anyone.

Arton slowly raised his chin off his chest plate—his physical appearance unchanged. Assisted by his mothers, he rose to his feet. After two steps, he gestured that he no longer needed their support. Arton addressed Liam and Lindor. "Please forgive me for the pain I caused you."

They exchanged expressions of disbelief. Was this the same misanthrope who tried to erase humanity from Earth? The same malevolent man who attempted to end their existence? Or was it another one of Arton's deceptions?

Willing to trust him, Lindor stepped forward first. Arton enveloped her petite body into his own. Lindor embraced the man she was deathly scared of confronting a short time ago. He released his hold.

Arton briefly hugged Liam and offered unimaginable words of compassion. "Take care of Lindor. She is a special Dropian."

"Yes, she is." Liam winked at Lindor.

Arton's eyes exuded total remorse. The transformation was complete—his soul cleansed from the exorcised evil.

"Ahhh!" Arton's eyes rolled back in his sockets.

"Arton!" Lindor shouted.

Arton writhed in pain. Four spears had penetrated his rear armor, into his rib cage, and out through the chest plate.

"They came from over there!" Nima indicated a location not too far in the distance.

The fog had entirely dissipated and Arton's army—that accompanied him from the vortex—was now visible.

Suspecting Arton's purified transmutation, they assumed control of the malicious undertaking. Tradon, the lead Darton and Arton's traitorous assassin, marched at the front of the pack. More frightening than the army's presence was the reappearance of the black cloud exorcised from Arton's body. The whirling evil mass penetrated the enemy in search of a new host. The entire army he had created absorbed his negative powers. This did not bode well for preserving the existence of Dropa.

Arton fell backward into the arms of his mothers. They carefully withdrew the spears and slowly lowered him as they knelt on the ground. Placing his head into Pricera's lap, they each gently stroked his cheeks.

"Liam," Vincora called, "he wishes to speak to you."

Liam knelt beside Arton's hip. "I am here, Arton."

"I possess the key you seek," Arton said in a raspy voice.

Liam glanced at Lindor who hunched over him. Her concentration never wavered from the stationary soldiers absorbing the black cloud like leeches sucking blood out of a human.

"You possess what key?"

Arton struggled to keep his eyes open as he explained. "There exists a set of entities...that can defeat mine. They were imprisoned...prior to my exile...from Dropa. The key that will free them...resides in my soul. The fo—" Arton was rapidly losing strength. "The fourth."

"Hurry, Liam," Lindor anxiously instructed, "they have almost finished the absorption process."

"The fourth what?" Liam lowered his ear closer to Arton's mouth.

"The fourth compartment...is for me," he whispered.

"For you? How will we get you in this compartment?"

Arton's mouth opened without any words escaping.

"Please, Arton," Liam pleaded. "I need more information. Hang on."

"Fill the... fourth compartment...with my dust and—"

"And what?"

"Concentrate Arton," Nima whispered encouragingly.

"It is almost complete, Liam!" Lindor shouted.

"And do what with it, Arton?"

"Send it...to Bandor...in the vor—" Arton's eyes closed for the last time as Liam deciphered Arton's final word.

"Send it to Bandor. We have to deliver his soul to the vortex."

Lindor rose abruptly. "Finished!"

"How do we get his soul into the fourth compartment?" Liam eyed Arton's mothers for an answer. He snapped his fingers. "That's it!"

"You better hurry, Liam," Lindor warned. "They are advancing."

"Can you each revert to your particle state?"

"Yes," Pricera answered.

"Help me lift him to his feet."

They hefted Arton's body. Liam wedged himself underneath Arton's left armpit and Lindor leaned her body against Arton's right side.

"You three must create the illusion of life."

"How do we do that?" Vincora inquired.

"Once in your particle state, hide behind Arton's body and manipulate him like a puppet. If they possess the amount of hate I expect them to have, they won't hesitate to completely exterminate him—allowing me to harness his soul in the medallion. You three must convince his army that he is alive."

They nodded in agreement.

"Hurry!"

The trio quickly transmuted behind Arton. To maximize the distance from the ensuing assault, Liam and Lindor retreated as the three souls guided Arton's body closer to the advancing soldiers. Liam and Lindor anxiously watched as he opened the medallion's fourth compartment. Arton's mothers admirably performed their roles by creating a convincing illusion of a living Arton.

"Hold on," Tradon ordered, "it's a trick!"

"What kind of trick?" Eci asked.

"No way Arton could have survived my attack," Tradon contended.

As Arton neared his renegade army, Nima, Pricera, and Vincora penetrated his body to present a more believable illusion. Arton's eyes opened and he spoke and gestured as if he were indeed alive.

"Why did you fire upon me?" Nima spoke in Arton's voice.

"Because you are one of them," Tradon responded, unconvinced of Arton's existence.

"Your spears failed, Tradon," Feri chided. "It's time for me to finish him."

"There is no need for you to enter Dropa," Arton admonished.

"This no longer concerns you, Arton," Eci ordered. "Choose not to interfere and we'll leave you be."

"Your effort is futile."

"You can't stop us, Arton," Tradon chuckled. "You handed us your scepter before your assault and now we possess it."

"I am in charge, Arton!" Feri raised the scepter over his head. "I have the key to the portal entrance and we will carry out the destruction of Dropa!"

"You will destroy yourselves in the process," Arton warned.

"Enough babble, Arton." Feri withdrew a fireball from his body and hurled it at Arton.

Arton's mothers waited as long as possible before leaving their son's body, but miscalculated the power of the flaming missile. It squarely struck Arton. His body instantly incinerated—leaving behind only ashes. The explosion consumed his mothers, whose courageous sacrifice allowed Arton's soul to escape.

"What's that drifting dust cloud?" Tradon inquired suspiciously.

"It's just smoke," Eci assured.

"It's more than smoke," Tradon argued.

"Open fire!" Feri ordered.

A familiar voice shouted from behind Liam and Lindor, "Head for the gateway!"

Athena, armed with her spear and shield, swiftly maneuvered in front of them. She intercepted the assault, and successfully deflected the projectiles away from Liam and Lindor who sprinted to the portal entrance. Arton's soul closely trailed. Liam watched the purified dust cloud funnel into the fourth compartment. Sadly, the other three would remain empty.

"Athena, I have him!" Liam shouted.

"Good! I cannot withstand this barrage much longer!"

Still fending off the attackers, Athena retreated with Liam and Lindor to the gateway. Spears, fireballs, and ice bombs flew overhead. The portal immediately closed behind Liam and Lindor as they exited and hurried down the stairs.

"How long before they make their way into Dropa? Athena?" Stopping midway on the steps, Liam glanced over his shoulder. "Lindor, what happened to Athena?"

"I am not sure, but we cannot wait for her. We must transport the medallion to Bandor."

Message of Fate

Liam and Lindor descended to the temple's lower level and into a clearing not far from the ruins. Lindor situated herself as Liam glanced at the portal. Neither Athena nor Arton's army had entered Dropa. He knelt beside Lindor and removed the medallion from around his neck.

A prone Lindor adjusted her shirt, exposing the pocket under her collarbone. She hastily guided the medallion to the small opening. "Please hurry, Liam."

About to insert it, Liam jerked his arm away, freeing his hand from her grip.

"Liam," Lindor insisted as she grasped his wrist again, "we have to send the medallion to Bandor."

"You are not completely healed," Liam cautioned.

"We do not have a choice," she said firmly.

"Lindor, I don't want to lose you too."

Lindor sat up, placed her hands on his face, and spoke in a softer tone. "Liam, we have exhausted all options."

"There must be one we haven't considered."

Lindor bowed her head before gazing into Liam's eyes. "I am afraid we only have two. You can save me, and we will both perish holding the key that might preserve all existence. Or, I must sacrifice my life and possibly save the living souls, here and on Earth."

Liam gently shook his head, not willing to accept either option. She was his soul mate and they were meant to be together—forever. He had loved and lost on Earth, and there in the most sacred of places, he will have loved and lost again. Liam mentally replayed the conversation with Ettepo. He would return to solitude—for eternity this time.

"Liam," Lindor whispered. "Liam."

The words Liam wanted to impart to Lindor would not leave his mouth. It was perhaps better that way, for no words could genuinely express his love for her. The words did not exist on Earth, nor did they exist in Dropa.

"Please say something, Liam," Lindor pleaded.

He couldn't. Instead, Liam responded from the depth of his inner spirit. He stared into Lindor's eyes before kissing her with his entire heart and soul. All the words he longed to speak, all the feelings he desired to share, and all the love he was destined to give were delivered in that kiss. He gently laid her on her back and slowly withdrew his lips from hers. "I will always love you, Lindor."

"And I will always love you, Liam. You are truly my soul mate."

Liam inserted the medallion in her pocket. "Good-bye, my precious one."

Lindor smiled peacefully.

He gently brushed her cheek with his right palm as her smile disappeared. And her beautiful eyes closed for the last time.

Liam looked skyward. "Noooo!" He buried his head in her bosom. "Don't leave me, Lindor. You can't leave me." Liam gazed at Lindor as he caressed her brow. "Please open your eyes. Please, Lindor, open your eyes." He kissed her lips. "I won't let this happen…not to you. I will find a way to revive you."

Liam rested his head on Lindor's chest but gradually elevated it after feeling a strange sensation on his cheek. He laid his head down a second time and experienced the identical sensation. The source? Her pocket. Upon further examination, it was closing, but gradually.

"As long as Athena and Arton's army are in the portal, I have time." Liam gently ran his fingers through Lindor's hair. "Until it is completely sealed, there's a chance. But how, Lindor?" Liam glanced at the portal, the city, and the mountains. "This is Dropa. There must be somewhere to revive you." Transfixed on the mountains, it came to him. "The river. The Eternal River!"

"I have done all I can for you, Athena. I must devote my effort to Lindor." Liam lifted Lindor into his arms, destined for the Eternal River.

"Clearcoat!" Bandor shouted. "Clearcoat!"

Stripes roared an accompanying call for the Dropa.

Bandor flinched, unable to cover his ears because his arms were pinned under Stripes' legs. "A tad loud, my furry friend."

Stripes licked Bandor's crown, slobbering on his hair and leaving excess saliva to trickle into his ears.

Bandor freed his arm from under Stripes' paw, wiped his head and the inside of his ears, and dried his palm on the cat's fur. "I should have kept quiet."

The Dropas arrived on Bandor's chest.

"Lindor is delivering something, but I sense she lacks the strength for it to arrive on its own." Bandor cringed. "You must retrieve it."

Clearcoat gibbered to Bandor, contending that the Dropas should not enter his pocket during his weakened state.

"I am better, my concerned little friend." Bandor gently tapped the transparent Dropa on the head. "Besides, it must be crucial, for I have not heard from Lindor since she departed."

Clearcoat offered no further resistance and beckoned the other Dropas to enter Bandor's pocket. One by one, they jumped into the chest opening. Several Dropas plugged their unseen noses as if plunging into a swimming pool. Others opted for a more athletic entry, performing somersaults and flips. Clearcoat shrugged at Bandor before diving into the pocket.

Lauren rushed to Bandor's side, curious as to why he had summoned the Dropas. Mason, Brian, Cooper, Ti, and many of the mended mural creatures closely trailed her.

Bandor brushed the crown of his head. "Please quit licking me, Stripes."

Mason laughed. "What's wrong, Bandor?"

"Stripes thinks I am its wounded cub."

"It's helping you heal," Ti added. "Where are the Dropas?"

"I sent them on a brief quest." Bandor gestured to the boys. "Please help me."

Brian and Cooper assisted Bandor into a comfortable sitting position, propped against Stripes' belly.

"You seem better, Bandor," Lauren acknowledged.

"I am, but I will weaken again if the Dropas do not return soon."

"What type of quest is it this time?" Mason sought more details.

Bandor wiped off the residual saliva from his neck. "Lindor is sending something to us."

"Have you communicated with her?" Ti asked.

"No, not since she and Liam left us."

"I hope they're all right," Mason said apprehensively.

"Any idea what it is?" Lauren gently scratched under Stripes' chin.

"Not a clue." Bandor glanced at his pocket. "It will be revealed upon the Dropas' return."

"How far do they have to travel once they're in there?"

"It is not a matter of distance, but rather of time. Size and distance are irrelevant once inside the pocket."

"I'm not following you," Brian admitted as he sat beside Bandor.

"Ti, do you remember when you were inside my pocket?"

"She was so tiny," Cooper chuckled.

Ti playfully elbowed Cooper after his wisecrack.

"Sorry, Ti, but you were."

"She seemed tiny inside my pocket, and my pocket is small when viewing it from out here. However, her true size never changed."

Everyone encircled Bandor. They were fascinated with the long-awaited explanation regarding his pocket.

"It is more of an energy state." Bandor circled his hands around a small imaginary ball in front of him. "Presently, the Dropas are attaining energy stasis with the incoming object. And the same progression is happening from the other direction. The quicker equilibrium is reached, the sooner the Dropas can retrieve the sent object and restore their initial state when they first entered my pocket."

Bandor considered everyone's glazed eyes. "Both Lindor and I exist in disparate energy states—a distinct form of uniqueness in Dropa. For something to travel through me to her, its own energy state must convert from that at the sending end to that at the receiving end before it can exit."

"Is that what happened to Liam?" Lauren asked.

"To a degree, but acquiring the energy state needed to exist in Dropa further complicated the transmutation. Consider a solid transforming into a liquid and then into a gas—like heating an ice cube. It first melts and, with steady heat, eventually becomes steam. For example, if the transported object is an ice cube, it must convert to steam before exiting my pocket. However, this is an example of transforming matter. The changing of energy states is more complex."

"Interesting," Brian whispered.

"That's pretty cool. Did we go through that when we entered the murals?"

"An excellent question, Ti. That is exactly what you did."

"What are the Dropas doing?" Mason inquired.

"They are speeding up the process because Lindor's pocket is not entirely healed. It cannot singly complete the transmutation of the sent item. It needs assistance from the receiving end. The Dropas are merely furnishing a catalyst."

A small periscope arose from within Bandor's pocket. The lens rotated, searching for acceptable clearance. When the lens dropped out of sight, Blue and Green's heads surfaced. They crawled out of the opening, as did the other Dropas—each holding a portion of the leather strap. Bandor assisted the Dropas as they completely dragged the object out of his opening.

"I've never seen anything like it." Mason admired the intricate detail of the medallion's simple design.

"What is it?" Brian asked.

Bandor rotated the medallion a few times. "If I am correct, you guys will be leaving soon."

"Good! No more twiddling our thumbs," Cooper said gratefully.

Bandor showed the medallion to the Dropas. "I believe I am."

The Dropas jumped up and down, gibbering ecstatically.

"One at a time," Bandor insisted, "one at a time."

Mason accepted the medallion from Bandor, inspected it, and handed it to Lauren. She subsequently passed it around for everyone to view. Bandor expressed both elation and urgency as he listened to Clearcoat clarify the purpose of the object. When Clearcoat finished, Mason and Cooper assisted Bandor to his feet. Bandor steadied himself, weakened from the recent event.

Bandor accepted the medallion from Cooper. "This, my friends, may help us defeat Arton's army."

Excitement abounded. The Dropas positioned themselves on Bandor's shoulders. Everyone, including the mural creatures, accompanied Bandor.

"Clearcoat says this holds the key to freeing the celestial prisoners."

"Celestial prisoners?" Lauren furrowed her brow. "Is that a good thing?"

"A very good thing. Before Arton's exile from Atlantis, he stole the single key the gods possessed that would free the constellations. Those starlit figures perceived in the night sky were imprisoned by either Proteus or his followers. Remember, Proteus is the shape-shifting god who taught and admired Arton."

They all nodded, recalling Bandor's explanation of Arton having been a disciple of Proteus.

"Zeus cleverly deceived Proteus into giving him the key. Arton must have stolen it from Zeus during his final plea to remain in Dropa. When it came time to free the constellations, the key was nowhere to be found."

"Where did Arton hide it?" Brian asked.

"In a place where no one would ever search and he would never lose it—in his soul."

A jubilant smile lit up on everyone and hugs of celebration ensued.

Bandor realized what they had concluded. "No, it is not over. Far from it."

"Isn't Arton dead?" Ti exclaimed.

"Yes, Arton is dead, but his soldiers must be alive! If it was over, Lindor would not have sent this medallion containing Arton's soul."

"How are they alive without Arton?" Cooper questioned.

"They must be separate entities. Perhaps, their malevolence likely assumed a life of its own. Regardless, we must assume the army is marching to Dropa. And, in order to prevent the invasion, we need to free the constellations."

"Will they emerge angry, knowing they should have been freed long ago?" Mason inquired.

"Perhaps. That is why the Dropas are accompanying you."

The Dropas on Bandor's shoulders cheered. Unable to assist in Dropa, they had grown restless in the vortex.

"How will the bitty Dropas convince potentially angry celestial beings to help us?" Cooper wondered aloud. "Ow!"

Yellow and Orange gibbered emphatically after playfully throwing their paintbrushes at Cooper. The other Dropas stood with hands on hips, disappointed that he doubted their abilities.

"Sorry." Cooper rubbed his cheek. "No need to explain, Bandor."

"Clearcoat, I need four mobile pods and a cockpit for Mason." Bandor relayed specifics to the lead Dropa as everyone gathered near Robohawk.

The Dropas climbed aboard its wing and Clearcoat beckoned them to commence their assigned task.

"Pods?" The kids asked in unison.

"Yes, you will each ride in a small spacecraft. A pair of mobile pods will be connected to both Robohawk's backside and underside. Two Dropas will assist each of you. Silver and Gold will stay with me. Robohawk and the dragons will fly in reverse direction of the spinning wall, as they did when freeing those imprisoned in it. Once stabilized, Robohawk will exit the vortex and navigate through the murals on the way to Earth."

"Earth?" Ti asked.

"Yes, the constellations are located in the skies seen from Earth."

Brian eyed Bandor in a puzzled way. "What if the murals are sealed?"

"Let us hope that Willie was able to keep torches lit in at least one."

"How will we survive in outer space, Bandor?" Lauren asked.

"Because you are securely encapsulated, your bodies will not seek reversion to your energy state on Earth. As long as you stay in the pods, you should have no problems."

"Should?" Ti contended.

"You will all survive this voyage," Bandor assured. "Once in outer space, you will free constellations seen in both the southern and northern hemispheres."

"Those constellations aren't next door neighbors, Bandor," Mason asserted.

"I am aware of their distance from one another. That is why the Dropas are creating pods capable of exceptionally high speeds."

"Do we get to drive the pods?" Lauren asked.

Bandor shook his head, prompting a disappointing moan from the teens. "Sorry. The Dropas will pilot the pods. You must ensure they stay connected to the dust trail."

Mason tilted his head. "What dust trail?"

Bandor tapped the medallion's fourth compartment. "When the pods detach from Robohawk, you will open this compartment, releasing the dust of Arton's soul. Robohawk and the Dropas will fly into the cloud, latch on to it, and spread the dust across the constellations."

"You indicated that we had to maintain a connection," Brian recalled.

"Because the spacecraft travel at tremendous speeds, you may lose contact with your dust cloud. If that happens, you must reconnect the pod to it."

"What happens after they're free, Bandor?" Lauren inquired.

"Lead them to the vortex."

"Assuming they don't rip our heads off thinking *we* imprisoned them," Cooper remarked nervously.

"Weren't two paintbrushes across your temple enough of a lesson for you." Brian reminded him. "We have the Dropas."

"Right, I keep forgetting that critical element."

The Dropas returned from Robohawk, their engineering project complete.

"Once in the vortex, how do we transport them to Dropa?" Mason asked.

"I will have the answer when you return," Bandor replied confidently.

"Do we have communication between the pods?"

Clearcoat offered Mason a thumbs-up.

"It is time to round up the constellations," Bandor ordered.

Brian and Lauren climbed onto Robohawk. Cooper and Ti boarded the pods underneath the giant bird with Black and White piloting Ti's pod and Green and Blue commanding Cooper's spaceship. Preparing to take his position on Robohawk, Mason felt a tug on his arm.

"Forgetting your keys?" Bandor winked.

"Even here."

Bandor placed the medallion around Mason's neck and embraced him. "Be swift and be safe." He smiled and backed away as Mason boarded Robohawk.

Clearcoat and Indigo accompanied Mason as he crawled inside the cockpit located between Robohawk's neck and breast. Orange and Red jumped into Brian's ship—Yellow and Violet joined Lauren.

Mason positioned the headset over his ears and made minor adjustments. He called to the others. "Ready, Lauren?"

"Ready, Mason."

"Brian?"

"All systems go."

"Ti?"

"Ready when you are."

"Cooper."

"I was born ready."

"You watch too many movies, Cooper. Let's do it, Robohawk."

Robohawk took flight with the dragons soaring above and below their squadron leader. Bandor, Silver, and Gold observed the giant creatures circle faster and faster near the spinning vortex wall. Once stabilized, Robohawk entered the gateway, resulting in a bright flash as its shiny armor disappeared.

"Good luck, my friends." Bandor waved farewell.

Silver and Gold saluted their companions.

The force of an electrical bomb rammed Athena into the visible portal entrance and interrupted her concentration. The unrelenting assault persisted on the lone warrior defending Dropa. Athena shook off the charge in time to raise her shield. Several Darton spears and Icic projectiles deflected off it.

The might of the invaders had significantly increased after absorbing the evil and negativity discharged from Arton. They had attained his god-like strength and, without resistance, Dropa would succumb to their malevolent force.

The weakened icon of Dropa struggled desperately to escape through the portal entrance, her attempt disrupted by the powerful Cycloton winds. They drove Athena further from her destination of temporary safety. Ultimately, the vacuum-like suction pulled the valiant goddess closer to her adversaries.

Beaten down, but unwilling to surrender, Athena utilized one last tactical maneuver to free herself from the shackles of death. She drew her spear behind her head and launched it at an oncoming Cycloton, resulting in immediate death for the whirling windstorm. The split second gained allowed Athena to slip through the gateway and escape another onslaught from the Pyrotons and Icics.

Athena dove out of the portal past the monoliths and rolled over the tile of the upper level. Her shield slid across the marble surface as the momentum carried her down the steps. Athena slowly opened her eyes. Portions of her armor were noticeably dented and the cloth under her metal plates was scorched from the fireballs. Struggling to sit, she removed the icicles from her hair. She had taken a minor shot from each of Arton's creatures, but managed to survive.

I hope Arton's key is not a trick. Athena glanced at the portal entrance before assessing the wound on her right thigh where a Darton spear had grazed it. She arose and retrieved her shield from the bottom step. "Lindor! Liam!"

No answer. Athena searched the area and called once more. Still, no response. She tried contacting Lindor telepathically, and received the same result. *Why does Lindor not respond?* Wasting no more time, Athena sprinted to the city.

"Athena," a concerned Dropian declared, "you are injured."

Additional Dropians gathered around Athena as she searched for Krolic. The disquieted crowd bombarded her with questions as she traversed the city streets and confirmed her well-being.

"Has anyone seen Krolic?" Athena inquired.

"Over here!" Krolic politely pushed his way through the throng of people with a hand above his head. He was shocked at her condition. "Athena, what happened?"

"I was attacked by Arton's army."

Krolic frantically searched behind her. "Where are they?"

"In the temple portal. They will enter Dropa once they unlock the gateway."

"How can you be certain they will get through?"

Athena expressed consternation Krolic had never seen. "Because they possess Arton's scepter."

"We cannot fight that army, Athena," Krolic reminded her.

"That is true, but we have to do everything we can to protect the Dropians, until help arrives." Athena peered at the distant mountains.

"What can I do?"

"Lead the citizens from the city to the Pillars of Solitude. I will notify the other villages to seek shelter. Keep them safe."

"What is your plan?"

"I have to prepare for the intruders."

"You cannot fight them alone," Krolic argued.

"I will fight until I can fight no longer." Athena surveyed her sacred land. "I will not let them take away our eternity."

"How will—"

"Enough, Krolic," Athena insisted as she gently nudged him away from her. "You have your assignment."

Athena instructed the crowd to join Krolic who escorted the Dropians to the edge of the city. Athena communicated to the messengers throughout Dropa to lead their fellow Dropians to the closest refuge.

Looking back, Krolic sighted Athena standing proudly on the top step of another temple, surveying her precious Dropa. "Be strong, our beloved Athena."

Clearcoat adeptly piloted Robohawk. The golden hawk flew with tremendous speed and agility, preventing Mason and the others from identifying any of the artwork.

"Most murals are sealed, Clearcoat," Mason relayed to his pilot.

Clearcoat gibbered confidently that it would find an unsealed one.

"I have never doubted you guys, have I?"

Clearcoat gibbered a response to Mason.

"Okay, maybe when you guys painted the murals and the time needed to paint cracks on the fortress wall." Mason laughed at Clearcoat's recollection. "Yes, I'm sure there are more instances. What's our destination?"

Clearcoat gibbered a reply.

"The North Star mural? How appropriate."

The Dropas prepared the pods for separation as Robohawk neared the exit. They discussed responsibilities with their human copilots and alerted them that further guidance would be given regarding how to sustain a grasp on Arton's dust cloud. The teens exuded confidence regarding their assigned tasks.

Clearcoat received confirmation from the pod pilots. All were ready. Robohawk accelerated to its final mural destination.

Willie and Roberto viewed the North Star mural from ground level. They had successfully lit the torches inside the walls.

"This is the last mural blackened by Arton," Willie confirmed. "That brings the total to twenty-two murals they can exit, if necessary."

The mural had Mason's signature steelcrete border, a combination of steel and concrete depending on the viewing angle. Depicted inside the border: an outer space scene, with the constellation of Orion in the center and semi-circles cut into the middle portion of the inner sections of the border. Placed inside those semi-circles, and stretching into the adjacent semi-circle of the mural, were images of Earth on the left side and a full harvest moon on the right side. In the upper left-hand corner was "carved" the logo of the school: "chiseled" stars and lettering of North Stars. Mason had painted his trademark peel in the upper right-hand corner, with blackened outer space and a shooting star behind the peel. Beneath that and the harvest moon, an Enter button was "chiseled" into the steelcrete. A second shooting star traveled from left to right inside the inner view of space.

"What is your obsession with that mural, Roberto?" Willie asked.

Roberto didn't respond.

"Roberto!"

"A shooting star is actually streaking across the artwork."

"Are you certain?"

"Check it out," Roberto insisted.

Willie studied the mural. "Are you sure it's not an optical illusion?" His eyes zeroed in on the anomaly.

"I'm positive, Willie. The longer I watch, the closer it appears."

"How is this possible?"

Roberto furrowed his brow. "After everything we've been through, I can't believe you said that."

"Me either." Willie rolled his eyes and sighed. "Let's see what happens next."

The shooting star grew larger.

"It's coming right at us!" Willie affirmed in amazement. "Get down!" Willie tackled Roberto and protected him with his body.

The ceiling and walls quaked violently as Robohawk reached the outer edge of the painting. The metallic Hawk rocketed out of the mural like a missile, crashing through the atrium entrance. Shattered glass flew everywhere and the steel doorframes collapsed as the giant bird revisited Earth, more dramatically than the first time.

By the time Willie and Roberto peered out of the gaping hole in the building, they saw nothing more than cumulus clouds swirling wildly along the path of the giant projectile.

"What in the world was that?" Willie asked, awestruck.

"I don't have the slightest idea," Roberto replied.

"And where is it heading?"

"I have no clue, but I wish you would kindly get off me."

"No problem." Willie boosted Roberto to his feet.

Two custodians scampered from around the corner and joined Willie and Roberto on the sidewalk.

"Holy mackerel!" Fred exclaimed, dumbfounded. "What happened out here?"

"Even if we knew, you probably wouldn't understand."

The four baffled onlookers stared at the vapor trail with hands shielding their eyes from the sunlight.

"Whatever it was, I hope it's on our side," Willie said.

Celestial Awakening

Robohawk cut through Earth's upper atmosphere and entered outer space. The titanium-winged missile destroyed numerous dismantled satellites, but with its precise navigational skills, avoided knocking the functional ones out of orbit.

Halfway through the solar system, Clearcoat instructed Robohawk where to stop. The giant bird broadened its wings into position and activated its newly-created thrusters to decrease its speed. Robohawk passed by the outer planets before coming to a rest, where it drifted freely in space.

The Dropas collectively entered coordinates of specific constellations into their pods after Clearcoat plotted each one's course. Of the eighty-eight imprisoned starred formations, the lead Dropa settled on amassing seventeen. Those celestial beings could be released in a timely manner and provide the highest possibility of victory against Arton's powerful army.

Mason engaged the microphone. "Listen up, everyone. Can you hear me?"

"Loud and clear," they all responded.

Mason removed the medallion from around his neck. "Before I release Arton's revitalized soul into space, the Dropas will disengage your pods."

Clearcoat transmitted the go-ahead to the pod pilots.

Ti blew her boyfriend a kiss. "I love you, Cooper."

"I love you too."

Gazing at one another, Lauren and Brian each pressed a palm to their window. The four pods drifted away from Robohawk's body. Black, Green, Orange, and Violet steadied their respective ships. White climbed onto Ti's shoulder, Blue onto Cooper's, Red onto Brian's, and Yellow perched itself on Lauren's.

After a short discussion with Clearcoat, Mason relayed instructions to the teen co-pilots regarding how to latch onto Arton's cloud when it appeared.

"Concentration is key to stay connected. Use any image you choose, one that is easy to visualize and maintain. Picture it attaching itself to the dust cloud and holding onto it. Does everyone understand?"

"Yes," they all replied.

"The Dropa on your shoulder will help you stay focused. Pay no attention to your pod pilot or what's happening outside the ship. That will be a distraction, causing you to relinquish your hold and us to lose precious time. Questions?"

"We're ready."

"Lauren, because of the way Clearcoat plotted the paths to release the prisoners, you will fly alongside me for a spell."

"Roger, squad leader."

Mason clicked open the fourth compartment. He placed the medallion in the cylindrical chute leading into space and sealed the hatch. Upon leaving the pod, the multi-colored dust particles drifted into the vast vacuum, but sustained a limited expansion. As the remaining specks escaped, the newly-released cloud reshaped itself into a nebula of Arton. His image no longer emanated a fomented wickedness, rather it radiated one of quiet strength and peace.

"Wow!" Ti exclaimed.

"He's huge," Cooper commented.

"Stay focused, you guys," Mason reminded them.

Unexpectedly, the image of Arton's soul bowed before them and spoke. "It is time for the celestial awakening."

Arton's colorful nebula violently swirled and his features dissipated. The key hidden in his soul was ready to unlock the future of Dropa.

"Start visualizing," Mason commanded.

The teens closed their eyes and imagined a device to capture the cloud. It was unnecessary for Mason to picture a latching mechanism, because Robohawk's talons served that purpose. The Dropas maneuvered the pods. Robohawk streaked for the nebula with the other Dropas closely trailing their leader.

Robohawk swooped into the gaseous formation and snatched a billowy section of the target. Brian, Ti, and Lauren's pods easily snared their designated sections. Cooper's pod flew straight through the cloud.

"Concentrate, Cooper," Mason encouraged. "You can do it."

Green redirected the pod, but Cooper failed a second time.

Mason assisted with Cooper's visualization. "Do you play sports, Cooper?"

"I fish."

"Fishing," Mason echoed. "Perfect. Pretend you're at your favorite spot. The pod is the hook and the cloud is the bait. Secure the bait on the hook, Cooper."

Cooper closed his eyes as Green steered the pod into the cloud.

"Good job, Cooper!" Ti encouraged.

"Did I get it?" Cooper asked.

"Nope. Ti, you lost yours too. You both must focus." Mason glanced at the other two pods, the connection intact. "Try it again, Cooper, and you too, Ti."

Green and Black guided the pods. This time Cooper and Ti successfully attached to the nebula.

As a result, Mason barked out the next order. "Let's move!"

Robohawk and the four pods flashed like spaceships entering warp speed. Lauren flanked Mason's right side as the other three vanished from sight. Blue knelt on Cooper's head, massaging his scalp to help him retain his concentration.

Arton's nebulous soul stretched across the galaxies as the pilots methodically weaved in and out of the celestial targets. Robohawk's speed allowed it to cover a larger area and gather more constellations. The cloud expansion aberrantly distorted space, drawing the entities in close proximity to one another.

The co-pilots adeptly sustained connections. Clearcoat issued the signal to release the cloud after encapsulating all seventeen constellations. White danced on Ti's nose to distract her and Yellow and Red tickled Brian and Lauren's ears with their paintbrushes. Blue attached its feet onto Cooper's hair and lowered itself in front of his head. It stretched his left eyelid away from his eyeball.

"What the heck?" Cooper instinctively swatted Blue off his face.

"Are you all right?" Mason asked.

"I'm fine, but I splattered Blue against the window," Cooper snickered.

Robohawk and the pods reunited, coming to a standstill near the freed constellations. The gaseous key of the nebula unlocked the prisoners.

The stars holding the celestial entities burned brighter as the captives escaped. Details of each constellation materialized as galactic clouds swirled around the bodies, exposing their prominent physical features. Solar flares erupted and tinted gases painted the darkened canvas. The prisoners shed their bindings and the stars restored their original brightness.

First to taste freedom from its celestial suppression was Draco. The dragon shot a fireball from its mouth to celebrate its release. Charging out of their "cells" came Aries the ram, Pegasus the winged horse, Taurus the bull, and Centaurus the centaur. Roaring out of its cage and following close behind the ungulates was Leo.

And right on the giant lion's tail, two enormous bears: Ursa Major and Ursa Minor.

Surprised by the constellations' appearances, everyone expected a lion with a golden mane, or bears with thick, brown fur. Instead, nebulous images of their natural form materialized. The prolonged existence in a celestial state affected their ability to re-establish true characteristics. Nonetheless, they maintained a mystical and transparent manifestation, and intermittently phased in and out of the features that they previously exhibited on Earth.

The water constellations appeared next, including Serpens the serpent, Cetus the whale, and Hydra the water snake. Cancer the crab and Scorpius the scorpion crawled out behind them.

Disrupting the peaceful release, Hercules and Aquila the eagle emerged angered. Hercules seized Ti's pod, ready to crush it in its giant hands. Aquila sunk its razor-sharp talons into Brian's pod. Robohawk reacted by emitting a screech that only the constellations could hear. The last two entities perfectly timed their appearance.

Orion the hunter and Sagittarius the archer freed themselves with bows already drawn. They each unleashed an arrow. Orion delivered a glancing blow off Hercules' wristband and Sagittarius nicked Aquila's talon—both harmless to the victims, but elicited the desired results. Black and Orange steered their pods away from the assailants and safely guided them out of reach.

Although outside its customary domain of the mural wall, Robohawk made its presence known and that it was clearly in charge. The constellations lethargically drifted away from their star-laden prison cells as if they crawled out of bed after a lengthy slumber. The distortion reversed, restoring the relative distances of the various galaxies from where the prisoners came. Because of the near-eternal incarceration, the starry outlines visible from Earth were preserved.

Each constellation methodically examined its own body to verify that all limbs functioned properly. Once satisfied, the celestial beings assembled around Robohawk. Acclimation to their new environment had begun.

Hercules gently gripped Ti's pod this time. The massive figure peered into the window, politely apologized, and set the aircraft free.

Viewing the constellations huddled around Robohawk, all were awestruck by their new allies—amazed at the enormity and astounded that each came to life.

"How will we transport them into and through the murals?" Cooper asked.

"Remember what Bandor told us," Mason reminded him, "about traveling through his pocket? Size is irrelevant."

"Will they be as intimidating in Dropa as they are here?" Brian questioned.

"That is yet to be seen," Mason replied.

Lauren peered out her window. "Will Arton's reformed soul return to Dropa?"

"Arton is gone," Mason concluded. "He sacrificed his soul to relinquish the key that freed the constellations. If we are successful in saving Dropa, his legendary story will likely be told for generations." Mason listened to Clearcoat. "Clearcoat says that remnants of Arton will probably coalesce with the Aurora Borealis."

"What a way to go," Cooper remarked.

"When you view the northern lights from Earth, remember what Arton's *true soul* did for us," Mason instructed.

"People truly can change." Lauren placed her hands over her heart.

"Arton represents the ultimate transformation of evil to good. He was proof that *everyone* is virtuous."

"Given all the evil he has spread, will people forgive him?" Brian inquired.

"Maybe not right away, but what he ultimately did for humanity will prevail." Mason refocused. "Bandor is waiting for us."

Black, Green, Orange and Violet maneuvered their aircraft near Robohawk and docked onto the mother ship. Clearcoat beckoned the constellations. Hercules formed the beginning of the chain as he clutched Robohawk's talons. The others followed, each supplying their own link. Every entity had boarded the "Robotrain" destined for Earth.

Willie and Roberto had finished sweeping up the glass. They tended to the steel beams that once made up the doorframes.

"What a mess this was, Roberto." Willie leaned his broom against the wall and checked in with the custodians. "How are you guys doing?"

"Almost done here," Fred replied.

"I'll retrieve the plastic to enclose this entrance," Wesley said.

"Let's drive these lifts over there," Willie instructed.

Willie and Roberto positioned the two hydraulic lifts as Wesley hurried from around the corner. The four men began attaching the plastic.

"Seems to be getting darker a bit sooner today," Fred commented as he glanced at his watch. "Is there an eclipse this afternoon?"

"I'm not sure." Roberto found no evidence near the sun, but a tiny flame appearing in the Earth's upper atmosphere sparked his curiosity. "Hey, Willie."

"Yeah, what's up?"

"It's...coming back."

"What is?"

"Whatever flew out of the mural."

Willie dropped his end of the plastic. "Please tell me you're kidding."

Willie and the two custodians fixated on the approaching object.

"I wish I was, and this one has a much longer tail."

"Get off the lift!" Willie ordered.

They all scrambled over the railings and dropped to the ground.

Roberto glanced at the artwork. "Willie, the mural has darkened again."

"Everyone inside! Roberto, grab the torches! We need to light this mural or they'll never make it to...wherever they're headed!"

"Willie!" Roberto tossed a torch in Willie's direction.

"Wesley!" Willie yelled. "Keep us updated on that trailblazer!"

"You bet." The custodian positioned himself on the sidewalk.

Roberto and Willie threw the torches at the mural. Both torches ricocheted off the wall and fell on the tile.

"Throw it harder, Roberto!"

They hurled the torches into the outer space portion. Nothing happened.

"It's getting bigger, guys!" Wesley nervously updated them.

"Again, Roberto!"

The torches caromed off the mural and dropped to the floor.

"It's no longer burning!" Wesley bellowed. "It's like a long snake, and it's speeding right for us!"

Fred tossed a torch to Roberto. "Catch!"

Roberto cleanly picked the torch out of the air. "As hard as you can, Willie!"

"Here it comes!" Wesley dove over the stack of beams.

Robohawk, with the constellations trailing like a kite tail dancing in the wind, veered in time to avoid clipping a water tower as it lined itself up with the targeted ingress.

Willie and Roberto launched the torches at the mural one last time. And one last time the torches failed to enter the wall. Before hitting the tile, the same adult and infant hands that had guided the mural travelers into the vortex appeared out of nowhere. The hands stretched into the atrium, snatched the torches, and retracted them into the mural—instantly lighting it. The "Robotrain" blasted through the half-hung plastic. The sheet burst into flames and melted before hitting the ground. This time, the building suffered no additional damage.

Roberto and Willie dropped to the floor as the constellations zipped into the mural behind Robohawk and vanished into space.

The four men rose to their feet.

"That was close," Roberto acknowledged.

"Too close," Willie admitted. "Fred, could you tell what it was?"

"It was traveling too fast."

Before another word was spoken, they heard a faint screech inside the darkened mural.

Roberto and Willie eyed each other. "Robohawk!"

Roberto scratched his head. "Why did they return to Earth?"

Willie gently slapped Roberto on the back. "I have no idea, but I trust that whatever they escorted into the mural is on our side."

Silver, Gold, and Bandor rounded up the remaining mural mascots.

"You and the other Dropas work exceedingly well with Mason," Bandor complimented his tiny companions, amazed that the creatures had been restored to their original states.

Silver and Gold modestly bowed their heads.

Bandor propped against a scorched palm tree, each Dropa perched atop a knee. With the exception of Stripes, the animals located pleasant spots to lie comfortably. The striped feline sauntered up to Bandor and roared.

Bandor covered his ear with one hand and gently pushed Stripes' head away with the other. "What is it, my furry friend?"

Stripes roared louder.

Bandor nestled Stripes' head against his chest. "I am sorry, but I cannot send you to Dropa through my pocket."

Stripes nuzzled its head into Bandor's abdomen, and purred loudly as Bandor stroked its forehead.

"I have to build up my strength to transport the constellations."

Stripes torpedoed its tongue at Silver. The huge, sandpapered muscle snatched the defenseless Dropa like a frog snaring a cricket. Laughing hysterically, Gold rolled down Bandor's leg.

Silver crawled into Stripes' throat, oozed into the prankster's nasal cavity, and emerged from the left nostril. Sensitive to the foreign object, Stripes sneezed the mucous-covered Dropa, somersaulting it across the sand. Silver examined its newly decorated body that resembled a fresh pastry rolled in cinnamon.

"You are making me hungry, Silver."

Gold belly-laughed at Bandor's amusing comment and pointed wildly at its friend. Silver hurled a handful of sand at its amused companion, but Gold ducked in time to avoid the crystal onslaught. Silver then rose to its feet and waggled its body like a wet dog, dispersing the sand.

The light from the torches extinguished as Robohawk and the constellations left behind the helping hands. Relying on its familiarity of traveling through the murals, Robohawk flawlessly demonstrated its mastered navigational skills on the return trip to the vortex. Clearcoat gibbered instructions into Mason's ear as Indigo closely monitored the trailing passengers.

"Attention!" Mason announced into his microphone. "Listen up pod riders." Mason upheld his playful role as squadron leader. "Ti, you are to break away from the mother ship and attach your vessel to Cetus."

"Yes, sir!" Ti replied.

"Cooper!" Mason called.

"Excuse me, sir," Ti politely interrupted.

"What is it, Ti?"

"What exactly is a Cetus?"

"Cetus…is the whale," Mason answered calmly.

"The whale?" Ti recalled her Lit class reading assignment of *Moby Dick.* "Captain Tihab is on her way, sir."

Black released its pod from Robohawk in search of Cetus.

"Cooper!"

"Ready and waiting."

"Go get Serpens," Mason ordered.

"We're on it, sir." Cooper motioned to Green.

"Hydra, sir?" Brian inquired, anticipating the next constellation.

"What?" Mason asked, confused at first.

"Hydra, sir," Brian repeated. "Are we to retrieve Hydra?"

"Yes, find Hydra. Once they're attached," Mason relayed, "you three will lead the marine constellations to Vortex Sea."

"Ahem, Mason," Lauren called. "What are Violet, Yellow, and I to do?"

"Follow the other pods and ensure reconnection after Serpens, Cetus, and Hydra leave the line."

"Aye, aye, sir."

Lauren's pod disembarked from Robohawk and Violet steered the ship to the tail end of the constellations. As the other vessels attached to the designated celestial life forms, Violet maneuvered its pod in position and guided the next entity to reconnect with the one in front of it. After the water beings had been retrieved and the others locked in place, the four pods realigned with Robohawk.

"Speaking for us all," Cooper bellowed, "we're ready when you are!"

Mason gestured to Clearcoat. "Here we—"

Before the last words left Mason's mouth, a small energy burst exploded underneath Robohawk. In defense, the giant bird's wings opened, casting three of the four pods behind it.

"What was that?" Lauren shouted.

Mason adjusted his headset. "No clue, but we must quickly enter the vortex!"

Black, Green, and Orange steadied the ships and returned to their original positions. Two more bursts exploded near the constellations.

"What's out there, Clearcoat?" Mason questioned.

The lead Dropa had no idea what type of creature was attacking them.

"Maybe it's a Gravalo, the gravity halo we battled earlier," Brian surmised.

"I don't think it is," Cooper claimed. "This creature's weapons are different."

"Clearcoat, we need to get to the vortex."

Clearcoat explained to Mason that the entity needed to be destroyed first. Its energy clusters were disrupting any chance they had to return to the vortex.

"Can we at least send the pods?"

Clearcoat consented but with the stipulation that a significant gap must occur between the bursting energy clusters. Mason peered out his window and saw nothing. Another set of clusters exploded near them. Cooper and Brian's pods spun out of control and away from the others.

"Mason, the constellations are disengaging!" Ti revealed.

The celestial guerilla was another one of Arton's evil manifestations trying to prevent the salvation of Dropa. The huge octopus-shaped Octula materialized out of the darkness. Unlike the Gravalos, its body was composed of a colorful nebula with tentacles able to fire negative energy clusters.

As it neared its prey, the appendages randomly shifted like eight large worms wriggling on pavement after a heavy rain. Although each could fire, the maximum number of clusters discharged at one time was four. A recharge was required after each assault.

Two more clusters exploded in front of Robohawk and another two aimed at the constellations. Aries, Taurus, Cancer, and Scorpius led the attack on the Octula. The colossal creature fired on its charging foes. Taurus and Aries dodged the initial wave of energy bombs and veered away from Scorpius, intending to attack the creature from multiple sides.

The Octula released a massive, black cloud at Scorpius before darting away from the attacker, its escape temporary. Taurus furiously blindsided the gaseous octopus with its horns. Upon impact, the powerful Taurus reared its head, launching the Octula over the bull's backside.

Aries subsequently attack the entity, but the Octula had recovered from the initial blow and entwined Aries in one of its large tentacles. Before Taurus could mount another strike, it too was entangled, tightly secured by the suction cups.

"Now!" Mason yelled.

At Mason's order, the four pods steered into the outer edge of the vortex. Robohawk stayed behind to lead the constellations into safety.

Termination loomed for the two horned allies, but the pods had escaped unharmed without a moment to spare. Grasping Taurus and Aries, the Octula steadied itself and fired another set of energy clusters that exploded near Pegasus and Centaurus, separating them from the others. This resulted in a major disruption to the intermittent phasing in and out of their earthly forms. Observing this, Orion left the others to tend to its wounded companions.

Sagittarius fired an arrow, administering a direct hit on the Octula's gaseous sac. This allowed Scorpius and Cancer barely enough time to commence their own attack. Scorpius reached the Octula first and thrust its stinger near its victim's mouth. Coming to the aid of its comrades, Cancer confronted the tentacles binding Taurus and Aries with open claws. The giant crab snipped the base of the two appendages and severed them from the writhing body. Taurus and Aries immediately darted away from their captor with the lifeless tentacles draped around them.

The Octula desperately fired multiple energy bursts that detonated in front of other attacking constellations. One struck Leo, temporarily collapsing the huge lion. The Octula entwined two attached tentacles around Scorpius and Cancer, securing the stinger and claws respectively and rendering them defenseless.

Draco launched its own counterattack before the Octula recharged. The enormous dragon discharged two blazing streams at the entity, burning off a pair of tentacles. The Octula hastily fired more clusters but hit nothing.

Concentrated on Draco, the frantic beast neglected to detect three assailants swooping in from the rear: Hercules, Ursa Major, and Ursa Minor. Hercules administered a stranglehold on the creature's giant sac. The Octula and nearest constellations briefly disappeared amidst the residual black cloud emission.

Once the gas dissipated, Ursa Major and Ursa Minor each clutched a tentacle. Sagittarius fired a second arrow with splendid accuracy, missing its own allies and striking the Octula in its mouth. It proved to be the fatal blow. The giant octopus exploded and nearly eradicated any constellation remotely close to it. The energy blast almost propelled them into the nearest adjacent mural.

Mason smiled, pleased with the performance of his new allies. "The enemy better be ready! C'mon, Clearcoat, let's round them up. Bandor is waiting for us."

Clearcoat directed Robohawk to retrieve each constellation—Taurus, Leo, and Aries, all needed extra time to stabilize their phasing. Orion signaled to Mason and Clearcoat that reconnection had completed. Robohawk sped to the vortex with the celestial mercenaries in tow.

"Here they come!" Bandor announced.

Four pods rocketed from the spinning surface. Violet steered its craft onto the beach and the other three led their attached constellations over the water.

Bandor, Silver, Gold, and the rejuvenated mascots hurried to Lauren's pod to greet her. Violet, Yellow, and Lauren emerged from the aircraft and met up with Bandor. As she explained what had occurred outside the vortex, the three pods flying over the sea released the cargo into the water. Cetus, Hydra, and Serpens, adept in their natural environment, rapidly swam to the portal where Arton escaped.

The three pods veered away from the entry point and came to rest ashore. Cooper, Ti, and their respective Dropas disembarked first, with Brian and his Dropas right behind them. They all reunited with the rest of the flight crew.

Concern for the others vanished when Robohawk made its appearance. The giant bird soared through the vortex wall, screeching to announce its arrival.

Down below, the onlookers cheered. Stripes roared loudly as it waggled its head. It was an awesome sight as Robohawk and the constellations arrived safely on the beach.

Bandor subdued his elation as he studied the phasing celestial soldiers. "The celebration is over. Mason, bring the constellations to me."

"On our way."

"Quickly!" Bandor insisted.

The kids perceived Bandor's anguish. Mason led the constellations to Bandor who had unbuttoned his shirt and positioned himself comfortably under the tree.

"Is everything all right, Bandor?"

"I am afraid it is not, Lauren. We need to send them to Dropa immediately!"

Lauren waved frantically at Mason. "Hurry!"

Mason arrived with the constellations. "What is it, Bandor?"

"Their phasing has me greatly concerned."

"They were just in battle," Mason contended.

"It has nothing to do with their involvement in a battle. It is from the prolonged period of imprisonment in that sustained energy state." Bandor closed his eyes and shifted his head into a better position.

"Do we have a chance?" Lauren inquired tentatively.

Bandor opened his eyes. "Yes, miniscule as it may be, we have a chance. Are they ready, Mason?"

"Say the word."

"What will happen to you, Bandor?" Lauren asked sadly.

"I am not sure."

"What exactly does that mean?" Ti inquired.

"I may not make it," Bandor admitted softly.

Clearcoat jumped to the front of the other Dropas positioned on Bandor's chest. The transparent Dropa enthusiastically waved its hands as it gibbered to Bandor.

"What's Clearcoat saying?" Lauren wondered aloud.

"The Dropas can improve the probability of my survival."

Brian leaned over Bandor. "How?"

"In layman's terms, they will hypnotize me to help stabilize my existing state. That will allow me to conserve energy and afford me a slightly better chance of withstanding the transport of all these phasing constellations."

"How do you feel presently?" Mason asked.

"I have recovered nicely since Lindor and Liam arrived in Dropa. I hope it was long enough."

The Dropas climbed onto Bandor's shoulders as he shifted himself to a sitting position. He hugged Lauren and her friends.

"I will miss you, Bandor," Mason prematurely bid farewell, troubled he might lose his best friend.

"Do not let go of me just yet." Bandor embraced Mason. He made eye contact with the others. "Keep thinking positively. Will you do that for me?"

They all nodded.

Bandor returned to his prone position. Lauren held Bandor's left hand and Ti his right. Unlike their other healing rituals, the Dropas aligned themselves along the center of Bandor's body, starting at his neck and ending at his waist.

"Keep me alive, my little friends," Bandor whispered.

The boys clasped hands as the Dropas commenced the hypnosis, a rather mundane display at that. They quietly chanted and waved their arms in synchronized motions. Bandor's cheek muscles and brow relaxed first.

Clearcoat briefly interrupted its chanting to signal Mason. He gently slid his fingers into Bandor's pocket, expanded the opening, and beckoned the first constellation.

Hercules stepped into the pocket. Then Draco. And Centaurus right behind them. One by one the constellations entered Bandor's portal to Dropa. Orion was the last to vanish from sight.

Stripes neared Bandor, making a second attempt to enter the pocket. The Dropas' chanting ceased.

"What is it, Clearcoat?"

Clearcoat offered a short explanation to Mason.

Ti grasped Mason's arm. "What's the matter?"

"The mural creatures are no match for those soldiers Arton created. Sending them through would not add any strength to the celestial entities and would simply prolong the inevitable for them."

"What about us?" Brian asked.

"Clearcoat also explained that dispatching us would not only jeopardize the constellations' passage to Dropa, but would definitely end Bandor's life."

Clearcoat gibbered additional instructions.

"I understand." Mason gestured to the kids to scoot closer and hold hands around Bandor. "As we did in the cave with Robohawk, direct positive thoughts at our good friend Bandor, and help him stay with us."

Everyone closed their eyes and visualized the wonderful experiences they had shared with Bandor. As they did, the Dropas danced in a circle on Bandor's bare chest.

Spiritual Plague

After Robohawk's disappearance into the North Star mural, Willie and Roberto rushed home to be with their families. At half past two, the skies had grown even darker. Willie found May and their two children huddled together on the couch.

"What's happening, Willie?"

Willie sat on a cushion next to his family. "I'm not sure, May."

"Daddy, why is it getting dark in the afternoon?" his six-year-old daughter asked.

"I don't know, sweetheart." Willie gently stroked his little girl's hair.

Willie and May stared at each other with dire trepidation. Willie drew his loved ones close to his chest.

"It's getting harder to breathe," Willie's son admitted.

"It'll be all right." Willie sighed, experiencing the same difficulty and not truly knowing if it would be all right. "I dearly love you all."

"We love you, Daddy," his children replied.

Tears streamed down May's cheeks. She wanted to stay strong, especially for the children, but she couldn't contain her emotions any longer.

"I love you, Willie," she whispered.

"I love you, too, May." He affectionately tightened his arms around everyone.

Across town, Roberto ran up the stairs inside his house and darted into the first bedroom. Four siblings silently snuggled next to his mother—the two youngest ones lay sound asleep. He and his mother exchanged worrisome expressions.

"Qué pasa, Roberto?" she asked.

"No sé," he replied disappointedly.

At a nearby hospital, a young man and his pregnant wife viewed the ultrasound monitor and listened to their child's heartbeat. Joyous smiles waned as the rhythm of life in the unborn baby unexpectedly slowed.

Phenomena of this magnitude occurred around the globe. Winds abated. Rain and snow stopped falling. Lava flows and river currents diminished. Waves flattened across the oceans. Flowers wilted and newly formed blossoms fell to the ground. The forest fires burning in the dense woodlands of the western United

States began extinguishing. Earth had almost come to a complete standstill. The souls of the planet would die soon, along with every other living organism.

Feri motioned to Dwin to examine the portal entrance to Dropa. Dwin blew low winds near the invisible opening, hoping to detect signs of its edges.

"Are we in the right place?" Tradon asked.

"This is where they exited." Feri noticed Ectorel's strange glare. "Any ideas?"

The principal Electromorph sparked its way near Feri. "Use the scepter."

"And Arton expected to preserve Dropa," Eci scoffed with a hideous laugh. "What a stupid man to give us the key to the front door."

Feri carefully examined the scepter's crystal. "Give me room."

Ectorel, Eci, Dwin, and Tradon stepped behind Feri. The Pyroton raised the scepter above its fiery head with both hands. The portal entrance materialized.

Carved in the middle was an image that resembled the artwork on the vase Liam had transported home from Athens. It comprised the Dropas painting, the harpist strumming its strings, and, of course, Athena. To the left of the image, an inscription of the lost continent of Atlantis before it disappeared from Earth. And to the right, the Pyramidic Islands.

Eci rubbed its fingers over the exposed gateway, leaving behind a path of ice wherever it touched. "What's this indentation below the middle carving?"

Feri craned its neck. "That, my friend, is the keyhole." Feri slowly inserted the crystal end of the scepter into the indentation.

The existence of the souls became visible as the solid entrance vanished.

"Let's go." Feri waved its burning arm and stepped into Dropa.

One by one the others followed—the effect of their presence already apparent via a blackened trail wherever any of the creatures walked. Feri's army marched down the temple steps and regrouped on the lower level. When the last malicious soldier entered Dropa, the portal closed, perhaps for the last time.

Tradon rubbed its hands together. "Where shall we begin?"

Feri scanned the unfamiliar landscape. "I suggest we split up."

"Why?" Eci questioned the tactic.

Feri placed its fiery hand on Eci's frozen shoulder. "We'll have more fun that way."

Eci smiled coldly as water briefly dripped from under Feri's palm, only to freeze as it contacted the rest of the ice-laden body. "I'm up for it."

"My Pyrotons and the Dartons are best suited for those buildings," the human-shaped inferno recommended. "Ectorel and Seduma, lead the Electromorphs and Medusamorphs to those pyramids floating in the water."

"Do you believe there's life in the water?" Ectorel asked.

"Not for long," Feri smirked.

"How right you are."

Both Ectorel and Seduma sparked with enthusiasm.

"Eci and Dwin," Feri called.

"Yes, sir," they answered.

"Take out the forest. After you finish, meet us at the shoreline. We'll travel across the water together."

"It'll be a pleasure, sir." Eci and Dwin saluted their new general.

Thus, began the devastation of Dropa. Feri and the Pyrotons initiated the destruction by setting the silky fibers of the meadow ablaze.

As the last soldiers left the temple, Tradon and the Dartons opened fire. Their spears catapulted into the columns, shattering them into pieces. Water that supported many of the pillars splashed onto the marble floors and ran off the edges. The water sizzled and emitted billowy steam clouds upon intercepting the blazing grassland.

The raging fire spread faster as the Cyclotons cut a wind-blown path to Musing Woodland. The flames rapidly engulfed the outer edge of trees. Sporadic snapping and popping sounds from the burning wood replaced the mesmerizing rhythmic music that emanated from the leaves.

The Icics refused to allow the Pyrotons to enjoy all the fun. They extinguished only the nearest flames as they advanced into the forest. Crystalizing the tree limbs and trunks, the Icics spread their liquid coolants throughout the woodland. The colorful array of leaves transmuted into crystal figurines of ice. And the frozen limbs and icicles shattering on the ground formed a duet with the crackling melody of the blazing timber.

The Cyclotons gave the Icics a sufficient head start. Satisfied with the gap, they increased their wind speed and unleashed miniature cyclones. The swirling winds leveled the forest right behind the Icics. Powerful gusts uprooted the smaller trees and obliterated the larger ones by discharging frozen wood fragments everywhere. If the icy structures withstood the initial ferocity of the Cyclotons, they inevitably exploded into tiny ice-covered kindling upon impact with the forest floor.

Adjacent to Musing Woodland, the Pyrotons engaged themselves in another form of barbaric entertainment by unleashing a barrage of fire bombs throughout the city. Trees, flowerbeds, and shrubbery in the beautiful gardens bloomed no longer. The pyromaniacs burned paths across the city streets. They attacked buildings with a fury, throwing fire bombs in, around, and on top of the magnificent structures.

Tradon and the Dartons marched closely behind their burning comrades. Using the standing monuments, statues, and buildings as targets, they bombarded the burning remnants with an onslaught of spears. Similar to the forest trees, if the structures didn't obliterate from the impact of the pointed projectiles, they shattered into fragments upon contact with the ground.

The Electromorphs and Medusamorphs had reached the water's edge. As Seduma led its forces into Mystic Sea, the Electromorphs initiated a destructive onslaught above the surface. Lining the gemstone shore, the masses launched a volley of electrical grenades at the pyramids. The ancient monuments withstood the first assault cast upon them despite their outer layers sparking like crossed wires. The Electromorphs used the initial volley of the unwelcome amusement to calibrate their targeting systems. After a few adjustments, they reloaded and hurled a second array of charged particle bombs. That wave of electrical missiles left little standing of the once-mystifying structures.

The giant jelly fish wasted little time commencing their own infernal entertainment under water. The colorful creatures below had no chance against the high voltage currents emitted by the Medusamorphs. They, too, made a game of the destruction. Several multi-tentacled creatures flushed their prey out of the coral reefs and directly into the path of termination from the fully-charged, electrical invaders.

Next to the messenger portal stood Athena, merely an observer of the senseless destruction of her beloved existence. The blunt end of her new spear rested on the marble tile as she pointed the other end away from her body. Strapped to her left arm, her shield hung even with her waist. Flames engulfed the city and two-thirds of Musing Woodland had already been leveled. And there was the blackness—the ebony trail that tracked the intruders deeper and deeper into Dropa.

Athena had seen enough devastation. She opened the portal entrance, anticipating help from Arton's redeemed soul. It remained empty. She spun around to identify the source of a tremendous explosion behind her. Blackness had replaced the last of the Pyramidic Islands. Athena could wait no longer, lifting her right leg to enter.

Hercules emerged from the gateway. "Aren't you a pleasant sight."

She dropped her spear and shield, and attempted to wrap her arms around the waist of the giant strongman. "I was about to search for you."

"That will not be necessary." Hercules gently picked her up and set her to the side. "We will need a little room here."

Centaurus closely trailed Draco. Next came Pegasus with Sagittarius astride the mighty winged horse. Leo roared into Dropa. And, with each ally that appeared, Athena grew more confident. Instinctively, she ducked as Aquila soared over her, barely missing her head.

Lastly, Orion emerged. "Ah, to be alive again."

Seeing no more reinforcements, Athena peered inside the opening. "Is this all of you?"

"This is it," Hercules replied confidently.

Athena sealed off the portal entrance, examined her newly recruited army, and tallied her troops. "Fourteen."

"Yes, there are fourteen of us, no, seventeen."

"What happened to the other three?"

"I believe Hydra, Cetus, and Serpens utilized another portal."

"Why?"

"Perhaps to preserve your friend who helped transport us here."

"We cannot wait for them." Athena assessed the initial destruction. "Our enemy is down there."

"What are we up against?" Sagittarius inquired.

"Extremely malevolent creatures that Arton spawned and assembled into a formidable adversary. Although he redeemed himself by helping us free you, that redemption did not spill over to his army. To make matters worse, the power he attained from his training and the evil he accumulated during his long existence on Earth has permeated to his soldiers, rendering them god-like. And, because Arton is originally from Atlantis, his powers have essentially returned home." Athena espied a strange anomaly. She paced in front of the constellations. Stopping at Leo, she investigated the peculiarity. "Hercules, what is wrong with this one?"

"It is an abnormality among all of us."

An alarmed Athena detected the same aberration with Hercules. "Please explain this."

"Because of our lengthy galactic imprisonment, our bodies periodically phase between energy states and render us more vulnerable when in battle."

"How big of a problem is this?"

"It could be a significant disadvantage," Hercules speculated, "but it depends on the weapons our opposition has at their disposal."

Athena's hope had diminished. "You are up against transcendent soldiers. They have fire, ice, high-velocity spears, and electrical bombs. Others can blow winds from here to the other side of Dropa."

"We cannot change what we are, Athena," Hercules reasoned. "These are the characteristics we possess, and we can only perform to the best of our abilities with what we have at the present time."

"You are right, Hercules," Athena admitted reluctantly. "I apologize to all of you."

Athena beckoned the constellations to join her. "We need to cut them off at Mystic Sea. It is that large body of water beyond the city. Pegasus, Draco, and Aquila will provide air support over the three groups I assign." Athena assessed her allies. "Sagittarius! You stay with Pegasus. Orion, you will ride Aquila."

"Yes, Athena," Sagittarius and Orion acknowledged.

"Centaurus." Athena considered the routes of the others. "Take Cancer and Scorpius to the left of the city, through the frozen tundra. Draco, you will fly over Centaurus. Because of your fire, concentrate your attack on the ice creatures."

"Hercules!"

"Yes, Athena."

"Escort the two bears to the right of the city."

"No problem."

"Orion, Aquila will hover over Hercules."

"What creatures should we concentrate on, Athena?"

"You and Sagittarius, snipe anything in your range."

Orion and Sagittarius clanked their bows.

"Leo, Taurus, and Aries will accompany me to the blackened city." Athena retrieved her spear and shield from near the portal entrance. "Pegasus will serve as our air protection. Expect the worst and watch each other's back."

Sagittarius stroked the mane of Pegasus as the winged horse bobbed its head in agreement of its mission. Centaurus and Hercules clasped one another's forearm with their hand.

"One more detail."

"What is that, Athena?" Centaurus asked.

"Maintain the element of surprise," Athena advised. "They are currently unaware of our presence. Keep it that way for as long as possible. It may be our only advantage."

Hercules relayed a conspiring wink to a grinning Centaurus.

"Pegasus. Draco. That means close proximity with the ground."

Pegasus whinnied at Athena and Draco emitted a puff of smoke, both in agreement.

Hercules immediately clamped his large hand over Aquila's beak, instantly muffling the sound from the screeching bird, and slowly guided the eagle's head closer. "Element of surprise," Hercules whispered into Aquila's ear before releasing its firm grasp.

"It is time," Athena ordered. She grasped Hercules' arm.

"What is it, Athena?"

"Someone is coming," Athena whispered.

Orion and Sagittarius drew their bows. Draco inhaled deeply and the other constellations readied themselves.

Although understanding their state of alarm, Athena loosened the grip on her shield. "No, it is not one of them."

"Who else could it be?" Centaurus inquired.

"Hercules, did you say there were three other constellations?"

"That is correct, Athena."

"They are here."

"Where?" Orion searched for the three late arrivals.

"The temple where the other portal is located."

"We do not have time to wait," Sagittarius alerted Athena.

"*We* do not." Athena eyed Pegasus, Draco, and Aquila. "These three do."

"One of them is a whale," Hercules alerted her.

"And presently, you are made of unstable energy," Athena reminded Hercules. "Change of plans. Sagittarius, lead Leo and Aries through the city."

Sagittarius slid down the side of Pegasus. "And what are you doing?"

"Recruiting additional soldiers." Athena climbed aboard the winged horse. "Move out, everyone!"

Hercules, Sagittarius, and Centaurus, with comrades alongside, advanced down the assigned paths to intercept Feri's army.

Athena kicked her heels into Pegasus. The winged horse took flight, closely flanked by Draco and Aquila. The airborne constellations flew low and swiftly to the scorched portal. Athena passed her shield in front of the entrance.

Cetus, Serpens, and Hydra maneuvered through the visible doorway into Dropa.

"Climb aboard," Athena commanded. "Hydra, take your nine heads over to Draco."

Hydra crawled across Draco's wings and rested atop the dragon. Serpens slithered its way onto Pegasus and draped itself around Athena. Transporting Cetus proved a bit trickier. Orion whispered instructions into Aquila's ear. Aquila took to the air at a low altitude and circled once. The eagle swooped down and snatched the whale's tail in its talons.

"Veer to the left," Athena instructed, the point of her spear indicating the destination.

"And the others?" Orion contested.

"We will catch up with them shortly. First, we need to drop the water creatures into a cove, hidden from the enemy."

"Does that feed into Mystic Sea?"

"It does," Athena replied boldly, "and I believe the Medusamorphs will be extremely shocked when our marine allies pay them an uninvited visit."

Orion scratched its head. "Medusamorphs?"

"Large, electrical jelly fish," Athena clarified.

Pegasus led the way with Draco right on its tail. The two constellations flanked themselves alongside Aquila. The transports released the aquatic constellations, changed direction, and readied themselves for the upcoming conflict.

Once in the water, Hydra and Serpens attached themselves to Cetus. The whale propelled itself to the devastated Pyramidic Islands.

Draco, Pegasus, and Aquila each assumed a position high above their assigned land troops, soon to be in range of the unsuspecting enemy. Athena smiled. They had all arrived as planned and unnoticed.

Inevitable End

Back on Earth, the sky above the beloved planet depicted an ebony canvas, sans a moon or stars. Willie and Roberto's family had lost consciousness and lay motionless, their breaths weak and shallow. And in the hospital examining room, the unborn infant's heartbeat slowed to one beat every two seconds.

The winds blew no more. Precipitation was nonexistent. Lava flows and river currents halted. The surface water of the vast oceans resembled sheets of glass, reflecting the nothingness above them. Plants and shrubbery blanketed the ground in a lifeless state. The once-blazing forest fires were nothing more than smoldering ash. Earth had almost completely ceased spinning on its axis.

In Dropa, the unwelcome intruders stood ready to cross Mystic Sea. Eci, with its band of icy comrades, unleashed a steady flow of streaming ice onto the liquid surface, forming an expansive frozen overlay to bridge the large body of water.

The once lush, vibrant Musing Woodland around the city stood no longer. The smoldering city filled the precious skies of Dropa with thick, inky smoke. From the black trails left on the surface and the dimming suns in the sky, permanent darkness in Dropa was imminent and preservation of the souls seemed unlikely.

The Electromorphs had destroyed the Pyramidic Islands in the middle of Mystic Sea and the Medusamorphs had nearly terminated all activity below the frozen surface.

"Well done, comrades," Feri commended.

"We're ready for more!" Tradon bellowed, starved for destruction.

"Indeed. Eci, is this ice strong enough to hold my Pyrotons?"

Eci smirked. "Don't insult me, Feri!"

"Good." Feri indicated the next destination with his scepter. "Onward!"

The Pyrotons and Icics led the way across the icy stratum. Marching on their heels was Tradon, accompanied by the Dartons. Cyclotons and Electromorphs finished off the formation.

From her perch on Pegasus, Athena witnessed the enemy unwittingly assist with its own demise. Attacking them on an unstable surface enhanced the possibility of positive results for her overmatched mercenaries. She waited patiently until the enemy reached the middle of the frozen sea, having no shelter to protect them and nowhere to retreat.

Athena propelled her spear at the center of Feri's army. From the ground, Hercules and Sagittarius commenced an attack with a barrage of arrows. Assisting with the air assault, Orion released its own set of deathly projectiles.

Athena's spear pierced through two Dartons, killing them instantly. Penetrating through the other side, the spear also wounded an unsuspecting Icic.

The arrows of the celestial hunters hit their targets with extreme precision. By the time Feri spotted the attackers, five additional invaders had been eliminated: two Dartons, two Icics, and an Electromorph. As the enemy concentrated on the air assault, the icy foundation trembled.

"What's happening?" Feri struggled to balance himself.

Tradon steadied its legs, but couldn't prevent its feet from sliding out from underneath its body. "I have no idea."

Cetus blasted its enormous body through the ice barrier. Clenching a half dozen sparking Medusamorphs in its powerful jaws, it hungered for more. Opening wider, the large whale swallowed three Cyclotons and a Darton before crashing into the water. Several Pyrotons lost footing and fell to an extinguishing peril below the surface water.

"Where did these beasts come from?" Eci yelled. "Look out!"

Hydra and Serpens emerged from the opening, enveloping their slithery bodies around whatever soldiers crossed their path. Darton spears decapitated three of Hydra's heads, but the damaged appendages quickly grew six more. From above, Draco zeroed in on its icy targets. Diving at them, the tenacious dragon unleashed a barrage of fireballs, incinerating multiple Icics.

By the time the enemy regrouped, it had already been reduced by one quarter, but still greatly outnumbered the celestial guerillas. When it initiated its retaliatory strike, the assault resulted in pure annihilation.

The Electromorphs countered first, spraying a shower of electrical bombs skyward. Their first strike shocked the phasing Aquila and Orion, hurling them both to a spiraling death. The explosions also propelled Pegasus into a tailspin and had Athena clinging to her own existence. Trying desperately to escape, the situation worsened as the disrupted flight carried them amidst numerous Cycloton offspring. The miniature whirlwinds incarcerated Athena and Pegasus inside a swirling wind funnel.

Draco avoided the electrical assault, but met a trio of Cyclotons that gyrated the helpless dragon into a frenzy. Its most powerful weapon proved suicidal when the dragon discharged three fireballs and the tremendously powerful winds redirected their flight. Two fireballs penetrated the dragon's exposed underside and the third blasted it between the eyes. Draco burst into flames and streaked away from the sea like a stray comet, its cremation concluding in the city center.

Aries, Taurus, and Leo mounted a united charge that yielded similar results. Aries and Taurus sustained fifty Darton spears throughout their bodies. Their phasing energy states withstood the initial attack but failed to withstand the next wave. The Pyrotons hurled fire bombs and the Electromorphs discharged electrical particle arrays. The negatively charged particles destabilized the horned constellations as the flying infernos disintegrated their bodies.

Leo also ignited, but decapitated a half dozen Dartons during the detonation. As its body struggled to fight off the flames, its energy shifted and the phasing lion met its fiery death.

Sidling low to the ground, Cancer and Scorpius avoided the incessant onslaught of bombs and spears. Masterfully coordinating their effort, Cancer captured a Pyroton as Scorpius applied its venomous sting. Their tandem attacks were short-lived, however. The force of the Cyclotons' winds launched the assailants from the icy surface against a dozen Dartons. Multiple spears protruded from their bodies as they violently struggled to escape. The Electromorphs applied the final strike, emitting negative particles throughout the already feeble mercenaries. Too much for them to withstand, the wave of negative energy exploded Cancer and Scorpius into oblivion.

Underneath the ceiling of ice, the Medusamorphs had also recovered from the surprise attack. Hydra, Serpens, and Cetus plunged to the depths after their surface assault and swam into Seduma's ambuscade. The jelly fish zapped the water constellations with an unimaginable wave of high voltage. The three celestial entities lit up like a stormy sky. Cetus surrendered first and exploded into a million particles. Serpens' demise was less dramatic as the giant serpent simply dissolved in the water. Tremendous amounts of negative electrical energy traveled through Hydra—its heads the single means of escape. Like popcorn kernels in hot oil, one by one Hydra's heads exploded and the headless body slowly sank to the bottom. Not expecting Hydra's kamikaze method of death, the Medusamorphs were also terminated, unable to escape the bursting appendages. Feri's troops had successfully crossed the frozen sea. There they waited for Athena's paltry troops to attack.

As they had performed at the onset, the remaining constellations executed another ambush. During the confusion of the first battle, Hercules led Centaurus, Sagittarius, Ursa Major, and Ursa Minor to the opposite shoreline. Carefully using the remnants from the decimated islands as cover, they traveled across the ice sheet undetected.

Another flurry of arrows struck the unsuspecting enemy in their backs. A dozen more egregious soldiers had been eliminated before they retaliated. Emerging from two large boulders were the giant bears. They each clamped their claws onto an Electromorph. The clash between positive and negative energy was a spectacular exhibition of physics. Rolling across the ground, they each struggled to overpower the other. Sparks filled the air, accelerating back into the source of combating particles. The persistent recycling resulted in the implosion of the enormous particulate of energy. The two bears and the two Electromorphs vanished from Dropa.

The Cyclotons effectively flushed out the last of the celestial warriors. Hercules, Centaurus, and Sagittarius emerged in concert. They each unleashed one last arrow before the Icics bombarded them with ice balls. Expending as much energy as they had and their bodies already phasing uncontrollably, they instantly transformed into frozen statues. The Dartons, with salvation the furthest thing from their evil minds, launched a barrage of spears into the frozen figures. Shattering upon impact, chunks of ice dispersed through the air and across the ground.

Feri and its soldiers readied for the next set of attackers. There were none.

"Is that it?" Feri wondered aloud.

Tradon surveyed the area. "I believe so."

Eci peered across the mostly frozen sea at the blackened city. "Nothing from this side."

"Let's proceed with our objective," Feri ordered. "Stay alert! There could be more!"

Eci stared at the huge hole exposing the water of Mystic Sea. "Are we abandoning the Medusamorphs?"

Feri gazed at the opening and waited for signs of life. "If there are any left, we'll retrieve them later."

Eci counted the visible troops. "I estimate half our army survived."

"More than enough to obliterate the rest of this place."

"What are we waiting for? Let's finish what we started." Eci accompanied Feri at the front of the formation.

The sky darkened further—the three suns had almost completely vanished. Feri's diabolical army seemed invincible. Restored to their humanoid shapes, the invasive creatures followed Feri and Eci to Butterfly Meadow.

Reacting to the evil and negativity, the lingering butterflies attempted to vacate their precious habitat. Flaunting his prowess, Tradon launched multiple miniature spears. The deadly projectiles intercepted the defenseless victims and shattered the colorful flying prisms. Tinted fragments, although dimly lit from the extinguishing suns, faded like the last trailing sparks of fireworks.

"Nice shot, Tradon," Dwin complimented his comrade.

"Easy targets," Tradon replied arrogantly.

"Feri, what are we waiting for?" Eci asked.

"Over there," Feri warned.

"Dwin," Tradon exclaimed, "stop the wind pipes from blowing for a second!"

Dwin signaled to the other Cyclotons, noticing its motionless troops. "They're not spinning."

"What's wrong, Feri?" Ectorel questioned.

"I don't like the way those blades of grass are swaying."

"Maybe there are more butterflies," Eci half-heartedly suggested.

"Doubtful. Tradon made sure of that." Feri crept closer to the meadow edge and lowered itself to the ground.

Tradon scratched its porcupine head. "What the heck is it?"

Ectorel, Dwin, and Eci leaned over to listen, all shaking their heads at Feri's paranoia.

Feri arose. "I don't understand."

"Did you hear something?" Eci inquired.

"Yeah, I did, but I can't make it out. There's one way to be sure." Feri broadened its arms. "Step back."

Feri stoked its inferno and set Butterfly Meadow ablaze. The flames spread and black smoke billowed skyward. Drier stalks snapped and crackled as the fire consumed them. The flames relinquished their ferocity, extinguishing at the nonflammable borders. The precious home of the butterflies had been reduced to a blackened carpet of dirt and smoldering ash.

"Satisfied, Feri?" Eci asked his suspicious commander.

"I'm satisfied."

"Good, let's have some more fun," Eci said in a spirited tone.

The nefarious soldiers marched onto the blackened, ashy ground. Awaiting them on the other side was the Eternal River. They trod confidently across the barren meadow when the ground quaked beneath their feet.

Tradon attempted to stabilize itself. "What's happening?"

Feri raised its arms. "Retreat!"

It was too late. The softened dirt foundation collapsed, swallowing Feri's troops into the twenty-foot pit of emptiness and covering them with a blanket of black soil and hot ashes.

After wiping the residue from their eyes, the enemy soldiers peered upward at tiny figures lining the edge of the massive crater. Hundreds of Quadropas, picks and shovels slung on their shoulders, quietly delighted in their adversary's misfortune. Others giggled hysterically or excitedly jumped up and down at the sight of their captives, impressed with the burrowing job they had completed underneath the meadow.

Their laughter ceased as a barrage of spears, fireballs, and ice spheroids rocketed at them from within the pit. The unharmed Quadropas scattered to the bank of the Eternal River.

"I told you there was something strange," Feri asserted.

"You did," Eci admitted, "but what are those miniature creatures?"

"I don't have the slightest idea. Ectorel!"

"Yes, Feri," the lead Electromorph responded promptly.

"Can you and the other morphs get out of here on your own?"

Ectorel considered the depth of the pit. "No problem."

"Good." Feri aimed its scepter at the top of the wall closest to the river. "Take your troops up there and find those tiny moles."

"I'm on it." Ectorel motioned to the other Electromorphs.

"Dwin, kick up a little wind and construct a ramp with this loose soil!"

"Right away, sir."

"You heard our leader, let's stir it up!" Dwin commanded.

The spinning Cyclotons and deployed smaller cyclones worked furiously, the dirt lifting and swirling before settling near the base of the closest wall. The larger Cyclotons gyrated around the pit, pushing dirt near the ramp. Dwin and the smaller cyclones whirled across the piles in a distinct pattern and with great precision, forming the desired means of escape.

Giant masses of negatively charged gases rose out of the crater and veered in the direction of the Eternal River. The Quadropas waited for the assailants at the riverbank. This time they were accompanied by a large contingent of Paldropas.

At the edge of the river, hundreds of miniature cannons, courtesy of the Paldropas, were loaded and ready to fire at the enemy. Like all creations in Dropa, these cannons were extraordinary, specifically designed to fight the Electromorphs as if the Dropas had obtained prior knowledge the electrical soldiers would exit the pit first. The Quadropas stood prepared to reload rocky cannonballs fueled with positive energy of the Eternal River.

The Electromorphs experienced strange, dangerous sensations as they cautiously drew closer to the river. Their fully charged bodies played right into the camouflaged protagonists' mitt-like hands. Ectorel led the fifteen remaining electrical entities. It didn't matter. There could have been fifteen hundred and they would not have survived the ambush.

The Dropas opened fire. Displaying uncanny accuracy, not a single cannonball missed its target. And as fast as the Paldropas fired, the Quadropas reloaded.

The Electromorphs exhibited an uncontrollable discharge. Particle by particle, each cannonball blasted through the gaseous bodies and meticulously picked apart the targets. The positively charged particles attached themselves to one of the Electromorph's negatively charged fragments and ripped it out of orbit. Again, and again, wave after wave, the relentless barrage of charged projectiles burst through the enemy. The Electromorphs writhed wildly from their disrupting orbits, sparking like a severed electrical wire in a summer storm.

The Dropas' uninterrupted volley demonstrated flawless targeting as they removed the Electromorphs' existence with surgical precision. The enemy failed to retaliate with a single electrical bomb.

Witnessing the imminent doom of its comrades, Feri led its troops into the foothills of the Prism Alps. As they retreated, leaving the Electromorphs to perish, a squadron of soaring bubblecraft homed in on them from Bubble Mountain.

The Dropas' bubbles were each armed with two guns, one on each side and an ample supply of ammunition stored in the rear of the iridescent spheres.

"Step aside boys," Tradon boldly commanded, "these gnats are mine! Dartons, fire at will!"

They launched a thousand spears. The Dropas adeptly maneuvered their bubblecraft without fear and avoided the land-to-air missiles.

"Impossible!" Tradon exclaimed.

The Cyclotons, Pyrotons, and Icics abandoned their pointy allies and rushed into the Prism Alps. Half the Dropas' squadron broke formation, ensuring the evil beasts maintained that course. The other half opened fire on the two-legged porcupines.

The Dropas fired razor-sharp projectiles with the same accuracy exercised by their companions near the river. The assault decimated the Dartons piece by piece. After penetrating the outer shell, the embedded projectiles released a positive charge inside the Dartons' bodies. Slowly, yet systematically, the forsaken troops disintegrated one small section at a time.

Unlike their counterparts, these Dropas were less fortunate. The Dartons battled the incoming bombers until their bodies could no longer function. Spears filled the air in a spasmodic frenzy, occasionally striking down an incoming bubblecraft and eliminating the Dropa pilot with it. A handful survived the loss of their aircraft, floating to safety strapped to a parachute.

The Dropas sustained the attack until there was nothing left of the targets. Dartons with partial arms or missing midsections shot wildly into the air. Their complete exposure left them unprotected from ensuing attacks. The Dropas fired wave after wave until the last of the Dartons had terminated. Abandoning their fallen foe, the bubblecraft pilots rejoined their companions that relentlessly guided the fleeing enemy into the mountains.

Feri's troops launched a counterattack with a volley of fire and ice bombs, achieving a higher success rate than the Dartons. Streaming fire explosives ignited the bubblecraft and, in many instances, incinerated the Dropas. Ice bombs instantly froze the bubbles and propelled them to the ground, where the craft and the Dropa pilot shattered into countless frozen fragments.

The diminishing army's assault was fierce, but short-lived, as the presence of the Prism Alps came into play. The Dropas had forced Feri's troops into Prism Pass. As the Icics and Pyrotons fired on the Dropas, the mountain opened and swallowed the remainder of the malevolent army. Transparent coffins encapsulated the bodies of the Pyrotons and Icics. Inevitably, the plight of the more elusive Cyclotons also ended in capture.

Once inside the individual tombs, the process of extinction commenced. The unwelcome bodies reverted to their most stable state: Pyrotons became ashes, Icics became water, and Cyclotons nothing more than harmless air. The prisms contracted, compressing its victims until they were one with the mountain. Their negative energy had successfully been converted to positive energy, and the last of Feri's army had been eliminated. Proof of their existence would be safely tucked away and mentioned only in the writings of the Dropa scrolls.

The eradication of the Cyclotons freed Athena and Pegasus from the shackles of the smaller cyclones. The swirling winds dissipated into the Dropian atmosphere once their spawners had vanished.

Unaware that the existence of Dropa had been preserved, Athena followed the path of the blackened landscape. She searched diligently for signs of her celestial allies. There were none, and no signs of the enemy either. The evil carpet of blackness ended near the edge of the Eternal River and within Prism Pass. Athena guided Pegasus to the Prism Alps. A large contingent of bubblecraft circled the pass and additional spheres soared amidst the brightening sky.

"Pegasus!"

Pegasus whinnied as an exalted Athena yanked on the horse's flowing mane.

"The Dropas! It is indeed…the Dropas!"

Athena gently pressed her hand against the right side of Pegasus' neck, guiding the winged equine away from the Prism Alps. She surveyed the valley near Bubble Mountain. The residual gray tones had disappeared as the landscape of the

Dropas' sacred procreation ground reassumed its normal vibrant colors. Athena spotted Liam and Lindor approaching Fog Canyon.

"Athena!" Lindor waved her arms to get Athena's attention.

Pegasus dove straight for them. Its wings opened prior to landing gracefully on the surface. Athena dismounted and broke into a sprint. The three embraced.

"We did it!" Athena said joyously. "We defeated the evil intruders!"

"All of them?" Liam stepped away from Athena and Lindor.

"Every last one." Athena's face expressed both satisfaction and overwhelming peace. "The fate of eternity has been preserved...and it is ours to cherish."

"Did the constellations defeat them?" Liam inquired.

"I am afraid not," Athena replied, dispirited. "Although they fought gallantly, the enemy was too powerful." She brought Pegasus' head close to hers. "Pegasus is the lone celestial survivor."

"Had they not held the invaders off for as long as they did, we would not be having this conversation," Liam commended.

Athena suspiciously eyed Liam due to his altered appearance before expressing confusion regarding his comment. "What do you mean by that?"

Lindor covered her mouth with her hands. "It was the Dropas, was it not?"

Athena dismissed Lindor's knowledge of the Dropas' participation. "Held them off?"

"The constellations bought the Dropas extra time," Liam clarified.

"We witnessed it!" Lindor proclaimed.

"Witnessed what?" Athena inquired, bemused by the dual conversation.

Lindor kissed Liam's cheek. "We saw it happen!"

"In the name of Dropa, what did you see, child?"

Lindor gazed into Athena's eyes. "The procreation of the Dropas."

"The procreation?" Athena was stunned. "How?"

"We did." Lindor embraced Athena. "It was magical in the truest sense."

Athena gently pushed Lindor away. "Tell me everything!"

Lindor gazed at Liam. "First of all, I would have never seen it without Liam."

"Of course not, he was with you," Athena declared.

"It is more than that, Athena. He preserved my existence."

Athena examined Liam from head to toe. "I thought there was something different about you."

He examined his arms and the rest of his body. "What do you find peculiar?"

Athena avoided the question. "Lindor, tell me what happened."

"I prefer you tell her the story, Liam," Lindor said elatedly.

Liam described the events after he sent the medallion to Bandor.

* * * * *

...'I have done all I can for you, Athena. I must devote my effort to Lindor."
Liam lifted Lindor into his arms, destined for the Eternal River.

Liam kept a close eye on the persistent shrinking of Lindor's pocket. Carrying her in his arms, he made his way through Musing Woodland. The enchanting music and the wave of colors emanating from the leaves presented Liam with a small glimmer of hope. Deep inside, he believed the power of Dropa would grant him a chance to save his soul mate, no matter how small it might be.

The fate of Lindor's existence consumed him—nothing else mattered. Images of their shared time filled his mind and warmed his heart. Never before had Liam experienced what they had together. And now he was wrought with despair at the possibility of losing her.

Leaving Musing Woodland in the rear, Liam impatiently waited at the water's edge. In front of him floated the Pyramidic Islands. *How will I get across?* He had no way of communicating with the dolphins as Lindor did. She exhibited no sign of life—a third of her pocket remained open. He stared at the islands, willing them to bestow him with a little magic.

He detected subtle movement amidst the foamy water in his peripheral vision. Liam waded the gentle disturbance up to his chest. His feet were suddenly swept out from under him. He tightened his hold on Lindor as they submerged. The pyramids had somehow answered his silent request.

A giant manta ray served as the emergency transportation. Sensing the urgency, its wings elegantly flapped in the water, propelling them gracefully, yet rapidly, to the other side of Mystic Sea. Laser-focused on Lindor's closing pocket—more than three quarters sealed—Liam was undistracted by the beauty of Fluorescent Valley.

Liam thanked the manta ray as he disembarked on the opposite shore. Wasting no time, he tenderly situated Lindor in his arms and hurried to Butterfly Meadow where the butterflies greeted him.

Flashbacks of Lindor's stories and their own recent visit to the meadow swirled in his head. A quartet of fluttering butterflies landed on Lindor's nose and cheeks. Their wings opened and closed slowly in an attempt to soothe their favorite Dropian. Preoccupied by their presence, Liam was unaware of how fast he had progressed through the grassland.

Upon reaching the other side, Liam darted to the river, the butterflies choosing to stay with him. He already felt the energy from the current. Once at the riverbank, he placed Lindor in the Eternal River.

Liam waited. And waited. Nothing happened—Lindor's facial expression remained unchanged. She showed no sign of life. Not in her face, her arms, or any other part of her body. He examined her almost completely sealed pocket.

"Lindor," Liam whispered, "what do I do?" He gently brushed his fingers over her soft cheeks. "What must I do, Lindor?"

No response. He frantically searched the area. *Is there a different part of the river I should take you?* Helpless, Liam couldn't tell.

Reminiscent of his freeing Connor from the cocoon, the answer he sought mystically presented itself. Two butterflies danced in the gentle breeze. They connected bodies and performed a beautiful ballet of shared life.

Liam guided Lindor into the middle. The energy encircled him and flowed through him. Lindor lay motionless. Comparable to the first time in the river, his body swirled with euphoria, sated with the energy of life—the energy of existence.

It coalesced with his own internal energy. The combined vitality engulfed his body. Unwittingly, he released Lindor. Her body remained afloat in front of him. Liam closed his eyes and inserted his hands into his chest, through his heart, and deep into his soul. He seized the energy and withdrew it. His body spasmed from its release. Examining his hands—a foot apart—he held an invisible ball of the same diameter. Liam lowered the sphere to an area barely above Lindor's abdomen. He slowly separated his hands further, extending the energy across the length of her body. She exuded a faint glimmer.

The shared life circulated through Lindor, traveling to her head and down to her feet. Liam watched, entranced. The pocket opened further—a quarter—a half—then three-quarters. Her faint internal light escaped as her pocket completely unsealed.

Slowly her eyelids opened. Lindor searched for something familiar and smiled when her and Liam's eyes met. "Where are we?"

Liam carried her to the far bank and positioned her against the same tree they sat by the first time they crossed the river. Her returning strength was evident.

"Where are we, Liam?"

"We are at the Eternal River." Liam grinned joyfully.

"Why...did you bring me here?"

"I told you I would never leave your side," Liam said softly.

"Yes, but why the Eternal River?"

"It was the only sensible place."

"The river alone cannot preserve one's existence."

Liam glanced at his crystal friends across the river. "A pair of butterflies provided guidance." He detailed the sharing of his soul with her.

Lindor lovingly drew Liam's face to hers. She leaned in close to his ear, and whispered, "We are truly one."

Liam assisted Lindor to her feet after she regained her strength.

"Liam! The city! And Musing Woodland!"

"The sky is darkening too! They are here."

Lindor buried her head in Liam's chest. "We cannot return."

"They need our help," Liam argued.

"There is nothing we can do against those powerful soldiers."

"You are probably right, but we must try."

"What is happening over there?" Lindor asked, distracted by a peculiarity behind Liam.

Liam pivoted. Gray tones they witnessed earlier in the valley near Bubble Mountain phased in and out of colors—gray—multi-colored—gray.

Lindor tugged on Liam's arm as she sprinted for Fog Canyon. "The Dropas!"

"Yes, the Dropas!"

Their excitement heightened in anticipation of viewing the momentous and jubilant event. Without hesitation and with assistance from the rolling cloud, they swiftly flew hand-in-hand, ricocheting across the canyon fog, and landed safely on the other side.

"Have you been practicing without me?" Lindor asked playfully.

"Perhaps."

Liam and Lindor arrived at the border of the valley—careful not to enter the sacred grounds—in time to witness the unimaginable rebirth of the Dropas. Mesmerized by the beautiful sight, they temporarily forgot the evil destruction near the city.

Hundreds of Quadropas and Paldropas had gathered. They had finished the initial ritual dance and their colors transitioned, as had those of the valley landscape. The multiplicity of vibrant tones transformed into corresponding grays.

The indistinguishable hues made it difficult for Liam and Lindor to discern one Dropa from another. Given that they had an unexpected audience, the Dropas' performance wasn't dedicated to onlookers, rather it was for themselves. As with all living species, the creation of a new generation was central to their existence.

Liam interpreted the transition to gray as a symbolic aspect of their rebirth. It reminded him that when one looks beyond the surface, everyone is the same—each having a mind, a heart, and a soul. And when it comes time for two life forms to share those three components, especially to procreate, that the surface is simply that. It is a shell that holds the true essence of one's self. The Dropas bestowed on him another precious lesson.

As Liam processed the true meaning of the ceremony, he was drawn to the one person who embodied the element of that lesson. Unaware of his enamored gaze, Lindor's face illuminated with exhilaration. Liam savored the joy in her eyes as she beheld the Dropas most sacred ritual.

The Dropas initiated their celebration of existence. Each paired with one other Dropa. They first joined hands and drew closer to each other. When they met, their bodies merged like a vanilla-chocolate swirl and displayed an indeterminant amount of colors. More amazing was the fact that it wasn't a different color for each pair, but rather each pair of Dropas exhibited a plethora of hues. Their globular bodies—fluctuating between grays and colors—arbitrarily joined and separated reminiscent of the "lava lamp effect" Liam witnessed with Connor during his ascent of Bubble Mountain.

The evolution perpetuated until each Dropa melded its precious characteristics with every other one. Only then did the Dropas collectively coalesce and commence their procreation.

The indistinct physical characteristics dematerialized as the hundreds of magical beings amalgamated into one large, gray pool of Dropas. A gray seedling sprouted from the union of life. As it grew, it absorbed the remnants of the pool until the green valley was prominent again.

Darkened clouds drifted down from the mountaintops to nourish the hungry, gray plant standing tall above the ground. The falling rain produced thousands of rainbows. A single gray blossom sprouted from the plant tip and stretched skyward. Hundreds of petals unfurled from its center, and from those petals, stalactite-like formations emerged.

Unlike the rainbows created from typical Dropa rain clouds, the ends of these colorful arches never contacted the valley floor. Instead, they terminated at the flower's stigma where their brilliant hues nourished the Dropa flower. Completely entranced by the spectacular event, Liam and Lindor watched the colors travel down the flower stem and out across the valley.

Initiating their own transformation, white cumulus clouds morphed from the rainclouds and swirled high above the terrain as the rainbows slowly faded. The billowy clouds intercepted one another and materialized into a huge cone before turning dark gray. Precipitation streamed out of the tapered end into the basin of the blossom until the cone eventually disappeared. As the water filled the cup of life, it overflowed onto the petals until dripping off the ends or rolling off the tips of the stalactite-like formations.

The water trickling off the petals gave birth to the Paldropas and the droplets from the stalactite-like formations created the Quadropas. In either case, the Dropas fully developed before settling on the ground. One single drop transmuted into a connected pair. Arms and legs emerged first, followed by hands and feet. And what started as hundreds of Quadropas and Paldropas had miraculously procreated into thousands. The Dropas had created a new generation for the first time in their new existence.

Lindor exhibited an emotional reaction unthinkable in Dropa—tears streamed down her cheeks. After contemplating this rarity, it made perfect sense to Liam, for they were not tears of pain or suffering or agony. Not in Dropa. Instead, they were tears of joy. The result of beholding the unimaginable evolution of life had exceeded the normal levels of elation that Dropians usually experience.

It truly was a magnificent spectacle and the most glorious one *they, or anyone,* had ever witnessed, individually...and together.

* * * * *

Athena embraced both Liam and Lindor. "If we were not in Dropa, I would certainly be covetous of you two."

Liam and Lindor exchanged smiles, understanding they shared something no one else might ever experience, and they would cherish it forever.

"It is time to congregate all Dropians to celebrate our renewed existence." Athena mounted Pegasus. "There is room for two additional passengers."

Liam and Lindor climbed aboard.

"What will happen to Pegasus now that Dropa has been preserved?" Liam asked as the winged horse took flight.

"Pegasus has communicated to me of its desire to exist here."

"What will people on Earth see when they gaze at the night sky?"

"The constellations remain visible. Their images still linger after the long incarceration."

"It is only fitting that way. The sacrifice they made to help preserve eternity will serve as an everlasting reminder to humanity."

"As with all involved in the preservation," Athena added.

Paradoxical Existence

On Earth, the blue sky re-emerged in all its glory. In the mountain ranges and tropical rain forests around the world, the snow and rain fell once more. Rivers and lava flowed. The wind danced again, rejuvenating the ocean waves. Across the prairies, wetlands, and forests, animals resumed grazing to nourish their bodies. Flowers elevated off the ground, greeted the sun, and opened their blossoms—exposing their beauty to anyone willing to admire them. Earth had awakened as had its soul.

Roberto's eyes opened. They darted back and forth across the ceiling and around the room. His mother and siblings remained asleep. He inhaled deeply and breathed effortlessly.

Roberto discerned the brightness in the window. Seeking certainty that he wasn't dreaming, he left the bedroom, scampered down the stairs and out into the street. Daylight had returned. He checked his watch and estimated that he had not been unconscious long.

"It's over!" Thrilled to be alive, Roberto danced and twirled. "Wake up, everybody! Wake up!"

"Roberto!" His mother yelled from the bedroom window. "Why are you carrying on like that in the middle of the street?"

Roberto stopped and waved his hands over his head. "Mama, don't you understand? It's over!"

His groggy mother peered skyward. Screaming with excitement, Roberto's siblings partook in the celebration.

A beaming Roberto ran to the bushes underneath her bedroom window. "Mama, we have been given another chance…"

Willie's eyes abruptly opened as he struggled to inhale through his nose. Staring at him was his daughter, her fingers plugging his nostrils.

"Hi, Daddy," she whispered, "it's wake-up time."

Squinting at the sunlight emanating through the window, Willie jumped to his feet with his daughter in his arms. "Wake up, you two!" He danced across the living room rug.

"I don't want to go to school, Dad," his son mumbled.

May awoke to her husband's booming voice. She excitedly shook her son. "Wake up."

He awoke as his mother planted a kiss on his forehead. "Why is everybody making all this noise?"

May hugged her son as she assisted him off the couch. She backed away and tightly enfolded Willie and their daughter in her arms. "Is it over, Willie?"

"Yes, it's over!" Willie reciprocated the embrace. "We have been given another chance…"

The young couple in the hospital awoke to the steady pulse of the ultrasound—the baby's rhythm had normalized.

The nurse proclaimed blissfully, "I don't know how, but your child has been given a second chance…"

And many miles from the hospital, in a gym where another mural had been painted, rose a custodian out of unconsciousness. Attempting to determine what had happened, he gazed at the painting on the wall. It had a circular, steel-looking border with a four-leaf clover opening. Behind the outer border, but intersecting the leaf openings, was a steel ring. A stained-glass mosaic filled each area between the ring and the outer border. Located in the large aperture of the mural, a white dove metamorphosed from a flame burning in the center of an evening sky. Accentuating the background shone a moon and a familiar shooting star.

The custodian leaned on his broom, his eyes fixated on the artwork. The dove flapped its wings amidst the flickering flame. As the shooting star traveled across the sky, the dove emerged from the flame and flew out of the wall. The beautiful, white bird circled the gym before resettling in the mural.

The custodian simply smiled and resumed sweeping. He stopped short of something on the floor, knelt, and retrieved a small branch from the dust pile. A single leaf remained. He held the branch up to the gym window and twirled it slowly in his fingertips. It was an olive branch…

During the return flight, the blackness of Dropa had almost completely receded. Pegasus landed near the outskirts of the city. The Dropas had already embarked on a new beginning, busily revitalizing their precious paradise.

Hundreds of Quadropas had initiated a renaissance of the city infrastructure—meticulously wielding their tools, as they resurrected buildings, chiseled statues, erected columns, or added ornamentation. Numerous fountains had already been restored and the "quality control" Dropas tested one finished product by riding atop the bubbles. Paldropas refashioned the city artwork and provided the finishing touches on various Quadropa creations.

Outside the city, a few hundred Dropas were "replanting" Musing Woodland. Unlike re-establishing timber on Earth, the miniature foresters replenished the area with full-grown trees.

Liam and Lindor gazed out into Mystic Sea where another thousand Dropas reconstructed the Pyramidic Islands. Below the surface, hundreds more restored the prominent Fluorescent Valley.

"Liam!" Krolic was leading the Dropians who sang joyfully behind him. "Lindor!"

"You survived!" Liam greeted him.

An elated Lindor hugged Krolic. "Where have you been?"

"Athena instructed me to escort everyone to the Pillars of Solitude." Krolic motioned to the Dropians to proceed into the city.

"Liam, we have to visit there."

"That will not be possible, Lindor."

Lindor's smile disappeared, recalling her conversation with Bandor in the desert. Her greatest fear of Liam choosing not to stay in Dropa had come to fruition. "Why not?"

"My purpose has been fulfilled. It is time for me—"

"You cannot return, Liam," Athena affirmed.

Liam whirled around. "Why can I not return?"

"Pure and simple—your premature arrival in Dropa allowed you to save Lindor's soul."

Liam glanced at Lindor who gratefully smiled at him. "I do not understand, Athena."

"Your body possessed both the energy of life and your soul, and you have shared them both with Lindor. You were the source. The Eternal River supplied the catalyst. The two of you are soul mates in the truest sense. You two cannot be separated. And *you* cannot return."

"Ever?"

"Not unless I send you on a mission," Athena replied with a wink.

Liam walked away from Lindor. Unsure of Liam's reaction—for no one had prematurely arrived in Dropa—Athena exchanged glances with Lindor and Krolic. The end of time on Earth customarily dictated when Dropians arrived. In Liam's instance, his life on Earth ended *before* its time. Or had it?

Liam stared at the Pyramidic Islands, oblivious to the reconstruction. Thoughts of his years on Earth and not seeing his friends or family played before him, but he understood he could visit one day. He held his head high and absorbed the mystical beauty.

Liam pivoted and made eye contact with Lindor. "In order for a new journey to begin, another must end. My journey on Earth is complete, and my existence in Dropa has commenced."

Lindor rushed into Liam's arms and kissed him.

"Welcome to Dropa," Krolic and Athena proclaimed in unison.

"Sounds like a celebration in the city center," Krolic announced.

Dropian musicians had gathered together to play instruments fashioned by the Dropas. Music filled the air. The Quadropas hammered rhythmically with the melody while Dropians danced in merriment.

"What do you say we join them?" Krolic suggested.

"We have friends waiting for us in the Nexus," Athena replied.

"Since that doesn't involve me, I will converse with you another time, Liam." Krolic left to join the festivities.

Athena, Liam, and Lindor detoured around the city to the portal. From there, the three set out on an excursion to the Nexus where they would celebrate a different reunion.

Bandor slowly opened his eyes. Mason and the kids, their eyes still shut, stood in a circle near his body. The Dropas, however, had finished their act of hypnosis. Some entertained themselves atop Bandor's head as others performed cartwheels on his chest. Indigo and Orange took liberty with their paintbrushes to give Bandor a makeover for his return trip to Dropa. Blue, Green, and Red lay on their backs with hands folded behind their heads and legs crossed.

Orange reacted first to Bandor's alertness and wasted no time informing the others. The Dropas reconvened on his chest, dancing and gibbering, but this time in celebration.

"Bandor," Lauren shouted joyfully, "you survived!"

He repeatedly twisted his hands in front of his face. "It sure seems that way."

Mason boosted Bandor to a sitting position. "How do you feel?"

"Terrific." Bandor rubbed his palms across his face. Seeing the discoloration, he playfully reprimanded the Dropas. "All right, who are the estheticians?"

Ti poked fun at her made-up companion. "It's totally you, Bandor. I wouldn't change a thing."

Ratting out their companions, ten Dropas pointed at Indigo and Orange. The two culprits came to Bandor's assistance and removed the leftover cosmetics.

Lauren observed the change in his facial expression. "Bandor, what is it?"

Distracted, Bandor peered over everyone's head. His jaw dropped slightly. Without uttering a word, he slowly rose to his feet as the Dropas scurried to his shoulders. Examining the vortex wall, he gingerly moseyed across the unblemished sand with Mason and the kids on his heels.

"Bandor!" Unwilling to wait any longer, Mason spun Bandor around. "Snap out of it!"

The Dropas danced and celebrated.

"Do you understand what has happened, Mason?" Bandor pointed at the wall.

"It's not spinning. Holy cow, the vortex exists no more!"

"How did we not see that?" Lauren asked rhetorically.

The wall had indeed stopped spinning. And replacing its state of fury was an expansion of the enchanting landscape they had seen before Arton wreaked havoc. The Nexus remained the center of the murals, but without the prevalent convergence of violence and turmoil. Its recent appearance of desolation no longer evident, the Nexus had restored the splendor, calmness, and serenity it once possessed. The vortex wall reverted to the blended scenes that revealed various mural gateways leading to and from that key intersection.

"What does this mean, Bandor?" Ti inquired.

"I am not sure, but if my feeling is correct—"

"Yessss?" The kids eagerly awaited his answer.

"If my feeling is correct, I surmise that the enemy has been defeated."

Everyone yelled and cheered. They hugged and danced, and congratulated one another for their part in preserving eternity. The celebration was short-lived, however, as Robohawk screeched loudly—not one of satisfaction, rather one of warning.

"Bandor!" Lauren alerted. "It's surfacing!"

What had been Arton's platform emerged from the bubbling center of the revitalized Nexus Sea.

"Man your stations!" Bandor ordered.

The Dropas boarded Robohawk and the dragons.

"Man our stations?" Brian asked, bewildered. "What stations?"

Stripes let out a deafening roar of dissatisfaction as the other mural creatures dispersed along the shoreline or hid behind boulders.

"Bandor, didn't you say the enemy had been defeated?" Cooper asked.

"Defeated, but apparently not eliminated."

Robohawk took to the air flanked by the dragons and birds. The platform completely surfaced and the force field deactivated. The Dropas readied their miniature bazookas and waited for the precise moment to attack the enemy.

"Clearcoat!" Bandor yelled as Athena, Liam, and Lindor waved from the watercraft. "Clearcoat! Hold your fire!"

"Take cover!" Athena commanded after perceiving the squadron's intent.

Robohawk and the dragons dove at the perceived enemy. Ignoring Bandor's warning, Clearcoat and the other Dropas fired. The three new arrivals had nowhere to hide.

Bandor, Mason, and the others couldn't bear to watch as they covered their eyes. Frozen, the three targeted individuals fixated on the bazooka shells approaching them. Considering all they had been through, they were about to be executed by their own friends.

The last sound they heard was Robohawk screeching as it and the dragons passed over them. Demonstrating incomparable precision, every shell hit its target.

"Un...believable!" Liam considered his new wardrobe.

"What is this stuff?" Lindor asked.

"They never stop," Athena commented.

The Dropas had attacked first with slime missiles before unleashing confetti bombs. As the watercraft neared the shore, the onlookers realized the prank the Dropas had accomplished and laughed hysterically. The Dropas' intense giggling caused them to roll off the landed aircraft.

Extending the mirth, Liam and Lindor leapt off the platform and rolled in the sand, becoming the sand creatures from the Nexus lagoon. Everyone questioned whether the Dropas would ever recover from their latest shenanigans.

"Who wants to hug me first?" Liam extended his arms.

Ti cringed and held up her hands in resistance. "Not even Pickle Fluff would touch you."

"You and Lindor hug each other," Lauren insisted.

Athena gibbered to Clearcoat. She enjoyed the practical joke, but it was time to end it. The giggling Dropas removed the slime, confetti, and sand.

When they finished, Liam opened his arms. "Any takers?"

"You look much better than when I last saw you." Ti hugged Liam first. "How was your visit to Dropa?"

"It unequivocally surpassed my expectations and imagination and, as Lindor alluded to in the murals, a verbal account will not do it justice."

"A picture is worth a thousand words," Lauren pleaded.

"For this special picture, a million words is not enough."

Everyone exchanged hugs. Liam and Mason made their way to each other.

"We did it," Mason said.

"An adventure for the ages."

They all relaxed for a short spell and communicated their stories. The teens were the most vocal, detailing the voyage into space, the entrapment in the vortex wall, and Ti's conquest of Bandor's mound of clutter. Lindor shared the adventure inside Bandor's pocket and Liam described his ascent of Bubble Mountain: the journey with Connor, Posaan, and Tesmar, and his conversation with Exott Ettepo.

After considerable pleading, Liam broke down and conveyed to his captive audience a condensed depiction of Dropa as best he could. Athena's subtle acknowledgment commended Liam for his more than acceptable portrayal. He stopped short of revealing the most important element. Athena understood Liam's omission and merely let the conversations run their natural course. On several occasions, she graciously thanked all involved for their collective role in preserving Dropa. Lindor capped off the storytelling with the most fascinating account of all—the Dropas' rebirth.

Clearcoat and the other Dropas listened intently, having missed the sacred event. One might have expected disappointment, but it wasn't their nature. They expressed happiness for the other Dropas in a solitary way, but were extremely proud and honored that their mission proved critical to everyone's survival.

A quietness overcame the tranquil reunion. The time had arrived to reunite with loved ones.

Lauren broke the silence. She glanced at Athena, Lindor, and Bandor. "Will you escort us through the murals?"

"I believe we can do that. That will allow me an opportunity to enjoy what you have painted, Mason."

"I would be honored to have you view my artwork, Athena."

They leisurely strolled through the murals. The lack of urgency during the return trip allowed everyone to let the magic inside Mason's paintings wash over them. They regaled each other with stories again and again. And each time, the tales sounded as exciting as the first.

The teens would be the envy of their friends and families for many years. The journey inside the murals was greater than the first trip they experienced together, but the first was no less vital. Because that initial mission to Barrow's Ridge was a critical facet, Liam reminded the four young adventurers to stress its significance with the others who partook in the collapse of Arton's fortress.

It became silent with the group's parting more imminent as they crossed the desert plain—the last segment before returning home, for most of them anyway. Unlike the completion of the first mission, no one greeted them upon their homecoming, including Willie. Memories of Willie played through Liam's mind for he wanted to bid farewell in person to his best friend.

Athena broke the silence. "Here we are."

They had arrived at the mural where Liam entered through his painted body. The sun setting behind them presented a storybook backdrop for the farewell.

Lauren gestured at the edge of the mural. "Liam, there you are in your headdress. Your real face looks different from the one facing us."

"Yes, there I am," Liam whispered, purposely avoiding Lauren's observation.

They all stared at each other. Had they not relinquished their emotions inside the walls, tears would have rained on the desert sand. Athena initiated the series of good-byes, starting with the adolescents and finishing with Mason. Bandor stepped forward next, followed by Lindor.

Bandor embraced Mason. "You are a good friend and I will never forget you."

"It will be lonely on the wall," Mason added.

"The students are good company," Bandor reminded him.

"It's not the same."

"It was worth a try," Bandor admitted.

Lauren and Ti hugged Bandor. "We will miss you, Bandor." The girls released their grips and returned alongside Brian and Cooper.

Realizing Liam failed to partake in the send-off, Mason eyed him suspiciously. "Are you ready?"

Silence prevailed as all eyes fixated on Liam.

"I will not be accompanying you," he said softly.

The kids were stunned by his response.

"When did you make this decision?" Mason hoped that Liam was kidding in his usual manner.

"It was made for me," Liam replied innocently.

After accepting the reality that he truly wasn't returning home, the kids moseyed over and said good-bye. Liam would miss them dearly—especially with all they had experienced together—yet he was at peace that they would safely reunite with their families and friends.

"What do you mean it was *made* for you?" Mason inquired.

Liam described the sequence of events after sending the medallion to Bandor. Lindor clutched his arm.

"Lindor's pocket had not completely healed. She sacrificed herself in hope of preserving our existence. *Our* meaning everyone." Liam recalled the chain of events. "Her pocket began closing."

"She was dying?" Lauren asked.

"Yes, her soul was dying. There was only one way to save her."

Lindor leaned her head on Liam's shoulder.

"I carried her to the Eternal River. Reaching deep inside myself, I shared my energy of life...and my soul with her. And because of that, I *cannot* return."

Mason and the kids expressed happiness for Liam. Although they wouldn't feel the sadness of his absence until outside the murals, he detected it in their eyes.

"Are you...dead, Liam?" Cooper asked naively.

"I am on Earth. But no, I am not dead."

"His soul lives on," Lindor added, "as does Bandor's and mine."

"In Dropa?" Ti inquired.

"Yes, in Dropa," Athena answered peacefully.

"I didn't expect we would part this way...or this soon," Mason admitted.

"Neither did I."

"They can visit," Athena suggested.

"What?" Mason asked, surprised.

"Like Bandor and Lindor visited Earth?" Lauren inquired.

"Yes," Athena acknowledged. "Liam, Bandor, Lindor, and the Dropas too."

"Speaking of the Dropas," Mason questioned, "has anyone seen them?"

They all scanned the area with no luck.

"I have no idea where they went," Bandor admitted.

"They were on all of our shoulders as we strolled across the desert," Lauren added disappointedly. "Déjà vu. This is like Barrow's Ridge all over again. No good-bye or anything?"

"Not to worry, I found them!" Brian pointed. "Up by the doorways in the sky."

"Yep, it's them all right," Mason concluded.

Eight Dropas flew into the desert through the doorways. Each Dropa had its own miniature biplane with a banner streaming behind it. And on each banner, an individual good-bye message to their friends.

"Where are the other four?" Athena asked.

"Here they come," Ti indicated, "by the dream catcher."

Exiting from outer space, painted behind the dream catcher, drifted the four remaining Dropas. They arrived on hot air balloons and each one had a single word painted on it. The tiny aviators had initially misaligned themselves, but they quickly reorganized.

Everyone read the message painted across the balloons. "**Always— Remember—The—Dropas!**"

"How could we ever forget them?" Mason asked.

The Dropas safely landed and bid farewell to Mason and the teens. Lauren and her friends embraced everyone again as the Dropas lined the mural ledge.

"The Dropas will prepare you for passage through the wall," Bandor advised.

Liam and Mason embraced one last time.

"Please pass along my regards to Willie and his family for me," Liam offered, "and the other kids."

"I will."

Bandor stood alongside Athena and Lindor held Liam's hand. They observed the Dropas ready Mason and the kids for the grand departure. One by one the five mural travelers exited the artwork with Mason waving as he left.

"Good-bye, my brother," Liam said.

They descended the platform the Dropas had painted for Liam's entry, and dropped to the floor beneath the artwork. Liam approached the front of the mural. When he arrived, the Dropas scurried up his arms and rested quietly on his shoulders. Peering up at Liam, Mason and the kids acknowledged their safe exit—each inhaled deeply and relayed a thumbs-up gesture.

"Hey, you guys."

"What is it, Liam?" Mason inquired.

Liam pressed his palms against the inside of the wall. "Spread the word that hope is alive and something spectacular awaits them. I have witnessed it. And we all partook in saving it. Something much, much greater exists. Something beyond what they possess on Earth."

Mason and the kids listened intently.

"It is magical, yet ever so precious, but they must do their part to safeguard it. It exists for everyone, but everyone is responsible for preserving it, both here and there. In order to preserve the fate of eternity—together—they must first nourish and preserve the existence of their souls on Earth—together."

Liam backed away, leaving one hand pressed against the inner wall. Mason and the four teens smiled, but this time, tears streamed from their eyes. Liam had imparted to them—as best he could—what was beyond. They all understood they had been given a second chance to discover it. It was up to those five to propagate that hope with everyone on Earth.

Liam gazed one last time at the people he was leaving behind before rejoining Lindor, Bandor, and Athena. They strolled hand-in-hand through the desert, into the mural sunset, and back to Dropa.

The journey continues...what will you do?